For Michael —
Thank you ahead of
time for your help on
this project

THE THREE

BOOK ONE
OF
THE ROAD TO THE REMEMBERING

by
Roberta Dawn McMorrow

Roberta Dawn
better known as Bobbie

Published by Lulu Publishing & Limelight Publishing.

Cover design @ Evan Walbridge

ISBN: 9781716397783

lulu.com
limelightpublishing.com

*for my grandsons
and the grandsons and granddaughters
of my heart*

"I don't tell you these stories to scare you.

I tell you these stories so you will choose a different path."

~Ray Bradbury

Contents

Thirty Days Ago

He rides as never before, as if the archangel of flying horses is within him. The night is darker and colder than any he can remember. He does not shiver or damn the dark; he spurs his horse on. Sweat and saliva from the animal's lathered mouth slops the boy's rawhide jacket. He ignores it.

He swivels from his waist to look behind him. It's too dense to see a soul.

Damn!

Smoke and fire swirl towards him in oppressively tight and heavy grey clouds, obscuring his vision further. Shadows fall forward, then rise at odd angles and collapse again.

Broken voices scream in Spanish, in English. Women, men, children. Voices call out in tears, in rage. Wretched, demanding.

"*Help!*"

"No!"

"Over here!"

"*Please... por favor!*"

The pleas assault him in circular echoes.

He navigates black walls of smoke framed by flashes of red-orange, red-blue flames. Fire, the only light the darkness will allow, licks its furious and relentless flame in front of him, above him, to his left and right.

A projectile spark sears his left cheek. His eyes sting and water, squinting open-shut-open. A flickering cinder stubbornly sticks to the skin that attaches jaw to neck. He swipes his leather riding glove over the burn, and the ember flares on the fabric, singeing his fingers. He rides on.

He's lost sight of his brother. Each of them had been ponying several horses into this town where the firestorms rage and people seek any protection from the winds that spur flames and leave them homeless.

They've been riding for more days than he can count. Two boys in their teens, they are; leading refugees out of this place of blistering destruction and into the rugged mountains. Each day the winds blow harder, and the fires grow hotter and faster and more devastating.

Hisss. Crrrack.

A stand of eucalyptus trees, the last wall of specious safety for the refugees, explodes in a rain of lethal sparks and accompanying ribbons of fire. Every animal and element in proximity moans with the new annihilation.

The boy yells to warn and direct the people in front of him, again and again, and to inspire his brother riding behind him. For a brief moment, a flaming branch hanging from a desolate tree illuminates the younger brother following at a gallop. The older boy yells courage, direction.

"We got this!"

Messages are lost in the thunderous wind-roar of the broken and dying around and between them.

Scorched concrete foundations are all that is left of homes. Broken chimney bricks, cracked from the excessive heat of cataclysmal flames, crumble and crash on anyone who wanders too close to their imminent collapse. Cars and trucks, useless and abandoned, explode around them, ignited by last drops of boiling fuel left in rusted engines.

The brothers ride to save the refugees. Their father had taught them to drive horses through the wind-whipped gauntlets of earthquakes, flash floods and fires. "Nothing stopped Dad," they had reminded one another this morning as they watched fire cinders whisk through the early sky. The now-common sight of these embers augurs daily foreboding, in a time when debris is carried from one end of the planet to the other by vicious tornadoes.

"Dad made necessary rounds. We make those rounds now. Saddle up." No matter the conditions, their father had pressed on — and they with him. The brothers have had little food to support their growing bodies for long months since, and only enough sleep to make sure they don't fall off their horses. No one had complained then, with Dad leading them. Or now.

They had lost their father months ago. But they are their father's sons; they don't turn away from duty even after he's gone.

Tonight, his brother is a shadowy image riding behind him. The smoke, compressed with the remnants of lives and lost human endeavors, flies past him, hotter and faster than a mere hour ago. Just a few miles outside their mountain camp, his sight and senses are blocked and blurred.

"Damn," he swears under his breath.

The older brother slows his horse to point the way. "That's where we're headed!" he shouts. He can't hear his brother's response over the wailing wind.

He trusts they stare into the same scene: the wretched and their children, fifty scorched yards ahead. All seek safety, refuge, as they shelter against a half-shattered concrete retaining wall. Frightened faces are turned towards them, lit by devil fingers of firelight that dance and tease and dare them to try escape. Hunched in agony and supplication, desperate for rescue, the people, day and night, beg the brothers for a miracle.

He smells the fear. It's even stronger than fire surrounding them. "Don't give *in* to it!" he shouts to no one, to everyone.

He leans over the ears of his horse, whispering courage and unity. "Me and you, old boy. Got to keep the youngsters calm as possible. Steady ... steady."

He's brave but not stupid. Years in the saddle had taught him the danger and risk of leading four too-young horses into a maelstrom. Not for a minute does he question duty. Not for a second does he deny crisis. But ponying extra horses is their single option, the only way to rescue these people from sure death.

His brother had agreed.

He pulls his red hat down on his forehead for the little protection it gives him against a crescendo of sparks. He spurs his horse on.

He prays to spirit guardians of horses and children. *Give me time to save them all.*

One. More. Time.

And then all goes dark.

Prologue

This is the story I tell my children's children and their children.

There was a time far more frightening than now, when the center did not hold. Icebergs melted, rainforests burned, thousand-year coral reefs died. Keystone species, from insects to giant mammals, declined from endangered to extinct in half a generation.

Everywhere were signs and warnings. Water rose from the fathomless depths of the four oceans and connected the Seven Seas in one gigantic, systemic, hydraulic surge. Commerce made excuses and shifted explanations until earthquakes cracked landmasses and rogue waves drowned coastlines. "Big business" could no longer force nature to its iron will.

"It won't get worse," the authorities said.

It did.

Emergencies, personal and public, ubiquitous and demanding, refused to be ignored. Illusions shattered like manifold mirrors thrown from a battlement.

Extinct volcanoes cascaded avalanches of lava. Temperatures thought beyond Earth's ability to produce, melted mountains. Endless drought created deserts from once-lush jungles while hailstones and snow fell on Pacific islands.

"Not me."

"Not mine."

"Not here!"

"Not fair!"

"Curses!"

"Blessings."

"Enough!"

Those who yearned for certainty took irresolute stands. Lines between fake-real, false-true grew more contested. Weary minds refused to grasp complexity. Networked systems, from grids to family units, broke down. Fingers pointed, but few pointed to truth. Greed, selfishness, disunity and stale compromise prevailed.

"God intervenes."

"My God is not your god."

"Build higher walls."

"No, tear them down!"

Millions screamed "enemy," over food, space and water. "Protection" was defined by who could pay for it. It didn't save them.

People blamed Wrong Old Gods, Bad and Evil New Gods, Government, Corporate Power, False Presidency. Many wanted a return to Rule-of-Law, Old Testament, New Testament, Koran, Torah.

"ALL holy books!"
"NO holy books!"
"Are we doomed?"
"It cannot be!"
Promises were made.
"Technology will save us!"
"New drugs!"
"New devices!"
"A final discovery!"
"Announcing the next-best-thing-invention!"
All led to dead ends.

Those who loved the fertile land and aggregate stars taught, "What choice does Mother Earth have but to save herself?"

Orthodoxy cried, "End times!"

Elders and Spiritual Warriors responded without judgment, "End times are for cowards who don't accept responsibility."

People cried, "Nothing more can go wrong!"

It did.

One night, the Earth clicked a hard notch out of its accordant, perfect-axis balance. The electromagnetics of our sweet and tortured, brave and wise planet wobbled, lurched, sizzled and roared.

The Three Days of Darkness, prophesied, prayed for and against for generations, descended.

Land and sea and, finally, our glorious Sun, foamed, spurted, flared and revolted. Those who rode that dark dragon of destruction saw the endless death of everything once reliable and trusted, known and loved.

Ancient mysteries awakened. Hostile and Light Forces ascended, descended, blessed or cursed old and new, together and equally.

Finally, on the fourth morning, the planet calmed into a shambolic semblance of its old self. Giant lakes plunged into sinkholes where cities had stood or tipped over and split into streams of smaller and more violent remnants of themselves. Entire populations, man and beast, farms, forests, towns and once-great continents were torn. No boundaries made by human mapmakers remained as they'd been drawn.

The Sun no longer rose in the east, but near west. The Moon no longer set in the west, but near east.

Dawn of Day Four, survivors woke to a tattered world, citizens of destruction and disorder. Few accepted their part in the undoing. Not set on righteous paths, they doomed themselves to repeat their downfall.

The Divine Immortal, Queen of Ascendant Masters, called Source Emanation, emerged from the Dreamtime and revealed herself to her closest kin: your grandparents, the young and brave of prophecy, and to the Elder Teachers who harbored secrets too important to die.

She charged them to enter *The Remembering.* It was the path, she promised, *for a future to be possible.* She hummed her myriad songs, singing *Understand and embrace The Vibration of Oneness forgotten for over ten thousand years. It lives in you, calls itself forward through you.*

The Source Emanation whispered to your grandparents, as I do to you now, *Each one of you must be the living definition of possibility itself.*

Our grandparents chose to live Her message.

Choose One-ness. Right-intention creates right-action.

At every curve and corner of their lives, deprivation and defeat dogged your grandparents. Did they also know adventure? Yes, and union, joy, love and laughter. And, yes, human heartbreak, loss, betrayal, pain and grief. All the rounds of birth, death, life!

You, like them, are children of Source Emanation herself, who was known by your grandparents as The Halfling Goddess, The Divine Bird-Girl. She guides you as she did your grandparents. She hums, *Trust. Faith. Compassion. Respect. Fearless and forgiving love.*

Your grandparents were heroic. But listen, children: they would never, ever, have called themselves heroes. What kept them alive? Courage. Unrelenting belief in one another and in the true name of source: The Oneness.

Their Unity defied separation.

I tell you their story now because I am an old woman in her final days. I am last of those who knew The Three who became The Four and those gathered around them. I am last to sit on their knees and hear your grandparents' wisdom. It wasn't Earth's rebellions destroyed so much and so many; it was the forgetfulness of the human species to hum the frequencies of this planet's elemental rhythm.

My Beloveds, your grandparents' story must not pass with me. I tell you in their words to inspire you to carry Teachings forward. *For a future to be possible, you, my children, must enter the mystery of The Remembering and be One with the Becoming.*

It all depends on you.

PART I

Chapter 1
Lost Girl

I am here as I have always been.
"I am alone."
Not alone. I am with you, always.
"Do not leave me, not again!"
Never. Not ever. Look to the river, sky, feathers, drumbeat ... darkness, water, eagle, moonlight, sun-flight. Look to fire, earth, elements. Where you are, I am there with you.
"Do not leave me!"
I won't leave you. Dare yourself to fly with me. Trust, my daughter. Trust, and fly with me. Dare yourself. Black wind, starless sky, sun-filled dark, boundless blue ... I am here and there, within you and without. Forever.
"Do not leave me."
I won't leave you. Promises made in lifetimes together refuse to die. Together forever.

*

Anna sleeps in a cradle of dreams — her faithful companions throughout a friendless childhood.

On the crest of First Morning, thoughts and melodies bend themselves into one-syllable words. Keys and octaves, tempos and frequencies sly-shift into half messages, almost-sentences. Familiar sounds spin around her. *My voice. Hers. Not hers. Hers again.*

The lost and alone girl dreams of inky-black, heavy river water. Eddies appear, disappear before changing color and becoming whitecaps that tumble around and over one another and then darkening again. A single shaft of light pierces a shadowed, liquid surface. And then her own voice interrupts and sings, *there you are.*

Assured, Anna exhales, *safe.*

Her inner dream screen clears to reveal a baby girl floating into view on the water, tucked Moses-like in a thatched grass basket.

This is her favorite dream, the baby in a basket on sea or river or lake. The baby who comforts, advises, sings and guides ... coaxing her to sanity, to *calm* in troubled times. Which are many. The baby's story ekes itself out, piece by piece, over years of Anna's life. But the story is never complete. Mystery hangs on the overlapping montage. It whispers of love and the intimacy of close friends. It promises mama-secrets and sorcerer's brew. The baby nudges Anna out of bad traps; it comforts her when she is caught. The dream-baby offers options and solutions without line-drawing conclusions. And it never, ever judges her.

Anna, anxious and lonely in this present moment, squeezes her mind for understanding as she sleeps and seeks comfort in the floating image. She admits it shames her, wanting so badly to own every hint of this consoling mystery.

Beware of over-attachment; a Teacher's warning. Grandchild of ancient traditions, of ceremony and ritual, the girl tells herself not to make demands of magical creatures kind enough to visit her.

Thank you, she mumbles dreamily, and curls deeper into her vision.

Anna's patience, short-fused with humans and ordinary life, is endless-wise with the complexities of altered states. Her heart, protected by the street-smart armor of city life and urban disgust, is grateful for the companionship of her sustaining dreams.

It is dawn, after three days of darkness.

She dreams the baby calls to her.

A threat of sudden, violent vortex in the water whisks Anna into illusory motion. She sees herself leap reflexively forward into a shaft of dream light, lifting the baby out of her basket.

And for the first time, she fully sees the infant. *Mop of hair — red like fire — orange-red, like sunset sparks.* Anna marvels at the cascades of tangled ringlets framing the baby's small face and falling past her tiny shoulders. *Enough hair,* Anna whispers in her dream-mind, *for a grown woman to be proud of.* She focuses on the baby's enormous emerald eyes. *Never picked you up, baby ... but the river, the force of undertow ...* Where irises should be, diamond-shaped crystals in the baby's eyes turn like variegated prisms. Thousands of points of glittering light illuminate the dream. *I know your eyes. I've seen them often — but never like this ...* The brilliant eyes speak silently yet powerfully of safety and love, guidance and protection.

Up close, the baby's mouth and nose are different. *Not quite human.* Anna now sees the features are actually ... birdlike. *Yes!* They form a tiny hard beak. At the same time Anna notices *wings* in place of arms, carefully tucked into the baby's body. Layer upon layer of multi-colored, exquisitely small, silk-fine feathers. The downy wings match the same prism of dancing rainbow sparkles as the eyes.

Anna catches her breath, shivers. The basket bobbles in her hands.

Full and glorious ... wings!

She recovers her grip. In her dream she tenderly caresses the feather-softness and beak-hardness. *So real. So close.*

Never seen this before, not in years of your presence with me! You are a ... a Bird-Girl! A Halfling, just like the myth! Part girl, part winged creature ... a Bird-Girl. A species of magic. Anna sighs, and in her dream-eyes and her sleeping, current-life eyes, tears sting. *You are a thing like me,* Anna coos, *a creature who doesn't fit into the world as one kind of being.*

In her dream, the girl gathers courage. She tucks the Halfling's wings back down, carefully and tenderly, and holds the baby tightly to her heart.

Bird-Girl speaks to Anna now, in an ancient foreign tongue. It's a trill and ripple of echoing sound that gurgles and billows, then changes to airy music evoking birdsong across a rain-soaked lagoon. Anna doesn't know how she learned this strange language, but she understands it, and has since the first baby dream came when she was four years old. The Bird-Girl messages don't come through Anna's ears; they radiate through her cellular make-up until her own body and mind, heart and blood vibrate with their meaning. With Bird-Girl up close to her, as she is now, the frequency enters Anna's heart — and ambient understanding is instant.

Find the boy in the red hat.

The Halfling bubbles strange words. Her wide, crystal-prism eyes hold Anna's, perfectly riveted.

Find him now. He will save you. You will save him. Then come for me. I will wait for you.

With Halfling's words fresh in her mind, Anna startles awake in the barren new world.

Chapter 2
Leo

Where?
Shallow, staggered breaths. Dry, choked cough.
What the ...?
Cough. Sneeze.
Ugh.

He wakes flat on his back and chokes on the sand in his mouth. Bone-dry, skin-cracking thirst sears his throat. His eyes tear from pain. He rolls onto his right shoulder, but can't force his body's young, aggressive adrenalin to push him up. He groans and flops back to prone.

He squints to see, but his vision blurs. Every fiber of his body's muscles ache. His mind and spirit scream, enraged.

He exhales a mighty *puff* to accelerate into a crouch, but collapses flat on his belly, stomach-punched.

His will argues with his body's suffering and demands. He moans, pulls knees to chest and rolls into a clutched-flesh fetal position. Minutes drag by. His breath is shallow. A vice of pain squeezes his skull.

He damns his weakness. "C'mon, dammit, *c'mon!*" He deepens his breathing to slow his mind. Coughs, clears his throat and exhales a raspy, short, sharp sputter.

Despite his stupor of exhaustion and pain, he forces memory. *Think! Think! THINK!* he yells inside his mind, and the skull-vice tightens.

He growls, "*Think!*" aloud in a crackled voice he doesn't recognize as his own. He rests a full minute, regulates his breath. One heartbeat of calm. Two. A third, and his nerves settle.

Eyes closed, he bends his mind to remember. "What? *What?*"

A grey shadow of memory-picture forms. A young child screams mere feet in front of him, pained, panicked, desperate.
Who? Girl? Boy? WHERE?

Before an answer comes, the two-inch lens frame that circles the child expands to wide-angle. He sees the visual memory as if he's still there in that moment. People — old, young — wait, shuffle, clutch loved ones. *They reach for me, for us,* he realizes. All are desperate and circled by flames.

"Winds," he whispers to himself. Powerful, tornado-force winds smash old oak trees and tear up bushes and debris, whipping his memory as they had in actuality that night, all around him.

"Cody!" His horse, veteran of dangerous runs, was leading young colts. He sees them spook, shy and try to break free. He feels the wild strength in their animal fear, and he feels how his hands shook with muscled effort to clamp down on the reins of several horses.

Then what? WHAT? He damns himself for not remembering more. *Horses ... fire ... wind ... rescue ... Where are they? Where AM I?*

Nothing more comes back to him.

He shakes from pounding pain, his brain on fire and his skin crawling with dread.

"Need ... *water.*"

Dehydration does this, he knows; it sends a brain into migraine-convulsions. His father's voice echoes a lesson he repeats to himself, logically, with no emotion or drama: *No use to anyone if you lose your own head!* He says it to himself again to force focus, chill nerves, and deflate fear.

"Don't think, *do!*"

He screams aloud. Forces his eyes open. Shuts them again. They are as scratched and sand-drenched as his throat. The little he sees is clouded with grime. His instinct is to rub his eyes to clear them, but he stops himself. He could dig sand, dust, or worse, into his eyeballs. He squints instead, then bends and straightens limbs. Shakes his fingers to force blood into them.

"*Water!*"

He hears panic in his own voice, primal and desperate; but he refuses it. He crawls to his knees, wobbles a minute, gathers strength, tries to stand on legs he hopes will hold him erect. They buckle once; he demands obedience, and they respond reluctantly. He sways side-to-side. Holds his beating head with both hands.

"Walk!" He commands his legs, afraid they've forgotten how. He moves robotically, then stumbles, falls to one bruised knee before his legs fully unravel and he can stand.

Cave? Shelter? Where?

His head grazes split lumber, earthen ceiling. He bends his back and notices surroundings but doesn't assign meaning to them. He feels weak, vulnerable, a feeling never known before in his young and capable body. He denies it, but when he straightens his shoulders, he shuffle-walks like a crippled sleepwalker toward a dim light. He forces back enormous fatigue.

Pain like a thousand razor-cuts doused in fire tells him his skin must be cut to the bone, muscles torn and shredded. He peers down at his hands, then at what he can see of his body. He sees a little swelling and some scrapes. Nothing more. He's confused, in semi-shock.

"Bruised, but whole," he half-sighs in bewildered relief.

His reliable mind refuses to bring any other valuable information. He stays riveted on the desperate need for water.

"*Walk*, dammit," he commands aloud to his rebelling body. "One. Foot. In. Front. Of. The. *Other!*" Feet pinch in cowboy boots he's slept in for "...what? *Days?*" He moans with each mincing step but doesn't pull them off. Swollen feet won't allow the boots back on.

Opening? Door?

Cloudy light draws him forward, out of whatever dugout he's in, enveloping him as he emerges to a daylight haze.

He smells water ... and stumbles toward it.

Twenty-five yards away he finds a noisy, narrow river. With vegetation gone, it whips like an angry rattlesnake over naked land.

He reminds himself, *test for poison*. But the warning is not loud, and his thirst overwhelms other senses. From a near-lost place in his memory a prayer comes to his lips, a prayer of blessing for the river and of protection for himself. He drinks. And hopes for the best.

Tired as he is, and thirsty as a desert, his years of training kick in. He sips slowly, barely balanced on shaky knees, and only allows himself short swallows when his body demands, *more ... more!*

He closes his eyes and insists, "Focus!"

He washes his lashes and lids with river water that stings, then cools. He dries his face with his torn right sleeve, relieved he can almost see again.

Hunkering back, he searches his mind.

He remembers anxiety that had built over the weeks before that last night of rescues. He sees himself ride through neighborhoods where towns, parks, community halls, shopping centers and churches once stood. Structures large and small had given up reluctantly at first. But eventually they'd collapsed into heaps and surrendered to the endless wind and rock-heavy dust that blew harder and heavier every day.

Firestorm. Fire tornado.

He remembers the flames, outrageous, indignant, ignited by wind that licked up the last traces of what the molten furnace had left behind. Fires had escalated day and night until wind-blown heat lived within every human cell, as sure as it burned and blew in the material world around them.

In the beginning, years ago now, they had driven trucks with their father and other volunteers and had joined professional fire and rescue crews. But when fuel ran out, so did most help. It was left to the few who could wrangle horses and ride to save whatever, whomever, was salvageable.

"Ugliest damn *posse* I ever saw," he remembers Dad saying.

Broken-down cowboys with angry dogs and worn-out horses had joined them. Teens raised in skate parks and in front of video screens came when their cities burned and parents went missing. They couldn't sit a horse without tilting left or right, and they couldn't saddle or throw a rope. But without anywhere else to go, they hauled hay and learned to nurse lost animals and cook eggs and beans for other city refugees. Migrant farm workers, too, who'd been trapped in the north because anywhere south was burning even faster, found them. Together, they'd fixed vehicles and used lawnmower engines to power smaller equipment. But soon every ranch hand had gone in search of home, wives and children. His dad had recruited anyone he could to help with the rescues. But after two years, those helpers were gone too.

"Just us three. Finally got me an A-team!" It was hangman's humor, but his dad meant it.

The boy tosses those memories over, resists his heart's longing, and stares into the restless, sullen river.

"Ok, get an *effing* grip!"

Behind closed eyes, he goes over details of the last night of rescues.

Geez, it was a freezing night, he remembers, *and there were refugees right in front of me, and my brother was right behind me. We ponied more horses than is ever safe, or sane.* He shivers at the memory. *Out of our fool minds!* The more horses they saddled and brought into the fires, the better odds they'd get people to safety. *But,* he admits now, *that night, we had too many young colts. ... We were still okay, we were riding towards people. We were almost right there! Flames behind 'em, around us, but chances were good we could get them out ... The people were right there ... so close, just feet away ... and then? Everything suddenly ... Disappeared.*

His memory strains. His head aches. Images swirl.

What, dammit? Everything...GONE?!

He trusts his visual memory and runs through images of the last night again. Slows down the camera of his mind, frame by frame.

Okay, be logical. Riding Cody ... holding the reins of too many young horses. Three for me, at least two for Conan.

He sees the horses shy and pull, rear and trip. Watches their nostrils flare in fear. His right hand tightens as it did that night to hold onto the panicked animals. His left hand grips Cody's bunched-up reins. *White-knuckled, but HELD.*

He shakes his head. *And?*

His eyes flash open. *It was a giant blast of wind!*

One enormous gust had crashed into him from the blackest, coldest night, attacking with vicious power. He sees it in his memory now. Cody, his horse was *blown* from under him.

Impossible! CAN'T BE. ... Tornado?

In a punch to his gut, the oxygen had been sucked from him. The gust had torn the reins from his hand as if he'd held a bouquet of dandelions.

Blown back through mid-air? How the HELL?

Think. It. OUT! He commands himself to capture the scene in his mind. *Couldn't breathe. No ... bearings. Feet, head, hands flying ... then what? WHAT?!*

No other memory warns or informs him. He checks himself for truthfulness.

Nothing.

For less than a quarter-second, he had flown into a black void. No bottom below him to land on, or ceiling above him to hang onto.

The true memory of it hits him in another nauseating slug to his gut. He chokes on bile, spits it out and squelches a scream of emotion. One heartbeat, two, to contain himself. And then a short gasp of pure fear.

"Conan!" His brother's name through cracked lips sears his burnt throat. "Conan!"

Tears sting his eyes. He yells at himself aloud, *"Get a hold of yourself!"* Desperate, he spins around left to right, searching, suddenly hyper-aware.

Memory tells him a fire had roared in front of him.

"Not here ... we weren't *here*. Fire wasn't *here* ... this isn't *home!*" Today's sky is thick and grey, cloudless. But with a blanket of damp overhang. Silent, dismal terrain stares back at him — but it's not seared land. It's not the fire-torn ground and sky of his last memory.

He tries again to make sense of things.

Okay, okay ... Blown from my horse. BLOWN. By a ferocious wind gust, maybe some fire-driven tornado. Right? And then what? And where? And for how long was I ... knocked out? Hours or ... DAYS?

Nothing, no one, inside or outside of his mind answers.

What of his younger brother? *Where's Conan?*

And where am I now?

Nothing familiar marks his view. He doesn't know this place, not the contour of land nor the snaking river.

He muscles up his intelligence, spirit and body against the fear that edges dangerously around his pounding head and shaking limbs.

He forces himself to follow simple rules he'd learned well. *Organize thought and take charge.* Next, he tracks his footsteps, easy to find in the light dust that covers the earth. He walks back to where he had woken, a wood-covered burrow in the side of an enormous, tumbled hill. He checks the split rail ceiling, the once-serviceable, rough construction surrounded by fallen earth on three sides. *Remnant of an old mining shaft, built into what musta' been a mountain,* he observes. *Most of which looks fallen into itself.* Stepping back shakily, he takes in the full picture of the mountain's collapse.

Whoa.

He runs through options of what could have caused such destruction: sinkholes, explosions, earthquakes. *Seen cave-ins ... but three-quarters of a big mountain? Never.* It doesn't add up, not in terms of what he knows of natural sciences, the Earth's terrain, or geology.

And — there are no rivers where he lives, and no mining was ever done there. So, where is he? How far has he been blown?

How could I possibly be picked up and moved by a ... wind gust? Even a super-powerful one? And — SURVIVE?

He shivers from the illogic, and a lightning-quick tease of being crazy.

Hold onto your damn brain! he demands of himself, asking aloud, "How, why, am I *alive? ...* Where is everyone *else?*"

No panic! Stay in your body, breathe. Center.

He rote-repeats lessons he's learned. *Anxiety, worry, desperation strangle courage. They choke mind and emotion. ... Breathe. Inhale. Exhale.*

He loses patience with himself. "Chill, dammit, *chill.*" He commands his thoughts to focus. A cool lungful of air fills him on his deliberate, ten-count breath pattern. *Ok,* he tells himself, *better.* Steadier, he analyzes.

How did this lean-to survive?

He crawls back into the tight shelter, peers around.

How could I have gotten here? Nothing is left from that last ride, no horses, no saddle, packs, or supplies ... no BROTHER.

Only his red driver's hat, crumpled in the dirt of the shelter, remains of what he'd carried and led that night. He picks it up, shakes some dust off the brim. His Dad had said, "Whatever you do, keep that hat on. It's what the refugees look for. *Boy in the red hat.*" He thinks of how Dad had held him at arm's length and laughed, exclaiming, "Seventeen, and six feet tall. Almost as tall as I am. 'Boy' isn't quite right, is it? Specially now you've taken on the responsibilities of a man."

He'd felt that truth, *boy and man,* within himself. And everything both words had meant to him. He'd felt proud and scared at once.

No time now to review the past. He shakes himself free of memory. Commands himself, *move.*

He duck-walks out of the shelter. In the open space he stretches his shoulders, lifts his arms straight above his head. Pulls his elbows in front of himself and across his chest. Winces at the tight soreness. Stretches his neck and rolls his shoulders. Tries again to clear his mind.

He sighs at the mystery of unfamiliar land and twisted river. A landscape torn and empty of life. He swears he won't get further confused. He does what he's trained to do: he kneels, ear to the ground, and listens.

Nothing.

Not a sound except the river.

He stands and marks distances: shelter to river; width of running water. He mind-maps the environs. Then he drops carefully to the ground, folds his cranky legs into a half lotus. He bows and lowers his head to meet his hands which are pressed together in front of his heart. He drops into slow meditation breaths.

It takes minutes to find inner stillness.

Finally, a picture of Conan forms. He feels his brother's presence, distant but distinct.

His heart leaps, his throat catches. He's *alive,* the boy is sure. *Thank God, Conan's alive. And close.*

Remaining in the interior stillness that brings insight, the thought crystallizes: *Must find Conan.* He must find his brother before they are further lost to each other.

He springs to his feet, damning the ache in his knees from the quick movement. *Stay centered!* Every cell in his body argues for immediate action. *Stay calm!*

His heavy canvas jacket hangs on him, he notices; it's full of holes and shredded threads. *It must've been torn by winds.* The dense air is muggy now, but he'll need protection at night. He takes the jacket off, ties what's left of it around his waist. Pulls his hat down over his short black curls. *Where is there anyone left who would look for the red hat?*

He chills, and refuses the fear licking at unanswerable questions. The boy moves back toward the river hoping the image of Conan will give him a sense of direction.

He'll wait. We always agreed. If we're separated, he waits where he is until I show.

But this isn't like any situation that's happened before, real or imagined. Fear could drive Conan to a dangerous search.

One more quick wish-prayer. *Wolf-brother*, he calls in his mind to Conan. And again, aloud, in a weak but clearer voice, "Stay *strong!*"

He presses two fingers, heart to sky.

"Stay whole. No fear."

His steps are uneven, his legs are still wobbly — but he wills himself to move as quickly as his feet can take him back towards the river.

Chapter 3
Branded

"What the *hell?*"

Halfway to the riverbank, he's stopped by a sharp hot pain that rips across his chest. He clutches his heart with both hands and reaches for a ragged breath.

A second blast, like a fire-hot poker, sears through him. It stabs left to right under his ribs.

"What the ..."

He gulps air and falls to his knees, catching himself with one hand, grinding his fingers into the pebbly river rock.

"This ... is *same!* ... This *burn!* ... It feels ... *the same!*" he pants.

Pain had collapsed his strong body that last morning in their mountain camp. It had thrown him to the ground. He hadn't known it was to be their last dawn before the night of complete darkness. Hadn't known he was destined to ride into a fire rescue and wake up — *what? days?* later.

A new shock of pain tears through him now, afresh. And another blind siege of sharp fire. He feels as if it shreds his body from inside out. "*Again?*" He gasps for an inhale.

Feels like it did that morning, he realizes. Below surface skin and muscle, deeper than bone, it's a hot knife-like *burn.* The fiery sear spreads across his chest into his lungs and punches into his heart muscle. It pierces through to his spine.

Fighting for oxygen, his shoulders roll forward, left hunching lower than the right to protect his heart. He struggles up to one knee, and his hands reflexively fold over each other and press his chest in an effort to stop the pain.

He pulls himself up to half stand. But the burn hits again and he stumbles. Swearing, forcing himself not to give into the stabbing spasm, he rises. He controls his breath in rattled gulps.

"*Breathe!*" the boy commands himself aloud. *Breath connects brain to body, to emotion, to spirit.* "Breathe *slow ... dammit!*"

Frustrated at his lack of self-discipline, his eyes tear. His face reddens and contorts from effort. Several heartbeats pass until he catches a steady wave of air into and out of strained lungs.

The pain recedes to a low throb.

He rocks back and forth. "I'm *okay.* I'm *okay.* I can. Handle. This."

He slides his right hand under his shirt, swearing at his own trembling and the worry in his touch. *Pathetic.* He probes the area that burns. *Yes,* he nods to himself. *It feels exactly the same as that last morning.*

He traces his fingers above his heart. The skin is raised up from his chest. *Like a brand.* It's the same thought he had had that first time. He fingers the pattern as he remembers it.

SCROLLS. Medieval-like. Bordering a rectangle five, six inches long ... three inches, maybe four, wide.

Stunned into silence that last camp morning, he had sucked sharp breath in and spit it out. For minutes he had shivered, teeth clenched, bent at the waist. Finally steady, he had lifted his shirt, inch-by-inch from the bottom of the torn hem, afraid the raw pain meant newly-burned skin would stick and tear. He remembers he had held his breath against the inevitable. But the shirt had pulled up without the tug of pain.

In California's sea-fog morning he'd stared dumbfounded in the cracked mirror hanging sideways on a tent pole. Reflected in the glass had been his own familiar wide mouth and edged jaw — but his lips were now caught in a grimace — as on his chest he had seen the graven *symbols.*

He closes his eyes now and brings back to mind his memory of the images. He fights back the fear of unsolved mystery.

"Symbols," he says aloud. "But *what? Why?* How the hell did it happen?"

Mythical lions. An eagle, wings spread. And wolves — four of them — scanning an invisible horizon, noses pointed in each cardinal direction. *And flying horses!* Above and below the rectangle, red horses flying through dark sky. *Like the ones I've seen in dreams?!* Dreams not shared with anyone except his brother and grandmother a childhood ago.

"What the hell?"

And a T-shaped cross, with a curved, hooked bottom — *an anchor?* — lying sideways in the scrolled frame. And on each corner of the framed rectangle, *dragons.*

What else? If he makes the images conscious again, he'll feel more in control, he tells himself. *Nothing makes sense!* He fights the shakiness of his mind and limbs. He breathes deeply and insists on clear-thought memory.

"Sword on fire. *Flaming sword ... Hell. ...* Enough! Don't have *time* for this now. *Gotta move!*"

He shuffles forward two, three steps. Imagines blue ice cooling the burn.

But the images won't release from his memory. In the interior center of the framed rectangle, under the flaming sword, geometric shapes zigzag across the inner screen of his mind. *Maze? No. Obstacle course? A cross-linked design of bridges?* The shapes seem to be hooked together in sequenced, odd connections. *What is that? Another mind-twisting mystery meant to scare me? ... I won't go there!*

He had insisted on sanity that morning the brand had first seared him — and wrestles for it again now.

On his last day in camp, he had woken an hour pre-dawn. Odd, conflicting dreams, both unfriendly and friendly, had jostled his sleep. He'd dreamt he was driving a chariot pulled by flying red horses. It was a dream he'd had a few times since early childhood. Always in the dream he flies above a forest filled with ageless wise men and women, mystics who seem to bring him to a council fire and teach him ancient secrets. The vision always carries him, head and heart, on wings of saffron and ruby-red benevolent fire, and he sees himself singing in a foreign language an ancient hymn of joy and victory.

Something like that, he says to himself as he strives for cogent thought.

He had woken happy that last morning. The dream had filled him with the peace of better days not touched by the destroying drought-winds and the relentless earthquakes and fires.

Usually, he'd tell Conan his dreams immediately upon waking. Conan, keeper of dreams, knows symbols and signs and magical lore much better than he. But the pain above his heart had hit fast, out of nowhere. *Like now.* It had shocked him to silence.

He'd told himself he'd show Conan the "brand" — the raised, tattooed symbols — later.

But there wasn't a later.

He doesn't have a name, even now, for the weirdness and shock of it. He and his brother slept side-by-side in sleeping bags. No one could have gotten past their guard dogs and horses unheard. Any slight twig-crack or dry leaf-crunch would always awaken Conan, anyway. And nothing had been disturbed. His knife, rifle, boots, saddle were untouched and within easy reach.

No WAY someone had snuck in and ... what? BURNED this into me?

Besides, he thinks, as he had then, *I couldn't let anything keep us from what the day demanded.*

Embers falling from the sky were harmless at the higher camp level, a few thousand feet up their mountain; but ashes would be wind-whipped an hour after sunrise, making the trek more difficult with every furnace-driven minute of the day. That had been the pattern of their daily experience, in recent months. Downhill from their camp, in the valleys below them, desperate, scared people waited for rescue. The firestorm there was brutal.

There was no time for the personal, or for questions that couldn't be answered. There was no time to risk fear making its mark.

He had put aside the dreams of forest teachers and chariot flights in the first shock and ravage of chest pain. And then all of it — the burn, the dreams, flying free — the mystery — was lost with the day's insistence. *Rescues, horses ... broken, lost, dead and retrieved things ... relentless fire and wind ... little rest or food ... the stench and sweat of human fear.* There never was time to do anything but prepare for the inevitable: another day to ride like hell and fight the elements. And to save what and who could be saved. Forgetfulness of the burn was curse and blessing.

But damn ... it's still here! And still BURNING.

A wave of nausea hits him. *Branded.* His throat closes and he spits out bile.

"*Branded!*" He yells it now. He holds the temples of his head to calm himself, hearing the shake in his voice. He can't dismiss anger. Images had been burned into his skin and memory. He tells himself to talk it out, to make it a thing he knows and does not deny.

"Okay, it's a *brand.* ... But with the detail and colors of a tattoo."

He presses his fingertips on his temples, shakes his head to clear his mind and commands himself to breathe normally.

Brands designate ownership, possession. "Am I *possessed?* Owned? No *way.* Not *ever!*" He shouts out in anger, refusing fear. "How ... *possible?* What does it mean? *Why me?*"

As he did that last morning, and must now, he grabs hold of the thoughts threatening to spin out of control.

"Why? How? It's *impossible!* — ENOUGH."

He's never felt victimized. Even if falsely blamed or punished by stresses that are part of being in service to life-and-death emergencies. But now the confusion and pain raise the possibility that he's been *marked.* Stamped and tagged. Burned and branded.

As payment or punishment?

He growls aloud at himself for asking questions without answers.

Thirst hits again, made worse by the fire in his chest. The boy focuses on the sound and smell of river water. Thoughts of his brother somewhere out there — and lost — push him into action.

"*CONAN! Wait for me!*" he yells into the lonely air.

Chapter 4
Strangers

A few yards short of the river, the boy's trained ear picks up soft whips of quiet weeping.

A kid!

He freezes.

A tearful, short moan is audible under the roars of the narrow, deep waterway. It seems to be coming from upriver.

His instincts, sharpened over months of living off the land and in the natural world of mountains, oceans and valleys, are hewn as sharp as those of the horses he wrangles and rides.

He moves forward, hare-quiet.

Another crackled, choked-back, sob.

Conan?!

His heart leaps. He wants to run toward the cry. Cautions himself. He crouches close to the ground. Closes his eyes and concentrates.

No, not Conan. His heart drops.

It's a girl's higher-octave cry. Sadness in it, he analyzes. But no anger and, surprisingly, no fear. Not the cries of a desperate animal.

It's a *kid.* A child resigned to grief and familiar loneliness.

His guess is that she's alone. No threat.

He prepares to advance with expert stealth — but stops himself. *Could be a trap.* A second person, a threat or criminal, could be hiding close by, using the girl as decoy.

The boy shifts his eyes in micro-slinks left and right. Decides he must take the risk.

Without shrubbery or trees to hide behind, he stays as close to the ground as his aching legs allow. He feels under the folds of the jacket tied around his waist for his Swiss Army knife. Unzips the pocket and feels for the case — but doesn't release the blade. He has no idea whether he could cause injury in self-defense. But if there's a girl alone and in trouble, he will act.

Every instinct he's ever known dictates protection of others. He doesn't think of it this way, he never worked out details or ethics. It's always been there: reflexive caretaking, guardianship, at his own risk. It's as natural to him as his hands, or green-blue eyes, or dark tight curls.

The girl doesn't hear him until he's a foot away.

She leaps up from her kneeling position at river's edge, spins towards him. She tries to stand but loses her balance and slips back sideways. The freezing water soaks the sleeve of her black cape as she looks up at the boy with fiercely defensive protectiveness.

He leans over and grasps her hand with gentle strength, pulling her out of the water to set her carefully on the rocky embankment.

*

Anna had gone to the river thirsty, yes. But more because she had hoped her dream was real. She prayed to see Halfling there, in her basket, waiting to be found.

But the Bird-Girl didn't materialize.

Anna exhales her angry disappointment. Rocks herself.

And she weeps. She allows herself to release the desperate emotions of pent-up fear. She thinks how easy it would be to fall into the depths of the freezing water. How easy to surrender to grief and disappear under the pounding froth.

It's a coward's thought, her grandfather had taught, *the wish for an easy death.*

She had drifted a minute, two minutes, between conscious and unconscious choices.

Buck-up, she says to herself, *and live. Or else I die, and lose my dream, my Halfling.* That fear, the loss of her dream, keeps her just short of the edge. Close enough, and far enough away, to remind her of the price of cowardice.

And then she hears a step.

She leaps up, turning in instinctive defense as she rises.

The shock of what she sees causes her to lose her balance.

A red hat!

Pulled from the river, she sees nothing else. Not water, dirt, or the haze of sky that spins and mixes with her own tears. She sees nothing, except ... *the red hat!*

With rapid, instinctive agility, she re-balances. Poised to run, she hears the dream refrain repeat.

The boy in the red hat. Find him!

Her heart pounds, and her mouth slacks open, speechless. She digs her threadbare shoes into the wet slimy ground. Her hands ball into boxer's fists.

Under no circumstances will she run. She'll play this out.

*

"Whoa," he says with a small laugh.

He sees the girl fully for the first time.

Probably thirteen or fourteen. Could pass for a twelve-year-old.

She's super-thin, with chiseled, impressive, muscles that define her shoulders and biceps and flex under her cape and leggings. Her tousled hair, cut short just below her chin, is a tawny dark brown. Flecks of gold sparkle through spiral curlicues that spring from the crown of her head like the petals of a layered chrysanthemum. Her dark brown skin, dotted with river water, shimmers with the same iridescent gold as the highlights of her dark curls.

"I'm not going to hurt you." The boy pitches his voice low, confident, controlled. He holds the knife out in front of him to show her it's folded. He deliberately tucks it into his Levi's pocket, then drops his hands to his sides, waggling his fingers loosely to indicate he's not a threat.

"*Not so quick!*" Her voice is sharp and strong. "Throw that knife at my feet."

He stares at her for one heartbeat. Then reaches back into his pocket and flicks the knife so it lands in front of her.

Anna doesn't lower her gaze from the boy's face. She's stock-still, wide-eyed. Only her chest rising and falling lets him know she's breathing hard. Her wet sleeve drips quiet splashes to the ground.

Her confused mind wobbles between options. She hasn't hoped for anything for so long, she doesn't recognize the urge, the possibility that one of her dreams might come true. The assault on her senses demands her to stay inside herself. *Do not show fear.*

She grounds her solar plexus and stares into the stranger's eyes.

He drops to his knees, his eyes remaining on hers. Slowly, he folds his legs into a half lotus. "No threat here." His voice is near-silent. "What's your name?"

Nothing.

"My name is Leo."

Nothing.

He tries again. "I have no idea where I am, how I got here, or how long I've been … I guess … *asleep?*" He shrugs, stifles a sigh. He waits for response, and asks again, "What's your name?"

Anna yells to take the quiver out of her voice. "*Where'd you get that hat?*" she blurts, her stance balanced for battle. The shrill tone of fear she hears embarrasses her.

Leo takes off the dirty, crumpled hat. He examines it, remembering how Conan had teased him about it. "Bruh! Not a ball-cap. Not a cowboy hat. It's not even a teen beanie! It's kinda like a backwards jockey's hat, Bro. Or one o' those old paperboy hats!"

Anna, as observant as he, and better-trained in picking up unspoken nuances, sees a wet glisten in Leo's eyes.

He rolls the hat in his chapped and cracked hands. "My grandmother." He smiles, sits up tall. "My Granny gave it to me. Right before she … went away. She, uh … had a dream of me wearing it while riding a horse."

Leo chooses not to tell her that Granny had dreamt of the troubles that were to come. But he can see that the girl needs assurance, so he allows himself to go on a riff.

"And then six months later, the same hat as in her dream showed up as a gift from a medicine man visiting our ranch. 'Don't lose it.' The guy was super serious about it. 'Keep it safe.' Granny told me that, too. She said, 'When the time comes, Leo — and you'll know when that is — put the hat on, and never take it off.'"

He thinks about this a minute. Then adds, "Seemed funny ... But, then, you know, the changes came, one after another. All those crazy rains. Then militias and uprisings in cities. And the damned winds." He stops and shifts eyes up and away from her, considering the sky.

The girl doesn't blink or move. She waits, still and attentive.

"And the earthquakes," he begins again, "shook us until the ground we walked on, *slept* on, cracked right under us. And, worse than rains, the drought. *Dry*, day after dry day, until even the effing native grasses were fried crisp. And then the fires started. We helped people escape out of the cities. With trucks, vans, even our motorcycles. Until fuel ran out and highways caved from the quakes. And then we had no choice. We rode horses to rescues. Only a few of us could ride."

She watches him gulp hard.

He forces a weak upturn of his full lips. He says, "That was when I remembered the hat. My dad and brother teased me at first, but Conan — my brother — and me were sure of Granny's dreams and stories. Wasn't long before even Dad realized people associated *help* with this hat. And, well, the three of us..." he shrugs, "...word spread somehow."

He is suddenly aware of the girl's sideways squint. It's as if she waits for someone else. Or listens for agreement.

"Nothing special about me. Not saying that. I'm just another helper. But people remembered the hat." His voice cracks from bits of dust and from not talking for days. He stops to cough and clear his throat.

Before he can continue, Anna blurts out, "My dream! ... I had this dream!" As if the dream that bumped and pushed her tired brain into action was somehow his fault.

He hears her confusion, doesn't get where she's headed, but doesn't move away.

"And ..." She tries insisting, "*Someone* in the dream said, 'Find the boy in the *red hat*.' And, and, you're *here* ... But how? ... And you're not a *boy!*" Anna is furious. Frustrated. She was wrenched from her dream. "You're ... *too damn big!*"

She doesn't say to Leo, *in my dream ... my Halfling baby said you'd save me.* Being *saved* is too dependent a thought to consider. *Trust* sounds a false scritch-scratch irritation on her acute internal hearing. Which is always tuned to self-defense. *Save me.* Those words scare her more than the emptiness and loss of everything familiar in the landscape. And more than the alone-ness she knows so well.

She keeps her fists clenched. She maintains her boxer's stance, balanced and resolute.

Leo nods, thinking to himself, *Yes. I'm too damn big.* The boy in him had given way to the man while still young.

To her, he says, "I'm seventeen, I think. But I have no idea what month or day it is, so I could've turned eighteen. And anyway … maybe boys have to be men in this time."

He means to engage her, but his words come out flat, and too adult and certain.

She doesn't respond.

"So, what's your name?" Leo asks again.

"*Anna!*" she barks.

"Good, okay." He ignores the aggressive tone. "Anna, I'm going to get up. Not going to hurt you. Don't want to leave a kid here alone, but I have to find my brother. He's close. Hopefully asleep. … I feel him alive." Leo shakes himself free of worry. "But no time to talk. So, look, I need you to come with me. Understand?"

Her face quivers. She tries to judge him, and the situation.

Gently but firmly, he presses her. "There's no one around. It's not safe to leave you alone. And look … I can't wait, either."

The situation is as impossible for her as it is for him. She stares.

He waits.

His reliable patience ebbs. He counts to ten, then says, "Are you in or out?" It's the question his Dad had asked before every single one of their rescue-rides. Meant to sound like a choice, but it was not a question either brother had ever seriously considered.

Leo isn't sure whether he or this girl Anna has any choice, either, but to be together.

She walks forward a step, bends down, picks up his knife and hands it to him. Her arm is extended as far as possible to give herself safe space from him.

"Good," he says aloud. Tells himself, *Maybe.*

He concludes she's a loner. *But … she's a fighter, too.* Useless as her boxing stance may be, he's impressed she doesn't run or surrender. *Right now, strong and independent is a plus.* Taking in her wiry, muscular frame, he thinks to himself, *she's like a deer. Same dark wide eyes. Twitchy. Not ready to run … but not really settled.*

He stands, slowly and deliberately.

Leo clocks her attire. She wears black leggings and turtleneck with frayed cuffs showing under the cape. Black skate sneakers, well-worn, one shoe laced with dirty white string and the other barely held together with brown cording catching every other hole. He categorizes his instinctual information in shutter-quick images.

"Have any food, or anything to carry river water in?"

She stares, as if she has to think hard.

"I don't know how I got here, either!" she finally spurts. Anna is combative, but wants him to know, too. "It's *crazy!* But I, I, think I was *blown* here, just lifted off my feet and … and *blown. Days* ago!"

"It doesn't sound crazy to me," Leo's agreement calms them both. "I was picked up off my horse. I was riding full speed and blown! Up? Forward? Back? No idea. So yeah, *crazy!*"

She doesn't altogether digest what he said. Her own words race ahead of her thoughts. "But I *know* this river, even without trees and the markers that were always here. For, like, forever-generations." She swirls around, amazed at the destruction and emptiness. She shrugs animatedly, shaking her head.

"Roaring Forks River, that's this one here, it's not too far from my Gramps' place, in Northeast Montana. Well, kinda' far if we were driving, just not too far if we were flying!" She doesn't intend humor, but he smiles, and she smiles back, tight-lipped. "My dream said to find 'the boy in the red hat.' ... Make any sense to you?" Her voice is high, shrill. Her look is anxious. This admission, repeated, is a big one for her. She damns her own shakiness but wants to believe in something or someone in this barren new world. She especially wants to believe in her own dream.

Northeast Montana. Leo's gaze lifts past her to the torn and tattered, unfamiliar landscape. "We helped people escape from burnt-out towns near our home in California." He exhales, his breath bigger and heavier than he intended. "People looked for this red hat to make sure they found the team with horses that could get them out of whatever hell was goin' on ..." He laughs ruefully, mindful of his confusion, and hers, too. "The hat became like a symbol of hope ..." he shuffles a toe in the dirt, "or, like, 'urban legend.' Maybe that somehow made it into your dreams?"

There is no flinch or squint of non-belief from her. She listens for something unnamed.

"We're a family of dreamers. We respect dreams," Leo ventures, "and the people they speak to." He waits a heartbeat, so she hears his sincerity. "Whether we understand them or not."

No comment.

Anna imagines Halfling and hears the immediacy and import of her message. But she can't tell Leo. The dreams are her one possession and true north. When she can't feel herself, when the night is over-long, and odds stack against her, the baby in the basket and her mystical messages are what she trusts.

He waits.

She doesn't tell him that dreams saved her life in the past. Just days before, the baby's strange voice had called to her with insistence, *"Run. Get out, now!"*

Anna had run from her mother's upside-down life for the last time.

She thinks, but doesn't say, *I know more about dreams, their movement and intrusion, their connections and symbols and messages, than you could know in two lifetimes.* But it is true.

Anna grits her teeth. "Okay. ... Yeah, I'm in." She slips her hands behind her back, so he won't see her crossed fingers. "No, no food, no water, no container. Just ... this."

From the folds of her cape, she takes a brown leather pouch and pulls loose the string that gathers it. The contents spill into her hands. Leo can see she's holding a pair of well-cut cylinder crystals, each two inches long. And a cobalt blue, egg-shaped rock nestles next to what looks like a whistle on a leather cord. A chunk of amethyst cut as if it just broke itself from the earth is curled in her palm, too, next to a miniature bronze statue Leo recognizes as Tara, goddess of compassion. Next, Anna pulls from the pouch a short, downy eagle feather, tied to a stick of sage. She rubs the feather until its ruffled edges flatten.

Last, she removes a red swatch of cloth wrapping a sticky, half-eaten fruit leather.

Leo laughs, "Same things my grandmother would have in her pocket. Well, not the fruit leather. But all the rest! She'd totally dig your cape, too."

It's an odd compliment, but he feels moved by commonalities, things that bridge strangeness. *We all touch the Oneness of connection,* he was taught. *Give mystery the right to declare its presence.*

Anna is confused as to why she shares her private talismans with this stranger. She stares at her hand with a stern scowl. Silently, she warns herself, *Stay alert. Vigilance!* Trust is a luxury for a lonely girl, especially this girl. She quickly puts the eagle whistle on its leather cord around her neck.

The boy considers that these tokens may be Anna's few treasures, her sole belongings. He senses her awkwardness in the ensuing silence. "Better save that fruit leather. It may be the only food you see for a while."

She stuffs everything back into their hiding place, her voluminous pockets. Then she licks the sugar from her fingers. Leo realizes she may be even younger than he thought.

He stifles a tired sigh. "Anyway, Anna. I love crystals, grew up with them, in the house and the garden. My family always said that the rock world blesses and stabilizes natural magic. Trees and rocks, especially crystallized ones, are the best citizens on the planet. My brother collects them." He waits for a response. Nothing. "Eagle feathers," he says, with a deliberate directness, "carry prayers to heaven. We'll need those, too."

Rattled by his intimacy, and fearful of closeness, she wants to defend herself with smart-ass-smack-talk confidence: *Heck yes, fool! Eagles are one of my totems! You know what a totem even is? I was raised with Eagle Dancers, slept on beds of eagle down. If I call on my spirits, they'll swoop down and gouge your eyes out!*

She wants the rush of a stinging, foul-mouthed response to bolster her wobbly position with this large, dark-haired boy with kind eyes. But she's been so alone, she's afraid of too many words. So, she swallows her nasty thoughts.

"Okay, yeah," she blurts. "I can find your brother. I'm good at finding stuff and people. I'm fast, you won't have to wait up for me." With a reflexive taunt, she adds, "Probably run faster than you anyway."

"Yeah? Good!" He laughs, "Probably right. No one ever asked me to be on the track team."

Leo likes her boldness. *She's more like an underfed mountain lion than scared prey.*

He studies the grey, sunless sky and landscape. Considers which direction they might take to look for Conan. He asks the girl whether she remembers other places, shelters, like the mining shack he found himself in.

Anna doesn't answer. She is scanning up and down the river. Abruptly she bends down, grabs a handful of dirt, and tosses it in the air. No wind picks it up.

She starts a fast-paced jog along the riverbank with her eyes on the distant mountain that can be made out even on this shrouded, murky day. Three jagged peaks, linked together, spike the sky on the far-left horizon.

The boy follows. He watches Anna stop several times to study the river flow and the mountains, muttering to herself. She's used to the outdoors, Leo silently assesses. That's clear from the way she uses her senses, and how she observes her environment.

But she seems confused, all of a sudden. Leo doesn't like not knowing *why*. Silent tears well the girl's eyes, and she turns her face from him. Her hands fidget inside her cape as she taps her treasures for support. Her tension creeps back, taut and angry.

"What's up, Anna?" He keeps his voice calm and low. His own inner anxiety warns him that something is terribly wrong.

She doesn't know what to say or how to say it. She fights back tears as she massages the crystals in her cape pocket, pacing. Suddenly she stops and faces Leo.

"Yeah." Her words come out in tight, worried bunches. "There were other mines, and plenty of hiding places. But now? Nothing is right! It's impossible ... but the river, *this* river ... something's wrong. I've spent tons of time on it ... I *know* it, like back-of-my-*hand* know it. Every eddy and turn. See the mountains over there?" Anna points at the far peaks. "Those are the Great Raggeds. I've hiked, camped, hunted, *lived* in 'em. But ... but ..." She stammers. Defensive, she half-yells, "They're on the *wrong* side of the river! ... You get it? They're on the *wrong side!*"

She scans past him. She knows she sounds crazy, because she feels crazy. "They should be on *this* side of the river. See? I mean," Anna shakes her head, "it ... can't be."

She paces again. Then stops, looking fixedly at the river. Gazes up at the peaks. Runs her tongue over her teeth, clenching and unclenching her fists habitually. Anna's cheeks burn, and she grits her jaw to fight childish frustration.

"And the river ... it's *crazy*, Leo, but it ran north to *south*. Now it runs south to *north*. And, like ... uphill? And the Sun is hidden, but rises in what I woulda' called the *northwest*, right? ... Dude, everything is in the *wrong place*. It's as if ... as if ... I don't *know* ..."

She hates the sound of her voice. *Crazy girl making up CRAP.* But she's lost for any rational explanation. Confusion over the one thing she was confident she knows — nature — pushes her to a shaky brink of desperation.

Leo tenses, not over her confusion, but because he knows she's right. He turns and tries to find the Sun through the haze and wind-borne debris. Leo, like Anna, is a graduate student of the natural world. He frowns at the sky.

She's right ... but how?

Anna searches aloud for an explanation. "I don't *understand* ... everything is ..."

In the twisted upset of moved mountains and backwards-flowing rivers, after her most recent weeks of aloneness, hiding out, sleeping wherever, eating whatever, Anna is now perilously close to exhausting her last defenses. She wants badly to be part of something; to help and belong. *Find the brother*, she tells herself. *Be valuable. Have someone think I am useful.*

Leo takes a slow, precise scan of the debris-strewn horizon... and finds the Sun's dirty haze, barely visible. "*Insane*, unbelievable, but ..." He shakes his head, squeezing his eyes to focus. "It's not in the east. Everything's ... wrong. Everything's almost ... upside down. It's as if the Earth ... half-flipped over. Or it made a weird wobble, or a slip. A shift ... of its axis?"

Anna seems relieved that Leo doesn't deny what she sees.

The boy walks a few feet towards the mountains and methodically measures the distance of open sky to Sun, back to the horizon, trying to determine cardinal directions.

He blows out his cheeks. Points. "*That* way would previously be identified as north. If that's north, then south..." He draws a direct line, finger in the air, tracing his sight. He narrows his eyes to the Great Ragged Mountains.

He's silent for minutes, causing Anna to shift onto the balls of her feet.

"What the hell. You're *not* crazy Anna. Look," he throws the palms of his hands up. "I heard once in school, not a prediction really, but ... ya' know ... an idea that some scientists had. They thought ... a hard click-*slip* of Earth on its axis *may* have happened, centuries ago. But it was, you know, someone's hypothesis."

He knows it's too bizarre a thought that such a thing could have happened again, if it ever happened at all in the first place. And certainly, a quick conclusion would be foolish. But after the last two years, nothing seems impossible.

"There was evidence, they said, that the Earth moved radically on its axis, like, I dunno, maybe twelve thousand years ago. Not the inch or two it does in a regular year, but like a 180-degree flip. Most scientists argued the theory down, said it was never proven … But my teacher said only a few feet of movement would cause devastating destruction. A *radical* shift would put oceans on land and pull mountains under water. At the very least, rivers would run backwards. Would the Sun and Moon change their rising and setting directions? That's disaster movie stuff. It didn't impress me at the time as possible. There was no real proof it could ever happen. But …" He scans the sky and the mountains again. "Something big, maybe terrible, would flip the directions. … And …"

He doesn't finish aloud the words in his mind.

It would kill billions.

Chapter 5
Phenomena

Leo turns his head to study the endless acres of gritty, barren, torn-up earth and the grey, unyielding sky that meets it all around. The river isn't blue or green, but a conforming steel-brown color, just like the tumbled earth.

Inestimable pounds of earth, shaken and thrown and blown in the air. That's what my teacher said about the giant quakes that split California.

Aloud, he says, "It looks like the mountains were thrown in the air!" *Blanketing the river and sky?* Clouds hang like a row of miner's overalls strung on an invisible line, seeming to make the sky heavy with black-smeared coal and the sweat of fossilized grime. "I've never seen the sky meet the mountains like this. The hills and rocks, they aren't separate, there's no line or demarcation."

Leo's thoughts drift back and forth between forgotten school lessons and the visible destruction around them in this new, near-unrecognizable, world.

He looks down at the girl, and then at his own hands.

"So, you don't know now which direction to search, right? Look, Anna, it's not your fault, I'm not angry. You're not responsible for what's happened. *Damn*, the earth's a *shambles* of itself! It's not our fault, whatever happened. … I just need to find Conan!" He hears his own anxiety. *Concern can turn to panic.* He has to control his breath and focus his mind. "Anna, here's what I do, when I don't understand… I meditate. Or at least pay attention, get mindful … and see what comes to me. Information, for me comes in pictures, word-messages. Even music. Kinda like pressing 'refresh' on a keyboard. Gets me focused. It's not perfect and may not work. But right now, it's all I've got."

She stares at him a beat too long for his comfort, but then nods slowly and closes her eyes. "My Gramps," Anna murmurs, then looks up at Leo. He sees a light in her dark irises, as if some confusion has cleared. "Gramps lives in those mountains. *He* taught me." She piles on her words in a rapid-fire stream. "And Nonny too. Not in the way other people meditate. They taught me to gather information from the natural world. And follow streams of energy threads. They taught me to trust my people's ancient knowledge, honor it in the Lakota way. And …"

She stops her slew of words before they lead her into trouble.

She wants to stay with Leo, and she wants to agree with the immediate emergency to find his brother. But she *can't* be tight and close to him. She's a loner, she knows it as her natural state of being.

Vigilance, she repeats to herself.

This screwed-up environment is her native land. Its upheaval adds to her uncertainty. She can't explain why, but Anna feels compelled to help set it right. At the same time, she feels oddly responsible for whatever Fate brings to Leo and his brother.

"*Anyway,* yeah." Anna stares into the silence. "Me too, I trained for times like this, too. ... Look Leo, I'm a helluva tracker. Big game, small game, people. Gramps taught me. But ..." She studies the windswept ground with its whispery squiggle-lines and colorless dust residue. "There's nothing left to track. The winds have blown every mark away."

After taking a quiet moment to acknowledge her anxiety and admit to himself his own, Leo shifts his attention inward. He sits on the ground, cross-legged, places his hands face up on his knees, closes his eyes and controls his breath. He glides into silent meditation.

Anna gazes at the boy, muttering in Lakota under her breath. She prays to Great Spirit, to Tunkashila, and to the ancestors. She bows at her waist to honor the spirits of the cardinal directions — but hesitates, squints, and rubs her eyes. She's not completely confident where east, west, north, south have moved.

She shivers from choked-back fear. *Please be alive, Gramps. Please hear me. Help!*

And then swiftly and fluidly, Anna drops into a cross-legged sit, facing Leo. She pulls her treasure bundle back out of the cape pocket and lays the talismans in front of her. She's done this meditation countless times, coming as she does from traditions and legacies of diverse spiritual cultures. But she's never before practiced in front of a stranger.

She resists unease. Breathes with conscious awareness. She slips with liquid grace out of her frenetic, frantic worry into welcome silence.

In seconds, the familiar cocoon widens. It welcomes her into an internal vastness never experienced until now. A flash of wonder tickles her curiosity. She deepens her breathing to *detach from emotion, be one with infinity*. That's the instruction her grandmother, a Zen teacher, had insisted upon.

One, two full-lung inhales and exhales. Stillness pervades her spirit ... for no longer than a minute.

Jolt! Sizzle!

An electric charge runs the length of her spine, from her tailbone to the crown of her head.

Shock!

Electricity flies down her limbs to her fingertips and toes. Anna's mouth slams shut before a gasp or cry can escape. She reels forward from her waist, shimmying with waves of energy. Tears fill her eyes. Her lips tremble, and heat rises in her neck and head. Her face flushes. Her fingers splay and then immediately clench without her command. Her mouth gapes open as if to scream, but no sound escapes.

Straight and sharp, a cobalt-blue light sparks above her head. Instantly it drops and expands into an aura that surrounds her. A tingling vortex throbs, encases and protects her.

Anna throws back her head and feels she *becomes* the cobalt, and it becomes her. She holds her place on Earth. She is solid. Heat flows into her chest and heart. Heavy golden warmth expands to fill the width, breadth and height of her lungs.

Her sloe-shaped dark eyes brim with hot tears. *Phenomena! A presence, a power.* She gasps silently, *Gramps? Bird-Girl? Are you here? Nonny, are you doing this?*

Zzzing!

Leo grabs the dirt around him to stay steady. The force of energy is strong enough to lift him straight off the ground, but he centers his core. His body quakes from skeleton to skin and back again. He feels as if an invisible hand straightens his spine and aligns his neck and head. His pulse quickens. His first-responder training tells him *too-rapid. A force.* The flow of energy feels like a river un-dammed. *But steady.*

Ow! Damn! Leo, nervous, confused, holds his breath and searches for calm — for one count, two, three — and then expels it in one giant puff.

Trust, an inner voice, not his own, commands.

Leo nods. *NO fear! I'm NOT scared ... I'm electrified.* But he's uninjured and centered. Calm, confident.

He can't pry his eyes open to more than slits. Anna is barely visible in the swarm of hazy blue smoke. The same cobalt energy surrounds her that swirls around and flies through Leo.

Time halts, as if the entire universe gathers within the two of them and draws a collective inhale. The strange energy builds, crescendos, ebbs and dissipates. In its wake, a visceral hum radiates around them, warm and supportive.

Slowly, groggily at first, then sharply awake, the two of them open their eyes and point in the same direction.

"He's *that* way! Close!"

Their jubilant laugh is a balm. The blue haze between them evaporates into a crystal clarity.

Anna shouts, "He's awake! It's *him,* right? Tall, skinny dude hiding behind some boulders thrown down from the mountain?"

Leo, with awe and wonder, shouts back "Yeah, *right!* On the other side of the river! He's closer to the peaked mountains! He's inside some kind of outcropping!"

"*Yes!*" cries Anna. "But ... how did we both see the *same* thing at the *same* time ... and, *together?* That's what just happened, right? How?!"

Leo stares at Anna for five seconds at least. He questions himself about this odd girl with her crystal talismans and unfamiliar familiarity, seeing the same surprise on Anna's face he feels on his own. Normally he's comfortable with uncertainty, fascinated by mystery and magic. But he likes answers and solutions.

Shaking his head slowly, he responds, "I have *no* idea." He extends a hand to help her up. "You felt that electric energy? Right?"

His voice, emphatic with the timber of incredulousness, makes Anna laugh again until the sound of her own rare joy shocks her to a self-conscious hiccup. She springs out of crossed legs straight onto her feet, ignoring the boy's offer of assistance.

"What *was* that we both felt?" Leo asks. "Coincidence?"

She throws her palms up. "My people don't believe in coincidence. And well ... I don't either!" She shakes her head, and the golden flecks in her dark curls sparkle and bounce.

He nods in agreement and wants to say more about the strange zaps of electricity — but a residual hum, a high-pitched current, suddenly spins through the foot of space between them.

Anna gasps, rising to her tiptoes. "You hear it, right? You felt that? *Damn,* Leo!"

He, too, feels indescribably elated by the bizarre frequency. His face lighting up, he directs, "Hurry, Anna, grab your things. Maybe your crystals and feather channeled that message." He grins. He half means it, half doesn't. With his wide-open, no-enemies smile — the one he's had his entire seventeen years — he tilts his head and tells her, "We'll work it out later. Right now, let's move. You need to meet my brother."

He looks forward and brings the rapid, roiling water into focus.

"As soon as we find a way across this river."

Chapter 6
The River

Move!

The word rings in Anna's ears. It's a relief to be in motion, with or without sufficient answers or a plan. Blood and adrenalin pump into her legs, heart, and mind. *Movement* is her passion.

She runs yards ahead of Leo along the riverbank for half an hour. She leaps over protrusions and glides across uneven ground, the same ground that causes Leo to trip and bump.

He huffs aloud, "*Ugh.*" Then catches up to her and asks how she's doing.

Anna squints at him sideways.

Leo laughs between gulps for air. "OK, yeah, you *move* girl!"

Move. She's strong-willed and focused in motion.

Her heart-mind becomes one active pulse in spite of food deprivation and the rapid pace. *This is it. A real adventure.* She breathes into the cells of her muscles. *Adventure with purpose.* The kind her grandparents spoke of. Someone needs saving in a strange land, and she and Leo have no supplies but their wits. No maps. Only her vivid dreams and their shared visions to show them the way.

Perfect, she thinks.

Anna loves adventure stories, real or imagined. *You'd be proud of me now, Gramps.* She sends that message out on psychic airwaves. And hopes it doesn't sound proud. *Gramps would hate that bragging shit ... And, oh yeah, swearing too!* Gramps reveres humility as equal to courage and integrity.

Leo calls over, "You say something?"

She shakes her head, *no.*

Humility is the True Way, Gramps always says. She punches her fist to her heart. *If we forget we are human, if we think we are better, bigger, wiser, than others, we're in a Grand Illusion. Be humble. Not with false humility but with true knowledge that we are all human, we are all one.* His words are etched in her heart and mind and memory.

"Gramps, you'd like Leo," she whispers into the ethers of family connection. She sneaks a sideways glance as they run along the rocky, tumbled and slippery bank. *He's not proud, but confident and brave. I can be too. Maybe I am. Is that true or false humility?*

Anna slows her pace to thank the Halfling dream, as her Native people do.

Leo asks again if she's okay as he catches up.

"*Yes!*" she shouts. She darts ahead. She doesn't want attention. "Just need *water!*"

She pivots mid-sprint and bends to drink. She thanks the river for its water and its enduring spirit. In her Lakota language, she thanks her grandparents. *Wopila*. She thanks them for lessons of river secrets. And for teaching her how to pay attention. She's learned to stay aware, to respect and honor and *be one* with the natural forces.

She blushes, suddenly self-conscious. She had stopped praying and singing the traditional songs in her rage years. *How long has it been?* She was pulled by her mother's constant addictions. And dragged through toxic cities. *Fucking dumps.* She was punished — no matter if her mother was up or down.

But now, driven by the promise of her dream, hanging with the red-hat boy, and being close to Gramps' mountain, she slips into the world of mystical traditions to which she was born. *I'm on it, Gramps! This is a true adventure. Wait for me!* Anna is convinced she feels his eyes on her. *Stay alive, I'm on my way!* She is certain that, in spite of the upside-down trees and shredded terrain, Gramps will know *exactly* where they are.

All at once, she stops short. Looking at the river, she is unexpectedly unsure of that, herself.

"*Leo!*" she shouts over the rumbling rocks.

A few paces ahead now, Leo stops, turns. He's impressed at how quickly she catches up to him. "Speed demon! You cover a lot of ground fast!" He laughs and slaps her outstretched palm.

"You were right!" She ignores his compliment, but he notices the pink blush under her amber skin. "The river somehow, like … shifted. It made a backward U-turn!" She steps back to get a better angle on the river. "See how it hooks?" She points. "Backs up a twist, then whips forward? The water is running the wrong way, south to north, like I thought before. But the mountains haven't moved — they're on the right side! I mean the *correct* side, where they're supposed to be! It's the *river* that's cut new ground. It *twisted*, backed up, and … dug itself … deeper."

She pauses a second, studying the impossible. Anna turns to Leo expectantly, inviting him to fill in the blanks.

He can't. But he nods. "Okay. Got it."

She stares at him a second before looking back to the water. "But now I see that, I know where we cross. There was a natural bridge of *humongous* boulders. That would be around the next bend."

She takes off, amped but not frazzled, before he has time to question her. He shrugs at his own lack of comparable speed and her effortless endurance. *Freakish.*

She stops a half mile ahead of him. "It's, like, totally jumbled and near gone … But they're here, alright," she calls over her shoulder to him. "And … they've moved!" Hands on her hips, nervy again, she searches the shoreline.

He catches up to her on the spongy riverbank. Anna is staring at a group of enormous boulders, scattered in a tumultuous stretch to the other side of the river. Her cape is pulled back, and Leo notices how reed-thin she is. But that particular boldness of hers is obvious, too. *She's got her take-command stance. Good. We'll need all the boldness we can get.*

"The boulders used to be in a perfect single file," she explains. Her grandfather had told her the legend of a lovesick giant who lifted these rocks from the mountains and created a bridge to help his beautiful Indian princess escape from the bad guys.

"That was one story I never believed," she adds cynically. "If the giant was so tough, why didn't he just wade in and save her? Ha! Probably afraid he'd break a pinky. Typical manly coward. *Anyway*, this is where we *shoulda'* been able to cross. But there's no lovesick giant to move these rocks into a perfect bridge."

Leo and Anna walk, trot, walk again. Up ten yards, back two. They eye every possible angle that allows a crossing. Debate the few options in quick phrases, then run back and forth along the embankment a last time.

A distance of at least half a dozen feet separates each jagged boulder, sometimes more. A natural, safe bridge no longer exists. It was blown apart by whatever moved the earth while they slept. What's left is an unevenly spaced and dangerous collection of slippery possibilities.

"No clear route," Leo mutters to himself.

Without ropes or guide tools, or smaller rocks or boards to fill the gaps, jumping from boulder to boulder may be possible in a few places. But not the entire way across. An unforgiving force of water rages around the rocks.

"Treacherous at best," Leo says under his breath. *If not utterly deadly*, he doesn't say.

They had traveled miles to get to this spot. The grey day, ominous and heavy, is receding with unnatural rapidity. Leo believes that if he doesn't find Conan before night's blindness, his brother will be tempted to break his promise and go searching for him. The chances of further separation are too great for Leo to risk.

"Conan n' me…" He swallows hard. "We're never really apart."

Leo doesn't tell her Conan's fear of abandonment is a greater threat than any fear for his own life. He's protective of Conan, proud of who his brother is. He won't give away Conan's vulnerabilities.

Anna's head is turned to study the boulders and river from every angle.

"Ok," Leo says to her. "We have to try it. Here's how it is. The water's freezing. Fall in, and we've got seconds before hypothermia sets in."

He squints across the river to assess the speed of the rushing water. The hydraulic force of downward swirls around the boulders creates a vortex of white caps. His brain clicks through fast and efficient measurements. He weighs options like the first responder he's become. Reminds himself, *don't dismiss dangers. Just don't let them stop you.*

He tells Anna, his voice flat, no drama, "If we don't immediately freeze, there's danger of being carried underwater by that deep, sucking churn. This is *damned fast* water. It can easily slam us into the boulders or pull us under."

The girl turns back to face him squarely and blinks once, unafraid.

Leo skips a handful of rocks across the river. They watch the turbulent froth pluck at the water-sprayed air and swallow the rocks before any of them can skip twice.

He purses his wide, thick, bowed lips and reasons strategy.

"Yup, strong velocity. ... So ... we cross solo. At least that way, there's a chance to help each other in case of a problem."

Leo had trained in swift-water rescue in the early days of the incessant rains. Storms had become El Ninos, and later tempests had turned into unprecedented monsoons. Droughts followed. Overgrown grasses had dried down past their roots, perfect feed for the next season of consuming fires. Two years later, torrential rains started again.

People had said, "It's *impossible!*"

It wasn't.

The best meteorologists hadn't predicted the deluge that washed mountain slopes into cities. Entire populations that for a century had rested serenely on gentle mountains were dumped, unmercifully, into the tsunami sea.

Leo learned that a dribble of lazy creek can unexpectedly overrun ten-foot-high banks in less time than it had taken him to hang a worm on a hook to fish that same water only a year before. He had studied oceans that defied tide schedules, and rogue waves that rose precipitously after polar ice melts.

He tells Anna now, "The drowning power of whirlpools in flash floods is ... unstoppable."

The boy had seen for himself the ways that water, in its beauty and majesty, can surprise the best oceanographers, boat captains, river runners, and hurricane chasers. But he'd had equipment, ropes, and other helpers. He'd had swift boats and pulleys, lifesavers with wave runners. And, better than any equipment, he'd trained rescue teams.

There's only one way across this river. And that's solo.

Leo weighs his options one more time. He looks at the landscape around them for anything helpful. Tree limbs left from years of incessant and powerful winds are bent and broken, too small for use, or half-buried under pounds of dirt. Tree stumps are all that's left of what must once have been thick forest.

Nothing.

He unzips his pockets. Rustles through them. Finds his Swiss Army knife. Wet matches. A bit of rope to repair a horse's reins. *Useless!*

His inhale sounds like a sigh to Anna.

The boy crouches low again to get as many views of the river terrain and its dangers as possible.

Anna is impatient to move. "Look, Leo! I can make it across those boulders!" Her nerves are stretched taut. She wants to say, but doesn't, *Enough already!* She is used to being on her own. She frazzles against her need to escape. "I've jumped worse gaps. *I swear!* Gramps gave me harder and higher jumps than these. They were super slippery! And wider than these. ... *Look.* It's scary, I know." She speaks fast, hoping to put his mind at ease. Wants him to know she's not a fool. "But I'm going for it, Leo! I'll show you how to follow me."

He hears confidence and exasperation, and her story rings true to him. He narrows and widens his eyes. "A river is true to only itself." He tells her that a fast-water expert told him that. And had drowned the next day. "He was pulling a family out of a van that went over a cliff. The day before, the river that killed him was a dry desert channel."

No response.

She's distracted, he thinks. He adds, "It was a flash flood."

She nods and shifts left, right, left. Bounces on the balls of her feet like a lightweight boxer.

He tells her he'd half-drowned, himself, during training and in rescues. It had taught him to respect natural forces.

She seems unimpressed.

He adds, "My trainer used to say, 'Wild rivers have no sympathy for human hopes and desires.'"

She shrugs.

He gives up the lesson. Leo blows out his cheeks. He bends over so they're eye-to-eye. "You up for this?"

"We don't have a choice, Leo. We *both* saw your brother on the other side of the river. There's no bridge left. We're lucky the boulders are here at all. How else do we get to him before dark?"

He hears her nerves, but no fear.

No other option, he says to himself. He doesn't like the odds. If either one of them should fall, there would be little chance of being saved by the other. Given his experience, he might have a chance to save *her*. But at her size, it would be impossible for her to return the favor.

"Geez, Leo, let's *move!*"

Leo hesitates. But without a better plan, he agrees to let her go first.

Before he can come up with a strategy, Anna has her cape off. She ties it around her waist and secures her pocket treasures, then removes her skate shoes. "Bare feet are the only way," she says. She tries to tie her shoes over the neck of her cape.

"I'll take the shoes," Leo tells her. "When I follow, I'll toss them across from the first or second boulder. This is one powerful river. But it's not so wide I can't throw 'em."

He scans up, down, across the river. Notes a braiding channel that connects a foot above one of the boulders they'll traverse. He calculates where tree debris juts out and the boulders make whirlpools. "If anything falls into the swirl, it's crushed." *Or anyone*, he doesn't say aloud.

He notes a series of rapids, yards before and after the boulders. "There are always hidden dangers in swift water."

Anna looks up, irritated. "You *always* worry this much?"

He laughs. "Okay, okay, I'll shut up!"

Anna, always ready for a confrontation, is surprised. But Leo knows that if he goes first and falls in, he won't be of any use to the thin, edgy, girl at his side. "I have to let you go first."

He says a silent prayer. *Whomever-Whatever, please be there for her.* He swears under his breath at the lack of perfect gods or safe choices.

Leo ties Anna's shoelaces together and hangs them around his neck. He wraps and re-ties the jacket around his waist. He argues and loses the fight to carry her cape. *She's small but mighty ... damn!* He rivets a serious focus straight into her exotic black eyes.

"I'll wait until you clear the other side, Anna, before I follow you. If you slip ..." She begins to protest. He cuts her off mid-sentence. "I know, I know, you won't. But still, we need a plan."

Anna wants to deliver another pushback, but she curbs her instinct. Dropping her argument, she breathes hard and tries to be as respectful to the boy as he is to her.

Trust. A growl in her mind startles her. It sounds like her Grandfather, strong and familiar. The word repeats. *Trust!* She blinks to focus.

Checking but not controlling the irritation in her voice, she says to Leo, "Okay, dude. Plan?"

Leo, happy to have her attention, answers, "Anything happens and you end up in the river, move away from the first few boulders as best you can. The third one doesn't have as dangerous a current around it. The others could suck a person into 'em. I've seen boats smash against boulders that big, so ..." She rolls her eyes. He ignores it. "... anything happens, swim out and away from the rocks. Or you'll be pulled under. Don't want to scare you, but ... Hey. You can swim, right?"

"Of course!" But a little hiccup in her tone warns him that swimming might be a weakness. *Not good*, he thinks. "Okay, I'm here if you fall. I'll be in the water before you can go down once. We're fish, Conan n' me. No worries."

He wants to sound confident. He thinks he could save her if he had to. But isn't sure. He wants to hug her or give her a big pat on the back that says, *Okay, let's go for it!* Instead, he squares her shoulders and dips his head to her eye level.

"We're in this together, right? I'll be there the minute you need me."

Anna can't take the closeness. This standing and talking, and Leo's attention and patience, make her irritable, anxious to move.

She's in motion before the sarcastic *"Right!"* she shouts over her shoulder reaches him.

Chapter 7
The Crossing

The first large river rock is two feet wide, and close to shore. Anna leaps to it easily by jumping off her right leg from a short three-foot run.

The second rock is higher, a true boulder. But it's close to the first. The girl barely crouches, and leaps with ease. She seems utterly unconscious of danger. Her long, lean legs look delicate, but she easily springs into the air and lands with grace and strength. Anna clears the divots in the rock without notice.

The third boulder starts the real ascent. She pauses to scan its angled, sharply slippery surface for the best place to land. She squints and mind-maps the geography, just as Gramps had taught her.

She'd learned every lesson her grandfather had schooled her in, albeit begrudgingly at times. Summers had been a chance to escape the insanity of her mother's life. Anna had dreamed of the warm-weather laziness and the pleasures of being with the tribe. She had looked forward to the ceremonial days of midsummer's traditions. *That was real life.*

She'd learned to make fires from flint, and weave horsehair ropes into halters and reins for her pony. She and Gramps had built tipis and wigwams and shelters of all kinds. They had used crazy-quilt materials, odd pieces of cloth and tender birch boughs. Fox and coyote skins, and scraps of string taken from abandoned bird's nests all proved useful. Gramps had advanced her bow-and-arrow hunting to bigger game, and he'd taught her to dress everything, from doves to young deer. Her grandfather's intensity, his focus on discipline and courage, his precision with "the ways of our people from before life on the rez" meant that nothing store-bought was ever used in her training. Anna had sometimes grumbled to Nonny, "His ways are *over the top!*" Most of their people had forgotten the details he insisted upon.

But his tutelage was her saving, then as now.

Poised on the second of the boulders, Anna admits to herself that Leo is right: this crossing is treacherous, and the river is now unfamiliar. There are larger gaps to jump than she's used to. And the higher, faster, deeper water creates slippery edges.

Rivers flow where they want, Gramps had taught her. In her tribal tradition, water spirits may bless, guide and protect, but are not necessarily beneficent to every soul who dares to cross.

Like all living things, every river has its story to tell.

Anna studies this new watercourse that has replaced, rewound and confused the one she'd grown to love as a friend. This river is more demanding, self-involved, and purposefully vicious. *Maybe it doesn't trust humans to care for it anymore.* She's suspicious of what story defines it. There is a darkness in the water that she can feel tugging at her as she regards the whirling eddies.

She focuses once more on her grandparents and the last summer they were all together, when she'd been taught to leap river rocks. *Was all that work for NOW? Did they know?* She tucks that question away for later consideration. She scrutinizes the boulder in front of her. Inhales. And imagines *energy* descending down her spinal column into the rock below her feet.

She needs perfect balance. Yet she can't be anchored to the rock. She needs a ballerina's spring, a gymnast's precise landing.

She prays to the spirits of boulder and river, sky and ancestors until no tremor runs through her. Anna targets her narrow landing strip. And then she springs up off her left foot with lithe agility. A soft *whoosh* of air glances off her cheek as she clears the chasm between the rocks and lands on her feet.

She calmly assesses the next stone. Visualization is the greatest asset to her athleticism as she calculates and concentrates. She leaps — and lands another flawless vault. Her quirky, nervous twitch is gone in the whisper that connects mind to muscle. Danger doesn't exist in her body's fluent and confident grace.

Her grandfather's directions are embedded in every movement. *Watch how pipers and cranes move effortlessly. They coordinate wind with wings to feel the lift. Think like a bird, Granddaughter. Dip your wings and propel.*

He had gifted her the small eagle feather that last day of the summer. *Eagles don't leap from rock to rock, but they fish rivers and know them well. This is your feather, sacred to our people. You've earned it with your hard work and quiet mind. Soon you will be gifted a larger feather, because you carry eagle medicine. Eagle Dancer calls your destiny. Soon, Granddaughter.*

Anna never questions magic, mystery, or tradition. At least not the kind taught by Gramps. She'd bowed her head in gratitude, though she was doubtful, still, whether she was destined anything but the chaos of her mother.

Leo watches Anna scale the fourth boulder. He's been holding his breath from the minute she started across, but the boy exhales now, recognizing that he is witnessing a unique phenomenon. *Beautiful. An athletic dance. Miraculous.* He's transfixed.

Anna closes her eyes, concentrating for a long, full meditative moment on visualizing the fifth boulder, the longest span of distance yet.

She opens her eyes, extends her arms like wings — and soars.

She flies! Leo gawks. Everything about her technique and grace is more bird-like than human. *It's as if she's part girl, part bird. Like a crane, or an egret. Amazing.*

The girl leaps to the last boulder as easily as she took the first one, and with one more bounding jump from the final rock she lands on the opposite bank, balancing her weight on both legs with her arms up and her feet precisely together. She opens her eyes wide and rejoins the world of two-legged creatures — then turns to face Leo from across the water.

He bursts into applause. Leo is somehow sincerely, elatedly *proud* of what he has just witnessed.

Chapter 8
Waterman

The boy yells, "You're AMAZING!"

But his words are lost in the river's roar. The wall of volume reminds him of the water's danger.

Anna's crossing seems just stupendous. Leo rewards her with a deeply formal bow. He comes up clapping again, arms stretched overhead, so she can see his applause from across the water.

She laughs, bows back. And points to the first boulder as if to say, "Your turn!"

Leo whoops. Then quiets. His senses quicken. The river is a loud distracting turbulence, a foaming, angry churn. He studies the uneven boulder path. He searches for signs of holds and slippery warnings. Confident of his wilderness water experience, he scrutinizes what's ahead and whispers to himself with a half-crooked grin, *One thing's for sure. I'm not a bird! If my Dad was here, he'd say, Bud, you'd better grow wings, 'cuz you gotta fly.*

Leo wishes he had Conan or Dad here to talk to him. Just to slap him on the back and tease him. Dad always acknowledged problems as problems. He'd say, *"I like talking shit as much as anyone. But that won't help us here."* Dad's truth talk gave Leo courage. A wry smile plays across his face, then dies out in concentration.

Steady! Leo commands himself.

He focuses specifically, inch by inch, on the rocky route, eyeing the territory and gauging distances. He takes in the rock-ruts denting the first few boulders. He assesses the violent splash of stinging, licking waves that slicken possible holds.

"Calm. Center. *Breathe*," he mutters into the noise. "Concentrate. Soft eyes … soft eyes." Leo reminds himself to estimate each step without attachment to fear. "Loose. Stay *loose*."

He takes three large breaths. Loosens up and rolls his shoulders, shakes out his limbs. Assessing the slipperiness, he takes off his boots and socks. His feet aren't as supple as Anna's, but he stands a better chance without his heavy-soled cowboy boots, so he ties the laces of the girl's skate shoes through the leather loops of his boot tops, then rebalances the precarious load around his neck. *Not perfect.* But he has to make do with the limitations.

Leo leaps easily to the first boulder, though the boots and shoes bang against his chest distractingly. He springs to the second rock, his toes gripping a divot in the stone's surface, and there he takes a moment to rebalance and reassess. The third boulder is higher and sharper than it looks from shore.

The boy adjusts his weight and neck burdens, keeps his eyes riveted on his goal — and jumps.

He lands with only a slight wobble.

Leo sees Anna standing, tight-lipped, at the shore. From atop the rock, he bows again to relax them both. She applauds. But doesn't smile.

Anna wants to say to him, *Stay alert!* But the words catch in her throat.

Leo studies the fourth boulder. It's off to his right by about three feet, and upstream from where he stands.

Harder ... but not impossible.

His stepfather had been the head of a team of fast-water rescuers. He had taught Leo to leap chasms between boulders strewn amidst the California Coastlines. *Not exactly the same ... but I learned enough.*

Leo closes his eyes. Imagines himself following the adult lifeguards. He studies his memory pictures of their calculated, bold moves. His stepfather, a powerful, quiet water-wizard in his own right, had promised, *Today, you become a waterman.* His faith had made the boy feel like a superhero.

He evaluates the upward trajectory. Catches his breath. *I never had to jump up that high. Or this wide. ... Damn.* The boulder's ledge is jagged with knife-sharp protrusions.

Leo remembers coastal rocks overhanging crashing waves. Remembers how small footholds or handholds offered protection from falling into the pounding surf and smashing against the unforgiving rock. He draws on his experience for courage and faith. *Halfway across. ... Steady!*

With knees slightly bent, he leaps.

No!

The load of shoes and boots swings around his neck, cutting into his skin and startling him so that his landing is off, and he hits the boulder sideways. His hands and right foot grip the edge of the rock. He's pitched against the jagged crown of the boulder at a dangerous, sideways tilt while his left foot dangles in the air. The tangle of shoes, boots and laces thumps against his neck and chest.

Leo pulls himself up on his right knee, his torso slamming against the side of the water-splashed rock. He gasps out half a lungful of breath — and slips on the lip of the boulder, losing his traction and his left grip.

One hand holding all his body weight now, he stares down into a cyclone of dark siren-song. A malevolent force swirling in the current seems to call to him. Gripping the sharp edges of the wet boulder, Leo commands himself not to let go. He grits his teeth and uses all his core strength to fling his left hand up to meet his right and grasp the rock ledge. Breathing in hard, shattered gasps, his face so close to the rock it hugs his cheek, he risks another look down.

The foaming, unforgiving churn below him rips and slams into the boulder, dashing away with equal force in a current that creates a vortex of deadly undertow.

Leo blinks. He inhales deeply, slowly, and forces calm. The fingertips of his hands are all that keep him from falling. If this river wasn't as fast, or turbulent — or if he was alone with no one else to be responsible for — he'd let go. He'd take his risks, and swim for the bank.

But this undertow swallows branches and sucks down bushes torn from their roots. Heavy rocks drown in its tight swirl. Any debris that survives the vortex smashes into smaller pieces against the granite boulder. Or becomes prey to the opposing whitecaps and competing currents.

Leo is a strong swimmer, and near-fearless in water. But he's no fool. *Can't risk it.*

With inestimable slowness, he turns his eyes an inch to his right — and sees Anna wading into the water.

Leo shouts, *"Move back!"*

She freezes, uncertain. She doesn't want to alarm or distract him.

The weight and tangle of shoes around his neck cuts off the boy's air. His arms are straining to hold the full weight of his body. He feels his fingers growing numb in the effort to maintain his grasp on the slippery rock.

Leo closes his eyes, dips his head, and wills himself into a dead man's stillness.

Focus.

He calls upon a primal roar of self-preservation, an iron reservoir of inner strength. Digging his fingertips into the rock, ignoring the razor-sharp pain as his nails tear, feeling the burn of his shaking arms, he heaves an enormous breath and pulls his entire body weight up. For one heartbeat, he hovers above the rock-rim. And then, arms rigid, shoulders locked, chest throbbing, he throws his left leg over the top of the boulder following it with a heave that brings his right leg up to safety.

Leo sits on his haunches on the water-sprayed rock. His face is splashed with river foam and sweat. He doesn't bother to wipe it off. He gasps in sharp, rattle-hard gulps.

But he knows that the ache in his shoulders and arms will set in and restrict movement if he rests a minute more. He quickly removes his neck baggage. Pulling on his jacket and reordering his burdens, he shoves them all under the tattered coat and zips it up tightly — swearing at himself for doing it wrong the first time.

Not looking at Anna, Leo steadies himself and eyes the fifth boulder. It's in a direct line from where he stands, but it's the longest jump so far. And it's onto the smallest rock ledge. He has to get leverage without the three-step take-off needed. And he has to land without a forward wobble … otherwise he risks being thrown off the other side.

Accuracy! Precision! he demands of himself. His nerves are fired up, but there's no shakiness. Adrenalin from the pull-up saved him. And he wills it to keep pumping.

Leo does a deep-knee bend for muscle certainty. He visualizes where his feet have to land. Under his breath, he commands himself, *take nothing for granted.*

He inhales … jumps … and lands.

Leo exhales. His feet quiver, his toes clench and relax. His hold is tenuous … but safe.

His relief is premature. One boulder stands in the way of securing the shore. *Last one. One more leap … up.* Leo studies the wet moss that clings to the boulder's dented rim. *Damn!*

Anna stands exactly where she was when Leo fell, up to her calves in water. She holds her hands in a triangle of prayer pressed under her chin. Mouth pursed, her words squash in her throat and choke her breath.

Leo almost shouts out to ask her advice, but stops himself, commanding self-attention. *It's too easy to lose focus this close to a goal.* He'd done that once, in the early rescues. It's a bad memory that sneaks into his mind at times like this…

He had been on one of his first rides with a team of pros. Fuel had gotten scarce and the ability to ride a horse had become a major asset. They were riding at a gallop towards a house on fire. At fifteen years old, he was a decade younger than any other man on the job, but he'd found the adventure exhilarating.

He'd been yards from the house with its front porch and roof ablaze. Above the whine of wind-driven fire, the screeching screams of young kids had grabbed Leo like a vice to his heart.

A sudden gust had driven the other rescuers back. Leo, anxiety and inexperience overwhelming his calculations, had burst through the last set of flaming trees. He'd jumped from his horse too soon. The animal had shied, and a second horse he'd brought to save the others had bolted and galloped off when Leo made a dash for the kids. He'd gotten the three kids out as the wood frame and shingle roof of the porch had collapsed behind them. Without horses, with licks of fire chasing them down, he'd been forced to shield himself and the evacuees in the water of a stagnant, algae-laden, bug-infested swimming pool.

Leo never forgot the feel of icy, terrified baby fingers digging into his neck and face. Never forgot the scared yelps of the kids' fear before the team reached them. And he never made the mistake of rushed judgment again. Leo became known for patience, purpose and attention. He doesn't ever fool himself that it's easy to keep vigilant in the midst of the predictable or the unpredictable. *Mindful,* is his mantra.

He studies the rock and its moss. A slip could sprain an ankle, bruise a knee. Or worse. *And, of course, there's this crazy-cold river water*. No emergency services will come. No chance of a water rescue team for him or for Anna.

He hisses under his breath. *Fear is our worst enemy.*

He gathers his nerves, crouches, and jumps.

Leo struggles for balance at the boulder crest. He wobbles. His left foot slips — but his right toes curl tight. *Safe.*

The last jump to shore is wider. The water is deeper than he'd gauged from the opposite bank. Jagged rocks and a forest of rotted timber stick out from the water, sharp and forbidding in contrast to the quieter waves lapping the embankment.

Thought drifts through him, detached from worry. *So close, yet so far away.* Anna's perfect landing had deceived him. *Her performance is even more impressive than I gave her credit for.*

He crouches. Stretches. Debates strategies. Decides he should jump off one foot, instead of out of his deep knee bend, for better control. He hopes it will give him enough leverage to clear the broken adversaries of rock and wood. He studies the landing zone a last time. And goes for it.

Leo clears the obstacles and hits the ground hard. He tucks and rolls to avoid injury. His boots break through his torn jacket and bang against his cheek. But he pops to his knees and bounces again onto his sore feet, breaking into a relieved grin as he rubs his skinned neck.

"Hey, Anna!" The boy strains to catch a full inhale. "Why the hell was I worried? You're a circus acrobat! An Olympic gymnast! A *bird!* And I'm a klutz!"

His ears ring, his legs shake and his lungs burn, but Leo hasn't lost his sense of humor.

Anna shouts in relief. She whoops a burst of energy, vibrating with the excitement of their achievement.

Leo hoots again, "I am such a clod! But *damn,* girl, you're the real deal!"

Chapter 9
The Secret Underwater

Anna blushes. Her thin arms flap up and down with nervous energy, and her feet bounce and pivot in a goofy dance. She splashes out of the shallow water to where Leo is standing on the embankment, letting go in a laugh of exhilaration.

"Didn't know if you were going to make it! I was so *freaked!* I shoulda' taught you to ground yourself and *then* lift." She flutters, settling her weight into her right leg and spreading her toes in balance. "Like, ya' know ... *sandpipers*!" She raises her left knee high, as if to take flight. "But *anyway*, I can't do a pull-up like you did over the side of the boulder! I mean, *wow*, that takes some serious muscle!"

Watching as the girl bounces and hops self-consciously, Leo muses that she looks like a sleek seabird, an egret, maybe, or a crane. But the way her black cape flaps around her, framing her shining, tawny skin, sends up images of a raven.

"You sure are graceful — like a dancer!" he tells her. "But you're a gnarly jock, too."

Anna babbles over the compliments, wringing her hands and then throwing them up nervously.

She's not used to company, or compliments, the boy thinks. *Maybe only her Gramps notices her.* He tucks that silent observation away, feeling somehow protective of her. Her jitteriness, the way her eyes flutter from left to right without settling on him, her sudden switch to shy-girl ... all these things don't match her superior skills. *That boulder jumping takes control, courage, training and steely confidence. But she's got these edgy, raw nerves. That doesn't fit together in the same person.*

"It's hard for me to just stand here," she blurts in a too-loud voice. Her face twitches. "Um, *anyway*, I have to talk and *move* at the same time!" She hears herself, knows she is booming her words. She snorts, and blushes again.

"Whatever!" Leo is happy to hear her laugh. He talks to diffuse her self-awareness. "It's cool to watch you. You can teach Conan n' me that series of moves. ... I was an *okay* jock, played lots of sports. Conan never liked anything regular, but he was good at martial arts and yoga, stuff like that. He'll *freak* at your moves! You'll have to show him."

Though the boy joins her laughter, the ache in his shoulders reminds him of the river's dangerous whirlpools. He hears again the loud roar of the water's surge. *Louder than a river this size warrants.* He sees himself dangling from the rock's ledge, the pull of the undercurrent beckoning him to let go.

"Anna," he ventures, "The river hydraulics were, like, ominous. Maybe it's just that its usual velocity is ... cramped-in tighter, narrower than its regular flow. But the circular motion, the sway of the river - and how it *slammed* into the rocks — indicates a more powerful undertow than I've seen before. It's like it's … trying to find a new course?" He watches the whitecaps build and disappear in jagged, chaotic waves. "Okay, I know that sounds dramatic, but there was a *pulling* action. … It felt — *evil*-ish, creepy. Like … it wanted to *grab* me!"

Turning to face Anna, Leo sees her grow suddenly pale. He realizes he's scared her.

"Damn, I sound like my brother, with his big imagination. *Crazy!*" He laughs and means to defuse the impact of his thoughts. "Ya' know, probably it's just adrenalin running my mouth, but when I was hanging from that boulder, I had a half-second to look down — and I swear there was like a, a …" His voice drifts off as he glances back at the rock where he'd slipped. But there is nothing more to be seen, now, than common fast-water dangers.

"I swear it looked like there was something *under* the surface, ready to rise up. Something that made the water … dark." He pauses. "Well. It doesn't make sense, right? But … yeah." He faces the river again, studying the current. "It's like a force was gonna grab me and pull me under." He shakes his head with another little laugh. "Probably it was just turbulence. Crap from underwater being dragged up by those waves."

Anna's black eyes widen, then narrow. She squints at the river. Then at the sky above and the bleak land surrounding them. When she looks back at Leo, her eyes appear more deeply set. The laughter has left her. She pulls her cape around her shoulders.

He waits two heartbeats for her to speak, but she remains silent. "Hey! I scared you." No response. "I usually leave drama to Conan. But anyway … Did you feel or see anything, like, ya' know … Odd? Especially in the whirlpools around those boulders?"

She stares at him. At the water, the sky. At her hands. She grounds her bare feet into the wet pebble-strewn dirt. Turns back to him, mouth open. If she means to respond, no sound escapes.

She's unresponsive, but not unaware, Leo thinks to himself. He notices the nuances in each eyelash-flicker of emotion, every bead of sweat before it breaks. He decides not to ask again. *Not now, anyway.*

Leo points to the gathering clouds. "Better move," he says. He unzips what's left of his jacket, unties the bundle around his neck. He tells her she'd better put her shoes on and be careful with those tattered laces.

Anna obeys in snuffed silence. She has one clear thought: *vigilance.*

Leo sees her neck and back stiffen with resolve. *Whatever, whoever, this girl is, she's not a coward*, he thinks. *She knows a helluva lot more than what she won't, or can't, say.* He tucks that observation into his mind, and with it a reminder not to assume he knows her at all.

Secrets, everyone's got 'em. Leo's dad used to say, "When your safety depends on others, find out what their secrets are. People hang onto secrets like they're some damn interesting mystery. But most times it's fear. Fear makes people do stupid stuff. Deny it, and fear gets you by the throat. Then there's no doubt it's your worst damn enemy."

Chapter 10
Little Wolf

Eager to get moving, Leo and Anna put on their shoes and boots as they walk, stumbling a bit but determined to press on quickly.

Anna has the security of her cape and its treasures. She feels for her crystal while she moves; she thinks of her Grandparents and asks them in her mind for help. It works. She is certain now that she knows exactly where Conan hides.

The girl points determinedly to the mountains.

"Yes," Leo answers, surprised again at how mutual their visions are. "It's amazing! We see the same thing! That's the exact direction!" He turns sideways to her without slowing down. "You know this area, right? How far from him are we?"

Anna stops briefly to answer the boy's question as accurately as possible. The landscape is transformed, so it's not an easy calculation. Trees are down, boulders have moved, and the river is all wrong. And she is struggling with an inner worry about the undertow Leo had spoken of, back where they'd crossed.

But she strengthens her resolve and makes an assessment. "About two, three miles. If we move fast, we can make it in twenty or thirty minutes. You think?" Anna looks sideways at Leo for approval.

"Okay." He moves into a trot and maintains that speed, slowing only when tree trunks or debris piled in their path create a temporary obstruction.

Anna easily keeps up with Leo's pace. His legs are long, but her speed is an equalizer.

After twenty minutes, she stops abruptly. Her breath punctuates her words. "Remember that mind-picture we saw together … That peak? It was in a straight line above the rock shelter where we saw your brother. It kinda' looked like a free-standing cave, right?" She points west toward the mountains. "That's *it*, right?"

Leo gasps, nods his head. "*Right!*"

Without another word, he sprints for the incongruous pile of enormous boulders and packed dirt. Hulking tree limbs poke through the toppled earth at strange angles from every side, slowing his progress. Nevertheless, he scrambles relentless and rapidly upward. Leo's heart pounds. He's learned from experience to be a silent investigator, to move with precision, to question in silence. But in this moment, expectation and worry threaten to override experience.

Anna slips behind Leo and whispers to him, "*Vigilance!* Stay alert!"

Leo nods, but can't help himself.

He shouts, "*Conan!*" and runs toward the outcropping.

Conan has always abided by his father's instruction.

If you get separated, stay PUT until I get to you or your brother finds you. That's the rule.

Right now, it takes all his sanity to remember his Dad's words. And every bit of the patience he wasn't gifted by nature.

He'd had that strange dream, last night. The one with the monk's face, and the robe, floating in the air. And when he woke up — he was in this unfamiliar, dark place, totally alone, totally confused, with no idea of his whereabouts or how he got there.

All day, Conan has allowed himself only a few short looks out of the dark enclosure, to see if Leo might be anywhere near. But with no idea how he got here or what has happened, how could he know what dangers would be prowling out there?

His body aches. He's cramped in this tight space. His long legs look for relief. However, he's not burned or broken. And he considers that a miracle.

His nerves are getting the best of him. Restless, angry at being alone and left behind, he tells himself Leo would always look out for him. But there's been no sign of Leo.

Hell, there's no sign of anything.

Until …

He hears a voice.

Fearful and tense, Conan doesn't trust his own mind. *Am I hallucinating?*

He crawls to the mouth of the enclosure. Listens.

Is that Leo's voice?

He holds his breath.

Goddammit, is that really Leo?

*

Leo whoops.

Tears the boy hasn't allowed himself to shed for anyone sting his eyes as he banks the first boulders and climbs to the top of the enclosure.

Conan, all senses alert, is climbing out of the rock cave in a low, stealth-like crouch.

"*Conan!*"

As Leo reaches him, his arms stretch out to bear-hug his brother.

Conan leaps from the boulders and, mid-air, punches Leo hard on his left shoulder.

Reflexively grabbing Conan's arm, Leo yelps, wobbles and falls to one knee.

"*Where the hell were you?!*" Conan shouts. "I've been waiting since like fucking *forever!* Another night, and I would've had to leave this rock pile for food and water! What were you *doing?!* You, you *left me here! ... I didn't know where you were!"*

Conan's face streaks with angry tears he doesn't brush away. His face is red, his voice cracks. His fists clutch and tremble at his sides.

Leo picks himself up and laughs in a short burst. He turns to Anna and says, "Now you see why I was in a hurry to find him. He *loves* me! And he's *so easy* to get along with!"

Anna has no idea how to respond. Conan's moist, narrowed, fuming eyes are drilled into his brother. He hasn't yet shown any recognition of her presence.

She steps back several feet.

Leo grabs Conan's shoulders. He looks squarely at his brother's puffed-up anger, waiting for him to simmer down. And then with formidable strength, he hugs the younger boy into his chest. He doesn't allow Conan's protests to separate them until he feels his brother's body relax.

Anna's eyes are lowered. Her heavy wide lids hide emotion. But she doesn't miss how shaken both boys are. She understands that neither knew when, or if, they'd see each other again.

They've lost so much, so many. She smells their grief in her wild, wary knowingness. She senses the full reality of their vital need for one another.

Her worry must show on her own face, she realizes. She flattens her expression into a scowl. Un-crinkles her eyes and buries any visible reactions deeper within. She's expert at hiding personal truth. *They only have one another,* Anna thinks to herself. *Separation, that's big-time scary, for both of them. Bond of brothers.*

She warns herself not to care. Her next thought will be that *she* has no one. *I don't have a sibling, or a parent, or a friend.* She rejects that thought before it's fully formed. It's self-indulgent. It's what her grandmother called, *the weakness of your separating mind. Do not separate, Granddaughter. It will hurt you, not protect you.*

Nonny's warning rubs against her obsessive need for separation.

She waits on the sideline of the brothers' relief. Shuffles her feet. Gazes across the endless shattering of forest and upturned, angry, landscape. Shudders at the clouds of darkening sky that gallop towards them, driven by unpredictable night. She disciplines her mind, reminding herself of the courage and stoicism of her people, and their traditions. She girds herself with their strength.

Leo is looking Conan over. "You in one piece?"

"Yeah! No thanks to you!"

"... Alone?"

"Alone?! Of course!! What, you think I'm throwing a party?!"
Conan's sputtered words and wordless spouts bump into one another.

Leo is interested only in whether his brother has any broken bones. "No gashes or wounds?" He ignores Conan's protests. Pats him down.

Anna can see that the younger boy's legs and arms are extra-long and thin. He doesn't have Leo's musculature. But she observes that he is as handsome as Leo in his own way. *He looks sly-eyed, harder to read or get to know. He's kinda mysterious, and wants it that way... like me,* she thinks to herself. The thought makes her nervous.

The brothers share the same near-black, curly hair and fair skin tanned from hours in the elements. Conan's baby-smooth face is rounder than his brother's, with a high forehead. His right-angled cheekbones are dotted with freckles. Both boys have bowed, red-lipped mouths. But Conan's isn't as wide or full as his brother's. It curls up slightly at the corners, *like a cat's after a satisfied lick of milk ... from somebody else's freakin' bowl!* the girl thinks to herself.

Leo motions her over.

"Conan, this is Anna. We found each other on the other side of the river."

In his brother's silence, Leo hears Conan's natural distrust of strangers. He speaks with direct, pointed words to get Conan's attention.

"If it wasn't for Anna, I wouldn't have made it over the river to find you. *She* knew the way, not me. Hell, she led. We were way down-river. No bridges or even ropes to help us cross. Boulders were scattered, uneven, slippery as hell. It took us all day."

Conan finally snaps to. He watches the seriousness on Leo's face, hears his directness. The younger brother turns and takes a step closer to Anna.

She keeps her distance. She takes in Conan's distinctive eyes. Instead of Leo's large round orbs that flash and twinkle, lighten and darken with every private thought, Conan's eyes are narrow, almond-shaped. *Almost Asian. Like mine. But deep-set. Easier to keep his own secrets. Can I trust eyes like that?*

Conan, with some reluctance, stretches out his hand to shake hers.

She looks at the ground.

Conan drops his hand. He warns himself, *She's frail, small, weak. Another refugee. Someone else to care for, dammit.*

Leo reads Conan's body language. And Anna's. He looms up behind Conan. "I gotta brag about Anna's prowess. Her strength and agility are awesome. She's like a ballerina-jaguar! Only with wings!" He laughs. "Hell, I was worried how I'd save her if she fell in that pissed-off river! But Anna got across without even a slight wobble! Me? Another story."

Conan is still shaken and confused from the endless night and solitary day in this foreign, shattered land. He makes Leo the receptacle of his dread. Abandonment is his greatest fear. He can't grasp the need for good manners. He offers Anna a quick, crookedly insincere smile, then turns back to Leo, unsatisfied with his brother's explanations and with his divided attention.

"Where the hell *are* we?! What happened to our horses and the rescue?! Shit, Leo, that fire was *intense!* Where the hell did it all *go?*" Conan's voice is loud and tight. He spits out his words.

Leo waits for his brother to exhaust his anger, then sighs and shrugs.

"I have no answers. I don't know. Anna says we're in Montana. Yeah, yeah, I *know!* I can't put it together either. What has anyone ever said about being carried by … What? Strange, weird *winds?* And this far! *How* far, anyway?" Leo looks at Anna for some guidance.

She says, "Far? … Where'd you say you're from? California? Then, like, maybe two thousand miles?" She looks left and right, and down at the ground again. She wishes she knew more. Wishes she could offer more.

Leo exhales, not asking for agreement. "It's insane! And on top of all that, we both landed *here?* In this place where the river runs backwards and the mountains shoot up in the wrong sky?"

Anna and Leo are certain only of what happened today — of what they saw together and how they found each other, and Conan. There are no answers for the rest of it, at least right now.

"It's all we got," Leo shrugs.

Conan is still indignant. He wants more, pushes back with overlapping unanswerable questions.

Leo says, "Whoa. Hold it. Look Conan, we're here now. I don't know much else. Sorry I wasn't here sooner, but I woke up when I woke up. Miles away and, like I said, *across the river.*" Leo's voice rises. He checks it with a short, impatient sigh. "We can't spend any time now feeling sorry for ourselves or trying to sort it out. We have to get a handle on our location and make a plan. Okay?"

Anna hears Leo's strength and command. But he's not being unkind. She relaxes her back and neck, takes a deep inhale. At the same time, she judges Conan's dark mood. She doesn't like his edgy distrust; it's too like her own. She sees how Leo takes charge, and how Conan snaps himself to order, in response. It tells her that their relationship strengthens them both. They expect it of each other, rely on it.

And maybe she can too.

That thought scares her. She doesn't count on anyone but herself. Hasn't since she was first forced from her grandparents' home. She isn't comfortable with anything close to dependence.

She straightens her spine. Reminds herself, *don't get stupid. Never forget the weakness of people.* Everyone but her grandparents has disappointed her. She resists a familiar signal, a shiver of chilling heat under her skin. She feels the urge to run. To be free of any restrictions. She controls her emotions for now but values their warnings. *Vigilance.*

Leo's voice cuts her inner dialogue.

"Where are we, Anna? Wait. First tell Conan what you told me about the river and mountains."

Anna startles a bit. Nervous as a cat, she looks around. "Well …" She doesn't want to seem weak or confused — especially in front of Conan. Instinctively she knows he'll judge her for it. "It's like Leo said, those are the Bitterroot Mountains. Those peaks are the Great Raggeds. The river we crossed is a tributary of the Bitterroot River, the Triple Creek. Or the Roaring Forks, to some …" She hears her voice rushed on the last syllables, and she slows her breath. "… *Anyway*," she begins again, better contained. "That's what I think, I mean *believe* … the river is way wilder and deeper. But narrower too, like the sides caved in. I've camped and fished this river with my Gramps since I was a baby. I don't remember it *ever* being this fast … and …"

She hesitates. Anna means to repeat what she told Leo, that the water runs in the opposite direction than it has for centuries. But she watches Conan's face and thinks better of it. *He doesn't trust me. He'll think I'm crazy. Well, screw him!* She narrows her eyes. *I don't trust him, either.*

On the other hand, she wants Leo to understand that she gets stuff *right*. She makes her voice mature and reasonable. "*Anyway*, things are turned around a lot, but for sure the base of those mountains is about another two miles away. There used to be some old Indian trails there. Tourists didn't know about them. Tracker's trails, Gramps called 'em, that weren't kept up by the forest service. No one cared. Fact is, mountain folks liked that strangers couldn't use them. Only old timers … like my Gramps … knew about 'em."

She stops. Both boys watch her. She doesn't know what to do with the sigh gathering in her chest.

"Look, when everything went dark, *whenever* that was, days ago, I guess, I was trying to make it to my grandfather's place in those mountains. I … uh … I …" She stops again. The terrible fear that her grandfather won't be there hits her full force. The fear that, like everything and everyone else, he will have disappeared into and under the rubble and fallen trees and loosened boulders.

She pushes back tears. The day's exhaustion crowds her heart and mind. Her legs are suddenly rubbery. Anna wills strength into her body and a granite resolve into her voice.

"Look, I … don't know if he's, uh …" She lifts her chin. "There's no way to know if Gramps is alive." There. It's out. The words make her head hot and her hands cold. She swallows dry tears that stick like coal nuggets in her throat. "… But if he's alive, and we can find his place, he'll have food and supplies. I have to go and find out. He may need me. He's very old. And, look, even torn-up, I *know* this land. And I can climb this mountain on my own."

Leo nods. "I understand."

Conan assesses the odds of whether Anna is trustworthy.

She pitches her voice an octave deeper to sound stalwart and certain. She wills any wobble out of it. "Hey, do what you want. But like I said, I know this land. There's no wild food left. No trees. The churn of that river means there's no fish, or they're too deep to find. No deer or wild rabbits or even ground squirrels. Shit, those rodents used to be everywhere."

She scans the territory. She is careful to grasp the truth of what was there and is now gone. Mounds of debris roll out for miles without end. She wishes there was a way to make sense of the once-abundant life that now looks to have completely disappeared.

Her legs twitch to move. She forces herself to stillness one more time.

Leo senses she's eager to run but afraid to leave them too. *She's tired*, he thinks. And, now that Conan's found, he admits to himself his own total exhaustion. It hits him full force.

"Okay, Anna. We stop right now. Rest. We need time to think out options." He's sure of Conan's agreement. "You need to get to your Gramps. Agreed. And we don't know this territory like you do. But we can't climb trails tonight, can we? Not unless you tell me we are less than a mile from him. Dark is coming in fast, which is really strange, but we have to accept it. I'm not seeing any rising moon or stars, either. And we don't have flashlights. We'll be blind out there."

The older boy observes a faint flicker of resolve slide across the girl's face.

"Anna, I'll bet you're as gnarly a tracker as you are a river bird, but *nothing* is going to be what you'd expect. The trees aren't just halved, some are stuck in weird angles and upside down, like, roots in air. It'd be easy to trip and break an ankle, or worse. Boulders are blocking trails, and the course of the mountain has changed, just like the river. The hill right behind the miner's cave I woke up in was just about collapsed. It could happen again — and who knows …" Leo catches a breath and punctuates what they haven't wanted to say to one another. "Who knows what else, or who else, is out there."

He understands that Anna's young-deer twitchiness could cause her to bolt, regardless of safety. She clearly values her independence, and he guesses she's not overly concerned with personal danger. And Leo knows his brother's silent evaluations of the situation will be close to his own. They don't know this place, but they are experienced outdoorsmen; they're alive because they've learned to take calculated, but rarely crazy, risks.

He looks briefly at Conan. His brother's narrowed eyes tell him they're on the same page.

When Leo looks back to Anna, he sees the twitch of her long fingers. The girl's back is rigid, and she bounces on her tiptoes. Leo guesses she's weighing her options. He's prepared to grab and hold her here if he has to, for her own welfare — but doesn't want it to come to that.

The brothers have a dozen silent signals they use between them, developed over their lifetime, and practiced in times of danger and uncertainty. Leo flicks a quick hand signal to his brother, now. He touches his right thigh with his index finger, pointing to the ground.

Catch her if I can't. Stay alert.

Conan meets Leo's eyes without nodding. The younger brother has an uncanny sense for seeing into the heart of anyone, young or old. But at the same time, he tends to distrust others until proven wrong, and he has a tendency to blurt out his suspicions. Leo hopes that their years of work with desperate people have prepared Conan for this exact moment, regardless.

He doesn't need to worry. Conan's right with him. His brother drops his gaze and dips his head to acknowledge he got Leo's signal.

Conan, for his part, watches both Leo and Anna without a muscle twinge or an eye shift. He hasn't seen Anna do anything special, but he notes that his brother seems to respect the girl. *She must have earned it*, he thinks. *She helped Leo find me. I can be patient for a minute.*

Anna balances on her toes. She shifts her eyes, poised to run or stay.

Leo tries to ease the moment. He looks past her. "Conan, have any food?"

His brother takes a second to adjust. "Huh? *Ahhh* ... yeah. Maybe." He brightens. "Wait here!"

Leo and Anna watch as Conan scrambles up the boulders to the cave.

Chapter 11
Part of the Journey

Watching his brother clamber up the rocks, Leo smiles.

Conan's gotten pretty agile since the troubles began, the older brother thinks to himself. To Anna, he says, "He used to love video games, cartoons, drawing, collecting junk, making bizarre inventions... not that any of that was bad, it's just that I'd have to beg his butt to get up and throw a football with me. But look at him now. He's turned into an athlete in cowboy boots!"

Anna, too, studies Conan as he scrambles into the cave. She's reminded of the gazelles she'd seen on Colorado prairies. Conan is very tall for his age — *whatever that is*, she thinks. *Maybe fifteen?*

She's glad to have a second's break to reflect. She needs space and time to assess this relationship between the brothers, in spite of her anxiousness to get to Gramps. Her disparate thoughts bombard her, all at once. *Go. Stay!* She is aware once more of how vulnerable she feels. And of how much she hates this feeling. She's nauseous from the inner struggle between her gut and her brain. Her skin itches. Her muscles ache to run up the mountain and find Gramps' cabin.

But she knows that Leo's right. The trails are wiped away. Soon there'll be no light. There are dangers known and unknown.

She is just not sure whether to trust these boys. *I hate being dependent on anyone!*

Her agitation rises and falls as she follows Leo's gaze to his brother's hide-out. She prays silently for guidance in the Lakota way of her grandfather. And in the Christian-Buddhist-Samurai way of her grandmother. She feels heat stain her cheeks. And then the familiar adrenalin chill as she fights to get her nerves under control. Anna can't command perfect calm, but at least she's able to stay put. An accomplishment.

Conan trots back towards them wearing an old drover's coat that falls in stiff canvas pleats to the top of his boots. It's the kind of coat that Australian outback cowboys wear. It's a size too big for his thin frame. The frayed collar stands up around his ears, and one sleeve is torn at the elbow while the other hangs past his wrist.

Anna sees his sly smile as he approaches them. She doesn't know yet how rare an open laugh is for Conan.

"So, *big brother*, what would you give me for some food right now?" A lip-licking cat smirk of satisfaction crinkles his eyes and the corners of his mouth.

There it is again! Anna thinks.

"I *knew* you had something, Conan! Come on! I haven't eaten for days! Whatcha got?" Leo grabs for Conan's pockets.

But Conan jumps aside. He turns his pockets inside out. "I've got *no* idea what you mean!" He turns his empty palms up.

Leo jabs left and right, trying to grab whatever his brother's hiding. "You don't know this sneak the way I do, Anna," he says, keeping his eye on Conan. "He'd never leave home without food. Sweets mostly. I'm pretty sure he has a stash somewhere…"

Abruptly Leo turns, as if done with this game. But then he swivels back, fast and low. He grabs Conan's coat, smiling sideways at Anna. "*C'mon*, Conan where is it?"

"Okay, *Okay!* Don't get so hyper! I *may* have something here…"

Leo refuses to release his brother's lapel.

Conan slips a hand inside the drover's hidden pockets, and Anna watches him intently. Conan's coat is like her cape. You have to keep track of your secret stashes, or spend frustrating minutes in a confusion of cloth, flaps, buttons and pockets.

As she touches the little Tara statue enfolded in her cape, she sees Conan's eyes narrow into an all-knowing squint.

"Okay, so what you gonna do for *me*?" Conan taunts his brother. The boy's right hand remains in a pocket of his coat.

"It's what I'm *not* going to do…"

Conan pulls out a small paper bag. Leo lunges at it.

"Hey, watch it!" Conan's voice rises as he struggles to push his stronger brother aside. "Here's what I've got. It's the last bag of that great trail mix that … Dad … made us."

Conan's voice loses its tease. Both boys stop as a flash of sadness passes between them. Conan's eyes widen, then darken. He glances away.

The older brother asks gently, "Saved it a long time, right Bro? Sure you want to give it up now? … Only thing to eat. … Right?" Conan and Leo both have one hand on the crumpled brown bag. Neither is letting go.

"Yeah," Conan sighs, "it's all we got left. The last of it. But we have to eat. Need to." He releases the bag.

Leo opens it with care. He crouches down, takes off his hat, and divides into three piles the handful of raisins, nuts, goji berries and dried fruit, then places the separate piles carefully into the crown of his red hat.

Anna sees that Leo's expression is heavy with a kind of tamped-down sorrow as he holds the hat out to her. The girl nods her thanks and takes one pile. She doesn't need an explanation of loss.

Leo passes the hat to Conan, who gazes at it a full minute before curling his fingers around the trail mix portion.

"Our Dad taught us to ride," the older boy reflects, "then dragged us along with him. He fed us, kept us clean. Kept us *kinda* safe," he smiles, "and protected — always. He never left us. Not when we were little." He shifts his eyes to Anna, including her in the reminiscence. "Not when we grew up, and not one hour when the troubles started."

He stares down now at the food in his palm. Then looks back up to Anna.

"We started every day before dawn. Slept on our horses, sometimes. We'd ride for hours, until the horses got too tired to lope anymore and we were beat — Conan and me, anyway. Dad pushed us on. He'd say, 'Be grateful, boys.' He'd remind us that we were among the few left who could help people escape the disasters ... the fires, and the collapse of towns, and the gangs that had started up. *We're the lucky ones,* he'd say. And one of his favorite lines was, *Anyway, boys, it's all about the journey.* Right, Bro?"

Conan doesn't immediately respond. Leo's smile is shadowed as he continues. "But ... one day, I don't know, months ago I guess ..." He stops and looks up again at Conan, who nods, eyes hooded. "Well, he just ... didn't come back."

Leo's voice fades out.

Anna takes a half step toward him, not sure how to respond, but anxious for the rest of the story.

The older brother goes on, considering an interpretation of his father that had not occurred to him before. "Ya know ... He was the happiest I'd ever seen him. The troubles and responsibility made him stronger and more ... centered, I guess, than he'd ever been."

Conan stays pulled into himself. His brother pushes on with his reflections, seizing the moment to talk out what hasn't been said before now.

"Dad would say, 'You want to know what being a real man is? *This.* Right now, right here. Being the ones who reach out and help. Being the ones who give a damn and do for others. Getting our boots on, saddling up. No complaints. Facing whatever God sends us today.'"

The younger brother's dark eyes don't betray his inner thoughts. He slips a small sigh, but still doesn't respond or add detail.

"We'd been out looking for stragglers," Leo tells Anna. "Heard rumors of trouble from a neighboring rancher who was chasing his last two cows over a ridge. He told us there were some kids who got separated from their parents, or were orphaned, out on the trails. He was telling us the kids would die out there alone, or be captured, who knows? Anything was possible, he said. Anything *bad*, anyway. So, we went in the direction he sent us. And ... late in the day, we came up on a large group of them ... kids, I mean."

Conan interrupts, "Kids of every age!" The younger boy speaks directly to Anna, his words almost overlapping, as if it suddenly matters that she's there to witness his flood of memory. "Some were as young as two or three, the oldest of the kids were probably in their teens, like us — and the big ones carried the littlest ones. School-age kids were dragging along sacks of whatever food they had, or thermoses of water or dirty blankets and beat-up sleeping bags ... It was fucking *intense.*" He takes a deliberate breath and his voice suddenly loses its thunder. "A lot of the kids were sick. There was dust everywhere — from fires, cave-ins, winds. They all looked starved for food, too. But the eeriest part was that … they were silent. Except for coughs or sneezes — or some whimpers from the babies." He shakes his head. After almost half a year, Conan is still unable to fathom the full impact of the last day they had seen their father.

Leo adds, "But no one cried or called out to us — or to each other."

"Yeah." Conan's attention shifts back and forth between Leo and Anna. "The older girls came right up to us, but they said *nothing*. That whole thing just felt like something out of a disaster movie. They all stared as if we were a mirage, like we couldn't be real." His voice evaporates in the memory.

Anna holds tight to her fist of trail mix. She moves closer to the boys. She spreads her cape behind her and sits next to where Leo stands facing his brother.

Leo takes her closeness and interest as a good sign. He relaxes a fraction and drops into a crouch next to her.

Conan remains standing. "Can't see the moon," he murmurs. Night blows towards them in bursts of grey-black, smoky clouds. "When we were little," he says to himself as much as to Anna, "our grandmother told us wolf stories. Myths, legends. At the ranch, we'd go outside with her and howl at every full moon rising over the ridge." Wistfulness hangs in his young man's voice. "Funny how we take stuff for granted. Like we'll always be able to see the moon."

Anna imagines the moon-howl nights and, for the second time today, extends part of herself into someone else's experience. She shivers from the uniqueness of this, the closeness to strangers, sharing thoughts. Being included.

Abruptly her self-judgment rises. She rejects the hint of neediness. Damns herself for weakness. Her inner voice hisses, *Vigilance!*

Her grandmother, Nonny, would ask her to name her feelings, not collapse emotions and ignore them or throw them out in rage, separating herself from whomever she was with. *We are not any of us so different, Granddaughter*, Nonny would teach. *Allow yourself to enter the mystery of shared experience.* Anna rolls those words around inside herself. Has she ever understood them? *No*, she growls, head down.

Leo dips his shoulder to get under her glance. She can't avoid his wide eyes. He smiles that wise, older-than-his-years smile directly at her, and then looks back to his brother. Anna thinks the glance they exchange must capture everything they know after a lifetime together.

A tremor of bumpy feeling runs through her, something she can't pinpoint.

"Yeah," Leo is saying, "It's sad how bare, how torn … how injured everything is, now, everywhere. It sucks. It was hard that day, and sorrowful every day after. But … we're here. We're alive. We don't know why *us* when so many are gone. But whatever's ahead, it's *part of the journey,* Dad would say." He smiles at his brother.

  Jealousy, Anna says to herself. *That's what it is. This feeling is fuckin' ... jealousy. I wish I had had ... this family ... thing. A sister, or a brother. Except for Nonny and Gramps, I'm alone. My journey is alone.*

  She coughs to hide her sigh.

Chapter 12
Visions

Anna knows that Leo is looking for her to be all in. She offers the only thing she can: a tight, insincere smile.

But then she's hit by a visceral lurch, a crunch inside that dumps her aching heart into her belly. She almost gasps.

An instant memory sparks. *I know this feeling.* It's just like the day she'd learned to slip the clutch on that battered stolen car. Anna had shoved her crackhead, jacked-up mom into the passenger seat. She'd grabbed the steering wheel and slammed the door on the pimp with the half-burned, twisted face. They had taken off, out of control, down the steep hill into San Francisco's fog, screeching like banshees.

Anna was thirteen years old, then, and so out-of-body that she'd seen the eyes of "The City" looking back right into her, from behind her mom's eyes and in front of her own, at the same time.

I know this feeling. Fear, insanity, panic, bump into the *whoop* memory of that night's rare victory. *Stop!* Anna screams in her wobbly brain. She wants to grab her chest to protect her heart, but resists. *Chill, dammit! Chill! Can't run. Not now.*

She drops her head and slides a foot away from the brothers before blurting aloud, "What happened when you found the kids?"

Conan sighs. He keeps watch on the fast-darkening horizon. Abruptly he sits, folding his coat under him to pad the hard ground.

Leo stirs the earth with his free hand. "Don't know. Gone over it a hundred times. Conan's right, the kids were burned out. Dad said, 'Jump down from the horses.' He was his usual self, he took charge, barked orders to us, but he was kind and funny and gentle with the kids. Real quick they trusted him, and us, too." Leo shakes his head. "They were so exhausted, especially the teen girls, and they just dropped everything once they realized they'd found the help they were looking for."

Conan picks at the story's thread, voice low and slow. "It turned out the teens rescued the little kids from what Dad called a 'shit-for-brains gang' who planned to ransom them back to their parents. Or worse, sell them to ... someone else."

"Some bad dudes roamed the abandoned towns," Leo adds. "Honestly a few of 'em were just scared kids themselves, but others were gun-toting, pissed-off freaks. The teen girls were scavenging for supplies and heard about these kidnappers, so they scouted the situation and figured out a plan to free the kids."

"I think it was the kind of rescue where everything goes wrong," says Conan. "Those girls were as battle-tested as us, but the rescue got completely out of control. Still, they'd managed to haul the little kids all the way up from the coast, between quakes and rock avalanches. They said they'd heard about three guys on horses who rode rescues. So they climbed at night, and hid during the day." He looks at Leo. "People told 'em to look for a dad and two sons, one wearing a red hat. Can you imagine? They were looking for *us?*"

Private thoughts, teased by aching grief and too much challenge at too young an age, run behind both brothers' eyes and pull them into the past together.

Anna is intensely engaged by the story of desperate children and dangerous escape. It's a life she knows well. *Without the hero parts*, she thinks. She studies the brothers. The boys' memory, she feels, isn't triggered by adventure — but by love for their dad. Her own yearning for family and salvation pulls at her ... but longing is a dangerous trap, in Anna's experience, one that threatens to unleash panic. She closes her dark eyes, turning them inside.

Whoosh!

Without warning, cobalt-blue electricity flashes behind her closed eyes. It skims a straight line across the black inner horizon. The sizzle rocks Anna forward and then thrusts her head back against her shoulder blades in a rave of psychedelic colors as the blue flame ignites like a string of neon firecrackers. Tremors shake the girl. She hugs herself against the jolts while her inner screen bursts into a 3D kaleidoscope of scenes. Her eyes fly open and shut again, torn between the frenzied need to focus and a desperation to escape the insistent rush of moving pictures.

All at once she realizes that everything, *everything* the boys see and hear in their memory comes alive in a diorama around her. Overlapping sights and sounds rush before Anna. Crisp and detailed images of people, landscape and sky connect their memories to her. Somehow, *somehow*, she's inside a rapid-motion reality of the brothers' individual and shared feelings and experiences.

Hot and cold shivers alternate throughout her nervous system. She's sucked into the motion as if she's flying forward at exhilarating speed. Jumbled thoughts — blame, shame, guilt at invading their privacy – embarrass and yet fascinate her.

The same thing that's happening for them ... is happening for me!

Each brother's internal camera, cued to perfect visual memory, connects emotion to sound and image. Information flows so easily neither is aware their two memories speak one narrative. Anna, along for the ride, hears their coordinated brains, hearts, emotions.

I'm inside their minds! ... How is it possible?!

She can't, won't draw attention to herself. *No way.* Leo might understand. He'd shared that vision of his brother's whereabouts with her. But Conan won't understand. He doesn't trust her. *Why should he?*

Uninvited, in their shared vision Anna sees Leo hand his canteen to a toddler. "Just a sip," she hears him say. "Slow, not too much." He sounds the same as when he found Anna at the river's edge — attentive and patient. More adult than boy.

As her dream eyes scan the wider scene, she sees Conan lift a heavy pack off a young teenage girl. Anna becomes aware, then, that she is seeing through Conan's own eyes as he bends down and slips each strap carefully off the girl's shoulders. *He's so ... kind ... and gentle. But in charge. This is too freaky!*

Her own inner words send another rattling tremor through her, and her mind takes her on a tangent of personal memory. *Freak!* She hears the shaming, haughty-cold cry in her mind. *Weirdo! Freak-Queen! Psycho!* The mean-girl voices from her chaotic city life, from her crisis-to-crisis street life, scream at her from a too recent past. They have no influence or authority over her now. But their loud and ugly disrespect haunts her.

Anna aches for understanding. But if she gives away what she sees and hears, the boys will reject her, she's sure of it. *The brothers aren't stupid. To them I'm a witchy outsider.*

She speaks Lakota prayers and Shinto mantras in a singsong string in her heart-mind. She begs the spirits to unlock whatever spell melds her to the boys' memories.

Her prayer doesn't deliver separation. She is whipped back to Conan's memory-perspective. On Anna's inner screen, the boy places the backpack next to a teen girl whose strawberry-blonde wisps of hair blow over her face as he kneels next to her, close enough for support but without insistence. He doesn't seem to require any "ask" of the willowy girl. Effortless, sincere, unworried, he's not the nervous boy of today. Anna silently admits, *he's a pro.* She twitches from that same spasm she hates to call jealousy, but she can't ignore the itch under her skin. A heated flush pinks her cheeks, and as she feels it, she dips her head to avoid scrutiny. But intimate small motions and whispered sounds wrangle themselves into her heightened heart-mind. She can't look away or turn down the volume.

In the next moment, both boys focus with a single eye of their memory as someone moves in front of Conan to dominate their shared movie screen.

It's their dad. Anna's internal whisper is a clear knowing. She sees him in his sons' mind-eye, taller and thicker than they are, but the resemblance is unmistakable. Neither boy looks exactly like him, but there are distinct pieces of him in each. He has fair, freckled skin, tanned by hours in the sun, and he has the same dancing green-blue eyes as Leo, offset by the red, bowed mouth shared by Conan.

Anna's guts wrench from the boys' heart-punch of loss. The sting of the brothers' choked-back pain threatens to betray her.

Then the internal shared camera moves up and to the right. Instead of their father, she sees Conan on that day. *Am I seeing through Leo's eyes? Or ... or — what?*

A stew of exhaustion and anxiety from swallowing her feelings and from the rapid eye-mind shifts between Conan and Leo jars her voice loose. Anna blurts, "Where'd your dad go?"

Snap! Her inner screen goes black.

Leo and Conan are flung back from the shove and tear of disconnected energy, ripped out of a recollected world into the cold, foreign present. Both boys gulp down painful jabs to their brains and chests, gaping at her in outright shock.

"We don't *know!*" Conan shouts, red-faced. "We don't know where he went!"

Leo stops his brother.

Conan swallows his anger while swatting away the restraining hand. He wraps himself back into his cloud of disquiet separation.

Anna's eyes fan right to Leo, fast, rat-a-tat. She stutters, "I'm sorry. The kids were so small, and … I dunno, I could feel how worried they were. And then that guy … that's your dad?"

She's gone too far. Her hand flies up to shut her mouth.

Both boys react viscerally. Conan is wary and alarmed. Leo is stunned — yet not completely surprised. "You *saw* him... right? Like we saw Conan together?"

Anna stammers, "Look … I … I …" She springs to her feet. "I gotta make it to my Gramps' place."

The hot California sun of shared memory has disappeared like the mirage it was, and in its place, grey emptiness surrounds them. Dark night is dropping like a shroud and fierce winds are picking up, howling down from the canyons to circle in siren-angry swirls.

She grabs at her cape and looks around for a possible exit route. She dodges the boys' stares with a twist and a hiccup, searching for a coherent strategy of escape.

"Wait, wait!" Leo jumps to his feet and puts his hands on Anna's shoulders. He feels her squirm, but maintains his firm grasp and forces eye contact. "We're not letting you go, Anna. Are we, Conan?"

Conan shifts from anger to disbelief and distrust. He wears his worst scowl.

Leo ignores him. "There aren't any easy choices anymore. Anywhere."

Anna's body aches to run fast and far, but she's without an option that feels safe and familiar. Rigid and reluctant, she allows Leo's carefully reassuring grip to keep her in place.

"Look, Anna …" Leo lowers his voice to a softer cadence. "Telling that story, some damned *weirdness* happened to me. You too, right?" He shifts his gaze to his defiant brother for confirmation. Conan's face remains hardened. Leo pretend-growls at him. He's ignored in turn. "My entire memory just ... *opened up*," Leo admits to Anna. He knits his brows. "I was thinking about stuff from that night we were talking about — but at the same time I saw and heard through *Conan's* eyes and ears.

It's crazy to say ... But ... it's not so different from earlier today when you and I saw Conan in his hiding place, both of us seeing the cave together — right?"

Anna's brain is stuck. She keeps her gaze fixed on the ground.

Leo gently tilts her chin up. "You're not the cause, Anna. It happened to all *three* of us at once."

She's confused by every bit of it, by her inability to run and the descending dark and her fears of being called all the hateful names she knows so well. She pushes down her sour stomach.

Afraid to look weak, she meets and returns Leo's direct gaze and forces a rattled response. "I don't know *either!*" Her words now fall over one another, high-pitched and nervous. "Yeah, it was like when we saw Conan. The same, but different too. More color and sound. Voices, even. And ... *details*. The real colors of things, from the girls' hair to the buttons on their shirts. ... You, too?"

Leo leans in, taking one hand off her shoulder. "You saw through *us*. It was the same for me. Not just reviewing old memories. I was *there* again, clearer than I could have remembered it. Anna, that's never happened to me before, or to Conan. For us, too, this is completely strange. It's scary, and damned weird." He releases her and walks in a small, slow circle of pacing. "Conan, help me on this!"

The younger boy shrugs. He remains edgy, moody, distant ... and silent.

Leo stops and throw his hands up. "Dude!"

Still getting no reaction, Leo turns from his exasperating brother. Calmly and analytically, he says to Anna, "It was sort of like a 'movie' of that day. We saw each kid, every horse. And ... Dad." He catches himself at the edge of a too-strong emotion. He clears his throat. "Also, I *felt* the same as I did that day. But I felt it more ... intensely. It was like this 'perfect recall.' But we couldn't have known then that it was our last day with Dad." His voice cracks in spite of his calm. With a shake of his head, he continues, "But on top of that, I sensed someone else right there with me, with us. Damn! It was like another person shared whatever camera was in my head." Leo is facing Anna, watching her closely. "It's okay," he says twice. "That was you, right?" His voice is authoritative, yet warm. "You were there with us."

She blushes, confused. She's worried about what they think of her, and worried about what she thinks of herself. And she knows she can't escape now.

"No judgment," Leo breathes. "Whatever this was, it happened to all three of us." She nods so slightly that he holds the look for a second to make sure she's with him. "But somehow ... you were in our memories."

She hates being out of control. Hates even more feeling dependent on anyone. A run into the night alone, even for a rebel who is used to risk, would be crazy-dangerous. But *not* to run free feels like prison. She shivers from cold sweat. Her connection to these boys makes no sense.

Except for the Bird-Girl's message. *Find the boy in the red hat.*

Anna is suddenly drained in mind and body. "I don't know what happened, Leo!" She can't check her runaway, angry exhale. "But I *have* to get to Gramps! I can't wait! I have to go! I'm, I'm ..."

"Scared!" Conan, stands. "You're scared, right? Well, guess what? We're *all* scared!"

His loud impatience shocks her. Leo's protective hand on her closes — but doesn't tighten.

Conan is glowering. "Hey, I don't know you, Anna," he says, ignoring his brother's look of warning. "But I don't like this weirdness at all. I mean, it was like I was awake while dreaming. And I saw myself through Leo's lens, yeah, and ..." Conan chokes on his words, waving a hand over his face. "I saw Dad. And everyone. In details I'd missed before ... with all the crisis bullshit of that day." His voice trails. "*And* I sensed someone else was able to hear, to see — *through* me." A spit of anger stings him and he's fired up again. "So, it's not exactly normal for us either! I have not got a goddamn *clue* what just happened!"

Leo growls, "Stand down, Bro."

Conan huffs at Leo. "No one warned us anything like this was possible, Leo. This Sci Fi brain-meld, this triple-sight VR, or whatever. Not even Granny's woo-woo friends talked about something like this." Conan glares back and forth between Anna and Leo. His high-pitched bark is meant for both of them. "It's *insane*! Who the *hell* is in my head and who the *hell* invited you?"

Anna is edgy for angry rebuttal. *What the fuck,* she wants to scream, *you think I WANT to be inside your messed-up stress brain?!*

But before she can blast him, the last of Conan's fire puffs out in a soft wail. "Leo. ... Dad. *Damn,* Bro. We saw *Dad.* We didn't ever ... didn't know. Haven't ..." Conan stops. His balled fists fall to his sides. "We haven't seen him since that day."

Leo holds the center between Conan's grief and Anna's disquiet. He senses that the girl is torn by her own stressors. He's been in too many conflicts not to recognize the signs of fear, freeze or flight.

His harmless grip on Anna's wrist makes her twitch all the more. "Let's get this clear," she says defiantly, shaking off his hand. "You and me? Earlier today? We saw the same picture of Conan at exactly the same minute."

Leo nods and explains to Conan the strange electric current that ran between himself and the girl. "It was tangible. It was at the *exact* same time. We saw you climb out between the boulders, Bro, and look up and down the river for me."

Anna's voice is sharp. "How did that happen? I don't *know.* Do *you?*"

The older boy murmurs, "Okay, let's just relax a minute. *Breathe.* When we saw Conan together, we'd just woken up. We'd been knocked goofy by winds. Maybe because we'd had no food or water, our brain circuitry was shaken up. And you know, what we saw happened so fast — hell, *everything's* happened so fast — it didn't seem that weird at the time. But now ... this happens. You share our past in a place you haven't been. *Whoa.* Scary? Yeah, sure! But, *damn ...*" He includes Conan in a wide arc of his eyes. "It was pretty cool, too! It's a miracle-mystery, right? Not all bad. Unexplainable. But amazing."

In the long pause that follows, he hears his father's voice. It warns, *Seers, prophets, fortune tellers and bullshit artists. Times like these bring strange fish up from the bottom of the sea. Takes time to know what you got on your hook, son. Keep your damn head.*

Is Anna a seer, a beneficial soul sister, a white witch or a bad omen?

"Look, we're freaked out. But — think about it. This triple-brain connection could actually help us. A shared wavelength is a connected energy field. We'll get more — and better — information than we could as individuals. That's how we found Conan, right?" Conan and Anna stare at him with the same skeptical scrutiny. He pushes past their distrust. "Ok, I agree. It's scary! But it's also a gift. Three brains are better than one." His voice is firm. "We have to take our chances with each other."

Anna drops her head to her chest and falls utterly silent. Hood up, she wraps her black cloak around herself like a bat wraps its wings in a fold of mammalian protection. The panic attack that had threatened seems to her to be ebbing somewhat, but Anna's inner dialogue runs hotly through her head. *Go ahead and run, you idiot.* Her mother's rage-filled voice teases and mocks her until tears gather.

These boys, schooled by the hardness of trails and endless rescues, are close and quick enough to grab her, she intuits. They can recognize the nerves that drive her, even without knowing her story.

She answers her mother's voice in her mind. *No! I can't run. I WON'T run.*

Then waits to hear the inevitable, familiar name-calling. *Witch! Weirdo!*

She dissolves further into the cape's folds.

Chapter 13
Teachers

The boys raise their eyebrows. Leo bends over Anna, gently and patiently waiting for her attention until she shifts her eyes up to him without unwrapping herself from the protective cape.

"Anna. There's more to this. It's not just the weird connection. You and I talked about how the river was all wrong, and we can't explain how we got here. And why no one else is here, or anywhere we've been so far. ... I just want to say ... Well, there's more to talk out. Teachers who came to our ranch when Conan n' me were kids, they taught us about a prophecy. A prophecy that the Earth would shift out of alignment."

Leo and Conan exchange a quick nod, a wide-eyed acknowledgement of their shared upbringing with its magic of tribal cultures and community gatherings.

"They talked about how a big enough shift of the planetary poles would cause common things to lose their identity and definition. Space-time might expand, contract. *Boom!* Magnetic poles would move feet instead of inches. And they said that, obviously, if that happens, we got problems!"

Conan is nodding his head. "I watched streams of weird science documentaries. If the axis tilted, *wham!* The Earth's entire electromagnetic field would change. Space-time boundaries might disappear. It'd feel like Earth was caught in huge, violent waves. Topography would get a serious overhaul — be dumped out and re-created. So, yeah, rivers would be likely to change flow and direction."

"New patterns," Leo adds, "could re- ... uh ..."

Conan fills in. "Reorient electromagnetics. Out-of-the-ordinary gravitational waves couldn't go on forever, I don't think. They would have to eventually anchor new, whatever ... new directions. If old patterns were shattered, new ones would be created."

At the homestead of their childhood, their Granny had hosted medicine men, white witches, lamas and priestesses alongside physicists and mathematicians and scientists of natural forces. The boys had always been surrounded by learned and venerable guests who came to be considered family.

"I mean, it's known that in ancient Paleo times, major polar shifts upset the planet," Leo reflects. "Could it happen again?" He shrugs. "No one knows. But if so, the Earth might redistribute all kinds of energy. Boundaries, man-made and natural, would be destroyed. It might encourage a rare kind of ... well, connectivity."

"Could it ... expand our brain's capacity to include other neural systems?" Conan enjoys this kind of theorizing. "Link us to other brains?" The younger boy scans the horizon.

"Exciting to consider, for sure!" Leo's fascination with scientific inquiry is triggered. "What about a sudden giant rift in the fabric of the universe? Dark energy sucking matter into a vortex? Maybe, it causes a gravitational singularity? How cool is that? It might mean that there are actually things like openings to other dimensions — portals, or black holes. Phenomena not yet named."

Conan leans in. "Yeah! It might be possible ... that a mega-shift would bring a new definition of physics. Like, a totally different energy connectivity that ... could ... connect the three of us together in boundary-evaporating dimensions."

Before Leo can chime in again, they are silenced by the wind's whip and whine through the desolate landscape. It's a high-pitched victory cry over anything that once banked its power. The brothers drop into a low huddle, crouching and encircling Anna, who shivers between them.

Leo surveys the turned-over land. It's bleak as far as he can see.

When a lull in the howl allows for talk, he whispers, "The wind feels heavy. I can feel ... the heft of it. It's like it's carrying something ... weighty." *With — regret. Or grief,* he doesn't say.

He folds his arms more tightly to his chest.

"More than one teacher said that 'openings' bring hoped-for miracles," he murmurs. He exhales a long, lonely sigh that fills the air between the three kids. His brother pulls his coat closer to his thin body, turning up the collar to warm his neck and ears.

"Could huge earth shifts be all to the good, at least eventually?" Leo wonders. No one offers an answer. "Can we even agree on what 'good' is?" he continues through their silence. "Sharing memory of that day was, well, *good* in its way. But ..." He hears a slice of anger in his own voice and cannot draw it back. "Everything we loved was *good*, to us. It was great. Beautiful! But everything we loved is now pretty much gone. Even if survivors, like us, have these new *gifts*, or whatever, like the teachers said — are they worth it for what we lost? I mean, who's left to value new knowledge? Or care?"

Conan follows his brother's gaze across the tumbled terrain. Childhood images float unbidden through his mind. The light of California's Central Coast, golden and warm, had suffused winter and summer days alike. It had pierced the valley fog and trickled into star-filled nights.

Leo snaps back to the present. He feels Conan drifting, and he's suddenly afraid his brother will latch onto the sad anger lacing Leo's words and spin into dangerous emotional territory. "Stay with me." His voice is a low command.

Conan turns to face his brother. Leo sees longing in his eyes. But no defeat.

"The teachers we met said, 'Gifts can usher in new ways to serve, heal and lead. They can create *One*-ness.' They made us memorize those words." Leo smiles crookedly, telling Anna, "Even then, Conan questioned them. He'd ask, 'But would that be good?' And the teachers would always answer something like, 'Service that brings Oneness is always considered the highest good.'"

The wind kicks up another brutal gust. In a two-heartbeat pause, Leo weighs the value and the complexity of supposed shift-changing gifts.

"*Any*way. The teachers said we'd be able to communicate in 'mystical ways.' I mean, could it be … that we traveled just now? To the past while alive in the present?"

Conan listens to Leo's subdued but deliberate words. *Even now*, he thinks, *without answers, with this strange girl in this strange place, Leo is direct, confident, strong. Dependable.* Conan relies on his brother's steadiness and courage. Leo can be surprisingly naïve, in Conan's view. Forgetful of details. His brother loses keys and tools, and he trusts everyone first - asks questions later. *Basically, the opposite of me.* His older brother, Conan reminds himself, leads naturally, with no bluster or bullshit.

The cowboys called it 'being easy in his heart.'

A tarot-throwing holy man the brothers had saved from tsunami-driven seas had told Conan, "Your brother is a rock of dependability. He has the fire of commitment. You're the cool water that surrounds fire. Water prevents fire from burning itself into complete destruction. Your brother," the old man was sure, "is a Golden Child. A spiritual warrior-king. But you're the king's alchemist. His soothsayer. He depends on your insight, on your art and truth-telling."

Conan had used that insight to influence Leo when his heroics seemed rash and dangerous. Or when his courage meant he didn't look out for his own or Conan's best interests. "Hell," he'd screamed at Leo over rainstorms, sliding down cliffs too slick to be safe, when Leo demanded more of himself than anyone else, "Put your *own* damn life on the line, but don't you dare risk *mine!*"

In their wind-whipped huddle, Conan coughs to clear his throat. "Leo's right. We had pieces of psychic-kinda' experiences off and on … But not like this."

"Shit, *never!*" Leo agrees.

A pause in the gusting wind makes the ensuing silence seem to echo.

"We never knew what was real or what was true," Conan admits. "Not a lot made sense about prediction and prophecy then."

"But," his older brother reminds him, "the teachers did say that 'others' could appear when and where the Universe decides. And then … 'gifts' would manifest, they told us."

Conan sits up with a smile. "Remember how Granny used to say when we were little, *the future will demand a completely different knowing? … People, events and knowledge …*"

Leo finishes with Conan, "… *will arrive unannounced in unusual ways.*"

Conan and Leo short-laugh, face to face, surprised to find they recall the precise words together.

"We were *so* little," says Leo wistfully.

Anna still crouches, face tilted down, hands wrapped tightly inside her cape's thick folds. She listens as only a child raised with Native ritual and multicultural ceremony can listen. With heart connected to mind and spirit, in her and around her and out into the larger rhythms of the Universe.

A cold gust brings Leo back to the present moment. He squints at the sky, now dark and empty. Planets, moon and stars, normally the night's means of navigation, hide behind thick, darkly dense clouds. There is no smell of impending rain.

The winds rise again in sharp, unpredictable punches and icy blasts.

Chapter 14
Run! Don't Run!

"Enough talk for tonight." Leo says in his adult voice. "What do we have to do, to bunk down? Nothing to light a fire with…"

Anna can start fires from flint. She can smell dry, useable wood from yards away. She knows how to coax tiny splinters of leaves into robust flames. But right now, she offers none of that. Her mind is a jumble of fear and anxiety.

Run! Run!

But *I can't!*

Conan digs into his drover's coat. He extracts his trusty Leatherman tool, then digs further until he finds two matches wrapped in dirty plastic. His brother gives him a fist-bump, and they start looking for dry twigs and branches. The barren ground has little usable wood; what they retrieve is damp with the river's shift.

"You'd think with the world torn to damn shreds, we'd find one good piece of kindling," Conan mutters. He strains against tree limbs buried under tumbled soil and boulders. "And it'd be a lot easier to look if we had more light!"

Leo leans for leverage against one half of a buried tree trunk so as to free another. He turns and observes that Anna has not moved. He walks to her, bends down to meet her crouch, and gently holds her elbow while guiding her to join them. The girl's hood slips back just enough for her to see without obstruction as she pitches in to look for firewood, moving robotically.

Conan glances over at Anna. His wariness of her returns. Leo pretends not to notice his brother's distrust.

It takes longer than it should to gather a pile of uninspiring sticks. They discuss whether a fire will alert predators of the four-legged or two-legged kind, in spite of the fact that they haven't seen a living soul, apart from themselves, since they awoke.

Leo says, "Well, there are no tracks to indicate anyone else has been around here. And we do need heat to stay alive."

He pulls out his Swiss Army knife. "Besides, if bad guys come, I have this — and Conan has his Leatherman sidekick!" He means it as a joke, but the others don't laugh. "We'll take turns at lookout." He pockets his knife again. "I'll go first. Conan, get some rest. I'll wake you when I can't keep my eyes open." Leo turns to Anna and says quietly, "I'll make a nature bed for you to sleep in. It'll be more like a dirt nest than a cushy comforter, though."

He gets to work digging a small burrow with a tree branch in the sandy soil a few feet inside Conan's boulder enclosure. "Better eat your fruit leather," he tells Anna. "And some trail mix."

She doesn't respond. The girl remains turned into herself, standing just outside the rock cave. Leo is surprised, and relieved, when Conan moves past her to enter the tight enclosure and place his own coat down in the dirt cradle.

The kindness startles Anna. Her eyes, nervous as a captured wild bird, widen. She manages a weak smile.

Leo's experience tells him she's disoriented. *But she won't run.*

Anna peers into the cave, taking in the boys' efforts to make her comfortable. She reaches into her pocket and takes a bite of fruit leather. Then she follows Leo's instruction and eats a spoonful of trail mix.

Shit happens to me, she thinks. *Strange things, can't be explained. Tonight was strangest of all. It makes me feel crazy. But — mostly I'm so tired, so beat-to-shit tired of everything. Of being alone. And different. And afraid.*

While she had listened to the boys wrestle in recall of the predictions they had heard, she did not want to participate in their musings. Prophecy was simply part of Anna's life. It was commonplace conversation around her grandparents' dinner table. Prophecy continually swims through her dreams on the music of pow wows, drums, flutes and the old songs of sweat lodges and ceremonies. None of the teachings were ever fear-based.

To be afraid of the future would be to deny the entire past and present of the songline, a visiting aboriginal Elder had taught. *There is no fear in the truth of the story, for it is the back-and-forward story of tribal life. Before you and beyond, it unfolds. It continues.*

The elders had been human containers for prophecies. In the presence of their storytelling, she'd always feel … calmed.

But — after her mother had stolen Anna from the safety of the traditions, *any* predictions spoken by strangers had caused her to fall headlong into a panic attack.

And now this new experience — this seeing and hearing through one another's minds — nibbles at her insides. It forces her to choose. Her mother's screech rings through her brain. *Run, you idiot! Fool! Dammit, run!*

Bolstering her threadbare self-control before familiar panic can capture her, she hears Nonny's voice. *Do not let fear control you. Deepen your breath. Use your mind.*

Tremors pound and push for dominance, but her rational mind fights to analyze her condition. *No fear! I can feel my skin is prickling, my eyes are burning a little … but I can see, I can hear. Anxiety is … gone.* Her panic begins to subside again. She's tired, hungry. Her muscles are strained. But she is strong, and her senses are clear. *I'm a normal and ordinary human.*

Leo is standing beside her again.

"The bed's not much, Anna, but it has to do. Tomorrow, we find your Gramps. And we get supplies." He's relieved she looks less anxious. "Better drink some river water before the night gets any darker."

The boy is suddenly aware of how compliant she's become. He's uncomfortable with the change in her. Going numb wouldn't serve any of them.

He sees that Conan has returned to stoking the feeble fire. Leo needs to let his younger brother know that he's fully aware of Anna's issues. *If Conan retreats into judgment, he isolates. Exactly when I need to trust him most.*

"Anna," Leo says deliberately, making sure Conan hears his words, too. "We'll need your agility and determination to get up that mountain. You're with us, right?"

She blurts, "I *want* to help. No matter what happens, I want to help. It's just…" Her voice lowers to a dry rasp. "Sometimes I, uh, see … in a, well, psychic way. But not like what just happened," she adds hastily. "That was different." She coughs. Swallows. Anna knows if she doesn't stay in control of her nerves, they will run away with her again. "It's just that you're talking about all these damn *prophecies!* The *same ones* that my grandparents told me!" She clutches at her throat as if to strangle the shrill sound of fear. When she's away from her grandparents, that very word makes her fear rise.

She's never told anyone but her grandparents about the things she sees. About the messages and dreams. Nonny and Gramps had already known anyway. *Your seeing is a gift,* Nonny had told her. *And gifts are blessings, unless you use them in a wrong way. Respect comes first, Granddaughter. Use your gifts to serve the people, and the respect is a circle from you to the people and back.*

She hadn't been fearful of her psychic abilities until her mother showed her off at drunken, drugged-out parties. Or when school kids picked up cues and bullied her.

Witch! Weirdo! Freak!

That's when the panic attacks had started.

Leo wants to reach out and remove her hand from her throat, unbind her voice. But instead, he simply moves an inch closer to her.

"Anna." Leo pauses, choosing his words carefully. "Here's all we really know: I was sucker-punched by a freak wind-gust powerful enough to blow me off my horse in California and end up in *Montana.* Then you and I get a psychic picture, and we find Conan together. … You think you're the only one who feels weird or afraid?"

He sees that their physical closeness scares her. But Leo takes a chance and gently clutches her left shoulder — at arm's length.

"And now we realize, we *all three* heard the same predictions, *years* ago. We never understood them, then. We just loved the stories. How can any of us explain that?"

He waits out her silence.

"Anna." Leo makes direct eye contact, closing the space between them a fraction more. "Your Gramps is a medicine man, right? You told me enough about him for me to guess that."

Anna nods.

"A billion other kids you could've met wouldn't have had a *clue* what that means. Medicine man? Don't you think it's amazing that Conan and I were raised with ritual and ceremony? When we're not Natives? We didn't get all of what *you* got, but we learned enough to love and have faith in those teachings."

Conan is looking up at him from the fireside. The brothers slip a nod to one another.

"So instead of being dumped upside down with people who think you're from another planet, you're here with us. We *respect* your ways. We trust that your Gramps is a special guy. And chances are, he'll understand what's happened. He'll know why we're together and alive. And — maybe he'll even know what's next."

Leo's relieved to note that Anna's breathing seems to have steadied again. His 911-trained mind appreciates the slight shift. He loosens up.

"Look," he says. "You told me a dream said to 'find the boy with the red hat.' Right?" He waits for her to agree.

She nods carefully, after a pause. "Yes, right."

Leo continues, "We have to believe those, whatever, coincidences — and also our little melding-mind experience — happened for a reason. Maybe an alchemy of prophecies brought us together. I'm not sure I'd have found Conan without you. Or made it across the river, if you hadn't led the way."

Behind him, Conan pokes at the small embers of flame.

Leo puts his other hand on her right shoulder. He doesn't pull her closer, but he wants her to know he is fully there with her. "Anna, there's more you're not telling us. I've seen lots of ..." A small sigh slips past Leo's lips, unintended. "I've seen a lot of crisis over the last few years. Enough to know how terrible it's probably been for you, too. We've been stripped of home, parents — and nearly everyone we love. But ... now the three of us are here. Together. That has to be a kind of miracle."

He waits again for her response. His patience, so reliable and resilient, is cracking. After the strain of this afternoon's boulder jumps, his knees are starting to tremble, and he feels his ligaments stiffening. His head seems too heavy for his neck, his swollen feet too big for his boots.

"Anna. Conan said it. We're scared, too. I just know we can't let fear control us. Not now, not ever. And we don't know whether the prophecies are right or not. But remembering them may help us understand and survive."

The girl's expression is unreadable.

Conan suddenly barks, "Hey! Enough! It's dark. Sleep! Leo, you've got first up, right?"

Leo tilts Anna's chin up. Her face is darkened by the lightless night. He stares his questions into her hooded eyes.

"I'm okay," she mumbles unconvincingly. He drops his hands.

Anna walks, head down, shoulders slumped, into the tight opening of the enclosure. She sighs at the drover-lined dugout. She's not used to the kindness of such a gesture. She wants to ask Conan, *are you sure it's okay if I lie on your coat?* But fierce exhaustion descends. She collapses into the bed the boys made for her, wrapping herself in the familiar black cape.

A trilling sweet wind flutters across her mind as her eyes close. A flickering picture of Halfling, poised above her earth nest, eases into the dreamscape.

Good. You found the red-hat boy. Good. Now rest.

In the next moment, Anna drops into a grateful sleep.

Chapter 15
Brothers

Conan thrashes on the cold ground a foot inside the rock formation. He pulls the wide collar of his down vest as far up as it will go to soften the gravel under his neck. He bends knees to chest and re-stretches his restless legs, cracks his knuckles and puffs out a rough exhale.

He wants everything to magically go back to *life understandable*. The way it was before wind, drought, quakes, fire and responsibilities. Before worry burned like hot bricks in his chest.

Conan grits his teeth. He hears Dad's command: *Courage! FOCUS.*

He squeezes his eyes shut and warms himself on his visuals. Puppies, kittens, foals, rabbits. Black Angus calves born in kitchens and showers and under beds and in barn lofts. *Litters of them.*

"That's ranch life," adults had explained when accidents or illnesses snuffed out the existence of a pet. Or when jobs needed doing after school or before school, sun or rain. When they were cold or tired or just a little sick, the hay still had to be hauled, the stalls had to be mucked. Horses, whether docile or ornery, had to be moved into or out of pastures. Cows needed to be shooed from the barn before they ate all the winter's hay.

A veteran ranch hand had sermonized, *we live the life cycles of the animals and plants, as well as the seasons.* Conan had come to understand those cycles. He was heartbroken when a beloved pony had to be put down, or when coyotes took away the curly-wool spring lambs. He was euphoric when riding fast after cattle or when tromping through marshy streams to collect frogs, lizards, rocks and river shells.

He reorders the chaos of the last two years, before life went completely awry, into simpler, safer buckets.

A Place in Space, a favorite poetry book, pops into his mind. *Is that what I am looking for? Am I looking for my place in space?*

He swims in the silver lake and deep blue ocean of his imagination. Feels his young boy's body slide through water like a seal, unencumbered by the challenges to come.

Leo sits a few yards away, outside the cave. He faces the dwindling fire, hunkered over to keep warm. He is lost in his practical concerns, speculating how — with an entire forest down — there are so few combustible leftovers. He throws the last twigs on the smoldering pile. And worries that dying embers won't keep them comfortable — or keep the predators away.

The boy thinks about how funny it is that he's a proud member of the tech-solves-everything generation. He's used to being totally wired, voice-activated, and socially-networked. Yet here he is wishing for a larger pile of sticks.

He hears a step. Looks up.

Conan comes to sit.

Leo exhales. "Hey." He deliberately collapses his worries. "So, what, are we *both* gonna stay up all night?" His brother nudges him away from the fragile warmth. "And stop hogging the heat!" he adds. He leans past Conan and stokes the fire.

The younger boy hasn't heard anything Leo said. His mind races from thought to thought, none in a straight line or tied to the last one. He flops backwards onto the ground, then quickly jumps up, jittery from lack of sleep and worry. The younger boy begins pacing back and forth in a two-foot square next to Leo.

"Bro! What the hell are we doing here?" Conan wants his brother to make sense of the senseless. But instead of waiting for an answer, he takes off on a riff he can't slow. "How the *hell* did this happen?!" he shouts. "And who the heck *is* Anna, anyway? Yeah, you found each other, *blah-blah*. But she's *odd!* I mean, really, her mind-reading is fucking *weird.* And, yeah, she's got more 'psychic insight' than what we experienced before. But we've seen shamans do shit like this, right?" Words bump up against words. "Is she one of *us?* Is she gonna be a help? Or another rescue? Does she really have a *Gramps* who's a medicine man? What if we can't find him? Or what if we do, and he's a charlatan dude? Or some dangerous crazy guy? Or — well — what if he's dead?"

Leo doesn't answer. He knows his brother has to ramble all this out.

Conan takes a half sip of breath and switches subjects. "Yeah, we heard stories about this *prophecy* time. But hell, we never planned for it. Never trained for it. Never actually knew what it all meant. We were little kids! No one asked us if we believed it, right? Am I missing something here?" Conan blurts an angry answer to his own question. "Hell, no! And *jeez*, where *is* everyone? There's no sign of life! And why fucking *Montana?* How could we have been *blown* here? That's like a bullshit *Halloween* movie."

The thoughts in his head for the past three days are cascading over each other.

"Hey! Remember that old TV show we watched with Papa, where all the survivors of a plane crash are really dead? But that's not revealed until the season finale?"

Leo rises up and pinches Conan's cheek.

"Ouch!" Conan flinches defensively. "Okay, Leo, I got it. We're alive, alright?" His voice cracks the dry question. "Guess we were saved. If 'saved' is the right word. Better to think we *survived.* But ... no one else? ... Why *us?*"

Conan slumps. Folds over like an abandoned beach chair in winter, emptied and worn out. His forehead droops two inches above the dented ground. He struggles to sigh — but has no air left in him.

After a long moment, he lifts his gaze high enough to stare into the fire. The dying flames calm his agitation. Two minutes pass in silence.

"Leo!" Conan's sharp bark catches Leo off guard. "Dude. You're made for this Armageddon hero-cowboy stuff, this football-captain crap. Not *me*! I went along with you and Dad because, what the hell ..."

His brother's choked cry rakes through Leo.

Conan, near breathless, continues. "... was there a *choice?* Ever? But — it's not *me*. I don't know if I've got anything *left* to do whatever we're supposed to do! Or supposed to *be!*"

The older boy moves closer so that he sits shoulder-to-shoulder with his brother as the cold begins to penetrate their thin clothes.

He can't answer the continuing barrage of Conan's queries.

"Home? Do you think it's still there?"

...

"If so, what's left? ... Who?"

...

"It's so far away. So far."

...

"What are the chances we're really alone this time, Leo?" His brother's runaway nervousness abates for a moment as he utters a hope. "So many times, it came down to you and me and Dad. But then someone would appear. Like, remember those hot shots who showed up? Those guys who were fighting fires all the way down from San Francisco? Or how about the time those refugees came up from L.A., the trained Army Rangers? They helped dig out that sinkhole that collapsed half the Valley. Other times, people showed up who brought equipment and medicine. At the exact right minute, we got support. But now ... it seems really alone out here."

We might be last two left — of our family, our tribe. Our pack. Leo hears that unspoken fear in Conan's words. He wants to give the worry an honest consideration. He wants to stay solid, not react. But his stomach growls violently. The stark reality of having no food, no light and no map forces his focus.

He says what is true for him.

"Conan, part of me believes we're just in the wrong place. That we'll hike up the mountain and find Anna's Gramps. Or start off for home, and others will show up to share whatever journey there is, and that, together, we'll understand whatever life is left. That part of me believes it'll be ... not perfect, but *okay*. But ... the other part of me knows there's way too much destruction. Anna n' me, we traveled miles to find you. There wasn't a sign that civilization had ever been here. There were no busted-up homes, there was no burned-out junk like in California.

There was nothing. And it's damn quiet now. Except for the wind and the river. It's way too quiet."

Leo glances up at the dark sky with its dense clouds defying the wind. He wants to call out whatever is unseen in the night, whatever refuses to be seen. He wants to know where truth is hidden.

"And I agree that it's totally bizarre, totally unreal that we could have been blown here, a thousand miles from home, and we're in one piece, with not even a cut, and my hat's still on my head, your stuff's still in your pockets." Leo shakes his head. "I don't know. I just don't know, and all that prophecy stuff is another mystery. It's weird we remembered those together, today. It's not like they were the only woo-woo we ever heard. But the predictions popped into both our minds at once."

Conan nods, digging in the dirt absently with a stick.

Leo says, "I think you were six or seven, so I'd have been eight or nine on that one day when I realized that we were hearing something really important. Remember that Navajo teacher? That really gentle, tall guy who told us our old pet sheep was our 'special protector?' Remember how funny we thought that was? But then he said we'd have other protectors coming who were even greater souls ..."

"Yeah." Conan smiles at the memory. "Then the white buffalo sisters came, just like the Navajo teacher told us they would."

The brothers lock eyes for a moment, recognizing a significance in the memory that had previously eluded them.

"*Synchronicity*, Aunt Sophia called it," Leo says.

Conan repeats, "Synchronicity." He gazes past Leo into the solid darkness.

Another long silence passes between them before the older boy continues his recollection of that childhood year.

"We lost our sheep, and my puppy Mo, and our first horse Sweet Pea within two weeks. Damn, that was a hard winter. But, you're right. Then the white buffalo sisters came. And we had celebrations with visitors from all over. Sophia told us it was the fulfillment of a prophecy. ... And that's when she started telling us the first stories."

Leo sits up as another thought strikes him.

"Funny. I didn't put those pieces together until now. But we built that sweat lodge and then the medicine men came, and ceremonies followed. Hey. You remember an old woman, wrapped in a star blanket?"

Conan smiles. "Yeah! A great-grandmother who was Pipe Keeper. She cried! Said she was so happy to have lived long enough to see the return of the white buffalo! She said, 'This is the Promised Time.' And ... what else did she say?"

Leo remembers it nearly word for word.

"Yeah, the Pipe Keeper told us that centuries ago, when the White Buffalo Calf Woman first appeared to the Lakota, she prophesied a time of Earth changes when most of the buffalo would be wiped out. Which is what happened. But not to worry because in time to come, they would reappear, and that would signify another big shift, and people who continued to follow the old ways of the Good Red Road would survive."

"Yeah, *Earth changes,* the grandma said," Conan whispers. The significance isn't lost on either of the boys.

Leo doesn't want to speak the next part. *Few survive*, the woman had prophesied.

Aloud, he says "Dad didn't want to hear it. He was like, 'Okay, partner, we're outta here.' He'd say, 'I think we have to go look for cattle at Red Rock.' As if there actually *were* any." The brothers hoot at the remembrance.

"Yeah, Dad! Jeez, he couldn't stand the *woo-woo*," Conan grins. "So, he took you along on his escapes. Said I was too little to sit a horse all day. That was okay by me. I got to stay in midst of whatever was going down. I was excited and curious. But … the day the white buffalo came was different. I felt the power of it, and prophecies didn't scare me. You know?" He asks figuratively. He doesn't really need an answer. "That otherworldly feeling came over me in ceremonies. Like I could feel the entire *cosmos* and I wanted to grab the magic. I loved it. But I was shy." He laughs at himself. "I'd hide in Granny's bedroom while the *boom boom* of the giant kettledrums made the roof shake! I couldn't resist watching when the big drums were calling."

Leo flashes on how different they've always been. He'd figured out the adult world using logic and a basic sense of how things should be — and then he'd translate for Conan. His little brother hadn't been driven by Leo's will for engagement. And he's never going to be, the older boy thinks now. Conan is an artist, a dreamer; before he'd learned to write, he was a poet in his heart. His brother, Leo knows, is tentative about real life but drawn to imagination, mystery, secrets and hidden treasures.

Far from the world they know, instincts heightened, brother-to-brother support intact, they have each other's backs, as they have always. Yet now, Leo hears Conan differently. *He won't tolerate being an observer. He wants to be right alongside the forces that move the Universe. He wants to be right inside them. I can see that now.* Aunt Sophia had always said, *Conan's our little Merlin.* But Leo didn't absorb it then the way he does in this moment.

He leans back and studies his brother.

"You want to practice it, right? You want to call in the spirit world? Mind read, interpret dreams. Be a medicine man. You want their *knowing.* You want to heal and bless. And make magic."

Conan turns a cocked head to his brother. "It's why I mostly remember those days in better detail than you do. Bro, the only thing I ever really loved was … the phenomena. And *abilities.* When we learned real science in school, I started to see, well … systems and patterns and connections. Information jumped off the page. It explained, you know, where evidence-based science crossed and blended with new science and alchemy *and* with the old ways. And how what we call magic actually has explanations and purpose!" Conan, realizing he's been talking too loudly, lowers his voice. "Science doesn't deny the power of traditions. It makes them real and practical, with proof and meaning. I believe that, Leo."

Leo says he's had the same thoughts. "But I wouldn't make much of a medicine man, myself."

His brother grins, glad to be validated. "Granny, Aunt Sophia, their friends... they *knew* stuff. They saw how patterns led to shifts and changes, way ahead of time. How did they know? Sophia used to say, *watch the earth signals.* And it came to me that she really could read the energy of people and places and things. And that was cool. Later I was like, *shit,* she can read people's thoughts, too!"

The boy pulls his flannel and vest tighter around him. He laughs. "Remember Sophia's guessing games? *What's the crow telling us, chattering in the tree? What's the story the wind wants us to know? What does it whisper?* We got pretty good at figuring stuff out. But we never put her games together with the prophecies. Now I get it, Leo. She and Granny were preparing us for *this* time. ... You think?"

Leo nods. "It seems obvious now. I mean, they made sure we had practical survival skills. Someone was always around to teach us to make bows, and skin wild rabbits, and set up tents. ... But, yeah, we never saw the prophecy angle." He thinks about it some more. "Definitely, they were preparing us."

Conan sighs deeply again, his excitement at their realization shifting. "It became a future to believe in, what they were all teaching. Now, well ... that won't exactly happen, not in the way I fantasized."

The awareness of dreams never to be fulfilled slams heart-first into a weariness, a new kind of grief. Sorrow for his unlived life engulfs the boy. Conan huffs in an attempt to clear his throat. But at last the tears he has withheld are let loose. He cries for a childhood gone too soon. He cries from the shock and grief of loneliness, of the loneliness of the last three days. And for being fifteen yet feeling like a used-up old man.

"Leo, my god. *Dad!*" He coughs. Shivers.

And Mom. Mom had lived a two-hour car ride away. When the freeways had cracked and caved in, they couldn't reach her.

"Leo, are we losing our minds?" Quick rejection erupts on his brother's face. "No!' Conan pushes on. "Listen, Leo! I mean, we did *nuts* stuff. We raced into firestorms, pulled people out of ocean waves and undertows and from cars sliding off fucking *cliffs.* Worst were the times we *couldn't* help because we already had too many people to drag to safety! Bro. *We saw people die.* DIE. That shit leaves scars we can't see."

Conan stares blankly at his shaky hands for too many seconds. Leo worries that his brother is lost in a freeze response. But he looks up at last, and Leo silently sighs his relief.

"Just months before hell broke loose," Conan continues, "... when was that? Two, three years ago? We were cruisin' life! I mean, we were semi-solid — but pretty much okay." His voice cracks. "Next, *boom!*

Craziness! But — we had a mission, then. And we had each other. So, we kept going. But ... were we sane? ... Crazy people don't *know* they're crazy, right?" He pokes the dying fire with the twig. "There wasn't ever time to break down, or cry, or give up. ... But — what now? Is fear gonna catch up to us? Are we in shock and denial?" He ducks his head and lowers his voice again. "I'm afraid I'll be a screamer, Leo. Like people we saw who went *psycho*. Normal one day, flipped-out the next. We saw people run in circles like headless chickens, freaked-out inside their own brains. They couldn't find their way out, they went *nuts*. Damn scary to watch! Remember?"

Leo puts an arm around his brother's shoulder. "It's okay, Bro. Don't rush. Say it all out. I'm not going anywhere."

Conan extends the silence, taking deep breaths of the night air.

"Are we in PTSD hell?" he finally utters hoarsely. "And we just don't know it?" Conan shakes his head and laughs chokingly. "That question scares the *crap* outta me!"

Chapter 16
Clouds

Leo leans sideways and pulls Conan against him until his brother's trembling quiets. The cry is cathartic, Leo knows.

Conan sucks in a last hard breath and begins to relax. But when he turns to face Leo, he startles, and his thoughts are intercepted.

A strange new swirl of dark clouds is circling overhead in the unillumined night sky.

"What are *those?*"

Leo looks up, and both boys scan the dark. The clouds appear extremely dense. They do not have the opacity or vapor of familiar clouds. This sky, they see, is different from the heavy air of an impending storm.

Conan whispers, "Wait, something's not right."

"Yeah. Those clouds are moving the way birds flock together. Or like … sardines, like fish that swim in precise patterns ..."

One formation now seems to suck and swallow the night's chemistry until ordinary wisps of heavy, moist air are replaced by a thick and dirty fog that gives form to the twisted oddness. And it's moving with a rapid flow and scurry towards them.

Intrigued, the boys study the phenomenon until a slight shift of heavier elements descends into the cloud from the thick night air. Eerily, the dark formation seems to have an organizing principal.

"It almost looks like it has a purpose." Leo whispers. "Yeah, something's not right …"

In the next moment, the dark cloud nosedives toward them.

The boys rear back as one, then duck. Arms reflexively covering their heads, they watch in astonishment as the cloud expands to twice its original size before morphing into a freakishly humanoid form. The brothers are horrified to see the features of the dark miasma blur, then sharpen into the warped reflection of a human face.

"What the f …?" Leo breathes.

At a stroke, the cloud drops directly in front of the brothers, and like a knife it deliberately slices them apart.

Conan, his eyes still wet from tears, jumps to his feet. As if choreographed, Leo instantly follows. They stand back-to-back. Both boys have their fists up, their legs planted in a fighting stance. The malevolent face flies up again above their heads, then plunges down to separate them a second time. The brothers press their backs together, determined to prevent the force from dividing them, moving in a coordinated circle as they defensively punch at their malignant attacker.

The force gathers into itself a third time before expanding into an even larger spawning and plunges at the boys again in a rapid fury.

Leo and Conan stumble, duck, sway and push — but stay together, back-to-back. Neither gives an inch in their coordinated effort against the enemy's demonic strength. Their knees buckle, their heads swivel and slam back, they stay standing only by the strength of each other's shoulders. The humanoid cloud dives towards them and dashes away again in dozens of attacks, sharpening its force and sending chilling, arctic shocks through the boys with each bone-chilling stab. A blinding dry-ice smoke envelops them as they fight the strikes and scream in solidarity.

"Dig your feet into the earth! Don't fold!"

"Look out! Hold your ground!"

Their shouts are muffled by the cold fog that engulfs them with every blow.

Then abruptly the cloud's denseness dissolves, diminishing to a thin, opaque wisp. Conan and Leo squint through the residual haze to understand what they're seeing. The vapor contracts. It sucks itself into a grey, puckered, fist-sized denseness — and holds itself still for long seconds.

"It'll pop or collapse," Conan whispers over his shoulder.

Instead, the cloud expands. It puffs out and re-forms into a crone's visage, crow-beaked and wretched. The face is wild, weepy, and grim, with eyes swimming in rings of overlapping wrinkles. The sickly face has a green hue, and its rage is deathly.

The brothers gasp in horror.

The hellishness of the visage turns suddenly into desperation. The witchy old woman's face becomes sad and needy. Clawing, cold fingers, disembodied from the cloud face, reach out tremblingly to grab for them. An ambient ache for her grief and pain whispers into the boys' joined consciousness. It's as if the cloud is whimpering. *H-e-l-p, please. Please, my darlings. Save me! If only you'd listen. Please listen!* The familiar call to answer an emergency makes the boys dizzy and momentarily confused, on the verge of self-blame and shame.

Conan rebounds first. He shakes his head clear of grief and guilt, and screams, "*Lie!* It's a lie!"

The cloud expands again, snarling. It drops pretense and renews its attack. Its weepy despair explodes, as if set afire by a stick of dynamite. A growling, vitriolic red-devil face emerges from the miasma.

The boys jump and swivel, still holding firm to their back-to-back circle, dodging a strike by stepping closer towards the fire. Leo acts on instinct. He leans sideways, keeping his back braced against Conan, and grabs a smoldering stick from the ebbing fire. "NOT FOOLED!" he thunders at the cloud.

Conan is caught by surprise, but quickly sees a chance and grabs a second stick straight from the fire, careless of the flames. "You *lie! Screw you!*" He hurls the blazing weapon at the descending cloud.

Otherworldly shrieks pierce the night. The boys' ears pound from the vibration. In a shuddering blast, the fiendish face collapses into its original grey, dense cloud formation — and pulls back into the night. The remaining clouds darken. They circle, seeming to watch and wait. The toxic fumes left in the air cause the boys' stomachs to churn, their knees to wobble.

And as rapidly as they had appeared, the outrider clouds dissolve into the dim penumbra.

The brothers hold their combative stance for a minute longer, their ears still ringing from the devilish shriek of the demon face.

"You okay?"

Conan gulps. "Yeah."

Slowly, methodically, they relax knees and fists, shake out stiff fingers, clear their eyes of the cold smoke.

"Stay alert," Leo warns.

Conan's fear has turned to defensive anger. "That *face!*" He shivers. "At first I thought she wanted help, like, *Help! My spirit is stuck in this crazy cloud and it sucks!* But that switch to the devil face, and her screech, damn! She was *evil* more than hurt."

His hands fly to his ears to shut down the echoes, then move across his forehead to clear the sweat. "That face had me by the damn throat! I mean, I felt this gut-clenching *guilt!* Was that cloud-woman someone we lost when we couldn't get through those walls of flame back in California? Was she someone ripped up in the tornado winds? Every scream for help we ever *heard* was in her cry! It was freakin' sad, desperate."

Conan's exhale releases a whistling whine. This is how it always is for him. Conan's hyper-intuitiveness — his hyper-sensitivity — causes him to feel first, process after.

"Breathe," Leo tells him.

"She acted desperate, Leo! … For *what?* Something we have that she wants? Those creepy claw fingers grasping at us for — for *what?* What the hell did she want? Did she want *us?*"

As Leo listens, he moves in a slow circle, his hands unclenched but reflexively alert, ready to defend them both. His attention is still on the dark sky overhead. Without changing his pace, the older boy eases forward in the direction where the cloud had receded. He waves his arms around in slow motion and tries to catch a vapor to examine. If he could see it more closely, he thinks, he might be able to understand…

Just as he had feared, the circling patrol clouds that the boys had thought departed suddenly reappear out of the shadows of the night. Again, the dense formations sweep toward the boys. But this time, instead of attacking, they stop short and hover. They converge into a poisonous, sickly green before mutating into chilly black wisps.

Leo's instinct is to stop, think. He will not allow himself to respond without analysis. *"They look … like that witchy cloud,"* Leo whispers. "They're made of that same odd, heavy air … Is it poison gas gathered into a semi-solid form?" He instinctively runs his mind through chemistry lessons and First Responder scenarios ranging from Anthrax to nuclear attack. Nothing makes sense.

Keeping an uneasy eye on the clouds, Conan follows Leo's thoughts. "Remember when smoke from the fires and volcanoes mixed with burning fuel? This feels and smells like that… But these clouds have form, and almost *weight* to them." The clouds spin, bump against and pass through one another, competing for space and proximity. "Are there liquid plastics that can form and re-form themselves at will?"

Leo nods carefully. "Plasticity? I remember studying how some elements can alter or modify themselves, but damn … to actually attack us?" He keeps his intention on analysis, staying deliberately cool in spite of his pounding heart.

"Do you think that witch cloud is coming back? Or did she give up?" Conan shivers.

Leo has no answer.

They watch in silence as the formations drop, dip, and finally retreat, the visage of hateful despair leaving a lingering pall on the mist of the lightless night.

Chapter 17
Gift of Fire

Half an hour goes by before the boys' tension eases and they remember that Anna has been inside the cave through the entire battle. A sudden terror that she, too, might have been attacked seizes Leo. He quickly moves to the mouth of the rock opening.

The girl is sound asleep under the protection of the boulders. Thankful that the screeches of the terrorizing cloud seem not to have reached her, Leo smiles in relief, shrugs and silently steps back to the fireside.

The fire is almost gone, now, except for small embers. The brothers have been plenty cold before; they've lain awake many nights together, wishing for home, for comfort, for familiar spaces and warm beds. But tonight's bitter cold is accompanied by a freezing disquietude.

Leo knows they have to get sleep, themselves, however. "Go settle in and get some shut-eye. I'll wake you in three hours," he tells his brother.

Conan doesn't object. But he curls up only two feet within the lip of the cave, ensuring the slightest sound will rouse him. "Not going far. Just in case..."

Leo deliberately does not respond.

Conan repeats, "Just ... in ... case ..."

In spite of his flighty nerves, Conan is asleep in a heartbeat, his arms wrapped tightly around himself for warmth.

The older boy walks a few feet away from the fireside. In the unforgiving blackness, he searches for anything combustible, swearing under his breath, "Too damn cold and damp." It's hard for him to believe that after all the fires he'd battled in California, he's now fighting to keep a small campfire burning. "Nothing to fuel it," he says to himself, disgusted.

The cold is settling more deeply in his bones. He kicks the dirt. He's walked only twenty steps from the cave, but already he can barely make out the shadow of the boulders. *Can't stray far.* Giving up his frustrating search for firewood, the boy circles back. He tries not to surrender to frustration and exhaustion.

A yard from the campfire, he jumps back, startled. A sharp burst from the embers catches his attention. He crouches down to take a closer look.

The ashes spontaneously flare into three tall peaks of flame.

"What the *hell?*" he almost shouts.

Must be some natural fuel suddenly caught, he thinks. *Maybe dried moss or plant residue. Okay, no big deal. It can happen.*

He relaxes. The flame gives new life to the small center of the campfire's heat, and the warmth draws Leo closer. He pokes the embers with a long, damp branch.

Not much here to cause that high a flame ... but, what the hell.

Wary but grateful, he lifts up his thanks in a low voice. "Whatever caused the heat to rise, I'm grateful. I've cursed fire, before now, for destroying California ... but right now, I'm thankful for this flame."

He watches the fire, with its hot, blue-orange flare, dance up and across the small campfire. In spite of his exhaustion and worry, he allows himself to laugh.

Was Aunt Sophia right? That elements have wisdom? Maybe you're listening, Sophia, and sending us warmth?

He walks toward the rocks that hide Anna and Conan. The heat from the fire reaches them, too. *No way!* Leo shakes his head, slowly and thoughtfully.

Total destruction. Geographical insanity. Anna appearing, with her mysteries and skills. Conan, lost and then saved. Noxious faces in the sky. There's no sense to any of it. It's all non-sense. But ... it's real.

He's bone-tired, in mind and body. But he has a strangely tingling sense that the flames are *listening*.

Leo faces the fire, his senses alert. And it flares higher and wider a second time.

He can only be wondrously, humbly grateful. *Honor the elements*, he repeats to himself.

Before the chaos, when the California drought had been pushing ten years, a Zuni medicine man had taught the boys about making rain. *Thank the spirits of earth, air, metal, wind, and fire*, the man had taught. *Honor all the elements in your prayers. Leave none out. Honor all.*

Leo holds that thought now.

Thank you, oxygen, hydrogen and carbon ... Damn, my brain is too tired to remember chemistry! Natives know how to respect and include the spirits of all the elements. *Ah, shit. I'm just an itinerant white guy.* Leo considers whether talking to the fire is an indication he's gone completely insane. Decides it's okay. As long as he doesn't discard science for magic, that is.

He listens to the soundless night and his rumbling hunger. He warms his hands, his legs. And pays close attention to his state of mind. *Confidence, not blind faith*, Leo reminds himself.

He accepts the obvious. The alone-ness and the distance from home. Their hunger, and the lifelessness of the land. He acknowledges the fear that threatens his courage. He examines all these realities coolly, and then repeats within himself the constant teaching of his family, the message that lives deep in his bones: *Face life as it is, straight-up. Face it the way it is right now, and how it shows itself in this moment. No fear, and no delusion. Stay strong.*

He settles into his own center, into the ambient chord of self-knowledge. It's what his grandmother called his "true north." It's the place, she had said, where his personal compass will always point. *This is your true direction, Leo. Confidence matched with humility and generosity. Courage to make honest choices and lead. True north is your personal inner compass. Let it guide you.*

True north, he repeats to himself. *Solid in the face of whatever happens. Here and now, no exceptions.* Granny's words are with him. *Gather your inner self. Be the rolling rock in a storm, able to settle and secure the others.*

He measures those words for accuracy. *Harmony is a "true north" for me too. People have to find ways to just stop the fighting and grasping and dividing. And learn to live together! Why is that so damned hard? What the hell! Look where it got the world.*

He kicks at a fist-sized rock. The rock rolls an inch, then stops.

Solid is good — but a rock is too rigid, even when it's rolling. Better for me to flex, to bend and adjust. I need to sync with what's coming down ...

Leo squints in the dark, scanning the desolation. He looks back at his brother, sleeping a few feet away in the cave, then up at the black and brooding sky absent of moon and stars.

Okay. Whatever is going on, we can find our centers, all three of us.

He stares thoughtfully into the flames that don't grow or die, but sustain a steady, warm burn. He decides it's a sign his confidence isn't foolhardy. *There are fires that destroy, and ones that give life.* He wonders if the source of both is the same; if fires, perhaps, themselves choose which definition to follow.

The boy touches the rectangle of branded skin above his heart. He had forgotten about it all day. But now he squirms two fingers up inside his shirt and feels the strange tattoo. He is half expecting that it will be gone — because maybe it was an illusion to start with.

Nope. It's just as he remembers, its length and width, the skin raised like a brand, but with intricate details the hot iron of a cattle brand couldn't create.

Is this thing another miracle? Or a crazy mystery he'll never understand? *Or,* he shudders against his will, *a curse?* Could it be a mark that distinguishes him, sets him apart in ways that augur trouble? And more suffering?

He deflects his worry. *Bullshit.* He can't allow his confidence to drain, replaced by fear. Strange as the mark is, he won't let it control his mind or disrupt his responsibilities. He's good at problem solving; he intuitively knows what to consider, discount and discard. He doesn't like strange happenings to be undiagnosed; he believes in his experience and believes there are no coincidences. Yet ... there are always bigger mysteries afoot, ones with meaning. His family had taught him that, too.

He stands, stretches his limbs and makes his way to the rock cave entrance. Looking in on where his brother and Anna are sleeping, Leo wishes he had blankets to cover them.

Waves of exhaustion suddenly enfold him, and thoughts of comfort are no longer pressing. He is simply too tired to care about anything but letting his eyes close and his mind rest for just a few moments. He settles on the ground outside the cave, pulls his knees up, and allows himself to quiet every instinct of his survival training and fall into an untroubled sleep.

Until the sunless day begins to dawn, and a strange sound of tinkling bells awakens him.

PART II

Chapter 18
Meera

Conan dreams of himself as a toddler.

He cranes his neck to look up at his grandmother. Her clear eyes capture his attention. She tells him the story he never tires of.

When you were born, your brother said, in his two-year old way, that he dreamt he called you down to earth. "Wolf-Brother, Wolf-Brother, it's time to come home," he called over and over again. "Brother Wolf." And so, we named you Conan. It means "brother to the wolf."

In his dream, the scene shifts from his grandmother's home to a forest of tall pine.

He runs with a wolf pack, his neck and face hot from their collective breath. He senses the power in their furred and muscled legs and feels the pack's accelerated rush, the sweat of their muzzles pressed together. Fearlessly, he meets their golden eyes, unafraid of the whetted fangs all around him. He feels their intelligence within himself. He trusts them.

He dreams of boys who become wolves, and brothers who live for the pack, all for one. Boys and wolves, wild cubs and howling adults are one tribe at the crest of a mountain. And he hears his grandmother's sing-song mantra.

Wolf-Brother, Wolf-Brother, it's time to come home.

Conan awakens from his dream and leaps straight onto his feet with such velocity that he slams his head on the ceiling of the rock enclosure.

"Shit!"

He rubs his eyes to see his brother standing at mouth of the cave.

Anna, behind him, whispers "What's that sound?"

"I dunno. Woke me, too," Conan responds, over his shoulder. He stares straight ahead past Leo.

Tinkling bells can be heard crystallizing on the thin wisps of foggy dawn air. Each note hangs as if balanced on molecules of morning dew. And each has a resonance, echoing a second chorus of cresting ripples and peals. After every third or fourth bar of the bell chorus, a lone Tibetan horn seems to echo in a far-off valley. It circles back to them before exploding in a baritone chorus of gongs. Trills of songbirds follow, as if a hundred-bird flock dives towards them through the thick, grey morning air over a splashing of river rocks. The crystal melody is tied together with the music of the elements, and the symphony is transcendent.

For Leo, Anna and Conan, the music knits together their thoughts and invites wonder, drawing them forward.

"You hear that?"

"What *is* that?"

Anna whispers, "Stay vigilant. Stay alert!"

Standing between the brothers, Anna's mind and muscles warm. There is no time to marvel that she's there and included, because of the bells soaring in the otherwise silent morning.

Leo signals them forward towards the fire that has miraculously burned true and steady all night. The majestic music beckons them, and any danger in the empty, torn land of riven rock is temporarily obscured. The bells pull them on invisible cords to the river's edge.

Leo's instincts kick in as they near the water. He signals Conan to step further to his left and for Anna to move to his right and a pace behind him. If they have to, they can encircle, and trap, whatever's ahead. No one runs or freezes. They take careful steps together. Yet not one of them feels any fear as the bells grow louder. The anticipation makes the hair on their arms and the backs of their necks tingle.

Anna, raised on Native ceremonial flutes and drums, forest sounds and bird song, thinks, *the music surrounds us ... but flows into and out of us at one time ... We are the music, too. It's a shared frequency.* The cascading notes merge with their bodies' cells.

The closer they draw to the river, the louder the music gets. It skitters and dives and matches the cadence of the white-capped waters dancing at the bank. The river's roar overlaps with the music, uniting with it, harmonizing around it.

Leo remembers his *true north.* He feels a kind of perfect gratitude echoing in this sweet symphony of sound.

Marveling, Conan whispers, "Is it one thing, the river and the music? Or are they separate ...?"

The music closes in more tightly around them. It's ethereal, yet earthy. It's gloriously unnatural, yet hyper-real.

Leo whispers, "It's like I can *feel* the music. It's like it's ... tangible." He fights the urge to reach out and touch the notes he can't see. "Vigilance." He repeats Anna's word of warning, then signals his companions to stay low to the ground. They baby-step, alert as woodland animals.

"Stealth." Anna calls the fox spirit to guide her.

It seems to them that the music emanates from the water. Yet closer to the river's edge, the sound dashes around them and transforms to a buzz and hum. It's like a swarm of bees soaring from a dozen hives, as if multiple queens lead winged subjects in one body of motion and sound. The seductive music still beckons and entices them to follow.

And then they see it.

They stop short, bump into one another and rock back, still in their crouch positions.

Before them, at the shore of the river, bright and beautiful against the endless background of empty land, stands a wide tree of abundant and vibrant green. Hanging from branches bent with their weight are enormous pendant pomegranates, ripe to the point of splitting their leathery skins. Seeds spill out their rich, thick, red juices onto the torn and tumbled dirt.

The kids freeze. They soak up the shocking sight of the red fruit against the glossy wide leaves.

Awe and wonder, Leo and Conan think to themselves. *How lucky are we?* Anna marvels.

The music lowers its volume into a steady syncopated drumming.

Conan rises out of his crouch, clutching his growling gut and glancing over at his brother to wait for a signal. All three kids gulp with the aching hunger of their several days without real food.

Leo does what he never allows himself to do. He sighs audibly at the sight before them. Anna's thin body rebels. Her stomach speaks loudly enough for the boys' bellies to respond.

Leo signals them forward. "Slow. Vigilance," he cautions. The incongruities of the color and the smell and the promise of taste warn their trained minds.

But any possibility of planning their approach is interrupted by the renewed tinkling of bells.

From around the side of the pomegranate tree there appears a ridiculously young, exotically beautiful little girl. The child is more shocking a sight to the three witnesses than the juicy pomegranates. Her bright pink Hello Kitty t-shirt with its wrinkled, ruffled cap sleeves is trimmed in tangerine; her short-shorts are as incongruous as the tempting fruit contrasted against the pounding, frothy river behind her. She wears thin leather thong sandals on her delicate feet and her toenails are painted a fuchsia that matches the *bindi* on her forehead. The bells on her toes, wrists and ankles ring out an unbounded, joyful welcome.

The young girl's open-mouthed, off-balance smile tilts left to right and back again like the grin of a bobble head, settling into a broad beam that radiates her warmth on all three observers.

Anna resists the temptation to fall to her knees in front of this child, to kiss her feet and weep. She's dizzy with a feeling like hope. Embarrassed, she hardens her face and disciplines her mind, glancing at Leo for a signal on how to proceed.

The emotion behind Leo's eyes tells her that he feels the same need to believe in something wondrous and rare.

Conan waits fifteen seconds. But when his brother doesn't act, his own self-preservation demands that he initiate some version of a commanding tone. He barks at the little girl, "Those okay to eat?"

The girl's laugh matches the tinkling bells.

"Of course! It grows for you. *We* grew it for you!" Her speech and laughter blend in a distinctive Indian-accented English lilt. Her smile is as radiant as what they remember of the sun.

"Grew it for you?" Leo asks.

But Conan lunges towards the fruit. He's past caring, since the girl is obviously too young and small to cause harm.

Leo reaches out to grab his brother's sleeve.

"Hey!" Conan's protest hangs in the heavy air.

Leo clings roughly to Conan's torn shirtsleeve. He growls, "Dammit, *think*. Do you know this fruit's okay?"

The girl's broad, giggling smile expresses her delight. Porcelain-white teeth shine against her pomegranate-stained mouth. Holding Leo's eyes, she reaches over and picks one of the spherical fruits, and then another. She peels back the skin and samples seeds from each, as if to say, *all are safe*. She licks her stained fingers, then leaps to the higher branches of the tree before twirling again to lower ones and springing back to the ground like the tree is a playground amusement. She doesn't trip on the rocks jutting from uneven soil, or from ragged roots pushing through the choppy dirt. Juice trickles down her chin. Her smile never wavers — and her eyes never leave the kids.

"Ooooh-kay," Leo laughs.

The little girl bends into a formal stage bow and gestures invitingly at the topiary.

Leo doesn't miss the obvious show she is putting on. Enthralled in spite of his caution, he signals a nod to Conan and Anna. They both charge the fruit tree.

Leo stays back and warns, "Eat slowly!" Their stomachs have all shrunken. He doesn't want any gulping, or their bodies will protest and sicken.

Conan catches his breath between bites, and nudges Anna, who startles out of a reverie of tangy sweetness to take an inhale. The joy of simply being alive is a rare and beautiful feeling for Anna. It sweeps over her now, and she smiles at the child who stands no higher than her waist.

The little girl turns to Leo. "And you, old king?" she asks. He flinches at the address. "Even the *king* must eat, no?"

"Whaddaya mean?" Coolly, Leo reaches for a large piece of fruit and strips away its skin. His appetite and thirst overwhelm his best intentions.

Between their slurps and swallows, Conan, Anna and Leo steal looks at the girl. Eventually they break their hungry silence and bombard her with overlapping questions.

"What's your name?"

"How old are you?"

"Where're you from, India? How did you get here?"

"How did this tree get here?"

"Where's your family?"

Leo tries to maintain a semblance of authority. His voice is level and mature as he questions her, which is hard to do with a mouthful of seeds.

The little girl points to the rips on the older boy's clothing and dissolves into a full belly laugh. The others join the joke at Leo's expense, until the older boy drops all pretense and grins along with them. Open, contagious enjoyment erupts from the child, her tinkling laugh matching the lyrical trill of her bells.

"Meera, my name is *Mee*-ra." The girl answers Leo's first question, only.

In succession, she approaches each of them. She presses her tiny hands into a triangle of prayer and bows her head. They smile at her solemnity and bow back to her. As they bend forward, she touches each forehead with her own.

"I've been waiting for you *forever*." Meera laughs as she scolds them. Her musical tone rings through the dense air, yet her voice is as light as the tender forehead she presses against theirs. "For forever! And also since you woke up after the Three Days of Darkness."

She bows last to Leo. He is astonished by her words, and amazed, too, to see that tears of emotion stream down her very round, very brown cheeks.

"You have been promised for so long, and now to meet you ..." she says.

Conan interrupts her words with another barrage of questions.

"Uh, *okay*, Meera, how'd you get here? You made the pomegranates appear? ... You a witch? Sorcerer? ... No, that's not possible, you're too small, too young." The younger boy's voice vacillates from plaintive to demanding. It's a jumble of insistence, curiosity and gratitude. "What do you know of the last few days? How did we — or you — *get* here? And how did this, this *tree* get here?"

The girl laughs melodiously. "Oh, Conan, your grandmother was right, you are 'the boy of the provocative questions!' This is the sign of great intelligence."

"Wait! Only Granny ever said that to me. ... Do you know her? Where is she?" Conan's angry suspicion floods back. "Hey! How'd you know my name?" *What right does this little girl have to know things about me?* he thinks. Things that remind him of a home and family he may never see again.

Meera tilts her head and looks delighted.

"Things are exactly as they should be, as prophesied. All is as was expected, my friends Leo and Conan and Anna."

She turns to Anna with innocent precociousness. "*Except*, of course ..." Meera cocks her head to one side, "*Anna* isn't your true name, is it? Your real, *soul* name, my darling?"

Whaaaa ...? Leo thinks. Meera rattles them all, he recognizes. First, she infers she knows the boys' grandmother. And now she accuses Anna of using a false name? With her childish, flimsy clothes, she appears so delicate and vulnerable — like another orphan. But she has the confidence of mature experience. Nothing about her fits together, Leo thinks. *Is something wrong here, is this a warning, a hint of something dangerous ahead?*

Conan is immediately wary. He knows that trust can be dangerous in distrustful times. But he holds the line, doesn't give away his concern. He scrutinizes the situation. He's confused by Meera, and suspicious of Anna.

He visibly stiffens as his older brother turns to the girl and asks gently, "Anna's not your true name?"

She trembles and blinks, as if caught in a flash of bright, direct light. But she doesn't take her eyes off Meera. Compassion shines from the child's entire being. Anna inhales deeply and directs her words to the boys.

"Nonny, my mother's mother, named me. My mother gave me up. She just handed me to Nonny when I was born." With the back of her hand, Anna wipes away a tear threatening to fall. "Nonny was an anthropologist who studied ancient cultures. She was mixed-race, part Japanese. She named me Inanna. I … loved her so much," the girl admits tremblingly. "But my mom came back. And my mom hated the name. So, she re-named me Anna."

She unlocks her eyes from Meera's and turns to the boys. "Sorry, it's just …" She looks down, struggling to find her voice. Almost inaudibly, she continues, "*Inanna,* goddess of ancient Sumeria. My grandparents insisted on calling me *Inanna.* But … well, my mom said it was *too big a name.*" Anna pauses, swallows. "And after she took me away from my grandparents, I didn't feel, well, important enough to carry the name anymore. I never used it."

What she doesn't say aloud is that her mother had beaten her black-and-blue, the first of many times, when she *had* used it. "*Inanna* is my real name," Anna had blurted to a group of her mother's party-going friends. She'd been defiant of the stranger-mother who rushed in and out of her life, the "mother" who had stolen her from her grandparents — and re-named her. Anna had rebelled, even as a four-year old.

But the sometimes-mother had travelled the country after every new man with new drugs, and her languid maternal interest would be easily diverted from the rebellious preschooler. At each turn of her parent's inevitable boredom, Anna would be returned to Nonny and Gramps. Until the next time that the woman would steal her daughter away all over again.

Tears tighten Anna's throat as she struggles to explain herself. Her parent's rage and depression fracture from a stuck place in her heart and threaten to consume her fragile self-confidence.

Chapter 19
Hungry Ghosts

On the heels of Anna's dark thoughts, the sky suddenly dims.

Huge swirls of black, dense clouds gallop towards them. They descend with a whine of cyclone force.

The watchers on the ground look up to see spectral faces in the shadows of the clouds, grotesque and enraged and menacing.

"They've come *back!*" Leo shouts a sharp warning, though his words are lost in the roar of the wind's blast. Both boys bring their fists up and reflexively stand shoulder to shoulder, protecting the girls and ready to fight the attacking force with all their strength.

But as Leo seeks to shield Meera, the little girl leaps away with a blur of unthinkable speed. Leo can't catch her. He's pushed back by vicious gusts as the clouds circle and punch at them with a cold, ugly fury. Fingers of icy vapor snake from the clouds, grabbing for them, clawing and seeming hungry to suck the children into the gaping mouths of the cloud faces.

Meera steps out into the open ground and holds her own space. She extends her arms above her head, throws her forehead back towards the sky, and locks her feet together in a dancer's parallel. Slowly at first, and then picking up speed until her form is a blur, the little girl spins like a whirlwind.

A tornado of colors, from silver to gold, tangerine to pink, explodes from the child in spiraling force. The strength of it blasts them all back. The shards of colored light grow wider, brighter. They spin faster and faster, until Meera becomes her own whirligig firework and her human form disappears in the whorl.

Leo holds onto Anna to anchor her, though he struggles to keep his own balance. Conan bends his knees to stay grounded, his back pushing against his brother.

Meera's centrifugal force matches the clouds' wind-whip offense. It expands until it is wide enough to capture the three of them in the eye of its cyclone. They are unable to move, unable to scream. The prismatic whirlwind grows in height, looming over them, roaring with deafening and unrelenting force.

The malignant clouds bear down, seeking an opening in the cyclone of light. They whine and fume in rapacious formations. The evil vapors maneuver as one force, then suddenly split into individual shapes each bearing Halloween's most horrifying faces, growing darker, condensing in satanically brutal strength.

Meera's spiral-lights become fiery rainbow swords. Her energy heats the color that she wields. She directs the beams of her bright fire directly into the center of the thundering, raging cloud coven.

The air quivers and convulses. Meera's energy, thick and hot, sears the clouds.

And all at once, they explode into icy, toxic plumes. With the tattered air sucked out of them, the malevolence diminishes into weak grey wisps.

In the next instant, Leo, Anna and Conan are stupefied to see the vapors disintegrate.

Meera twirls and slows to a vibrating spiral, gathering the wind into herself with hand-over-hand movements. She becomes a gentle circle of radiant light — and in the glow, the boys and Anna begin to see her human form again. When her spinning stills, little Meera stands serenely before them once more with her colorful Hello Kitty t-shirt and fuchsia nails.

She smiles with full-toothed delight and tilts her head to gaze composedly into the faces of the three kids who now cluster around her. Astonished, unable to find words yet to express their wonder, they are bursting with heart-expanding love for the tiny miracle who is Meera.

She brushes off her shoulders and arms, flicking away any leftovers of dark energy. Disdainfully, she spits out, "*Ugh*, Hungry Ghosts."

The three kids look at her, open-mouthed.

"No? No? You don't remember Hungry Ghosts? Yes, yes, I insist you do!" Meera punches her small fists onto her hips and glares at them.

They're still speechless.

Meera slaps her palm to her forehead and laughs at their stares. The bells at her wrists and ankles tinkle in rhythm with her giggles. Her baby belly, sticking out from under the tee shirt, bounces up and down.

"You are surprised? Why? *Think!*" Her insistence penetrates their astounded minds. "*Hungry Ghosts!* Ahh! There is much for you to remember, and right now! *Quickly!* Nothing must surprise you, or we will be slowed down."

Meera studies each face, then huffs out a breath.
A chorus of vastly deep gongs follows her exhalation, enveloping them like the deepest tones of the bells that had led them to the riverbank.

The kids swivel to search for the source of the sound. The gongs seem to respond to their need — by settling into an earthy thrum of *calm*.

Conan shifts his weight to study the sky where the cloud force just vaporized. He squints. A memory sparks across his vision.

"Hungry Ghosts … Okay… okay, wait I *do* remember something." Snippets of stories nudge his recall. "Spirits of people who died…" he searches for the words, "… *unsatisfied.* … Is that right? They didn't accomplish what they came to do in their earth life, and they died angry, dissatisfied. So, their spirits are still … hungry, they're still attached to their failures. They feel cheated, like they deserved more." He snaps his fingers as a specific term comes back to him. "*Despairing*, that's the word I remember. These ghosts are the dead who never got what they wanted most. And now they blame someone else for their failures."

His voice trails off.

"Yes, yes!" Meera claps her hands. "And, what else?" she teases, as if playing a guessing game. "Come on, I *know* you know." She belly-laughs again.

Anna joins in her laugh and responds to the prompt. "Well, Nonny told me that Hungry Ghosts are the spirits of the newly dead. Spirit forms who, like, grasp for that *one thing* they didn't get in life. They died blaming 'fate' and the world of people who got more than they did." Anna crosses her arms protectively across her chest. "*Attachment*. That's what keeps souls lost in the space between earth and an afterlife. They're in limbo. At least that's what Nonny said. There's no heaven, no peace, no reincarnation when there is *attachment*."

Anna shudders. "And, uh, something else ..." She now realizes how close to despair she has often come, herself. She feels convicted by the loneliness and sadness that so often cling to her. She drops her head and studies the ground.

"Despair ... *driven by despair*. Hungry Ghosts are doomed to find *living* persons who also give up hope. Those people become hosts for the gross, deadly ... energy suckers ... They feed the dark spirits."

Conan is nodding. "Vampires are pretend things. But Hungry Ghosts really do move among us. They don't suck blood, but they suck human energy. Granny taught us that our fear and despair are their sources of life. And then ..."

Conan, Anna and Leo glance at one another uneasily.

Conan finishes his thought.

"The Hungry Ghosts can destroy human life."

Chapter 20
The Grand Illusions

Conan wonders how he had forgotten these lessons, last night, when the crone-cloud had attacked.

Anna gulps. She hadn't seen what the boys saw the night before, but she had had the same lessons about the dark spirits from her own grandmother. And she knows that *fear* had grabbed her all the times she had refused to be called Inanna. *So, she realizes now, it must be obvious to the Hungry Ghosts! My bullshit could have hurt everyone. Goddamn it, I need to remember to stay vigilant!*

Leo and Conan don't deny their fears. Both of the boys ask within themselves, *how close was I to despair?* Loss, betrayal and abandonment had been heaped on them when their nightmares had become realities in the earthquakes and firestorms. Could the two of them now fall prey to the dark parasites? Each boy bears private witness to the places in his heart where he had fallen victim to anxiety, despair and worry.

"Fear makes you *dinner* for dark forces.'" Conan suddenly remembers those words and speaks them aloud. "Who was it said that?"

Leo breaks his silence. "Hungry Ghosts believe in the Grand Illusions. It's why they die in despair. Nothing's ever good enough, including themselves."

The mature timbre of his own voice actually gives him confidence that his inner knowledge is dependable. It merges with a power outside himself he's barely aware of, but now feels like a supportive breeze. He stands at his full height, head erect, and speaks aloud a memory of words without any idea how they come to him.

"The Hungry Ghosts leave their earth bodies believing the Grand Illusions are real. So, they're doomed to repeat destructive illusions. They search for humans with the same delusional thinking, still living here on Earth. They then pull on that shared darkness. And then that evil poisons the next generation, and the next."

Meera leaps, twirls, and shouts triumphantly.

"Good, good, you remember!"

Anna and Conan spin around from Leo to Meera. Bouncing on her tiptoes, she bows to them all and claps. She bellows a laugh louder than her small body should be able to hold. Gold light pours out from her and showers them with glittering sparkles.

"Yes, yes … oh, very good! And remember now, what are the Grand Illusions?"

Conan speaks up again, seizing at a recall. "Ah! Okay … *Separation* is the first of the Grand Illusions. Yeah! And *control* is an illusion. Believing humans control everything, nature, the planet, each other. Wow. Whoever believed *that* bullshit should see the world now!"

Leo bends to meet Meera's eyes. "I don't know how I remember the Hungry Ghosts. But … are you an illusion of some sort, too?"

"No!" Meera puffs out her cheeks in fake indignation. "We are those who were promised. We chose this life, this time and path. We chose and were *chosen*. We lead together." She studies their faces, each in turn. "That is why The Remembering is so important. You *must* remember like I remember."

The three kids look at her, then at each other, puzzled.

"You saw that woman's greedy face in the cloud? Yes? She was a richy-rich woman, a victim of Grand Illusions who believed that love can only be had through *things*, possessions, the very Illusions that push love away. She left a fortune to her squandering, selfish children — spoiled by *her!*" Her little nose wrinkles in disgust. "She died greedy. She needs the energy from living beings to search for her spoiled children. She *drains* whomever she finds. Right now, that's you three. She wants your energy so she can get strong enough to reincarnate and grab back what she thinks was denied her and come back as a selfish human being all over again. That's what keeps the Grand Illusions going, generation after generation, poisoning human hearts."

Meera makes an ugly twisted mouth, flaring her nostrils and eyebrows, mimicking the cloud. Then she sputters in distaste. "*Bleccch!* Sickening!"

The kids swallow their laughs because of her fierce determination.

"Conan is right." She bobs her head. "Vampires aren't real. People created those stories to explain the blood-sucking greed that poisons and kills the body and spirit, feeding the bloodless predators of the Illusions. The Hungry Ghosts have no limits, no care for what is fair. They attack who they find."

The three look nervously side-to-side. Meera laughs again, breaking the serious mood. But her laughter does not dismiss the truth.

"Isn't this *fun?* Knowing true things and finding right-action together! We are on a quest, a mission! Soon you will remember as I do, and so much more!"

The little girl turns pointedly to face the older boy. She rivets him with her startling gaze.

"Isn't that right, Leo?"

Chapter 21
True Name, True Self

Leo jolts out of his self-reflection. Somewhat alarmed, he meets Meera's gaze.

She laughs, "Of course, I know your name, Leo, because I *remember* everything, all of it. I was born *Remembering* my karmic past across centuries. And yours. And each of your true names — yours, Inanna's and Conan's, too."

She reaches for his hand. "Leo."

Upon her touch, the boy is flooded with sensory recall. Rolling images of past tender seasons run across his memory. The clinging of his toddler cousin's fingers wrapped in his own work-roughened grasp. The intimate touch of his cherished first girlfriend.

An enormous wave of long-buried emotion washes over him.

Meera reaches her arms out to Leo, gesturing to be picked up the way children do, without guile. He grasps her under the arms of her ruffled shirt and lifts her to his chest. She's light as a feather. *Wow*, he thinks. Her powerful spirit had led him to expect she'd be heavy. *Nothing about her is as it seems.*

He holds her on his right side, but she shifts to lean against his left shoulder — and places the palm of her hand on the branded skin above his heart. Leo blushes, feeling as if a fearsome secret has been exposed. With her eyes closed, Meera smiles, and her tiny palm gently heats the burn of his brand.

When she opens her eyes, Leo sees that they are wet with tears.

"Of course, I know your name," she says in a hushed, twinkling voice. Her smile is radiant. "Leo, the name of the High King. The *lion of the gods*. This sign," she presses the hand on his heart, "says that, too, Leo. *The king of the jungle, of men and beasts.* No one put it there. It *grew* from within you."

It takes a moment for Leo to absorb her impossible words.

"Your own spirit gave rise to these images above your heart, to remind you of your karma," Meera murmurs. "The symbols are clear if you remember how to read them. ... No? ... Not yet? Soon you will, Leo. And you *must!*"

Leo, holding Meera in his arms, feels a rush of memory from the morning he had woken with his branded skin. "Yes. I was dreaming of dragons. My chest was on fire. I felt hot energy running through me ... and dream-images of these five strange dragons came charging out — of a cave, or a den, or something. They came roaring forward at full speed, as if they could bust right through me."

Meera nods gravely. "Leo," she tells him in her childish voice with its ageless wisdom, "in The Remembering, this time that we're in, first we recall *who we are.* We remember the true name of the *true self* which has been carried forth through the ages. That's the name that marks your karmic path. Past, present and future."

She moves her head so that only he can hear her next words.

"Listen, Leo," she whispers, "The mark above your heart is the story of your *true self.* It links to *all* the other stories."

Meera raises her voice now to include the others. Her words ping a surge of connection, heart to heart, Meera to Leo to Anna and Conan.

"The prophecies teach, *Now is the time for the oldest stories to birth new ones which will take us all forward.*"

The young girl breathes three long inhales and exhales and draws the children into the center of her knowing. The rhythm of her breath both calms and awakens them.

"We live by the stories we remember and tell. It's time to understand the old stories and birth new ones. Only those who enter The Remembering, with a true heart, understanding their true name and true self, can lead us forward."

Meera removes her warm palm from Leo's chest and places it on his forehead, between his eyes. Under her silent, steadfast gaze, pictures flash across the broad landscape of his mind in a cavalcade of memory. Fire-red horses descend from a dark night sky. They gallop, pulling golden chariots. The high-definition visuals and wrap-around stereo are so real that Leo feels he can leap onto the horses' backs and fly across the embattled skies where he challenges unseen enemies.

At the height of the heart-pounding action, the images dissolve into scenes from a different time and place. Startled by the sudden shift, Leo reels back on his heels. He steadies himself, keeping his hold on Meera. His inner screen shifts to reveal a river of great length and width, fog sliding off its forested bank. Beyond the river, a bold castle commands a hilly horizon. In the next moment he sees knights in feather-plumed helmets mounting armored horses. Multi-colored battle-flags flap in an early morning breeze.

The scene widens to unveil a vast battleground. Leo is stunned by the visual power of the scene. Battalions of men, moveable fortresses, trebuchets, carts, weaponry, tents, legions of horses all spring up in one panoramic view. Leo whispers, "It's a war camp at dawn." He can't linger on any single image. Pictures tumble, transform, shift and re-form.

As the battleground fades, a proud, bold armada of sailing ships comes into focus, diving into and out of enormous waves on a white-capped, turbulent sea. On the prow of the flagship stands a commander. His rugged profile is as determined as the waves that push his ship forward.

"Yes," Meera interrupts. She takes her hand away from his charged forehead. "Be fully open to the past and its meaning. Accept who you are, and step into the responsibility to *lead.*"

She places her palm over the brand again, and whispers close to his ear, "To be the author of a new story, you must claim your entire past and future. Your true name, your *true self.* And you must *lead.*" Her gaze is penetrating, unblinking.

As she removes her hand from his chest, the images on Leo's inner screen wash away like watercolors in drizzle.

Meera points to be let down. Leo leans over and places her gently on the ground. The little girl puts her hands together in a delicate prayer triangle and bows deeply. As he bends in gratitude, returning the bow, Meera reaches out with both hands to touch the temples of his head.

"Leo," she whispers, "Never forget. The Darkness and the Light are forever in equal proportions to each other. To know one, is to know both."

Chapter 22
Merlin

Before Leo can find his voice to form the countless questions peppering his brain, Meera skips over to the others and stops in front of Conan. The younger boy is clearly uneasy at the child's approach, but her beatific smile disarms him. From a few paces away, Anna watches the exchange with nervous curiosity.

"What … just happened?" Conan is shaking his head. His throat is dry, his voice's indignant edge is gone. He is restless to understand *how* the little girl can create her phenomena – the pomegranates, the tree, the music, the prismatic tornado. *Does she contain it within and unleash it at will?*

Meera addresses him with her beaming smile.

"*Merlin*, isn't it? Your Aunt Sophia and your Granny called you 'Merlin,' correct?"

Conan startles. He doesn't like surprises, especially by strangers, and most especially surprises about himself. He has an instinctive suspicion of "psychic insight," underlined by his certitude that people are morally tenuous and untrustworthy most of the time, anyway. Conan is often misunderstood by people, in return. "An enigma," they'd say. He doesn't much care. Even his best-loved family and friends, like Leo, tell him, "Don't be so critical," or "That's too negative," because his intuition, when unchecked and spoken aloud, can sound harsh. But he respects his own gifts and feels they protect him from life's shocks and disappointments. He's okay with criticism as a by-product.

The surprise of hearing Meera use the name *Merlin* makes him reel, and he finds himself struggling to appear poised. Not at all comfortable with emotional exposure, he's conflicted about whether to trust her or keep his guard up.

After taking a moment to recover, he bends to her level in order to make clear eye contact. Then abruptly he changes his mind and stands straight up to his full height, deciding it might be an advantage.

"So what? Merlin. It's only a name." He can't hide the shake in his voice. He crosses his arms on his chest, unconsciously protecting his heart chakra.

Meera's response is so soft that Conan has to lean forward to hear her.

"Merlin carries the prophecies and promises of the high king," she almost whispers. "He remembers the alchemy of lost generations. The king and his people need Merlin's gifts of sight, wisdom, knowledge and magic." She turns now to include Anna and Leo, her voice rising in resonance. "*Everyone* has gifts, and ways of special knowing."

After a pause, Meera returns her gaze to Conan, smiling broadly again. "Yet only *Merlin* penetrates the ancient mists. Only *he* can connect old secrets to new futures. Merlin deepens the traditions and combines them with new science. Yes?"

Meera claps once, and a thunderous boom resounds through the atmosphere.

Conan drops to one knee, suddenly plunged into a staggering sea of images washing across his inner screen. Complex scenes of unimaginable scope and setting float behind his eyes. One particular landscape starts to emerge most prominently: an enormous lake, moonlight glimmering off its cool water, wooded mountains surrounding its misty stillness. With his eyes open, Conan sees radiant light begin to rise from the depths of the water in an expanding incandescence. The lake appears to *glow.* It spreads its platinum light from shore to shore, sending ripples of shimmering glitter across the water.

As the light radiates outward, Conan's vision starts to focus on the water's forested shore. He watches with a sense of prescient wonder as a single golden-brown acorn drops from a tree and nestles itself into the loam. With the speed of a fast-motion cinema reel, the acorn grows from the ground to a seedling, then a sapling, then a wondrously massive English oak. The light from the lake turns to a golden brilliance and seems to center its resplendence on the tree as the oaken leaves turn gold. Its limbs, its bark, and the surrounding grasses glimmer with threads of intertwined metallic luminosity.

Crack!

The oak splits right up its center, roots to treetop. From the center of the just-hewn hollow emerges a velvet-cloaked wizard. He's as gnarled as the tree itself. The hood of the wizard's cobalt cape falls to his shoulders to reveal penetrating lavender eyes set deep in his creased face. A grey tangle of long, thick hair half covers his proud forehead.

The tall unearthly man extends his right arm directly towards Conan. It's as if the limb reaches out across time and space. He points at the boy with a thin, crooked, inhumanly long finger. "You, boy, are *me.* And I, boy, am *you.*" The wizard's voice rumbles with a resonance that could cleave the very air. "These things are dictated from the time of legend, and *cannot* be broken by sword or vow, nor by magic, nor trickery. *Remember.*"

The light on the lake trembles. And the picture disappears. Conan still kneels in front of Meera, spellbound, transfixed.

Meera is nodding. "You are him, and he is you. That is so, is it not, Conan?"

He does not speak. His gaze stretches past the visible.

Leo tenses. He knows his brother. When Conan goes to this place of semi-trance, Leo has no option but to wait until the kid comes back to him. It can be — frightening.

But Conan surprises them. He straightens his back, shifts his balance, and folds to sit cross-legged in front of Meera, whispering, "Yes, I … I have … always known."

Meera leaps on Conan, squeezing him with a child-sized bear hug. He falls onto an elbow, laughing as he rebalances himself.

"I know!" She laughs, squeezing him harder, not caring at all about his embarrassed surprise. "I *know* you know, of course you do! It is hard to accept it all, yes?" She doesn't wait for an answer. "Yes, it's so true. They will clear the way, the others. I mean, on the *other side*. They love you very much! But you must do the work of The Remembering!"

She jumps up and stands before him, grasping his shoulders.

"Do not deny this gift. Do *not* doubt yourself. Yes?"

Conan doesn't leap into unknowns unguarded. He isn't a natural volunteer. But Meera knows secrets he's never whispered to anyone, other than to Leo just last night. *She produced the druid Merlin right out of the ancient oak!* He's shocked but also validated. He wants *more*.

"I don't know what I'm agreeing to, Meera." His quiet voice has a shaky, raspy edge. But his gaze stays steady. "Merlin, the magician *trickster?* Or Merlin, the wizard, *wise and seeing?* 'Merlin' means a lot of things. Different things, often dangerous, to lots of people."

Meera meets him nose-to-nose, so close that Conan sees tiny flecks of gold in her otherwise black fathomless eyes. She folds her hand under her chin and sighs, meeting his contrariness with a lop-sided grin.

"Oh, *Conan!* It's not whether *this Merlin or that Merlin*, no, no, no! You can contain *all* of who you are and have been. 'Merlin' has myriad meanings, ones known to you now, and many others that you cannot yet know. But Conan, *you* are real. You are here. You are needed. You must decide whether many definitions of 'Merlin' live in you today. In this life you were named Conan, *brother to the wolf.* One of Merlin's spirit guides is the wolf. The wolf lives for the pack, for his clan, for family. The wolf is a shapeshifter, yes? Merlin is known by many definitions. Yet he has the same energy, one life to another."

Conan squirms and frowns. He can't agree or disagree.

Meera laughs, "It is much to think about!" As she did with Leo, she places her chubby fingers with their glittery-pink nails on each of his temples.

"Alchemy begins by transforming the alchemist. The alchemist and alchemy are one."

Leo and Anna can't see what Conan has seen. But they hang on Meera's words and count their questions.

Meera jumps up and stands as tall as her small body can measure. "Any-*wayyy*, Conan-Merlin. Later. More, later."

Her eyes still on Conan, Meera addresses Anna before she even turns to the girl.

"And you, *Inanna.* You know everything there is to know about alchemy, yes?"

Chapter 23
Inanna

Anna's eyes widen. She looks left, right and behind her, seeking space to flee.

Meera dances sideways towards her. The child reaches out and holds Anna's hands together in her own tiny palms, her smile unwavering, her manifest care enveloping the nervous girl.

"*Inanna*. To find Halfling, the Bird-Girl of your dreams, you must enter The Remembering. And you must admit your true name. Inanna, your very name is key, the clue to mysteries that fulfill the prophecies. You receive dreams we all wait to understand! Don't deny this truth. Claim it! You are *not* Anna, the victim of this life's story, but *Inanna*, of the Golden Era. Inanna is the name that Halfling knows you by, from eons ago. Bird-Girl knows the path to the mysteries of survival and redemption."

Anna is speechless, confused — and somewhat scared. Until yesterday, she didn't even know to call her muse "Halfling." But at the same time, Meera's confidence begins to calm her. The extreme warmth of her hands starts to melt away her nervous tremors.

The two girls stand face to face for a full minute. The boys stay in place, processing their own revelations while observing Anna's. The only sound that fills the silence is the crashing of the river's waves against an uneven shore.

Meera repeats the name *Inanna*. She emphasizes each vowel and consonant. She doesn't release Anna's eyes until the girl's instinct for flight fully ebbs.

"Inanna," Anna whispers. And in the next moment, she vows to herself never to return to the other name.

Meera's full-body laugh explodes from her parted lips and rolls over her round belly all the way to the ground under her sandaled feet. She's engulfed in tears of laughter. The others catch the contagion of joy. They laugh for whatever reason moves Meera.

Abruptly Meera bows, serious again. She repeats her ritual. Her hands tingle against Inanna's temples, her eyes fixed into the girl's very soul.

"Inanna. Remember ... Those unafraid of entering the abyss are given wings to rise above it."

For a fleeting instant, Inanna can sense Halfling's iridescent wings flutter near her as she sees her own self hanging by her arms above an infinite chasm. She can feel herself holding on, grasping for salvation, aware her very life hangs in the balance between faith and fear.

Before she can understand what she sees, however, the spirit wings disappear.

Then Meera lets go of Inanna's face. The child claps her hands together, jumps up and down with spontaneous glee, and becomes the precocious urchin once more.

Leo, Conan and Inanna forget the penetrating cold and bleak sky. They forget their desperate aloneness. And for long minutes, they revel in Meera's joy. They have been in their memories along with her, and now she pulls them back to their present, where for a brief and bright while they feel their youth and hilarity and exuberance, and the simple celebration of just being alive.

Chapter 24
Last Instructions

Leo gulps down his laughter, wipes the mirth from his eyes, and ventures a question.

"Meera. You never told us where you're from! Or how old you are! Or — how you know so much about us!"

Meera scrunches up her little face.

"Oh Leo, questions, questions! I cannot answer all now, no, no, no! Just this. I am, hmmm … Ah! I am six years-old, I think. I am not good at counting time. *Irrelevant!*" Her head bobbles right, left, center. "But, ahhh … yes, *six* years-old. Here, today. Maybe."

Meera laughs as if she is surprised as they are. "I come from far away. In this life, it's a place you call India. It's my favorite place to come from, for hundreds of lives. But I have *always* been close to you. That's irrelevant too, right now — there will be time for stories soon. Let's see. Oh, yes! I found you because I knew where you were, silly! *Here!* I helped put you here. *Whew!* That was a hard job! Inanna was not so hard because she was nearer."

Meera doesn't wait for more queries. "I know your true names because I was born remembering. I was born speaking. I didn't have to re-learn, I just Remembered what I was reborn to be and to do. My karmic map, the one inside my soul and spirit, was open for me to read. And so, I did." She looks one to the other, seeming not to notice their stupefaction. "Yes? Understand?"

"No," Leo laughs, "Am I supposed to?"

"Yes, yes, very soon! You three must work on it, *together!* It's your job! It's what you were born to do, so don't be lazy!" She releases a raft of tinkling giggles. "Oh Leo, you look so serious. I know you won't be lazy. But, um, Conan … *hmmm.*" She wags a finger at the tall boy. Then pivots to Inanna, hands on her hips. "And you, Inanna. You are not lazy, really. But, too worried."

She turns back to Leo. "Leo, remember what a teacher once said to you. *Know yourself best. Know your friends as well as yourself. And know those who choose to be enemy. Then, lead!*"

Leo is attentive — but uncertain. Before he can express his doubt, Meera again wags a finger at them. "There is little time," she warns. "Go now!" Her blunt-cut raven hair swings back and forth with the motion of her emphatic gestures. "Inanna, the pathway to Gramps is covered in rocks and roots and fallen trees. The ground is difficult, covered with ash from earthquakes and fires. Do not falter! No matter what happens, be brave! Gramps waits for you."

At these words, Inanna falls to her knees in front of Meera. She grasps the little girl's shoulders. "Meera, he's alive? Gramps is *alive?*"

she gasps. She had so feared his death. She'll climb the mountain alone if she has to. No amount of destruction can dissuade her.

"Oh, yes, Inanna, alive! But you know that he is old. He is very old. He will not be on the earth plane much longer. He knows you are on your way, and so he waits. But he must pass, soon. And he must see you before he does."

Meera places both palms over Inanna's trembling hands, then turns her head to the boys. "Gramps waits for *you*, also. Yes, he knows you two." They gulp.

The child releases Inanna's hands, spins around, and flings her arms out. "Isn't today wonderful? For centuries, we have prepared for this inspiring time! Most wonderful, hopeful, *promised* time. *Dawn!* We are excited, yes?" Her bells ring and her belly bounces. Her head bobbles and her black hair swings. Her unmitigated joy is evident. "Leo, Conan, Inanna. You have the courage to embrace the prophecies and enter The Remembering. Together we will help create a time *not* ruled by the Grand Illusions, by the greed, separation, and control, that brought us destruction! This is our chance. *Hooray* for us!"

The three kids are at a loss for words. The chilled, empty landscape creeps closer.

Meera doesn't seem to notice. "Now," she exclaims, "no more talking!" She tells them to pick a few pomegranates. "They are filled with goodness, yes? Food and drink in one! Inanna, higher up, the river flows straight out of the mountain and is clean to drink, too. I climbed it yesterday. I sipped and sipped. Ah, *delicious!* Now, time to start!"

She turns to Leo. "Follow Inanna. Don't let her slip into *Anna!* This is important! Use only her true name. We need Bird-Girl, and the Halfling responds only to the true name."

Meera touches Inanna's shoulder, motioning for her to rise and get moving. "No more 'blah-blah,' no time to explain. But soon you will see. Now, pick the fruit and leave."

Her shooing gestures are almost comical, but her tone is an unmistakably direct command.

Leo and Conan begin to protest. "No, wait — aren't you coming?"

"We can't leave without you!"

They want to insist that she come along with them. They cannot fathom how she could possibly stay safe and protected here.

Leo sinks down on one knee to entreat the girl. "I won't leave you here. None of this makes sense! Least of all, abandoning a six-year-old while we climb a mountain to see a guy we aren't even sure is there!"

Meera remains firm. "Gramps helps to start your journey. Much has changed and much more needs to be learned. And old ways need to be relearned." The boy starts to interrupt, but the child holds up her hand. "Gramps has instructions and supplies. And he knows secrets to get you home and keep you safe."

Conan and Inanna move to either side of Leo. All of them look entreatingly at Meera.

"Do not worry about me. I will be safeguarded. No more questions now!"

She casts her arms out in a wide arc. From her upturned palms, smoky wisps of spontaneous energy, silky as spider's threads, swirl into the thin fog. The vapors wrap around her like a pulsing cocoon.

She drops her head. She seems to listen to something — or someone — the others can't hear. Then she lifts her eyes, fixing them on the sky, and, in an utterance quite unlike her childish lilt — in an otherworldly voice - she speaks aloud.

"This is the dawn of prophecy. This is the promise of a new day. Everything that has ever existed in time and space, in the hearts of sentient beings and in the relational universe of thought and elemental manifestation, is NOW. Good and evil, danger and redemption. Positive and negative. Light and creative force. Everything exists NOW, in this time. Stay awake!"

She looks back at the three. Her eyes seem to drill into theirs. *"Stay awake!"*

The cocoon disappears. The baritone *gongs* that had announced her arrival a short time ago now reverberate anew, as if cued from her wrists and ankles. She claps her hands, the gongs recede, and the irrepressible six-year-old child is back.

Meera motions the three of them to get a move on. "Time to go now! No worries, I know my way! And I have others to visit. Do as I say, and pick fruit. Trust! Start at once, before it is too late! Move!"

Too late for what? Leo doesn't dare to ask. Meera won't be denied. She is insistent.

Leo, Conan and Inanna nod their thanks. Conan speaks for all three of them. "Okay. We got it. We hear you."

They stuff their pockets with pomegranates. They can't help but notice that the fruit has slated their hunger *and* thirst. "Is this fruit, uh, special?" Conan asks. "Or are our stomachs walnut-sized from near starvation?" The three of them busily gather as much as their pockets can hold.

As he is picking, Leo calls over his shoulder to Meera, "You totally sure you'll be safe? Where are you going? You said there are others you have to see, so that must mean that more people are alive, right?" He receives no answer.

Leo spins around to where Meera had stood — and finds her gone.

"Hey! She's not here! Where the hell did she *go?*"

Conan, Inanna and Leo run in opposite directions, up the mountain and down to riverbank and back to the cave, searching for the tiny conjurer, calling out for her.

"Meera! *Meera!*"

There is no response.

The three convene again at the pomegranate tree, desperate to make a plan and find her. But as he takes a breath to speak, Leo is shocked by a burning stab of the brand on his chest. The pain shoots through him as deeply as if he had been cauterized. He turns his back so the others can't see him tremble.

Too late. Conan and Inanna have already seen the warm aura that spreads from Leo's heart and now radiates out to encircle all three of them.

"What the…?" Conan exclaims.

Tinkling bells begin to chime above the nimbus circle. The light appears to dance in rhythm to the gentle carillon.

Leo hears Meera speaking directly into his head. *You must go. Now!*

"She's insisting!" Leo tells them.

Conan and Inanna stand shock-still, incredulous.

"She's somehow … talking directly into my *brain!*" Leo reaches searchingly into the golden aura, trying to grasp it. He almost believes he'll find Meera there. The light slips through his fingers and disappears.

The boy drops to the ground. He lowers his head, closes his eyes. "She says… she'll find us. She says … *Don't worry.*" He brings one hand to his chest, covering the area where the pain has receded. "*How* is she speaking directly into my *brain?*"

He looks at the others.

They don't have an answer for him.

Rising to his feet again, Leo takes a deep lungful of air. "But I can tell you this. I know she's right. We have to go."

Chapter 25
The Climb

Leo scans the territory one last time, needing to relieve any doubt that Meera is not with them.

Conan runs up the hill to grab his coat from the cave. He shakes off the dirt and twigs, checks its inner and outer pockets and secret folds for his few possessions. Meeting his brother back at the pomegranate tree, he secures two more pieces of fruit per pocket, then nods to Leo that he's ready.

Inanna, a tight bundle of longing and worry, starts up the old tracker's trail. The once-secret route has been wiped out, but she leads the boys steadily upward in the direction her instinct guides her. She grumbles a spit of frustration. There are damn few landmarks left. *Can't lose the way. Can't disappoint them. Can't make any mistakes.*

Meera's voice, razor-sharp, shouts straight into Inanna's brain. *INANNA! Do not falter!*

Inanna's hands fly up to her head, covering her ears with a wince. "*Ouch!* Damn!" Meera's message echoes with an insistent clarity.

Remember your true name! You are a granddaughter of warriors and medicine people! Fear is a useless trap!

Inanna, red-faced, curses her own anxious thoughts. Reaching within for the ember of confidence that Meera had ignited, she repeats to herself, *No despair. No fear.* She shifts her precision-coordinated, swift-twitch muscles into over-long strides, leaving the boys behind.

Several minutes later, Conan and Leo catch up with Inanna at a bend that veers up and away from the river. They can see that the river disappears into boulders on the path ahead.

All three stop and look back. None of them expect to see Meera, but they can't help themselves. Her confidence in them and her telling of their true names fills each with a mixture of astonishment, reassurance and encouragement.

"Awe and wonder," Conan sighs.

Leo grips his brother's shoulder and smiles at Inanna.

But she is looking up the mountain again, assessing their progress, impatient to keep moving. "The river switches back again a mile up. Or, it used to." Inanna shakes her head. "But we'd better drink here. Or else wait a half hour more."

The boys nod. They both kneel at the river's edge and swallow mouthfuls of the cold, crisp water. They all take a few bites of pomegranate. The fruit seems almost supernaturally to fill their bellies. Conan sighs happily, "This fruit is *magic.*"

With a last glance over her shoulder, Inanna starts up the steeper grade. She studies the broken ground with its disheveled rocks. She looks to the water, the sky, and the slope and pitch of the mountain for anything familiar to guide her. It takes perfect concentration and her best hiking skills to climb without a trail.

Yet her thoughts return to Meera's promise. *Was it a promise? Yes,* she decides. *Gramps is alive! And — I will find Bird-Girl, she will be real and materialized.*

She disciplines herself to pay strict attention to the terrain, even as her thoughts revolve around Meera's words. *Halfling only incarnates for ME, she said! But — how does Meera know about her? And about me? And Gramps?* She wants to ask the boys, *Was Meera right about YOU?*

Inanna backtracks where tumbled rocks and fallen trees mar the way. She swears and stifles her worry about what is ahead. But she doesn't talk.

Neither do Leo and Conan.

Each of the three is charged and changed by Meera's personal and mysterious messages. It's as if her faith in them insinuates their every inhale and exhale.

From their earliest days, the boys had been schooled by their Aunt Sophia that to be seen and acknowledged is the greatest gift we can give to one another. Unknowingly, both boys remember this message at the exact same moment.

For Inanna, too, having been *seen* is the most powerful impact of Meera's visit. Behind her the boys climb, paying close attention to the terrain even as their thoughts continue to revolve around Meera's revelations.

Hearing a huff of exertion, Conan looks up from the convoluted trail to see Leo bound determinedly past Inanna. The older boy wraps his arms around an enormous fallen tree trunk and heaves it to the side of their path to clear their way, though the chunk of timber is clearly twice his weight. Conan smiles. *High king in a lineage of high kings,* Meera had said. He had always known that Leo was born to lead. *But royal lineage? Laughable.* He mulls on that as he climbs past the fallen tree. *But, there's a thing about Leo. He's not selfish. And he knows shit, but never brags. Other guys, even crusty old cowboys, follow him. People remember Leo. They want his help and advice. Noble? I guess he is, in a way.*

Conan pauses for a breath. *And me?* He squints up at the far mountain top and considers Meera's message to him. *Alchemy, new science and old magic. Damn! That's a plan I can get behind! Merlin? That's a whole lot better than being king!*

At the same time, Leo, too, broods on Meera's words. As he continues the punishing ascent, he thinks about the vividly etched images he had seen on his inner screen. *What did Meera call this time we're in? The Remembering? And ... I'm supposed to be a leader? Like that commander on the ship?* Yet Meera had referred to *others.* He breathes hard. *Meaning — more humans?*

He deliberately rejects the thought. *Fantasy wishing can be a dangerous diversion.* He refocuses.

Inanna only admitted her true name when Meera insisted. He asks himself if that's a signal he needs to consider. Should he trust her? Not trust? Conan, Leo knows, will argue the same issues. *I can hear him now.* "*Trust a skater-shoe runaway who can get inside our heads and read our thoughts, share our memories? Dude, you outta your mind?*" Conan won't simply accept something about someone because Leo does.

But — Leo wants to believe in Inanna. And he's sure Meera does. *What did Meera say about a Bird-Girl? Or a "Halfling?" It seemed super significant to them. ... But why?*

Leo does not allow himself to slip into tiresome worry. *Meera trusts Inanna. And Meera is believable. I mean, hell, she annihilated the Hungry Ghosts! And — she knew about this mark on me, she knew about my goddamned brand!* Leo lightly touches his chest, grateful to feel no pain there, no fire.

And he respects Meera for understanding Conan so well. She had used almost the same references that Conan had, himself, last night. *I mean, she blew Conan's fear and stubbornness away! That is hard to do.*

He rubs his hand over his shirt. It lingers over the hidden tattoo. *Crazy! But what isn't?*

He rambles on inside his own thoughts, reviewing the inexplicable events. He wonders how it is possible that they had slept — or had been unconscious — for three whole days, as Meera specified. And he wonders if it could be true, what she said about helping "bring" them to this location.

Impossible.

His ruminations begin to tumble and crash together as he climbs. He catches a long inhale-exhale to shut down his worry. *Chill, dammit!*

The time would come, he was taught, when he would understand things that are mysteries in the present. *And you will understand the need of mystery itself.* He whispers his gratitude to all who had tutored him in patience and perseverance; and a greater ease sweeps through him, though the rocks slip under his boots and the steep path challenges his balance.

Meera's message and the images of his own past lives had brought him something he'd forgotten how to feel: *hope.*

No.

That's a word he doesn't allow himself. He hasn't wanted to think about any promise of tomorrow. His dad had said, "Shoulda, coulda, woulda' brings you *nada.*" Dad believed that *hope* was a shitty strategy in the midst of inestimable, unpredictable change.

Leo snaps himself out of his inner talk. He readjusts his stride. The slope is pitched to a high-degree grade. It would be difficult to navigate under all circumstances. But strewn with slippery rocks and ravaged trees, it is grueling.

Stay focused!

Leo, Conan and Inanna climb for two hours straight without speaking. Their thighs burn, their shoulders ache. The passage of time is impossible to discern, with the Sun burning so faintly behind the clouds of dust and devastation.

"Nature's clock is not a help," Inanna gasps aloud as she trudges upward.

Chapter 26
Elk

The three kids round the bend of their climb and reach the point where Inanna said the narrowed river would reappear.

It's not there.

"Oh, man. I'm telling you it used to be right here." Inanna struggles to quell her frustration and anxiety.

The boys shrug it off. "It's okay. You didn't move it."

"I'm really sorry. I could have sworn this is where it would show up." She swears under her breath. The path has been tortuous to navigate with so much debris confusing the routes and causing delays. Yet there's no choice but to keep trudging on.

After a few more miles of climbing, they're rewarded by the sound of rushing water splashing over boulders. They pick up their pace — then stop and exhale, marveling at the sight before them. Higher and closer to its source, the wildness of the river has increased. It curves deeply through the ravaged vista and splashes into small waterfalls. Farther up, they can see water rockets above boulders thrashed together by quakes, sending sparkling plumes straight into the air. The deadness of the land is blessed by this river that cuts across it like a silver snake.

"*Wow*. Let's stop a minute," Leo suggests, kneeling at the bank to drink.

The other two clamber down to the river's edge and run their hands through the freezing water. They toss handfuls over their heads. They drink greedily from cupped hands.

Conan is close to dehydration. It's a lifelong problem, the way he forgets to drink. Now he gulps the clear water. He chides himself to slow down — but no stomach cramps follow.

And then he remembers. "Hey, the pomegranates!"

He digs into his pockets. Laughs out loud for the crazy miracle of it. "Can you believe that green bush, the red fruit, in the middle of this wasteland?"

The others can't hear his garbled words over their own hunger and the river's blast.

Inanna is tired of the questions she's been rattling to herself these hours up the mountain, so she voices them at last. "Who do you think she is? Meera, I mean. How did she get to us? She's so *small*. And why did she disappear?" The girl spills her questions in between slurps of water and crunches of seeds. "She was gone before we finished telling her to stay! And — how did she know so much about us?"

Inanna sits perfectly balanced, her heels flat on the uneven ground, her knees bent in a deep crouch. She shows no apparent sign of fatigue or discomfort. Conan is impressed with her flexibility and athleticism. Leo was right, he thinks to himself. *She's a phenom.*

"Hey. You're a pretty fast climber," he says to her somewhat grudgingly.

She nods, preoccupied. Her attention is drawn to the river.

A flicker of unease suddenly prompts Conan to ask, "Why'd you call yourself Anna?" His voice is not actually combative, but it leans that way. "Meera got you to admit your *true* name, whatever that means."

Leo tries to catch his brother's eye, to quiet him. But Conan has turned suspicious and cold. "So, is it Anna or Inanna? And if it's Inanna, why'd you lie to us?"

His brother glares a withering, wide-eyed, incredulous look at him, perfected for times like this. It's meaning is clear: *Are you effing kidding me? She explained it once already. Back off!*

Conan returns a nearly perfect mimic of Leo's wide-eyed stare in reply. *What?*

The older boy turns to Inanna, his voice kind and soft. He tries to save the moment. "Meera said to make sure we call you Inanna. That okay?"

She isn't listening, and she hasn't noticed the brothers' exchange. She stares up at the river boulders ahead. Shifts her weight slightly to rise from her crouch so smoothly the air around her doesn't stir. She takes tiny, inch-by-inch steps to Leo's right side. Silently, she nods upriver a dozen yards.

Leo's eyes follow hers to a rock ledge that juts horizontally from a jagged outcropping of steep stones. The giant granite slab must have tumbled downriver only recently; torn moss and wet algae drip from the rock.

Her wilderness instincts afire, Inanna senses movement before she sees it. She flattens her belly to the ground, places her finger on her lips to silence the boys, and points with her upturned chin.

There.

Leo and Conan drop down and army-crawl into position before looking up to regard the miraculous sight of a living, wild creature — a yearling elk.

"Whoa. Doe, I think," Leo whispers.

"Wow," Conan murmurs in hushed reverence.

The beautiful creature shivers, clearly disoriented. The three kids are simply astonished that anything wild and young still survives. They hold their collective breaths.

Their awe abruptly changes to active wariness when the doe's ears twitch — and she dashes forward. She darts too quickly on the wet rock. She skids, stumbles, slides to a precarious stop near the boulder's ledge. In a panic, the elk judges a dangerous leap, furtive wide eyes scanning behind her and forward. She slips again on a splash of river and rights herself, trembling head to foot.

Her three human watchers know that if they move, the elk will jump from the ledge and certainly be injured. They want to reassure it. *We're not your enemy.*

In the next moment, collectively, they realize it is not them she fears.

From the broken ground behind the elk, an inky, oozing mass emerges, undulating and creeping toward the rock's edge. Amorphous in shape, its venom steams and emits a rancid smell. It burns the kids' nostrils from yards away.

Alarm bells inside their heads scream siren warnings. In horror, they watch as the mass percolates and shifts in color from obsidian to bruising purple to plasma-red, and back to dense ebony. The excrescence seeps across the tumbled dirt and wet river-rocks with extraordinary velocity. It expands its width and height as it rolls. In mere seconds it grows from an oozing menace to a monstrous, vertical wave. It rises to a height of ten, then twelve, then fifteen feet above the highest point of the boulders. Its silent muscular force matches its appalling speed.

Before the kids can scream a warning, the wave engulfs the doe, swallowing the elk whole. A thrash of one piteous hoof hangs in the air before it disappears into the blackness.

Then as quickly as it had risen, the monster flattens itself onto the river rocks with a sickening suck. In the blink of an eye, any sign of life that had stood on the outcropped boulder is obliterated except for a dribble of blood that falls with a sad *ping, ping* from the rock ledge into the river below.

The three witnesses dare not blink or breathe. Conan squeezes his right hand over his mouth, trying not to wretch.

Before they can exhale their shock, the muculent horror surges back to a twelve-foot-high wave. As dark as a starless night, its oily shine ripples and undulates and splits itself into three identical swells that split again into twelve billows. A brotherhood of black destroyers hovers above the boulder. The coordinated forms ripple as if to calibrate, assess.

If words form at all in the minds of the three watchers, those words are the stuff of childhood nightmares. Their breath is frozen in their lungs. Fear grabs and stifles their exhales.

After hovering a moment in an eerily sentient wave formation, the dozen viscous columns collapse into one monstrous glob. Flattening itself again, it slithers and snakes backward into a crevice between the rocks.

As it aligns itself with the aperture, though, it seems to hesitate. With the kids looking on in horror, the mass starts to joggle and oscillate. It shimmies, palpitates. Then it flings itself straight up to its tallest height. It widens to a thickness matching its peak and shapes itself into a wave-sword of glistening power.

Leo's heart is pounding. *My God, it's weaponized to kill.*

Conan's stomach twists. *It's ... it's intent, aware!*

Inanna closes her eyes and fists, then opens them again sharply.
It knows we are here!

The monster coils and turns until the face of the wave is smoothly angled towards them. Its ebony sheen seems to scrutinize them, eyeless but … intelligent.

Leo reaches left and right to keep Inanna and Conan from separating or stirring, inciting the predator to attack. But the two are frozen in shocked torpor, unable to move.

In the moment before Leo decides they must run or die, a gossamer mist stirs the air, gently, swiftly and entirely encircling the trio. Sparkling with tiny beads of energy and silver streaks of light, the dewy particles start to grow into bigger fragments and then shards, and then lightning beams that splinter and shimmer into a gleaming vertical energy wall.

A warping, flexing, electrified zone now stands between them and the dark mass.

The kids gasp, unsure at first whether they face another unstoppable threat — or whether the energy field is in fact shielding them from their attacker.

On the other side of the towering shaft of light, the malevolent killer draws back. It compresses, then expands again and forms itself into a series of hostile, menacing waves. It ripples and thickens as if gathering force. The kids see its power through the electrified warp-shield. But the black wave's bold aggression seems agitated, confused. It withdraws into its center, then catapults in full force towards them.

The killer is slammed back as it hits the wall, shuddering as if struck by a thunderous blow. The protective wall sizzles with radiant heat to fend off the mass, and the three witnesses feel the heat blister their skin. They look down at themselves reflexively — and are horror-struck to see their own bones. It's as if X-ray images reveal their skeletal system in shocking visibility through their clothes, skin, sinew and muscle.

They stare open-mouthed at their bodies. Conan's screech freezes in his throat. Leo sways towards Inanna in an irrational urge to shelter her. Impulsively she rolls sideways, listing dangerously close to a rockfall. She is intercepted by the screen of electric energy. It creates a palisade of heat that crackles, warps, bends, and lifts her up from the ledge to stand shakily at Leo's side.

Shocked, the kids are dangerously light-headed from loss of oxygen. The radiating heat, too, begins to drain their own energy. Yet they now see that the heat wall is a protective curtain holding its guardian position against the attacker. Behind it, the wave shivers in place, seeming to scrutinize or evaluate a course of action.

It bends in their direction again, as though preparing to fling itself towards them in a renewed assault. Instead, it widens — then collapses and shrinks into its original viscous, oozing mass. The ugly mire, effulgent with a crimson sheen, skulks away, disappearing into the rocks.

The scorching heat of the radiated energy wall starts to dissipate. Leo, Conan and Inanna release their breath in a whopping collective exhale. They gulp fresh air, feeding their lungs and heads with oxygen.

They look down. Their skeleton x-rays have disappeared.

But before they have time to utter a single whoop of survival victory, the charged protective veil *flips* and flattens from vertical to horizontal. In the next moment it reassembles itself into a formation resembling a 3D moving puzzle with incalculable height and depth. Shards of blue light twist, dive, link and connect into horizontal scaffolding. The electrified field creates a structure of bridges and planks that connect to one another, vibrant with tangible, cobalt energy.

The kids are looking into a vast pattern of interlaced, variegated, connected lines.

Conan, awed, murmurs, "A hologram?"

"*What the...?*" Leo gasps.

Inanna is riveted. "Stunning. Endless ... *stunning*," she murmurs. "It's ... a *labyrinth*."

Chapter 27
The Labyrinth

As if set on an immense, invisible craftsman's table, the labyrinth builds into circuitous overlaps of shimmering silver and blue. Multi-dimensional geometric bridges of cobalt, paths and hallways of towering iridescent beams cross over each other in vertical and horizontal assemblage. The intricate maze widens, lengthens, grows and folds over itself. Spires and towers shoot up, complex tetrahedrons plunge down. The entirety of it hangs in space, a glorious fairy-like construction.

Soft steam rises below the labyrinth and pirouettes between the planks; it emits a radiant heat that casts warmth without enervating the amazed watchers. The labyrinth builds itself without human hands or visible blueprint. It is perfectly executed, transparent, crystalline. The structure seems infinite, its bladelike beams glowing blue and silver, it's jewel-like contours sparkling like an ice palace.

Conan asks, "But ... what *is* it?"

The finished construction glistens and sparkles as the kids gaze into it. And then a concurrent shiver of energy lifts the three of them off their feet, floating their bodies mere inches above the river. They feel a charge of vitalizing effervescence course through them, removing their fear and fatigue, filling them with healing strength ... before they are gently placed back onto the solid ground.

In the next moment, the labyrinth folds into itself like a dancing origami — and disappears in a puff of cobalt smoke.

Conan, Leo and Inanna reel with the series of back-to-back shocks. From the beautiful hope of seeing the wild baby elk, to the agony of witnessing it being swallowed by the hideous black wave, to encountering the searing energy field and the curtain of its protective force; to staring straight through their own bodies at their own skeletons, and being scorched by the radiating heat ... and now facing this mystical super-construction, and feeling the marvel of their physical rejuvenation ... the succession of astounding events leaves them stunned.

Their whispered questions tumble over one another.

"Is it magic? Or ... or what?"

"It saved us, right? The same energy protected us, and then ... made the labyrinth?"

"Is this what's called a miracle?"

None of them ventures an answer.

Conan pinches his own arms and legs. "Seeing our skeletons *really* freaked me out. I thought we were *fried!* But ... we're okay, right?" He can hear his own heart pumping.

Leo nods. "We're alive." He bends to a crouch. He won't let his relief override keeping a wary eye on their surroundings.

Inanna drops to her knees and scans the boulders, river, sky and earth. She reaches out, trying to catch a wisp of a last blue vapor for clues. "The black-death ooze is gone."

"Yeah, what the hell *was* that ... or, or any of it?" Conan wonders. "Okay, well, our bones are covered by muscle, our skin is intact." He shivers. "And, *damn!* I feel *woke!* But — I never want to see my skeleton again!"

Inanna puffs out a long slow breath. "That black stuff wasn't a Hungry Ghost. They're spirit vampires, they need their victims alive. That blackness was really bad, really evil. It was even more powerful than the Ghosts." She is almost talking to herself, processing what she knows, balancing Nonny's teachings with all the that they have just seen. The boys listen while assessing their own understanding of the events. "That black killing machine split and *grew*, right? And — did the labyrinth-maze seem *alive* to you guys, too? I mean, how did it just ... *make itself up*, in seconds — and then disappear, like, *poof?*"

The day's cold returns in biting draughts. The kids fill their lungs with the bracing air. Leo and Conan share a glance. They stand slowly. They no longer trust the day's silence.

Leo turns in a careful circle. He narrows his eyes and analyzes the terrain. He sees nothing.

Conan grabs his brother's wrist. "Leo, everything that just happened *can't* happen." His whole body shivers. "But it did, right?" Troubled by his own fear, he fixes his gaze on the rock where the elk was swallowed. He knows they will have to pass around the edge of that killing-boulder on the trail ahead. He asks Inanna, "It's the only way up, right? There isn't another way?" He steels his voice but can't keep the tremors out of his hands.

She scans the mountain. Scrutinizes the riverbank. "There's hardly *this* way, let alone another." She straightens her back. Her resolve renews Leo's confidence in her.

"Ok, *Inanna*." Leo stresses her true name. "Meera said *get to Gramps*. We can't focus on questions with no answers. And we can't stop moving. Meera said, *trust* and *move*. We'd better make it to your Gramps before nightfall. Agreed?"

Leo respects the rebel athlete in Inanna. And he is intrigued by the hints of her "psychic powers" and the prophecies that Meera hinted at. But Inanna's testy nerves and combative edge also make her a risk. He moves closer to her, gently touching her arm.

"Inanna, we'd better *own* our true names. Because if Meera's right, we each have the skills and knowledge necessary to survive. We need to embrace those gifts right now. Odds are pretty much against us, otherwise."

Inanna shies away from him instinctively. But the saying of her name, *Inanna*, reassures her. "Yeah, before nightfall." Her voice is stronger. "There's lots of phenomena in Native ceremonies. But I never heard of *anything* like that scary gunge. I don't want to be out here with that death thing roaming around hungry."

She stops. Conan is looking at her. *He's not convinced I can get them to Gramps. He thinks maybe I'm too scared. And too much of a freak. — Like, HE'S normal?*

She squares her chin, hikes her cloak up and ties it over one shoulder. Without a glance back, she calls out, "If you can keep up, I can get us to Gramps!"

Inanna leaps from her foothold to the next rock. She doesn't stop for pomegranate seeds or additional water. She doesn't even glance at the killing ground. She grits her teeth, steels her eyes, and silences her raspy mind.

Conan shudders when he passes the place of the elk's death. He's seen too many innocents suffer in the past two years. Forcing his attention away from terrible endings, he observes the absence of blood on the boulder-ledge. Swipes his hands in the air to test if it's electrified. But he doesn't slow his step.

Leo half turns, looking back at his brother as he hikes. He reads Conan's mood. The boys' eyes meet; they nod a brief understanding. Then speed their pace to keep up with Inanna's accelerated strides.

It's one thing to lead in hard times, in fires and winds, Leo thinks. *But how do I protect anyone from THESE kinds of nightmares?* The things they've seen this day aren't the kinds of disaster he has trained for. *Who do I have to ... be? How do I show up? The electric field protected us. I think. But we can't count on it appearing again. We can't count on anything.*

Stop! Leo commands immediate discipline of himself. He damns his scattered internal questions. *Stop!* He blocks out doubt. *FEAR puts us all at risk.*

The magical little Meera pops into his mind. He feels her warm palm on his heart and her forehead pressed on his Third Eye.

He thanks her under his breath.

In one heartbeat, he hears Meera answer. *You are welcome, Leo.* Her voice, in the aftermath of death, rescue, and unanswered questions, strengthens him.

Lead! Meera commands.

And he knows to obey.

Chapter 28
Mountain Guards

Two or three hours pass in silence as the three climb the rough terrain of the mountain. They need water and rest, their stomachs growl, their mouths are dry. But not one of them wants to stop.

Night closes in, intent on shrouding any light that helps them find their way. Inanna trips on a rock, swearing under her breath. She shakes off the boys' concern. "I'm fine, I'm fine." She waves them on.

Conan and Leo also fall over several hazards on their path. They, too, grimace and then deflect.

At different times and places, all three kids force themselves free from obsessive thoughts.

... *Impossible, that electrified warp field. But we all saw it, felt it.*

... *Death, too damn much death.*

... *That baby elk. Did it suffer? Too much suffering, too much.*

Are we safe? they all wonder. *What happened to the world, the Earth, the people? Where IS everyone? What the hell happened?* No one shares an anxiety aloud, however. They do not allow fear to slow their pace.

Leo says he wants the rear guard for a while. Conan shrugs his assent. He trots forward to close the gap with Inanna, calling over his shoulder, "No heroics. We're in this together."

Leo holds a fist above his head. *Got it.*

Forest damage forces Inanna into detours. They have to stop too often to push trees out of the way. Inanna curses at the barriers to ascent. The boys don't question her choice of path, but she bristles at the mountain, and the slip-slide of mini avalanches tumbling underfoot. She hates her lack of alternative, her lack of control.

"These getting bigger the higher we get?" Conan huffs and hurls aside a large pine bough, limp with heavy needles. He negotiates a tight turn.

Leo grunts a reply as he climbs a boulder, only to slide off the wrong side. He's forced to circle back, repeat the climb again.

An occasional cuss word fills the otherwise silent dusk as they navigate the terrain, but they are resolute.

Inanna quickens her pace. Conan trots to keep up. His thighs ache, his feet are sore, his breath grows shallow. Leo insists that they stop and eat the last of the pomegranate seeds. Inanna disagrees. "We're losing the little light there is. We still have a long way to go." She scans the boulders ahead. "The earth looks *rototilled*." The river is clogged with more debris than she'd expect at this altitude. "We need to eat and hike at the same time." She's up and moving before the boys even register her directive.

The mountain is relentless. Slopes turn into ever-higher inclines. *Brutal.* Leo wishes silently for ropes and hiking boots instead of slippery cowboy boots made for other adventures, other times. Conan can't help thinking how much easier this climb would be if he were actually a wolf.

But no one sees any use in mentioning aloud what they are missing, what could make things better. *After all,* Conan considers, *that list is endless.*

The last licks of light suck away into the soundless, blackest night. They're forced to pick their way ahead without stars or moon as beacon. Until after what seems like hours more of climbing, Inanna abruptly stops.

Hands on her hips, the girl waves for the boys to join her. Silently, she points to an angled bend in the mountain grade ahead. It's a direction that takes them farther off the river route, deeper into the broken forest.

The boys know they've got to trust her. But exhaustion creeps up to meet them, and their uncertainty seems to grow straight out of the troubled ground.

Conan shivers from the cold, consuming dark. He raises his eyebrows behind Inanna's back. Leo places a confident hand on his brother's shoulder, without comment.

They see it at the same time.

About a hundred yards ahead, a thin billow of smoke wafts above the shadow of two enormous, tumbled mountain boulders.

Inanna places an index finger to her lips. Points directly at each boy. *You. And you. Silence!*

She gestures for them to separate left and right. Stays between them, but trots twenty feet ahead.

Leo and Conan glance at one another, eyebrows raised. They follow her, wary and alert. Night blinds them to any dangers that might lie ahead.

About fifty feet up the grade, Inanna stops before the wall formed by the twin gigantic boulders. The rocks seem to have been dug deeply into the ground, the earth around them exposing a two-foot trench. It appears to be a sort of dugout, or dirt moat.

Inanna allows herself a small smile. She crouches behind one of the monolithic boulders. She leans her weight into it. Then quickly gestures for the boys to join her.

They all three jump down into the dirt trough. Inanna's whisper is urgent. "Stay down!"

And just in time.

A fleeting instant later, they hear a deep-earth growl rumbling from above them. An avalanche is unleashed on the mountain. The rolling earth cascades, taking trees, roots, shrubs, and dirt heavy with crags, rocks, slabs and rubble. The groundswell of debris hurls overhead and past them.

The three are shielded from the barrage by the defensive bulwark of the twin boulders.

In the dust of the last free-fall of debris, the boys unfold from their head-covering crouch and look cautiously out from the safety of their position.

Inanna growls in a loud whisper, "Can't hide here long!" She leaps up, motioning firmly for the boys to fall behind her. Neither brother likes seeing the wiry girl run lead, but her skill in navigating the mountain is undeniable.

In a tightly connected column, the three break into a fifty-yard sprint toward the next protective barrier in sight: a massive fallen tree. Inanna reaches the shield of timber first. She jumps onto the limb to make sure it's completely stable in the soft ground. And then with swift insistence, Inanna yanks on the boys' sleeves, pulling them down to a shielded position behind the tree trunk. "Take cover *now*!"

Wrraacck!

They hear the forest above them ripping and splintering as the mountain rolls in another burst of bombardment. "Cover your heads!" Inanna shouts.

Boulders skim left and right and fly overhead. The ground under their feet shakes and shudders for what seems like long minutes before coming to rest with a settling of loosened dirt.

In the second of silence that follows the last rumble, Inanna is up again. "Follow me!" she yells, as she vaults over the log barrier and bolts up the hill. The boys move in rapid pace behind her, running in a military crouch up the sharp incline slippery with rock debris.

A third round of mountain tremblers knocks Leo to his knees. He's able to catch Conan before the younger boy slides too far backwards. Inanna's legs buckle, and she throws out her arm to brace the fall before her face hits the dirt.

The three kids stay low as the ridge rolls with a series of small aftershocks. They are breathing heavily, coughing spasmodically from the settling dust. Inanna rolls to her side. She wobbles to a standing position, legs wide to balance herself on the unsteady ground. She reaches under her cape to retrieve the eagle whistle hanging from around her neck, then puts the instrument to her lips and blasts a resounding war cry identical to that of a descending raptor. She repeats the furious screeches, once, twice, a third time in close succession. The sound pierces the night.

The boulders around them seem to shiver, sigh and settle in response to the signal. The dust and dirt and debris ease into rest. The mountain tremors cease.

A wispy tendril of smoke reappears over the ridge ahead of them. It widens and rises into an expansive plume reaching far into the inky sky. Inanna whoops and raises her arms in a victory cheer. She pivots to the boys, pointing in triumph to the smoke signal.

The boys peer through the darkness. Their eyes gradually adjust to the shadows as an outline of a timbered cabin comes into focus. The ramshackle dwelling is perched in a tight valley between two forested hills, completely surrounded by fallen trees. Smoke swirls from a cracked chimney.

As dilapidated as the cabin appears to be, it emits an aura of radiance. Brilliant, golden, ethereal light pours from the two crooked, cross-beamed windows framing its open wooden door.

"Miracle." Conan exhales. He shakes his head and turns to Leo. "Damn ... Meera was right! It's still standing." His voice, dry and sore, cracks. He rubs his throat. "How? How could it be the only thing saved?"

Leo swipes a hand across his forehead. "Miracle."

Inanna doesn't hear their exchange. She is already running towards the cabin door.

Leo puts a hand on Conan's arm, signaling for him to let the girl go first. The boys trail her a few steps behind, their relief and wonder pushing away exhaustion.

Light pours from the wide-open doorway, creating luminescent circles around the house like the rings of Saturn. The glow expands as they approach, reaching out to greet them.

"Gramps, Gramps!" Inanna calls, running to the door.

In return, a gravelly laugh, warm and filled with welcome, hails them. The boys can't see the old man from whom the laugh issues until their steps take them to the door. They cross the cabin's threshold to find Inanna enveloped in her grandfather's loving arms.

Chapter 29
Gramps

Finally releasing each other from their mutually adoring and grateful embrace, Gramps and Inanna stand cheek-to-cheek in the middle of the cabin's compact central room. Not three inches taller than she, the old man is almost as sinewy, wiry, and muscled as his granddaughter. His weathered pecan skin stretches across his high cheekbones and forehead in feathered cobwebs. His erect and noble posture belies his years.

Placing his hands on Inanna's shoulders, Gramps smiles broadly, taking in the full measure of her. "You look fine, girl. Skinny but healthy. Good. No, beautiful." He shifts to Native blessing words, grandparent to grandchild. She lowers her head, letting her tears of relief and joy fall without embarrassment.

Leo and Conan stand apart from them, somewhat awkwardly. An identical yearning for family and home hits them forcefully. Waves of nostalgia and longing ripple through each of them.

When at last Gramps turns to the boys, his smile for them is genuine, and deeply warm. He tightens his arm on Inanna's shoulders.

"Who are these young braves you have brought me, Granddaughter?" His belly laugh crackles his thin ribs.

Before Inanna can answer, Gramps stretches out to grasp the boys' nearer hands in each one of his. "Conan. Leo." The old man's grip is strong and sure. Time stops for the boys as the venerable warrior studies their faces. Even Inanna, used to her grandfather's surprises and insights, is stunned by his use of their names.

Gramps nods gently, his eyes smiling. His focus remains on Leo and Conan. He deepens the cadence of his voice into that of Native teacher. *"The White Buffalo Brothers who are also Wolf Brothers enter the mountains as boys and leave the mountains as men. They come forward to lead the people out of the wilderness."*

He measures a slow exhale. "Prophecy comes true this day." His emotion is evident. "I believed I would live to meet you. And here you are in my home." Gramps bends forward to hug each boy closely, one at a time. Leo and Conan are taken by surprise. But they lean into the embrace. "Gratitude." The old man inclines his head. "Gratitude to the ancestors and to you both, from myself and all who promised this moment." He blesses them in Lakota, as he did his granddaughter.

He turns to Inanna. "Wise daughter, you wore your eagle whistle." He nods to her. "You are true medicine child. You didn't forget the boulder-guardians and protections put down by us long ago."

He apologizes to the boys for the challenging approach. He explains that the quakes and bombardments are natural alarms of earthly guards. "They are our security system, meant to deter those who carry bad medicine. But you had Secret Keeper with you. Inanna knows where the protections are laid. Eagle call assures mountain spirits that she's family." He raises an eyebrow. "Sorry for the scare."

Conan and Leo look at each other.

"Prophecy?"

"Boulder-guards?"

But they don't pursue the questions. They are incredibly relieved to have found Gramps, astounded that he knows who they are, and filled with gratitude that he welcomes them here into his home. That's enough for now.

More than enough, Leo says to himself.

Gramps' presence stirs in the boys a yearning for what they had lost when their father disappeared: the respect and warmth of an older man, a mentor. They're happy for *whatever* he thinks of them, *whoever* he believes they are. *If it's the last place in the world*, Leo thinks of the humble space, *it's okay by me.*

Gramps' contagious belly laughs burst from him.

"Food! Water! *Aiyee*, Inanna, your grandmother would be angry with me for waiting even a minute to feed you all, isn't that right?"

He's in motion before he finishes his query. His movements are astonishingly quick and agile considering his agedness. Gramps calls directions to Inanna as he stirs a small black cauldron atop what he calls a "first-generation" wood-burning stove. He speaks in sentences that sometimes seem to have no need of pronouns.

"Boys, it's old as me, but this stove heats the house. No need for jackets. Yes, take off boots, put them there, good. Inanna, bring chair from bedroom. Boys, spoons and forks in that cabinet, dishes above. Get bowls down and stoke fire. Use bucket of water in bathroom to fill kitchen sink and wash up. And mind you don't waste a drop."

Gramps' tears of emotion run freely into the creases on his cheeks as he speaks. He seems ageless in his energy; vibrance emanates from him in the same concentric circles of light that drew them to the cabin.

He speaks over his shoulder as he spoons large ladles of steaming stew into their bowls.

"Bean soup. My grandmother's recipe." The rich smell of garlic and herbs fills the house. The kids realize, as if they have one united stomach, that they're starved. The pomegranates finally can't satisfy their appetites. "I had some dried beans and just enough onion from the root cellar. No fresh meat, I'm afraid, but the deer jerky has simmered for hours. Hopefully it won't be so tough that it pulls my last teeth out."

The old man convulses in laughter again, bold and unrestricted. The boys crack up, too. They double over. It's suddenly as funny as anything they've ever heard.

Gramps shoos them all into three chairs. He cautions them to eat slowly, to make sure their famished constitutions "break in." The kids wrap their hands around the hot bowls and let the heat flow through them, their mouths watering. But the boys' good manners hold firm in the midst of their starvation, and they wait.

The medicine man stands over them and holds up a spirit plate with a spoonful from each of their bowls. He prays in a low rumble of indigenous tongue. When he is finished speaking, he puts the plate in the center of the table and then places his hands on the boys' heads.

"Great Spirit understands that in this case, food must come first, so I said blessing words in your names. You'll pray thanksgiving when you realize this is best meal you've ever had."

Inanna rolls her eyes while the boys grin. The old man takes a chair at the table, watching with satisfaction as the kids start on the soup hungrily. They are mindful of Gramps' warning and try not to gobble it too quickly — but it's hard to pace themselves. Conan and Leo have not had a hot meal prepared for them in months, and after one spoonful they nod with ecstatic appreciation of the flavors. "Best meal ever!"

It's not until their bowls are nearly empty and their initial hunger has eased that Leo ventures a question. "Gramps, how's it possible you're here? How's this house standing? We walked for miles yesterday, and more today. There's hardly a tree alive. And outside of a little slime on rocks, there's no green. But you — and this house — are saved. And your root cellar is in place?"

Gramps studies each child. A grin cuts over the creased folds of his cheeks and chin. "Well, not everything stayed put. Never had electricity but had running water from well. Wasn't able to save that. Think I forgot to do it, actually." He thinks this over solemnly. And then laughs again, full of conspiratorial goodwill.

"It's same way you were saved. Spirit world used winds to lift you to safety, and spirit world safeguarded this cabin. And me. Mountain protections were laid to assure as much stability as possible from predators and inevitable damage of quakes. The promise was, I'd survive, and you'd find your way."

He muses about that a second.

"Was easier to move Inanna. She was close by. You two had to be taken from *so* far. That was very hard work. But — here you are." The boys stop, spoons in mid-air. "Anyone for more soup?"

"Wait!" Leo seizes on the apparently nonchalant comment. "We were *moved?* Saved?" Meera had said that too. But had he believed her?

He hesitates. Then risks more questions. "It was … deliberate? How? And from what? Fires? Were they going to … take over?" Leo swallows a hard lump. "And, why us?"

In his mind he can see faces, old and young, surround him from that last night of rescues, screaming in terror. He forces himself back to the present moment. "What happened to the people waiting for us …?" He can't finish the sentence.

Conan is listening intently, his mind spinning around the same questions. He almost interjects, but Gramps' hand is raised in a halt from across the table.

"Leo, Conan, Inanna. You weren't saved because of the fires. Those you might have survived yourselves."

The old man stops to ask himself how much teaching is tolerable before these young ones are rested and have time to pray. Clearly their questions haunt them, and he knows the weight of that feeling. He closely regards each of them. Takes a breath. Then pitches his voice into teaching tone.

"We knew you had to be moved before Three Days of Darkness fell. We didn't know it would be that night, but when nuclear explosions began, we had to act."

The three kids are suddenly wide awake. "Wait ... *what?*" Leo interjects.

Gramps knows his own words sound crazy. "You wouldn't have seen what happened, where you were," he says, "but in places around the world, there were flash fire-in-sky explosions. Nuclear devices of some kind. Maybe you saw that sort of thing in old movies, or heard about them in school?" He waits for them to respond.

Caught between shock and fear, the kids' minds jumble-rush questions, but no words form. Gramps drills his gaze into Leo, then Conan. He reaches across the table for both boys' hands.

"A series of dirty bombs, I believe, were scattered here, there, in different hemispheres. They caused fires, winds, and even worse destruction than seen in these last years. Our planet shook from eruptions of ice, water, earth. The last of our glaciers blew up. Avalanches and sinkholes swallowed vast landmasses. The Great Lakes spilled over like dumped cereal bowls. Darkness hooded the entire planet."

Leo struggles to put Gramps' words into perspective, context. To align them with what he knows from science and nature — as well as from myths and legends. He attempts to speak, but his questions drown in swirls of confusion as no one piece of information hooks to another. Only, he feels certain that more information will surely bring more sorrow.

Gramps nods to agree with Leo's unsaid thought. *It's too much for now.* "Many things need saying and understanding. Many things beg for teaching and learning and practice. That's why I am here, and why you have joined me."

He looks directly into Leo's wide green eyes and sees an unusual depth of understanding for a man so young. "Leo, Conan. There wasn't a way to fully prepare you two, or Inanna, over recent years. We, the elders, had to trust that, when time came, your own legacies of courage, service, stewardship, integrity and sacrifice would be revealed to you. We trusted you would come to see for yourselves your souls' code and accept *choice and chosen*. We trusted you would know what was asked of you." He is a person of few words and much action. But tonight, words are required. Impactful words.

He stands and offers more soup all around. "We prayed your past lives would awaken in this moment of catastrophic change and lead you to your highest purpose. Who you three are, hearts-minds-spirits, past and present, will be needed, as it was taught to us, *for a future to be possible.*"

None of this makes sense to the brothers. Inanna doesn't understand completely, either. But she has lived this life of mysterious teachings, ancient and esoteric. She accepts what Gramps says with the faith of one who has witnessed miracles.

The three eat slowly, thoughtfully.

They ask themselves silently, *in my life, did I have courage? Have I served? Did I choose responsibility?*

Is this a continuation of Meera's messages? Am I Merlin? Am I a leader?

Am I a companion to Halfling? A carrier of traditions forward?

"We, the elders," Gramps continues, "in body on this side, in spirit on the other, have been learning how to save *what* and *who* we could. But especially you Three. Our instructions were transposed from many languages, from ancient texts and wisdom schools. It was never completely clear, it was ..." he searches for the right words, "... *demanding* to understand how best to save you. Even for us who practiced medicine ways all our lives. Then the warning came. *Three Days of Darkness, soon.* We weren't given more time or instruction. We had to act."

He drops his eyes, remembering the terrible decisions the elders had had to make, their human worry and sleepless nights. The pain of learning how much would be destroyed. Plant life, animal life, and human life too. How many would be lost, including loved ones — no matter the best intentions of his small and dedicated community.

The old medicine man forces himself back to the present.

"We studied until we came to understand exactly which elements were necessary to save and rescue what we could. Yes, you felt wind lifting you. A host of spirit elders, and a few more on this side, like myself, gathered and spun the elements of air, fire, earth, minerals, and water, to move you." He pauses. "We had to learn and relearn old ways. And create new methods, to assure your survival. To bring you as close to me as possible." His face softens into a smile. "Meera played an important part. Yes, Conan, she is only young child, but that is now, this life. Meera is old, old soul, reborn at her own request — to serve. She *chose* and was *chosen*. She's called saint by some, avatar or *bodhisattva*, by others. She laughs at lofty titles. Whatever she thinks of herself, her power is far greater than her size and few years in current earth life."

Gramps stands and goes to a cupboard. The boys allow their eyes to roam the room as he does so. Conan is particularly impressed with what looks like a samurai sword hanging over the fireplace. Leo notices the Eye of Providence pinned to a closet door. But mostly the cabin is furnished with Native American blankets, talismans, totems and instruments.

The grandfather shuffles through the shelves stuffed with papers, loose photos, official looking documents and books. He returns to the table with a red leather-bound photo album.

"You see, others also work, even now, for your safety, for unfolding of prophecies." He opens the album and points to a photograph of two laughing women. "Inanna, tell the boys. This is your Nonny, my wife, yes?"

Emotion clutches her throat as she stares at the snapshot. Inanna nods a solemn *yes*.

"Tell them," Gramps lays his hand over Inanna's, "who this woman is, here, next to her? You recall meeting her?"

Inanna remembers well. "Nonny's friend. The one who came with many gifts."

Both boys suck in their breath as their eyes fall on the image.

Gramps goes on, "Leo and Conan's grandmother. The one they call *Granny*. Your Nonny and their Granny were close friends, many years. They sat in council of elders, those who came together from varied races, religions, and backgrounds. They learned together. They continue to work for us. As I will, soon, from the other side."

The boys reach out tentative fingers to touch the image. Conan holds his breath. Leo's posture betrays his grief. They had not allowed themselves to hope their Granny had survived the fires and devastation, but to learn she is truly gone is a blow they can hardly process.

"Not gone," Gramps says to the sadness invading their tired minds. "On the other side. Not gone."

The old man removes the photo from the album and places it reverently on the mantle. Celluloid images, locked in time, smile down at them. He moves back to the table and takes a seat with the kids again.

"When you needed to be lifted out of the destruction, your Nonny and Granny were both there for you, on the other side. United with other spirits, they used elements, helped create winds to bring you here."

He allows a long pause of respect for the emotions filling the room. "It's difficult, I know, to discover this and accept it in short time. But it cannot be helped. The world has turned over, north and south upended. And so suddenly. Even those who knew it was coming…"

His naturally unpunctuated voice fades. He walks to a window and stares out into the night, his reflection flickering in the candlelight. After a long silence, he turns back with a half-smile on his creased lips.

"*Three Days of Darkness*, that was prophecy. "*The Three* named in the prophecies are *you* three, here, now." With great respect, he whispers, "*Incredible*." He glances down at his hands, notes the repetition of that number. "*Three*. I have *three* days here to teach you, before you start your journey."

Anger flushes Inanna's cheeks. Leo and Conan glance at her uneasily. Gramps studies their serious faces. His own features impart a crinkly compassion.

"The way ahead is the crest of a journey spanning many centuries, coming to fruition in this time. You are blessed. Your Granny used to say to you, *awe and wonder of your shared path matches any challenge thrown at you* — yes?"

Gramps tilts Inanna's resistant face towards him. "Meera inspired your true names. *The Remembering* she spoke of awakens oldest, deepest memories, and sets your journey's course. Do not resist. All will be revealed. Lessons we bring forward together from distant past will enlighten the present and make the future possible."

Inanna has heard only one part of her grandfather's message. She growls, "No! I'm not leaving. I won't leave! I don't want another effing 'journey.' Bullshit! I'm staying with you!" She leans back, arms crossed, with a tough-talking, narrow-eyed vehemence. Yet they all recognize that at the heart of her protest is an anguished plea.

Leaning over in his chair to place his hands on her shoulders, Gramps says, "We each have our paths, Granddaughter." His countenance is rueful but determined. "Our journeys, fate, choices and destiny twist around themselves like snakes making love. Destiny is written by your soul's choice. *The Remembering* awakens your karmic contract with the Universe."

He doesn't wait for agreement. Keeping Inanna in his gentle hold, he looks over to the boys, making sure all three kids hear the importance of his instruction. "Preparation for this journey is demanding. Tonight, you need food and rest for strength. Tomorrow we start the teachings."

Inanna tries another protest. Gramps shakes his head with a smile, chuckling. "Inanna." He changes the mood, gives her shoulders a squeeze. "Here, look, I saved some honey from the spring — before last of the bees wisely disappeared."

He steps over to a blue-and-white utilitarian cooler squeezed amidst the furnishings on the crowded floor. He returns with a large jar and three spoons. "Sorry, no cookies or toast to go with it. Oh, Nonny," he cries theatrically, hand on his heart, eyes to the ceiling. "If you are looking down from Heaven, don't punish me for being a poor host!" His laugh lightens the room.

The honey is golden and rich, sprinkled with hints of wild blueberries and sunflowers, and so thick a half-teaspoon takes minutes to lick. The sugar rush buzzes their brains.

"Wait, what's in this?" Conan mumbles. His tongue is heavy with the perfect sweetness. "Magic elixir? Spring-time … high?"

After a tranquil pause, Gramps sits back down and reaches for Inanna's hand. He includes the boys in the wide, collective force of his voice. "You slept through Three Days of Darkness. We needed time to protect you from destruction and terrors. On fourth day, yesterday, you woke. As was predicted."

Gramps isn't given to drama or histrionics. Silence is comfortable for him. He's a medicine man. The wisdom of his ancestors and teachers emanates from his very being. Generations of working the natural elements in forms unfathomable to dabblers or laymen are embedded in every molecule of his existence.

"Leo. Conan." He turns to the boys. "As you rode that last night, you saw effect of first explosions, the blackness that covered Earth. You felt beginning of the great winds. Yes, boys? What do you remember?"

The honey's buzz fills the kids' brains. It trickles through their bodies and transports them to a space between material and ethereal. Leo has to half close his eyes in order to focus. "It was late afternoon. We had a couple of hours for rescues." His brother nods. "But night didn't just ease in ... it *fell*," he adds.

The sugar buzz now wakens Conan's tired brain. He jumps up animatedly, and in the next moment sits back down. "It was so *weird*!" he exclaims. "The freakish weather wasn't new, there were plenty of times that big weather shifts changed the patterns. But this was *bizarre*! At first, I thought the smoky wind was creating a fire-tornado. I've been in 'em, they are the effing worst! There's no time to think or change direction. But, I thought, we can handle this, we're used to riding hard and fast, we fight winds and fires, we rescue who we can. Shit, a super black night wasn't going to stop us."

In a mock TV reporter's voice, Leo cuts in. "*Never before-seen weather conditions. Unprecedented.* I mean, that was our *every* damn day! Fires didn't just burn, anymore, they raged. Blazes were hotter, higher up the mountains and deeper into the canyons, all the time. Until the flames got locked in and we'd have to wait days for them to burn themselves out."

"The smoke was sticky from chaparral burning," Conan interjects, "and from gas tanks blowing up. Old crap like asbestos or kerosene — in houses, cars, or dumped in forests — was toxic, and so thick we kept wet scarves on our faces. Horses charged around, itching to escape. Can't blame 'em. Some got so anxious we couldn't coax them to calm. Especially that last night."

The boy feels the noxious elements charge through his system all over again. Talking about the smoke makes his nostrils cringe and his eyes burn exactly as if he's back in the center of the firestorm. He checks himself, shakes off the sense memory. "Anyway. We had to ride." Punching his brother's shoulder with a smile, he mimics, "*Bring more horses, get more people out!* Leo has these damn *hero* ideas."

Conan's smile becomes serious again. "We had no choice, right? If we didn't show up for them ... they'd die." He stands and limps around the room, muttering at his bruised feet. He hobbles back, wincing, and sits again with a weary sigh. "I got totally freaked out. The winds were deafening, like being right under a landing jumbo jet." He places his hands on his temples. "Those winds squeezed my brain. And separated me from Leo like a solid brick wall."

After a moment, he confesses quietly, "Bro. I couldn't reach you." Both boys feel their chests tighten. Their shared visceral reactions are identical.

To Gramps, Conan affirms, "Leo's right. It was like a heavy weight pulled the sky down. There were no stars or moonlight. We could only see these little red spits of flame ahead."

They sit in silence while the candles flicker. The brothers are afraid to ask the old man whether he knows of anyone else who might be alive or dead, lost or saved.

Steeling himself, Leo ventures the question. "So ... we were 'saved' ... as part of some prophecy?"

Gramps slowly nods. *"The Three are saved to go on together."* Closing his eyes, he seeks words from the curves and crossroads of his ageless mind. Every one of the many days of his life careens before him. The inner windows and doors of his knowledge creak open and urge him, *teach.*

He pushes himself up from the chair and walks back to the window. The face of his beloved wife appears before him in the dark pane, just as he had seen her at that last Sun Dance ceremony on Pine Ridge Reservation. Warm, gentle, serene and yet so strong. She covers him with her love and compassion as she affirms, *Yes. It is time now.*

Inanna moves to him and wraps her arms around her grandfather's shoulders. Any remaining hesitation or misgiving he still harbors fades in the glow of Nonny's vision and the tender affection of their granddaughter.

Chapter 30
Prophecy

Giving her grandfather an encouraging squeeze, Inanna rejoins the boys where they sit at the table awaiting their teacher's guidance. Gramps shakes his head and sighs ruefully, "*Aiyee.* The young. Too much energy for an old man!" He pulls his chair closer to the hearth and composes himself.

"All right. Prophecies aren't revealed to just one people, or only once in history of humans and the planet. Deep truths cut across space and time. Teachings are revealed in language of each place and culture."

The kids nod. They shift in their chairs, leaning into his voice.

Gramps says, "Meera insisted you start by knowing prophecies from her tradition. And so, I'd better start as she instructs." He smiles. His words are more formal than his usual staccato speech as he delivers the teachings.

"Several thousand years ago, in part of world we call India, lived teachers of astounding esoteric knowledge and practical methods. They called themselves the *Rishi.* Common people called them *Forest Kings.* They were doctors of herbs and healing, astronomy and physics. Warriors of martial arts, mysticism and magic.

"They lived in places inaccessible to normal people: jungles, fog-shrouded mountain canyons, forests of impossibly tangled vines where dangerous species prowled. Rishi lived, studied and taught in homes hidden to the world. They ventured out only when Spirit directed them to aid villagers in times of pestilence, natural disasters or war.

"At such times, Rishi came unannounced. And when their work was done, they vanished into the fog of forests or the mists of mountains. An entire tribe of Forest Kings … *gone.*" Gramps snaps his fingers, waves a hand over his head as if dismissing a thought.

"Over time, organized religions developed, caste system divided people, and villages grew into towns. Battles were fought for land, tribal rivalries tore families and allies apart. The Rishi teachings, which were *for the benefit of all*, were ignored. And so, the Rishi themselves disappeared altogether where humans couldn't follow."

Gramps rises and moves to a wooden cabinet next to the mantle. He takes out a heavy book so parched with age that it crackles; dust flies from its pages as he sets it in the middle of the table.

Conan is immediately fascinated. "Was this printed in those ancient forests?" Leo gives him a look. "I'm not joking!"

The old medicine man smooths his hand over the book's brittle pages. "Oral traditions were written and copied decades after they were spoken. Printing was created another thousand years later, after the traditions were first taught. This book is as close to original teaching as could have been documented."

Conan and Leo lean across the table, bumping shoulders with Inanna.

Gramps gazes down at the volume. "These sacred writings came to be called The Vedas. I'm sure it's not *all* of what was taught, yet still it is powerful. At the back are 'First Teachings.' These are what we have come to call Yoga and Ayurveda medicine." He lifts his head in their direction. "Who gave this to me?"

"Meera!" Conan shouts the answer.

The old man's smile broadens. "That's right, *young Merlin.*" He winks at Conan. "Funny little girl she is, six years old and ageless at once."

The boy blushes and his eyes grow wide as he realizes the medicine man knows about their true names.

Returning to his chair near the hearth, Gramps continues his lesson.

"The Rishi Prophecy dates back to the Rishi's disappearance. Wiser students retold Rishi Prophecy in order to search for clues. The loss of their Forest Kings was incalculable. It was the one chance these people had to create an enlightened civilization."

Gramps hits a nerve. *Disappearance. Incalculable loss.* That kind of grief is close to home with these kids, he knows. *Betrayal, abandonment, loss, isolation ... They know the big hurts, too young.* He gives them a moment to assimilate.

"Even rival royalties knew they needed the Rishi. They sent search teams into extreme terrain. But no remnant of Rishi existence remained." He leans back in his chair. "Just as search was given up, a visitor arrived among the seekers. In a remote village that bordered a thick forest, an ancient monk appeared one day at dawn. The nearby forest was filled with tigers, rogue elephants and dangerous cobras. Few dared to venture near it. But the ancient monk appeared at dawn from its borders, without even a stick in hand for defense.

"Clothed in a threadbare saffron robe pockmarked with holes, the aged monk made his way into center of village square. His eyes shone with golden fire as he came among the people. And then the ancient man folded himself into lotus pose, *one within himself.* And whole village gathered. They sat and meditated with him silently for hours. Until, at last, he spoke."

The three kids are listening with such rapt attention that they have forgotten their exhaustion.

"The monk's voice was cracked from years of silence," Gramps says in his own timeworn rasp. "He told them that he was *Rishi.* He spoke to the gathered people about the importance of long-forgotten teachings."

Gramps leans forward, placing his hands on the arms of the chair.

"By and by, as the ancient man spoke, a scrawny beggar boy, unknown in that village, stood up from the circle. He stepped over to the well, tipped a ladle into the well's bucket, and brought water to venerable monk.

"An astonishing golden aura sprang all at once from the old man. It circled the boy and drew entire assemblage together. The light radiated a love and strength so complete it didn't require explanation.

"The Rishi monk told those listening, *People are not ready for Rishi Teachings. The selfishness of man has led to war and greed. Rishi will return long from now, when drowning rains and quakes cause lakes and seas to overwhelm the shores. When long-standing mountains fall, and new ones rise. From the ashes of destruction, the Rishi teaching of Oneness will awaken The Remembering in the few who survive the ruination. Only then will our wisdom once again be taught.*"

Gramps pauses. He trusts that his words will spark recognition in his three young listeners.

Inanna, for one, has been holding her breath. She is relieved to find that this "prophecy" doesn't send her into a panic. She peeks at the boys to gauge their thoughts and sees that the brothers are sitting in utter stillness, assimilating Gramps' teaching.

The old man gets up and goes to the next room. The boys can see it's a bedroom crowded with tools of the Native medicine trade. The old warrior comes back carrying a small, plain cedar container that Inanna at once recognizes as the box holding the sacred pipe her grandfather has used in Native ceremonies for over eight decades. He sits back down with the box held reverently in his lap.

Give silence its space, his wife would say.

After a charged few minutes of reflection, Conan breaks the quiet. He can't contain his questions a moment longer. He blurts out a stream of brain-peppering worries.

"And so — what's the end of the story? I mean, do the Rishi return? And when? Like, is that *now*? We used to hear people talk about prophecies, when we were growing up — and they said things like *Armageddon*, and *Apocalypse*, or *End Times*. Or *the Mayan calendar predicts* ... Are they all actually the same prophecy from different traditions, like you said? Or do all these different prophecies just sort of *sync up* at the right time? It seems like they all predict the same thing! *Disaster*. But we're not to worry, because — the Rishi will be *back*?!" Conan slumps in his chair, trembling in spite of the energy of his questions.

The others remain silent, waiting for Gramps' response. But the old man continues to simply hold the sacred pipe box in his lap, looking at them all with patient serenity.

Eventually Conan speaks up again, but this time he is more subdued.

"It happened so fast … ya' know, Gramps? It took years for the Earth to burn, shatter, flood. It just got worse and worse. But that last day, *slam*. Everything was gone in seconds. But we're *here*. So, it's not over. It's not, like, *over*-over … right?" He shivers.

The old medicine man opens the pipe box, smoothing the folds of the leather pouch inside.

The boys respect the ways that indigenous teachers impart lessons. They know that Native mentors often use oblique, unique patterns of story-speech, with artistic pauses, lilts and drifts. And few direct answers.

Minutes go by.

Eventually, Gramps closes the lid of the ceremonial box, then rises and puts it carefully on the mantle before resettling himself to go on with the teaching.

"Entire village was bathed in glow of Rishi monk's aura. He stayed there, in lotus position, until the moon rose. The villagers had been attentive to his Rishi Prophecy — although I suppose they hoped for more words. But you see, humans worry about immediate needs rather than welfare of future generations. And his prophecies seemed like they told of a time a long way off.

"When the moon waxed in evening sky directly over heads of those assembled, the monk looked up at the villagers and smiled. His beam was pure radiance. Then, *poof.* In a single spiral of cobalt smoke that burst from within him, he evaporated.

"The villagers rushed forward, tearing through the vapors, crying to one another. The monk's tattered robes dropped empty to the ground, discarded. Unnecessary."

Leo sits rooted, focused on his private thoughts, his hands laid flat on the table.

Conan gets up from his chair and circles the room. Absentmindedly, he pauses at the table and lifts the honey spoon, watching the drips fall back into the jar. Then he moves to crouch by the cabin door and get some air.

Leo breaks the silence. "Meera told us to *remember*. When she first said that, I saw these scenes swirling around me, like a rolling history lesson — not like a dream, but more like a 360-degree diorama." He wants to report this exactly right. "Meera put her little hand on my Third Eye, and I was, well, *transported* into a virtual reality. It was like the memories wanted to be known." He shakes his head. "And then just now, when you were telling the story of the monk, Gramps, it happened again. It was as if then and now were one experience."

A sudden, fiery stab sears Leo's chest. *The brand*, he registers, even as the spasm of pain seizes hold. *Why now?* He turns away so that no one sees his face contort or his hand clutch his heart. The pain shoots up from the boy's chest, heat spreading outward through his fingertips. He almost moans but catches the wail before it crosses his lips.

"*The Remembering Time.*" Leo coughs to cover his groan. The stabbing heat starts to cool and release its grip. "Meera said it starts here with you, Gramps."

The old man's face is benign.

"*This* is the Prophecy time isn't it? *We're* the Rishi - or were. Their story is our story. *Past meeting present to lead the future.*" It's a statement, not a question.

Gramps leans towards him. "Go on."

Leo pivots to Conan. "Can't say how I know, but I'm pretty sure *you* were the boy who gave the monk water. Listen, Conan. Maybe it's a weird across-generations connection — but remember that monk dream you had, a long time ago? You were five, maybe six years old? You ran to Granny's house as soon as you woke up, to tell her about the dream. What you dreamt made you kind of afraid — but you were excited, too."

"Oh my God, yeah, yeah!" Conan jumps up from his perch by the door. "And I almost forgot, but just before you and Inanna found me, I was waking up and half-dreaming, and I didn't remember *all* of it — but I saw that same *robe* floating in the air above me!" He turns to Gramps and Inanna, exuberant. "This dream is amazing! It seems like it's just so real, like I could touch this monk's robe."

He slips back and forth between his six and nearly sixteen year-old self.

"So, here's how it goes." He paces again, gesturing in the air. "There's an old, old man. Asian, or Indian. Exotic, dark-golden skin, eyes kinda like mine — sorta cat-eyes. He's dressed in these orange robes, with huge holes in the thin material. That silky material. The robe just hangs on him, he's so thin, too. And like Leo said, I was a just a kid, that first time I saw him in my dream. I woke up and freaked! More in awe than fear. The monk was floating *over my head.* As a whole person! And then, *zoom!* His round face was suddenly right in front of me."

Conan moves his palm to his face, an inch from his nose, to show them. "This monk is so eerie — but not scary — just real. He always seems to me like he's whispering secrets."

He blinks at the image in his memory-mind of the monk's face so near his own, startled awake on the top bunk with Leo asleep below him.

"The monk waved a hand over me." Conan sweeps his arm in a wide arc out to them and back to himself. "It felt like he pulled the covers up and tucked me into invisible clouds of, like, *calm.* It felt cozy, safe."

Leo adds quietly, "The next day, Granny taught us about spirit guides and guardians, remember?"

"Yes! She told us that we're cared for by 'energy forms' on the other side. People call them angels, ancestor spirits or guides. She said this 'venerable monk' came to remind us that the other side always watches over us." Conan feels that same soft air of safety wrap around his shoulders as he speaks. "Leo, how did you ever remember my dream?"

Leo shrugs, throws his palms up. "I have no idea! But when Gramps told the Rishi story, I straight up remembered it. It's like a movie camera inside my head scanned the village scene that Gramps talked about. It just came into my head, like, *oh yeah, that's right.* Like I knew it all along."

Conan is all fired up. "Is it possible that the Rishi monk in your story, Gramps, was, well, the same monk as in my dream? Is Leo right? … Is it possible that … *I* was the boy with the water?"

Gramps smiles. "I'm not teaching you anything you don't already know." He cups his hands under his heart. "During this *time of growing winds*, or the Kali Yuga, the prophecies tell us that gates open between worlds. These openings allow *the chosen who choose* to enter *The Remembering.*"

The kids are silent again, studying their own flickers of awakened understanding.

"Knowledge may come unexpectedly now," Gramps continues, "and as Leo said, you will know it to be so. This is sign *The Remembering* has begun.

"The Divine Force, God, or Great Spirit. *Sacred Energy of Source.* All give name to same force. Light, breath, the *word* abides in smallest elements and binds the disparate together. Medicine people teach, *we are one,*" the old man nods in answer to Conan's question. "But we small, scared people create opposing camps. Fear walks Earth by many names but always makes us deaf and dumb in rounds of illusion, delusion and denial. Greed, rage, disunion grow on the toxicity of fear. And then hatred becomes acceptable.

"Oneness," Gramps reminds them, "is music of Source. Oneness hums in birdsong and rain, in roar of crashing waves and soft patter of snowfall. It sings in flourish of flute and soft beat of drum. It speaks across cultures and generations in music, art and the natural world, through all the chemical elements, and throughout the human story."

Gramps growls a sigh. "Awake, we understand that universal intelligence isn't purchased by a single religion, nation, corporation, political or economic system. But people, bought off by distraction and consumption, did not awaken in time to change. Even the prophecies became a tool for exploitation."

Inanna, who has been silent, speaks up. "Nonny taught, 'Prophecy in the hands and mouths of false prophets creates falsehoods.'"

Gramps nods to her, glad for her recollection. "Gurus, CEOs, priests and celebrities, even some among our Native medicine people, used their skills to sell destructive, selfish messages. Trying to convince people 'only *we* know the truth.'"

Leo chimes in. "We all got hooked on delusions, whether addictions, drugs, tech or gaming, or, I don't know — stuff to *buy*, I guess. Adults ran the world, and their delusions were worse. Conan and I saw that. Poor ranchers gave up years of working farms and building towns to help the financially powerful because their delusion was that they would get rich too. So, they allowed oil pipelines to cut through their land. They started fracking and clear-cutting. And they poisoned the Earth with toxic chemicals to raise crops no one wanted! They just did shit that was against their own best interests."

Leo sighs. His voice is suddenly tired and sad.

"For *what?* Money? Where the hell is all that money now?"

Chapter 31
To Be the Light

Gramps studies Leo, taking in the boy's shrewd blue-green eyes and steady voice. He recalls himself at the same age. Eager to prove his manhood in a white man's war, he had turned away from the traditional teachings of his tribe.

Leo, he believes, has none of that false ego. "Son, you are wise. You have proven yourself a leader able to rescue, heal the injured and weary-hearted, and expect nothing in return." His words are strong and direct, but don't draw a hard exclamation point. He believes it's better for truth to find its own mark. "Do you wonder how it is these greater truths are easily known to you?"

Leo's face reddens. He holds Gramps' eyes with respect.

"Soon you will come to the answer for yourself."

The medicine man tells them all that there will be no spurious positivity or sunny disposition to enlighten their understanding. "I am so greatly saddened by all the corrupted teachings and twisted truths." He spits out each syllable. He stops himself and takes a breath to calm and caution himself against his own anger and judgments. "The task before you, creating a new world," he goes on, "takes so much heart."

Memories of suffering, poverty and the illnesses of his tribe flash through him. Memories of watching men die in a distant Vietnam jungle — his own son among them. All for false power, for *lies*.

Gramps bows his head to gather himself. At length, he looks up and whispers, "Who am I to unleash my rage?" He admits to himself that he's struggled with the demons of self-righteousness his entire life.

Collecting his thoughts, the old warrior resumes his lyrical teaching in a rolling, deep-throated cadence. "True teachings in all belief systems are the same. Be One with Spirit, Source. Seek union, balance, compassion. Be righteous and just. Yet true words must be *lived* for truth to take root, to grow and guide us."

Inanna is moved to speak again. "Only right-intention can direct right-action. Right-action creates a living mandate with lasting value."

Gramps kisses the top of her head. "It is a gift to hear Nonny's teachings spoken by the child who carries her spirit forward."

He unclasps his parched, work-stiffened hands. "Right-intention is the clear spoken heart of Oneness. But when we forget this underlying truth, the prophecies can't manifest." His fists clench. "Our world has seen so much death and suffering to satisfy the prejudice and ignorance of the masses. The true word of the Creator has been trampled. People have jumped from conspiracy theories to dogma, from *my nation, my religion, my God over yours*, to isolation. Humankind has feared change, instead of grabbing for opportunities to change. And they have blamed the *other*."

Nonny's warning rings in his ear a second time. *Succumb to rage, and you are as culpable as the corruption you argue against.* He closes his eyes and answers in his interior voice, *Aho, Nonny. Yes. Teach, don't preach. Inspire, don't conspire. Good wife, you know me too well!*

He opens his eyes and crinkles them in a smile.

"To forge your futures, leave all resentments behind. I cannot now, at my life's end, with responsibility for you three living manifestations of the prophecies, be captured by revenge and retribution. My selfish urge to condemn those who brought us to this brink only continues the worst patterns of the past."

Gramps goes to the cupboard and takes down three brass candleholders. He carries them all together to the table and sets one in front of each of his three listeners. Going back to the hearth, he searches out three fireplace matches and then brings them back to the table along with his chair. The old man eases himself back into the seat and gestures for the kids to strike the matches on the rough-hewn table to light their candles, which they do, each in turn.

"*Light dispels darkness.* Refuse to be captured by the dark poisons of fear, rage and polarization. Vow to be the light. The light of understanding, wisdom, forgiveness. Go forward without burdens of old hatreds." The candle glow illuminates his proud features, chiseled with timeworn experience and crossed with the wrinkles of well-lived years. "Three candles." His voice is low and soft. "One Light." *The truth of Oneness is embedded in the shared karmic consciousness of these three souls*, he knows.

To them, he says, "Many paths, myriad ways, centuries of understanding will be revealed." And yet, the sheer complexity of what's ahead for them staggers him.

He pushes away his worry. "Drawn together, your three intelligent minds will work as *one*." He won't overwhelm them with the recitation of their daunting challenges. *In spite of all that's hanging on their shared destiny, they're very young, very human.*

Gramps quietly but firmly cuts through his own thoughts. His love-filled voice reflects no disquiet. "Have another sip of honey. Then let's get some rest. I'll pray with the pipe for your memories to awaken while you sleep."

Chapter 32
Return of The Rishi

Before Gramps can turn their attention in the direction of sleep, Leo interjects a question.

"But … the Rishi Prophecy - what's our part?"

Inanna and Conan immediately echo the query that has been lingering in their own thoughts.

Gramps demurs, "Better to dream on what's already been said. I have spoken too long. Let's call it a day. Tomorrow we will have an early start."

The three kids shake their heads in unison. "We know some stuff about what happened over the past few years across the planet, Gramps," says Leo. "But we don't know much about what went down that last night. And we literally know nothing about the part we slept through. Or about what's out there now — or, like, what's left. I'm just saying, if knowing our part in Rishi Prophecy helps us to understand … and begin The Remembering … Why not know *now*?"

These kids hadn't observed their world's worsening times at a safe distance. They had lived in its midst. The boys' childhood had been abruptly torn from them and exchanged for duty. While Inanna had gone from personal chaos into the slip and slide of betrayal and abandonment.

But when global networks had collapsed, news of the widespread destruction had been limited. The kids were not made aware of the universal crisis.

Grief lingers in the unknowing, as well as the known.

Conan speaks up. "Honestly Gramps, how bad *is* it out there?" He is feeling himself grow jumpy again. "What part can we possibly play that could…"

Leo finishes his brother's thought, "… make any sense of it?"

Scrrreeech!

A sharp whiplash of wind startles them all, sending a rush of bitter cold flying down the chimney. The blast of air spins around the room and blows out the three candles. It tears at the peeling windowpanes, knocks over loose furnishings and sends the photo from the mantle flying into the air.

The bone-chilling wind attacks Gramps with biting force. The old man leans into the assault, one hand on the table next to him, the other on Inanna's arm. His granddaughter wedges her shoulder against his.

"Gramps!" Inanna gasps into her grandfather's ear. "Stay strong! The ancestors protect the teachings!"

The medicine man closes his eyes and reaches for Nonny in his thoughts. *It's fallen to me as you said it would, wife. Help me to fight my doubt. Strengthen me against my human worry and emotion.*

As the wind rages and Gramps steels his resolve, Leo hears a voice in his head. *One day you'll be like this old man. One day you will prepare the next generation.* Bracing himself against the table stained with years of loving meals and close family, the boy reaches out to squeeze Gramps' hand. He feels confidence in the old man's small but strong grip. Leo returns the encouragement in unequivocal measure.

The relentless wind diminishes, and finally calms.

Gramps' eyes are bright with tears. He straightens himself and looks around the room. Seeing the photograph of his wife and Granny on the floor, he moves to pick it up and tenderly replace it on the mantle. He lights another match, steps back to the table, and relights the three tapers.

"All right then. Tomorrow we start in earnest. Tonight, I will give you one more important piece of information to help you begin The Remembering."

He stands in front of the hearth, arms folded.

"The teachers who prepared me for you, Meera among them, felt the story of Rishi origins was essential to stir your shared memory of links between you Three and prophecies. And tonight, Leo connected Conan's childhood dream to the Rishi story."

He bends over his granddaughter so she can't avoid his eyes. "Now, Inanna. We need your help." The old man holds her gaze with firm intention. "Your gift of sight is not a choice, daughter. It is demanded by this moment." The girl is holding her breath. "Now, Inanna. As Nonny taught you."

Unvoiced questions flash across her face. She shakes her head once, curls bouncing over her blushed cheeks. Her hands stay steadily pressed together under her heart. "I'm not sure …"

Gramps blesses her with a smile of assurance.

Inanna sputters, "I never practiced this. I don't know … what … I can do."

"The prophecies say, *The Three.* Each of you must use your gifts for the benefit of all Three. What better time? Here and now."

She puffs a nervous exhale.

Conan studies Inanna under half-closed eyes. Privately, he relates to her embarrassment and nervousness, having often felt that way when asked to use his "intuition." But he knows that Gramps wouldn't demand something she couldn't do. *What is it he's asking? Why is she scared?* he wonders. Exhaustion curls into his bone and muscle. He resists a yawn, and picks at a rough patch on the splintered table.

Leo, too, is watching Inanna closely. He saw the spark that passed between grandfather and granddaughter. He doesn't know what Gramps is asking of Inanna, but he sees that even though she's embarrassed, she's lost her deer-in-headlights tension. *She has ability,* he observes, *but she's stubborn and proud and she doesn't want to screw up. Still, here with him, she shines.*

Gramps' direct command interrupts their thoughts. He stands resolute from his position at the hearth. "Granddaughter. In our sharing, we become powerful — and ONE. It is time to act!"

With a last shy sigh, and a quick side-glance at the boys, Inanna closes her eyes. She sends out silent prayers to Nonny, Bird-Girl and the ancestors. She inhales, exhales, settles herself into the back of the bentwood chair. Hands folded in her lap, she rubs her shoeless feet on the floor.

As taught, she directs the energy from the Earth's core up into her legs and spinal column and out her slender shoulders to her arms, hands and fingers. Her eyes flicker open, then shut loosely. Her black irises slide from side to side beneath her eyelids. Every cell of her consciousness sways into a soft and fluid wakefulness. Her personal aura, naturally flecked with gold, radiates out to them.

Minutes go by in expectant silence.

At last, Inanna speaks. Her voice is strangely resonant with a new maturity.

"*The forest teachers,*" she intones, "*the Rishi, were able to move their spirits out of their human bodies and sail on universal winds without peril. They gathered esoteric wisdom from the entire cosmos. They were able to return from out-of-body journeys to teach and heal.*"

Inanna's cadence is trance-like. There is an ageless echo in her tone. She reports exactly what she hears in a strange language she can't identify, yet she translates with ease and enunciates each word.

"*The Rishi cured bodies and minds by understanding the vibrations of Source energy. They manipulated cells and atoms.*" Inanna waves her right hand in a slow half-circle in front of her face, as if clearing away smoke. She tilts her head to hear the words. "*The Rishi saw past-present-future as one constant unfolding story, like a tapestry of endlessly connected patterns.*"

On Inanna's inner screen, a fast-moving tableau of watercolor animation passes by, clear and quick. Flowing human-like figures, young and old, female and male, run in warm winds. Orange robes flitter like heaven-hanging silks behind laughing human shapes. Images ascend and form, descend and dissolve into pools of liquid color. "*The Rishi moved as lightly as kites through the dense, iridescent forests they inhabited when in earthly form.*"

Behind Inanna's eyes, beautiful and ferocious animals, large and small, on four legs or slithering across the matted earth, pounce or slide or glide. Open-mouthed creatures plunge and pivot; disappear, then reappear and rear up. They grow the wings of multi-colored parrots or golden eagles and speed across the high jungle canopy. "*The Rishi befriended and merged with man and beast.*"

Sunlight dapples the shadows over and above the images that blend into one another in the lens of Inanna's trance-eye. The girl's graceful fingers cross one another, mid-air, as if she tracks musical notes that dance before her eyes. *"Rishi healers were spiritual warriors. They were able to become one with molecules of soul, spirit, and material bodies. They merged and exchanged electromagnetics with anyone or anything at will, in wide auras and in the tiniest particles, too, without losing their own life force."*

Zap! Pop! Sizzle!

A silver and cobalt ribbon of electric current jolts Conan, then Leo. *Like last night!* Both boys startle, but don't cry out. They immediately recognize the pulse. The cobalt light links The Three by a thin thread.

The boys can suddenly hear what Inanna hears, and even glimpse, shockingly, suddenly, what she is seeing too. Color-flashes of half-man, half-spirit liquid shapes dash across the night winds of majestic snow-covered mountain peaks or fly through densely tangled foliage. The boys hear tinkling bells, the thunder of hoofs, and rushes of soft wind.

Conan is transported, euphoric. *Let me see more! Let me hear, let me feel MORE!*

Leo breathes in shallow and concentrated gasps. *Awe and wonder.* He composes himself with deliberation.

Inanna continues as the spirit speaks through her.

"The Rishi sat meditation. They would expand their souls and spirits into limitless vibrations of sea, earth, sky. They created new frequencies. They found 'right' vibrations. They merged them with sentient bodies and with trees, rocks, and earth. All became ... One."

"Yes!" Conan speaks in an excited whisper, *"All knowledge is known to them by becoming One with each vibration,"* he repeats. He is validated by the inner knowledge he recognizes but couldn't claim before now.

Inanna startles. She realizes with Conan's words that the boys are connected inside her mind. Her voice quivers for a moment, but her sight remains true to Source within.

"Tuned beyond the five senses, beyond the sixth sense, the Rishi developed abilities over bridges of time and dimensions of space. From the earth's core to the farthest star nations, all knowledge ever secured was known to them."

The boys and the old man breathe in rhythm to Inanna's words. The candles on the table flicker gently. Inanna's inner screen widens to allow the vast night firmament of stars and planets. A parade of fiery red horses crosses the sky, galloping with celestial beauty among the blue-white stars.

"They carry the Rishi into the highest, farthest vibrations of the cosmos," Conan intones along with Inanna. The spirit voice that proclaims through Inanna speaks as lucidly to Conan as if it joins their memories together.

Whoosh! At the moment his brother speaks, the floor falls away beneath Leo's feet. The cabin walls fold out and flatten like a deconstructed cardboard box. Leo flies into the night, past the mountains, higher than the stars. *NO — I can't...* He feels the air rush into his lungs. *Stop!* He nearly chokes with the shock of it. Centrifugal force throws him further out and up. *What is happening?* His speed slows into wide loops and twirls, and he sails into the unbounded cosmos. Red horses fly around him in the inky-black night, across the star carpet of the Milky Way. He cries, "Gramps!" No one answers. Leo hears Conan's voice coinciding with Inanna's, obscured and far off. He tries to scream, but the wail gets caught in his throat. *Do you hear me? Am I here? Do you see me?* An acceleration of flight forces him farther out into the cosmos. His eyes slam shut. His bursting heart expands and soars him past fear, past worry or any need to know where he is and what's happening.

In that same wink of time, Inanna hears Conan speaking along with her — and then she hears the echo of Leo's call to them. She does not pause or waver. She continues the descant of the spirit's words. *"The Giants, as they were called by our ancestors, were visitors from another dimension who chose select earth creatures to train, teach and mate with. Those few, and their children and grandchildren, became the Rishi, men and women who shared equally the knowledge of the Oneness, whether leading or healing, whether in combat or compassion."*

Inanna takes a deep breath and listens to the secrets that inform her.

"The knowledge that the Rishi taught was crafted from a perfect understanding of Oneness. Seeking harmony between planets and galaxies, stars and sentient beings, the vibration of Oneness creates and maintains the balance and equanimity of the galaxy, and beyond. Without it, no life, NO life anywhere can continue."

Inanna's eyes flare open, unfocused, then flutter shut. Her hands fold over one another as she presses them to her heart.

"The Rishi, being part human, understood the temptations of earthly life forms. They knew that the Grand Illusions could take hold. And so, the Rishi chose to remain hidden after their Giant ancestors left. When the dark forces of the cosmos descend to fight for control of the Earth, the Rishi will return. And when the Rishi reveal themselves again, they, like their ancestors, will take to the skies on chariots of fire."

As Inanna speaks the last sentence of the Rishi prophecy, Leo joins in from his mind's soaring vision. He proclaims in unison with the spirit voice, *"When the Rishi reveal themselves again, they, like their ancestors, will take to the skies on chariots of fire."*

Though seated in the humble chair of the tiny cabin room, Leo is flying through the star-filled sky. He proclaims what he sees, directly from his stratospheric experience, confirming the message that Spirit speaks through Inanna.

"The Rishi!" Leo declares. "They FLY on chariots of fire pulled by massive flying red horses! They battle the Dark forces, flinging comets and asteroids like they're star-fired Frisbees! Why?" Transported by the breathtaking vision, Leo lowers his voice to a whisper. "For the preservation of the balance and the survival of the Oneness … the original breath of God."

Silence falls in the small cabin. The candles continue to flicker.

In the next moment, the line of mind-connection between Conan, Leo and Inanna shivers, tenses — and then loosens. Inanna's shoulders slump. She protectively wraps her arms around her chest. Conan lurches, heaving a huge gulp of air as he grasps the sides of his chair. Leo is suddenly thrown from the exhilaration of his mind-flight. His head slams forward and straight back as the floor rises to meet his feet and the walls fold back into place.

As quickly as it had started, the scene that has captured them all for these long minutes, collapses. In the same moment of time, the electric thread between Leo, Conan and Inanna is cut.

A vibrating aura of violet-gold light circles Inanna. The Spirit's voice quiets and the girl's seeing vision lifts.

A long sixty seconds ticks off in exaggerated silence.

Humming a Lakota flute melody under her breath, Inanna finally stands. She bows her gratitude, hands at her heart in a prayer-triangle. The aura that has spun around her hovers, then absorbs itself wholly into her.

She leaps into her grandfather's arms. "It worked! Exactly as Nonny taught me!!"

Chapter 33
Part of A Really Old Story

Inanna hugs her grandfather. She hiccups and laughs, her emotional enthusiasm riding high.

Conan is still sitting at the table, trying to process all that he has seen and heard. He asks her self-consciously, "Did you see any of that, while you were ... speaking?"

Inanna rushes over to hug Conan, too. But her shyness returns. She stops herself, heart pounding, deep pink glow to cheeks. "Yes!" she bounces on her toes, hands clasped together. She is back to her kinetic, nervy self, the maturity of the spirit voice giving way to Inanna's familiar pace.

"Yes! You were the little boy, Conan, just as Leo said. You lived in the forest with the Rishi and were a student. And the monk — this'll sound crazy, but I'm pretty sure that was *Meera*! Not the Meera we know, but another form of her, from another lifetime!" She turns to Leo. "And — *you* were a Rishi warrior-king! A man, but, well, not fully human. Closer to the energy of the Giants. And you were able to ride those fire chariots! Oh *damn*. It's hard to explain!"

She turns to Gramps for help, clearly wanting him to intercede and elucidate her vision.

Gramps, gently smiling at his granddaughter, remains silent, his lips curling patiently.

Inanna looks around at the boys again. She starts to pace. She wants to get this right. She wants them *all* to understand the spirit's message — including herself.

"The Rishi were descendants from celestial beings called the Giants, who were like ETs, I guess, from another galaxy! The Lakota and the other tribes have those stories too." She nods her head vigorously. "I mean, I know about the Star Nation descendants, and all that. But this is a sort of ... validation!"

The strange security of having been connected in her mind-sight with the boys, again, gives Inanna confidence. The boys, too, feel the resonance of the woven energy.

"It must have been some weird thing on our linked connection," Leo says, "when you were speaking in that sort of trance-voice, Inanna — I was here, but also in the night sky. I can't explain it, but ..."

"I totally felt you above me, Leo!" she interjects at once. "It was like an enormous wing sort of *whisked* the air overhead! You saw the chariots, too? The red horses? Constellations?"

The entire experience has been a validation of not just what Inanna had seen, but of who she is. For the moment, her nagging fears of what the world has become are tolerable. And for the boys, the shared vision of a mystical past lifts them out of their routine devastation and sense of loss.

Conan stands. He winces from the soreness of his muscles, the aches of months of endurance riding, deprivation, and extreme conditions. "I feel like an old man."

Gramps grunts. "You have no idea."

The kids laugh softly with him. A long, reflective silence ensues.

Conan crosses to the hearth behind the medicine man. He stares into the dwindling fire. His innate instinct to guard his own emotions would normally keep him from being too completely raw and honest with people he's just met. But the magic of this evening, combined with his physical exhaustion — and his newly found trust in Gramps — loosens his reflexive guard. He feels compelled, now, to express some of the long-held frustrations and disquietudes he has long harbored — and which the night's events have cast light upon.

"I'm still not sure how me n' Leo and Inanna fit into these prophecies. But I can see that it's bigger than any of us," he begins. "I've always accepted that I'm ... different. And you know what, fuck it, I don't care. But I don't understand myself well enough to know *why* I'm so different. ... Leo, you know I think you feel the same disappointment about some people that I feel. But somehow you dismiss it and rise above it, or maybe ignore the truth about them ... sometimes to your own detriment."

Conan turns to Gramps. "You know, people tell lies, Gramps. They can be deceitful. Our Aunt Sophia used to say that most human beings have moral inconsistencies. But what I see about them is they can be ugly and cruel. And when people are mean like that, when they are lying and cheating and unkind, it sounds in my mind like a hundred sharp fingernails scratching a blackboard." He winces. "And at times like that, I just want to shut down and isolate."

He sits back at the table and slips an unintended sigh. "But ... I can see that my, um, complicated emotions and understandings might, well ... Maybe they can help other people too, some day." He smiles self-consciously.

Gramps pats Conan's back. "Good, son. Continue."

Leo eyes his little brother with approval.

Conan puts his hands on his knees, searching for the right words to sum up his meditations. "Now that all this has happened ... now that we met you, and Meera made herself known to us ... it just seems to me that we're part of a really old story. Like a legend or a myth or something. Whatever it is ... like I said, it's bigger than any of us. And it just sounds, strangely, so — right. And familiar."

Gramps squeezes the hand on Conan's shoulder. *Patience, old man*, he tells himself. *Now is not the time to push his memory into full awakening.* He smiles at Conan. "I am proud of you, son. These are good, important thoughts. And what you are telling me, all of you, gives me hope The Remembering is possible."

He turns to the others. "But it is late now. And while there is still much to learn in very short time, we must get rest. We will start afresh in the morning."

In spite of their fatigue, the three kids still have questions. They are reluctant to end the teaching. Gramps can see their eagerness to continue. He holds up his hand, laughing gently.

"We will start again in the morning."

He moves around the tight cabin space, uncovering pillows, blankets and sleeping bags tucked into every crevice and cubby. "Boys, take space in front of fireplace. It will keep you warm all night. Move table back, make room for those long legs. Yes, that's the way. Good, good. Inanna, take that lumpy old bed in the other room. I'll use my army bedroll and sleep on floor next to you."

Inanna does not appear to be listening. She stares into space, not moving from her position at the table. Her awakened psyche demands attention.

"Gramps? There's more we have to tell you. More you need to know ... about what we saw today. And — yeah, it needs to be before we go to bed," she insists.

Gramps guffaws. "In one night, we have traveled very far. We went to ancient India and the forests of Rishi. Conan took us to his past and the world of his dreamscape. Inanna opened to us the universe of the Giants. While Leo sailed on chariots of fire! Enough! *Rest*, now." The old man smiles. *The young. They can be so exhausting!*

Inanna ignores his deflection. "Meera explained the Hungry Ghosts. But, Gramps, we saw something else. And I don't know how to explain it. I only know it was *bad*. Sinister. Evil. ... Something really scary happened."

The boys glance at each other, then turn towards Inanna. They want answers as much as she does — though without giving voice to the thought, they had almost hoped *not* talking about what they had seen this afternoon would somehow diminish it.

Gramps folds his arms. After a moment, he sighs and throws another log on the fire.

Inanna stays in her chair. The boys stand near the table, on either side of Inanna, waiting to hear her account, and preparing themselves to add their own perspective.

"About a third of the way up the mountain," Inanna begins, tracing the route in her mind, "there's a giant boulder with a sort of outcropping."

In staccato detail she tells of the elk's death. She speaks deliberately, not allowing emotion to color the telling of facts. "Something — or someone — rose, like a foul, dark *ooze*, right out of the ground."

Leo corroborates. "It grew with incredible speed, and thickened into, well, sort of a shiny, black *wave*."

These children are witnesses to pain, injury and death. In the lexicon of human suffering, they are not innocents. Yet, the dark, rising *thing*, and the destruction of the baby animal life form, created a confusing stew of anger and shock that had settled into a sense of foreboding. That unease had stayed with them — until this moment, when they could speak of it for the first time.

"It was this creepy, gelatinous material. But — it didn't have a face, like the Hungry Ghosts." Leo searches for words. "It seemed — malleable. It bent, stretched, grew and shrunk back, like, at will. It wasn't an animal; it had no limbs, and I don't think it could have had internal organs. But it had an organizing principle of some kind, like the Hungry Ghosts. And ... it was really disturbingly scary."

In the next instant, Conan and Inanna begin to barrage Gramps with overlapping qualms and questions.

"Have you ever seen it, Gramps?"

"It rose up and gobbled the elk! There wasn't even crunch of bone, not a cry from the poor thing!"

"Gone! In a single, horrible swallow."

"Then that, that, *thing* split into *parts!* So many ... a dozen."

"More!"

They shake their heads. Their eyes widen, their pulses race.

"Gramps." Inanna chooses her words with care, striving for accuracy in her account. "Within seconds, this thing shot into the air and swallowed the elk, right in front of us." She shivers. "And then the blob just slid back down into the ground, sort of like it was ... waiting for the next victim." Inanna turns her palms up and shakes her head at the boys for help.

"This is the first time the three of us have talked it out," Leo adds. "But, yeah, the speed of it, the viciousness, was gruesome, and really scary. Its evil power was clear — that part isn't a mystery."

Inanna's impressed that Leo can be honest about his fear. She's trained herself not to express her true feelings. And she's learned there is a price to pay for hiding those feelings. Conversely, she guesses there's a price that Leo pays for the expression of his feelings. But she can now see the reward: his emotional courage. She tucks that recognition away for later, private rumination.

Conan jumps to his feet, gesturing with his arms energetically. "And then all of a sudden, the air between us and the thing just *warped* — like a, a shimmery, vertical, see-through mirror, or a sci-fi force-field was right there in front of us!"

"Like a shield of pulsing electricity!" Inanna agrees.

Conan is nodding. "It rippled in front of us. And then it ..." He sweeps his arms straight out, "... flattened out into this complex maze, and then it built up these steep grades and passages, like tunnels and bridges!"

"It was like a Harry Potter-fantastical, self-constructing *labyrinth!*" Leo concludes.

The three kids look at each other. And abruptly they all start speaking at once. Now that they're talking it out, they have so much to say their voices scramble over and across one another, noting every detail.

"It was so *eerie!*"

"But weirdly beautiful, too!"

"Did you see the shades of blue in it, and a sort of icy silver?"

Inanna declares, "I felt for a minute like I was running along the labyrinth bridges!"

"But wait," Conan interrupts. "What about that heat? That burning, intense heat that came before we saw the labyrinth? We saw our *bones!*"

Inanna is shaking her hands, her arms flailing at her sides as she flashes back to the moment. "Our bodies were like an *x-ray!*"

Leo confirms, "Gramps, we saw our own skeletons!"

Inanna, suddenly chilled, pulls a blanket around her.

Conan, too, feels almost numb as he recalls the phenomenon. "It came out of nowhere."

After a moment, Leo continues, "Then – *snap!* It was gone. I felt scared, later, but in that moment, I just felt shock. There was no time to investigate. And we shouldn't have, really. So, we kept going. We headed up the mountain again."

Conan studies his big brother. "Leo took up the rear, behind me, after that. The whole way up. I knew you had my back, Bro."

Leo examines his feet for a moment, then looks up with a tight smile. "Tried to keep watch over things. But not sure I could've protected anyone from that thing."

A contemplative silence ensues, broken only by the gusts of wind outside the cabin.

Finally, Conan looks to Gramps. "So … the warp-field? It sure seemed like it saved us from that black slime. *Did* it, do you think, Gramps?"

The old warrior stands by the hearth, completely still. He has held the same position throughout the kids' narration, clutching an unstrapped bedroll under one arm. He remains silent with his thoughts for a full minute.

At length, Gramps responds slowly. "Anything else you remember?"

Inanna turns to Leo. "What about what happened at the river? You felt something there, right? A hostile force around the whirlpools?" She turns to her grandfather. "I didn't tell Leo about the spirit that supposedly haunts that rock crossing. Not until after. But — he sensed it."

Leo shudders. "Yeah. It looked like a ... well, a dark whirlpool was trying to pull me into the river. It felt like something evil. ... And now that I think about it, maybe it was trying to form a wave? Same as what got the elk?"

Gramps closes his eyes and lowers his head. When he looks up, his voice is low and direct. "That all of it?"

The three kids think hard, calling to mind every detail as trained observers. They exchange looks, then nod agreement. "Yeah, that's pretty much it."

Gramps responds, "Think hard." He tightens his grip on the bedroll. "Was there any sign of a red color in the black wave? Or in the river whirlpools?"

Inanna and Leo shake their heads.

But Conan stares past them. He flashes on a recognition. "Yes. Yes ... there was! That killer wave rose up black, then there was this red sheen for less than an eye-blink. And then it was black again. I remembered the red later, when we were climbing. I had a freaky feeling I knew what that red was ... but I couldn't pinpoint it ..."

Gramps emits no sigh to indicate shock or opinion. He remains impassive.

The kids' quiet attention is equal to their bold action at other times. Thrust from the carelessness of childhood into harsh reality, into responsibility and loss of innocence, the three of them have learned patience. They wait for Gramps to speak.

At length, Inanna moves to him and gently uncurls his gnarled fingers from the bedroll. Leo pulls up a chair for him. Conan moves to the table and lifts the honey spoon from the jar. He carries it to Gramps, one hand cupped to catch any drips, and offers the precious honey to the old man's cracked lips. Then reaches for a mug of fresh water to chase the sweetness down.

Gramps' tight-skinned face crinkles in thanks. He eases into the chair, waves them to sit close.

And speaks.

Chapter 34
The Darkness

"The lines between Light and Dark are razor thin. Light and Dark
are meant to be in relationship with one another. But when one or the
other gains too much control, chaos results."

Gramps takes a deep breath. "I thought we had more time, my
young and beautiful and brave relatives."

The old medicine man projects the gift of truly and fully *seeing*
them all, each in turn. His overwhelming warmth draws them into a circle.

"It was my ... *plan* to wait until the next few days to tell you this.
Foolish old warrior, to think the Darkness would stay away until my *plan*
unfolded." He shakes his head. "Those who help us from other side —
Meera, and others — didn't warn me that the Dark would come so soon.
This means that even they thought there was time. There is not." He gets
up from his chair, too restless to settle yet. "Better to face truth than give
evil any advantage."

He circles the small room, wrestling with his unease. *How much
to say? Their hearts and minds have already been so greatly tested, this
day.* He stops again at the hearth. Stokes the dwindling fire. When he
faces them, his jaw is set and his expression is resolute.

The boys see the fire of determination and commitment. They
see the brave of his youth, spine tall, head erect, shoulders back. He is
ready for battle.

The old warrior addresses his council.

"You witnessed power of the Darkness recreating its most raw,
earthly presence." Leo, Conan, and Inanna sit in a semi-circle on the floor
around Gramps. "Nothing, no one, is completely devoid of the Light. The
Darkness defines itself by its relation to the Light. It is only when it goes
into opposition against Light, however, that you must arm yourself.
Because then chaos reigns." Gramps stands behind his chair, his hands
gripping its slatted back. "Darkness is more complex, harder to penetrate
than what is taught in human laws and religions. Because the
manifestation of evil generates from the essence of evil itself."

He pauses. He knows the difficulty of understanding this concept
and wants to give them time to process his words.

"Darkness understands human weakness. It seeks to coerce us
with the language of our own ego, with our own fears and delusions and
competitive natures. Darkness creates the very illusions we think give us
meaning: wealth, beauty, ownership, control. Our very *words* — our
poetry, political slogans, rallying cries, and self-focused prayers — can be
evil's own influence!

"The Darkness obscures simple facts in science and history, so
that personal fears and prejudices dictate new laws and create institutions,

governments, and idolatrous religions. Borders and boundaries are erected to possess and dominate. The world of man, poisoned by the Darkness of the Grand Illusions, serves the worst, most pervasive, evil."

Wrrrack! Rrrrippp!

An enormous mountain rock, hefted by a sudden cyclone of wind, slams into the cabin directly above the doorframe.

The kids gasp, turning. Leo is on his feet at once.

A second rock-blow hits the wood-shingled roof. Splinters fly down the chimney, dust and ash surge through the room. Fire embers spin in a funnel, like a cinder tornado. The sheltered cabin suddenly feels as if it's caught in the coil of a viper's spitting assault.

Conan covers his ears as the pressure of the wind makes them pop. Leo kicks his chair aside and reaches to help his brother, but he's caught off balance in the spinning wind. He stumbles without anchor. Inanna rocks sideways, her eyes locked on Gramps, who stands upright in the center of the cyclone. Her faith is concentrated on the power of his sacred knowledge.

She grasps the edge of the table and screams into the wind. *"No panic!"*

Gramps stares ahead, his high-carved cheekbones gleaming in the reflected fire. His deep-set eyes throw off their own flame. The old warrior growls a deep, full-throated invocation in Lakota. He cantillates in octaves that jump and sing in a multi-tonal chorus of prayer. The wind lashes harder, and Gramps sings louder. He raises one hand over his head, defiant, commanding. And at last, the gusts start to dip and dash and fall under his control. After what seems long minutes of battle, the tempest gives a final full-throated wail, and twists back, curving itself up the chimney. Ashes, dust and cinders waft to the wooden floor. The little room grows still.

He lowers his head for a moment. When he looks up, his chest rises in a deep inhale of breath.

"This errant wind-attack is an envoy of the Dark. And the black form you saw on mountain is another primal form of Dark. Both are rough harbingers in search of us." He looks fixedly at Leo, Conan, and Inanna, each in turn. "Especially you Three. Sophisticated forms of malevolence are *far* more subtle. And more dangerous."

Hands on his temples, Conan tries to ease the painful sound of the squall from his brain. Leo steadies his brother, knowing he is prone to crashing headaches. He pours him a cup of lukewarm tea from a heavy pot that had escaped toppling in the winds. Leo nods respectfully to Gramps and whispers, "Please, go ahead." He keeps his hand tight on Conan's forearm.

Gramps warns them not to be distracted by the shock of the wind and the pummeling of rocks against the cabin. "Darkness throws fear. It messes with spirits and minds. But it's never stronger than our commitment to Light. Darkness can't hide from you and it is *not* stronger than you are when you are fully awake."

The medicine man's eyes burn with a golden sheen. He stares so deeply at Conan in particular that, in spite of his fearsome words, the boy's headache eases and his body calms.

"Darkness," Gramps continues, "draws every ache of the dissatisfied world to itself. Together, Light and Dark are a dance of union, of reflection, mirroring one another — but when out of balance, all horror and mayhem are born. Battles for territory, histories of gold, silver and money — and of religious wars — all these are the ugly work of the Darkness. You know story of the Inquisition? Supposedly done to protect the Church? And the burning of 'witches,' the Crusades, persecutions against Jews, Muslims, 'heretics;' the genocide holocausts that destroyed indigenous people in the Americas and Africa, and eliminated entire cultures; and Christians on opposing sides of Christianity who practiced cruelties beyond description to rid us of 'evil' — were all committed by evil itself."

His fierce words demand attention, but they are tinged with a compassion as strong as his grief for the sins of the past.

Nonny's voice pierces his heart-mind. *Don't be just another preacher.*

"The 'faithful' were deafened by falsehoods, blinded by misinformed hopes or our human weakness for fame, fortune, and, yes, 'patriotism.' We unknowingly empowered another, more pervasive evil."

Gramps drops his head to his chest. "I know because I was one of those young braves. I'm no stranger to corrupting power of ego. Self-righteous rage is never far from me."

He lifts his eyes and goes on to tell them that denial and delusion had dragged him in and out of *right-intention* and away from his people's *Good Red Road of right-action.*

"After the Korean War, I vowed never again to pick up arms against another man. I turned to the old ways of my people. I studied medicine traditions. I left the cities and white man's rules behind." The old warrior closes his eyes. "But then came Vietnam, and my son's deployment. I volunteered, a second time." He opens them again, looking straight ahead. "*Twice*," Gramps continues, swallowing hard, "the horrors of war taught me that evil poisons the hearts and minds of good men with promises of glory. *Twice*, it took terrible loss for me to awaken and stand for *peace* and the rights of common people." His voice rises. "Twice before, I called out the Darkness by its true name, no matter where it hid." He lowers his voice again. "Including in my own heart."

The three kids feel the tears of his pain prick at their own eyes.

"It took two wars, and uncountable horrors, before I understood that Dark power hides its evil intent wherever humans gather. The spiritual warrior caste, traditions from which you Three and I come, must always be alert, awake to evil's corrupting, subtle influence. We must choose righteous action over self-righteousness. Inclusion over enemy. Oneness over false teachings of glory. The spiritual warrior is fearless in his or her quest for truth, balance, equal and fair justice for all, no matter religious beliefs or government policies."

Gramps abruptly throws his head back, expands his lungs until his ribs flare wide. His arms extend outward, palms facing the sky.

Whooosssh!

The fire contained within the fireplace now erupts. Tongues of flame shoot out behind Gramps' back. The fire licks at the ceiling and plunges with rocket-dive speed to his feet.

The old man, framed by crackling flames, doesn't flinch.

Inanna, Leo and Conan suck in their breath, thrown back onto their elbows by the force of the fire's wind. Conan reflexively looks to Leo. *Do something!* Leo scrambles up, runs to the sink for water to douse the flames. But a glance at the medicine man's steady posture stops him. In the same moment, he hears Inanna's gruff whisper, *"No threat!"*

The boys swallow their alarm. They carefully reclaim their seats on the floor next to Inanna. They abide the mystery of the fire's respect for the medicine man it guards.

Gramps' eyelids flutter. They close, open again and focus on the distant sights beyond the cabin walls, beyond the mountain and the night.

A golden light, tinged with a blue as bright as the red-hued flames of the fire, fans out from the old warrior and dances around The Three. The light warms them all but doesn't burn. It licks innocently at their feet and faces, encircling Gramps.

Light guards against Darkness. Abide the mystery. They all three hear the voice speaking to their heart-minds.

Inanna whispers, "Golden Light commands the fire. I've seen Gramps be one with this force before, but…" Her eyes are wide.

An immense sense of well-being emanates from the Light. Its safety is layered in concentric circles.

Conan sighs. "Gold fire. Protective flames. It feels … alive."

Leo eases back into his chair at the table while Conan and Inanna remain cross-legged on the floor. Each of them feels the wordless message of the Light: courage, power, compassion and passionate joy. They reach out tentative fingers towards the drifts of glimmering. It sifts over their hands, sparkling, casting a glow on their arms and shoulders. They tilt their faces up and the Light cascades over them.

Leo whispers, *"Awe and wonder."*

Inanna exhales, *"Blessing."*

Gramps speaks from within the golden ring of rays. "Light is Source and genesis, always, forever, within us and around us and near." His palms are held up, his Lakota prayer voice is steady. "Darkness resists, opposes the highest intent of Light from Source. What occurred to create this opposition? Who can say?" It's an observation, not a question. "Perhaps an innocent need for safety, home, or perhaps a fear of death or ruin of family, drew a first dangerous promise. Perhaps a parent hoping to save a child, or a man whose wife was dying, reached out in grief and fear to whatever energies promised life — and then the first bond was made, first agreement struck between the Darkness and an unsuspicious, innocent human."

The flaming circles around the old warrior vibrate to a rhythm, a beat of low drums. Gramps is motionless and unblinking for long seconds in his prayer stance. He nods to a silent internal message, his grey-black braids following his movements. He tenses his muscles, digs his moccasin-covered feet into the knotted and curled floorboards. He stands his ground as the fire erupts three times around him in elegantly surging circles of flame. The fire leaps and rises, spreads and curls, twists to the notched and aged rafters of the cabin. It descends and licks again at the old man's feet and body.

He blinks three times. When he speaks again, his voice resumes its sonorous tone.

"Malevolence roams the Universe in myriad manifestations. The Darkness that ate the elk is an earthly manifestation, an ugly, deadly form of Darkness. That Dark wave feeds on raw animal energy, with or without a kill. But without doubt, in any form, Dark's greatest feed is our fear." The flames at his feet do not trouble the old man. He continues, "*Red* is a defining characteristic of this particular Dark energy. And it grows stronger with death of its prey. Red is color of blood-passion, of battle, of hatred, of rage moved by heat of war. But red is also a symbol of love's passion and heart's desire. Red signifies Sun's rising and setting, the light without which no life is viable. Tonight, you saw the red flames of fire's protection. You also know too well that flames can kill."

The boys exchange a glance.

"Always be sure *which* red you recognize. The guises of the Light and the Dark as fire energy are many. Never mistake one for other."

Gramps' obsidian irises, so like his granddaughter's, sparkle with his intensity. The force of his words and warrior's stance sizzle the air. The Golden Light pulses in place behind him now; its fiery grace reflects back the lessons The Three are learning. The old man knows that these teachings must be absorbed, carved on the interior stone of their personal history, made real and repeated.

At last, he lowers his arms and cups his hands under his heart.

"It is good you recognized the *red*, Conan. Your ability to diagnose threat is essential to survival." Gramps shifts his gaze between the brothers. "Leo needs you as extra ears and eyes. Your insight gives him advantage in journeys ahead. You're his psychic advance team. His spiritual scout." Gramps is gratified to see their nods of agreement.

"I have to readjust my teaching because of today's new threat." He narrows his eyes. "And possibility of more killings."

He doesn't say aloud, *Three days. Not enough time.* But his penetrating stare clouds over long enough for Inanna and the boys to notice. He blinks back his worry and smiles his wide, white-toothed grin.

"You're a serious tribe, young relatives. And no wonder. Much behind you, much ahead. If Meera were here, she'd lecture me. She'd say *you teach about no-fear and then you scare them! This is the time of greatest possibility!*"

The old man sits in the chair again, placing his hands on his knees. "You should trust Meera, above all others. She's lived longer and wiser lives than any of us, and in better ways."

Conan exclaims, "She's a little scary! I mean, damn! She *knows* stuff about us…"

The kids share a self-conscious giggle. Gramps looks on indulgently, then governs their attention again.

"Know this: even in darkening times, that black death-form is rare for human eyes to see in its horrific … glory. Yet, even more rare was the mysterious gift of the saving shield. It rose to protect you Three, I have no doubt. It shielded your fear from the black wave's radar."

Gramps pauses. He needs them to understand that it's the heart of his message.

"*Fear* is the greatest enemy. Never, ever doubt that. Know your own fears. Don't let them nibble at your heart-mind, unchecked. Call them out. Call them by name, and they lose their power."

Whoooosssh!

More wind gusts fly uphill from the valley floor and viciously pound the door, loosening hinges, slamming windows and peeling away sashes. Another ferocious roar races down the chimney.

Leo and Conan jump, alarmed. Inanna, too, is startled, but she quickly recovers, keeping her attention on Gramps, who stays grounded, unperturbed.

The golden flame around him is not moved by the wind's resistance.

Leo rises from his chair to sit on the floor next to Conan, shoulder to shoulder. The boys' alarm shifts to careful attention. The three kids sit together watching the wind rush around the room. This time they do not feel the same foreboding.

Conan whispers, "Cold wind and hot flame know each other, oppose each other. Light and Darkness."

The Light around Gramps circles and pulses into a warmth that expands to every nook of the cabin. The threatening wind pushes against the Light — but finds no opening.

After a few minutes of raging, the gale blows out of the cabin in a furious retreat up the hearth.

Gramps is concentrating on Conan's observation. He nods. "That is right. It is good you know this, son."

Conan feels his eyes fill with tears.

"Leo. Conan." Gramps regards the boys with utter fullness. He projects his love and respect for these boys who are soon to be men. He turns his gaze upon his granddaughter. "Inanna."

The Three can't yet know how precious the memory of Gramps' simple utterance of their names will be, in years to come, when even greater burdens mark their days. But Gramps knows. He balances between worlds and listens to the old and new messages of his teachers.

"The lines between Light and Dark are razor thin. The Light always wins in the end. But Darkness will always return to try again."

He studies their young faces and sees no fear. "Meera's right," he avows. "You need only to be reminded of what you already know."

The old man throws his arms out in a graceful arc. He tilts his head back. He looks to the roof and, seemingly, beyond it to the night sky. Light and fire merge behind him, and around and above him, and blow back through Gramps with a singing roar before disappearing into the hearth and up the flue as mysteriously as the elements had first appeared.

A glittering dance of red-gold azure shimmers through the little room, covering them in serenity and soundless grace.

Chapter 35
Why Don't We Learn?

They stay in that calmed silence, in the peace of the Light, for a long while. The day's battles are temporarily forgotten, as is their exhaustion.

After a time, Leo gets up and crosses to one of the cabin's small windows. The presence of the Darkness beyond the sheltering walls of the cabin is palpable. Yet Gramps' attention and compassion, his trust, and the guardian fire's presence breathes into Leo a quiet that strengthens his faith.

The boy doesn't want to break the majesty of the moment. But his private thoughts nag him and squeeze his chest. The human history of genocides, cultural cataclysm, chaos and confusion — the Earth itself torn apart — these devastations oppress his mind.

"Why don't we learn?" he almost wails, pressing his hands against his temples. "The useless, brainless *repetition*," he protests. "Why doesn't someone say *Stop! We've done this before!* Why do we repeat the story? If fear is the real enemy, why do we all get scared at once, give up, join in, collude?"

He flashes back on all those who were left homeless, forgotten, maimed, killed, in the years leading up to that last night, when only he and Conan remained.

"Even if we're not deliberately evil, still, in personal and small ways, *why* do we go along with insanity? Does Darkness feed off not just the cruelest of humanity, but also those who simply put up with it? Why don't we learn?" The boy pulls his tattered jacket tighter around him.

Small sparkles of light remain in the room. They expand and encircle them all in tangible warmth, relieving the chill of Leo's despondency.

The Three breathe rhythmically.

Gramps makes plain his approval. "My boy. My good *man*. You are wise as you are courageous. As was promised in the prophecies. Physical courage many have, but you have emotional courage. To cultivate emotional courage, we must be willing, again and again, to face our own darkness."

Leo returns a soft nod.

"The future depends on your willingness, *each* of you, to search for answers to this question, *why don't we learn?*"

Gramps instructs them that they should see the eternal question as an opportunity.

"Among different cultures, in different places and ages, humans enjoyed generations of peace, unity, love and prosperity. What did those peaceful and loving people know that humankind seems now to have forgotten? The Rishi, the Tibetan Kingdom of Shambala, the Desert Fathers, the early Gnostic Christian communities, the Iroquois Confederation, the Sufis of Islam — why weren't their sacred teachings sustained and spread to secure our future?" He sighs. "You're right, Leo. Why don't we learn? Why, indeed?"

Gramps' tone is deliberately even. He means to impress upon them the importance of this question, and its only answer.

"Conan's dream revealed the identity of the Rishi monk and listening boy. Inanna's Sight gave us history of the Giants. And Leo's flight on chariots of fire connected these revelations. Perhaps all your visions and insights contain clues. They are promises that point in same direction. The answer to your question, Leo, lies in unraveling the memory of your past lives … and finding truths to create a different future."

The Three sit again in their chairs at the table, eager and attentive to the old warrior's words, their backs straight and resolute.

"See your question as opportunity, not burden. Soon you'll understand your shared destinies and connections, past to present. The Remembering will awaken, and you will relearn The Oneness, the eternal potential when division can be healed, and war is made obsolete."

Gramps hears the obliqueness of his message, however. He worries that his time with them is short.

Trust, old man, that they're strong and smart enough. Trust that they chose to be here, as surely as they were chosen to return at this time — together.

Chapter 36
Divine Protector

"Now, what explains the rest of it?"

Gramps still stands in front of the fireplace. He crosses his arms and looks down at his moccasin-clad feet, contemplating the question.

"Warp Fields," he begins again, "were spoken of among teachers. When Nonny saw her first video game, on one of those original big screens, she said it reminded her of a 'warp field.' She said the game looked like a shimmering wave, separating and joining dimensions of space and time! What do you think of that?" He shakes his head.

"Conan, you're right to call the phenomenon a *force field*. Perhaps a dynamic shift of energies — like the upheaval that has wracked the planet — opened a multidimensional portal of maze-like structures? Which can shield and guard?" The old medicine man turns up his palms. "My generation saw such things in trance, in dreams and ceremonies, but never as manifested personal experience. And for you to see it all together? Unexplainable, except as a true *gift of the gods*."

The Three sit in the wonder of that statement for long minutes, until finally Leo ventures a question.

He shifts his legs out from under him, leaning back on his arms. "Gramps, here's a thought. Could *Meera* do that? Can she open an electromagnetic field, create a labyrinth? We didn't see her there on the mountain, but ..."

Gramps considers. Then moves his head in dissent. "No, not even Meera could throw down a force-field at will. The only explanation for the phenomenon of the shield, sent at exact second you needed saving, is that you are under protection of a Divine Guardian." The old medicine man's voice is almost a whisper at the suggestion. "Which means a greater energy formation than angels or spirit guides must have been given to you Three. Divine Immortals, also called in some traditions Divine Emanations, are believed to be direct manifestations of Great Spirit, Source ... and to have helped create the known Universe."

The long-serving Elder feels the weight of his task even more fully, in light of this possibility. "Meera may know." He nods solemnly to himself. "Let's put hold on this discussion until Meera can add what we know. Remember that whatever it is came as protection. Be grateful. But — don't attach to any certainty. Divine intervention or not, we walk a human path. Miracles or not, being human is the greatest test and burden."

He leans over and puts his hands onto Leo's shoulders, looking him squarely in the eye.

"Leo, you asked, *when* will humans learn? Here is at least part of answer: When we stop excuses. And collectively strive for a unified way of being and understanding greater than our selfish desires."

The boy returns Gramps' steady gaze and affirms what he's hearing with a determined inclination of his chin.

"Enough talk, now." The old man straightens and addresses all three kids. "You know now what killed the elk, you know as much as I about the rest. Much will be demanded of us in next few days. Time we rest."

The kids get up and stretch their legs while the old man retrieves his pipe from its sacred box. He unrolls the leather pouch, adds tobacco to the bowl, and lights it. Puffing to fire it up, Gramps then lifts the pipe over his head, arms held high as he intones his Lakota prayers. Inanna repeats the prayers she was raised on and settles the blessings into her mind and body. Leo and Conan bend their heads.

When the prayers are finished, Gramps slowly brings his arms down. He carries the pipe forward to touch its head to each heart of The Three.

It's just enough, he says to himself. The ritual is abbreviated, but enough.

Grateful, is the word that comes to Leo. He repeats it aloud. "Gratitude. I mean, in spite of the sad and scary truths shared tonight, I feel gratitude. For the Light, the fire, the memories. For Meera, Conan and Inanna … and for you, Gramps."

The other kids bob their heads in agreement.

"I guess … I already knew some of what we've learned tonight. Now I feel … understood. And it mostly makes sense in new ways."

Conan affirms his brother's statement. "Unexplainable, but I feel the same."

"Gramps," Leo says directly to the medicine man, "I know the power of evil."

Conan interrupts, "*We*, Bro. We were there together. We know evil. It's menacing and brainless-cruel."

Leo nods. "But, I've — we've —" he turns to his brother, "seen too much, lost too many, to be fooled. It was a shock how that black mass came out of nowhere and ate the elk. But after a while, we knew it was, like you said, another expression of evil." Inanna and Conan exchange a look of agreement. Leo adds, "What I'm grateful for, Gramps, is that in spite of mystery, we have at least some explanations. We're safer knowing there *is* a Darkness, an evil that can contaminate everything it touches."

Gesticulating, Conan adds, "Leo's right! Darkness is like … something that bubbles up from inside people. It's like this toxic *shit*. People and situations turn effing out-of-control — terrible and deadly in seconds. I mean, evil can be mysterious — but it's not a mystery!"

His brother reaches out to give Conan an arm-squeeze, then looks back to Gramps.

"I just know that once I see something for what it is, no matter how bad, I can handle it and feel safer. Even if the odds are against me, knowing what's real and what's not gives me a fighting chance."

Inanna, observing the brothers standing together, thinks about how different they are in the way they process their feelings. But, she realizes, in how they face reality and find truth in that examination, they are very alike.

I am not so cool-tempered as Leo, she thinks. *And maybe Conan isn't, either. But somehow, together, they share a better brain and understanding. They're not just brothers; they're friends. They've learned to share problems and solutions.*

Will I ever have that kind of companionship? she asks herself.

Chapter 37
Beginnings

"Good." Gramps regards the children with satisfaction. *So much said. Enough said.* "Good."

He picks up an abandoned bedroll, dropped an hour ago. He casually tosses it to Leo, as if nothing of consequence has occurred this evening. The boys release their breath. They are happy to follow Gramps' straightforward instructions.

"Stoke fire. Add logs. Keep pot-bellied stove hot through night."

Gramps insists that Inanna take his bed. He dismisses her concern for his own rest and hands her the pillow he'd saved for her.

"Damn! My old *Moana* pillowcase?"

The boys hoot. She gives them back some smack they'd not dare utter to her.

"Hey, jerk-offs! A decorated army vet, Lakota medicine man, is in the *house*! With his witchy granddaughter by his side! You cowboys *did* see the fire come right out of the fireplace to protect him? Think twice before you go all wise-ass, yo' *big hat, no cattle* wannabees." She dances around them, gesticulating.

The boys whine a weak protest but can't — or won't — match her drubbing.

Gramps guffaws, "That's my girl!"

Abruptly the old man holds up a finger, seeming to remember something he'd forgotten. He turns to a corner cupboard and removes a small black velvet bag. Holding it out to his granddaughter, he smiles and uses his favorite endearment. "Open it, *Chunkshi.*"

Somewhat awkwardly, shifting from her taunts to this sudden moment of gifting, the girl gulps and wipes her hands. She accepts the bag with questioning look. Then she unties the cords of the dark velvet pouch to reveal Nonny's favorite necklace constructed of tiers of talismans, medals and crystals.

"Nonny wanted you to have it. Wear it when you are ready to leave the mountain. It will help protect, inform, and guide you." The old medicine man's smile lights his pride in her.

Inanna's emotions are running high, in all directions. Gramps' approval and the blessing of her Nonny's necklace fill her with a kind of unfamiliar serenity. She hugs her grandfather, holds the necklace up to her cheek for a moment to honor the power and memory of her grandmother, then tucks the jewelry back into its pouch and stashes it in a cape pocket. After throwing the boys a last sardonic look, she settles into the plain wooden bed in the next room.

Dusty, earthy, herb-infused smells fill her nostrils. She sighs and whispers to herself, *Home. Family. Gratitude.* Her bouncy pulse slows.

Her mind relaxes. She allows herself the indulgence of feeling comfort …
and safety.

Gramps blows out the candles, leaving just one burning in the
bedroom. He props the door between rooms open, watching with
amusement as the boys arrange their bodies among the legs of chairs and
table, squirming to get comfortable.

"You two are tallest people ever to sleep under my roof."

Before the boys can emit a snicker, Gramps retreats to the
bedroom and tucks himself in on the floor next to Inanna's bed.

Within minutes, the old brave is asleep.

Snuggling her pillow, Inanna remembers how her grandparents
had shared this far-off cabin whenever they could break from the demands
of the desolate, often freezing, windy frontier of South Dakota. Inanna had
once asked her grandmother why she, an accomplished academic from a
notable Japanese-Korean family, had joined the demanding journey of the
medicine people of The Lakota.

"Belonging," Nonny had answered Inanna. "I belonged here."

This was the final destination of her own true path, she had told
Inanna. The one that had called to her, her whole life.

"I knew even before I arrived in the United States that this would
be *home.* I knew this would be the place where my knowledge and
interests and spiritual beliefs could meet. Before I came here, I studied
what I loved. Here, I live it. I practice what I preach. True, I miss the
people of my birthplace whose teachings live in my heart-mind, yet for
me, this life was and is the great adventure. It's a perfect place of
belonging."

To *belong,* Inanna thinks now. That's how she feels here in
Montana, or on the reservation of her birth. Or anywhere Native tradition
and family come together.

And, for the first time, a sliver of possibility opens inside her.
Might she belong, too, with Conan and Leo?

Immediately, her head warns her, *don't be a damned fool!* Any
fantasy idea of herself being included seems impossible. *But if we ARE
The Three? Does that mean we're friends, too? Fuck! That's a concept
that's too weird.*

She nestles more deeply into the lumpy, cozy mattress. Still, the
notion within her tugs for recognition: *belonging.*

She tumbles into a dreamless, child-like slumber.

Her dreamlessness gives way, after a time, to soothing imagery, a
gentle ripple crossing a blue-black pool of water. The water seems to have
no boundaries or limits of any kind. Without hesitation, Inanna the
dreamer leaps above, slips under, floats, paddles and strokes on warm,
silky, onyx-black water. *Happy.* The sleeping girl recognizes the rare
feeling. *Infinity.* She sighs, skimming across the endless, silent sea in her
reverie.

Bird-Girl emerges, drifting into Inanna's dream-view. The muse floats down an aquamarine stream that crosses the black water. Halfling's enormous eyes shine with a turquoise iridescence; her flowing red hair is dappled with gold. Tucked into her sides, her multi-colored wings ruffle in a sweet, forgiving wind that propels her basket towards Inanna. Bird-Girl whispers in her odd click and hum language, *Inanna. Stay with the boy in the red hat. Keep the other brother close. Call in the Light, and don't fear the Dark. Truth is in both. I am guiding, protecting. We will be together. Soon.*

Inanna breathes. *No fear.* A sense of belonging spars gently with her familiar solitude. The outcome seems undecided ... but untroubled, too. *Light, Dark. Alone, together.* She watches the lush black water engulf the turquoise river and surrenders into the lazy comfort of calm.

Until a shock of colors — golden beads, cobalt stars and ice-blue comets, vibrating liquid-silver moons — explodes in a dazzle against the velvety dark background.

Halfling, Inanna sighs. *Bird-Girl.* The mystical creature slides across the black water. Her unique language sings a melody from ancient time, before time, a time lost for eons. A symphony of bells, cymbals, and intricate chimes crescendos in the foreground, while a background of deep-throated kettledrums grounds and supports the higher-pitched, lighter frequencies. Together, they form a choir of alternating earth bellows and air sprites. The music courses through Inanna's heart and mind. Her spirit expands and hums along.

The song tells of the eternal unfolding and refolding of creation. Bird-Girl hums in every octave of the earth, every voice of the angels. She reveals to Inanna the dimensions that spiral and cycle within one another, expanding and contracting, creating spinning universes and exploding stars and dying suns and luminescent moons. In dazzling illumination, amidst a chorus sung in colors, she weaves the infinite symphony of the Universe. In a thousand voices that are all the voices of Halfling, she weaves the perfect web of Origins and Love in which all things are possible.

Remember, Inanna hears. *This is the story of First Creation.*

The mystery, sparkling with vibrant splashes of iridescence, reverberates around, above and below Inanna. She repeats in her dreamer's lucid voice, *Remember.* Alert and unafraid, she breathes into the mystery of the Bird-Girl's message:

Inanna, I am the voice that calls you to The Remembering.

I begin this at the dawn of all beginnings. This is the story of the Origins. This is the story of all future Becomings, soon to be revealed. It is for you, Inanna, so that you never doubt the great unfolding, the great realization of Source, Great Spirit, God. For you must have faith in the beneficence and continuation of the Universe.

You must know this story for a future to be possible.

Before the boundaries of memory, before limitations of past, present and future, before even the elements were yet named or known or bound together to create the cosmos, there was the presence of the Black Velvet.

In the space known as sky, ether, solar system, galaxy, Universe, before any sentient and insentient beings were named, divided, extolled or cast out, the exquisite, pulsing Black Velvet breathed itself.

The Black Velvet shivered and shimmered, a fathomless drapery rippling across a boundless stage, a mighty bed of rolling waves on a measureless, silent sea. The Black Velvet floated freely in the endless timelessness we came to call space.

Not yet manifested, the Black Velvet was integral, and satisfied. Whole within itself. Undifferentiated, it breathed the promise of what would be Life. The Black Velvet contained the possibility of all the worlds and universes. All manifestations destined to come that could be imagined in the minds of the creator gods who were to follow, throbbed within the potentiality of The Black Velvet.

Before the limited notions of humans, or the troubles they created, or the goodness they sought or the dreams they explored, there was the presence of the Black Velvet.

Before oceans, trees, suns and moons, before the definitions of animals or life forms, before the divisions of beliefs or nations, It thrived within itself.

Before sensations of joy and hopes of salvation, before the betrayals of loss and hatred, before the glories of love and devotion, before civilizations created armies, cultures, and religions, before human forgiveness, there were eons of the Black Velvet knowing Itself.

The Mystery of Its Consciousness was no mystery to the Black Velvet. Perfect awareness was contained within Itself, until within Its pure potentiality, the Black Velvet Itself chose Its course.

In the great gathering of Its own volition, in a singular composition, a miniscule, white hot Point became realized in the center of the Blackness. Over millennia uncounted, the Point lingered. Its intense white-hot beauty shone against the Black Velvet. It shimmered with astounding possibility.

The Point was the Black Velvet's first creation.

The Black Velvet gave Itself up to Its child. The Point pulled power from the Velvet in an enormous inhale, whose singular intention was its outbreath. The inhale, exhale of the Point was a binding, a contract, a vow of the enduring love of the Black Velvet for all creations that were to follow.

The Point breathed out the first particles. Those glimmers spun and whirled from the Point and celebrated their existence. Bound together, they danced themselves into a new being, the first small sea of what has become known as energy.

The Point's first children, now called the elements helium and hydrogen, burst forth and spread, and in time birthed their own elemental children. The becoming of the elements was realized as a constant, inviolable choice of relating: the endless quest that would be forever embedded in all interactions and relationships yet to follow.

Together, bound by devotion to Origins, by what we have come to call love, these primary elements matched and connected, breathed life into one another and gave birth to the creator gods who crafted what we experience now as the known Universe. All was manifested, dreamed, imagined and born out of the Black Velvet's choice to know Itself as pure potentiality.

The Velvet lived on through Its myriad elemental children. To them, and to all who followed after, it is known as Source. Divine. Great Spirit. God. Physics. Krishna. Allah. Chemistry. The potential of Its origins is unlimited and eternal. All wholeness and holiness pulses with Its blessing.

For a future to be possible, one must depend on the perfect Knowing of the Black Velvet. All past, present and future, across all boundaries of dimensions, known and unknown, must reflect Its choice to create a connected web of love and understanding.

Choose as the Black Velvet chose.

For a future to be possible, manifest the never-ending Oneness.

*

The silence that follows the transmission of this Halfling-inspired dream floats through and around, above and below Inanna.

Deep within, her heart speaks to her mind. Her spirit, *one* with the ancient traditions of family, tribe and legacy, sings its forever song to awaken her soul's promise.

Not yet conscious of all that the message implies, Inanna begins to *Remember*.

Chapter 38
Dark and Light

Conan groans, rolls over onto his back. He sighs, loudly and pointedly.

Leo's body cries for rest. But he knows this routine.

"Okay." Leo grumbles, "What's up?" If he ignores Conan's hard-shelled thought-nut, he invites a long night of one-more-word interruptions until his brother is satisfied.

Conan doesn't have to wonder if Leo will put up with his questions. He's confident of his brother's unqualified support. He sits up and squints to adjust his focus, looking past his sibling toward the flickering candlelight of the bedroom.

Pushing away his uneasiness at the wind banging and lashing the cabin's fragile exterior, Conan whispers, "Remember that time, a lotta years ago, when I asked Granny about how, if God created the Universe — which includes evil — then, can evil exist without God?"

Leo nods. He remembers well. "She said you'd asked a question about the very existence of ... well, *reality*, right? And she took us for hot chocolate at that little café in town, said we could miss school for an hour. So, that was cool! She said your question was such a big one, she'd call it an *existential* question. Granny wrote 'existential' on the back of my spiral notebook, I totally remember that — and she asked if we saw the small word inside the big one. We found *exist*. Granny said that was a 'good start.'"

Conan snaps his fingers, pointing in the direction of his brother's sleeping bag. "*Yeah!* And Granny's opinion was that not even evil can exist without the possibility of goodness. She said everything that ever was, started in the same Source." Conan tucks his arms back into the warmth. "Gramps just said that, too. Right?"

After a long silence, Conan adds, "I'm just thinking that maybe ... we're getting closer to knowing the answer to that question I asked Granny."

Startled, Leo realizes that Conan's been thinking about that long-ago question ever since. *For how long? Seven, eight, nine years?*

He considers again how, close as they are — in fact inseparable most of their lives — Conan still surprises him. Dad would say, *In the baseball game of life, Conan is the curve ball. He'll throw you a mind curve just when you were sure you were getting a slow, straight pitch down the middle.*

Conan continues his whispered musings. "You know what else, Bro? When we were climbing today, I remembered a poem Granny taught us before she left. That day she gave us ... last instructions." He can't keep a wobble out of his voice. "It ended:

For it is important that awake people be awake,
or a breaking line may discourage them back to sleep;
the signals we give — yes or no, or maybe —
should be clear: the darkness around us is deep.

Leo smiles in the darkened room, remembering how they had practiced saying that poem with their grandmother. In his memory he hears Granny's voice overlay his own quavering recitation in his much younger boy's voice.

"Yeah," he murmurs. "And I remember the first lines, too:

If you don't know the kind of person I am
and I don't know the kind of person you are
a pattern that others made may prevail in the world
and following the wrong god home we may miss our star.

Leo had always felt it to be a challenge, not a warning. "I believe there's a possibility in it. And a *choice.*"

"Yes," Conan replies, his voice gravelly as sleep overwhelms him. His body feels heavy, and he's cold. He hunkers into the folds of his sleeping bag. "Yes." The boy's yawn is so wide, his jaw aches. His eyelids feel infinitely heavy.

"I need ... to know ... true name. I hear that ... But, Leo ..."

Conan gives his head a shake, trying to clear his head for one last refrain.

"The Darkness around us ... is ... so ... deep."

PART III

Chapter 39
Ceremony

Towards the uncertain dawn, Conan dreams.
Five riders. Warriors. Braves. The last rider is their medicine man.

His own voice narrates the details.
They're riding along a narrow ledge. It's nearly dawn, and they've ridden all night. The sun will rise ahead of them over the distant, low horizon. They scan the ground for dust clouds tossed up by the hooves of the enemy's horses.

In his dream voice, he warns the braves, *don't stop.* He doesn't wonder whose side he's on. *Marauders came at dusk the night before, burned down the camp. While the warriors were away hunting. Killed their relatives. Innocents. The youngest already asleep.*

Conan rolls over in the sleeping bag. He speaks to himself as the lucid dreamer and the reporter at once. Asks himself, is he sure? *Yes,* he whispers. He flicks at an itch on his cheek and pulls the warm sleeping bag up to his chin. He slips back to the scene.

A sudden sting of impending violence and vengeance prickles Conan's skin. His mind wants a prologue. *Who are they? Where are they? Why...?*

He slips back into the past.
Marauders raided the camp when its protectors were gone. The enemy knew there'd be no one to fight back. Cowards. Conan feels anger churn his gut. He shifts his sleep position from one side to the other. *The invaders captured their leader's new bride. She's the daughter of the medicine man. And they took her mother too, the medicine man's wife.*

A slow action camera in his dreamer's mind scans the entire scene from an otherworldly vantage. *Yes,* he tells himself. *Their leader is a young chief. The last rider is the medicine man. I see them now.*

Conan's dream vision narrows to study the enigmatic faces.
All five braves wear crow bonnets. Not just feathered headdresses. The entire body of the crow is crafted into their bonnets. The dead crows seem to know he is there, on the outskirts of the dream about them. They watch him as they perch on the heads of their riders. Their orange-gold glassy eyes slide sideways, as if they can lock Conan's gaze through the ages and dimensions of space-time. Their yellow beaks are polished to a shine; the tips of their sharpened talons are barely visible under folded black wings.

Crow Bonnet Warriors.

Sleeping on the floor of the cabin, yet present with his dream, Conan feels a thrum of power awakening in him.

They are a secret band. Secret even among their own people. Because to wear the crow bonnet is a privilege. Even among their tribe's hunters and warrior-braves, few are skilled or strong enough to ride with the Crow Bonnet Warriors.

They had seen from afar the smoke swirling above their burned-out hunting camp. Not one of them had spoken. They did not stop to bury their dead. The five braves had blackened their faces crow-dark with soot.

Conan sinks his current consciousness into the hearts of these men. He knows this space, lucid and yet sleeping.

Their rage is shuttered and controlled. Their revenge is ice-hot. The five warriors ride until the Sun is almost up. When the dust ahead of them has settled, they slide off their ponies and jog alongside. They slip into a ravine where no shadow gives them away. The enemy, setting up their own night camp, is in sight.

Before each fire rescue, Conan's mind had raced, his belly had twisted, and he'd have to ask himself, *is this real, or not real?* The same restless anticipation, the same nervy edginess had rattled through him then, as it does now. Each time the same questions would pellet his mind: *Am I really going to do this? Are we? Again?*

But Leo or his Dad would yell for him, then. And they'd all be off to the next fire, or the next rescue from a sinkhole that had swallowed an entire neighborhood. Or they'd be rushing through stormy surf to save a boat overloaded with kids trying to find safety. And he had dreaded it, every time. Conan clutches his belly. Does he want to wake from this?

Perfect concentration. Taut, ropey tendons. Muscles in bas relief against carved ligaments. They crouch low beside the horse's necks, in stride with them. They are silent, unified in stealth and precision. He feels himself with the Crow Bonnet Warriors. He feels the violence that is preparing to explode.

The thick grey mist of early morning intrudes.

Stay lucid! Suddenly Granny's voice is in his head.

He commands himself to stay with the images. Wakefulness tempts him to the twenty-first century. He has to pee, and his shoulders are sore. It's as if he carries the weight of both worlds, now and then.

Had this dream before. No idea how, why, it comes ... but it always ends at this exact point. He's eager for the rest of the story. But the scene is starting to ebb.

Dammit, buck the fuck up!

He argues with himself and tries to reenter the picture. He balances there, between realities, between centuries, for minutes more.

Until, through a pause in the passion of the dream, a mesmerizing rhythm intrudes.

Conan is awake.

Chapter 40
Grandfather, Granddaughter

Thrrumm. Beat. *Thrrumm.*

Blended voices hum and sing a deep invocation, imbuing Conan's waking consciousness with a new frequency, one that is today. Present. Drawing him out of the past.

He sighs. *Not a dream.* He won't be able to reenter the lucid dreamscape. *Damn!* The tones of harmonic accordance pull him to the surface. *Lost the thread of the story.* The dream images fade. Conan flattens his back and emits a weary moan.

Damn! Awake!

His bones feel stiff and heavy, but his tight muscles demand he stretch himself and move.

The music fully claims his attention. *Singing.* He rolls onto his side, lifts up onto an elbow.

His brother, always first up, stands peering out the window near the cabin door. Leo has wrapped himself in his sleeping bag, clutching it under his arms.

Conan squints into the weak dawn light. "What the heck …?"

Leo turns and smiles. He tilts his head, indicating that Conan should join him at the window.

Conan heaves himself up with reluctance. Pulling his sleeping bag to his shoulders, he shuffles to the window to join his brother.

The boys look through the dusty pane to see Gramps and Inanna standing together on the weathered porch, absorbed in their morning prayers. Grandfather and granddaughter face the direction of what was, for countless millennia, the eastern sunrise — but now seems closer to northeast. The girl is wrapped in an exquisitely detailed star blanket and wears simple buffalo skin moccasins on her feet in place of her battered skater shoes. The boys, familiar with Native artifacts, note the vibrant, multi-pointed stars and hand-sewn luminaries on the blanket. The vivid gold and blue colors contrast with the cloudy grey dawn and tumbled, somber earth.

The old man and the young girl follow the traditions set for their people for centuries, apparently unfazed by the radical shift of the planet. Inanna holds Gramps' ceremonial Indian pipe over her head as the medicine man sings a prayer. Her rich alto descant joins the chant, casting a circle of sound around Gramps' deep intonations. The familiar flighty tension of the girl, her uncertainty, is completely gone, replaced by a sweetly elegant confidence.

The boys are transfixed. They are seeing Inanna in an entirely new aspect. Her back is to them, and her long neck rises from the star blanket in a straight sweep to her still and proud head. Eagle feathers are laced into her careless curls and tucked behind her small, shell-shaped ears. Her beauty is a promise that both boys perceive. They would be completely perturbed to admit it, however.

What they do recognize, in that sunrise moment, is that they are witnessing a rare glimpse into the past and present as one reality. Grandfather and granddaughter are carrying the traditions of an honored past into the unknown future. Conan and Leo are moved by the ceremony. They are unexpectedly infused with hope and faith in a life affirmed at the dawn of a broken world.

With a pause in the prayer, the boys open the rickety door and shuffle onto the porch, still holding their sleeping bags up under their arms. They lean against the cabin walls and listen silently as the singers begin a second round.

Inanna turns slowly and fluidly to acknowledge the listeners. Gramps steps in pace alongside her. Their graceful movements form a compass honoring first the four and then the eight directions. Inanna's high cheekbones shine above the cobalt blue and sharp yellow of the star-bursting blanket as the two celebrants continue their chant.

The girl extends blessings to each direction. To the earth below her feet, to the heavens above, to the ancestors and to those yet to come. Then she hands the pipe to her Gramps. She moves to pick up a conch shell that glows with burning sage. Inanna blows into the small fire. Smoke flames out from the shell in thin concentric rings. As casually as if she expected them to be there all along, Inanna waves the aromatic smoke over the boys. She conducts the air with a long eagle feather in her other hand so that the boys are covered head to toe in the fragrancy of the herb.

The brothers each free a hand from their covering, and, as they'd been taught to do since childhood, they pass their hands over their heads, whisking the smoke over themselves. They tip their foreheads in a small bow of thanks.

Inanna's eyes widen and deepen. To the boys, this morning, the girl appears ageless and wise, mature and confident. She reminds them of an antique drawing of an Indian princess. Older, fantastical books with stereotypical stories about Pocahontas and Sacajawea had always seemed to include drawings that, the boys knew, were mostly the uneducated fantasies of white settlers. But, now, it seems in different ways to both of them that there was a certain truth to the artist's impressions. Inanna looks like a vision out of another world, come to anoint them.

"She's ... like, someone else, right now." Conan whispers to Leo.

The older boy nods solemnly. He leans in to murmur, "And some*where* else, too. Like from another time."

Conan recognizes an uncommon quality in Inanna. He sees that it's not just the unique golden flecks that highlight her dark skin, or the matching gold sparks in her green-black eyes that distinguish her; he realizes that she's a human expression of myriad rituals and ancient voices that span the cultures of her woven genetic heritage.

In that moment, she is beautiful beyond compare.

The boy doesn't admit that to himself — he couldn't. Not yet. But still, he assimilates the recognition.

Inanna prays, "*Mitakuye Oyasin.*"

Drawn into the ageless ties of belonging, the brothers repeat the prayer they know well.

"*Mitakuye Oyasin.*" *We are all related.*

On this cold and sunless morning, memory's sights and sounds are kindled. The brothers feel a longing for days past. They can smell the cracking clay dirt of a distant summer's soil, and the floating scent of the night-blooming jasmine that grew along the pathways to their home. This morning ceremony evokes family traditions of years past, when ritual was accompanied by the croak of frogs dominating a spring night, or sea fog slipping into the California canyons on a fall afternoon.

Weighty breath, heavy with yearning, squeezes their lungs. Both boys feel it, and they both push it out in deliberate exhales.

Leo won't allow memories to overtake his present awareness. Or, he tries not to. When he does indulge memory, he's never sure if those reflections serve or hurt him. *We have to face the reality that everything, everyone from our past could be gone. We have to face that possibility, if we have any chance of going on.*

His chest aches to remember the devastation that had assaulted them in their last years in California, every day with no exception. There had been no time to wallow in sadness. *Wake up! Suit up! Get on that damn horse and show up!* Those words had been their daily mantra. The boys had never whined or wimped out. Dad's voice would shift in a nano-second from gruff demand to joyous whoop. His laugh was always contagious. *We're lucky to be here, boys! Cowboy up!*

After Dad was gone, they had moved on automatic pilot. They rode, hiked, swam, climbed from one group of city-refugees to another. They clear-cut trees and shrubs, set backfires, and dug trenches to stop the next conflagration. They stopped asking *why* or *what* or *how* or *when.* They did what was asking to be done, what had to be done.

Leo asks himself now, *did we ever admit fatigue or fear — or defeat?* He knows the answer. *Nah. Wouldn't have thought it would do us any good.*

He studies his brother's face, alight now with the music of Inanna's voice. The older boy is reminded of Conan's emotion just two nights ago, before they'd started their journey up the mountain. He'd asked whether indulging in a longing for their past would weaken them.

I was always pushing him hard. Too hard. The thought makes his chest feel heavy. Their Aunt Sophia had taught them, "*Name what you feel.* It's what's unexpressed that festers and causes sickness." She would sit patiently with them. When satisfied with their breathing, she'd ask them, "Do you know a word that describes what you feel? What's your body telling you?"

Leo sighs and feels into his body … and decides it's not the right time to answer that question. He can't risk emotional weakness. And he can't lock feeling away *or* allow it to roam free and unchecked by duty. *Not yet.* Not until he knows which choice makes him stronger. "Courage and vulnerability balance one another," Aunt Sophia had told them. "Say the words, own your feelings. Let nothing and no one else define you."

He slides his eyes over to Conan again. He decides their thoughts are likely the same.

Leo whispers to his brother, "Remember the Native ceremonies when the buffalo arrived? When the medicine men visited?"

Conan's smile is wistful. His eyes glisten.

The boys join the prayer song of gratitude to *Tunkashila,* the grandfather spirits. They are grateful for this morning, this moment, wherever they are, however the day unfolds. *Truly grateful,* Leo thinks. Grateful for Conan's presence by his side. Grateful that Gramps is here, blessing them. Grateful for Inanna, who led the dangerous mountain journey and brought them to this cabin safely. He closes his eyes briefly and wills away his lingering sense of longing.

Conan catches his brother's sigh. He repeats in Leo's ear, "*Love home, but don't attach to what was.*" He smiles ruefully, knowing their Granny's words are especially relevant to their mutual melancholy.

Leo mutters, "Thanks for the reminder." He's proud of his brother.

The prayer song shifts from lyrical recitation to Lakota benediction. It seems to Leo that Gramps identifies the three of them to the Lakota spirits; he says their names in English, each pronounced slowly, syllable by syllable. And then each name is also iterated in Lakota.

Gramps fills the pipe's bowl with new tobacco from his leather pouch. He strikes a match and puffs deeply. The old medicine man touches its stem to his heart, tilts his face to the sky and utters a few words in each direction. Then he turns the pipe in a semi-circle and hands it to Inanna. She follows the ritual. At the end of her prayer she turns and hands the pipe to Leo.

Leo receives it in both hands, respecting the traditions. He loosens his grip on the sleeping bag for a moment. As he takes the pipe, the cover slips a few inches, revealing the brand burnished above his heart. He doesn't notice.

Inanna, standing in front of him, cannot help but see the mark. Her eyes, chest-high with Leo, fall on the scrolls and symbols of the raised tattoo. She freezes in place. She quickly lowers her gaze and bows her head as the boy continues the pipe ritual.

Taking a puff, Leo prays for protection and guidance, and hoarsely echoes, "*Mitakuye Oyasin.*" He clears his throat, touches the pipe to his heart and passes it to his brother.

Conan reaches out for it respectfully. And sees the brand on Leo's chest.

His shock is evident.

All at once, Leo realizes his chest is bare. He blushes, hikes the blanket up to his shoulders, and shakes his head to Conan, signaling, *not now!*

Conan quickly nods, swallows, and bows his head. After a moment, he looks up, repeats the prayer — and adds aloud in a clear, confident voice, "Whatever spirits are watching, please help me, help all of us, to *Remember.*" He hands the pipe to Gramps again.

The medicine man smiles at Conan, then intones the same prayerful words, "*Help us to Remember,*" in the fluid simple elegance of Lakota.

The old man takes the smoking pipe from Conan and holds it out in front of him, palms flat. He carefully regards the young man destined to take a similar medicine path as the one he's lived. *Fate and destiny will come together in Conan in his own way and time,* he knows. He lifts the pipe in the traditional offering above his head, once again. And, in a voice resounding with his years of wisdom and mastery, he sings a Strong Heart prayer in his native language.

Chapter 41
Light, Blessing, Life As It Is

On the final syllable of Gramps' prayer, the kids collectively gasp.

As if rendering the heavens from east to west, a single slice of luminescent light splits the sky directly over their heads. The beam pierces the clouds and shines its brilliance directly towards them, casting its illumination further as it descends — seemingly reaching out to them.

"*What the ...?*" Leo's mouth falls open at the stunning approach.

Conan steps back, his neck and head craned to the horizon - and then he looks to Inanna, as if she might have an explanation.

Inanna is as startled as the boys, and as full of wonder, but she has a better understanding of mysteries and enigmata to ground her. She slides her black eyes sideways to Conan and holds his questioning look with the same satisfied cat smile that she had observed on Conan himself only a day earlier.

They are all stupefied — yet none of them is fearful. The spectacle is too beautiful to induce anything other than wonder. The magnificent radiant shaft illumines the dark day like an astronomical searchlight.

Leo is openmouthed. "It's pointing straight at us. Coming our way." Still, he feels sure the light is not predatory, not threatening. He doesn't know how he knows that, but he's certain of it. He keeps his eyes riveted on the laser as its descent slows.

"Where's it *from?*" Conan exhales.

Awe overwhelms analysis. They can see particles in the light, like sparkling electrons that dance and swirl and dazzle.

The three kids step back as the beam draws close. When it reaches them a breath later, the light appears to focus itself centrally above the bowl of the sacred pipe in Gramps' hand, before widening into a circular glow that draws the four of them together into its radiance.

The old medicine man drops his chin to his chest. Keeping his head low, yet with his eyes lifted to the light, his voice rises in a thunderingly plangent prayer. Intoning his gratitude for the wondrous display of guidance, the warrior's invocation is filled with a deep resonance of faith and veneration.

When the prayer is complete, Gramps lifts his smiling eyes to The Three.

"Miracles amid devastation. How can mystical portals and dire catastrophes come into being, at the same time?"

Inanna meets her grandfather's gaze. "*Abide and respect the mystery.*" To the boys, she says, "That's another of Nonny's prophecy teachings. *Abide the mystery.*"

In this moment, the beam of supernal light confirms their faith in the power of mystical guidance.

Conan's sigh is audible. *"Awe and wonder."*

In the past few years of the Earth's rapid revolt and rebellion, kids everywhere on the troubled globe had grown up very quickly. They had made brave stands, wrestled dangers, failed, won, learned, lost and eked love and acceptance from the remnants of what was left. Too many had suffered cruelties without the protection of their elders — protectors who were lost early in the crisis and chaos.

The laser-light, in this moment a perfect halo that visibly extends from stratospheres beyond their vision, brings these three kids new hope that a brighter future can still exist.

Gramps knows this Light. He knows it is there to inspire his counsel and teaching. And to bless the insights and learning of these children he calls The Three. *Do not despair for their futures*, he reminds himself. *Face the teachings to come this day with courage, old man. With grace and humility.*

Gramps dips his head to listen to his heart. When he looks up at Inanna, Leo and Conan, the iridescent light still circling him, he says, "Inanna's right. Nonny taught that there are always *miracles amid devastation.* My children, remember that the courage to accept life as it is, not as we want it to be, is the greatest courage of all."

The beam's burnished blessing lingers for another heartbeat, then collapses into a silvered pinpoint. It spins in front of the four of them before blinking back up into the clouds in one streak, its silent luminary path folded into the heavens.

The four stand looking at the filmy gray cloudbank on the horizon.

Inanna flashes for a brief moment on her dream of last night, the white-hot point exploding from the Black Velvet. *Awe and wonder.*

The sacred pipe pressed to his chest, Gramps turns to face the three kids. He fixes his penetrating gaze on Leo. "Acceptance of *life as it is* begins with acceptance of our true selves."

Leo blushes, aware again of the brand which, he now realizes, Gramps must have seen and registered. He self-consciously tugs his sleeping bag tightly against his chest.

Gramps smiles gently. "Lessons must begin this morning. But," he adds, starting to move towards the cabin door, "you need energy to face this day. So, first we eat."

A squawk erupts from Conan. "Wait! Gramps, that light! What *was* it? Did it come because of the prayers …? Was it like last night's light, just sort of in another form? … Will it come *back?*"

"Light," Gramps opens the door and shoos them back into the cabin, "is *always* inside and always outside you. Will it manifest again, in this form or another? Answers come with the Remembering."

Inside the cabin, the old man moves to put away the ceremonial pipe and sacraments. "You Three have learned at other times, in other lives, to work the vibrations of Light. Conan is perhaps the most skilled."

Conan twirls from where he was warming himself at the stove, with a boyishly eager and hopeful look on his face.

Still smiling, the old man growls to Conan, *"Remember!"*

Having folded away the star blanket and donned her cape again, Inanna sets the table with swift efficiency. She tests the sweet potatoes baking in the potbellied stove. She puts Nonny's bright blue pitcher decorated with yellow cornflowers in the middle of the table. She scrubs the mismatched cups and lines them up with the plates. Pleased with herself, domesticity never being until now of interest, she stands back to inspect her work.

The boys take turns in the bathroom. They dribble water on their hair and pat down the unruly, tight curls growing out from years of buzz cuts. Clean socks, mix-matched but warm and without holes, are provided by Gramps, along with a couple of roomy flannel shirts.

The old man surveys the boys' freshened appearance, hand to his chin. "Soon enough, your hair will be long enough to braid."

"No way!" Conan snorts. "*Dreads* are what we get, with all these damn curls!"

The boys laugh at themselves, somewhat sheepishly. Inanna giggles as they sit at the table and the old medicine man passes around the Spirit Plate.

After they have all lifted up a portion of their food and joined in a prayer of gratitude, Gramps continues dishing out more breakfast while muttering about the kids' growing bodies and lack of proper nutrition.

"But," he says, "I have sweet potatoes for you, and some nuts and seeds and honey sticks, and some terrible dried milk and powdered eggs. Don't be polite, *ha*! Eat as much as possible." He cheers their efforts to gnaw down the tough jerky. "That's probably the batch Inanna dried, before she got the knack."

"Ignoring you!" Inanna scowls at her grandfather, covering on her ears.

Gramps grins. "Might not be such good pickins' along the journey."

They eat thoughtfully, but Conan gobbles what he can, faster than he should, then stuffs a couple of honey sticks in his pocket for a later fix, catching Inanna's disapproving eye as he does so. With a good-natured shrug, he pushes his chair back to continue his exhortation.

"Why do we only have 'three days' to learn what you need to tell us? And why does there have to be a 'journey'? The magic is *here!"*

Leo leans over and lays a hand on Conan's forearm. He hears his brother's longing — and he's certain Inanna feels the same reluctance to leave her grandfather. Yet, he knows, they have to press forward from worry to understanding.

He says to Gramps, "There's more you haven't told us, Gramps. We feel it." Leo speaks with respectful maturity. "We sure learned a lot last night, and we can agree that there are 'no mistakes in the Universe.' We saw that fire burst around you like it … well, sort of *agreed.* Crazy as that sounds. And now, that laser of light, coming out of nowhere …"

Leo squeezes his brother's arm before leaning back in his chair. "We're older than our birthday years, Gramps. We can take whatever anyone else can, maybe more. Don't protect us from any of it. We need to know what's out there — and what we're being asked to do." He nods toward his brother next to him. "We learned, Conan n' me, there's always shit we don't know, maybe can't know until we're up close and confront it. But the more we know ahead of time, the better we're prepared." Leo hears Meera's voice in his head. *The Old King.* He looks at his feet, blushing.

Inanna listens with her head slightly bowed. Her eyes sting from old betrayals and new hurts. *No prophecy is going to take me away from here, unless I CHOOSE it. "Stay!" "Go!" It's the effing story of my stupid, pulled-apart life.*

She turns away from the boys and Gramps, and towards her fury. *I'm done with everyone else's demands!*

Immediately, Halfling appears on Inanna's inner screen. The muse's multi-colored wings are closed, as if in prayer – and then they unfurl. Halfling lifts her head to Inanna. Her dazzling prism eyes meet the young girl's in unwavering regard.

Inanna is confronted by the fear she knows is always lying in wait under her rage. *Halfling, if you tell me I must go, I will. But, it's SO hard to leave Gramps. And … I wonder if out there, away from him … if … the boys will leave me.*

In Bird-Girl's click-and-hum strange, mystical language, Inanna hears, *No fear. Fly on wings of Oneness.* Spontaneous warmth flows from the Halfling straight into Inanna's heart. The girl feels the compassion, the connection that she's only known with Nonny and Gramps. And it melts her resistance to what she intuits will be her destiny.

Halfling, she silently sighs, her denial slipping away. *Me, with the wrong name — no true name until now; and you, without a proper name. You and I are one in our heart-of-hearts.*

With a sudden rush of humility and calm, she repeats to herself Nonny's words of long ago. *A prophecy mission can't be denied. There are lives that don't belong to our small, selfish desires, Inanna. We are here, we take this incarnation, to serve a mission greater than ourselves.*

When Inanna lifts her head and opens her eyes, she finds Gramps staring directly at her. Inanna can't hide her thoughts from him. He values both her rebel spirit and her mystic promise.

"*Wowicala,*" he says to her under his breath, without hesitation, as if he's heard and seen and remembered with her. "*Wowicala,* Granddaughter. *Faith.*"

Conan, lost in his own thoughts, hears the Lakota word. It brings him back to the present. Like Leo, he wants the rest of the story, and he's eager for Gramps to continue. For the boy, prophecy is a wholly acceptable intrigue. He had grown up with his own family's teachings in the matter, after all. "The real power of the Universe, the Divine Spirit, binds all of life together. Don't fear it, Conan. Stay humble. And trust it." His Aunt Sophia had whispered to him with every bedtime kiss, "Trust that you are connected to mystery."

A chill of fear suddenly shudders through him. She had said "stay humble." She had told the boys to live for something greater than themselves, so they could better manage the selfishness of human ego. *But now I understand that I want this medicine power, these psychic skills, like Gramps and Sophia have. I want them SO much that my ego could pull me to the Dark edge.*

Prickles of hair stand up on the back of his neck.

The Remembering, Meera had told him, would reveal how Merlin had perpetually walked the razor's edge between Light and Dark, the dangerous — yet enlightened — edge where opposite energies meet.

He looks at his brother, who is clearly ready to pick up the thread of his questions to Gramps. The boys exchange a nod.

Leo's chest rises in a deep breath. "If we're who you say we are, Gramps, and this is our *journey*, whatever that means ... we have to face all the news, good *and* bad, as soon as possible. Trust us, Gramps. We trust you. What," he finishes, "do we need to know?"

Chapter 42
Teachings

Gramps hears Leo's voice-within-his-voice, the unsaid that speaks with the steadfastness of ancient echoes. The old medicine man gets up and moves to the hearth, assuming a prayer stance, releasing his powerful auric field to include The Three. In Lakota, he asks the spirits to recognize them by their true names.

"These are The Three who were promised. They stand before you as humble spiritual warriors."

Inanna translates for the boys, tells them that Gramps is praying for courage to teach them right and well. "And for our own courage, so we do not fear past, present or future."

Gramps' energy pulses with the eternal breath of the informed, intelligent, relational Universe. He reaches into the living vibrations of The Three as they are today, in this moment. He is quietly assured. *The Remembering is beginning.*

Aloud, he thanks the spirit world and, satisfied that the three kids can hear into the realms of the many dimensions, he returns to the present.

Inanna brings him a chair. The kids sit around him on the floor, as they had the night before, ready.

"Leo," says Gramps at length, "I too, like you Three, *chose and was chosen.* For us all, teacher and students, there are, as said last night, *no coincidences and no mistakes.*" The Three sit up straight, legs crossed, hands on knees. "Teachers assist destiny by the choices of what we pass on to our students. A true teacher can't fear the fates of his students. He or she teaches *not* for himself, or herself, but to inspire, awaken, and preserve deepest truths. In teachings that help create destinies of spiritual warriors, we learn there are students today who were yesterday's teachers. And there are those who are today's students who become teachers of tomorrow."

Gramps waits three heartbeats. His attention is on Leo as he unwaveringly holds the boy's eyes to his. "Under all circumstances, teacher and student hold themselves and one another to responsibilities of the teaching."

Gramps shifts his gaze to pull Inanna and Conan closer.

"You Three, and a few others you are yet to know, are the best of teachers and students of many generations. The ones who chose right-intention more times than not. Ones who acted upon those intentions, no matter the outcome. Even in face of your own suffering. And, you must not be the last."

When Gramps is sure they have taken in as much of that message as possible, each in his or her own way, he walks to the cupboard. Gingerly he opens a creaking drawer secreted inside the lopsided cubbies.

The medicine man brings out three leather pouches tied with leather strings.

He holds them up. "Beginning a journey into past lives welcomes *The Remembering.* Like many journeys, there is no single, exact starting point. And a search into past is never a linear path. Truth lies in what some traditions call the Akashian records, what others call songlines, or what Native peoples call vibration of the ancestors. These beginnings of a soul's journey are not easy to access. They are hidden in layers of mystery and in the fog of time. But last night through Inanna's Sight, Leo's memory of flying red horses and Conan's dream of the Rishi monk, you brought back teachings that are centuries old."

The kids don't shift under his penetrating gaze. No one questions him or expresses doubt. It is as if they absorb his words through their skin, breathing them into the center of their beings.

"You sensed yourselves that you had lived over many past lives." He looks one to the other. "Do you understand so far? This is what is known as Continuum, or the Golden Thread."

The three kids nod. Inspired by the morning ritual of prayer and singing, they are centered and held in the reassuring resonance of Gramps' empathy and generosity. They feel as well as hear the right-intention of Gramps' teachings as gift *and* a course of action.

"Last night," Gramps begins again, "we followed Meera's traditions. Today we will follow those of indigenous people of this continent. Your own Granny, boys, taught about ways to open what she called *the celestial gates.* It's an understanding that cuts through diverse traditions and what might be called physics of space and time. Last night, your link to one another opened a celestial gate."

He holds the small leather bags. "Today, memories come forward with aid of these medicine pouches. If the pouches are as powerful as I have been led to believe, they will hold memories for you from your own ancient lives, and celestial gates will open for you."

Conan glances at Leo with a quick smile, then transfers his eyes back to Gramps. "Granny said the gate opens where it opens. We can't dictate its course of discovery. But if a person knows how to question the past, *great secrets of the Universe can be revealed,* she said."

Gramps threads the leather strings of the bags through his fingers. He takes silent measure of each of the kids and their individual energetic fields.

"Clinging to the past can be a dangerous anchor. Overly attached to what once was, we may close our minds to the exact things that could help us find better ways. Yet the past also has power to be our greatest teacher, if we vow to understand its deeper lessons. The Council of Elders saw in meditations and ceremonies that you Three earned *abilities* from past lives. Not because of magic or blessings or personal accomplishments, but because you learned greater truths that will help you now, in this life, to be courageous."

He closes his eyes and tilts his head down, listening carefully, closely to the interior messages that inform him. Syllable by syllable, slowly, rhythmically, with respect, he translates what he hears. *"Your journey to this mountain awakens The Remembering, as an intact and whole, living landscape of experiences. And now it is your time to re-experience the lives of your greatest learning."*

He lifts his head and opens his eyes. The old man focuses on each of them, singularly and at length, before finishing his message.

"Granddaughter, you know that in this life you brought with you gifts from past lives. It was evident to Nonny and later to Council that you could see and hear and remember things that you had not learned in *this* life." He winks at the boys. "When visitors came, as they often did, to ask toddler Inanna how she saw or remembered what she did, she would say, *I was borned this way.*"

Gramps smiles at Inanna as proud grandfather and fellow mystic, both. Inanna blushes but doesn't deny either his words or the intent behind them.

She does catch, out of the corner of her eye, Conan's suspicious squint. She understands that particular scrutiny. It's the same not-easily-convinced look she'd have, if their roles were reversed. She hardens her face and returns his sly glance with her own cold, slant-eyed stare.

Conan blushes and looks away. She smiles to herself. *Gotcha.*

Leo nods in rhythm with Gramps's phrases. "Our Aunt Sophia also warned about attachment and ego. She said that a Seer needs confidence and humility in equal parts."

Conan corroborates, relieved to be distracted from Inanna's dark eyes. *"Respect and protect gifts, or lose them,* she'd say."

"Nonny," Gramps goes on, his arm around Inanna's shoulder, "your Granny, boys, and Elders of many paths and traditions, all studied ancient teachings in long and demanding meditations. They predicted there would come a day of reckoning, a day that would call forward ancient souls. They said Inanna was part of this, and that two brothers would join her — and survive the Three Days of Darkness. It was said, *They must remember lessons of the past to save the Earth, themselves and others."*

"Three days." Conan's shoulders slump for a moment, then straighten again. "Well, *that* part's true. We survived, and we did find each other." An unexpected wave of responsibility washes over his sensitive heart. "Beyond any lucky chance or good reason, we're here. I guess, like the elders said, as prophesied." He looks at the others. "Was it chance, or a miracle?"

No answer is ventured by Leo or Inanna.

Gramps waits for them to understand the terrible beauty of their survival. "Leo," he says gently, after a moment, "you were right when you said to me, 'we must be prepared.'"

The joined response of The Three is audible, as if they have been waiting for those exact words; they breathe in unison.

The old man teases, "Didn't you trust me to take care of you?"

The kids speak up at once in protest, though they know he's joking. Gramps holds his hand up to stop them. He laughs, "No worries. Events and challenges you have now, and will face again, would make anyone eager to be prepared."

He tells them they must accept that the timing of each teaching is known to him and to their guides on the other side. "But the *plan* has to be accelerated by circumstances we didn't foresee. So now we must give our fullest attention to bringing your pasts forward. So that you may understand and reimagine them. And learn."

For reasons he can't explain, what Gramps is saying reminds Leo of an accepted truth he heard often repeated in his family. "*What you bring forward has the power to save you,*" he quotes aloud. "*And what you refuse to bring forward...*" He hesitates. The ending of the precept suddenly seems heavy with meaning and challenge.

Inanna looks directly at him and finishes, "*has the power to destroy you.*"

Leo returns her linear gaze and matches her steadiness. He adds, "And the power to destroy *us* and the *future.*"

"*Aho!*" Gramps is pleased that they understand the intention of his lesson. He allows a short space of energetic flow to connect thoughts and memory. "Today," he begins again, "surrounded by deep teachings of natural world, we search your pasts through Native American lives. These were lives that were inhabited not so very long ago — not as long ago as the Rishi, though they are important to understand together."

The old warrior draws their attention back to the leather pouches in his hand. "These are medicine bags. You have worn similar ones over your childhoods. These are passed down for generations, saved by many relatives who believed the day would come for you to claim them."

He doesn't wait for further questions. The old man gestures to the door. "We start outdoors. We need space for what must make itself known."

He pulls jackets and vests from tucked-in places. "Yup, bought and saved for you." Gramps directs them to grab several of the large, multi-colored Indian blankets from the floor and from shelves. "Inanna, bring the conch shell. And sage and sweet grass."

He's out the creaky door before them, nimble and quick, completely belying his age. They climb up a sharply steep slope until a flat meadow opens with a view of the teeming, clamorous strip of river snaking above and behind the terrain. The cold air leaves a frost on nearby rocks that line the clearing.

Gramps places the colorful blankets close together, overlapping the edges to form a circle. He carefully sets the three leather pouches on a bright red blanket in the center.

The pouches are similar, two or three inches by four or five, and hung from long rawhide strings. Each bag is beaded on one side. The patterns and faded colors vary; the fabric, scuffed and worn but carefully preserved, is deer or elk skin, hand-prepared in the old and careful ways of the tribe.

Gramps instructs The Three to sit cross-legged on the blanket. "Pick up each pouch, rub fabric across your fingers and palm. Study beading. Close your eyes and take deep breaths. Smell the rawhide, and let pouches speak secrets to you."

Chapter 43
Initiation: Reluctant Warrior

Wilderness trained, The Three intuitively use their every sense, taking in every detail.

They find the pouches to be smooth from age, yet still sturdy. The precise seaming holding the bags together isn't common thread, but something stronger. One of the pouches is best maintained, another more colorful; all are beaded with petrified seeds. Their leather lanyards are the same length and equally faded, yet two are greasier from dried sweat than the third.

Leo inhales. "Smells old, but not moth-bally. More earthy. Sage, maybe, and sweet grass. Tobacco's inside, for sure. And maybe dried musk."

The kids reach out to touch each bag lightly, tentatively at first.

A ripple of intense emotional pull stings Leo's eyes. Conan's throat clutches, and his stomach drops. Inanna doesn't hide the sensations that trickle across her face, as she lets go in a rapid-heartbeat response.

Gramps allows himself a smile. "You're feeling each bag's energy."

The three kids glance at each other quickly, almost giddily, eager to discover which bag most calls to them.

The old medicine man tells them, "Your lives crossed and influenced one another's in past, so all the pouches stir emotion for you at some level and bring up images. Your personal medicine bag is different. It will call to you, separately."

Standing in front of them, hands clasped behind his back, Gramps looks at each with import, emphasizing his words. "Do not influence another's choice. Imperative that the right pouch find you."

With a wave of his hand, Gramps indicates that it's time for the first part of the choosing. He instructs Conan and Inanna to sit farther back at the edge of the wide blanketed circle. He himself sits cross-legged next to the pouches. He takes the rawhide bags in his hands again, holds them to his heart and lays them back down in a new order. He lights some sage, then blows on it so that the herb gently smokes. He intones a prayer to help center thoughts and intentions.

The old warrior says quietly to Leo, positioned in front of the pouches, "Gonna hand you each one separately. Only one belongs to *you*. The Elders instructed, '*One for each True Name.*' You will know which is truly yours. Trust that it will reach for you."

A thrill courses through Leo. He asks in a low voice, "Do all the bags have some … well, reminder of the past? From our past? Like, we … *owned* it?"

Gramps nods yes.

Another time, Leo might be skeptical, drill questions. But right now, everything is anomalous, changed, and extraordinary. He won't challenge this wise man who has earned his trust.

He picks up the first bag.

Immediately, a pressing need to possess it tugs his heart. A mystical space infused with gold and ruby-colored flames spins around him. Flute music trills and thumps. A thrum of two-beat drumming swells his heart with ambient safety and protection.

"It says *courage*," Leo leans into the space, reverent, "and also … this bag breathes, hums with the words *no fear*."

Gramps whispers, "Keep your voice private, just between us. Stay with message."

Leo, eyes wide, whispers back, directly into Gramps' ear. "I want this pouch to be mine. I want to own *no-fear* ... but …"

Leo rejects the instantaneous impulse. He places the bag back down on the blanket with swift deliberation.

Gramps hands him the second, more colorful pouch.

"*Healing*." Leo breathes in herbs and musk. "It's got … medicine in it. Maybe a doctor's pouch? It has guardian energy, too." And he can feel *flight* in the bag. "It feels sort of as if there could be … bird energy. And it's strong. Like a raptor, maybe. But it's light, too – like dove's feathers." Leo tilts his head, assessing. "It's got, I think, a powerful healer energy, but with wings."

Leo draws it near, examining the bag more closely. A strong, pungent aroma of herbs dominates his senses. He studies his heart's response; it is nostalgic, tender, gentle. He does not feel threatened by the immediate, impulsive demand that had pulled him with the first pouch.

As he strokes the colorful beading of the second bag, allowing its vitalizing essence to fill him, Leo's attention is suddenly grabbed sideways to the third pouch on the blanket.

And with an overpowering, screaming inner call, his entire consciousness is invaded by a fire of possession. An acute, integral and profound pull of longing dominates his reason. He moves impulsively to grab it.

Gramps swiftly lays his hand over Leo's, before the boy can lift the pouch. He gently withdraws the second bag from Leo's right hand, setting it down next to the first. The old man whispers in Leo's ear, "Do not influence the others who are yet to choose, son." He removes his hand from over the boy's grasp of the third pouch, allowing Leo to fully experience its energy.

"This one pulls you to itself? What do you feel?"

Leo is trembling. "It's like a powerful magnet inside the pouch is drawing itself to a magnet embedded in my hand!" The pull is acute, vital. Leo's heartbeat is racing. "It reaches for me! Like it *knows* me!"

A drumming pulse of blood beats in his temples. Tremors shock his entire arm. Leo switches hands, and the sensations intensify, as if he's been picked up and thrown across an electrified fence.

He gasps. "I can't ... let *go*."

A visual memory hums in the finest margin between this moment and a past just out of reach. Pictures pop without warning before Leo's closed eyes, like wild blots of bright paint thrown at an empty canvas. His mind grasps after understanding, but the images are still indistinguishable; they are wild, yet uncontrollably compelling.

His body clutches, releases. He is propelled forward, back. Leo sucks in air as a phantasmal wind stings his face. *I know this feeling.* He recognizes the thrill of break-neck speed, the unmitigated joy of a heady ride, racing bent over the neck of a galloping horse. He smells dirt and sweat mixed with the acrid scent of human adrenalin and horseflesh. The quarry he chases is still unknown; his entire focus is *pursuit.* Leo's muscles tighten and strengthen. He tries to stay in control, tries to analyze the experience instead of giving into it. *It feels like I'm racing to catch a runaway steer, or dodge out-of-control wildfires ... But this ride is much tougher, faster.* He begs his mind for disciplined analysis. *When was this? Where? Is this memory of myself? Or someone I knew?*

His whole being yearns to jump headlong into the commotion and emotion. *But how does a simple, antique pouch contain so much power? How does this feel so alive, so real?*

He steadies his breath. He forces his eyes open.

The boy gapes at the bag he is holding. "It feels like I've seen this pouch before. *How?*"

He hears a whisper from Gramps, who sits cross-legged in front of him. "Stay with it, boy."

In a sudden, violent rush, Leo falls headlong into a speeding cross-current of whirlwind, a well of turbulent, unfamiliar energy, as if he's tumbling head over feet into the center of a tornado. Images explode around him. Furious blows crash into him. He thrashes left-right to grab anything stable.

Instead he's thrust into the furor and chaos of battle.

Leo leaps to his feet and screams, "Watch *out! Take cover!*" His heart beats past the restrictions of his rib cage. But he can't hold back from the forces pulling at him. Vaporous energy forms, grey outlines, appear and disappear, unidentified. He shouts commands in two languages from past-to-present-to-past again in one flow of translation. "Full charge, *battle!*" He hears his voice pierce the atmosphere. Adrenalin pounds. His chest swells. *Where the hell am I? Here, there, where?*

As if to answer Leo's question, a three-dimensional landscape fills his inner screen. The scarred land and clouded atmosphere are replaced by fertile grassland and azure sky. A wide, lazy prairie river, benign and gracious, cuts through cottonwood trees. Tranquil clouds drift on a stormless horizon.

A copper-skinned young man, short and lithe, appears for a half-heartbeat in front of Leo. *Who?* Leo tries to grasp the image, aware but unaware.

Trembling, he gives himself up into the body of this other, so real and familiar, tightly-muscled stranger. *Arms, back, chest ... not me, but mine? Now? Then? When? What the HELL?* The power of the talisman-pouch projects Leo into another dimension of space-time, but on a parallel path to *here, now.*

Impossible!

He tries to claw his way out of the man's body — but falls to his knees.

He is in the center of battle. From the spectral ground, he thrashes at unknown enemies. He's hit by penetrating blasts of undefined force. He hears the screech of an eagle whistle. Men scream and demand in every direction. Horses roar. He sees their mouths foaming spit, their nostrils flaring.

Leo's consciousness, past and present together, charges forward into the cacophony of war. *My people. My battle.* Spirit bodies, alive and immediate, push and fall and pin sweaty flesh, human and animal, against him. He doesn't resist. He fights on. Metallic bile fills his mouth. He is flooded with *hatred* for the enemy. Leo consciously rejects those words, even as he realizes the acrid taste in his mouth isn't hate – it's worse. *It's the taste of fresh blood.* He spits out the horror of it, twice, to rid himself of disgust. *Is it my blood?!*

The strain of his over-filled veins thumps his forehead. Afraid he'll slip into a distant time and not find his way back, he demands himself to *stay here, now! Goddammit! Today, here! Not WAR! Not blood!* Leo wrestles down panic. But peace and war, equally compelling, both seductive, vie for attention. *Is this my past?* If he drops out of the battle, he fears he'll relinquish insight into his history and karma. But this *violence? It cannot be right!*

Fighting with his own rage, Leo slashes at the air — and feels his fingers curl around the hewn wood of a lance. The ghostly weapon is so real to him that his fingers reflexively tighten in a death grip.

He recognizes a man's voice in a foreign language. *It's my own!* He hears the brave whose body he shares shout orders. Screams congeal into an earsplitting war cry.

He throws the lance.

His thrust is answered by spurts of blood that hit him, sting his eyes and splash into his open mouth.

"Blood ... *not my blood!*"

Fully embodied in the warrior brave, Leo is locked in a life and death battle on the high plains, three centuries ago. *Slash!* He wields a hatchet left, right. Spins his ghostly mount around and gallops head-first into the center of the enemy charge. Bodies hit the ground. He drops his hatchet and pulls up another lance. Climbs up to stand on the horse's back. Without a whisper of fear, he throws the weapon. *Sure kill!*

He leaps to the ground and pulls off three perfect shots with his bow from the arrows slung across his shoulder. His war pony gallops up next to him and he jumps onto its back. Holding himself astride the horse with the strength of his tensors, he notches another arrow. He rides at ridiculous speed, with no concern for danger. Fellow braves fight all around him, their howls of victory drowning out thought.

Leo, oblivious to the present moment, is in the center of a mercilessly violent vortex. The brutal onslaught shakes every cell of his body; the press and power of bloodthirsty rage shatters his innate need for balance and calm.

Conan is watching his brother wrestle and attack the empty air. His heart clutches in horror. "He's out of *control! Stop him*, Gramps!" His steady, dependable, always-centered older brother is unknown to him in that moment, and Conan is terrified.

Gramps growls a decisive command. "Stand down."

Conan screams. "It's like he's in a fight for his life! *Why*, Gramps? What's going on? What does he *see?*"

Conan lunges for his brother across the circle. Gramps throws his arm up and out, hitting Conan's chest like a battering ram. The boy falls to one knee.

Gramps' eyes do not waver from Leo.

Conan sits, trembling, wary, looking from the old man to his brother, breathing hard.

Drawn into the fury of hand-to-hand battle, Leo inwardly recoils from the horror of the bloody scene in front of him. His nerves split and splay, as if stretched and unthreaded from their braided core. *Harmony* is what his soul had always sought, he felt. Yet, here and now, slip-sliding between past and present, the duality of his own character shocks him. He revolts at the tension of opposites. *Me? CAN'T be me! Never war, NEVER! Revenge never brings peace!*

He uses all his strength to throw the pouch in his hand to the blanketed ground.

As quickly and unexpectedly as it had appeared, the vast prairie and endless blue sky recede into a horizontal slant. Like an antique Chinese fan, the vista folds itself into a flat line of dark and doleful grey.

The current day comes back into Leo's view. His brother and Inanna, their faces strained and nervous, watch him anxiously. Gramps sits cross-legged next to where he had first laid the pouches. He remains perfectly calm.

The war scene blurs on the corners of Leo's vision. He sweats through his warm clothes; his breathing is staggeringly labored. He puts his hands to his head, shaking it roughly.

"That man, his *battle* ... how could he — could *I* — be that *violent?* And *why?*" Even as he rejects the ferocity of what he saw, he senses that the story holds deeper truth. "It's why we're here," he mumbles aloud.

And right then, he determines that he must know the truths of the past.

He turns to face his brother and Inanna.

"I have to try to understand this. Granny always told us," he pants, "*all your wisdom comes to nothing, unless understanding comes first.*"

Gramps lays a quiet hand on the boy's shoulder. At the medicine man's touch, Leo trembles with an overwhelming release of tension.

Very quietly, turning so the others cannot hear his words, he tells Gramps, "I'm just ... so confused. The other bags, the first two I held, felt like they were filled with harmony and ... fearlessness and ... healing. Those vibes just seem more like me, Gramps, than the bloody warrior energy of the bag that called to me above the ... sensations, the energy of the first two!" Under his breath, the boy asks, "Am I losing my mind?"

The old brave half-smiles and answers, "Or finding it?"

Exhausted from what he thought would be a simple process, Leo nods.

"No worries, son. It will soon make sense."

Gramps drapes a woven blanket around the boy's shoulders before motioning for Leo to sit at the edge of the circle with the other two. Leo shivers in spite of its warmth. His face is ashen.

Conan punches his brother's shoulder, laughing in relief. "Hey, you *scared* me!"

Leo blinks, shakes his head again. "No worries, I'm here."

The other two kids share a nervous crack-up.

Seating himself again at the center of the circle, Gramps places the pouches in a new order in front of him before turning to Inanna and Conan. "When it's your turn, hold each bag. Take your time. Study each carefully. Notice differences."

He can see that the two who have not yet felt the power of the choosing are intensely curious about which pouch had spoken so profoundly to Leo. The old medicine man won't allow them to ask the question or discern an answer.

"Don't rush. Let the messages come *to* and *through* you. Allow each pouch to reveal itself."

Chapter 44
Initiation: Eagle Dancer

"Inanna, daughter, are you ready?"

Nonny had exposed her granddaughter to a wealth of practical, spiritual and mystical traditions of the East. Inanna had learned nearly all of Nonny's secrets of the healer trade. But she has never before seen these pouches. She'd only heard about them, and always in the hushed tones of mysteries and secrets.

As she gets up, she quotes her Nonny, proud to show off her learning in front of Gramps and the boys. *"The Choosing ritual helps untie the knots of karma and uncovers secret legacies and histories."*

Nonny had taught that it takes equal amounts of faith and courage to free the voices of the past. "It's fundamental to remember that we are influenced by what once was, but at the same time we are not determined by it," she'd taught, inculcating in her granddaughter that "once choices are made, the past starts informing the present — and then the journey to the future begins."

Many were frightened by Nonny's ability to excavate mystical diversity. They were especially wary about what their pasts could reveal to others who might judge them, their families and societies. Nonny was fearless. "And so are you, Granddaughter," she'd assured Inanna.

"Ready?" Gramps asks now, as she takes her seat in front of the pouches.

Inanna grins. "Ya' know I was *born* ready, Gramps!"

She drops her head and closes her eyes to center her rebel energy. Gramps lights the sage again and passes it over the three pouches to clear the energy of Leo's experience.

Inanna moves her right hand slowly over the space above the medicine bags. Energy flows from them into her open palm, then up her arm in tickling electric bristles. She opens her eyes, extending both of her hands an inch above each pouch.

She tilts her chin up and glances at Gramps from under her thick eyelashes.

He whispers, "Found it?"

She smiles.

Like Leo before her, a magnetic force pulls Inanna towards one particular pouch. Unlike him, she knows and trusts the process.

She places her palm down on the one that draws her. But doesn't pick it up.

"Legacy," she whispers so only Gramps can hear. "Nonny taught, *No fear, the object calls its rightful owner. Choose and chosen.*"

Gramps nods, grateful and proud that she remembers.

Beyond the boys' listening, Inanna continues, "The healer's power is gifted to me with this bag?" She doesn't expect her grandfather to answer. She breathes in the pouch's mixed elements. "I feel a woman's vibration, a mother, sister, daughter … a … *family* vibration."

She considers what she's learned. Each healer uses different and specific elements, knowledge and traditions.

"It's too old a pouch to be the one Nonny created for her own work. Right? She knew I didn't want the responsibility of the healer's path, but … could it be hers, that she left to me? Or is it … from another healer's lineage?"

Suddenly flushed with awakening vibrations, she rocks forward. Inanna leans in close to Gramps and asks in a low voice, "What's that energy?" She shudders from the force, rocks back. "Whoa, it's healing, but not sweet. It's more like, in my *face*."

Closing her eyes, Inanna regains a rhythmic pattern of breath. But in the next instant, she gasps as an unseen force slaps her full in the back. Her shoulder blades tremble, twitch, contract and lift, then … *expand* outward. Her vertebrae align, her spinal column lengthens, and she feels a powerful urge to soar.

Wings!

She's pulled straight up onto her feet into an erect stance by the weight and spread of spirit wings. Her trapezius muscles draw down, her rhomboids draw back. Her torso flexes to balance the ethereal burden. Her ribs widen and her lungs fill with a sweet flush of air — and the grace of flight.

"*Aho!* No way! Yes! ... *Wings!*"

A soft tickle of feathers touches her cheeks while sharp talons grow from her toes and an inhuman power forms within her.

"Shapeshift!" She exhales her last fears. "*Take wing!*" She voices the words of her teachers, as she did in ceremony. "*Fly with eagle.*"

Medicine people, righteous keepers of mysticism and secrets and the oldest traditions, do just that. They fly with hawk or owl. They roam night's jungles with jaguar, hunt with wolf pack or coyote. They shapeshift. They bring messages of the Universe on wings of the messenger hawk, they hunt with the mountain lion, they climb with bear and elk. Animal spirit and human body become one. Spirits are transmigrated, transmuted, transformed and wholly integrated.

Shapeshifter!

Inanna had studied rituals, she had learned the dances and songs that breathe life into animal, fish, bird, and insect energy. But she had never truly transformed into spirit form — until today.

Her people had recognized Inanna's gift of bringing animal spirits into ceremony. The spirits had whispered: *I call you to take my form. Learn my medicine.* An old Auntie had blessed her in Sweat Lodge, assuring her, "It's a rare gift to be called." Inanna had loved the idea and had learned from each spirit, yet she longed for the mystical connection to one specific totem.

"Eagle!" The majestic bird's cry awakens her nascent gifts. As she speaks its name and hears its call, the eagle vibration enters her being. With the medicine bag clutched to her heart, standing tall on her grandfather's blanket in the dust-grey morning, a fresh wind lifts her spirit wings. Present life to past, human form to bird, all merge into one reality.

"Eagle Dancer!"

Her senses, her mind, her memories carry her back centuries to when the Eagle Dancer she had been wore her ceremonial buckskin dress. Inanna sees now each eagle feather and seed-bead the Eagle Dancer carries, preserved and saved for generations in honor of this dance, worn by the healer called to express it in this lifetime.

Slipping into trance, Inanna dances to the ancient rhythms, her head keeping time to the music only she hears. Flutes, rattles, bird-calls trill over river rushes and sing through her. She dips her knees, sways and swirls. She hears feathers rustle, and her feet dance, stepping toe to heel in a two-beat perfect rhythm. Her talons stretch and claw the stirred air, her wings beat in time to the awakening elements. The thrilling call of the eagle cries out in her mind's ear, and Inanna's human spirit soars on the wings of the bird, flying into an endless sky, penetrating the clouds. She stretches her range to rise over mountain peaks and dive over meadowlands as an ancestor chorus lifts up the prayers of her people.

When Inanna was four years old, her birth mother had kidnapped her from her grandparents. She had prayed to Eagle Spirit to be rescued. Months went by. Lonely and scared, the four-year old had stopped believing that the spirits cared.

Then one day, Bird-Girl appeared in her dreams, and became her solace and escape.

Now, inside the deep sanctuary of the dance, Halfling appears in the sky above her. Bird-Girl's prism eyes bore into Inanna. Her message is manifest: *You are healer, teacher, guide and spiritual warrior. You are medicine woman-eagle dancer sent to initiate the future that must Become.* Halfling sings songs of the Black Velvet and of the First Day burst of creation. The elements crackle and sparkle across Inanna's inner screen. *We are One, forever together.*

With a dip of her rainbow wings, Bird-Girl disappears into the curve of the horizon. And in the next moment, Inanna is back in human form, floating to solid earth.

Her desire to remain in the eagle form is so consuming that she almost collapses. Tears course down her face, stinging her cheeks, and she lets them fall, unashamed. She prays to the spirits, *let me fly to whatever highest heaven receives eagle prayers, into the arms of Great Spirit.*

Inanna bows her head and falls to her knees.

Gramps is watching her closely, his emotions shrouded. He understands the temptation to free oneself forever from the density of the human body. He has taken the spirit of birds and animals, himself; he has shapeshifted hundreds of times. And he knows her challenges, her story, who and what she ran from to make today possible.

He knows, too, what she must learn in order to temper her hatred for those injustices and turn to the blessings that now call her to Remember.

Gramps folds his arms around his beloved granddaughter as he sees an eagle fly above them, circling the grey sky. He gently takes the pouch from her clasped hands.

"Flight of Eagle Spirit is not in clouds, it is *within* you, Inanna. You know that." He taps an index finger above her heart. "Eagle is within you, as it was in the distant past," he tells her in a near whisper. "Meera said, *Remember.*"

Inanna wouldn't allow anyone else to guide her surrender. "*Within me.*" She lifts her chin. "I do remember."

"Eagle never left you. Nonny and I never left you, even when you were far away. The Remembering is your time. Don't fly from life's sadness. Use it to heal yourself. One day soon you will be able to use your grief to heal others."

Inanna squares her shoulders and connects directly to the depth of Gramps' eyes. The eagle image shimmers above her.

"Gramps, I claim Eagle as my medicine, and ask to be its servant." The worlds of past and present grow still, listening. Inanna repeats the words with grace and dignity, more loudly now so that the boys can witness her oath.

"I claim the medicine I was gifted."

Gramps sees in Inanna the Eagle Dancer, healer, spiritual warrior and medicine woman she was hundreds of years ago. *This is the promise of her life's destiny.* The emotion on his crinkled brown cheeks is evident.

Inanna's beautiful aura shines out over the barren land and warms the day.

Leo stands and bows his head to Inanna, acknowledging the significance of the moment. Conan, too, rises. He is moved beyond his own understanding by what he has witnessed.

Gramps says to the three of them, "You must guard the gifts that return to you now. In all traditions, healers must learn to *own* the medicine and not be owned *by* it. Otherwise, its power will turn against you." His look lingers on Conan for a brief moment. "Medicine *never owns you* unless you betray its spirit or use it for personal gain. Only then can we be taken over by the shadow side of its power."

Still seated in the middle of the circle, the old man gathers the three bags and keeps them cupped in his palms as he speaks.

"Each of you was a person very much *of* the time in which you lived. You made human mistakes. But none of you traded away your gifts, your medicine or integrity. Not one of you deceived others, or clung to personal gain, or chose power over service."

Gramps places the three pouches on the blanket again, in a new order.

"Stay in the space of inquiry until *all* the stories are known to you, *all* the lessons are gathered."

Leo repeats Gramps' words to himself. He thinks, if battle leadership was his past fate, the core piece of his true self — well, then, he wants to know and understand the complete story.

Conan is absorbed by every nuance of what is unfolding. He scrutinizes the others through his cat-slant eyes. Not a flicker of eyelash or hint of a tear is lost on him. Meera's words drift back. He hears them in her special lilt: *Merlin, master of alchemical magic, king-whisperer.*

Conan studies the pouches from a cautious distance as Gramps prepares the sage. Then the old medicine man turns to him and nods.

"Your turn."

Chapter 45
Initiation: Medicine Man

Conan is nervous.

He had watched his brother, the "I got you! No worries!" *sane* leader, thrash, scream, and struggle with invisible enemies. *Fighting his own memories? I don't get it.*

And Inanna? She had seemed to soar above them, whatever she had experienced was so real to her. *I felt the energy of her flight! But ...was it safe? It was like she wouldn't care if she actually flew away ...*

He doesn't share these observations aloud.

Conan trusts Gramps' words. He believes that the three of them do have gifts from an undetermined past. And Conan fervently hopes that his gifts will awaken here and now. But he's also wary. *Leo got so damned scared! I've never seen him that scared. ... Inanna doesn't need to be afraid. She knows she's safe here, and she's more familiar with all this mystical stuff ... But me? I am NOT cool with this.*

Breathing in the rawhide scent of the pouches, Conan almost itches to feel every nub of each bag's fabric. He examines the differences and similarities of the faded leather and beading as he leans over the pouches in front of him on the blanket.

When he's ready to touch the bags, he begins methodically. He shakes each bag lightly, quickly. He bends his ear over them to catch a hint of the secrets within.

But a fierce, sharp, sting vibrates inside his brain, accelerating the connections from mind to senses to spirit.

Conan flinches. He warns himself, *go slow, be careful!* Yet he can't. Won't. Just the opposite. His tall body convulses in full-height shivers. Surrendering to the rush of energy, his entire consciousness kicks into the highest gear. He feels thrown into space, thrust into a tsunami-surge of accelerated force; he finds himself panting from the explosion to his senses, overwhelmed with the electric charge.

He closes his eyes and begs for guidance and courage.

On the assurance of his commitment, the three pouches recognize a master. They speak their elemental language to him.

He picks up the first pouch.

The boy whispers to the old medicine man, "I hear it telling me it *heals wounds of heart, body, mind.* It's a healer's medicine bag. But also, it says *flight, air, wind ...* and *bone* and *feather.* I hear, *Take flight!*"

Gramps cautions him to stay calm. Conan has been holding his breath. He exhales, now, and tries to settle his nerves.

He put down the first bag carefully. His right hand moves to the second pouch and Conan picks it up with care, inhaling its fundamental elements.

Damn! Fierce! Scary-brave. Maybe a soldier's bag? He drops the bag instinctively, lifting his head to Gramps. I hear *"Belonged to a warrior.* There are elements of something like iron, earth-power, firepower. There's flint in it — to start fire, or make arrowhead?"

Gramps tilts his head but does not otherwise respond.

"Are words just *popping up* around me?" Conan presses him. "Or are they in my head, like, sort of, speaking memories?"

Gramps raises an eyebrow, clearly impressed. But he gestures for Conan to return his attention to the pouches.

"I think," the boy begins again, "that the first one has to be Inanna's. Because it made Inanna feel like she could fly. And it said to me, *Take flight.*"

He holds his hand above the first pouch and risks a glance over at Inanna, sitting next to Leo a few yards away. All at once, his perception winds around hers and Conan feels within his own person the girl's exhilarating flight. His senses heightened, his heart fluttering with a new poignancy, he sighs for the beauty and magic of it.

The knowledge that each bag can speak to him, that its essence can be felt by him, reassures Conan of his latent, untested abilities. He sputters, "I've been sleep-walking through life! But now ... I feel woke! *Alive!* I am NOT going back asleep," he hoots. His bowed lips curl into what Aunt Sophia had called his *baby-wise, old-guy-secret smile.* His inscrutable, mysterious, ticked-up grin of kept secrets.

Conan composes himself. He whispers to Gramps, "I love this."

Years ago, Granny had given both boys a pair of medicine pouches filled with elements. She'd told them the bags were meant *"for adventure to find you."* She didn't say, *for protection and guidance*, but they had felt that, too. Conan, as a little boy, had trusted that the crow feathers attached to the lanyard of the pouch would bring magic, and the carved shark stone would keep him safe in the ocean, while the bear tooth and scrap of rough horse fur would bring him strength.

Both he and Leo had lost their pouches over the course of that summer. They'd tried to recreate them. They'd pieced together fragments of fabric, stuck special rocks in pockets, and strung feathers around their necks. But the magic of the originals, like so many precious talismans of childhood, was lost.

Conan had never forgotten the "sixth sense" Granny's pouch had given him. As he grew older, his love for science and art had grown, as had his passion for tech, tools and inventions. He'd sought to combine them all in a sort of mystic desire for what he called "provable magic."

Today on Gramps' mountain, hundreds of miles from home, the three pouches in front of Conan bring back sensations of those early childhood years. He is fleetingly flooded with a sense of sweet nostalgia.

However, the power of these three medicine bags pulls him back to the present moment and the need to *choose.*

He looks up at Gramps, who is patiently waiting for the boy to lift the third bag. Conan feels himself wrestling between a desire for careful, cautious inquiry and an overwhelming need to believe in possibilities beyond the hard cruelty of these Days of Darkness. His rambling thoughts erupt in a torrent of new questions.

"It's … like meeting relatives I used to know and still recognize, you know?" Conan keeps his voice very low, for Gramps' ears only. "But — were the bags lost by whoever we were, ages ago, and then were — I don't know, somehow found and saved, until we … came back for them? Or — can objects time travel? I mean, I love Sci Fi, but … *really?*"

Gramps still gives no response.

"I just … Gramps, are these really *ours?*"

The old man looks back at him impassively.

Conan shakes his head, looking down now at the three pouches placed side-by-side on the red blanket. "This one and that one," he points to the first two bags, "I *know* them. But they don't actually feel like mine."

A flicker of excitement sends a shiver through the boy. Taking a long inhale, he picks up the third pouch.

Instantly, a heat as intense as a direct flame scorches his hand. "*Aarrgh!*" He pitches the bag from hand-to-hand, sure it must be singeing his skin.

Yet within seconds, it cools to a comforting warmth.

Conan cradles the bag in his right hand and lifts it to his face. The pouch speaks to him. *Wings of many birds.*

"That was *loud!*" Conan looks around him. "Did you hear it?" he asks Gramps quietly. "Who is that speaking?"

Fearless.

He spins, stares behind him. Turns back, looking left and right.

Gramps murmurs, "Stay with the energy, my boy."

Holding the pouch in the palm of his hand, Conan feels that its warmth emits a healing element. *I feel some of the same energy as in the first pouch. I think this one has equal healing power. But it's more direct, fierce. It has different elements of protection.* Conan closes his eyes and intuits the pouch's contents. "Small smooth stone. Fur and … bone." He recoils a half beat. "*Human* and animal. And dried blood."

The truth of it tightens his chest and spins his mind. He squeezes his fist around the bag and grasps it to his heart. He feels an urgent need to place it around his neck. If he does it quickly enough, he tells himself, he'll possess everything it contains. *Secrets. Elements of flight — but earthy warrior, too. Grounded power.* He hears ceremony songs, drums and rattles. He smells burning sage.

Conan opens his eyes and rasps, "*No fear!* I hear those words. Am I right?"

Gramps says quietly, "The forces of medicine want your attention. Listen."

No fear!

"This pouch *calls* me, Gramps," he whispers. "It wants to tell me a story. So — it chooses me, right?"

Gramps lifts his chin and focuses a stern eye on the boy.

Conan wills himself to place the pouch back down on the blanket. He feels feverishly the need for its ownership.

It's mine!

He doesn't want the old man — or the others — to see the excitement crowding his mind. The boy gets up reluctantly and moves to a nearby boulder. He sits and hoods his eyes. He suppresses the heavy sigh gathered in his chest.

Conan lives in a complicated cosmos of imagination and wonder folded into a love of the material world. He is passionate about mysteries; he can endlessly examine, assess, and analyze the most profound riddles of the universe. But now, in the midst of these secrets yearning to reveal themselves, he questions his own sanity with the same ferocity that tempted him to claim the pouch despite Gramps' directive.

After a few minutes of inner turmoil, Conan masters his nerves and walks back to Gramps. He sits in front of the pouches again and whispers to the old teacher, "I was afraid if I let go of it, I wouldn't find my way back into The Remembering, or forward into a medicine man future."

Gramps nods once, his eyes gently holding the boy's. "Proud of you, son," he whispers.

Conan drops his head to his chest, grateful.

The medicine man gathers the three pouches again while he lights the sage to clear the energies. He motions for Conan to join Leo and Inanna, who are sitting watchfully on the far end of the blankets. Once more he places the bags in a new order. Then he lifts his head, straightens his back, and fills his lungs with the cleared air.

"The pouches have called you. Now it is time for you to claim them," he announces to The Three.

Then Gramps focuses on Leo.

"Which bag is yours? Do not hesitate. The others will know if you decide wrongly. Leo, it is time for you to *choose*."

Chapter 46
Choice and Consequence

As Leo steels himself to reapproach the center of the circle, Inanna and Conan instinctively give him the space to make his choice. Conan moves back to the boulder, and Inanna takes a seat on a log across the blanketed circle.

Leo can't deny his anxiety. In spite of whatever gifts and ability might be carried in the pouch, he worries it's also filled with negative energies of war and rage. He tries to assure his restless mind. *Calm down. It's only leather and old beads. It's just herbs inside.* But a doubt nags him. *Does it contain something dark? More sinister?*

He asks himself whether a "choosing game" even fits with the choiceless-ness of their circumstances. *What does "choice" mean anymore, when so much of what was real to us is gone?*

Leo walks to Gramps and stands in front of the three pouches, his hands at his sides. He looks from the old medicine man to the bags, and then centers his gaze on the pouch that calls to him, even now.

And can we be defined by a certain place and time, as warrior-healer or medicine man, in only one life — or over many lives?

His internal struggle causes the veins on the sides of his head to overheat and pound.

Gramps, in a low and even tone, reassures him, "The bag carries mystery and magic, and also the real, elemental potions of your legacy. It's not *all* of who you were, are, or will be. But it is fundamental key to unravelling entire thread of karma. It has chosen you already, Leo. *Courage.*"

Inanna and Conan, from their more distant vantage, still have a clear view of Leo as he deliberates. They glance at each other quickly, both finding it hard to remain completely patient and placid.

At last, Leo bends to one knee and reaches for the pouch with the faded yellow and red beaded lightning bolt.

Conan expels a noisy breath. Gramps chuckles, shaking his head. "That's a sigh of *relief* from your brother."

Leo is only half listening. He clasps his fingers around the pouch, but before he lifts it, he looks up to search the old man's face for any hint of caution.

The medicine man tilts his head, still smiling, and gives Leo a brief nod.

Courage is carried to the boy on tremors of surging electricity. His own muscular strength upwells in him as he raises the bag high. His spirit and mind merge and focus. His entire being awakens.

"Share what you see and feel, son," Gramps encourages him softly.

Water-colored images, peaceful and serene, float in front of Leo's vision. He sees none of the violence and battle of his previous memory. "I'm joined to something. I see … men training horses, notching arrows. They're stoking a fire and shaping wood." No image is perfectly distinct.

He rises from the blanket. He is drawn into the placid scene. He sees Indian ponies galloping across open plains. The horses' unshod hooves barely touch the earth. He sees *himself* — but his skin is chestnut brown, his eyes are darker. He turns his hands over to examine them and finds that his legs and body are bare save for a breechcloth.

Leo barks a laugh at himself, from who he is now to who he was then, present to past.

"I'm part of what feels like … a team. I mean, there are jobs to do. But it's fun, it's not urgent. Men are organizing and planning a hunt. I hear, *in protection of others.* But there's no rage and no …" Leo almost sickens at the word, "killing."

The boy inhales the aromatic scents of the pouch. He feels calm, now. And he is suffused with a deep confidence. He closes his eyes, steeped in the spirit of the brave and his fulsome power.

He's quiet for several minutes. When he opens his eyes, the watercolor scenes disappear.

Gramps breaks the silence, gently observing, "You see your role of warrior leader, Leo?"

The boy hesitates. His humility is so innate, it's hard for him to claim a leadership title. "It's as if …" He stammers, then finds his voice. "I have come into my true name."

The defining qualities of Leo's spirit, in this life and in the past life he has glimpsed, breathe themselves into awareness.

He slips the pouch's lanyard around his neck.

"Know the truth of it, Leo," the old man murmurs. "You are a spiritual warrior. Protector, leader, and also one of a team." Gramps nods solemnly. "You understand now."

Leo nods back. The heaviness of responsibility is light on his neck. The pouch feels so totally *his* that to deny it wouldn't now occur to him.

Gramps lays a supportive hand on Leo's shoulder.

"Understanding, knowledge of each past life journey will unfold. You are who you are Leo, who you've been all along. Many roles and abilities are contained in definition of your true name, true self. *For a future to be possible*, that truth must be owned."

Leo inhales Gramps' words. He creates space inside his heart-mind for their expression.

Choices and consequences, his Dad had taught. *Show up, suit up, let God do the rest.*

Chapter 47
Legacy

Inanna waits her turn with contained excitement.

This process of "choosing" is not Native American, she knows. She had learned that it's the way Tibetan Buddhists select reincarnated lamas to lead the next generation. Relics and ordinary objects of a deceased Lama's life are laid before a child as young as three or four years old, while ordinary playthings are also spread before him, scattered on the table or floor, meant to distract. The child is instructed to choose.

Most kids are happy to find a new toy or grab a candy. Few choose the exact belongings and sacred objects of a deceased teacher. For those few, the die of their future is cast.

Nonny had instigated this *choosing* game. She'd set out treasures, bird's nests and pebbles, feather headdresses and sage bundles, dried wasps' nests or beaded rattles among common and distracting toys. "Nature uses everything," Nonny would say, "there is purpose in all. Look carefully, hold each gift. Decide which is yours."

Her grandmother never acknowledged right or wrong choices. Inanna felt successful each time. Each choice was perfect in the moment.

Nonny had told free-flowing stories about the responsibilities of choosing. She'd instruct, "Wear the eagle headdress, and your message to the people is responsibility as spiritual leader and healer. Or choose the messenger hawk's bundle and serve the tribe as Seer and messenger. Shells in your medicine bag will tell the tribe that you are a daughter of the sea, able to swim in dark waters without fear." And she had always finished the same way. "Choose wisely, daughter. Choose wisely."

Today, kneeling in front of the pouches laid in front of her, Inanna asks herself, *can I step into Eagle Dancer? That's big medicine, and I ...* She can't finish the sentence, even in her own head. She searches her heart for reassurance and sees Halfling fly next to the same wide, complacent dream-world river that Inanna flew over only minutes ago, in eagle form.

Can I choose, be chosen? Me, the crazy runaway? After all the crap I've done, pretty much rejecting most everyone in my world? She speaks in her heart to Bird-Girl. *Am I brave and strong enough to get over my own bullshit and accept these gifts?*

Bird-Girl is silent, but Gramps answers.

"Minutes ago, you danced and flew. You whistled and sang with Eagle. Now you question yourself. Can you turn away from what you know is your call, because of fear?"

"Gramps," Inanna's voice is low and choked. "I know what this means. Gifts must be shared. Responsibility to tribe comes first." She looks up at her grandfather. "In order to be Eagle Dancer, I have to —

grow up. And be strong enough to serve." Inanna swallows hard. "Am I really going to be able to do this?"

Halfling fades in her mind's eye to the far distance, and a second image appears. Her grandmother comes into view, standing directly behind her husband's shoulder.

Nonny!

With an aura as beautifully serene as the beloved woman herself, her warm intelligence radiating with quiet poise, Nonny waits for her granddaughter to choose. She hovers there behind Gramps for several moments before lifting her hands, her arms outstretched to Inanna. With cupped palms, she offers her granddaughter a ghostly ceremonial pipe.

Gramps is watching her face. "Choose, daughter."

Afraid a wrong word will cause her grandmother's image to fade, Inanna rises to her feet. She rolls her shoulders up to her ears and back down again. Straightening her back and holding her head high, she refuses a nostalgic sigh.

"Nonny is … here," she whispers, fighting tears.

The old man inclines his head, then raises his chin ever so slightly in the direction of his wife's spectral presence. "And she always will be with you, Inanna. Whether she's seen or unseen. Never forget that." He keeps his voice steady and low, yet his love and longing for his wife are evident in the untended moisture in his eyes.

Standing at the boulders, the boys can't see Nonny the way Inanna and Gramps can — but they can sense that the presence of a beloved spirit has entered the circle. The brothers are moved by what they see in their faces — and they are flooded with a yearning for their own close family, now lost.

With her grandmother's image looking on and holding out the sacred pipe, and with her grandfather seated in front of her, Inanna finally chooses the pouch she knows is hers.

"My pouch. My legacy."

Inanna grasps the timeworn medicine bag to her heart. Its moss-green rawhide is decorated with a single crimson feather. "The bag chooses me as I choose it."

The vision of Nonny softly nods, then dissolves in the sunless grey of the sky.

In the silence, Gramps holds Inanna's eyes. "Choice is legacy and future too. You know why Nonny held out the pipe to you?"

The girl glances down at the feather symbol on the pouch, faded and worn but alive with meaning. She fights for the right words. If she admits that she knows the meaning of the pipe, she'll be agreeing to another step of responsibility even beyond that of becoming Eagle Dancer.

But — can she disappoint Gramps or Nonny by saying *No?*

At length, she looks up. "Yes. This is the pouch of the last Pipe Carrier of the Crow Bonnet Warriors."

Though the old man's creased face is impassive, his eyes smile with love and approval.

"My daughter, I believe that you are the reincarnation of that woman healer. A woman warrior, spoken of for generations. There were eagle dancers — and pipe carriers — in every tribe. But the one who owned this pouch is the center of an ancient story."

With utter respect and reverence, Inanna studies the medicine bag carried by the legendary woman she had heard stories of since she was old enough to listen. She prays for strength, clarity, and humility.

The girl meets her grandfather's eyes. "I — I think now that I have seen this pouch before."

The sound of the river can be heard from the valley below them. The boys hold the stillness of Inanna's remembrance.

"It was when … I was a part of Nonny's choosing game. I was about four-years-old, I think. Nonny laid out rattles and toys and my favorite cookies … but I grabbed this pouch." She looks at the bag in her hand. "I — I totally understood that it was *mine*. But — I had completely forgotten about that, until now. I guess … holding this bag brought back that memory, too."

Leo and Conan slide off the boulder where they have been sitting and move closer, concentrating on Inanna's story.

"Nonny hugged me, she cried real tears. I never saw her cry before or after. She said, 'This is the Eagle Dancer pouch.' She said it had belonged to a woman who was both Pipe Carrier and Eagle Dancer."

Gramps gestures for the boys to join Inanna in the middle of the circle. "Yes, Nonny was truly overwhelmed that day of Choosing Ceremony. It was rare day when Nonny couldn't hide emotion, but that day was special to her."

Inanna, suddenly self-conscious about too much attention on herself, turns to Leo and Conan. "The Crow Bonnets were a sort of secret society. Even among the tribes, few knew about them. I guess you could say they were a crack team of killers — but only when attacked." She turns to Gramps. "And the woman who wore this pouch, she was the wife of a Crow Bonnet Warrior, and, yeah … she was both Eagle Dancer and Pipe Carrier." She looks at the boys again. "That's … a *big* deal."

She laughs nervously, and the boys follow suit. It feels good. The morning's events have given them all a great deal to process.

Inanna rattles on, a bit giddy now.

"The Lakota don't have teachings on past lives. That's Eastern, Buddhist, Hindu, Shinto, other traditions …" Her ruddy cheeks are flushed, her smile is full and wide and quietly joyous. "Nonny had her own ways of putting stories and traditions together, but somehow they always made sense."

Chapter 48
Crow Warrior

The day is darkening early again. Though it's impossible to gauge exact time, with no visible sun for reference, the kids feel as if it might be approaching midday. Their appetites are certainly growing ready for another meal.

They all take draughts from a canteen Gramps has packed, watching silently as the wind whips small dust devils up from the ground around them.

Gramps waits for minds to settle back to here and now. It is clear he means to press on until the choosing is complete. He motions for Inanna and Leo to give Conan the center space.

"My boy. I left your choosing for last, because your choice was clear. So come, son, and claim your medicine bag."

Conan sideways-smiles to Gramps, then drops to his knees on the blanket, eager to own what is his. Without hesitation, he reaches for the faded blue pouch with the whirlwind totem. Its medicine power returns instantly. He can feel an even stronger adrenalin rush fill him with the energy of its healing current. His head buzzes with voices, messages he can't quite distinguish — but they reverberate with a sense of sanctuary and strength. The bag's elements speak to him about a *revelation*, an assurance of something to come.

But revealing what ...?

The boy stands now, holding the blue pouch in both his hands. He looks up to meet Gramps' eyes — and hangs the frayed lanyard around his neck.

A jolt of energy rocks him from side to side. He throws his arms out in an effort to balance, but the force of the voltage knocks him off his feet. He slams forward and bangs his chin on the hard ground under the blanket, grinding his jaw and knocking out his breath.

As Leo and Inanna rush towards him, Conan spits blood and sour water. He draws his knees to his chest in a fetal tuck before being jerked straight up onto his knees like a marionette on invisible strings. Another lurch pulls him to his quaking feet before depositing him down again, this time onto his rear. The other two kids drop to either side of him as he sits trembling, his back rigid, limbs quivering, and moaning a terrible, wounded-animal cry.

But as Leo and Inanna reach out to help Conan, Gramps growls, "Back off!"

Leo yells, "He's having a seizure!"

Conan slams forward again, tugged by something unseen. He groans as he's pulled back up into a shaking, rigid standing position, legs stiffened straight, his eyes bulging and his heart thumping.

Leo jumps up and tries to grab Conan away from whatever force controls his erratic movements and obvious pain. Gramps stands as rapidly as the much-younger man — and holds his flat hand in front of Leo's face.

"Halt!"

Leo spins around to Gramps, questioning him with wild eyes.

Gramps stands firmly between the brothers.

Leo's eyes dart from Gramps to Conan and back again. Dust devils flail them with pebbles of sharp sand. Anxiety rising, Leo is about to turn back to his brother when he feels Inanna's tight grasp on his wrist. The boy stares down at the girl's clenched hand, then back up to meet Gramps' piercing gaze.

Reluctantly, he turns away from all three of them. He drops down to the ground and puts his hands to his head in an effort to control his overwhelming desire to intervene.

Conan shivers violently. He bursts into another cry of pain.

And then, as suddenly as the unknown forces had manifested, they release him. His body recalibrates its electrical systems and his senses slow. He heaves a cavernous breath … and begins to grow calm.

Eyes closed, he settles into a space between then and now. Behind slammed-shut eyes, Conan sees he's in the exact scene where his early morning dream broke off. He whispers to himself, not trying to tell a story, just trying to make sense of what he sees. "Five warrior-riders creep inside a gully, crouched next to ponies, and…" He grabs his pouch to his heart. He blurts aloud its message. *"Fearless."*

Gramps' ravaged Montana mountain disappears from Conan's inner and outer sight. In its place is the warrior's experience. *Not a dream. Two realities. Here and there together.*

The five warriors move silently towards unsuspecting enemies. Crow Bonnets are predatory; their focused strategy is precise and unemotional. Conan whispers, "That dream … it's *alive!*" His chest thumps with the brave's heartbeat. His eyes see, ears hear with the man's senses and instincts. His dual mind turns cold as ice. Space-time bends, boundaries evaporate, and multiple dimensions open like a fan of 3D cards with photomontage images.

The lens of the scene widens. *Dusk.* He slinks down the rocky gully of the past. His heart-mind stretches as if he speeds on the invisible air that accelerates under him, lifts him out, up and into the forgotten history.

Gramps, his voice as deep as ceremonial drums, commands Conan, "Tell us what you see." The old warrior has folded himself into a sitting position at Conan's feet. He seems to move as easily as a man decades younger than he. He reaches for a small flute tucked into his belt and commences piping an uncanny melody that echoes distant war drums. The frequency carries a blend of today and yesterday refrains in one harmonious rhythm.

Eyes closed, Conan focuses on the ghostly drama filling his inner screen. A song-like Native mantra rises within him. He wants to fly into past and mystery. Yet he's afraid he'll lose his place in the present world.

Inanna and Leo hear him whisper, "*No fear ... No fear.*"

Sweat pours from Conan, in spite of the day's chill. His chest expands to allow a maximum amount of oxygen to empower him.

Gramps, decisive and direct, commands, "Speak to us, Conan. Bring us with you. *Remember.*" He repeats the word twice. The flute never seems to leave his lips; the music is uninterrupted.

Conan's eyes flicker open and close, his words sputter in short gasps. "I am on ... my horse." In his trance state, he looks down at the horse's bare back and the warrior's plain, worn moccasins. He feels the weight of the crow bonnet with its preserved eyes and sharpened yellow talons. He feels the man's fingers grip the wood-handled tomahawk. He sees ...

Conan shouts, "This exact *pouch!*" The pouch he clutches to his heart today is the same as the one worn around the neck of the warrior. "I *see* it!" *Same elements. I smell them. And feel the same energy!*

Adrenalin surges through him. Mystical knowledge awakens him. His consciousness focuses into a sharp, detailed lens and narrows onto a clear image of the five forbidding Crow Warriors.

Leo, Inanna and Gramps see Conan as he is in present time — the skinny, tall fifteen-year-old with freckled fair skin and uneven dark curls. But for Conan, today's picture disappears. He's shorter and a couple of decades older; sable-bodied and well-muscled, he's a warrior-clan medicine man. Black braids skim his back. His war pony trots on his left side.

Conan releases all vestige of fear, and his emotion is replaced by an ageless, disciplined grace unknown to the boy he is today. Fires of controlled rage course through his Native limbs and create a circuit of deadly calm within him. His courage intensifies to meet the ferocity of the medicine man's concentration on the enemy ahead.

"Tell us what you see." Gramps's voice pierces the dimensions of long-ago centuries.

Conan reports the dream from last night as he relives it here, awake.

"I am the last of five riders. I am staring in front and behind me, at once." He guards his fellow warriors. They creep along on their horses, ahead of him. The first rider is the young leader, who narrows his eyes back to the medicine man. "I am the medicine man, the last rider."

Time crawls to a careful, detail-by-detail unfolding as Conan watches the slow-motion reel of pixelated action.

The young leader spots the dust of the enemy's trail. At his signal, the warriors dismount silently and walk alongside their horses. With finely-honed stealth, the medicine man opens his pouch and removes a pinch of blue-grey powder. He ritually blesses it, then throws it into the air above their heads. The powder thickens even as it disperses and grows into a fog of smoke that screens his four warriors. The braves continue their silent progression through the blue fog that obliterates the last of the day's sun. They had expected the cover. No one, nothing sees or hears them coming.

As the four other Crow Bonnets move quietly forward beside their horses, weapons ready, the medicine man sees the bird in the sky waiting for him. Pausing in his steps behind the other braves, he deconstructs the physical cells of his body and stretches his limbs to match the magnificent ebony crow wings of the bird above him in a breathtaking *unfolding*. He shapeshifts. The man's spirit releases into crow form, and the two spirits, man and bird, become one being.

Conan sees the shapeshifter even as he feels the transition, physically. His own body ripples with a violent tremor, then straightens. To Leo, it looks as if his brother shivers into a tighter, invisible skin.

Conan tells them what he sees. "The medicine man's spirit enters crow, and crow awakens to the man within him." The tall boy's chest expands; his arms fling out right and left, shoulders pinning back and forehead tilting to the sky.

The flute music surges and continues its own telling of Conan's story.

"I'm flying over the enemy camp." The enemy is unaware. They are setting up their temporary base for the night, undistracted by the blue fog. They are blind and deaf to the riders and flying crow that stalk them. "I see the two prisoners. One is the medicine man's wife, and the other is their daughter." Conan realizes the shape-shifter's daughter is also wife to their young leader; and his own wife is the tribe's Pipe Carrier.

The women are seated with knees drawn, hands and feet bound. They are alert, however. The mother scans the sky and sniffs the descending grey-blue fog. She nods carefully to her daughter, who responds with only the slightest quickening of breath. The women bow their heads.

Their enemy captors laugh at their weak prisoners, these women who think prayers will help them.

A hint of a smile plays on Conan's lips. "That's a mistake," he reports aloud, without emotion or emphasis. "Another one."

Leo and Inanna exchange a glance at Conan's words, not yet sure what they signify.

In the enemy camp, Conan sees the mother and daughter go utterly still, eyes cast down. The women breathe a united circle of vibration, sharing the same hum of prayer with the medicine man who is Crow. The shapeshifter circles once, casting blue vapors from the tips of his wingspan. His flight is smooth and deliberate as he spreads the fog curtain over his braves who are moving unseen towards the enemy. The fog grows thicker and wider, and on the Crow's second circle, the enemy warriors notice that a blue cloud hides the setting sun.

But it's too late for them.

The shapeshifter circles a third time, then drops into a screaming dive, shrieking with a piercing *caw-caw-scree* as his four companion riders explode out of the fog in a single attack force, their bloody war cries matching that of the Crow.

Conan, his voice strong and controlled, tells his listeners, "The Crow dives like an arrow, straight down from the sky. He's a giant raptor!" Wings tucked tight, he attacks with his fiery talons and weaponized beak. He is accurate — and deadly. His Crow Warriors are outnumbered by triple, but the enemy has no chance. The power of surprise, the Crow Bonnet Warriors' skill with tomahawk and lance, and the perfect timing of the shapeshifter's descent combine to slaughter the enemy forces.

"*Stealth and grace ...*" Conan reports in a hiss. "The enemy screams their death cries before they see their attackers coming. They drown in their own blood."

The Crow Bonnet Warriors, impossibly silent, take what was stolen from their camp. Death is their coup, revenge their reward. Slaughter is due to those who had burned their encampment, stolen their horses, and killed their innocents. "*Fools*," Conan hears - and repeats. He shakes his head, as if he judges the silly actions of naughty children. "They took the young leader's wife captive. *No mercy*."

The leader cuts the ties that bind the women. The medicine man's wife, the Pipe Carrier, swings up and onto the waiting horse as the shapeshifter releases the crow energy and reclaims his human form; the crow bonnet sits securely again on his head, feathers unruffled. He leaps onto the horse with his wife, and she puts her arms around his waist. Chill air embraces the five warriors and their two women. No words are spoken.

Dream stars appear in Conan's vision of the war party's night sky.

"The riders take the reins of their stolen ponies, and they round up the enemy's horses. The Crow Bonnet Warriors follow their leader at full gallop. No one looks back." The horses' hooves kick up dust in the evening sky as they run at full pace with their riders. Birch trees shine against moonlit hills, then sink, roots first, behind Conan's closed eyes into the earth as it was on that day, never tilled or broken by man. "They ride until their burned-out camp is in sight."

Conan's view widens to see the entire story. His voice chokes with emotion. Their dead are his dead. Loss and victory are all part of him, as the medicine man he was then, and the young man he is today, now and forever.

Minutes pass in a silence broken only by small currents of wind that come and go across the meadow. Conan's heart pounds, his hands sweat even on this chillingly cold day. He breathes in dry gulps and stretches to ease his cramped muscles.

A last, lost embrace from the small woman seated on the horse behind him propels him to spin around, expecting to see her. Even as he turns, he feels the arms of the medicine man's Pipe Carrier release from around his waist.

A lurch of volitional upheaval brings the boy back to the present time. Staggered, he looks around him. He takes in the present-day Montana mountain, the meadow, the chill grey day, and the three who watch him.

Breaking the expectant silence, Conan gasps, "*Oh*. Oh…" He puts a careful hand on his abdomen. "I feel … the warp field … closing up again … *inside* me!" He fights his emotion, bending in an effort to hold onto the diminishing sensation.

Leo stands near his brother, rapt — and full of respect for what he has witnessed. Inanna leaps to her feet in readiness to move in and support whatever comes next.

And Gramps plays the flute in a final cadence that sounds to The Three like the winged power of a metaphysical flock of birds taking flight in unison. The final notes drift on the wind that skims below the ending words of Conan's story.

Chapter 49
The Golden Thread

The old medicine man tucks his flute back into his belt and eases himself onto his feet. The Three stand before him in the center of the blanket circle, holding their chosen pouches.

Gramps encourages them all to drink. He removes two more water canteens from his rucksack. Conan thirstily obliges, then uses his sleeve to wipe water from his mouth and beads of sweat from his forehead. His flushed face is streaked with grime from the dusty cold wind. Leo is still reflective, and visibly moved. He turns slightly to look down at the river while he drinks from his canteen. Inanna starts to fold the blankets.

Complicated emotions from their experience with the Choosing Ceremony linger, for all three kids.

Conan is the first to speak his thoughts. "That was amazing! And I feel so ... so charged! And part of some shared thing, too ... a pattern, a continuum."

Inanna agrees. The word *trust* resonates, tucked in her heart-mind.

"It started this morning ... near dawn," Conan continues. He is physically exhausted, and his chin and jaw ache from the tumble he took, but he has an overwhelming need to share his dream from last night, now that the images are so aligned with his pouch's message. "I had this dream this morning, just before I woke up, that ... sort of insisted I pay attention. But I forgot about it, with everything else that was happening — until the Choosing. The dream was about the same Native warriors that I saw with the pouch's vision! And now I get it. My dream was telling me to Remember!"

Leo and Inanna nod their heads in understanding and recognition. They, too, have had dreams that seemed to be calling them to a consciousness that is only beginning to make some sort of sense. The day is darkening early, but the kids all feel a dawning awakening that contrasts with the sunless, cold atmosphere.

Conan now admits that he'd been afraid to speak about some of his questions and fears.

"I was, ya' know, desperate to know the kinds of things Gramps does." He thinks about that word for a moment. "*Desperate*. And I always wanted so much to understand what my grandmother and my aunt knew, for instance — all their spiritual and philosophical and mystical knowledge. And now ... I feel like it's coming together somehow."

He rubs his dry throat.

"I guess knowing about old, old past lives," he pauses, "helps us figure out ... what matters. I mean, no school could have taught us the things we've been learning these past few days."

Leo turns back, giving his brother a wry smile.

Conan guffaws and gives Leo a shoulder-punch. "Right? New energy is waking inside and around us. Maybe we feel, see, hear past lives because we're traveling through space-time! Or maybe we're traveling *within* a dimension. Who knows? But I do know that stuff that's been bubbling inside me for years is starting to ... *relate*. And I'm starting to understand what the Golden Thread really means."

Leo pats his brother's back. "Big thoughts, bro! I've been rambling questions inside my head too — but, damn, this is another level. *You're* at another level!"

Conan looks a little sheepish. He slides a quick look to Inanna, who is still folding blankets. He guesses that she can relate to what he is trying to say. He and Inanna share a distrust of people outside the immediate community they were each raised in. But now a new current connecting Crow and Eagle, medicine man to pipe carrier, is felt by both, he is sure.

Inanna, too, senses that she and the boy can hear one another without their individual prickliness and judgments, at least for the moment. Their sensibilities and sensitivities are so alike; they both crave and reject closeness — and they both need and fear intimacy. Through the relationship their pouches have revealed, they are momentarily at peace with shared experiences.

Conan's head burns from exhaustion. He gulps water. The mountain air is whipping up a brisker chill in more frequent gusts as the dim sunlight recedes. When a sudden roaring wind threatens to scatter all their gathered gear, Gramps yells over the howl, "Let's get inside!"

They grab canteens, rucksacks, and blankets, and jog to the cabin. Inside, it is hardly less cold than on the mountain. All four busy themselves with stoking the hearth fire, getting out provisions, stacking logs, and putting on water for tea.

Gramps pauses by the window to listen to the wind. He measures the whirl of its whine across the near-barren mountain slopes that were once rich with vegetation.

He turns away, stretches his thin angular body and moves as silently as a catamount to the hearth. From a cross-legged sitting position, he coaxes the weak fire. The rising flames compete with the wind snaking down the flue, but the old man is patient, and the fire's warmth begins to spread around the small room.

He pushes himself up to stand next to Conan, who is seated at the little table.

"Brave," he says with respect. He repeats the word in both English and Lakota. "Brave, to stay in the experience, son. Brave to share vision and yourself too."

Conan blushes, shyness creeping back. He's unused to being noticed, uncomfortable with compliments. "Gramps," he asks quietly, "were these mysteries *asking* to be found, like the pouches were? Is that why all three of us are Remembering and finding our pasts, at the same time, together? Does all this relate?"

"You are right," Gramps softly smiles and places a hand on the boy's shoulder. "The pouches are, after all, reminders. Yes, they carry powerful medicine. But it's you, your soul-level *true self*, that matters. Bag chooses its owner. Why? Because medicine, magic, traditions, and knowledge already exist within you and in one another."

Gramps looks to Leo and Inanna who are listening from across the table. "You call each other across ages in this way. You relate, element-to-element; memory-to-memory. Golden Thread weaves to Golden Thread. Teachings connect then and now, knowledge to tradition to discovery. Understood?"

The Three nod.

Conan adds, "I mean, *starting* to understand."

Gramps laughs. Then his tone changes, and he shifts so that all three kids can see his message is meant for each one of them.

"There is much we don't understand, not any of us. But starting now, you learn together." His tone implies a command. "It's *shared* destiny, relationship, that matters most. Shared. That's yet another mystery, but it is one that holds the Universe together."

Chapter 50
Memories

Leo has been silent since they returned to the cabin. Now he moves to where Conan is seated with Gramps standing beside him. He gives both of them a signature bear hug, and he includes Inanna in the scope of his gratitude by giving her a tender smile from across the room as she busies herself amidst the kitchen pots.

The others feel Leo's love and support. But his distant look and faded smile aren't lost on them, either. They watch as he crosses to the cabin door and goes out to the rickety porch.

He stares into the windswept, darkening sky, stretching his arms and shoulders, cracking his fingers and rotating his neck. He knows how to drop within himself. Find peace and direction. He just needs a moment to do that, he figures.

In spite of having fully accepted and owned his medicine bag experiences, he remains unsettled. The blood he spilled in that past, and the responsibility he feels for taking life even in that long-ago reality, creates in him an inner struggle. He's wrestling with whether he has to own the violence. He is a tender young man, sensitive to everyone else's needs. He can be forceful, decisive in a solid way, though he's never flashy or self-aggrandizing. And he has *never, ever* condoned violence.

He admires and envies Inanna and Conan's trust and faith. They had found truth and purpose with ownership of their medicine bags. His own pouch doesn't bring grace or anchoring truth. Instead, he doubts himself. *Who am I, really? If Meera and Gramps are right, what will I be asked to do in times ahead? Am I a warrior? I want to be, have always been, a peace seeker. I don't want to be someone I'm not sure I'll like.*

Silently, Gramps is at his side a second later. The old man wraps an Indian blanket around Leo's shoulders, then zips his own jacket against the cold.

Conan, standing just inside the open cabin door, can't follow what's going on with his brother. *It's just totally unlike Leo to seem confused or sad*, the younger boy observes.

Gramps gestures with a flat palm for Conan to stay inside.

He hesitates, looking behind him at Inanna. She is rinsing plates left from breakfast and searching for something to eat. She putters, humming to herself. Conan watches her for a moment. He doesn't understand who this girl is to him. But he knows that his brother is essential.

Conan turns back to face the porch. The brothers understand one another in ways no one else can. *He's freaked by the memories of his pouch. Is it to do with that brand above his heart? What the hell is that about, anyway?!* He steps back a pace into the shadow of the doorway.

Acting on instinct, he opens the buttons of his flannel shirt and presses his medicine bag against his bare chest, inhaling its herbal essence.

In the next moment, Conan is back in the realm of the Crow. It happens that quickly, in one breath. Eyes shut, he focuses his mind-lens, this time, on the leader of the Crow Bonnet Warriors.

With heightened perception, Conan concentrates his inner sight on the very young leader — *barely out of his teens*, he thinks. And this recognition stirs in Conan an awareness of the leader's humanity.

The young chief needs his medicine man. He can see, now, how the older man's wisdom, his experience — and his shapeshifting — are necessary. *He has to have the support of his medicine man, in order to lead.*

Opening his eyes to look at his brother standing on the porch, Conan reflects how ironic it is that he never thinks of himself as necessary to Leo. He has always looked up to his big brother. Leo has infallibly been the leader, the one making sure his younger brother has the right horse, the right tack. *Leo is Dad's second-in-command. He takes over when Dad's gone — sometimes he did that even when Dad was around. Me? I'm his helper. But this past life was ... different.*

Standing in the shadows, Conan closes his eyes again. He drifts back to the images of the Crow Bonnets in his memory-mind. This time, a sacramental ritual appears before him, full of motion, color, sound. *Blessing ceremony*, he hears in an echoing voice. *How the hell do I know that?* he quizzes himself. *For protection and guidance*, comes the answering voice. *For the leader who will be Chief.*

Conan recognizes with a dawning awakening that he needs to change his perception of his role as younger brother. It's time to learn how to be a true medicine man because Leo will rely upon it.

He repeats what Gramps and Meera have said. *The secrets I most need live inside me. They have been there all along.*

Outside, Gramps stands silently next to Leo. Long minutes pass before the old man finally speaks.

"Leo, you said this morning, '*time is now.*' My son, you need as many answers as I can provide. You're right."

Leo turns, surveying Gramps' compassionate, creased face. He considers all that the venerable old man has experienced in his many decades of life, what he's learned of war, blood and death.

The boy swallows hard. He has come to trust Gramps completely. He is desperate to understand, while also afraid of what he will find. Emotional courage is emblematic of Leo. While he doesn't consciously acknowledge the fact, it's truly as natural to him as the way he walks.

So, he runs a hand through his hair, wraps the blanket a little more firmly around himself, and follows the old man back through the doorway.

Conan throws an arm around his brother's shoulder.

Inanna is at the fireplace. "Found a cast iron skillet," she hums as she moves food to the table. The meal is leftovers from last night's dinner, but the hungry boys are grateful for it, and grateful to Inanna for preparing it for them. She scoops the heated stew onto their plates and winks at Gramps. "Bet you didn't think I could do this."

"Complete faith in you, girl." Smiling, the old medicine man motions for the boys to sit as he helps Inanna with the serving. He pulls up a fourth chair so they can all sit together, then asks that they each add a portion to the Spirit Plate. He says a blessing, and they tuck into the meal.

After a few minutes of appreciative silence, Leo steals an expectant look at the old man.

Gramps nods, still eating.

"1950, Korean War broke out." He takes a few more bites and pushes out his chair, wiping his mouth with the frayed cloth napkin.

"Seems like ancient history to you kids," Gramps begins, "but it's yesterday to me. I was about your age, just turned sixteen, felt cheated of the life of a Lakota warrior. It's as fresh to me even today as then. I was troubled and crazy-brave, taking every foolish risk. Bar fights, knives and beer are volatile mix. We fought mostly over girls, or something someone said about something someone else said. Any excuse. We fought for who was toughest, who was more skilled with knife or bow or fists. We fought over stuff we couldn't remember next day. There weren't enough ways to prove ourselves." He reconsiders. "For *me* to prove myself." Gramps pictures the young man he was, wrapped in fool's bravery and false sense of self. "Useless," he mumbles.

The boys put down their forks and wait for him to continue.

"Indians have many tales, old stories, about why we have to, or had to, prove manhood. Brave-heart stories, warrior legends. Well, don't matter anymore. But very real to us then. Enough to give our lives up for."

He stares past them to the window. *Day is turning to night too early*, he notes. Beyond today's setting grey sun, he views his history. He sees the frustrations of his youth and what had seemed important, what defined life itself in a different time at a different age.

"I felt that life as I knew it couldn't bring me excitement, glory, sense of purpose in the way of hero-legends told by our Elders. I was looking for something big enough to die for. … Didn't occur to any of us to have something big enough to *live* for. Not yet, anyway." He shakes his head at the insanity of it. "Hell, I couldn't find Korea on a map, but it didn't matter. One day a soldier, Cherokee, came to the rez. Walked right into our high school class. He had on real Marine dress uniform, when not one of our fathers or uncles even owned a suit. Sharpshooter, he was. Had been a sniper in World War II. Gosh-darn, he had real fancy, shiny medals to prove it. One was a Purple Heart, other was shaped like a rifle he'd won when he'd taken out entire platoon of bad guys by himself. Said it respectful, like a true Native warrior, not bragging."

He looks out past them again, seesawing between his memories and those present.

"Damned if half a dozen of us didn't just go and sign up, right then."

Inanna gets up from her chair to stand by her grandfather. She knows what the boys don't: there's more sorrow in this story than glory. She leans down, hugs Gramps' shoulders. She knows the end too well.

The girl moves to the fireplace and returns with a plate of Johnnycakes. "Nonny's recipe, made it by heart," she says proudly. She bites her lip, hoping her concoction is palatable. "Had to use powdered eggs, and there wasn't enough butter, but I sprinkled brown sugar on top." She looks hopefully at Leo and Conan.

They examine the pancakes.

She makes a wry face. "Go ahead, I didn't poison you. I hope not, anyway!" She giggles nervously.

Leo picks up the cue. "Yum!" He doesn't have to pretend. Not having had any food at all for days before they arrived on the mountain, to them the cakes are the best treat imaginable.

"Hey, these are really good!" Conan's surprise, along with the brown sugar dripping off his chin, makes them all laugh.

Gramps sits in the center of the laughter, buoyed by it. *So brief. Like much happiness, too brief.* He shakes off worries, and says aloud, "No, no more for me. Tastes wonderful, but you have growing bodies, and me, I have my story to tell."

He puts down his fork. Leo and Conan encourage him to return to the story.

"I'm not sure what we boys thought we were signing up for. Knew nothing about Marine Corps life," he resumes. "What we were chasing was heroic adventure, something that called us to 'be' someone. We thought going to war could pull us like magic out of poverty, the dullness of our just-getting-by life. The rez held no promise of glory." He sighs. "Indians fought and served bravely in every American war. That was not ever really recognized until Vietnam, but it didn't matter to us then."

He pictures himself as a skinny teenage kid, and half-laughs at the memory.

"Being a brave was part of the culture of our people ... proof of courage. Fast horses, skill in hand-to-hand combat with ax or bow and arrow, lance or tomahawk — these things dominated our history. Hell, my generation hunted food for our families since we could walk. As young as five or six years old, we'd camp on snow and ice, had none of them duck down sleeping bags that came later. We had cheap rifles that backfired, and often only small birds to shoot in frigid winters of North and South Dakota. Boys who couldn't sit still indoors five minutes stayed quiet on the hunt for hours. Became skilled sharpshooters, or we didn't eat. Best of us, the Army turned into snipers. Probably they'd planned that all along."

Gramps stands, goes to the corner cupboard, and takes out an old carboard box. He lifts the lid and shows the boys his medals and discharge papers. He sets the box on the table and returns to his telling.

"But there are many parts to real stories, aren't there boys? You learned this, fighting fires. Glory stories and brave stands carry grief along with them." Gramps doesn't wait for their answers; he knows what they've seen for themselves. "You've learned there are some you save, but others you have to leave behind. You've learned when you're called 'hero,' you're never comfortable because you see in your memory-eye what didn't get taken care of and who couldn't be saved."

Leo wipes his face with his napkin, moves his chair back. He bends forward at the waist and stares down at his rough, callused hands, turning his palms up, back again, and then together in prayer shape under his chin. His eyes hooded, he looks at Conan, who reflects back a mirror of compassion for the old man's story. They both know how feeble even courageous acts can be. They know these things from real life.

Gramps watches their eyes find one another's. "You wouldn't think twice of going back into the fight to rescue or heal whatever is next. 'To serve' is its own reality, it takes on its own life. It was my time to serve, and so I served. It was time to make a stand, and I stood. Nothing more, nothing less."

Inanna pulls into herself, nervous hands quiet, bouncing feet still. She realizes that, though they are separated chronologically by nearly a century, the boys understand courage as Gramps does. They take responsibility for granted. She feels her own lack of experience in this realm; the only suffering she has known well is her own.

Gramps hears his personal thoughts mix with the boys' and takes a short breath to adjust his emotions. "Someone told the Marines I was sixteen, so they made me wait and not leave with others. They'd wink at a year, but not two. I stayed home another twelve months and goofed around and practiced shooting, and oh yeah, found out my girlfriend was pregnant. No, not Inanna's grandmother. This was a young rez girl I barely knew who was always around; sweet thing, as I remember. She was crazed to get away from her alcoholic father. I barely noticed when we got married. I stayed wedding-drunk for days. Not proud of that, neither. I turned seventeen and couldn't wait for war. She didn't care much if I left, what with me sending back my military paycheck. More money than she'd ever dreamed of."

Gramps closes the worn edges of cloth that hold his medals, rises again, and puts the entire package back inside the cupboard. He turns to the boys and shakes his head *no* to unasked questions. "No, sons, don't let those medals fool you. I was no hero. I was just an over-eager boy who needed to prove manhood. But 'manhood' is many things, right? Like your father, standing tall for the two of you, caring for you. I didn't do that. I left a baby son with his mom and went to war. And I went for myself. I suppose I 'served.' But served my ego most of all, with fuzzy thoughts of glory."

He tells them there's no word for "hero" in Lakota, or any other Indian language he knows of. "To earn the title 'Brave' was honor plenty in the tribes. No one went to battle for medals. We went to prove we were brave enough to die 'for the people,' and we meant it. Everyone for all. No other way for tribe to continue. In old days, survival of all depended on courage and skill of all."

Chuckling, he sits down heavily. "You both make good Indians, don't you think?"

Leo jumps up to help Gramps ease into the ladder-back chair. He doesn't know if the creak he hears comes from the cracking wood or from Gramps' knees. The old warrior smiles his thanks and continues to tell them about his training, and about how all his Native American unit had the best marksmen. "Except for some very good squirrel-hunting white boys from Tennessee." They'd competed with each other, he says, the Indians especially. He tells them how much fun it was. "Until targets were real men."

He had lost his best friend, "a boy, really," his classmate since kindergarten who had kept traditional ways and played drums at ceremonies.

"Lost him. Leonard was his name. He shouldn't have died, when I had his back, and he had mine too. Lost him when no enemy was supposed to be anywhere that threatened our position. But someone was ... and someone did kill him." The old man shakes his head solemnly, not able to hide his sadness. "Probably just another kid from a Korean tribe of some kind who thought he was doing his job, too."

Gramps stops for excruciating minutes. In his memory-mind, he tracks images of men and war and friends gone. His forehead wrinkles fold over each other in long furrows.

Conan observes the bulging veins in the back of Gramps' hands. Inanna reaches for her grandfather's palm. Leo is thinking that every rivulet of blood in those veins has a story to tell.

"Well," the old man finally says, and pushes aside the past, grasping Inanna's hand with his. He leans in. "You'll hear this from those who fight wars: shoot small game, graduate to big game, and then to men. Watching things die can damage you or twist you... or make you want to be a better person. But watch a friend die, someone you know, man you love, who laughed and shared history ... you snap."

Gramps leans back. Another full minute goes by before he speaks again.

"Didn't see Leonard die," he finally says. "Knew where he was, he knew where I was. We were moving towards our targets, silent as snow falling. We had each other's backs ... tribal brothers. More than soldiers fighting together, we were blood." He draws in a low breath. "Didn't see him die, snipers are well hidden even from each other. Just heard a *pop.*

Heard lots of them *pops* in war, but that one I never forgot, knew immediately what happened, like I'd been standing right next to him." He pauses. "I went crazy, Indian-crazy. Loaded and reloaded, hunted and shot until I killed everything on two legs. Whole time thinking *What happened to all those thoughts in his head?* Leonard was the smartest boy in our class: spelling, geography, history. Memorized baseball scores from radio, learned percentages when the rest of us were still at simple addition."

For a heartbeat, the old warrior is fighting in a jungle again. His voice is distant and reflective. He asks of his floating visions, "Who vanished his ideas for building a house on the rez, and better life for his family? Where did his dreams go? Did they spill out? Vaporize or bleed into Korean soil with his blood? Where did it all go when he died?"

His pain weighs on them as heavily as his laughter had lifted them. Leo glances at Inanna, hoping for her to say or do something to change her grandfather's mood.

Inanna doesn't take her hand from Gramps'. Leo shifts his eyes from granddaughter to grandfather and realizes that the girl doesn't look worried or scared. He envies their closeness, and swallows the grief of his own losses, family and tender moments. He silently squeezes his brother's shoulder.

At length, Gramps raises his eyes to Leo. His soft smile carries an intrinsic light that unburdens sadness. "Nothing of the world's distress must cling. We carry it in our hearts forever, but we don't let it determine our choices," he says gently. "My boy, I started on Korea because of your confrontation with your medicine bag and memories. I have plenty of stories of battle and war, blood and death. They don't end in Korea. Swore never to pick up a weapon again … but," he looks up at Inanna, "I went to Vietnam, too. It's a complicated story." He looks back to Leo. "You only need to know I speak from experience of war. And something else, Leo: I know what's in your medicine bag."

Leo straightens. He lifts his head and meets Gramps' eye.

"What we call *medicine*," Gramps continues, "Nonny and your grandmother called *karma*. Your soul's history, your story, personal to you. Your pouch brought powerful memory-images of hand-to-hand battle, yes? The violence and emotions known to those who fight in wars showed on your face and body, Leo. I don't know the entire mystery of your pouch and your karma, and where they cross. But I know enough to see the junction is not … an easy understanding."

Leo takes in a breath. *Do I really want understanding? If I get enough support, will that settle my mind over the scenes that were in that vision?*

Gramps turns to Conan, without losing his eye contact with Leo.

"Conan, tell your brother about the young chief of your Crow vision. Tell him what you were just seeing. And what you can see right now."

The younger boy blinks, taken by surprise. He didn't realize the old man was aware of what he had been thinking and seeing while his brother and Gramps were on the porch. But after a moment of consideration, he recognizes the conjunction between his own thoughts and the old warrior's message.

He swallows hard and leans into the table, face in hands for the space of three deliberate breaths before he sits up and holds his pouch to his heart.

The inner scene opens to him anew, a mystical moving photomontage. Conan's young voice becomes more mature as he speaks, deeper. With his eyes closed, he tells his three listeners what he is seeing. He observes the past as if he's a part of it, but removed, too, by space and time.

Seeing the young Crow Bonnet leader before him once again, Conan studies him closely. Aloud, he tells the others of the brave's sadness over the loss of their innocents in the enemy's raid. "The young brave is looking around him at the burned-out encampment."

The innocents who were slaughtered by the enemy lie all around them. They were the children, the families of his warriors. What had been a hunting foray had turned into tragedy for these souls who were lost. His sorrow is unbounded. That his own wife had been spared is a blessing for which he feels infinite gratitude, yet his grief and sense of responsibility for the loss of his men is incalculable.

Conan tells his listeners, "But the leader is strong-minded as well as strong-willed." Even in sorrow and rage, he is commanding, in control. He wears his authority as comfortably as he does the medicine bag around his neck.

As Conan speaks, he becomes aware that the young chief has turned his spectral eyes and supernatural focus directly on him. This warrior of the past sees him as he is *today*. And he sees him as the tribal medicine man he, Conan, was then, at the same time.

Conan dips his head in deference. The leader nods back to him. Their eyes meet in mutual recognition and respect.

The boy looks away, his awareness returning momentarily to the cabin room. He straightens his back in the chair. When he returns to the vision of the long-ago scene, the young leader is attending to his men.

Conan resumes his reporting, aware he is conveying what the man he *was* is seeing.

"The medicine man ... lights some sage. He ... I ... am waving the smoke to cleanse and pray over the leader and the other four riders, right there among our dead. We take off our Crow Bonnets. I clean each man of blood, so the enemy's vengeful spirits don't return. I bless my wife and daughter. We load our dead onto the travois pulled by horses designated for hunting booty. And we ride out of camp. We don't look back."

The boy makes sure he's seen everything important to report. He allows a last, uninterrupted look at the young leader from the watchful perspective of the medicine man. He doesn't want to be swayed by any emotion or context of his current life — or persuaded by ego. *I have to be,* he tells himself, *absolutely true to the gift of this vision.*

When he's confident he has told all there is, for now, he opens his eyes and looks into his brother's expectant face. "Can't tell you how I know ... but Leo, I think you know it's true ... I was that medicine man. And you were the leader." He doesn't shy away from what he's witnessed and believes true.

Gramps assesses Conan's control and assurance. "You're coming to understand responsibility for Third Sight. Remembering awakens this rare and powerful gift." Gramps adds silently to himself, *as promised.*

Conan's emotions are close to the surface in the aftermath of his memory's fusion with his brother's past. He doesn't really understand why Leo fights within himself over the visions his pouch evokes. But he believes it's his role to help his older brother step into the future by accepting the truth of the past. Conan wishes for the perfect words to give Leo peace and confidence.

Leo *does* feel a kind of healing with Conan's perspective of the Crow leader's story. While the heartache of the tribe's loss crushes his chest, and the images of the cruelty of the destroyed camp cause his teeth to clench, there is a concord in knowing the leader's heart. It's deeply important to Leo to have this assurance of the leader's humanity.

Leo reaches out to squeeze Conan's forearm in wordless acknowledgement. The younger brother grips Leo's hand in return.

Gramps nods. "War is hell, Leo. Let's hope the day comes soon when it's obsolete. When people will recollect war as part of evolution, beast to elevated man. Pray for that day. But in that warrior time, tribal men had two jobs: protect and hunt. Both skills were more than necessary. They were life itself."

For hunter-gatherers, he tells the kids, wild food was spotty. The nomadic tribes had to depend upon rain and elements out of their control for provision. Hunters were essential to the survival of the tribe, because each buffalo or deer or bear they culled would provide more than merely the meat; every part of the animal was used to sustain them. Thus, the better the hunter, the more valuable he was to all.

"No one can deny their medicine history, Leo. Through past life memory, we come to understand we're capable of much more than we know."

He turns to Inanna and wraps his arm around her shoulders. She nestles into the comfort of his strength.

"The pouches, which were here waiting for you until you could claim them, are your first opportunities to awaken your heart-mind-spirits and tie you to the path ahead, *for a future to be possible*, as was prophesied."

The day is almost fully dark, now, yet they can still see wisps of smoky clouds passing by the cabin window.

Leo walks to the fireplace and idly pokes it with a stick. He sinks his mind into the awakening memories. "I do get it. I see that they — we — were hunters for survival, and I even understand they had to, well, seek revenge on the murderers. It's just that … when the lance was in my hand, I *felt* all the rage and power I was going to unleash." A shuddering passes over Leo. "And the way the other warriors gathered around … me …"

"You thought," Gramps finishes his words, "if you were their leader, then you were the one responsible for the violence. Am I right, my boy?"

Chapter 51
Trust the Process

"Yes! I understand about protecting people," Leo says. "If I was that leader who lost people in a raid, or whatever, and maybe we would've lost more if I didn't act …?" He shakes his head. "Well, he — *I* did the thing that had to be done, right? It's more like … I feel responsibility for things gone wrong, too. Violence shouldn't have gotten to that point."

Leo pauses. He shoves his hands in his pockets abruptly.

"I worry that battle creates love for battle, for the fight itself. Just holding the medicine bag, I felt that destructive energy calling me. It was *way* bigger than me." He looks over at Gramps with questioning eyes. "Was *choice* gone? I mean, during the last few years, Conan n' me, we faced some pretty bad guys. And we saw how those people can attach to revenge and hatred. I mean … if humans feel like they have to get *even*, violence becomes the way to settle anything and everything."

The old medicine man eases himself up from his chair and moves to join Leo in front of the hearth. "Leo. Yours are words of a philosopher-spiritual-warrior. Seems like you were learning this in your present life, too, in midst of crisis and chaos."

Gramps puts a hand on the boy's shoulder. "Our Elders taught that no soul progresses without having lived as conqueror and conquered, victor and vanquished." He gently guides the boy back to the table. "Now. Sit down, hold your pouch. Tell me about its beading."

Leo allows himself to be led back to his chair. He looks down at the pouch hanging from his neck. He takes it in hand, twisting the lanyard.

And all at once, he is transported. The boy's eyes flutter shut, then wide open, before closing again. He inwardly steels himself against the threat of battle scenes, blood and death. But this landscape is different. He relaxes as an unexpected tranquility spreads over him. A wide expanse of serene land and sky appears before his closed eyes.

Gramps instructs him to narrate what he sees as he holds the pouch.

A vision comes up almost immediately that makes Leo smile with the surprise of it. "A … healing ceremony," Leo begins, his fingers on the beading of his bag. No blood or death or confrontation. Instead, a wave of powerful caring imbues the scene. "A child follows as older men make their rounds, caring for small injuries, and illnesses, and warrior wounds..."

Leo watches as the men set bones, prepare herbs, wrap poultices. They talk with one another, and to those they tend; they sing, they pray. The healing seems to occur as much in their careful listening and interpretation of dreams as it does in their material care.

With growing awareness, Leo realizes that the scene he is witnessing is seen through the eyes of the young Native boy. Through the child's perspective, Leo tracks the movement and connection of the others in the tribal circle. They move with smooth efficiency, like choreography danced a thousand times. The boy runs ahead of the medicine men, burning sage, assembling healing tools, stirring pots of herbs he's gathered. The child is attentive, watchful, deeply respectful.

"The boy learned the medicine from his father and uncles." Leo is reporting what he knows from the little boy's vantage. "But he also learned to ride, hunt, shoot and fight. He chased buffalo, started colts and fillies, trained them."

But there's something different here, he senses.

"This ... is not the same group of men we have seen before. This is not the same ... time frame as the Crow Bonnet visions. This ... is later, like more than a century later ... But ... somehow, it's related, there's a similarity of spirit, or energies, here. It's ... part of the Continuum, part of The Golden Thread." Leo doesn't know how this scene and the information it transports comes to him with such certainty. He searches for the right words to convey the intangible perception of similar vibrations between this life and that of the Crow Bonnet warrior.

"I think this guy has the same *energy* as the Crow Bonnet leader. Like it was ... regenerated, maybe, and carried over in this later guy."

Leo is immersed in the circle of healers. He observes the caring regard the medicine men have for the ill, and their total lack of judgment. His heart aches for the closeness and understanding that encircles this group of healers. "They are as physically strong as they are spiritually." When the path of medicine calls, these men turn from fighting and hunting. Their lives are devoted to the spirit-mind-body of tribe.

The images of the serene circle blur, fade and shift in Leo's vision. Now the boy appears older — fourteen or fifteen, perhaps. He is singing, and there are drums. The scene he regards is another kind of ceremony; he stands in front of warriors who wait to be cleansed and blessed after battle. Within himself, Leo feels ... *proud* of the Native boy, of his earnestness and devotion and maturity. Leo longs for something he can't name and didn't know, until now, that he missed.

The montage shifts and the boy grows into a young man not much older than Leo is now.

"He mounts a horse. A muscled animal, lean, with kind eyes. A mare ... who is painted with ... *wait!*"

Leo opens his eyes and studies his bag's beading. He lets out a gasp of air.

"Horse and man, *there*, are painted with the same symbols that are *here*, on this medicine bag. The one right here in my hands!" He closes his eyes again, studies the renewed scene, makes sure he's right. He shakes his head briefly. *The message speaks itself in my head and heart at one time.*

Leo's eyes fly open. Breath held, he studies his pouch. "This bag, I think, had the lightning bolt on it when it belonged to the Crow Bonnet Warrior — I mean, to *me* — if we're right about this — when I was the leader of the Crow Bonnets. But this blue beading here came later. I think it was added for the guy I'm seeing now. And new elements were added to the pouch, new minerals ... Is it a star, this blue design?"

"Steady." Gramps's voice is close to Leo's ear.

"Right," Leo nods. He breathes into the energy. "It's not a star — it's a comet, a cobalt-blue *comet*." Just the saying of the word, comet, loosens some poignant rush of energy within Leo. He closes his eyes again, calibrating his excitement, reaching within for the elusive understanding nagging his memory.

Still touching the antique beading of the pouch, Leo sees the warrior riding into view. "The comet is ... a protection symbol, like a god's eye. Except ... an arrow flies through it ... or *from* it. Protection and prophecy are symbolized in these beads."

A light beading of sweat appears on Leo's brow as he continues relating what fills his inner screen. "I can see other riders joining the leader from every direction. He raises his spear over his head ..."

The riders are gathering in countless number, and they are all silent. Not a word is uttered. Not a horse whinnies. All those gathered seem to acknowledge the leadership of the blue comet warrior.

"He's older now, wears ... what, a special shirt? A buffalo hide shawl, sort of thing." Leo hears the words *Shirt Wearer* in his mind's ear. *The Shirt Wearer is a man among men*, he hears. "It's a great honor to be Shirt Wearer. It's a mark of respect signifying the bravest warrior of the tribe." Leo speaks fluidly, more confidently. "I see him join other riders. He will be leading them into battle. He is fierce but focused, calm. And ... his face paint matches the horse's symbols: lightning bolts, comets."

The warrior's hands are quiet on the loose reins; he sits his horse without a saddle, just a blanket. He scans the distant hill, where he is leading his men.

A shadow falls by his side. "He reins in his horse to look down at a young woman ... wearing a black shawl ... who is ... holding a spear up for him. He reaches out ... takes it from her hands."

Leo's chest aches. He's touched in a deep, forgotten place in his heart he can't share with the others. In one heartbeat, their entire story, the warrior's and the young woman's, all their feelings and who they were to each other, streams before Leo's internal movie screen.

He opens his eyes, blinks, swallows hard. "Couldn't see the woman's face. A cloud passed over her." He wipes a hand in front of his eyes, almost as if to wipe the screen clean. "Or a thin veil, like I wasn't supposed to see her clearly."

The boy closes his eyes again.

Without spurs or boots, the blue-comet leader heels his horse and gallops off. He rides to the front of his warriors. The braves are battle-ready, and the warrior leads hundreds of men in a war-cry, singing as they ride out of the camp. As they gallop towards the distant hills, the battle cry silences as if it's one voice, ceasing as suddenly as it had started, so that the braves ride over the hill in unbroken silence before they disappear on the horizon.

Trust the process, Aunt Sophia's meditation floats to him. *Stay right where you are. Live the entire experience. Truth is revealed in silence and concentration.*

Leo straightens his back, takes a deep breath, and flutters his eyes open. Without looking yet at the others, he moves to the window. He peers into the outer edges of what was once robust forest. The story that is unfolding is still unclear to him – but he feels its import to his core.

He turns back to the others, who are sitting around the little table, plates pushed away, ruminating on all they have heard.

"How did an apprentice medicine man become the leader of those braves going to war?" Leo asks them. "Can someone who *saves* lives and *takes* lives be the same person? I know it was a different time, context, but ..."

His brother finishes his thoughts. "But tribe stands together. We do what's needed to serve the whole, right? If we are, well, listening, if we give a damn, I mean." Conan smiles at Leo and glances a little self-consciously at Inanna and Gramps.

"Dad used that word, 'tribe.'" Leo agrees. "He'd say, 'Family are people who will stand with you, who hold the same integrity.' Even pissed with each other, 'tribe' stays together and strong."

Conan nods. The boys' father had found his tribe in the cattle-ranching families he wasn't born to. Tribe, they had learned, wasn't necessarily blood; it was the firm belief in right-action for the good of all.

Silent for a long while, Gramps now reaches for each of the boys' hands. They are astonished by the strength and confidence of his grip.

Inanna frowns and squeezes her thoughts together in gnarled tight strangles. *Tribe* is a sacred word for her. *Can I? Can I surrender my ... self-doubt?* she asks herself. Can she belong to a new tribe with a new definition of family?

Leo sees the girl look down. He reaches out with his free hand to place it on Inanna's forearm. He recognizes that family — in all of its definitions — is a rock bed trust for him. But for Inanna, the concept carries much more complex emotions.

"We were all together in some form in the past, I feel confident in my bones," he assures her. "But what's really important is that the *tribe* is being put back together. In this life, I think we're called to wake up to the entire story. We need to understand our paths and travel the Continuum together — that path that is travelled over many lifetimes, right?"

Getting up from the table, Conan starts clearing the plates. "It's what you're teaching us, isn't it, Gramps? Past lives, not just our personal ones but all of them together, prepared us for here and now?"

Leo sits across from Gramps. "The winds, fires, earthquakes … *whatever* the shift was that happened to the planet, terrible as it is and, hell, *will be* — still, in a weird way, it's an opportunity. It seems crazy to say, but it's like the collapse itself gave us a way to this Remembering. To find and continue the good work of family and unity and respect that was started *eons* ago."

Conan has finished stacking the plates in the sink. He turns back to the table and reflects, "My physics teacher said, 'The Continuum opens and closes like a wave.' Not sure how the Golden Thread fits in with that physics wave, but maybe that open-close, fold-over of waves bring the best from the past, to the present? That what you're thinking?"

"Damn!" Leo shakes his head with a smile. "Not sure about physics, Bro. I stopped studying science and math when the schools closed and the internet went down!" He smiles ruefully, mumbling, "…But what was I talking about, anyway? ... Oh yeah. Okay. Lots of things went really bad, and now we're here. And maybe there's an 'opportunity.' But one question keeps recycling in my head: why does change come so *hard* for people? Why does it take so long, and so much suffering, to change?"

"Why don't we learn?" Conan ventures that same repeated question.

Gramps pushes for clarity. "Leo, you rejected battle scenes, were frightened, denied them. So, battle is what you must come to understand. Does that make sense to you? The hardest lesson of *my* life … is being honest about fears. I believe all people share this challenge. Fear keeps us in old patterns. If we can't face fears, we don't, *can't*, learn from the past."

Inanna gets up and joins Conan at the sink. But she can't avoid her grandfather's thoughtful gaze. His eyes seem to drill a hole in her back. Because he knows that what she fears is her own rage — and the constant dread of abandonment that her rage hides. Being abandoned by her mother had stolen the faith and trust right out of her. And she fears, too, the responsibilities for the traditions and teachings that fall to her as the last of many generations. *Maybe*, the thought flickers across her mind, *those traditions should by right have been bestowed on my mother*.

Grandfather and granddaughter meet eyes. Inanna is embarrassed that Gramps can read her thoughts so easily. She quickly looks down.

The old medicine man turns his gaze to Conan. "Son. With almost no effort except aid of your pouch, you are able to slip into past life as medicine man. Deepen your vision; test your skills. You Three must be your own medicine people, find your own truth."

"Yes!" Leo realizes first. "Inanna, let's try what worked before. We should go outside, sit in a circle, meditate together. We found Conan that way. You've seen our lives with Dad, and you've seen into our Rishi lives so clearly, you're already connected to our shared past. You've seen what we couldn't."

Inanna appears startled, and newly uncomfortable. She darts a look at her grandfather to gauge his expectations. Leo looks from Inanna to Conan, hoping his brother will join him in persuading the girl. But Conan seems as edgy as she does. *They're so alike*, Leo grunts to himself. *Both unwilling to trust completely.*

He tires of their reluctance. Leo wraps a blanket around himself and steps outside.

The sky is fully dark. The sound of the rushing river reaches him from down the mountain. He stretches and fights a yawn. He's determined to try his idea, and confident the others will join him when they are ready. He finds some matches on the porch from the morning's ceremony, and the conch with its stash of sage. He lights the herb and blows until soft puffs of smoke rise. The aroma, sweet and pungent and earthy, fills his nostrils.

The smell of burning sage reminds him vividly of the day of his Aunt Sophia's wedding. He had been very young when he and his little brother Conan had been given the job of "smudging" the guests, one by one, as they sat waiting for the bride to come up the mountain trail. She walked on the arm of her brother, their father, her path strewn with September wildflowers. The memory seems exquisitely close and yet so distant. Those days had been rich with the light of love. His heart twists for what is forever lost. *Gone so fast.*

The cabin door squeaks on its hinges. He turns, sees Inanna following Conan out onto the porch. The sound of the door's resistance is a suitable underscore to their reluctance.

With a silent smile, Leo picks up the conch and "smudges" both their backs, and their feet and palms, too. And then he spreads his blanket on the porch and motions for them to sit. A light drizzle sprinkles through the heavy fog, but no one complains. Without working out form or protocol, they sit cross-legged in a small circle, knees almost — but not quite — touching. Shy of each other's space, Conan and Inanna inch away a bit until they are finally settled. Leo notices the adjustment, smiles to himself, drops his gaze.

Respectful of her traditions, the older boy asks Inanna to say a prayer.

The power and mystery of their minds opening to one another is seductive and frightening. They all take conscious breaths as they close their eyes and focus.

Conan hasn't forgotten that Inanna saw their Dad in the shared visions. He knows she felt his pain, and Leo's … their grief, love and loss. But to allow her access into his heart-mind as he is today, in this moment? It feels too invasive, too personal. It rattles vulnerabilities that have plagued his young life. Yet — the boy also knows that his brother is right. Secrets hidden in their shared pasts must be remembered collectively.

Conan sneaks a side-glance at Inanna. *But why do we need her? We've made it this far alone, just us, the two of us.* Then a freakish thought occurs to him. *Or have we been alone?* If Inanna was with them in past lives, was she somehow lingering in the shadows, along the ridges and edges of *this* life?

All three shiver in silence as the connection of blue current lights their circle — and their shared memory-vision flows between them.

Chapter 52
The Last Encampment

The scene they share behind closed eyes turns vibrant and real. It's different from the other visions they've had today. The energy fills a space where personal needs and wants could otherwise argue, cause conflicts, and pull them into individual silos. Separate waves of sizzling Golden Threads braid into one. Beginnings and endings can no longer be distinguished, as moving pictures appear and fill the shared vision.

Conan's inner eye focuses with astounding clarity. It hooks his energy, drags him swiftly in a direction that feels beyond control. He gasps for air. He is dizzy, his palms sweat, his stomach cramps. He fights his instinct to return to the present time and place. And then Conan remembers that he's going to have to allow himself to be more vulnerable, and trust, with Inanna sharing the vision along with Leo.

He inhales the sage and the moist air. He commands his body to stop trembling and drifts into trance.

Trust, a warm wellspring of comfort he's rarely known, fills him. *Trust*, he hears in his own voice. *Trust this small circle of woven energy*, he hears in another's voice, inside and outside him. *Woven energy makes it safe to cross boundaries of time and space.* The words drift freely, like balsam wood on moving water.

The connection links their bodies and minds in energetic fusion. Each person's vibration and frequency, light and movement, flows through The Three as one river of space-time.

"*Mitakuye Oyasin*," Inanna's prayer hums around the circle.

The curtain of their shared memory-image opens on a large circle of tipis. It's near twilight. Preparations are being made to feed many. Leo eases into the anticipatory tension of the camp he recognizes from just minutes ago, but now with Conan and Inanna accompanying him. He breathes in the courage to immerse himself, to dispel his dread for any role he may have played in battle. He commands himself not to delete or deny any message or memory.

"Let it flow," he whispers aloud. "Inanna, name the things you know. We'll follow you."

The girl completely surrenders to the electric tension. She's lived in the heart-soul of Native ceremony, and welcomes melting into the edges between the mysterious and the known. With the wide-angle lens of dream-image, she watches scenes of riders readying mounts, of cooking pots being set upon fires, men gearing up for battle and women filling their every action with intention and commitment. Preparation for life-giving and life-taking coincide.

"Tribe." Inanna sighs the words aloud with envy and longing. The colors are vibrant, but the sounds are subdued. No one yells or shouts orders. Without direction being asked or given, even the very young carry out chores. No child protests, no play gets in the way of duty.

She asks the boys to let her know if they see what she is seeing. "One rider gallops up," Inanna murmurs, "from around the back of camp, from the east gate. He's dressed in full battle regalia." His pace is so fast that mothers grasp children to them for fear they'll be trampled.

Their fears, Inanna can see, are ill-placed. The rider is the most conscientious of men. *This is the leader.* Once his people see him, confidence courses through the tribe on a current of courage. There are many warriors, but *he* is the one to follow.

The boys are with Inanna, captured by the sheer clarity of their shared vision. "It's as if we're there." Conan's words are soft, filled with wonder.

Leaders arise from each camp within the larger tribe, but everyone knows the bravest of the brave, as revered for his strategy as he is for his warrior skills. As he rides around the perimeter of the camp, other braves rush to mount horses and follow him, until there are hundreds of warriors riding together. This man has no selfish need for glory. He lives for the people. Many call him, *The One.*

Inanna sucks in her breath as she fully recognizes what she is seeing. Stories from the rez, and her grandparents' teachings of Lakota history ring in her mind. "This is the day — the last enormous encampment of the People, *my* people!"

The present and past hum into a single stream of thought and narrative. The braves ride so fast, there's no beginning or end of the galloping horses. The circle is continuous. Watchers of all ages gather in the middle. The Three hear the entire camp encourage the riders, pray for them, sing. The boom of the kettledrums and cry of the eagle whistles resonate throughout the encampment.

"I *love* that sound, the trilling of Native women!" Inanna whispers.

Conan adds, "Tremolo. Eerie, powerful. Sad ... and empowering, right?"

Inanna agrees. "These are the Strong Heart songs."

The tribe sings to instill courage, bravery. To remind one another that this battle is what they were raised for.

Inanna observes, "See the man who initiated the ride around the encampment? He's revived this war ritual from generations before. It was abandoned until this day we're seeing, which would have been June 25th, 1876. The ritual circle of galloping riders surprised everyone there that day. Once he starts ..." Her voices catches. "Every warrior follows."

The warriors circle the camp four times to honor the four directions. The thunderous power of hundreds of flying hooves, the energy and adrenalin — the commitment of it — pulses through Inanna. She yearns to *be* there with her whole being.

"See his spear and banner with the colored flags and the feathers? My grandparents tell this story. And *to see it, him, alive…*" her voice trails. She has no words to describe how moving this scene is to her.

A thousand horses with a thousand riders keep a perfect cadence, nose to tail in the circling of the encampment. It's a parade of perfect precision. Leo and Conan both know the skills needed to ride this way: no space between war ponies, every rider at full gallop. The brothers, both experienced riders, exhale across the link that connects them.

No sign of a slip or misstep.

Near impossible.

Mesmerizing.

The wide expanse of the Greasy Grass River flows behind the last great encampment of the Lakota and their allies in the tranquil beauty of the plains. Inanna, Conan and Leo are there as one connected consciousness in the dusty light and warmth of that historic day.

All at once, Inanna's memory zooms in on a detail of the images they are seeing. She gasps as she recognizes the yellow lightening totem painted on the lead rider's face and on the flanks of his horse. The same symbol as the yellow beading on Leo's medicine bag.

And on the brand above Leo's heart.

Inanna directs herself to *stay calm.*

When her breathing is even, she speaks from tribal memory: *"Mounted on the horse with yellow streaks of lightning on each flank … the cobalt blue hailstones spread across his horse's hind quarters match those painted on the warrior's right cheek … one line of red paint streaks from his forehead to his chin."*

Inanna's eyes fly open to meet Leo's wide, shocked gaze. Conan, sensing alarm, opens his eyes, too, and sees Inanna's open-mouthed amazement.

With the awe of revelation filling her voice, she whispers, *"Crazy Horse."*

Leo quickly looks down. "Crazy Horse," he murmurs, shaking his head.

The Three are still connected; they close their eyes as Inanna returns to her report of what they all see. It's a story known to her by heart. "Crazy Horse sings a Strong Heart chant as he rides." The fierce words of the song are an encouragement for Crazy Horse's men, the bravest of an entire nation of warrior souls.

The leader's hair is tied with a small brown stone behind his left ear. A similar one is tied to his horse's tail. The stone is a symbol, as are the lightning streaks and painted hailstones, of a dream that set his warrior's course. Crazy Horse wears the calfskin cape of the Shirt Wearer. His pouch is filled with medicine-magic elements created for him by Horn Chips, the warrior-medicine man of his tribe.

Inanna's voice carries the cadence of her people as she tells the legendary story she's heard a hundred times over. "As a boy, Crazy Horse was teased for his surprisingly light hair and eyes. *Light Hair* was his first name. It was often used to tease and separate him. But he turned the hurtful words into silent strength." While other boys dreamed of battle glory or of beautiful women and horses, Light Hair dreamt of glory for his people. "He had a *thunder dream* of lightning bolts and hailstones. My people say, *the dream chose him*. His dream called and committed him to *tribe* in bigger ways than it did for others. It became his future. His destiny."

High Back Bone, a most accomplished warrior and hunter, saw greatness in the boy, and chose him as apprentice. And soon the boy's father, a medicine man, gave Light Hair his new name, Crazy Horse, when the young man proved himself matchlessly brave in battle.

Inanna's speaking is almost lyrical, dancing with their shared vision of this singular event in the history of her people. "Crazy Horse became the greatest brave of his time. Yet he never asked for any honor."

The warriors are all around The Three in their shared vision. Dust flies from the horses; feathers and flags color the sky. Faces, faraway and yet familiar, alight and dim and then alight again.

A meditative silence falls.

Until Leo finds his voice. "He couldn't ignore the call. It drew him forward into the rest of his life … and the tribe, his people, with him."

Gathered in the middle of the circle of warriors are the women of the tribe, holding their children to witness the moment. They pick up the Strong Heart song. The chanting melody grows louder, matching the speed of the riders as they gallop in a circling ring of flying animals. The colors painted on men and horses mirror the colors painted on flags and tipis and the beaded ceremonial gowns of their women. Vibrant bird feathers adorn headdresses and warrior lances; colorful ribbons are braided in the hair of girls and small boys. The braves atop their painted horses manifest invincibility in the perfection of their unified parade.

"Never to be seen again," Inanna murmurs. To be witnessing the story she knows so well, to be *there*, fills her with an ineffable longing and sorrow.

The Strong Heart song ends with a final chorus. As Crazy Horse turns his mount, without any signal or command, the warrior riders follow him in majestic parade, filing in a single line, hundreds upon hundreds, out of the camp, in silence.

If this is the last, it will be the best of what we have, of who we are. These are the words The Three hear together in their heart-minds.

"The Last Encampment. Right, Inanna?" whispers Conan, his voice choked. "The dream that day wasn't to *take* anything from any other people. It was to protect what they had."

Emotions swelling, they watch as a thousand riders clear the distant hills. From the Last Encampment, the women and children and old men wounded from battles of the past watch the braves ride until they can see nothing more than dust settling on the far horizon.

Then the entire assemblage wordlessly packs up their camp, preparing the final journey of the nomadic tribes.

Conan whispers, "Are *we* the last of someone else's future dream?"

There isn't an answer.

The Greasy Grass Encampment images dissolve. The golden setting sun fades away, along with the languorous river and peaceful smoke of a thousand tipis. Montana's ravaged mountain reappears, with its fallen forests and exploded boulders and hardened sky.

The Three hold their own circle in the palpable wonder of shared memory.

*

Inside the cabin, Gramps sits cross-legged by the old hearth. He meditates as the children join together outside. He doesn't see what they do; he doesn't have to. He knows this story intimately. He's seen it in sweat lodges of South Dakota and Sun Dance ceremonies of the Black Hills. He's heard it in the martial drumroll of the Korean Peninsula and the screaming bullets shot through the Vietnamese jungle.

He prays to all their spirit guides for the memories of The Three to fully revive. He prays, too, to his ancestors that the two days he has left in this earthly realm will be enough to send these children as safely as possible into the unsafe and perilous future. The one he can never fully know.

Gramps reaches behind the fireplace to dislodge an old river rock from its secret place of protection. From the space behind the rock, he takes out a very small, smooth-edged brown stone. The old man rubs the stone, rounded with age, and raises it close to his tired eyes. In the gleam of its polish, he sees his wife's face. She appears as she was the day they'd first met: fragile and exotic, her intelligent eyes laughing at the jokes he told so awkwardly in his very bad Japanese. He'd never understood whether she laughed at him or at his joke. It didn't matter then, or now.

As he looks on her image, another picture forms, this one of the day she left this world. She had laughed that day, too. Her merriment at the absurdity of life and her human failings had always carried her through challenging times. "Husband," she had said, "when Inanna and the boys come, you must be here. *Three days* is the time you will have. Only that. And then you will come to me. I will be waiting to take you home."

His heart aches inside his thin chest. His ribs creak and expand from the rush of air into his lungs, from the need to see and hold her and put his tired head against hers, and weep.

"I am a weak, old, sentimental man," he says quietly to the luminous image.

"Soon," she sighs, smiling. "Fine work almost done, my old man. Soon."

And then she is gone.

Chapter 53
Chaos

The Three huddle inside the final notes of their unified circle of memory song, oblivious to the cold night air clawing up and around them like an inky sidewinder.

Leo is the first to shake himself back to present. *Today is reality.* He climbs to his feet. Inanna and Conan follow suit reluctantly, not yet looking at one another, not yet ready to talk out what they have witnessed.

"We'd better get firewood."

None of them has any idea how much time has passed since they first sat down in their connected vision. The cabin light is dim from the porch, and they can see little in the dark, but the kids scan the nearby ground and find a scattering of tumbled logs and sodden timber, damp with the mist of the darkened days, a little way down the hill.

"Vigilance," Inanna warns aloud. "Don't catch a foot on any upturned roots."

Conan pauses in his wood-gathering to take in the destroyed terrain. "*Forests* of trees are down, everywhere we've been, since we … woke up in this darkness. Are there any left standing, anywhere?"

They speak now in short sentences, still avoiding talk of their collective vision, instead musing about their hike up the mountain just yesterday. On range after range, as far as they had seen then — or see now — the vegetation and trees had been wiped away.

Inanna says it barely looks like home.

"It grows back," Leo assures her. "California's mountains burned down to the dirt."

Conan interjects, "*Past* the dirt, into the roots of the dirt, into the minerals. And then it burned the minerals. But eventually, rains came and regrew new life."

Leo nods, "Count on it."

What they don't tell her is that it all burned twice again.

"Anyway," the boys both say in overlapping reasoning, "we don't actually, know…"

"…not really, we don't really know what went so wrong in the end."

And they review again their possible explanations for the complete mystery of what could have happened while they slept through the Three Days of Darkness. They indulge in subdued speculations about geographical upheavals. Earthquakes, sinkholes, hurricanes, tornadoes, mudslides, avalanches, and multiple pandemics had all been predicted effects of the stubborn denial of environmental destruction.

They agree, because they had all heard it repeated so often, that humans had remained in denial and had perpetuated claims that environmental fears were a *hoax*, or a *leftist plot*, or *bad for the economy*. The kids wonder privately what those people must think now … that is, if they survived.

"Dad said people followed 'bright, shiny object' distractions from the obvious. He'd laugh and say, 'Maybe an asteroid fell? Maybe the Old Testament God is mad about transgender bathroom rights?' That kind of stuff drove him crazy!" Conan retorts.

Teachers the boys had liked best said, "Follow the science." But no one conclusion satisfied all. Selfish, power-hungry leaders were motivated by greed and what their Dad had called *chasing chaos*.

"Insane! They're running with scissors and refusing solutions!" he'd rant. The only political strategy seemed to be to distract the masses, or to bully, damn, and deny. Never accepting responsibility was the theme of weak leadership.

One for all, the mission of men like Crazy Horse, had become a lost hope.

Conan scans the acres of unexplained wreckage. He reflects, "I used to watch a lot of nature and science documentaries … But actually, I should've watched more on survival techniques."

Leo bends to mock-whisper in Inanna's ear. "He's a *tech nerd!* Technology and gadgets. VR and AI. You shoulda' seen Conan. I mean, he was glued to any screen!"

Conan spins around, clutching a log like it's a baseball bat. He pretends to threaten his brother. "Well at least I didn't get thumb paralysis messaging adoring social media fans twenty-four, seven!"

Leo grins and kicks a rock. "It was just yesterday, right? Well, okay, maybe a year or two ago — but still." Before cell towers went down, before signals sputtered, before the deluge of floods and the wild appetite of fires. Before everything had … gone out. "Feels like just minutes ago that we swiped, snapped, signaled on our devices to anyone and everyone in the world, right?"

The three kids sigh in unison from the crush of everything they've buried and carried. But they are intrepid, and they set themselves to the common chores of what must be done. They heft and drag their collected wood towards the cabin, having managed to find enough dry pieces to add heat to the fire, provide light and boil water.

"We need food. Let's get warm," Leo directs a nod towards the cabin.

Before they can take a step towards the light, a low, deep tear of thunderous inner-earth movement stops The Three in their tracks.

A second, louder *CRRAAACKKK* splits the heavy night. The sound seems to come from miles down, as if it originates below the valley floor under compressed layers of earth. In the next instant, the mountain just below the hillock on which the cabin stands rips open in a slashing slice of riven rock.

A third *CRRraaackkk, RRRRIPPP* assaults their ears. The river at the bottom of the hill roars a crashing warning, its white caps flying through the dark sky; while at the same time the rips in the ground widen and deepen, as if violent hands tear at the very seams of earthen fabric.

Inanna shrieks, whirls around, and slides backwards. The overloaded wood in her arms bobbles, then tumbles to the shaken earth. Leo reaches out to grab her and she steadies herself on his arm, one foot on a beam of fallen timber.

Silence drops with a thud, interrupted only by their heavy breaths. The earth recovers control.

Leo gasps out an "Okay?" He nods to assure them — and himself.

The three kids stay in place, waiting for another shake or maybe an aftershock. Within seconds, a low, gradual roll ruffles the split earth ... followed by another totally still minute.

"No worries ... small quake," Conan breathes, rebalancing his log bundle.

They all three exhale deliberately, turning in slow circles to be sure of their ground. They wait a few more moments.

With nervous grins, the kids nod to one another. No further tremors. They trot up towards the cabin, laughing in relief. Conan elbows Leo. "Shoulda' seen the look on your face!" Leo retorts, "Yeah? ... Did I ask?"

But before they can progress even a few yards, the settling stillness of the atmosphere is pierced by a head-rattling, high-pitched, cacophonous shrieking sound.

The Three freeze, dropping the remaining firewood they'd collected. The terrible ululation seems to emanate from the terrain where the ground split open just behind them.

Wordlessly, Leo drops into a crouch and signals for the others to do the same. He eases towards the caterwauling, waving at the others to stay back, but Conan and Inanna creep directly behind him, wanting to stay together. And then they see the creatures.

Hordes. Thousands, millions of extremely large *ants*.

The kids let loose a torrent of horrified words, speaking over each other.

"What the hell? ... *shit!* ... Army of ... are those *ants?*"

"Can't be! Too big!"

"*Giant* ... what the hell?!"

In the next minute, there's no doubt.

Squadron upon squadron of red insects emerge from the split earth, ten times larger than any ants The Three have ever seen. They are as big as cockroaches, each over an inch in size. Their mandibles are visibly opening and screaming as they snarl their deafening insect messages. The ants swarm out of the shredded earth, scramble in confusion and then re-form into organized lines before flailing and scattering again, disoriented and enraged.

Conan and Inanna, slightly behind Leo, move to tighten the distance between them. The ant columns, drawn blindly towards the movement, hiss and charge.

Leo yells, "Scatter! Don't give them one target!"

Obeying his directive, Inanna races toward the cabin to get Gramps' help.

Inside the house, the old man doesn't immediately hear the kids' muffled cries. He is well used to the shifting terrain on this mountain. Tonight, he is lost in his meditations on the challenges ahead for The Three.

"Gramps!" Inanna's scream cuts through his thoughts. Startled, he swivels towards the door and simultaneously hears Nonny's echoing spirit voice. "*Grab FIRE!*" he hears.

Without hesitation, he moves to the hearth, grabs a stick, wraps a rag around it and dips the tip into a pot of kerosene — and then into the smoldering fire. He races out the cabin door with the fire stick, yelling in full-throated Lakota and in English, "Move *back*! Move *slowly*, so they don't follow you!"

He himself runs, swift and direct, towards the infestation. He measures each move instinctively.

Leo sees Gramps' fire stick and makes a dash for his discarded blanket. Disoriented ants switch their attention from Inanna to Gramps, and then scramble after Leo. Their pace is so rapid, the creatures gobble up yards of ground within seconds. Their screech and hiss fill the mountain's canyons and valleys.

Quickly Leo holds the blanket out to Gramps. The fabric catches with a dangerous *swoosh* and Leo drags the flaming weapon over the ground just as an ant column starts to climb his pant leg. He raises the fiery blanket and throws it over the parading column just inches away from himself. Soldier ants are extinguished under the smoking blanket, but more of them run awry. They try to re-form columns — only to surrender position, dash in opposite directions, turn again and crash into one another. They rear on their back legs, mandibles raised in battle against their own ant relatives. Confusion leads to more chaos. Thousands of the red giants throw themselves headlong onto the burning blanket instead of away from it.

"Leo! Your *pants!*" Conan screams. "*Ants!* Shake them off … they're African Driver Ants! They will eat *everything* they catch!"

Gramps waves his fire stick close to Leo's pant leg, but the relentless, blinded, enraged insects tenaciously cling to his boots and jeans.

Inanna, at Conan's side, screams to him, "You have those honey sticks in your pocket?"

Conan's eyes register, widen. He grabs for the honey, pulls off one plastic tip with his teeth, and flings it near enough to Leo to confuse and distract the insects, who scramble toward the siren sweetness. The giant red devils devour the honey and plastic, both. He repeats the bait with the second honey stick, and the sweet lure calls to other columns. The lines of ant soldiers crash into one another; their age-old instincts gone awry, the huge insects attack in tribal inter-warfare.

The flaming torch in Gramps' hand burns dangerously close to his sleeve. Heedless, he waves the kids towards the cabin. Inanna and Conan move backwards in quarter-inch paces. Leo shakes his pant leg with furious strength, still trying to fend off a few stubborn creatures. He yelps at a hard-stinging bite, while Gramps brushes as close as possible to his leg with the fire stick in another effort to distract the ants.

Meanwhile Conan has cleared a path with his honey bait, and now runs to help Leo. The brothers kick and swipe at the red soldiers until just one enormous biter remains, only to be shorn in half as Leo strikes it to the ground.

In the midst of the fiery, screeching chaos, Gramps brandishes his stick, commands his lungs to expand, and hoarsely begins a chant to the Ant Nation. The old medicine man sings a crazy-quilt song in loud and purposefully offbeat vocalizations. The tune dives low, rises to a high-pitch run-on riff, and skids to a sharp stop before starting again in a discordantly high frequency. No note seems connected to the last. In the midst of the random sounds, the old man command-sings Inanna's name, and she comprehends his intention at once. Taking the path cleared by Conan's honey bait, she races to the cabin and grabs Gramps' flute, then runs back into the chaos to give the medicine man the instrument. Still holding the torch in his other hand, Gramps takes the flute and continues the crazy, off-kilter tune on the instrument while Inanna accompanies her grandfather by singing the deliberately irregular song.

To Leo and Conan's amazement, some of the ant lines react to the confusion of Gramps' tune. Whole armies of the parading red giants fall back into the fissure of split earth. Others screech and clamor at the sides of the crevice, trying to emerge, but destroying their own reinforcements in the attempt. Millions die — yet millions more scramble up and out, hissing and wailing over the lip of the mile-deep crack in the earth's surface.

Leo, eyes squeezed against the pain of his bite, sputters, "They're crazy-confused, their instincts are gone!" He bends to ease the seared heat of his burnt skin with a fistful of spit-soaked dirt.

Seeing what has worked, Conan opts to get more fire. He traces a deliberate path up to the cabin, taking care not to draw the attention of the distracted insect hordes. Following Gramps' example, he wraps a log with a kitchen towel, dips it into kerosene, then into the fireplace with a flash of blue-red ignition. Conan prays that the same protections that safeguard the mountain will cover the cabin from destruction by fire as they fight the outraged armies.

He grabs the kerosene bucket in his other hand and races from the cabin to reenter the battle.

Without pausing in her chant, Inanna helps Conan slosh some of the flammable fluid toward a new line of ants. The boy ignites the kerosene with his torch and the sudden flaring blaze sizzles the teeming red driver ants in a death scream. Leo joins the battle, using a log to scoop up what's left of the blanket and swirl it toward the flames. He swings his burning weapon in a red arc of falling sparks, back and forth over the squadrons. Ants fall back and circle wildly, then loosely reassemble to repeat their attack. The blanket is burned to a cinder and the flames are dying out as Leo brandishes the remnants to defend himself from yet another squadron.

"Throw it!" Gramps pauses in his flute playing to scream at Leo. "Back to cabin for more cloth!"

Dizzy from the venomous bite to his leg, Leo hurls the blanket, then scrambles back to the cabin just as an insect column nears the porch. He manages to reel past the line, heading directly for the fireplace to grab a discarded shirt left over a chair. He wraps the cloth on an age-twisted walking stick leaning against the bricks before hobbling outside to dip the stick into the kerosene bucket that Inanna brings him.

The ants have nearly climbed the porch when Leo plunges the stick towards the enemy legions. A dry plank ignites along with the insects. Flames erupt in Leo's face and scorch his jacket. He jumps back and stomps out the embers as angry mounds of the creatures topple over their own dead and run right into the burn set along the singed plank. Seeing the ants regroup for another attack, Inanna jumps onto the porch, and she and Leo fight the flames and the burning insects, shoulder to shoulder.

"*Damn*, how many more of 'em?!" Leo shouts above the roar.

With a new defense in mind, Inanna hops off the porch and pours more kerosene from the bucket in two rows about a yard away from the cabin, stridently singing along with Gramps' deconstructed, no-verse tune. Leo dips his fire stick and ignites the two lines of kerosene, creating a barrier — and death trap — for the ant armies.

"Inanna, we need another!" he directs. "Hook the ends together, circle them in fire!" Inanna follows his orders while Leo lights the kerosene and Conan backs her, lighting a fourth line with his fire stick to close the circle. Leo allows himself a moment of relief as the flames form a death pyre for the encircled attackers.

Gramps waves his torch as he plays his flute. A guerrilla insect column splits from their army and chases him across the short space. The red giants leap at the old man, but he spins, pivots, stamps his feet together and confuses them with a new and sudden twist of his song. He switches the tone and tempo of his off-beat music in rapid shifts. The song's pitch distracts the insects' efforts to regroup and charge. Their self-defeating civil war intensifies with every erratic movement of music, fueling their enraged confusion.

Inches from the gash of black earth from which the ants are still streaming and hissing, Gramps stops. The Three line up behind him, torches in the boys' hands. The old medicine man switches his melody, now, and sings a mournful Lakota dirge of death.

Totally disoriented, the multiple columns of surviving African driver ants rise on hind legs, snarl and spit. Some turn to fight one another to the death, but most turn back and try a last assault on the humans gathered at the ravine.

Gramps doesn't hesitate. He waves his flute to indicate his intention, which The Three grasp at once. Inanna moves to Gramps' side with the kerosene bucket. The old man gives Inanna his lighted torch and takes the kerosene pot from her. Hanging his toes over the chasm, still playing his instrument, he uses his free hand to pour the remaining kerosene into the ragged canyon of torn earth. In one breath between the notes of his continued melody, Gramps shouts to the kids, "Throw fire in! And jump back *fast!*"

Conan, Leo and Inanna hurl their lighted torches into the earth's opening.

The kerosene explodes in a rushing roar, flames spreading up and over the lip of the ravine where the ants are still attempting another charge. The fire erupts into the sky overhead and fans out in a blinding blaze. The dampness of the air and surrounding terrain contains the fire to the crevice, but the power of the flames throws the three kids back in their struggle to maintain balance. The giant African driver ants are incinerated as the fire obliterates the insects' shrieks.

The old medicine man slowly draws his flute from his mouth. Wordlessly he directs The Three to move themselves to the cabin. They walk backwards with careful deliberation, keeping their eyes on the smoking ground to avoid any residual ant soldiers.

The flames from the riven ground are starting to diminish when they feel the earth beneath them tremble again. The three kids take Gramps' cue and crouch to keep their balance while the terrain under their feet shifts, cracks, and splits out in a web of tears from the ravine. The incisions snake across the scarred land, twisting and drilling down into shallow gorges as the incinerated ant-infested gash widens and deepens. Separated on fractured islands of dirt, all four of them turn and leap towards the cabin's light. Jets of acrid smoke and fire explode ahead of them where the circle of kerosene is dying, and behind them where the ravine is smoldering. Leo drags his bitten leg. Conan slips once, banging his knee and shoulder on the rocky, scorched dirt. Inanna takes her grandfather's arm, unsure which of them needs more support.

Gramps grits his teeth but keeps his steps light. He reaches the porch just behind Conan, and they both turn to help the wounded Leo up the step while Gramps keeps an arm around Inanna. The girl leans against her grandfather, fighting to keep herself from retching from the smell of fumes.

They line up shakily on the edge of the porch and survey the battleground, breathing hard, coughing and attempting to reassure each other — but they have no words for the decimation before them.

Long minutes pass before their tension and trembling starts to ease. Gramps holds the silence, giving a prayer of thanks for the protections that kept his cabin safe from fire and infestation.

Then he moves to open the door with a quiet smile and a gesture of welcome, as if nothing at all had happened since he first greeted The Three with his serene warmth, the night before. The kids are just about ready to collapse with exhaustion and relief — and an overpowering sense of gratitude to be in each other's company, alive.

Inside, Gramps directs Leo to shake his pants out, just to be sure there aren't any stubborn stray ants still clinging to the fabric. "You'll find some sweatpants that should fit. Laundry box is behind bathroom door. And we need to dry that kerosene off your cuffs."

He hands Inanna his flute, asking her to get out the First Aid tin. He checks Conan's knee and shoulder. "Bruised bad, but no cut." He dabs salve on the welt, then inspects both Conan and Inanna for any burns that might have gone unnoticed. They take turns at the kitchen sink while Gramps examines Leo's bite.

The medicine man digs gently with a small scalpel, extracting the ant's head lodged half an inch into Leo's swollen shin. Leo grunts and his face reddens through the pain, but he doesn't complain. Gramps repeats his salve treatment, telling the kids all the while about Nonny's secrets for healing tinctures and medicinal herbs.

"Nonny was a wonderful healer. She made natural plant salves, like this one. She knew every root and herb. And she always sang through her healings." His voice is warm and supportive, as soothing a medicine for their embattled psyches as the salve is for their wounds.

Easing his bandage-wrapped leg onto the floor from where he had propped it on a chair, Leo smiles crookedly at his brother.

"Bro! Really? *African driver ants?* Where the hell did you pull out that one? Oh wait, of course." He puts on the voice of TV news reporter. "*Hours of documentaries pay off for boy-savior of Montana mountain ANT attack! Only he, red-eyed from hours of TV, could save these mountain survivors from the devilish attack of AFRICAN DRIVERS!*"

"Hey!" Conan retorts. "I was still partly in a trance from the Encampment vision! But in spite of being totally freaked out, a documentary *did* actually come back to me. It was like watching a TV screen off to the side of my vision, I swear!"

Leo's jocularity wanes. "Hey. Bro. Those insects were out to kill. I'm grateful to you, to all of you." He shivers. "If they'd attacked me in a horde, without your backup, I don't know…"

"They were *insane*," Conan responds. "And where the hell did they *come* from? Driver ants are from East Africa. How did they get *here*?"

Leo looks at the old medicine man. "Gramps, your flute, your singing, made them run out of control. Am I right?"

Without answering directly, Gramps motions for Inanna and Conan to stoke the fire and start a kettle of boiling water, gently pushing Leo back into his chair when the boy starts to get up and help. "Not yet. Rest," he says, and sits down across the table.

"A crack in Earth. Deep," the old man begins. "… Anyone know geography? Where East Africa is, *was*, in relation to us? Of course, poor old Montana isn't where it's supposed to be, either." He coughs, and Conan brings him a glass of water. They are all gaspingly thirsty, and their eyes sting from the oily smoke.

With fuzzy recall from school lessons, they try to figure what might be the longitude and latitude of their location, finally agreeing that East Africa would be "under" them — on the other side of the globe.

Gramps sighs heavily. "Ant Nation lives for tribe, order. Instinct is to unite in community, to save their queen. But now? Earth is out of kilter. Africa ants explode from beneath quaking mountains in North America?" He shakes his head slowly. "They come here from a tectonic crack deep enough to reach other side of globe? Doesn't make sense to me. But much does not."

He takes a long drink of water and dabs more water into his burning eyes. "I played music to confuse vibrations, yes. Ancient tribal war trick, long forgotten. Weakens them. But ants killing each other? Not nature of Ant Nation or spirits of ant species. Native peoples respect life in all forms." He bows his head for a moment. "I spoke prayer, at the earth's crack, for their journey into afterlife."

Inanna kisses the top of her grandfather's head as she sets a fresh jug of water on the table. He smiles at her.

"My role is to prepare you Three for what's ahead. Hard to do when what's ahead proves to be … unexpected. Lots of surprises can happen when world is turned inside out." He forces a laugh. "Think *we* were surprised? What about poor ants?!"

The three kids return abbreviated laughs, but the air in the room defies buoyancy.

Chapter 54
A Story Wants to Tell Itself

Gramps changes the mood with a playful slap to the table. "Food."

He gets to his feet and goes to the sink. While Inanna washes the cracked cups from her grandmother's collection and searches the cupboard for treats, the old man pours cooking oil into a large pot of water on the pot-bellied stove. He adds a small bag of herbs and dehydrated soup along with pieces of buffalo jerky and chunks of potato. He stirs with great care, as if each turn of the spoon is a meditation.

"Something to go with soup," Inanna mutters under her breath. She finds saltines. Tests them, "Hmm … little stale, but okay…" and places a dish in the middle of the table. Conan grabs a handful before noticing he's only left a few for the others. Looking a little hangdog, he puts a couple back.

Conan and Inanna join Leo and Gramps at the table. They each make an effort to put the night's horrors at a distance, for the time being. "Breathe. Stay present," the medicine man directs. "Only way to avoid …" He doesn't finish the sentence, but they know his intention.

"PTSD," Conan exhales. "Right." The three of them press their shoulders and backs into the chairs, reminding themselves to breathe deeply and stay in the here and now. Their injuries are throbbing, and their exhaustion is heavy; yet Leo, Conan and Inanna are still eager to learn. Whatever the ant attack indicated about the state of the world, one thing is clear: the lessons, whatever they are, must be known. Must be learned, for that elusive future to be possible.

"Ready?" Clasping his hands together, Gramps begins. "Describe the meditation you did together on the porch, before the Ant Nation battle." He leans forward slightly. "This is our main purpose together," he reminds them, "to uncover the past in order to take essential lessons forward into the future."

The kids are quiet for long moments. Recalibrating the cross currents of opposing energies of the day and now the night. Shedding the ant chaos.

"Take the important lesson forward, Gramps reminds them. *"Leave the rest behind."*

They steal glances at one another. Inanna's sadness for what was lost at the Last Encampment rocks her anew. Leo's face reddens, the black-shawled woman's touch haunting his memory. Conan looks away, his artist's mind drawing him back to the spectacle of flying colors and painted faces.

After another moment of awkward adjustment, Leo takes the lead and pushes his chair back from the table to get a modicum of space. The two others follow suit, and they all bow their heads to focus.

Leo begins the narration of what they saw in their shared circle. "Inanna recognized the Last Encampment on the Greasy Grass River."

The beauty of what they experienced — the soft, sepia-colored native grasses, the water-colored birch trees swaying below a crystal blue sky, the beehive *hum-thrum* of the tribe — still moves them. Every frame of the motion picture images is infused with their sad knowledge of what lay ahead for the tribe after that day.

Conan speaks up. "Yeah. Gramps, we saw even more than in my Crow Warrior vision." He wonders whether, when their minds link, the shared energy creates a new frequency. "I don't know enough physics." He admits with a laugh, "I don't know *any* really! But our connection, this strange link we somehow share, changed the entire experience. It's obvious," he lifts his head to Inanna and Leo, "we see and hear more when we're together."

"Our connection made every scene more alive," Leo agrees. "Literally, more energy flows when we experience something — anything — together, and so I guess that's why the images are bigger, brighter."

"I don't know about you guys, but I wanted to stay." Conan tries to sound funny, but his emotion betrays him. "We didn't see war, but I think if we had wanted to, the connection between us was so great, we could have just dropped back together into that space and the battle scene would have opened for us, too."

Leo whispers, "Hadn't thought of that possibility, but…" His voice drifts off.

Inanna vehemently shakes her head. "It was already enough to handle in one night."

"We got the story," Conan presses. "Better than just a visual memory, we got the *feeling* of it. And an understanding that we couldn't have gotten in any other way. Or on our own. We *felt* what it meant to be there that day. We felt it in the hearts of the people of the tribe … the unity, the determination, the … love. And it meant the same in ours, too."

Gramps catches his eye. "Conan, no story ever needing to be told could be better expressed than in the words you just spoke."

Conan reddens, a smile twitching the corners of his mouth.

"You saw the leader?" Gramps asks. "Young man, lightning bolt and blue hailstones painted on his cheek? Match the paint on his horse?"

The boy is open-mouthed. "How did you know? Did you … see it with us?

Gramps moves his head in a soft denial. "That was your special blessing, meant just for The Three." He watches the weight of that statement register on their faces. "You see a red-paint, jagged line, forehead to chin?"

Conan whistles quietly. "Knew it!" He glances at Leo, who diverts his eyes. "*Knew* it!" He leans forward. "We watched history, real history, right, Gramps? *So cool!* It's not just woo-woo coming at us through the ethers! Although," he snorts a laugh, "I love the woo-woo."

The old man turns to Inanna. "Granddaughter, you tell them who that young leader was?"

She looks at Leo, who can't avoid her direct gaze. "Crazy Horse," she murmurs. "He was the brave who led the warriors into what our people call the 'Fight on the Greasy Grass.' What the whites call Little Big Horn. Native warriors of several nations together won that battle. But … they lost the war."

She measures her grief, magnified now by the immediacy of the encampment experience, against her rage at what can only be called the genocide of the Native people.

Straightening in her chair, she allows anger to color her words. "After their loss, Americans threw thousands of their cavalry against our people until they, *we*, were overwhelmed by numbers. In a few short years, Crazy Horse was," Inanna swallows, "… murdered. Lakota were forced onto reservations. Buffalo were hunted to near extinction."

Her words hold Gramps, Leo and Conan in the history's soft-slide, emotional grip.

Leo stands and goes to the window to watch the cold, unforgiving night claw at the door. "Are massacred ant bodies swept away by the dark wind? Just like the Greasy Grass camp was gone in seconds?" He pushes away a cold shiver and turns to Gramps.

"Look. I know where this is all going. We've discussed this. The truth is, I would *know* if I'd been Crazy Horse. I mean, it's … outrageous! All these years, Gramps … stories and celebrations at our ranch, talk of Crazy Horse … I would have *known.*" Leo doesn't like the sound of his too-fervent voice. He huffs a heavy exhale and drops his gaze, waiting until he's calmer to continue.

"If this is his medicine bag, and it came to me …" He reaches for the right words. "Okay, I admit it feels like it *chose* me … and I chose the medicine, too. But not because I *was* Crazy Horse … That would just be so arrogant. We were raised to question 'ego-attachment.' It's impossible for me to believe that it's good for anyone to attach to any famous identity, especially of someone we learned to revere, like Crazy Horse."

Leo paces, shaking his head. His ownership of the pouch feels so right ... but claiming a history that is not his own feels so very wrong.

"Believing I was anyone important, at any time, is screwy nonsense," he continues. "I mean, I get that there may be reasons Conan n' me are alive. And reasons Inanna and I were at the same place, same time. It seemed random. But then Meera," he waves his arms, "and her Third Eye magic, and life-saving pomegranates, and you calling us 'White Buffalo Brothers,' and knowing our grandmother … well, it's unexplainable. But … maybe we three are exactly where we're supposed to be."

He trails off. The others wait in silence. At length, Leo stops pacing, turns his palms up.

"If we're actually seeing into dimensions, retrieving memories, then, *damn*, big stuff's come down. One thing seems clear: there's purpose behind everything, even if the purpose isn't clear."

Conan agrees. "Like, there's purpose even in the mysteries we can't unravel…yet."

Leo nods energetically. "I don't have answers. But I can't agree with things I don't believe to be true just because it's hard work to keep thinking. I have to keep digging for what the meaning really is, and what purpose it serves."

The old medicine man listens carefully to the boy's understanding.

"Gramps," Leo says, "I want you to know how grateful I am for these pouches, your teachings — and mostly just for you. But it's disrespectful of me, an ordinary, generic white guy, to think, geez … 'I'm *Crazy Horse?*' I just can't go there."

Leo won't allow delusion. He works to find dependable truth no matter the struggle.

"As far as I know, this is a never-before-known, *effed-up* time we're in. It's hard to find anything reliable." He sits at the table again and allows a laugh. "Dad used to say, when everybody called everything 'unprecedented,' it was just an excuse to avoid truths we don't want to face."

The conflict of logic versus emotion registers with them all. Conan grumbles, "Attachment, non-attachment … ego and wanting … I can relate, bruh." He clutches his bag possessively.

Yet Inanna senses she is more at peace than the boys are, if just for tonight. She has no worries about hidden meanings or where they lead. She feels secure in the snug safety of traditions and memory. She lowers her gaze and silently thanks the mountain for folding the insect-intruders and their deadly frenzy back into Mother Earth's internal, eternal, envelope.

"I admit," says Leo, instinctively touching his own pouch, "it felt perfect in the moment of being there, in the encampment … but too damn much is unexplained. I don't want to cling to anything that narrows my ability to understand."

Gramps lifts his chin high, closes his eyes, and searches for threads that connect him to their unified past. He finds the right vibration. He weaves it into a low two-beat rhythm that hums the Strong Heart song within him. He picks up the narrative of the Last Encampment story at midpoint, strengthens the connection and sends his voice out into the room.

Page | 262

A fresh, alive frequency circles them, filling the cabin and easing its message into their heart-minds. The wind outside begins to whine again, but no one pays it any attention. The three kids lean back in their chairs. The old medicine man waits until he's sure Leo is centered within himself before lowering the frequency to a near-silent hum. The peace of the room fills them for long minutes.

Then Conan starts to fidget. He isn't as patient as his brother. He itches to ask a thousand questions. *Attachment poisons*, he knows. But the younger boy yearns for the certainty of a medicine man, a Merlin — and for the magic and Sight he feels he's been promised.

He moves to the fireplace. Gramps' palm-sized carving knife is on the mantle. The boy picks it up absently, turns it over in his hand. After a moment, he fumbles in the log pile until he finds a suitable piece for whittling. He's hampered by gusts of wind that splay down the chimney and irritate his tired eyes. He coughs at the grit, frowning. But he finds a piece of wood he likes and takes it, along with the knife, back to the table.

Inanna remembers the soup. She gets up now to lift the kettle's lid and start spooning the broth into earthenware bowls, as Conan begins to scrape the sharp knife blade down the stick.

"You have quick, gifted fingers, son," observes Gramps, after a minute. "Deft hand of a born artist. Good." He turns to Inanna as she sets bowls of steaming soup in front of them. Its salty, pungent aroma fills the room. The old man mock-moans at the stale saltine crackers accompanying the meal. He rubs a finger over a chip on the edge of his bowl.

"Ah, little one," he smiles to Inanna, "Such thin fare? Your friends do not know the bountiful table your grandmother set. She always made sure, even in hardest times, that healthy, delicious food graced these chipped, mis-matched dishes."

Inanna reaches across the table and squeezes Gramps' hand while she pops a saltine into her mouth with a grin.

"*Starving!*" She blurts, eyes wide. "Tastes good to me!"

Conan puts his whittling down while Gramps prays over the food and puts up a spirit plate. They each add a small portion of food to the offering and follow his prayer of gratitude with their own murmurs.

When he's satisfied enough time has elapsed for stomachs to be at least partially full, Gramps begins his lesson.

"You Three were born with all knowledge you will ever need," he says. "We are all born this way, with direction of our lives embedded in our spirits and souls, if not in our immediate minds." He puts down his spoon, letting his soup cool a little longer. "You Three," he tells them slowly, "are precious on multiple levels of cosmos. You must live into the future. I can protect you right here, for right now; but you must learn to self-protect, physically and psychically, spiritually and emotionally."

They absorb his lesson, the vibration of his song still resonating in them.

"Much as I know of your mission, history, future, I have only a small piece of much larger story. Meera knows more — but not everything. There are other teachers ahead to assist you. But you must discover much on your own."

Conan pushes back his finished bowl and picks up his whittling again as he listens.

"What Native people brought forward of old traditions saved us: songs, prayers, secrets of healing kept our hearts open even in the special hell of captured people. What we *couldn't* remember of our heritage … and what we couldn't forgive or forget, what we refused or denied … destroyed us." Gramps sighs, rests his hand on Leo's broad shoulder. "Keeping Good Red Road of my people is not an easy journey. Yet it will never be the hardest one either. It's just what it is."

Gramps tilts his head. "Leo. Decades before you were born, the pouch you wear now was gifted to me by a dying medicine man. The old man was last direct descendent of Crazy Horse, warrior among warriors. *Care for it*, he said. *A young man will come to you*, he told me. *The pouch itself chooses him.*"

Leo blinks, looks up. He wonders if Gramps sees into the four and eight and sixteen directions of every endless road, his obsidian eyes are so deeply acute.

The old man holds up a finger, as if to let Leo know that he must be patient with a digression. "Now, choosing these pouches is actually a 'mixing of medicine,' and not a practice my people recommend. We respect other traditions, but we are also taught not to upset the spirits that serve us. Mixing medicine can confuse spirit world. Cross purposes cause conflicting energies. Spirit world is as diverse as the materialized world. There can be jealous energies. You don't ever want to upset them by being disrespectful."

Yet, he tells them, the elders of his tribe had to be dedicated to work that would challenge their tribal legacies.

"Our dreams and spirit messages told us to rediscover *oldest* spiritual ways that had been largely abandoned, while also adding to our knowledge of other prophecies."

He describes to his three listeners how the Lakota Elders had fanned out and met with multiple Native American tribes, and with First Nations of Canada. They had worked with, prayed with and held ceremonies with many tribal nations. They had travelled to the Inuit of Siberia, to the Yanomami of Brazil.

"When word spread, others came forward. We added to our band of knowledge seekers with the Sami people of Northern Hemisphere, the Mayans and Aztecs of Mexico and Central America. The Romani of Europe. And the Aborigine, Maori, Native Hawaiians … and more. Nonny renewed her scholarly contacts in other countries and cultures. Those scholars joined our efforts. Together, we came to understand that within each of our traditions there were secrets not known beyond our own cultural borders. And, some very important memories, like Conan's Crow Bonnet society, and deep secrets hidden in the oldest Daoists tracts, had only been hinted at, even among their own. And so — prophecies were shared. Histories were examined, oldest languages and ceremonies explored. Shamans, priests and priestesses, scholars of lost languages all searched for ancient, shared visions and teachings. Our search of prophecies was always focused on uncovering the clues and keys to the Oneness."

The old medicine man looks around the table slowly at each of The Three in turn.

"We learned that a time of prophecy was coming soon."

He pauses to underscore what he's tasked to impress on them.

"New understandings would finally tie old and disparate teachings together. There were physicists and cosmologists, brain scientists and chemists among us who reviewed the mystical teachings with respect. Sometimes with shock, because of … ways our truths and their research pieced together. In time, we started to think of our discoveries as … instructions. It became clear that all the prophecies pointed in one direction."

Gramps sits straight in his chair. "It was predicted, as Nonny said, that *The Three, known to one another from the most ancient times, will come together in this lifetime and will find the Fourth, their sacred companion. Many will join them to renew the Oneness.*"

The kids are silent, absorbing the very personal implications of the old man's words. Conan has whittled his piece of wood to a smooth cone shape on one end.

Gramps picks up the empty plate of saltines, turns it over. He smiles to remember how cherished these assorted plates had been for Nonny. His eyes focus on the brush strokes of this one he holds, green sprouts of bamboo leaves dancing in a sea breeze.

"My wife was raised a devout Japanese Shinto. Her father was descendent of countless generations of Samurai. Nonny's mother was Zen Buddhist, and Nonny followed in her mother's footsteps to become an anthropologist." He tells them that his young Japanese-Korean wife, with her enormous gifts as healer, scholar, mystical teacher, singer and keeper of traditions, had become legendary before her fortieth birthday.

He puts the plate back down with loving tenderness.

"Yet, she was a better-educated and more respectful Christian scholar than most Catholics and Evangelicals. And she was a more diligent student of Judaism, especially Kabbalah, than most born to those traditions." Nonny could translate the ancient languages, he tells them with pride. "Pali, Coptic, Sanskrit and more. I think she fell in love with me," Gramps smiles, "because I was another culture for her to study. And I spoke a language she didn't yet know." He barks a short laugh. "Inanna is right, my wife made her own 'spiritual soup.' No one but me ever challenged her medicine!"

Inanna moves her head vigorously in agreement.

"So." The warrior looks pointedly at the older boy again. "The first medicine bag was gifted to me by my old teacher, descendent of Crazy Horse, before he passed, Leo. And the next two came from diverse indigenous backgrounds who knew we were searching through old traditions to understand the prophecies." He looks in turn at Conan and Inanna. "When all three came together, we saw that the time of Great Change was coming."

The creases on the old man's face reflect the glow of warmth from the fire. "Nonny was first of the Elders to understand that the three of you would come together after Three Days of Darkness. She knew a girl child was to be born to our family, 'Eagle Dancer returned,' as she said. And two young men would find her, she told us, *Buffalo keepers and wolf brothers, destined to climb this mountain and claim these pouches as their own.*"

Leo watches his brother whittle as he listens. Not a word of Gramps' teaching is lost on any of The Three.

"Just as Nonny gathered the last pieces of mystical knowledge found in her travels to indigenous peoples, she met your grandmother, boys. Their friendship was deepened by shared visions. Together they connected disparate pieces of prophecies."

Leo lightly touches Gramps' arm. "Do you know our Aunt Sophia, Gramps? Our father's sister?"

A sweet smile lightens Gramps' face. "Yes, I met her at Sun Dance in Black Hills. U.S government allowed Sun Dance ceremony at our most sacred ancestral ground for first time in hundreds of years. Your grandmother and Sophia were with us. I remember Sophia well, a tall young woman as beautiful on the inside as outside."

The old man recalls that medicine men at the ceremony had seen spirits of white buffalo walking with Sophia, one on either side of her, as she gently, patiently, made her way through camp. "And, then, of course, a year later, those two white buffalo sisters were born and came to live at your ranch, protected by your family."

Conan puts down his knife and looks at Gramps with a grin. "Our ranch, even before the white buffalo came, always had tons going on, parties and big meals, so many visitors all the time. Medicine people, healers, mystics, business leaders and refugees, pre-school teachers and ranchers ... And, well." he laughs, "it was always interesting. Then the white buffalo sisters came and ... *more* celebrations!"

They all share in his laughter. But Gramps leads them back to the point. Doubt was gone, he tells them, when the white buffalo sisters arrived.

"Prophecies had said, *when the Sacred White Buffalo return, the Earth will shift, and a new time will emerge.* And so ... we knew. The medicine people, North and South American tribes and indigenous people well beyond our borders ... we all knew." Gramps looks one to the other. "The time had come."

The Three exchange quick self-conscious looks

Leo puts his hands on the table and takes a breath. His leg is still throbbing, but the food, water and rest — and the voicing of memories — has quieted his discomfort.

"Aunt Sophia," Leo says wistfully, "used to play a guessing game with us. About who we were in past lives. We would guess whether we were pirates, or astronauts, soldiers or saints. Sophia always reminded us 'a story wants to tell itself.' She said not to attach to some 'maybe story' of a past life, or else we'd be caught up in a character, like '*I was he or she.*' And once we attached to an identity, we might miss the lesson of the story that needed telling."

Conan cracks up. "Granny always said most people decided they were famous or wise or a hero. No one ever thought they were the bad guy or the loser!"

The boys share a grin. Leo turns back to Gramps. "I've been thinking about Aunt Sophia's lessons, especially, today. She wanted us to know, even though we were just kids playing games and imagining past lives, that what's important is the *intention*, the energy coming through. We learned to wait for the story we needed to hear."

Conan pushes away from the table, crossing an ankle over his knee to prop his whittling. "So, what you're saying, Leo, is that we don't need to *be* that person whose past life we see. We need the lessons, the energy, from the past life story. Right?"

The older boy nods, then looks back to Gramps. "Maybe Crazy Horse himself calls us. Sends lessons from his life through this pouch, or through Inanna's and Conan's. The understanding came through our shared visions."

He touches his medicine bag.

"Conan and I had an uncle, adopted into our family in the Lakota way. He was a very young medicine man then. We called him Bear. You remember, Conan?" His brother smiles as he carves. "Bear taught us *total* respect for Crazy Horse and the time in which he lived. 'Honor his memory and the story it teaches,' he always said. Because it's a story about personal responsibility and how to live for something greater than ourselves."

Conan looks up and adds, "Like Bear lived."

Leo is nodding. "We were taught to pass on that same legacy, the *Oneness*, to anyone who, well, joins our family, our tribe."

Gramps sits, eyes half closed, listening and watching as Leo finishes his thought.

"The story of Crazy Horse calls us to pay attention, here and now, to right-intention and right-action. His spirit-story, the *energy* of it, and the message — that's what matters. Like Sophia said, that's the story that wants to tell itself."

"I get it!" Conan puts down his carving. "Crazy Horse's story teaches what Bear called *reverence*. Bear was about the age Leo is now, eighteen or nineteen. Reverence, Bear said, was one of the meanings of the white buffalo, which teaches a respect for Oneness. Right? I'll sign up for that! I'd be honored to carry the reverence for right-intention forward alongside you, Bro."

The boy's cat smile curls the corners of his mouth as he turns to the old man.

"But by the way, Gramps, I'm not my humble brother. I'd rather *own* that I was the Crow medicine man, and also maybe the medicine man to Crazy Horse — who knows?"

He winks at his brother.

"Just sayin'…"

Chapter 55
The Spirit World Slices Open

Leo walks to the window again. He likes the meditative aspect the black-blanketed night brings.

"No stars or moon."

His injured leg chills and heats anew, a reminder of the insect chaos. Just thinking of their over-large bodies and crazed death-fervor makes his blood run cold. Whatever caused their centuries-old instincts to freak out, whatever thrust them into a foreign territory the entire length and width of the Earth away from their African home, was not their fault. He's angry for their helplessness.

Pushing away his agitation, he focuses on the unconditional, humble bravery of Crazy Horse. And an instant fire of courage rises in his chest. Warmth radiates from the brand above his heart. Leo again hears the tribe singing; again, he sees the braves riding off together, a thousand strong. The image of the beautiful black-haired woman handing Crazy Horse his spear, the touch of her fingers grazing his, causes Leo's heart to ache. He wishes to know her through the veils of the past that separate them. And this stirs a longing for those he recently left behind.

He turns from the window.

"It seems pretty clear," Leo starts again, "that responsibility for something greater than our own selves has to be the focus. Like it was for the tribes. But not just for one tribe, or family, or religion or whatever. We have to find ways to include everyone, whoever is left. Otherwise, why did we survive? Why would Crazy Horse and Eagle Dancer and the medicine man who wore your bag, Conan, *why* would the messages of the Rishi — and *all* of them — come together and remind us now? Has to be a reason." Leo puts his hand on his pouch. "These medicine bags carry a vibration, an energy of old knowledge. Whatever elements are in this pouch, I swear they push words into my mind."

Setting down his whittling, Conan moves to the hearth. "Yeah. The purpose of the medicine pouches, I think, is that … they are meant to help us with the Remembering."

A change has come over Conan, since arriving on this mountain, that he feels himself wanting to own. His entire life, Conan had been happy to be second lieutenant to Leo. Their father was a gregarious, edgy, forceful and opinionated leader. Dad could switch from commander to comedian at will. Physically large, strong and dominant, he was a force drawn to the limelight, the center of attention. Unless he wasn't there at all.

Conan had never tried to compete with his brother or his father.

But those hours waiting for Leo to find him after the Three Days of Darkness had been a lonely, heart-stopping ordeal. He had doubted his own sanity. He had wondered, if Leo didn't show, whether he could care for himself, whether he could go on. His choice had been to dig deep for courage. In that boulder cave, facing his greatest fears, he had found strength he didn't know he had. And he's beginning to realize now that it was the beginning of his call to medicine ways.

Gifts of psychic-seeing and magic had coursed through his unconscious during the Three Days of Darkness. He had heard his grandmother and aunt's voices reassuring him, *you have the Gift.* Those dreams, those words, had kept him alive, he now realizes. When Conan had fully woken, he'd stayed hidden — and he'd felt Leo moving towards him on the threads of the energetic flow of unity, brother-to-brother.

And tonight, Conan feels the growing awareness that the medicine bag he wears is a testament to his shamanic history and legacy. And to other lives with Leo, in whatever form each of them took.

He moves back to his chair and slaps his brother's knee.

"Hell, who are we to say *no* to that call?" Conan leans in. "Look, Leo. I think it's great of you, really, to be so humble. But right now, we may have to rethink that humility. It's time to move into what calls us. You have to admit it's like, what …?" He looks around him, searching for the right word. "It's like a *miracle* that we can see into the past together. Maybe this is a sign that these things couldn't happen until now."

Throughout the boys' theorizing, Inanna has kept her silence. But suddenly she starts bouncing in her seat and blurts, "Yes! Yes!" She jumps to her feet. Her buoyancy and enthusiasm refresh them all, after all the complexity of the day. "That's what I keep thinking, too! Look, I never shared thoughts like we did today … it's so cool and, like, eerie and mysterious too." Inanna has avoided looking directly at Conan, but now she forgets her natural self-protection as she touches his arm. "It's like a message from the past calls us to the future. And a message from the future tells us, 'find the knowledge you need, then come find me, the next puzzle piece.' It's awesome!"

She drops her hand. Suddenly the confidence she spoke of abandons her. *Damn!* She thinks to herself. *Said too much.* She sits back down and looks at her feet. Yet even as she does, Inanna feels a flick of feathers skim her blushed cheek.

Bird-girl!

The realization hits her in the same moment that she feels an inner fire heat her Third Eye. She talks to the Halfling in her thoughts. *You are an important piece of the stories! Old and new. That's why you keep coming to me, is that right? You're here to help us find the answers to these mysteries?*

A flash of the Black Velvet she saw in her dream floats tranquilly, majestically in front of her mind's eye. She recognizes the unending, enduring cosmic curtain and the gentle breath that waves it. She closes her eyes and feels her own energy float into the endless expanse of Velvet.

A sudden explosion of Light pierces the curtain, a sharp, clear laser that seeks and finds her. Inanna feels an immense, soothing calm permeate her being.

I understand. We need faith to accept the truth, and courage to answer the call.

She opens her eyes. Only a moment has passed, though it seemed an endless respite. She can't speak aloud what she saw, and she has no words for the sureness of her vision.

The girl instinctively looks at her grandfather — and finds that the old man is gazing at her with utter awareness. She gets out of her chair to wrap her arms around him. He rests his head, cheek to cheek, against hers for a full minute before pulling her chair closer and motioning for her to sit again.

Leo and Conan observe this exchange without understanding what has passed, but they are moved to see the familial expression of empathetic regard, nonetheless.

Outside the cabin, the night winds pick up. Swirls of black clouds can be seen crossing the windows. Leo jumps up and stokes the fire. Flames fan up, and he is glad for the warmth. Moving back to the table, he sees that Gramps' soup is uneaten, now cold. He removes the bowl, dumps it back into the cook pot and refills it with warm broth.

Conan picks up his whittling once again and watches from under hooded eyes while Inanna lifts Gramps' spoon and tries to get her grandfather to eat some. The old man smiles and allows her to feed him baby portions while Leo wraps a woven Pendleton blanket around his shoulders.

Unfolding an arm from the blanket, Gramps reaches out to touch Conan's hand. He turns the whittling knife slowly so that the boy's thumb and forefinger move less than an eighth of an inch around the hilt of the knife. "Hold knife like this, son. You'll get more leverage without pressure ruining fine edge."

Conan nods, but doesn't resume his woodwork. He is looking at the old medicine man with eager expectancy. Gramps crinkles his eyes, eases more deeply into the chair and exhales a hum of pure melody. They all lean back in their own chairs, loosen their limbs, close their eyes and take a deep breath.

Images of the Last Encampment ignite across their inner screens, just as they had seen it before. In their shared vision, swirls of pastel colors, like paints drenched in water, surround the scene. Yet, for the first time, the hills above the teeming camp come into sharper focus. The lens of their united vision narrows, and they see a lone medicine man who squats at the top of a prominence above the circling parade of horses and riders.

The man kneels in front of a deerskin bedroll. He is creased and bent with age, dressed in the ceremonial regalia of a venerable prayer warrior. As they watch, the man leans over to unroll his bundle, revealing the relics of a lifetime of dreams: animal bones, tobacco, sage, powders, herbs, feather, and a sacred pipe.

Rapt in his prayer ritual, the man blesses the warriors from his high vantage point. His medicine song rings through bottomless canyons and soars up to the prairie clouds. Inanna, Leo and Conan hear the same message: *The spirit world slices open.*

Downhill, young men vibrate with the frequencies of song, drum, prayer, and turn them into the energy needed for battle. A moon of gold rises behind the praying man on the hill, sharing the sky with the setting sun.

Conan is struck with an instant knowing. He swivels to Gramps. "YOU were there, weren't you?" The boy's mouth hangs open. "That medicine man … on the hill above the Last Encampment …"

He reaches for Leo and Inanna's hands. Breathing together, the sizzle of cobalt connection links their minds.

"*Look!*" Conan breathes excitedly. "The old guy's medicine bundle, right there in front of him … you see that buffalo skull? He's painted the skull with the same yellow lightning bolts as on the cheeks of Crazy Horse!"

Gramps acknowledges that the spirit of that medicine man lives within him — and in them. "That man's prayers were for victory and protection. But he also said greater prayer for survival of Lakota traditions, Seven Sacred Ceremonies and return of White Buffalo."

His hum switches to the same song the medicine man on the hill performs. He sings louder, and the rhythmic intent of his prayer-song reverberates through The Three. Individual spirits relinquish all separation.

Gramps' voice drops back to a low, rumbling hum. "Everyone you love, everyone who challenges you as teacher or 'enemy,' those who move you in important ways in this life, have played a role, often significant, in a past life. No one is here for first time."

He bows his head.

"That man on the hill came to Encampment because he'd had vision telling him *this would be the last great victory.* This fight was the end of their time as they knew it."

Gramps returns to his humming for short minutes, then resumes his lesson. "He prayed for leader, Crazy Horse, to leave the battlefield whether dead or alive knowing he'd done everything possible to save what was sacred: family, tribe, preservation of the Earth we call Mother. After battles are won or lost, my children, it's medicine ways that give us our true path to Great Spirit. Every ancient tradition knows this: animal and human, rock, plant, mineral and spirit are One. *What happens to the whole, happens to me.*"

Unexpectedly Gramps bursts a laugh. He says, "Now I must sound foolish, for I am only reminding you of what you already know."

The hands of The Three are still connected; they squeeze them more tightly.

"Leo." Gramps sounds like a patient old lion growling last testament verses to his cubs. "Crow Bonnet leader, his courage and calm inspired generations. Was he eventually *reborn* as Crazy Horse? We can't know. But that young leader had same spiritual energy as the Shirt Wearer. And Conan's Crow Bonnet medicine man, he learned wisdom so profound as to become shapeshifter. He, too, may have come again, maybe reincarnated as Crazy Horse's mentor, Horn Chips." He watches their expectant faces. "Or not."

The importance, he instructs The Three, is to find the patterns that connect. "Patterns in you, and patterns that connect you to others. In that way you will come to understand you earned the lessons, gifts and responsibilities you bring forward now."

Conan touches his medicine bag. He understands now that mysticism is his Golden Thread. *I want to know what the really old medicine men knew.* The spiritual warriors who practiced the medicine ways truly 'lived for the people.' He wonders whether he can give up enough ego to fully realize his spirit power.

"Okay," Gramps' voice easily shifts from visionary to practical keeper of the house. "Enough for tonight." It startles all three kids. They drop hands awkwardly.

Gramps says he'll clean up the dishes. He directs them to grab flashlights and gather up the logs they'd dropped when the ants attacked. He shoos them out. He needs a minute to collect his thoughts and settle his energy.

Great medicine man. White Whirlwind. Gramps cracks himself up as he remembers the name he was given by his teachers. And he chuckles to recollect the adoration of his many students, even after he had proven over and over to them the fragility of his own humanity.

He studies his gnarled hands. Glances at his thin legs. He presses his lips together in remembrance of how proud he once was of his muscled, youthful, physique. *I'm so old and shriveled, it'll be a miracle if I have energy enough for two more days of teaching.*

He catches himself and remembers the lessons on hope that he was taught by a Tibetan Rinpoche. *Faith is more powerful than hope.*

The old man sighs as finishes cleaning the last dishes. *I must have faith that our traditions and legacy will guide me when my memory and body fail. And I must have faith that The Three will be guided by those on the other side who support them.*

He whispers aloud, "*And, faith they will survive, as was planned — but not promised.*"

The door to the cabin bursts open, pushed by gales of wind and laughter. Inanna and Conan knock dirt off their boots and the gathered wood. Leo is last, and as he jokes with Conan, he turns to step off the porch for a last armful of logs.

He freezes. An unexpected rustling sound prickles the hair on the back of his neck. A low crackling of dry dirt, a stirring of fallen leaves.

Leo crouches, pretends to pick up wood. He doesn't want to alarm the others.

At a distance of fifty feet from where he kneels, a slow gelatinous slime oozes in the cabin's direction. The threat undulates with sentient pulsation.

The dark mass. Elk killer! ... On the hunt?

The oily thickness slinks sideways. It hesitates, quivers in place, and then recedes into the jagged, fire-torn split of open earth.

Leo holds his breath. He feels suspended, momentarily rootless. He looks back to the cabin where Gramps' wave beckons him. Glances once more at the crack in the ground and satisfies himself that the oozing Darkness is gone.

He decides he doesn't need to mention it to the others yet.

Enough confrontation of fears and worries for one day, he thinks.

Returning Gramps' smile, he calls, "On my way!"

There'll be enough time to tell him about this, later.

Chapter 56
Remember Who You Are

They prepare the cabin for sleep in low-key teases, laughter and exhausted reviews of the day.

"... can't get over the power of these medicine pouches ..."

"... mountains shifting into prairies...."

"... those Crow Bonnet Warriors were frickin' *awesome* ..."

Inanna hums the melody of the Strong Heart song sung at the Last Encampment.

Gramps asks, "You know that song, *Chunkshi*, the lyrics?"

"Yes," she answers. But she doesn't recall when she heard them, or how she remembers them now. Gramps doesn't offer an explanation.

Conan asks, "What the hell is a Chunk-shee?"

Inanna repeats his mispronunciation mockingly, and huffs at him, "Just like a white boy to mess up a beautiful Native word!"

Conan huffs back, "It must mean *cranky witch child.*"

Inanna glares. "It means *daughter.* When Gramps says it, he puts that spin on it that's pure Lakota. *Obviously* above your pay grade."

Conan sniffs. Gramps laughs.

Leo ignores them. "I'm still thinking about the horsemen at the Last Encampment, racing in a circle with no beginning or end. I was just ... blown away by their skills. And the complete trust of those ponies."

Gramps agrees. His own visions of that famous ride in the Last Encampment have always filled him with awe. And yes, skills then were beyond what Indians could do now.

Leo reflects, "Gramps, we rode with the best, but I haven't ever seen anything like it."

After a half-minute pause, their combined exhaustion begins to be acknowledged.

"*Damned* tired," Leo admits. He is met with silent nods of agreement. Gramps says he's glad to know it's not just his old man's temptation to take a long snooze.

Inanna turns from putting away Nonny's dishes, intent on teasing Conan about the loudness of his yawn. But she loses her balance for a moment and is tossed hard against the cracked corner of the white enamel sink.

Before anyone can ask if she's okay, a slow-rolling quake of the earth ripples the cabin.

Leo shrugs as if to say, *No biggie!* Conan opens his mouth to reply — but is stopped sharply.

Boom-boom!

Two jabs, one on the left side of the room, a second on the right, explode like high velocity rockets under the floorboards. The earth growls and rumbles around them. Another *boom* sends the dish rack clattering to the floor. Utensils and plates slide. Water sprays from the toppled jug and dishpan.

"What the *fu* ...?!" someone shouts.

The mountain sucks an enormous inhale. Silence descends for the length of one heartbeat. The four of them hold onto chair backs, walls, tabletops as they wait for a next breath.

With an ear-popping shift, an avalanche of rocky earth descends upon and around the cabin.

The Three hold onto whatever's close and semi-stable. They try to assess the level of threat as the ground settles into gentler rolls. But before they can relax, a violent upset pitches the ground under them. It feels like the whiptail of a roller coaster gone off its rails.

The cabin floors were built two centuries previously, with timber and nails from the first railroads that connected Montana to a new nation. They've been stalwart guardians of the home ever since. But no building materials could withstand the earth's violent thrust, this time.

"HOLD ON!"

The floor buckles. Old iron spikes shoot out of the wood in several places near the door. The kids duck, leap or are pinned against walls. Splinters attack them while the ground shakes. *BANG!* Sounds like ballistic corn popped at a too-high temperature scream in their ears. Projectiles of rock *ping, ping* against the windowpanes. A loud *crraaack* announces the first window to break.

Gramps goes into action. He throws off his blanket and shouts orders.

"*Inanna*, Seven Sacred Stones — under floorboards in bedroom, put 'em into fire. Conan, help her! Leo, throw everything loose into sink. See that board under it? Nail it down. Hammer and nails are next to firewood. Help me push table and chairs against door. Tie furniture down! Secure cabinets. *Go, GO!*" Gramps moves the entire time he talks. "Inanna, Conan, push *all seven rocks* deep as possible into fireplace. Cover 'em with logs and ashes. NOW! Bury them ...Yes! All seven! Fan that fire. Put iron grate in front. And secure it. Find way! Grate can't move!" His voice is strong, commanding and immediate. "*Good!* Now you two, nail shutters closed! You hear? Good. No wind and no light can get in ... *None!* Cover 'em all, bedroom too, bathroom."

No one drops a tool. No one misses a cue, or freezes. No one admits fear.

"*Leo!*" Gramps yells over the hammering and staccato shouts. "Grab iron pot!"

Leo drags the empty soup cauldron away from the fireplace and wedges it tightly into a secure corner of the room, so it can't budge. Gramps runs to help him cover the large water urns securely and position them under cupboards. The old man is suddenly moving with as much agility and confident strength as the boy.

The loudest *thud* yet hits the cabin with train engine speed. Giant boulders, the size of small cars, explode out of their long-secure holds and tumble downhill past the cabin. The fury of the enraged earth buckles the mountain. The wind-driven echo of blasts and bursts circles them while a chorus of flying dirt deafens their ears.

"*Move! Do NOT stop!*" Gramps shouts. "Leo, Conan! Turn off gas lamplight, bring all candles you can find. Cabinets and shutters secured? *Double check.* Inanna, grab my sacred bundle. And yours. And the pipe! Conan, take that drum off wall. Leo, all secure? *Good!*"

Before he sits in front of the bedroom door, the north direction of the room, Gramps scans the interior a last time. He makes sure every inch of space is secure. Remembering their comfort at the last minute, he throws a few Indian blankets on the floor for cushioning. He whispers to himself, *Not perfect!* He knows the impact of the natural world slamming against them will be greater than they can prepare for.

He doesn't say that. Instead, he encourages them. "Good job! Okay, yes, okay."

Gramps opens the pipe-box, lifts out three feathers. He gives a Red Tail Hawk feather to Leo. He extends to Conan a blue-black Crow feather. For Inanna, an Eagle's tail feather with black tip.

Conan screams above the bangs and clatters of the mountain attacking the cabin, "What's *happening?*"

Gramps shakes his head, no time to explain. He yells to Inanna, "Tie feathers into their hair and yours, with tipped points down. Like bird diving into battle. *Quick…* Conan, grab conch, and light sage. Crawl if you need. Smudge everyone. Yes, me too *and yourself.* Right!"

They scramble to follow directions. Leo holds Inanna's trembling fingers so she can secure the string that ties the feathers to their hair. Conan falls sideways once but keeps the conch shell steady. He blows on the sage, and its aromatic smoke fills the cabin.

Gramps blesses the tobacco with a quick prayer. He loads the pipe, holds it above his head and calls for the aid of generations of Spirits who honor the traditions. His chest-deep baritone rings out, rising above the cascade of falling boulders, "*Tunkashila*, hear me." He assures himself silently, *they will come. They must! Not for me, but for these Three.*

"Whatever happens," he roars to The Three above the cacophony, "*do not* leave the places I put you. The four directions must be honored!" His tone, unequivocal, is the command of a fierce war leader and powerful medicine man. The part of him that is old grandfather seems to disappear.

"Leo, sit there, in West, your back to the fireplace. Conan, honor the Wolf, take South. Yes, cross-legged. Inanna, your place is in East. I hold the North Gate. Conan, put conch in middle of our circle. Listen, son, you must keep sage burning at *all costs!*"

Conan wants to assure Gramps he has this, that he isn't scared. But when he goes to speak, his throat shuts and a weak nod has to do.

The medicine man doesn't wait for a response. He leans as far toward his granddaughter as he can. "*Inanna!*" He yells over the tumult around the cabin. "Daughter, *you* are Pipe Carrier now."

Inanna's eyes widen and sting. She shudders and vigorously shakes her head. But she knows Gramps won't abide denial or weakness. Bending her chin to her chest, she whispers to herself, "Strength. Humility. Respect."

Her grandfather remains solid, present and confident even in the maelstrom, and his strength anchors her resolve. Initiation under her grandparents' guidance and under the tutelage of her tribe will have to be enough. She knows the medicine. It's her time, even if young. Her usual defenses, said to her family for years, *not deserving, not ready, it's too much,* bounce around her inner ear as semi-formed cruelties.

She bows her head to her grandfather. He bows back solemnly, respectfully.

Gramps lights the pipe and sings Lakota blessings before handing it in the sacred manner to Inanna. She smokes, prays and tries to stand — but wobbles from yet another punch and roll of the mountain. Dropping to her knees, she bows to Conan, who stays seated as he takes the pipe and returns the bow. He short-puffs and prays scattered words of his own creation. Inanna bows again to him, takes the smoking pipe and inches over to Leo.

This morning's prayer flows back to the boy in a flood of lyrical vowels and hard-edged consonants. He's not surprised Lakota words pour out of him; only that they come without effort as he passes the pipe back to Gramps. But there's no time to reflect on that miracle before the next series of jolts strike.

"*Earthquake!*" Conan screams, to his own immediate embarrassment. *As if they don't know!*

The big quakes had come with more and more frequency in the last California years. Reports that the state was rocking and rolling had spread across America. But when the Earth split and tore huge gaps around the globe, everyone stopped praying for California. And stopped criticizing what false judges called "their liberal ways."

Riding to rescues, the earth would suddenly bulge and convulse beneath the boys' shying horses. Conan never got used to the tremblers. "The fires are bad enough!" he'd say, grinding his teeth and enduring the next wave.

Tonight is worse.

A direct slam of boulders against the cabin accompanies a rattle-thrust of earth below them, throwing all four up, back and sideways. They lean into the sickening motion like drunk sailors in a storm. The pitch settles for a few precious seconds. Each of them takes a half inhale. It's all the mountain allows. In the next moment a quake picks them up like rag dolls and slams them in the other direction.

"Get your butts and backs into place," Gramps yells. "Now! *Do NOT leave your Gate.*"

The earth rolls a series of heavy undulations, punctuated by sharp thrusts. *BANG-BANG-BANG.* Inanna and Conan, both too light to stay steady in the jolt and sway of the cabin, are thrown forward. Inanna feels the skin on her elbow break open, and Conan's forehead smacks the floorboards. His fear shines wildly in his eyes as he tries to scramble to his feet. His heart races, hands sweat. His brain begs for a breath of open air. A stomach-turning urgency to *run* overtakes him. He takes one step towards the cabin door — forgetting that outside, chaos reigns.

"*STOP!*" Gramps warns. "Stop! *DO NOT open door!*" Gramps' spine is rigid, the pipe in his hands. He screams over the roars. "*Listen!* Under no conditions, NONE! No matter what happens, DO NOT any of you open that *damn* door or *any* window!"

Gramps' eyes dart to each of them. He sets a glare on Conan's startled face. The boy's heart pounds under his thick jacket. Instinctively he latches onto his medicine bag. He sways to his knees, then finally drops back down, trembling.

The medicine man nods when Conan shivers into position, then shouts to each and all, "*Remember* who you *are* … Your *only* defense is to anchor your *TRUE SELF within you.*" He waits to make sure each kid registers the full intent of his severe warning. It takes a mighty effort for Gramps to out-roar the mountain's rebellion. He pants, grabs an inhale that fills both lungs to capacity. And drops his eyes from them.

The old warrior prays silently as he unwraps his bundle. Inanna follows suit and lays hers closely in front of her, wanting to protect it against the next jolt that could scatter its contents. She sets the pipe in the center of her own sacred treasures as the medicine man prays aloud in a rumble of song that matches the deepest echoes of the earth's canyons.

He looks up at The Three and says loudly enough for each to hear above the cacophony, "*The ONLY enemy is within!*" He demands they repeat his words. He can't hear their nervous whispers, and he shouts again, louder still, "The Darkness lives and grows on energy of *HIDDEN FEARS. Know this!* This is your last warning!!"

A howling wind picks up outside the cabin, battering against the ragged porch. Planks can be heard splitting, nails loosening; a board bangs with a crash against the front wall and debris slaps the siding and roof. Rocks swept up in the furious gusts attack the cabin's doors and windows. The gale force drives shattered wood out into the night to be swallowed in the black wind.

Gramps scans each face, feels each possible doubt The Three might harbor. His vocal chords are scratched and stretched from screaming over the discordant racket, but he persists. "Past lives prepared you. This life's lessons awakened you!" He gathers the breath and strength to drill his words into them. "Tonight's lesson is fear itself! If any image, memory, pain, real or imagined, enters your mind, immediately throw that attack into the sage. Burn your fear thoughts as if they are thin paper! *No exceptions!* Burn them! You hear me?"

They nod in unison, but the medicine man, knowing the terrible temptations ahead, growls, "*Repeat* what I said!" He commands in his loudest, most powerful voice, "*Commit to it!*"

Quick to obey, their voices muffled by nature's rage, they each call back to him.

"NO fear!"

"Enemy within is *not* real. Stay One."

"Stay together!"

Gramps commands, "Fear is both friend and foe. Tonight, it tests you. Do not allow it to capture you!" His strained voice cracks over the wind's agonized wail. "Or, the possible future is lost!" He doesn't wait for response. "Conan, you'll be tested as apprentice medicine man, too. Understood?"

Conan nods. But he has no idea what Gramps means. The old man asks the boy if he knows the work of the Seven Sacred Stones placed in the fire. Conan shrugs, again unsure.

Inanna, her voice shrill above the roar, yells to Conan, "Seven Stones are *relatives,* here to *facilitate connection with Spirit World* – just like in Sweat Lodge!"

Conan nods his head more vigorously, "Okay, *yes!*"

Gramps calls, "The relatives will teach you what to do. But you *must* keep fire going."

Leo and Conan have vague memories of Sweat Lodge ceremonies, and the power and influence of sacred earth elements. But the belching mountain and pounding wind distract and confuse them. It's all they can do to remain upright.

Gramps leans towards Inanna. "Any fear that betrays your heritage must be cast into conch-fire! Then return attention to vibration of the drum. And call your ancestors! They support your True Selves and strengthen us. But your *own* fear, enemy within, is *your* responsibility." He reaches out his arms to make sure the boys pay attention to his words. "Some fears that show themselves will feel real. You must not be fooled! Linked minds make you stronger, braver. *Use link.* You need all strength available to prevail against fear."

His throat burns from the effort of screamed words. He won't let it keep him from a last warning, "You are *The Three.* If you die, lose your minds or succumb to fear, the Darkness wins ... *fear* is the way Darkness wins."

Gramps takes an eagle whistle from his bundle items. His hands shake as he touches Inanna's stretched-out fingers. With humility and respect, she acknowledges Gramps and accepts her own legacy. She places the whistle alongside the items in her bundle.

Next, Gramps lifts up a small, half-dollar-size leather pouch. He says to Conan, "For you." And he pinches a small crush of powder from the pouch, tossing it into the conch. Tendrils of silver-blue, cobalt smoke erupt from the fire. The wisps swirl into themselves and form a spiral of ascending and descending smoke before dividing to dance in four helixes above each of their heads. The kids look up in wonder. It seems to Conan that the blue, smoky spiral is a conscious pattern mapped by invisible hands. He whispers aloud, "I — I … can't explain that."

The spiral widens and unthreads itself into a cloud that dances above them. Conan wants to reach out and let the smoke play through his fingers. The Three are mesmerized, momentarily forgetting the maelstrom outside.

The smoke completes its journey and gathers its many threads back into itself. As if it has physical breath, the single spiral sighs and then descends back into the conch. The sage flares into a warm flame, ignited by the soft blue wind.

Chapter 57
The Long Night: Conan, True Medicine

Conan can't take his eyes away from the spiral of blue smoke. *This is it!* He realizes now he's being given the same powder that the Crow Bonnet medicine man had carried. *The same.*

Gramps hands the small bag to the boy. Conan manages to bow his head and grasp the treasure, clutching his medicine pouch in his other hand. He presses both to his chest.

The fear that had surged through him and urged him to run now quells and subsides. The mystical, magical quality of the powder and what it can conjure fills him with both wonder and calm. As if the roar of the natural world is a reflection of The Three's inner journey, the sounds and movements of the earth surrounding them seem to quiet for a time.

Gramps, seated cross-legged in his North Gate position on the cabin floor, reaches up to untie a hemp thread from his left braid. He carefully removes a small stone from the aged binding. Worn smooth over many years, the small rock had gone unnoticed by the boys. Gramps reaches out to Inanna, giving her the stone — but looking at Leo.

"Tie into Leo's hawk feather, Granddaughter."

The lull in the shake and howl of the world outside enables Inanna to inch over to Leo and, through a pinprick hole laced with the hemp, tie Gramps' sacred stone onto Leo's feather. Inanna's fingers are shaking as the emotions of the moment and the concentration of avoiding fear cause her to tremble. She can only meet the boy's gaze for a brief moment, their eyes just inches apart. The significance of the gesture is not yet fully known by either of them, but it is felt by all. The girl blushes and tilts her head in respect. Leo returns her nod.

For an instant, a cobalt current of energy runs through her to him and binds them in mutual wonder.

Inanna drops to all fours and crawls back to her East Gate position.

Leo rubs the stone tied to his feather. He feels a profound sense of security just in touching it, and he's grateful for the grounding of this small essential element.

The old medicine man locks eyes with him. Touching the stone with his fingers, feeling centered even in the midst of the chaos and tumult surrounding them, Leo is stunned by a sudden revelation piercing his core.

This belonged to Crazy Horse.

His heart expands and fills his chest with a kind of serenity. The past infuses the present with peaceableness, even in the midst of mayhem.

Gramps pulls the drum to him and begins to beat the taut leather with a pounding stroke of his buffalo-bone drumstick. The bright feathers of the stick fly in rhythm; the two-beat drumming sings a song of enduring elements. The old man sings his Lakota medicine song of protection, filling the entire cabin and beyond it into the dark closing curtain of night. Pitched in a reverberant contralto, his voice cries out to their Spirit Guides for protection. And he sings to the very earth a chord of shared vibrations — breathing with earth and spirit both, *we are one.*

His song is of White Buffalo Calf Woman and of these two brothers, Conan and Leo, who protected her children; it's of the Eagle Dancer lineages from time immemorial and the heritage that falls to his granddaughter. He sings of promises to these Three.

The wind outside the cabin picks up again, whipping the windows. The ground under them feels as if it's waiting, held in a temporary pause of movement as its sister element rages.

"The wind is the Darkness." Conan ventures. "It's angry. It's trying to outcry the medicine man."

Inanna boldly adds her voice to Gramps' song. Leo begins a hum, allowing it to deepen and grow louder within the cascading vibration. Conan hears the shift in voices and joins the chant. Their bodies reverberate and echo with the drum's earth tone, tapping reservoirs of resilience within their spirits, minds and bodies.

The winds outside roar with catastrophic velocity.

The four inside the relative security of the cabin keep their song going, even while the air blows the doors and windows and walls with the strength of a cyclone. Conan tries to keep his hand steady as he leans forward to check the flame inside the conch. He blows on the twigs with a quiet prayer; the sage flares and responds. Its earthy herbal aroma inspires them all with images of rain-laden clouds, of the Sun's hot glory and the Moon's cool reflection.

And then a new wave of rocking tumult from the earth's core sends debris pummeling against the cabin from seemingly every direction. Winds howl in accompaniment to the ground surging under them, and the four seated in their circle instinctively curl inward to ground themselves, throwing out arms to prevent toppling.

Conan commands himself to *stay present!* He notices the quaver in his inner voice, and stops singing long enough to growl to himself, *stay strong!*

But as the floor lurches again, he flings out an arm to catch himself, and a forgotten memory charges into his mind. He's a small child, an infant. His baby cheeks are red and doused in tears, his chubby infant arms reach and flail through dry air for a secure hand or the beat of a warm breast. *No one is there.* Desperate to be held, his heart crushes in his newborn chest. *Left ... alone. I'm all ... alone.*

Abandoned.

The fear, greater than any reality, punches his solar plexus.

Conan grabs his stomach, dropping the pouch protecting the precious powder as he rocks to his side with the physical and psychic pain of his most dreaded terror. *"No!"* he screams aloud. The boy's guts twist. Bile fills his mouth. He slaps his hands on the floor, flailing, feeling around him for the fallen bag.

Inanna and Leo, doing their best to hold their seats to the roiling floorboards, both look at Gramps in panic over Conan's obvious torment. But the old man holds up a hard hand, motioning them to stay in their places and let Conan fight his own demons.

Conan swallows the bile, retches, and doubles over. Whispered, tightly-locked files in drawers of scattered, secreted memories are now thrown open wide to his view.

Crumpled in a fetal ball, the boy sees a dense forest of ancient trees dripping with wet, fermented vines. A murky fog rises from the forest floor and blows towards his mind's eye. A tall, pinched and spindly figure stands hunched over in front of a tree, hands clasped.

Sorcerer. Shaman. Unjustly ... blamed. Shamed.

Conan feels in his very intestines the wrong of the man's burdens. He knows in his very core that the shaman is accused unjustly of ill deeds, of failing to heal a plague even though *he had tried, he had tried* ... He really had *tried* to cure his people ... but he had failed.

So, he was tied ...

"Oh my god!"

Conan screams at the scene, his cries matching the wind's shrill roar.

Gramps calls above the din, "Stay with the story Conan! What do you see?"

Conan is rolling, cradling himself. "He's tied to a horse, his hands are bound ... There is a ... *noose* around his neck. OH my god, there is *no one to HELP him!"*

As the lean stallion is kicked out from under the would-be healer, Conan cries out in horror and anguish. The sound of his torment pierces the pandemonium surrounding them all. *ABANDONED! There was no one there to defend him.*

He feels the man's spirit leave his body in a rush of tortured release. Conan's heart burns, his ribs ache. *Why did you abandon me?* The words catch in Conan's choked throat. He can't speak them. Black-and-grey images swirl in front of Conan's bulging eyes. The bedlam of the quaking, shaking present is replaced in his mind by a clear, full-screen moving image.

"Dad! DAD!"

He sees his father as he saw him last, on that terrible day of rescuing those kids in the high mountain pass. *Where are you going? DON'T LEAVE!*

His father turns in his saddle to look at his son. His familiar, sardonic smile seems to Conan resolved, set on his face as if he understood all that would follow that day. His dad tilts his head just slightly to Conan. He touches the brim of his dirty black cowboy hat.

But he doesn't stop. His father's red flannel shirt fades into the distance as he rides away for the last time.

"*Dad!* No! NO! *Don't leave me!*" the boy screams aloud. Conan's chest collapses in one strangled exhale. His heart is imprisoned between ribs refusing to expand.

The visions are unrelenting. Before he can take a saving breath, Conan is plunged headlong down a silver-black slide of time again. *Healer, medicine man.* A different man than that of the doomed, hanged soul. This man is younger, broad-shouldered, standing tall. His hair is wild and long, his skin russet-brown and seared with injury. Three long exotic bird feathers announce him as shaman.

Behind the man a village burns. Enraged, the shaman tears an amulet necklace from his neck. With furious strength, he throws the talisman into the fire, cursing his gods and spirits. He drops to his knees, his face twisted in despair. *Alone. Last one standing.*

Conan doesn't have strength to uncouple grief. His fear of abandonment captures him as if he's an animal caught in the jaws of a steel trap.

Leo screams to him, "Fear ... *not real!* Stay *strong!*"

The boy is dragged into an avalanche of lonely and pain-filled memories — as healer, sorcerer, merlin, shaman. One after another they insinuate themselves, haunting and taunting him from every direction. The litany of failures screams for control of his consciousness, echoing the self-blame that has plagued him his entire present life. Conan digs raw fingertips into the cracked floorboards, then claps his hands tightly over his ears and screams aloud, "Everyone *left* me! EVERY time!"

Inanna and Leo hear his cries above the howling wind and shaking ground. They're completely torn, fearful for Conan's safety but hampered by the knowledge that he must be fighting spirits of which only he can wrest himself free. They strengthen their resolve to maintain their chanted support of Gramps' Strong Heart song.

"I *never* gave up!" Conan is shouting into the air. "I *never* ran away from what was expected, never surrendered. I lived to heal and protect you! But... you gave up on me, *left* me. *Why?*"

"CONAN!" Leo stops his hum to yell over the mountain's uproar. "Dammit! Listen! FEAR is the ENEMY within!" He reaches out an arm to his brother's curled-up body.

Gramps breaks from his drum-song and commands, "STAY PUT! *Fear will take ANY form to grab a soul.*"

Leo quickly nods his understanding. He holds his balance in the West Gate position and leans out just far enough to touch his brother's back. Conan recoils, but Leo shouts again, "*FEAR* is the enemy!"

The floorboards wave under them. Conan rolls and scrambles to regain position. He gulps, coughs and sputters. He's no longer sure which life or whose story he's in. Unable to find a solid sense of present time, the heart-stopping fear of being abandoned overwhelms him. "*Please ...*"

he begs, "*please* ... don't leave me!" His handsome young head burns as if feverish.

Inanna knows what must be done. Still singing, she motions to Leo. *The conch!* She can't reach across the circle to touch Conan without leaving her place at the East Gate. She pauses in her singing to shout, "Breathe! No fear ... *NO* fear! Conan, you are the Medicine Man!" Inanna knows this wild, out-of-control terror. It drives people over cliffs, real or imagined. She screams, "*No fear! Focus on the conch!*"

The boy's eyes dart around the darkened room. He ducks his head and fights capture by imaginary punishers dashing across his mind's inner screen, even as very real dangers punish the cabin's walls.

She screams again, "*The conch!*"

Leo leans into his brother, just able to keep a hand on his arm. He prays Conan can hear their words and feel their presence.

The younger boy becomes aware of his brother's touch. This time he does not shake it off. The current that connects The Three is still imperceptibly present, supported by Gramps' drum-song, and Conan can hear Leo and Inanna's voices through the dark babel. "*Leo,*" he whispers. Leo is there for him. *Always. Leo ... wouldn't ... abandon me.* "Leo ..." Conan calls out to his brother.

And the energy of hope and faith that attaches to the calling of his brother's name lights a silent, sacred space within him. Without being conscious of his knowing, he feels the presence of the little bag filled with blue powder. It calls to him. He knows where to find it, now — and he reaches for it through the dark.

He feels the soft leather of it on the rough floorboards. He folds it into his palm.

Leo and Inanna continue their humming and singing, as the world outside the temporary haven of this circle continues its furor.

Conan opens the bag as familiarly as if he's done so a million times before. He murmurs a prayer. His fingers close on a pinch of blue powder. He tosses it onto the sage burning in the conch shell.

Three lazy spirals of smoke rise from the conch, all together, as if in preordained communication. They wind themselves into one tornado-shaped swirl, twisting and turning, ascending above the shell. The blue smoke gathers its energy and rises higher, winding around itself before exploding into a dozen shimmering cobalt tendrils.

A hurricane-force wind pounds the walls of the little cabin. The porch boards screech. They can hear the old nails hitting the windows as another plank tears away from the front of the cabin and is swept up in the cyclone, smashing against the shuttered panes. With a shattering crack, glass splinters against the wooden barrier. Boulders bang against the house. The mountain is whiplashed by the force of the wind. But these four humans, alone in the midst of the massive destruction, hold their Gates. They sing and pray to the beat of Gramps' drum, strengthened by the protection of the cobalt spirals of smoke.

The blue spirits that had exploded into tendrils now fly into each corner of the room, up and down walls and across the fire grate. They skim across the shuttered windows and door. They dash to the ceiling, only to descend and circle one another in pirouettes of dancing smoke.

Conan whispers, "The powder … it's a protective force."

He basks in the miracle of it. His being is infused with the mystical, powerful elements that pulled his fear away from him with the rising smoke. Conan is tempted to throw more powder on the fire to ensure his courage. He puts fingers into the leather bag — and stops his own hand. The bag is no bigger than a half dollar. The reserve of powder is thin and shallow.

His chest tightens, his mouth goes dry. But he fights against the panic. *I am not a scared child! I can control my fear!* Aloud he shouts, "I am *not* alone! I refuse fear! I am *not* abandoned. *My people* are with me!"

Conan picks up the melody of the Strong Heart song. Holding his South Gate position, he adds his voice to the strengthening melody. His words of affirmation resonate within him and send the vibration of his resolve around the circle.

Into his mind's eye, new images replace those of fear. The boy's inner view is overspread with a picture of the medicine man Horn Chips, riding with Crazy Horse into battle. The power and conviction of his bravery swells Conan's soul.

And in the next instant, he feels the Crow Bonnet on his head — and in the next, the wings of his shapeshifted Crow expand his shoulders. Yet another image floods his inner vision, that of a Merlin, staff in one hand and a prism-topped wand in the other, leading students into a crystal cave of ancient ceremony.

I am courage, Conan sees now. *I am magic. I am my True Self.* "*One!*" He calls out to the others. "We're *all* part of one another's past. We're all ONE!" The true call of his purpose has been circling him all this time. *All my life.*

Inanna sings louder, her voice rising with grave and mature emotion as she responds to the change that's come over Conan. Leo closes his eyes, smiling in spite of the furor outside. His brother has beaten the enemy *inside.*

Inanna's chest swells and fills with the frequency of the song. Their united energy blesses the circle. The girl knows that there is always a lesson in fear. She had always been taught that, and she had lived it, too.

She looks over at her Gramps as he drums and sings through the rattle and roar shaking their world. His proud head is a silhouette that brims her being with love.

From deep within herself, a chord of alarm strikes, ringing with disquietude. *Soon the drum and drummer will be silent.*

Dread shudders through her body. *GRAMPS!*

Her singing voice is snuffed out as if it is a candle hit by a chilling draft. An icy blast freezes her blood.

Don't leave me, Gramps! Inanna's mind screams.

Chapter 58
The Long Night: Inanna, Eagle Spirit

Inanna struggles to revive her senses.

Enemy within ... stomach twisted, mouth dry. It's fear I'm feeling. The cold I feel is FEAR. Get a hold of yourself!

Her words of warning don't find their mark. Her terror of losing Gramps tears at her intestines. She shivers violently. *Don't leave me, Gramps.* She yells inside herself, *STOP allowing fear.* She yells it aloud.

"Toughen the fuck up!"

The words bounce hollowly around her troubled being, inside and out, and bring no comfort. Inanna instinctively reaches for Gramps. *Too far! He's too far away.* This is how she felt when she was separated, too often and for too long, from her grandparents. As if the miles between them had been ten thousand instead of hundreds. *I can't reach him!*

Gramps sings on. He beats the drum louder. His right arm is raised well above his head. He drives the beaded drum stick down in unwavering rhythm.

Inanna reaches through the space that separates them, longing to physically feel Gramps' steady grace. But the Strong Heart song that had filled and fulfilled her now runs through Inanna without effect. She cries out, "Leo! Conan! Gramps will be lost if we don't grab him. *Help* me!" The girl searches, gropes for any piece of him, any touch of the fabric of his shirt or a brush of his skin. But he slips farther away. It's as if he's an apparition, a figment of imagination. Angrily she questions herself, *has he gone to spirit too soon?* "*NO!*" Gramps is inches away from her out-stretched hand, but her fingers slip through air. Fear wraps her in its tight, malevolent swaddling. Aloud and loud, she hears her own voice. "Stop! Inanna! *NO FEAR!*"

The wind roars and whines. The mountain kicks and bucks.

In the next instant, the last of the candles, tucked into a corner behind Gramps and protected by a flimsy glass dome, flares. They hear a quiet *tinkle, tinkle* of glass cracking. And then, *whoosh* the wick blows out.

The thinnest spark of fireplace glow maintains a wisp of red-blue light. And a vaporous form emerges in the dark of the cabin.

"NONNY!" Inanna gasps. Her grandmother's image floats through the blackened room. Inanna sees through Nonny's ghostly ceremonial gown, but she recognizes its shape and the familiar, intricate beading. She reaches for her grandmother — but Nonny is nebulous. The much-taller-than-real form slips left, right, back, as if carried by a whisper of breeze. She dissolves into black empty space, leaving only her ghostly fingers fully visible. The apparition's hand beckons Inanna forward.

Still holding her East Gate, Inanna follows Nonny in her dream-mind. She silently calls to her grandmother. She sees herself run harder and faster to reach her side. Nonny silently floats backwards over a chimera cliff that appears out of the emptiness. Just as Inanna reaches her, she dissolves again, this time into what seems like a canyon, or a sinkhole. Inanna, in her vision, runs on tiptoes after Nonny. She shudders to a stop at the lip of a sharp, sheer cliff. Her grandmother reappears, floating above the cliff's edge, rising higher and higher above the canyon. Inanna dream-sprints after the vision, over the abyss.

Suddenly her interior screen goes completely black, as if a curtain has dropped. The darkness lasts for only an eye blink. Inanna sees herself in the next moment inside a decayed, dimly grey Gothic mansion. There's a warning ringing in her dreamer's ear, but she can't make out the message. She screams aloud, "Where *am* I? Where *now?* Nonny, stop! *Come back!*"

Nonny appears again, floating just yards ahead of Inanna, skipping inches above a cold, marbled purple floor. *Nonny, stop!* She leaps to grab the hem of her grandmother's gown.

Before there's a chance to understand what's happening, she's catapulted forward to slide helter-skelter on a hard, slippery, polished floor. A descending spiral staircase appears, free-floating in the air. She falls, hurtling down the curling steps. *"Noooo!"* Inanna hears her own high-pitched shriek. She slaps a hand across her mouth. But her fingers are immediately ripped away from her face by the speed of her descent. *What have I done? I lost you! Nonnnyyy!*

The ephemeral stairs collapse like dominoes knocked over by a careless child. Inanna turns end-to-end in a forward plunge. Her stomach crunches between ribs and hip bones. She falls down and down into a tight, dark-then-darker abyss. She reaches out for help, but the ghostly stair rail has no attachment. Her dream hands flail, unable to grab anything but air. *"Nonnnyyy!"* Inanna's scream reverberates in empty circles of sound.

In a final forward tumble, Inanna lands, standing on her dream feet. The spectral stairs reappear under her, inviting her to descend them upright. She sets one foot down at a time, with care, and continues until she balances on the last of the dreamscape steps. *It's a trick ... a trap!* Anxiety spreads through her limbs. She tells her feet to *RUN!* They don't move. She screams again, *"Run!"* Her knees tremble. Her legs refuse to obey. "Nonny! *GRAMPS!*" she calls, desperate for their salvation.

In front of her, apparitions suddenly pop up. They are close, a foot or two away from her, grotesque humanoid figures, misshapen and horrific. An entire crowd of them circle her. Some have horns like devils, others have staffs with dead animal parts hanging from them. She can't tell females from males; their grossness belies identification. Inanna drops her head to chest, swallowing her fear. *They're just spirits, just dead people. This must be Hell*, she thinks. She gathers courage to ask them,

"Are we in Hell?" The spirits whine and howl, but don't answer. Instead, they change form. Some shrink to dumpling-bodied, bulbous-nosed gargoyles. Others grow to the heights of hollow-eyed giants. Two of the most aggressive break off from their gang to sneak up behind Inanna. She swirls around with a gasp and then growls back at them. One angular spirit, witchy and gaunt, crawls up to her right. Another watery giant with an ornate crucifix plastered across his bony chest looms on her left. Two others rise up in front of Inanna in a rush attack.

She drops into a kickboxing crouch. She breathes into her core and, with elbows drawn back and fists clenched, she's ready to defend herself. The ghouls circle her again, scowling, spitting venomous sprays of humid air. Inanna swivels left and right, ready to run or fight. She screams, "If I'm on the Other Side, then this is *Hell!* And you're all *damned!*" They sway and shimmy, menacing, staring hungrily from empty eye sockets.

Inanna digs for her courage and leaps off the last stair. She charges the spirits. They scatter, howl, grunt - but fall back. They seem to attempt re-organization but fail to rally in strength. As the specters inch towards her, Inanna holds herself steady. *Vigilance*, she commands herself.

And then she hears a voice. *Remember.* The word radiates like an ethereal, circular surround-sound. Inanna doesn't recognize the voice, but it has a warmth that speaks of courage. She leans into it. *Tell me.* The voice answers, *Remember.*

Before she can make sense of any message, the spirits lunge. Like a malevolent choir, their mouths hang open wide as they scream in assault. Inanna's hands lose their resolve to fight; she clasps them against her ears and howls, "*Courage, damnit!*" before her tremors defeat her. But when her own cry dies out, she realizes none of the ghouls have actually reached out to strike her. Yet every ghostly visage is so twisted, so filled with hate, that she feels violated. She glares at them. *Hateful.* She's outnumbered by a legion of ugly, lost souls. *They're not REAL!* she tells herself. *Vigilance!*

She hears the voice again. It seems closer, clearer now. *Inanna, look into the past! Remember!* As she repeats the word, a single flash of cobalt light zings through her brain.

She rocks back on her heels. And she begins to Remember.

First within herself and then aloud, her voice fuller and filled with heat and passion, she blasts a message to the grisly spirits. "*Betrayers!* Selfish *liars.* You are *enemies of what's real and true! That's* who you are ..." The words are Inanna's, spoken by her, in her own voice. But they also sound like a profound revelation from outside her personal mind. *I knew this once before. Ages and ages ago.* But she couldn't hear it in this life before this very moment.

She wants now to laugh in the faces of the spirit army. She wants to run them down and celebrate a soulful victory. But she keeps up her tirade. "*Liars!* You who destroyed the great truths and created the *Grand Illusions!* Thieves of goodness, power hogs, betrayers of souls!" Inanna screams at the monsters and inches towards them. She is unafraid. "*You're* the souls that betrayed the Traditions. The ones who lied about the teachings of my people, of my grandparents' people, through the ages. You lied and cheated to protect yourselves. You were priests and witches, medicine people and politicians. You were scribes and trusted advisors, kings and lords and princesses, who attached your power to the Grand Illusions. You had the chance to do *good*, but you turned against us. You betrayed the secrets of *The Way*, and the Good Red Road, the Vedas and the Universal laws of *Oneness*."

She calls aloud to Gramps and Nonny, "*I Remember!*" Her heart fills with strength and her mind is perfectly clear. "We defeated you before, we will again. YOU are gone! *I am here!* The traditions will live on through me!"

The monsters pull themselves up to their full heights. They loom and leer, inches away from her frail dream form. But Inanna holds her place and the monsters begin to fold, fall back and collapse, melting as though heated wax. *Just like the Wicked Witch, they liquefy into the product of their own evil. But it's not water dissolving them. No, it's me, saying the Truth.*

Joyous and exhausted, she wants to run from this place. She is ready to return to Gramps, to the cabin, to the boys.

But when she tries to grab a healthy breath of air, she coughs. Her lungs won't fill. She feels dizzy from lack of oxygen. *What the hell!* The air around her has turned into a heavy fog. It thickens and begins to weave itself into thick veils. It's as if the fog is consciously dropping from an invisible ceiling in order to wrap and drape itself into endless curtains of fabric. As she tries to push one veil aside, another one drops down to replace it. Inanna plunges ahead, and the infinite veils seem to coax her, tease her to enter their folds. *What is on the other side?* She can't tell if they guard an entrance or lead to an exit. They seem to get heavier, harder to move.

She hears in her mind, *these are the veils of illusion.*

Inanna tries to push them away, but they continue to multiply, twirling around her until she's completely wrapped inside their infinite folds, spinning her from one to another. She's like a lost and lonely ballerina being spun between duplicitous partners. One veil feels like it's made of expensive silk, the next is as scratchy and coarse as horsehair. The next two are warm and inviting, velvet and satin. They twirl her between themselves and then pass her into the center of a new touch, another infinite swath of fabric.

The last veil spins around her fast and then propels her onto a darkened stage. Her instinct is to laugh. But she hears indistinct voices murmuring, menacing. Inanna realizes she's no longer alone. *Vigilance.*

She breathes deeply to center and guard her mind and strengthen her will. She balances on the balls of her feet, ready to run.

New apparitions appear between the curtains of the backstage which are also veils. These ghosts are more vivid than the last, younger, hiding and then peeking out, only to be swirled again within the curtain folds just as she was. *Maybe they were also victims of the veils.* The elusive figures come alive as if they know Inanna's paying attention. They call to her, tempt her to come forward to join them. *Play with us! Run!* They call to her. *Try to stop me,* one of them taunts. The voices have a teasing quality. *Look here! Follow me!* She knows where this will go.

But before she can run, the messages turn ugly. *You're an idiot! Weirdo! Crazy bitch!* The voices grow louder and more vicious. The taunting turns to screaming attacks of hateful words. Inanna tells herself *don't listen!* She doesn't know any of them! *But did I? Some other time and place?* Inanna tries to turn away, but spectral fingers reach out from the veils and from the dark places on the stage to pull her back. Her heart flutters. She feels the too-familiar signs of a looming panic attack. She grabs a breath, and hears Gramps' voice in her head, *don't empower whatever is hiding!*

"Come out, you freakin' cowards! I can face you! Can you face me?" she yells.

These aren't apparitions of past lives, or evildoers from ancient times. These are her enemies of *this* life. The ones she never wants to see again. Never wants to remember. A terrible bone-deep weariness floods her mind and spirit. But she can't let them know. *Show no weakness.* "Screw you!" she yells, but her voice is thin and too shrill. She damns herself for not being strong enough to make these spirits disappear forever. She can't help being different and odd. She's *glad* she's not exactly like them, like anyone else, actually.

A vicious gaggle of middle-school girls crowds her inner screen, darting across the stage. Inanna holds her place. She forces herself to see them, to hear them. They are the same girls who laughed at her not-right, not-hip clothes, her rundown shoes and her "no-address-available" homes. Just as they did at every school and on every playground, they pretend to be Inanna's friends. But only to set her up. Her history of abuse from their meanness, her confusion with their intentions, fills her heart-mind with self-loathing.

Her face heats with the rage and shame of those terrible days. Her body goes rigid remembering the constant moves, another school, *another set of fucking ins and outs!* She never got the social rules right. She'd lived in back alleys and rundown motels and on the living-room couches of strangers' homes. She was lost, awkward and alone. Fear and rage were her only companions.

Poisonous anger builds inside her now as it did then. Every move had turned out the same. New faces, apathetic teachers, other girls and different boys — but the screech of cruel names thrown at her were, are, the same. *Half-breed! Crazy-freak! Native American? Is that even a THING? Are you kidding? With that 'fro? You're nothin' but a black bitch-chink!*

She claws at their faces as they taunt her from the veils. She screams back at them, the gangs of inner-city or farm-country bullies, whether in Vegas or Brooklyn or Dallas or wherever, the unfairness and judgments were always the same. It didn't matter where she lived, where her mother dragged her. Cruelty and prejudice seemed destined to find her. "No!" she screams to the memories growing bolder with her upset, with her inability to scare them away. "NOT again!" Familiar and not-familiar and too-familiar faces come out of hiding to laugh at her. The playground slurs, the classroom disses fill the stage in hissing refrain.

Until the scene changes again. Inanna sees herself in rapid-fire montages, running with her mother from debt collectors who bang at thin doors, lying to unpaid drug dealers, escaping to the homes and lives of yet other men. Drunken party scenes appear, faces leer, drooling drunks and ragged addicts threaten and retreat. She is stung by a flat-handed slap, spit on by a lecherous sot, pawed by an alcohol-infused masher. *Pretty baby, sweet baby*, the men say. She smells old beer cans stuffed with smashed cigarette butts, and her mother's rancid breath competing with a waft of cheap perfume.

Inanna screams at her dream-self, *Run, damnit! Run!* Her mother screeches as she flies ahead of her. *Run faster!* She struggles to keep up, running down more flights of stairs, across fields, over fences, into city shelters or fast-moving cars. Her mother now moves behind Inanna, pushing her with gusts of ghostly air. She laughs with a shrieking growl. *Better run faster, baby girl! You know what they'll do to us if they catch us!* Flying ahead of Inanna in the next moment, her mother's long sleek hair appears to wave like an ebony flag.

"*Mother!*" Inanna cries. The longing in her voice for something she can't name scares the girl. She picks up speed but her mother teases and turns to run backwards, laughing in her face, her painted red lips garish, her white teeth gleaming. Her eyes are filled with joyful malice, her angled cheekbones are shadowed with spite. She hoots, *THIS man is better! He's richer, handsomer, braver! THIS one will save us, pay for us, help us escape the last one! Run FASTER, you little bitch! CATCH me! Or else you're on your own!!* Her mother's uncontrolled laughter is laced with booze or drugs, or both. She turns, her hand on an out-thrust hip. A ubiquitous cigarette hangs from parted, pouty lips and disdain drips from her like sweat.

Her beautiful, crazy-charismatic, outrageous and brilliant, obsessively dangerous mother. A woman born to profound lineages of Native medicine and sacred traditions, and taught the scholarship, languages and warrior ways of her Asian family, too. *She never respected any of it.* "She's a *Rebel Without a Cause*," one man had told Inanna. "It's the title of a book," he had sighed, this man who was much older than her

mother — the only man in her mother's long history of lovers that Inanna
had liked. His patience was as abundant as his library. "It's not a book
about your mother," he had said to Inanna, "but the title suits her."

Mother didn't show up one day, which became a weekend and
then whole weeks. The library man had sent Inanna to Gramps and Nonny
by train, consequently, which had led to a long stretch of salvation time
with her grandparents. Until inevitably her mother had shown up again,
demanding fealty, promising sobriety, threatening suicide if Inanna didn't
come back to her.

In this moment, Inanna feels afresh the pain of every new escape.
There never was a *someone else* who was better; there was always just
another man, crueler maybe, kinder perhaps, but not a savior. *Not ever.*
She sees again the countless towns and rugged backcountry hideouts. She
sees herself at five years old, at ten, at twelve, scene after scene of
dangerous street-play. She's with kids too big to confront and too scared
themselves to offer solace to a strange younger child. She hides from them
or joins them. Plays with matches and knives and sharp scissors. She's on
the streets at night, sneaking into and out of windows and through holes in
screen doors. She's fighting with fists or bricks or rocks or a kitchen
knife.

She can't remember having a friend. But she remembers needing
one. Over and over again, Inanna sees kids she no longer can name jeer at
her Salvation Army clothes and second-hand shoes. *Retard! Idiot! Freak!
Ya' gonna scalp me?* Her mother yelled at her when she came home with
yet another black eye. *Never trust anyone!* And she didn't. Not ever again.

The chorus of voices grows louder as the phantoms squeeze in.
Her mother, the bullying kids, the leering men, the ghouls and gargoyles
descend upon her all at once. Inanna's fear, rage and anxiety close in on
her at the same time. She can't scream the images away, she can't fight
back, and the circle of bullies closes in, bombarding her in a cacophony
louder than the boulders crashing against the Montana mountain. Her
dream legs feel like they're slogging through heavy mud. Fast as she is,
she can't run fast enough to get away. She slips as she tries, landing on
her back. The apparitions surround her fallen figure. She punches and
kicks at them. They dive at her like hungry vultures waiting for prey to
give up or die.

As Inanna struggles to release herself from the monsters, any
success or blessing that helped her survive those fearful years seems to be
out of reach. The voices are a deafening chorus, a raging maelstrom that
overwhelms the amazing grace of her grandparents' myriad teachings. She
commands herself to *face the fear*, but she feels more lost than ever before
in her life. She can't sense the floor of the cabin beneath her or see how
the light of the fireplace burns low. She doesn't sense Gramps and the
boys are worried for her as she screams to the ghosts of her past. She
doesn't know that their courage is focused on her.

"Gramps! Nonny!" she calls out. "You *promised* you'd always be here! *Help* me! *I am lost. Lost, lost!*" Exhausted, her will to fight drained, she rolls into a fetal position.

Whoosh! A flash of Halfling's rainbow-feathered wings sweeps across Inanna's vision. Curled into herself, the girl holds her breath. *Is it you?* she dares to ask. Inanna hears the click, hum of the ancient, mysterious language she understands but can't speak. *You are never alone. Remember.* The magnified prisms of Bird-Girl's iridescent eyes sparkle with cobalt and gold, appearing to see into her very soul. *Remember*, she hears. "Remember," she whispers.

Bird-Girl turns in profile, and the single iris in view now widens like the aperture of a camera lens. It draws all the light Inanna cannot see into its center. Her ghostly attackers lose their individual shape and contour; all the bodies, men, women, old and young, spin together like a fairground color whirl, blending into each other until they are one pin-point dot in the center of Halfling's eye.

And behind that color-filled eye, a new image emerges.

Inanna gasps aloud. *Labyrinth!*

Ice-blue and silver-white bridges, planks and tunnels self-construct before her field of vision in perfect multi-dimensional construction. It's as if an unseen hand builds in rapid motion a puzzle of complex cosmic formations, just as Inanna and the boys had witnessed on the mountain. The entire beautiful construction radiates with a pulsing heat of energy.

She rises to her knees. Her lungs fill with air. Her fear begins to subside as she releases into a faith she thought she'd lost.

Labyrinth!

The incalculably stunning construction fills the space all around Inanna, while the eye of Halfling continues to swirl.

She calls aloud, "I am *not* lost! *Not* alone! I *will not* be a victim of hatred! I am Inanna, daughter of the medicine traditions of my People, the Lakota and the Samurai. I carry forward the ancient lineage of the Shinto and the Horse Nation and the Wolf Pack. I am a granddaughter to the Rishi and the Giants who birthed them. I am cousin to the Halfling. I am *protected* in the past and in the present!"

The Labyrinth seems to call to her, tempting her to travel *deeper* into its mystery. Inanna wants to let go of all restrictions of the past, present and future and travel across all boundaries. She yearns to run into its mystical, endless caverns.

But even as she yearns to sprout wings and fly into its mystical depths, Bird Girl rises in front of her, wings unfurled. Halfling's spinning iris contracts into a dark, liquid pool of stillness.

Inanna hears an echoing command.

Not now. Do not ever enter the Labyrinth alone.

She suddenly awakens to present time. She rocks from the cabin's roller coaster ride and the rebellion of the mountain. She loses balance. Tumbles from her knees to her side. Without knowing where she is, without sensing those around her, she loses her emotional center. Only one word insinuates in her mind. *Alone!*

Above the punishing noise of the mountain, Leo and Conan hear Inanna scream.

"INANNA! We're *here!*" Leo calls out to her. "NO FEAR, Inanna!" Conan picks up Leo's insistence. "We're all here, right here! Gramps is here!"

The girl moans from her curled-up position on the floor.

Conan yells above the confusion of noise, "Inanna! *Listen!* It's *me*, Conan. Leo's here. And Gramps. We're *all* here, Montana, the cabin, together!" But her moans grow into cries and again she wails. Fear has its own ragged voice. *It cripples her*, he thinks. *Fools her. Like it did me.* Conan closes his eyes in humble acceptance of his need for the expression of a personal truth. *Like it does me.*

It was Inanna who had first handed him the small pouch with the blue powder. *Right-intention, right-action*, he repeats. His mind races, *but how do I know what's right, right NOW?*

Conan fixates on Gramps' gift of the eagle whistle. He holds his South Gate position and stretches out his long arm, feeling around on the splintered floor. He worries the chance of finding the whistle in the dusky-dark of the pummeled cabin is almost nil. He argues back his growing anxiety and screams, "No *fear!* Inanna, the right-intention is *NO FEAR!*"

He prays aloud to the spirit guides Gramps told them to rely upon. He prays to the venerable monk in the tattered robes of his childhood dream, and to the one in his Rishi life. He prays to every Merlin from any lifetime and he prays to his grandparents who loved him, "and anyone else," he says aloud, "out there," to please *help* him.

A feather-light breeze skims across the back of his right hand. A guiding current seems to pull his fingers in wider circular hunting ... until they close around the sacred object on the bundle.

He does then the only thing he can think to do. He brings the whistle to his lips and blows as if their lives depend on it.

The whistle releases its distinctive, piercing cry. Certain as Eagle itself, it slices through the destructive dissonance that rolls from the mountain's threatening destruction. Conan blows the whistle until his mouth is sore. He fills his lungs again and again until he hasn't any breath left. His soul rides the soaring vibration that connects lung to breath to whistle.

The eagle's call pierces the nightmare dark of the cabin, and rising through the gloom, a sublime span of Eagle Spirit appears before them. The chimera wings unfurl from strong, feathered human shoulders, and under them a fleet-footed spirit dancer twirls and dips and lifts into the shadowy air, heels together, toes turned out en pointe. *Eagle Dancer*, shapeshifting from human girl to majestic raptor, rises before them in a vision.

If Conan had to give himself up to this vibration, be a sacrifice to Eagle, he would, he thinks, in this moment, gladly and without fear relinquish his life.

"Don't stop!" Leo shouts to his brother. Conan continues to blow into the whistle, his energy increasing with the spirit's presence. As he whistles, he reaches out again, his free hand searching the black space between them in search of Inanna's fingers.

The Spirit Eagle's wings flutter and pulse, and as the current of air brushes his hand, he feels Inanna's cupped palm.

Conan exhales a long, heavy breath ... and he places the eagle whistle in Inanna's hand. He can't see her, but the feel of her alert touch encourages him. He senses her energy shift as the protective shell of her panic begins to release. He knows the frequencies of fear too well inside himself not to recognize the change.

Trembling, Inanna pulls the whistle to her dry lips, draws in a breath that stretches her lungs to capacity, and blows her entire being into the small instrument.

She shifts to a kneeling position, finding Conan's hand again and giving it a grateful press. Inanna blows the whistle without stopping, as Conan did. Its resplendent call sounds as if it circles the heavens.

The Spirit of Eagle, still fluttering in the shadows, responds with a proud and fearless flap of its wings before passing up into the shadows and vanishing.

"It worked!" Conan shouts. "*It worked! Eagle Dancer...* Inanna, it's your *True Self!*" His voice raspy from the effort of blowing the instrument, he yells, "Gramps, Leo, do you get it? Right-intention is *no fear!*"

The mountain's revolt plummets Conan forward again. He braces himself against the floor with both hands. The sharp jolts bounce him around but don't topple him. He hears a grunt from Leo, but the drumbeat continues. There is no way to see anyone clearly through the dark.

In the ensuing lull in the tumult, Conan wonders if the night's uproar is ever going to stop. It's more unsettling than any they had endured in California, longer and louder and stronger — and seemingly never-ending. The boy wonders for a moment if it's more than they can survive. But quickly he warns himself not to ask questions that could tease fear.

True Self, he hears his strongest inner voice speaking. He pulls himself up straight and grips the small pouch. He brings it to his chest, pressing it against the bag of the Crow Bonnet medicine man he wears around his neck. *It's the Eagle power that saved her.*

"Thank you," he hears Inanna whisper in the dark.

She wants to ask Conan, *how did you know to give me the whistle?* But in the jostle of the rocking cabin and her own emotions, she doesn't yet try to give voice to all her thoughts.

Despair had been calling her to its icy, unforgiving edge.

Only by facing fear are we fearless.
She's glad they can't see her tears in the dark.

Chapter 59
The Long Night: Leo, One Smooth Stone

Leo is brave by nature. The mountain's continuous and rolling uproar hasn't really scared him, exactly.

Yet, he admits in his mind and heart, *I can't anchor into my own solid center. This time, this quake — or whatever it is — is different.*

In the brief lulls when the mountain settles for even a few minutes, Leo tries to feel for the truths that always sustain him. But the reliable pieces seem to tumble with the worst crashes.

He can't help himself when it comes to worry. He's an expert at it. He may not actually know it, and certainly wouldn't claim it. He's the first child in a hyper-responsible family line of first children and caretakers, so worry for others wipes out any personal concern. His focus right now, in the midst of chaos, is on his brother, Inanna, and Gramps.

His heart had leapt when the eagle whistle rang out. He couldn't see all the motions or hear all the words between Conan and Inanna, or what went around their haphazard circle. But he's pretty sure Conan whistled first and then gave the instrument to Inanna. *Damn smart of him.* And when Inanna blew the Eagle call, it had been truly inspiring. *She makes that wild screech sound like music. I guess that's the gift of being Eagle Dancer.*

His way to deal with any challenge, even facing stress and fear, is to talks things out. He wants to ask, *what happened to you both? What fears did you face, and how did you overcome them? The Eagle energy saved Inanna, right? And the blue smoke helped Conan?*

Leo's questions, tossed and jumbled by the intermittent quakes and tumbles, bounce in and out of him, unanswered. He whispers aloud, "We're safe." Though he does not feel the truth of those words in his heart of hearts.

The young man takes his first measured, conscious inhale in an hour. He reaches out in the dark to find his brother's shoulder, nudging it to warn him that the conch fire is low.

Conan leans over and blows carefully. Tiny wisps of smoke float free. A small red glow nestles deeper into the shell. They all welcome a minute of semi-quiet grace.

Until a new jolt propels Leo forward. He lands hard on his elbow in the center of the circle. Struggling to regain balance, his fingers sear when his hand fumbles into the conch. He stifles a yell, catching himself before his stumble can snuff the fire out. He leans over and blows on the sage, unsure of his brother's whereabouts in the dark. "Stay alive, stay alive!" he whispers to the conch.

Resettling himself backward in his West Gate position, wringing his hand to cool the burn, the boy has an instinctive urge to feel for the stone tied to his hair. It's hanging loosely, and he catches it before it falls out of the curl at the back of his neck. He closes it inside his burned hand, glad for the security it seems to bring him.

Leo rejoins the song with Gramps. The old man has not ceased in his drumming and chanting since he first picked up the feathered stick. Leo sings for his own life and for the lives of Gramps, Inanna and Conan. Though he can't imagine that anyone, anywhere, could help them now. The mountain is too mighty in its revolt, too powerful and enraged to stop. Even if they could risk leaving the cabin they would be destroyed, crushed by the cascade of a collapsing mountain.

Stay strong, he tells himself. The power of the smooth stone in his hand encourages the fire of fortitude in his heart and cools the burn on his fingertips. Thin vapors of blue powder wind into the tendrils of smoke that escape from the sage.

Inanna blows her whistle once more. Leo breathes deeply, as if he can inhale the Eagle Spirit to help him ground his own faith and courage. *Go within! No fear!* He's surprised to find his hands are trembling. He squeezes the small stone harder.

Shimmering into form in the black air before him, an image of Crazy Horse rises.

Leo gasps. His first response to what he sees is that he wants it to *go away*. But it demands his attention. He wants to blot it out, to make it disappear. Because he knows in his core that this is an image of the warrior riding to his death.

The image insists to be known. It doesn't care about his fear. The death scene floats up as if it rises from the floorboards of the splintering cabin. Consciously, it's a story Leo barely knows. But when it forms itself so distinctly before him, there in the smoky cabin, his emotions guide his thoughts.

Betrayal. The truth insinuates itself into his mind, as if it's been in hiding there all along. *Crazy Horse was betrayed.* The truth rings in his ears so loudly, so clearly that Leo is sure it must have been the last thought of the warrior hero before he died. It's as if their spirits, heart and memories are connected, woven together across space-time.

Betrayed.

The picture expands and the last scenes of the Lakota Shirt Wearer's life come alive in the dark before his eyes. "*Lies! Liars!*" Leo screams aloud. People had lied. Trusted people on whom Crazy Horse had *relied* had betrayed him. Close advisors who had told him to trust them, had lied. *Betrayed!* The word chokes his dry throat. He tries to control his mind and temper. As the scene gains clarity and detail, Leo regains his voice and yells into the dark cabin, "Cowards!"

He sees the warrior dismount from the same horse he'd ridden into battle. But this isn't a battle day. This is a day made of lies and false promises. *This is Crazy Horse's death walk.*

Leo watches as Crazy Horse relinquishes his weapons, as promised. *What the fuck was he doing there?* But the boy knows the answer. The Lakota warrior had come in from the cold. He had turned in his weapons and agreed to end his relentless skirmishes against the growing strength of the U.S Army. *He didn't give up! He didn't surrender because he lost. He turned himself in for his people. Not to save himself. NEVER for himself.* His people had asked him to go to Fort Robinson in order to attempt a peaceful resolution for the sake of his tribe. They wanted peace. They needed food. Their children were sick.

He, who had led their greatest victories, stood alone.

The images that revolve around Leo now reverse time and history. He's whisked away from the lost world of the Lakota and into the further past. Through the dark of the cabin's interior, a montage forms, a rush of kaleidoscope shadows. The images shower down on Leo as the Crazy Horse scene gives way to new places, other pictures racing past him, encircling him, taunting him. Leo sees strange versions of himself, older, shorter or taller, heavier or leaner, as king and warrior, leader, peacemaker, and captain.

In the cabin, sitting on the floor of old railroad ties, he unconsciously draws his hand to his chest. He feels his legs, then slaps his cheek in an effort to bring himself back to the present. *I'm here. I'm Leo. In the cabin, in Montana, with Gramps, Inanna, Conan!*

But the chorus of past-life images begs him for help, for forgiveness, for an army to support them, for money to unite them! They demand new laws, rules, commandments that will bring death to their enemies! And salvation to them. They praise him, as if they can see Leo as he is today alongside the figure of authority he was then. They smile, they cheer false praise. They say how *good* and *brave* and *wise* he is.

And when he doesn't respond, they yell their hatred, they blame him for their woes. When he still doesn't respond, they call for his death.

Leo feels a visceral twist of rage and anguish at the scenes rising and falling before him. *Betrayal. I fear it. But why? When did this become such a fear?* Betrayal wasn't a word they had ever used, day-to-day, in his family. Yet — he knows fear. *I know how afraid I am of losing Conan. I know the horrible feelings of loss ... mom, dad, so many others.*

Struggling to maintain objectivity, trying to brace himself against the onslaught of this test of faith, Leo asks himself what he is most afraid of. *Failure*, he thinks. *If I fail, someone else suffers.* He knows this about himself. He's determined not to let people down. He's seen the result when he wasn't fast enough to ride to a rescue.

Flashes of memories from his current life skim by. He remembers small things first, little boy disappointments. Broken promises of people who said one thing and did another. Adults who didn't show up when he needed them. *Hurt feelings, nothing more!*

Then an image of himself, only eight years ago, pops up on his inner screen. A third-grade teacher makes Leo the butt of a joke to cover her own embarrassing screw-up. A middle school football coach blames him for a teammate's injury, clearly the result of adult mistakes. Leo sees these memories of finger-pointing and shrinks into himself. *Scapegoat. Everyone laughed. Or judged me. It sucked. But betrayal? Maybe, but crap like that happens all the time to kids.* He tries to slough it off.

Yet something bigger continues to nag him. A warning from Gramps that had underlined his sensei's teaching pops into his mind: *There's only one way to be fearless. Don't run away. Don't deny or hide it away. Turn and face the fear.* Karmic memory can poison the present and destroy the future, if it's locked away. *Find the key,* Sensei had said. *Unlock your own jail.*

Leo settles himself with deliberate breathing. *Am I so brave? Then, buck up!* He closes his eyes and blinks them open again suddenly, surprised by the nauseous chill that grips his guts. He tells himself it must be the intermittent undulation under the floorboards making him feel queasy.

Betrayal! He hears the word echoing, circling in the smoky air around him. He wonders for a half-heartbeat whose voice that could be. Before he can finish the thought, he staggers from a piercing pain in his abdomen. A sharp lance of anguish seems to rip a hole through his resilient spirit. Tears sting his eyes. He can't deny the truth again. *"Okay! I got it! I can face it!"*

Betrayal, the same voice speaks again. The spectral words are pronounced in slow, accented English. *The praise begets the blame that tilts the other side of the scale.*

Leo, clutching his stomach as the sharp pain subsides, wonders if the voice is warning him to expect a weighing of debts. *Praise and betrayal? Wherever, whenever someone's praised, honored, there's more chance of betrayal?* He's never really trusted praise. People say he's humble. But maybe he just knows, somewhere inside himself, that praise can so easily give rise to blame.

Before his eyes, the onslaught of moving diorama quickens, wrapping more tightly around him. The non-stop carousel of scenes and characters plays out relentlessly. *Face it!* he yells to himself. He cranes his neck and swivels his shoulders in three-sixty arcs to witness the moving collage of fearsome images.

Scenes on ancient battlefields, as warrior-king, as captain and commander, in private and public spaces, open and flit past him. He sees men whose lives were dedicated to leading others. They make stands as royal protectors and defenders, or as simple fathers and common men who took control in dangerous times. There are others, in ages and memories past Leo's understanding, who are scholars, scientists, judges and messengers. All these men defend truth and fight for justice. They protect who they can. And they are human. They win some. And lose some.

The overlapping images revolve around again to Crazy Horse's last day. *Betrayal.* The warrior hero had laid down his arms. He'd been imprisoned, though he had been promised peaceful negotiation. And then he was ambushed. *Betrayed. He had turned himself in — in order to serve his people. To bring peace and end the fighting. He was the one they praised. But punished.* In the exact moment the Shirt Wearer feels the blow of betrayal, Leo screams out loud. His anguished cry rips through the cabin's eerie space. The physical pain of it, sharp, shocking and raw, nearly shatters Leo's young heart.

He knew! Leo realizes. Crazy Horse had *known* he would be killed.

Crazy Horse, who was never injured in battle, whom no enemy could bring down, was fatally bayoneted after he allowed himself to be taken into "safe" custody. With his last breath, the warrior saw all of it: the brilliant past and the sad present of his people. He saw their tortured future in the tomorrow he would never see. *Failure. Betrayal. He knew he could never save them all.*

Leo rises to his knees as new scenes open to view, some the same as he had seen when Meera pressed her small palm to his Third Eye. He is captain of a fleet of naval sailing ships crashing through the high grey waves of a winter sea. He sees scenes of knights and warriors donning armor in the courtyard of a castle, sun glittering on its surrounding moat. Leo can hear the easy flap-slap of wind furling the military flags. He's dazzled and seduced by the glory of it.

But he's not fooled. He says to himself, *Service and failure. Praise and betrayal. They're all interwoven.* He strains his vocal chords to shout above the roar of the mountain: "Meera showed me the *same memories!* But now I see the back-story of leadership. The harshness and … the hardness of it!" Leo sways on his knees in an effort to keep his balance. *It's as if … as if there's always an undertow. Always a dragging down of the leader.* "Undertow," he whispers aloud. The word itself wants to pull him down. *Like the darkness under the river boulder.*

Leo is suddenly ferociously angry.

"He *tried!*" he shouts. "Just like I tried … to save them, help them, show them the way out! To lead, to tell the truth!" This man and that one too, this life and in another, in all of them, he fights for something bigger than himself. "Conan, Inanna! Gramps! Can you see this too?" He wants someone else to witness the *truth* of these lives.

Stay clear! He demands of himself, *no drama!* Leaders sometimes make terrible sacrifices. Aloud, he yells "You know they suffered! But they knew happiness, too! And satisfaction! Because they were true to their word!"

There is no response but the wind.

"Gramps, Inanna, Conan, *are you here?*"

Nothing.

Leo holds his throat and gulps for air. *Leaders. Warriors. Saviors. Everyday heroes. Not for glory. Never for himself, never for themselves.*

He tries again to touch the shadows inside the cabin that he hopes are Inanna and Conan. He's desperate for understanding, especially from Gramps. *We all say that, right? We try to live for something greater than ourselves! I feel it inside myself. All the way THROUGH myself.*

Leo wants desperately to understand what he sees in the stories unfolding around him. He wants to know who these men are, were. He wants to know what is *happening*. But he doesn't want to feel the suffering, the rawness of betrayal. The unfairness done to these men, and the pain of those left behind, is searing.

"*Meera!*" he calls out in the dark. *Is she here? Did she make these memories come alive?* Gasping, his head spinning as fast as the diorama of history spinning around him, he screams aloud, "I *understand.* I get it! *Meera! Please* make the pictures stop! You want me to face the betrayals of the past. But it's *too much* now! *Where are you?*"

No one answers.

The swirl of moving images slows. An undefined gathering, an army of smoky, topsy-turvy men of the past circles inside the first swirling series, with stories even harder to understand. The ghostly figures all seem to know him. *Face whatever fear this is,* he demands of himself. "Do you *know* me?" he asks aloud of the spinning images. "*Me,* Leo? Who I am today? Did I ever know you? Was it another time and place? I'm not *him* ... or if I was, I'm not now. Maybe you think I am the men in these stories. Or was. But, I'm NOT. Not commander or captain or warrior or leader." Inside his revolving mind, he asks himself, *but was I? Sometime ... longer ago than the history I know ... Was I HIM?*

The faces all turn to Leo. They are twisted in rage, in pouting disappointment. They hiss at him. He shrinks back, stunned. He yells aloud, "I didn't fail you. I didn't abandon you. I tried, I always *tried!*" The voices of blame are loud, threatening. But there are also haunting voices of weak praise, of tender, fake concern. All sound the same to him. They push and whine for help. They demand favors and insist they will take favors away. They whimper to him, *not ME, I loved you!* The voices and images blend together. The stress and pressure of leadership, of standing up for right-intention, for good over evil, pulses hot blood against his temples. *No way to do right for all.* Leo's heart pounds.

Leo doesn't feel the renewed buckling of the floorboards. He doesn't flinch at splintering windows. But he thrashes and near-drowns in an ocean of vile memory.

He sees a man that may be him, *so real, so familiar.* The man has been captured. He can't save an entire village of beloved family, children and old grandparents. Leo, as he is now, as he was then, watches the homes burn, sees the young being carried off. His mind doubles over itself with grief and anxiety. Without the boundaries of space-time, consumed by memory and story, he damns himself. In one life and then another he screams aloud, "*I failed! I lost them. My fault. I swore to protect them. I couldn't! I didn't!*"

The faces leer at him from opaque history: he's an African leader shackled in the bowels of a ship, captured while trying to protect his people from the slavers. In the next scene he's a young ship owner, seeking to help runaways; but pox-ridden dockworkers turn him into authorities to pay off their gambling debts.

Betrayed. Vicious cunning lingers on faces of magisterial judges, priests, ministers, who use laws of societies and religions bent on greed, power, or revenge to punish innocence. The man he was then fights them as a young lawyer, a writer, a soldier, a judge himself. In another life, he's a military commander who faces down other officers. They've used positions of authority to lie and cheat for their own gain. They trumped up charges. They sent him to prisons, or far countries where he couldn't escape. They lied to his followers. They burned his books. They raped his women and stole his children. They used him as an example and stopped his followers. They would, did, trade everything, anyone, for their greed.

Leo thrusts arms and legs out to hit and kick against enemies that press in from all sides. They feel, look, sound, so real. The raw and sharp deception is like a rusty handsaw scraping his heart-mind. He can't tell any longer who he is, Leo himself or these other men of the past. Bondages both of love and hate grapple with Leo's mind. He tears at his wrists that feel gripped in the bondage of tight ropes. He's sure he's tethered to a wall by iron cuffs; he feels his skin rendered, flesh to bone.

He has a vague notion that there's another reality. Another place and time he's supposed to be. But he's lost in complicated stories of the past. Gramps, Inanna and Conan are so far from his immediate consciousness now that he can't fathom their existence.

Ghostly images continue to fall and rise in front of him. They flicker, dilute into watery puddles or die out in bursts of gunfire, cannons and loud screams — only to flame alive again in new forms and memories. Leo tosses from side to side as the floor becomes liquid beneath him. He damns himself for trusting the distrustful. For believing in false prophets. *I put others at risk because I couldn't imagine evil. Couldn't understand the hatred and greed that boils in the hearts of men and women. Some I trusted with my life. With my love for them.* An avalanche of raw, toxic, self-blame matches the horrors of betrayal. The rage of emotion is as dangerous as the rock and earth slide outside. Confusion, anxiety, and a deep and abiding sadness fall over and around him. It's a deluge of self-blame and shame.

Betrayal. Leo's heart throbs with self-doubt. He can't find his reliable positivity, his True Self, which always chooses right-intention. His inner life, his pure spirit, is fueled by duty and responsibility. He knows that. Counts on it to guide him. He listens for its voice and message.

It's silent. Leo no longer knows himself.
KaaahhBOOOOM!

The mountain explodes again like a bomb is detonated below its crust. The previously sturdy ridge under the cabin begins to buckle. The small house rocks and the floor tilts. The four of them slide a foot right, then left, scrambling to stay in their honoring directions, east, west, north and south. Gramps plays on, his drum hardly missing a beat.

As fear whines in his ears and threatens his nerves, the fingers of Leo's right hand warm and tingle. *The stone!* Still clutched between tight knuckles, the small, ancient talisman radiates a golden heat. It glows through his fingers, lighting itself from within. It seems to Leo that the simple brown stone *sings* to him. Its words are, *Fear is the only enemy. The enemy within is the only enemy. No fear. No fear.*

Leo recognizes it as The Strong Heart song, Crazy Horse's song of the Last Encampment. The music breaks through his worry and self-blame and fear of failure. The song reminds him that Crazy Horse's personal beliefs and ideals were trampled, discarded, destroyed — but his spirit could not be killed. The memory of Crazy Horse, of all those who live and die for something greater than self, outlives the tragedy that brought their downfall. *He could have saved himself. He could have refused to go. But he didn't. Even then, facing death, knowing he'd been betrayed, Crazy Horse never lost his own right-intention.*

The rumbling mountain sends stronger and stronger tremors throughout the cabin. Leo falls sideways and slams his forehead against the floorboards. But he does not lose his grip on the small, warm stone glowing in his hand. *Here! Now! Fear is the enemy! Stay strong!*

Leo hears the lyrics of the song. Gramps is still singing, yet the words the boy recognizes come from deep within his soul's voice. And behind his tightly-closed eyes, he sees the men he was centuries ago fall into the hands of jailors, former allies, lovers and haters. He sees these men who hold his memories stand bravely, refuse blindfolds, *face* betrayers. And in that way redeem the truth of who they are.

Other voices, those who would destroy higher ethics, whine, "Don't stand up against them! Don't be a hero-fool-self-righteous-victim! Save yourself. Swallow their lies and go along. Be afraid for *yourself!* Save your own skin!"

"No!" Leo screams back at the cowards who play across his inner screen. "I will not be a coward! I will not be afraid."

The golden halo that pulses from the stone grows wider as its warmth deepens. The stone hums. It says, *refuse fear.* In the face of punishment and threat of death, *stand tall, face betrayers. Right-intention, right-action.*

Instead of scenes of betrayal and punishment, Leo sees the man he was in lifetime after lifetime, guardian-protector-caretaker, courageous leader of his people. These men that he was, or may have been, were understood, revered, loved. They stood for justice and equality. In small and big ways, whatever their lives brought them, they kept to the course of what Leo today believes is his true path. *Unity. Truth. Oneness.*

Leo stares down at his hand. He's amazed by the enduring golden warmth of the small stone. And inspired by the man who had first tied it in his own hair. Inspired by all the others, courageous and bold men and women who held steady to their tribe, their village, one another and the integrity of their beliefs.

Leo shouts into the darkness, "You can kill my body, betray me, but you can't take my mind! You can't destroy my heart! Strong hearts are never lost or betrayed. And true hearts never die!"

The cabin shudders, then stills for a fragile instant.

In the next moment, it slides off its moorings and plunges down the hill.

Chapter 60
Light Beings

"Stay in your directional positions!" Leo screams the command as Gramps continues his drumming. "All directions must be honored, for spirit protection!"

The rocks on the mountain shatter as the explosive force of boulders toppling from above turns the sliding earth into a dry-mud river. Downhill from the cabin, the torrent merges with the snake of water nearby, and the dual rivers become one catastrophic deluge. The house is a helpless skiff in a sea of earth, tossed in a rolling wave of groundswell that hurtles them towards the mudflow.

Leo can't see through the shuttered windows and closed door. But he feels the treacherous shift as surely as if the streams run through him. The cabin slides what feels like a hundred yards before skidding to a shuddering stop against a sheer wall of tumbled boulder. The little house shakes and trembles. The humans inside are aware of the rising torrent around them, sluicing and slushing with annihilating strength, surely trapping and burying them if the dirt continues to rise.

Gramps plays on. The Strong Heart song is unstoppable.

Leo hugs the splintered floor and belly crawls to find Conan and Inanna. They are both flung to the center of their disheveled circle. He grabs them by arms and shoulders, pulling them back into their directional positions before crawling back to his West Gate. He steels his courage, sits up crossed-legged in the vulnerable cabin, and directs himself to throw off any residual fear of old betrayals and new terrors, and stay true to this moment.

A cobalt comet flies out of the dark towards him, radiating in wide shimmering rings and throwing off sparks of blue light.

Leo sees at once what The Three must do. "The *link!*" he shouts to Conan and Inanna, while Gramps continues his drum song. "*We need to link our minds!*" Feeling for his medicine pouch, he tucks the small, warm stone securely into the bag around his neck. He then reaches out his hands to the others. The Three spread their arms, swallowing their anxiety over the cabin and the growing deluge of dirt surrounding it, trying to touch fingers. They can't reach.

Until the electrified connection comes to life, flowing from the comet hovering in the air above the conch embers and linking their outstretched hands with the radiant blue light. Three minds speak to one another as if they are one shared consciousness. And then the cobalt expands, embracing their four-person circle, even as the river of mud rises around the feeble walls of the cabin.

Gramps maintains his song as the blue light grows. The comet hovers above them in the center of their circle, emanating its energy into their very souls. Leo looks up into the densest portion of the comet and focuses his heart-mind into the nucleus of the Light. Without conscious direction, he wills the blue bolt to circle inward even as it stretches outward. It folds back to close the circle in a symbol of infinity that dances itself into a giant mobius, glowing in a never-ending cross of streaming Light.

Leo, Conan, Inanna and Gramps visualize themselves in the center of the infinity symbol where the endless loop intersects. The mobius picks up speed, swirling and twisting and curling without cessation. It rises through the roof of the fragile cabin and flings itself up and out into the dark sky. The four humans seated on the floorboards in their directional positions of North, South, East and West raise their heads up as one and gaze into the starless night. The silver-blue threads of Light illuminate the Universe itself.

The cobalt sings its own universal hum. The sound is a sonorous roll of *om*, the widest, deepest, breath of the Universe. It's the sound of creation. It's the music of Source, the exhale that split the Black Velvet.

Awe and wonder.

In the sky above them, images of their grandmothers, great aunts and others who sang and taught and prayed with them circle The Three. The women have beads woven into their long and loose hair, they are softly laughing, their eyes radiate with beatitude. And then another circle grows within those pictures; the kids can see beloved grandfathers, uncles, and great grandfathers — even ancestors met previously only in vintage photograph albums. Images of cousins and friends who had passed too early come into view, standing together in circles within circles. Serene or serious, gentle or mighty, every one of them glows with love and approbation.

Leo whispers into their linked minds, *True hearts never die.* Conan and Inanna try to repeat his mantra, but the emotion of the moment renders them wordless.

Dozens more of those who've passed from the earthly realm begins to materialize. Old medicine men and fine braves of many nations awaken from legends. Rishi teachers, men and women, come forward into the circles. A tight, saffron-robed cluster of Tibetan monks floats forward and bows, and the resonance of their deep voices reverberates to bring Daoist healers, Buddhist monks and nuns. On a high precipice an Imam's luminous voice calls the entire Universe to prayer. Priestesses, holy women lost to memory slip through the crowd in long silver-white, diaphanous gowns. They bow to The Three and take their place among lamas, shamans and healers of forgotten generations.

Every nation of believers in love, right-action, and integrity who are themselves the brothers and sisters of the Source, Great Spirit, the Divine order, is represented.

Warrior leaders and wise queens smile and bow heads to one another and to all. Merlins stand tall among white witches. Amazon women rise next to and above kings and knights. Multiple circles form within one another and spread farther into distant multi-colored and iridescent spiral rainbows. They are ageless, endless, unbent by time. Their faces are eager and warm as they bow to honor the children of the prophecies. They pour love and memory, healing and protection into the past, present and future of The Three.

Innately, the children know they are being asked and inspired to Remember. And to believe in a future they cannot yet know.

The spirit choir circles closer, singing and drumming and chanting as they wrap the four humans huddled together into their center. The vibration of their collected wisdom weaves into one frequency. The languages of the spirit choir must have been different when they were in earthly lives, and their traditions, their cultures and beliefs too, were lived in their own time and place; yet, in this moment of coming together, the hum of their unified purpose is the music of One.

At the very center point where the spirit circle is complete, centered over Gramps, The Three see a golden orb emerge through the cobalt essence of the vibration. The gold pulses as the gathered ancestors and beloveds seem to make way for the growing energy, circling out and around until, with a unified breath, the Light Beings step forward.

With a universal inhale, all those who witness the emergence of these Beings who embody the very vibration of Oneness recognize they are seeing that most rare of all miracles, the physical manifestation of pure Light.

The Light Beings are clothed in an indefinable spectrum of scarlet, purple, lavender luminosity. Their features have no corporeal density or specific form, their limbs are pure extensions of incandescence.

They are unalloyed, illuminated, stunning beauty.

The Beings expand themselves, growing to infinite height. A vast feeling of palpable protection radiates from their glow, embracing all it touches. They shine in a united consciousness, spreading their arms around the entire collection of spirits.

Their forms merge into one continuous spinning and dancing Light. The cabin is the eye of a vortex, a helix of golden, cobalt, silver and white threads of energy. The small home, torn ragged, pummeled and pounded, barely held together by its loosened beams as the earth comes up around it, is held safe inside the halo of Light.

And as the mountain thunders its revolution of rock and dirt, and mud mounts from the furious, roiled river, and ash falls from the eruption of cracked earth, the cabin begins to moan. Its wood screams, nails pop, windows crack and shatter while the maelstrom roars around its fragile walls.

At the point of the embattled cabin's sure physical destruction, a cobalt comet explodes above them, behind the Light Beings. From its spark, a shining Golden Thread spins out and ropes itself around the corners of the home that holds the four humans. Flashes of gold light braid together, winding and encompassing the entire tenuous structure.

As the Light Beings cover them in luminosity and the Spirits sing, and as Gramps plays on, the Golden Thread lifts the cabin off its perilous mooring.

The old house rises straight up, free from any roots of the mountain's ownership. The massive amount of dirt and debris that had near-buried it falls away, showering the ground below. The cabin holds its position in the air, not swaying with wind or resisting the Thread. It's unburdened of any contact with the mountain's turbulent landscape.

The human inhabitants, connected by the cobalt current, close their eyes as one.

Below the cabin, the mountain's destruction begins to slow. It breathes a final heave, as if disgruntled that the humble domicile, a target of its fury, is unperturbed. The earth settles, redistributes its weight, and falls silent.

At the same moment, the celestial Spirits circle and swirl with increasing rapidity until they become one stream of energy that whirls itself into the center of the comet from which the Golden Thread is spinning. The four — Gramps, Leo, Conan and Inanna — open their eyes as they feel the little home float down again to land in its original place, atop the same spot that Gramps and Nonny had chosen to build it decades ago. Even amidst the newly tumbled terrain, the cabin lands softly, gently, onto the redistributed ground.

The interior of the cabin tilts slightly as it lands on the debris; it slides a foot but rebalances itself. Into the ensuing silence an earthly sigh of culmination is palpable. The mountain and the cabin are at peace again for this miraculous moment.

The Golden Thread whips itself away from the outside walls of the little home. It flies in through its cracks and its flue, whips through and around the small room, casting a Light so bright it's almost blinding. Leo, Inanna, Gramps and Conan are aglow. And then it spirals once more, spinning at lightning speed until it emits an ear-popping roar, compresses back to one fist-sized ball — and shoots through the roof like the comet that announced it and disappears into the night sky.

The cabin is dark again. Gramps' drum has finally stilled. The light from the fireplace is low, with embers still burning only faintly. The sage is miraculously still wafting its smoke. Conan, Leo and Inanna's ears are ringing, they are bruised from the fights with their fears, their eyes are strained and their throats are dry from flying dust. But they manage to sit up.

The cobalt connecting The Three becomes one with the elements, humming with their vibrations until it blinks itself out.

PART IV

Chapter 61
Medicine Dreams

Exhausted beyond all ability to analyze the miracles they have witnessed, The Three fall into an unconscious sleep. For hours, they slumber like newborns, sacked out on the ravaged floor of the little cabin, oblivious to each other in the interim.

Towards the quiet of the dim-sky dawn, Conan tumbles into a medicine dream. It pulls him into its rhythm. It's as if the dream has been there, in the folds and curtains of space-time, telling its story all of Conan's life. Waiting for him to Remember.

He follows a message he hears in Gramps' rumbling voice, deep within him. *Wolf brother, you dream this dream for us all.* In his sleep, Conan sees the back of his own head as he faces Gramps. The old man is speaking in a low murmur of indistinguishable Lakota. Conan nods to Gramps. Although he doesn't understand the medicine man's specific words, he's sure of the intent.

The medicine man wants this vision, he seems to tell Conan. And the boy, beginning to realize his True Self, will dream it for him.

*

On the last morning of the Sun Dance, in a year of the great Sioux Nation migration to the plains, long before the appearance of horses among the tribe, the apprentice wakes in the darkest pre-dawn and prepares the medicine man's sacred instruments. The boy doesn't untie the bundle that contains the personal power elements gathered over many years by his teacher and other teachers before him, all the way back to the First Teacher beyond known time. To open the bundle would dishonor the man and his medicine.

The boy doesn't prepare breakfast because for the fifth day the holy man will fast. Instead, the apprentice heats water over the fire he's built, and brews a thick tea of herbs. The aromatic smells tingle his nostrils and lungs.

When he goes to wake his mentor, he finds the medicine man in silent prayer, wisps of smoke from sage and pipe circling the air. The apprentice tilts his head in respect, then retreats, as silent as the smoke.

The boy walks slowly, deliberately, reverently, to the center of the circle where the Sun Dance Tree stands in the shadow of the Black Hills. He ties a piece of red-dyed deer hide to the tree. He places his forehead to the bark and prays for the strength to serve. He prays, too, for his teacher's life — more fervently than he does his own. He asks Great Spirit for wisdom and courage. He asks to be worthy enough to grow into a medicine man himself, one who serves the people as his teacher does.

He backs up and bows to the tree. Then sits and waits.

This very young boy is serious, resolute beyond his few years. Twin ebony braids hang to his shoulders on either side of his thin face with its aquiline nose and high cheekbones.

He listens to the first rustle of prairie grass bending under the dew of pending dawn. He smiles at the mew of a distant bobcat cub. He smells a waft of sage as someone nudges its sparks to life, somewhere in the camp.

At one second before dawn, before the new day rises over the promontories of the Black Hills, a cobalt blue light explodes across the horizon. It spreads like seven arrows piercing the sky in every direction.

"Aho," the boy says under his breath. He's startled at the sight. As quickly as the cobalt light appears, it disappears. The sun crests the mountains and drums call the people to the Sun Dance circle.

The camp awakens at the first arresting words of the medicine man's song. For hours the boy watches the man sacrifice for their people, circling the Sun Dance Tree. At the heat of midday, and for hours after on this cruel, rainless and dry summer, the old man pulls the buffalo skulls behind him. They're tied to him through incisions cut into his leathery skin slicing right through to the muscles and ligaments of the man's back and shoulders. The gashes bleed for a time, then scab over and are cut afresh each day. Rawhide tethers, bloody and grimy from use, are tied to the very sinew of the man's body. And the skulls to the ends of the cords.

The apprentice counts the skulls as the day progresses. One at first, at dawn; as many as five by the end of the day. He helps tie them on his teacher. Some are as wide as a foot across. He's had to teach himself not to react, not to cry or worry for the man he reveres.

Throughout the day, the people weep and pray, dance and sing to the rhythm of the kettledrum. Its stretched buffalo hide is so large it takes three men to beat it in unison, four to carry the drum home each night.

Other men tie their prayers to the tree. They are the year's Sun Dancers. They pray for their families. For an end to suffering. For an abundance of animals to hunt and babies to be born. They pray for their sick and dying. And for courage in battle and on the hunt.

The boy's eyes never leave the silent stoicism carved into his teacher's face. Without complaint, the man makes a sacrifice of himself worthy enough for the Spirit world to answer the prayers of his people. He suffers that others be spared.

The viciously hot afternoon wears the camp down. Dancers fall, braves and chiefs struggle to keep their feet. As dusk whispers along the edges of day, a hot whining wind begins to rise. A white dust devil starts a dangerous spin at the Western Gate of the Thunder Beings.

With frightening rapidity, the dust devil gathers power. In the blink of an eye, it grows into a small white whirlwind. The swirling force, unmoved by human fear, unconcerned with human suffering, builds into a tornado. The storm's roaring voice deafens the boy. He screams into the gust as it moves with quick determination towards the Sun Dance circle. The tornado ignores the apprentice's prayer.

The tribe turns to run, as one. They dive to the ground and cling to rocks, covering their heads. The wind blows them left and right, showering them with leaves and tree limbs. The young and strong protect the small and weak. Children hide under the skirts of mothers and grandmothers who run to secure what isn't blown asunder. A few people stumble down the steep gully and fall into the cold stream, clinging to large boulders that resist the wind.

The boy hears the cries and screams of his people. He knows these are the voices of fear. Many risk losing the courage that defines their lives.

But, not the medicine man.

The teacher bends lower and his steps are slower as he circles the Sun Dance Tree. He's determined to finish the number of rounds that he committed to walk, "for the people."

Drummers refuse to leave him. They beat louder, their arms lifted high above their heads, their hands descending with as much power as the spirits allow them. They don't fear the tornado even as it whips sand, pebbles, rocks and tree limbs into itself. The faithful see and hear the whirlwind as a message. Not a good or bad omen, but only as nature's harsh song of change and transformation.

The whirling wind gathers speed. It whips the hide-covered tipis, pulling out poles, scattering the tools of food making, and spilling precious water. Healers have their baskets and bowls ripped from their hands as the wind's velocity sprays the collected herbs into clouds of colorful sprinkles. The bright flags of yellow, white, black and red that mark the four directions are torn from their poles, along with the Sun Dance Tree prayer ribbons, to be consumed by the gathering force.

Nothing can withstand the tornado. Nothing can keep it from its designated path.

By the time the whirlwind reaches the Sun Dance circle, its power is ferociously destructive and unrelenting.

The boy flattens his thin body to the ground. In the center of the circle one drummer falls, swept away by the wind. The other two are battered and struggle to stay close to the drum. They, too, are soon lifted and thrown from the circle like rag dolls. Only five dancers of the dozens who committed to be here today remain. They are big men, warriors all, and strong enough to turn their backs to the gale. They tether themselves to the Sacred Tree, kneeling to face its grey bark. One by one they fall to their faces, wrapped shoulder and hip to one another.

The boy clings to the ground. In torturous, inch-by-inch movements, he crawls on his belly toward his teacher, worming his way forward. The drum beats once, twice to challenge the wind. But the howl snuffs it out.

The boy doesn't give up. His belly is raw from sharp sands that whip around, above and under him. He coughs as dust cracks his throat. He bleeds as his fingernails rip the ground. He doesn't feel the pain. The apprentice barely makes out the shadowy figure of his mentor in the circle ahead. But, inch by hard-won inch, he continues his crawl towards the teacher.

A black shawl of chilling wind descends and tightens around the curling tornado. The black wind circles left, as the white spinning wind twists right. The tornado feeds off the competing energy and grows larger still.

The medicine man's hair falls loose from his braids and whips his craggy face. His eagle feathers loosen and fall victim to the ferocious gulps of white whirlwind. Yet he abides the beating of the tornado. His steps are excruciatingly slow. He is dogged, determined to complete his prayer. With his back bent and his concentrated weight as low to the ground as possible, he pushes relentlessly into the wind.

The roar of storm responds with a surge of savagery, and the old teacher is forced to drop to a crawl. Still he refuses to surrender to the roiling sky. The white whirlwind roars its fury and surrounds the aged medicine man, enveloping him completely until he becomes the eye itself.

The boy looks on helplessly from under the protective crook of his arm as the medicine man is sucked from his crawling position onto his wobbly knees. In the next moment, the most violent spirits of the air pull the medicine man to his feet. His buffalo skulls lash his body, his skin is ripped to the bone from the whirling elements.

Seemingly undaunted, the teacher uses all his remaining strength to throw his head back and turn his face to the heavens, shaking arms outstretched in a benediction.

It's his last prayer. The man the boy loves gives up his life and spirit to the whirlwind.

The boy, an already wise child who has seen many unexplainable things in the company of a man who calls in the spirits, cries aloud. He watches as the aged mentor's soul flies from his body. Out of the medicine man's chest, seven arrows of cobalt blue pierce the spinning sky, followed by a Golden Thread that whips from the heart of the beloved teacher towards the center of the cosmos. He becomes one with sky and wind.

His broken body, no longer needed by his flying spirit, drops, lifeless, to the ground.

In the apprentice's young mind, he hears, no fear. In his heart he hears, no regret. In his teacher's voice, a refrain repeats: For the people, that they not suffer. For the people, that the traditions survive.

These are the last words of his teacher that the apprentice, who will grow to be a medicine man himself, hears before he falls into a heavy sleep of many days.

And dreams himself to be a white whirlwind.

Chapter 62
Courage

Huddled on the splintered floor of the battered cabin, for a few precious hours, The Three find rest from their physical and spiritual turmoil.

In each individual consciousness, the Golden Thread weaves itself alongside rivers of cobalt and silver. In each dreamscape, they revolve unanswerable questions of awe and wonder.

Conan is vaguely aware of a buzzing throughout the frayed wire of his body's electrical system as he sleeps. The tingles and shivers eventually awaken him. He doesn't try to sit up. He opens heavy-lidded eyes and peers through the dim morning light falling through the cracks of the cabin at his hands, expecting them to be scratched and bleeding. He realizes he had a dream that he was clinging to earth and assaulted by flying rocks and dirt. He rolls over onto his back and stares at the rickety ceiling, trembling slightly, before his mind relaxes and he falls asleep again.

He dreams of a boy and his teacher, a medicine man of centuries ago, stirring a pot of healing herbs over an open fire. *Cobalt blue. Golden Thread. Ceremony.* The words spin in his unconscious. Conan wants to touch the magic itself. He longs, as he has since he can recall first cognition, to stand, dance and sing in the ceremonies.

A true medicine man knows the mystical, the spirit world, is never his. It can't be owned. It belongs to Source, to the same power that burst the stars into existence. The pursuit of its ownership, even for powerful seers and healers, is foolish seduction. That knowledge settles into the buzzing of Conan's sleeping white noise.

Leo rolls over onto his side, trying to find a more comfortable position on the floor. He dreams of fire ants, of hot and painful bites, of hissing insects disappearing in spinning winds. He pulls his blanket over his head. Inside the comfort, he watches a dance of ancestral images and Beings made of pure Light dazzle his inner screen. He feels the warmth of the smooth brown stone hum to him from his medicine pouch. Its power comforts and calms him.

Inanna moans as she starts to waken. She gingerly fingers her eyes, rubbing the grit embedded in her lashes. She knows she should get up and rinse her face but can't make herself move. Instead, she tugs the old quilt to her shoulders and squints at the shrouded daylight emerging through the loose beams of the house, wondering if the Sun has found a place to appear.

She feels for her feather, tied in the tangles of her hair, and unties it. Eyes still half closed, she finds Conan's and Leo's feathers close to where they lie. She tucks them next to their sleeping heads.

A mixed tape of crisis and miracle, fear and fearlessness rolls inside her mind. She questions all they've seen since yesterday's laser pierced the sky at dawn. In her mind, she hears a distant eagle whistle. But her bones feel heavy with fatigue, and she allows herself to curl up in the blanket again for long minutes more.

Until Bird-Girl appears, her prism eyes glittering, their crystalline centers reflecting amethyst, rose and gold. The iridescent shafts of refracted light pierce the steely dawn. Inanna smiles in her sleep. She wants to reach out and touch Halfling, but instead the muse comes closer to Inanna, and the sharp message penetrates her heart-mind. *Your grandfather, Inanna. Go to your grandfather! Go. Now!*

Inanna jumps straight up on wobbly legs. She feels dizzy, confused, light-headed. Nausea races from her stomach to her throat. Suddenly desperate, she searches around her for Gramps. He is no longer in front of the bedroom door in his North Gate position. Her heart skips a beat before she sees him lying near the hearth. Inanna realizes he must have been thrown out of the circle when the house settled back onto the ground. The old man's arms and legs appear to be twisted at odd angles, but the buffalo-skin drum is still tightly held under one arm. His head is half-covered in ash from the fireplace.

Inanna steps over the sleeping boys to gently touch his shoulder. He doesn't respond.

"*Gramps!*" Her voice, tight with panic, is a muffled scream.

Both boys jar awake. Leo jumps to her side. Inanna kneels, trembling, afraid to check for his breathing. Shock reddens her eyes as she looks to Leo for help.

The boy moves her gently aside. He pulls back the old man's jacket and shirt to press his ear closely to Gramps' thin chest.

Nothing.

He peels back Gramps' shirtsleeve and searches for a pulse with both his hands.

Nothing.

He feels at the medicine man's neck for the carotid artery.

Conan, now fully awake, crawls to Leo and crouches beside him. He glances over at Inanna's tense face. Reaches out to squeeze her hand.

Carefully keeping one hand on Gramps' neck, Leo sits back on his heels. "Okay," he breathes. "Got a pulse." His eyes shift to Inanna. "It's weak, but there. Conan, get a pillow off the bed. Inanna, some water for him to drink, and a washcloth or towel of some kind. We need to get the dust and junk off of him, so he can breathe."

Conan notices that he's kept hold of Inanna's hand. He lets it go now, slightly embarrassed. She doesn't notice. Her attention is riveted on her grandfather. Together, they listen to the soft catches, the bare whispers of Gramps' exhales.

Too weak, Leo thinks but doesn't say. Conan feels for any broken ribs, following Leo's instruction. In spite of his purposefully light

touch, a tiny whimper escapes from Gramps. It sends shivers of relief —
and worry - through The Three.

Leo murmurs, "Badly bruised ribs, at least one broken." He looks
up at the others. "Let's move him when we've gotten some water in him."

Leo cradles Gramps' head as he would a newborn baby's, with
tender firmness. Conan finds the covered jugs of water in their secure
cabinet near the sink. They were spared from the tumble of the cabin, to
his relief; he says a silent prayer of thanks for their foresight on that count,
anyway, and he brings a chipped cup to Gramps.

Inanna shakes her head. "Can't drink." Conan finds a teaspoon in
the clutter of dishes and cutlery, and hands it to Leo, who purses the
man's cracked dry lips and dribbles water into his mouth. The kids'
anxious hearts pound in unison, willing life into Gramps' weak body.

With the emerging dawn light, dim as it is, they can now see the
grey dust and mountain dirt that must have flown in from cracks in the
cabin's walls, settling on everything and everyone in the small, jumbled
space. The normally rich reds and browns of Indian artifacts hanging on
walls or clustered on the floor are subdued under the debris left by the
mountain's vomiting.

Leo blows or wipes off as much dust and grime from Gramps
and himself as he is able to clean, with Inanna's help. He tries not to
disturb the old man as he again attempts to spoon water into his mouth,
with Conan shifting position to cradle Gramps' head. With tender strokes,
Inanna washes the ashes from Gramps' cheeks. Inanna's tears wash her
own gritty eyes.

At length, Gramps coughs. The water bubbles up in drops that
linger on his lips. He opens one eye a mere slit, and croaks, "… Tryin' to
drown me?"

The kids catch their breath, then laugh in an exhale of long,
whistling relief.

Leo asks him whether he wants more water. Gramps nods. The
boys spoon a few additional drips from the cracked cup into his mouth.
Inanna leans over and kisses his forehead. She's alarmed by how cold his
brow is. She kisses him again, caressing his head, straightening his dusty
braids, and speaking her prayers of healing in Lakota.

Conan wraps another blanket around the medicine man, and Leo
asks him if he might be able to sit up. The old man nods a faint reply.

Slowly, gingerly, the boys wrap their arms around Gramps, Leo
taking the head and Conan taking the feet. But as they lift him, the old
man grimaces and emits a faint, hollow moan. Alarmed, Leo and Conan
look at each other. With a wordless signal, the boys ease him back down
onto the blankets.

Leo whispers to Gramps, "It's your shoulder or arm, right?" He's
seen this before in rescues. Busted ribs can cause extreme pain, a sharp
jabbing sear when movement occurs. He knows Gramps is so stoic that he
would only cry out if something was broken. "We have to get you out of a

prone position, to clear your lungs." Leo is gentle, confident, reassuring. "Have to make sure there's no chance of a cough developing from dust or whatever blew in last night." The boy considers his options. "I'm going to lift your shoulders, elevate your chest some, but keep you here on the floor … okay?"

Gramps attempts a smile in response.

Leo lowers his eyes to gather strength and give the old man a breather before they try again to lift him. With help from the blankets wedged under his shoulders, they get his chest up. His breathing remains shallow, but they can all tell it's more even and steady in a raised position.

Leo counts Gramps' inhales and exhales until he's satisfied. "We'll get you into bed as soon as you're stronger, Gramps."

The old warrior nods, *yes*. His physical energy is at its lowest ebb. Yet his spiritual center holds. He focuses on the hum of vibration that circles through The Three and back to him. *They're Remembering*, he assures himself in-between small spasms that filter through his lungs and ligaments. No self-pity can claim him. But he worries the teachings, what he's been tasked by so many to impart, will be lost if his health fails. *They must survive. Teachings must survive.*

Gramps closes his eyes and silently prays for guidance.

When he opens them an hour later, he realizes he had fallen asleep – and that he was moved to the bed in the meantime. He is grateful that the soft blankets of the bed he'd shared with his wife for decades had welcomed his tired old bones.

Inanna and Conan have gathered up the fireplace logs that had rolled around the room. They've taken down the grate and renewed the fire in the hearth. Conan drags the cauldron from its corner and sets the water to boil. He asks whether he should remove the seven rocks they'd placed in the hearth last night.

Inanna considers this for a moment, then shakes her head, *No*, as she adds pungent herbs to the pot for a poultice, muttering Nonny's directions to herself. The boy joins in the stirring and asks specific questions about twigs and pieces of leaves and roots she's using.

"Just so you know, I see anything crawl or wag a tail, I'm outta here!" he says with utter seriousness.

Gramps can hear their exchange from where he lies in the bedroom. He smiles to himself, relieved to know the children are getting on with the important matters of their survival. And he approves their decision to let the Spirit Rocks remain in their protected position. *The grandfather stones came to this home with me*, he thinks, *and they will leave with me*. He drops back into a doze.

Leo reorders the shambolic cabin. He takes ropes off tethered furniture, rights the table, hammers back any legs that have loosened. He removes nails that were torn from shutters by the onslaught of the mountain. He takes the planks from the sink top and washes the dirty dishes they had piled there the night before. He shakes off the broom, then sweeps up a pile of two-inch thick debris.

But when he opens the cabin door to sweep the collected grime outside, two of the hinges tear away as the pile of rocks and dirt that had settled against the door upon the cabin's landing shudders into the room. The torn door slams into Leo before he can try to shove it closed again.

Conan and Inanna rush to help him. The boys muscle the door in place while Inanna moves to sweep, brush and heave the rubble into a corner. Conan and Inanna then hold the door shut so Leo can screw in the hinges, using Conan's trusty Leatherman tool kit. Done, the kids step back, wiping their brows. They laugh at the surprise, the shock of it – and how handy that damned Leatherman kit can be when they least expect to need it.

Gramps awakens from his doze, hearing their laughter. "Leo," he whispers through parched lips.

Leo and Inanna run to the bedroom as Conan fills another cup from the urn. Before allowing Gramps to speak, Leo insists that the old man sip more water. The effort exhausts but quenches him. With a gravelly voice, he directs The Three to shift the rocks outside the cabin.

"Climb out bedroom window …" He pauses, sucking in a small breath. "… move rocks off porch, away from door … before more fall … And remember ants. Can't know if gone for sure. Have to keep enemies out." He tries to wave them off then, but winces when he moves his arm.

"Not before I look at that shoulder," Leo insists.

The boys ease Gramps to a better sitting position, and immediately notice his right arm hangs useless. They nod tightly to each other before Leo works his hands gently down Gramps' shoulder and upper arm.

"Broken," Leo murmurs. He's able to control his expressive face so as not to show concern, but he can see Gramps already knows.

"Listen, Leo," Gramps' voice is subdued, slow, but unafraid. "Not going skiing or bear wrestlin' any time soon. Maybe it's broken. But could also be just my old rotator cuff injury, which hurts like hell. Just lift my shoulder best you can and wrap it front to back. Put in sling. Inanna knows where bandages are. Enough to push these bones into … useable shape."

Leo eyes him. The boy wonders if the old man can handle the pain of wrapping the shoulder. He doesn't like the odds. Pain weakens everyone, and at Gramps' age, he thinks, *it might kill him.*

Chapter 63
The Long Trail of Fear

Gramps' gaze remains steady as Leo peels back as much of the old man's shirt as he can without disturbing the shoulder. The boy feels the bruise, taking an extra minute to rehearse in his mind the steps of resetting a dislocation. Leo instructs Gramps, "Look straight forward."

In the early days of the increasing natural disasters, Leo had trained and worked with medics. He'd helped put shoulders back into sockets and had learned to wrap them. But Gramps' shoulder is more injured than in the boy's previous experience; it's twisted forward and down.

"You guys hold him here, and here," Leo directs to Conan and Inanna, indicating positions of support. To Gramps, he warns, "This'll hurt some."

The medicine man doesn't change his focus from Leo's eyes. "Okay," he says. "Go ahead."

Leo takes a deep breath and lifts Gramps' shoulder. He quickly slides it up towards the chest and pops it back into place. Gramps' eyes close; tears appear at the corners. His chin falls forward. He takes several long moments before opening his watery eyes and seeking Leo's.

"Good ... job," he whispers.

The boys ease him into a more comfortable position.

Inanna runs to the fireplace. She returns with the bandages and foul-smelling poultice. It's turned a hot, noxious, greenish brown. She squeezes water from the herbs; steam rises from her hands as she packs the herbs on the right side of Gramps' chest and layers the poultice over his shoulder, crooning to him in Lakota.

She and Leo switch positions without speaking. As if they've done this together for years, they work in partnership. Inanna holds first the herb mixture in place, and then assists Leo in layering the gauze and cleaned bandages. Finally, Inanna tears some old sheets into a sling, measuring and propping Gramps' shoulder and arm until she's satisfied.

No one fools himself or herself. Gramps' body is amazingly strong for his age, and limber too, but his bones are brittle, the ligaments and tendons fragile.

When the kids had first arrived, the medicine man had said he would have three days to teach them. They don't know why he doesn't have more time. But they know there are less than two full days left. And even if he were to survive this injury, how could they leave him like this? How could he heal fast enough to care for himself up here on this mountain?

For his part, Gramps knows what stresses their hearts. Nothing is lost on him. He slips in and out of consciousness, praying silently, asking the spirit world for guidance.

The kids shift to the main room, moving quietly so as not to disturb the old man. Inanna busies herself with finding some food, keeping herself distracted from her anxiety over Gramps. The contents of the cupboard are completely overturned, but the girl picks through the mess to find a large, dented tin of oatmeal. Checking first to make sure it hasn't gone rancid or been a magnet for weevils, she digs out an old Coleman stove. The Bunsen burners still have their lids intact; she's satisfied. She sets water on to boil next to the porridge.

While the cereal cooks, the boys check all the windows to determine which one will make the best exit route for the time being. Leo soon finds that Gramps is right; the bedroom window will be the easiest access. He removes the nailed shutters, and the boys squeeze themselves out onto what's left of the porch.

Inanna quietly follows to the window and looks out after them. She can see that the chasm where the ants had been destroyed has doubled in width since the mountain's quakes, while other areas of ripped ground appear to have filled in with last night's avalanche.

She looks over her shoulder at the bed where Gramps lies sleeping. Swallows the fear that pushes up to claim her. *I am Pipe Carrier and Eagle Dancer, granddaughter of medicine people, born of the Star Nation. I must go forward with courage.*

She looks out the window again, watching for a moment as the boys begin the task of clearing the night's debris from the cabin entrance.

There is no logical way the cabin stands. Boulders equal to the size of the house itself block the view of most of the mountain. Debris, mud, tree limbs and stumps, roots, rocks, and dirt are piled high. The miracle of the cabin being lifted from where it had come to a stop further down the slope had clearly saved it from total burial under the mountain of rubble. Even so, when it had "landed" back in this spot — whatever fantastical saving force had set it there — the surrounding debris had shifted to block the front of the house.

The entrance porch has been shattered except for a few planks and tenacious clinging remnants. Leo pauses in his work and stands back to take in the scene, laughing when he spies Inanna's face framed in the open window. He widens his eyes and holds up his arms, as if to say, *can you believe this?*

Inanna shakes her head back and forth slowly. She wonders again at the miracle of this rickety structure of logs and nails that is their splintered refuge. *Still intact.*

The boys pick up and throw whatever timber and rocks they can over the taller boulders that surround the porch, and they use tree limbs to sweep and scrape enough dirt from in front of the cabin door to make it passable.

The boiling water and simmering oatmeal pull Inanna's attention back to task. She returns to the front room, pushes the chairs away from the fireplace, wipes off the accumulated dust and goes back to stir the cereal. She wrinkles her nose at the aroma. *Damn!* It's the same pot she'd used to cook the poultice. She shakes in an extra dose of cinnamon and crosses her sticky fingers.

She hears Gramps groan in his sleep, thinking he whispers her name. She flits to his side. Her grandfather opens his eyes fully for the first time this morning. Inanna holds her breath. She recognizes the look she sees in his eyes. It's the same gaze he has when in ceremony, or at the side of the dying: half in the world and halfway moved to the other side.

At first glance he looks right through her. But after a few moments, he re-focuses — and smiles.

Inanna lets flow the tears that were hiding behind her bravery all morning. She nestles her head tenderly, gingerly against the uninjured side of his chest. Gramps' raw voice scratches the ear she's tucked up to his heart. "You and Nonny are greatest gifts of my entire … too-*long* life." He nudges her head up with his chin and looks into her almond eyes. "Courage, daughter. You … are promised one in our lineage."

He closes his eyes again. When he inhales too deeply, he coughs. But he continues. "Inanna, you carry forth Nonny's blood and spirit, and mine. You carry promise of our people. You will remember, always, true meaning of the four directions of medicine wheel. And you will honor teachings of White Buffalo Calf Woman."

Inanna wants to ease his mind, save him breath. She sputters, "I *know* Gramps. Please, *please* rest. I know what you're trying to say."

Touching her lips with the crooked fingers of his good hand, Gramps murmurs, "Yes, you know in your mind and sometimes in heart, but in future you must Remember all of it … and more. The braiding river of who you are, of who we are, must be so strong in you, Inanna, that nothing can stop you from your prophetic course."

She loves this and hates it. Each word has meanings and memories, sounds, smells, images … beauty and terror.

Gramps knows every inlet in her consciousness stream. He wants to relieve her pain and extend her joy. *But*, he says to himself, *not enough time.* "Inanna," his voice cracks. His granddaughter shakes her head and moves to bring the cup of water to his parched lips. He gently waves her objections away. "Inanna … you were named for the first Goddess."

"Gramps, I *know!*"

He overrides her protest. "*Inanna, she who lived at the juncture of east and west. Inanna, who fought personal demons in order to save her people … all of that is in you. Is you!*"

The cabin door groans on its battered hinges as the boys come back in with logs and sticks piled high in their arms. They stop short to listen when they hear Gramps' low rumbling words. Leo exhales, *Whew*, and tosses wood into the fireplace. Conan drops his load on the hearth and leans as far as he can towards the bedroom door without being intrusive. He can only catch a word or two.

Inanna doesn't notice the boys. Under Gramps' pointed reminders, she hears her heart warn, *it's the beginning of his goodbye. I can't stop him from crossing over. I don't know how I can be strong enough to face losing him.*

What she does know in the marrow of her bones is that she is her grandparents' true heir. It's as if the blended legacy of her diverse backgrounds had sprung from the original wishes and dreams of thousands of years of knowledge; as if she belonged to Gramps and Nonny and all the ancestors and storytellers, healers and seekers, teachers and believers that spoke through their shared space-time. *You will live for all of us,* her grandmother had said.

But right now, Inanna only wants what she can't have: to stay with Gramps. To guard him from dying. To believe in a future where they still hold one another up against the storm.

Conan inhales the spicy aroma of Inanna's simmering oatmeal and lifts the lid to stir it. His thoughts, complex and hidden, circle now around images of goddesses. Like those on the necklace Gramps had given her — Nonny's necklace. Venus, Aphrodite, Tara, Quan Yin, and, of course, White Calf Buffalo Woman. These legendary women were sprinkled through the myths and stories their aunt and grandmother had told them when they were young.

Gramps pets his granddaughter's mop of spiral curls, and in a voice weakened by pain, he calls the boys to his side.

Conan brings a bowl of oatmeal and a drizzle of honey to sweeten the cereal. Gramps waves it away. But the boy insists on feeding him a few spoonsful before allowing the old man to speak.

Leo, meanwhile, finds a small pot to make tea. He brings everyone a mismatched cup. Gramps insists on holding his himself, balancing it awkwardly in his left hand.

They find that Inanna has cooked enough oatmeal for a small army, but the kids are famished, and they don't seem to notice the medicinal aftertaste.

The old warrior allows himself to be fed a few spoonsful of cereal, then takes some sips of the tea in his shaky hand. The kids nestle around him and wait until he can speak.

He focuses his mind, his entire being, onto them. He commands his voice to have the strength to impart what he must teach them. *Time is short, now*, he thinks.

"Today," Gramps starts, "is only the second day ... we, my teachers, your ancestors, weren't prepared for last night. None of us anticipated that final blast of mountain. We knew it could come. Dark winds threatened for many years. More quakes are always possible. But we hoped the mountain would hold tight until … after you'd left." *Hope can be an expensive delusion,* Nonny had taught.

Leo notices how short Gramps' inhales are, and how his ragged exhales rattle his hollowed chest. He tries to keep his assessment clinical. *Fractured and bruised ribs hurt like hell. Maybe there's a collapsing lung, though.* He tells Gramps to rest, to wait.

But the medicine man is determined to prompt their reflections on the night's events. "You saw your grandmothers … yes?" The Three smile almost shyly, not sure how to begin to encapsulate all they saw. "They are always with you," Gramps goes on. "Pay attention. The spirits who were once in human bodies have personal karma to attend to on other side. Time and space mean nothing in their worlds. But they are there for you. In whatever way your message comes to them, they will be wherever you need them … to protect, guide and teach. Pay attention." Gramps coughs abruptly. But he refuses the concern forming on Leo's face. "Fine," he coughs, "I'm fine."

"Gramps …" Leo hesitates. "We haven't had time to think about last night. We wanted to wait until you could talk with us. But … there were those *beings*, made … well, made completely of light, it looked like. It was like a white light shined inside them. I guess they were spirits?"

"The Light Beings? Ahhh …" the old man lets his eyes close for a moment. "So rare to see them." He looks at The Three now, scanning their faces. "You are blessed. They have only come to me in dreams. Light Beings are direct manifestations of Source. They are … Light itself."

The cup in Gramps' hand begins to tremble more violently. Inanna folds her hand over his and tilts the tea to his lips. He takes a tiny sip, his eyes half shut as if he's receiving information from somewhere else. "Listen carefully. Last night … in hour before the Spirits came to support us … you each faced your own demons. Trust … that spirits came to us at exact right moment."

The effort to speak depletes the old medicine man's breath. Inanna caresses his brow. She asks him somewhat hesitantly, "The Spirits lifted the cabin, right, Gramps? That's what happened?... and that blue light, isn't that what's called 'First Light?' It appears when we…link our minds." She blinks shyly at Conan, directly at Leo. "And – Leo, you somehow called the cobalt in… right?"

The boy gives a brief nod, but he has no idea how the instinct or ability came to him, so he lets Inanna continue to speak for them all.

"Then it kinda' *exploded!*" Her palms form a bowl in front of her flushed face. She throws them up and open, as if she's tossing handfuls of confetti into the air. "And formed into this giant infinity symbol!" She dances her long fingers and flowing hands over and under one another. "There were so many ribbons of light, I think they must have been some form of energy." Inanna's cheeks are flushed. She stops, seeing Leo looking away.

A long pause ensues.

Finally, Leo gives voice to his thoughts. "Each of us had to experience our worst fears, last night, before the Spirits came." His grief and his fears of betrayal bubble up in his head afresh. It's easier to refuse them now, in daylight, when the mountain is eerily still. But he isn't fooled. He knows that fear calls in whatever medium it chooses. "Fear wants to own us. We were *all* afraid, during that circle." He slides his eyes to Gramps. "Fear *can* be a friend, right? A warning. Like, Conan n' me would be riding in the mountains, hear a rattlesnake threaten attack." He looks over at his brother. "Once you hear that rattle, you never forget it, right, Bro?"

Conan guffaws. "*Shit*, no!"

"Our fears may be different, at one time or another," Leo finishes. "But in whatever way it comes, and for whatever reason, we have to pay attention. We have to turn and face it."

Leo's honesty and humility open a door for the younger kids to admit without shame or pretense that they, too, had almost lost courage. Slowly, one by one, The Three, exchanging the stories of last's nights fears, begin to realize that what had attacked each in their personal battles had happened to the other two. The stories were different, but the intent of fear and the lessons were the same. Gathered in the understanding that they had shared so similar an experience of fears — old, cosmic, or current — is in itself empowering. They realize that whatever battle they each had fought, they had survived. Each had found a pathway out of fear.

And so, they acknowledge each other.

Inanna looks sideways at Conan, blushing in spite of herself. "Conan, uh, *dude*, not sure how you thought to blow the eagle whistle ..." She shakes her head, a cascade of hair sweeping her cheeks. "But you did. It brought me back. Felt like I was spiraling out of control. And I saw that labyrinth ... and it was like ... it knew I was there ... but I was falling into it, before you ..." She stops, brushes the hair aside. Straightens up. "Anyway. Conan. Ya' know — thanks."

Conan wags his head. After an almost-awkward silence, he says to Gramps, "And it was your message that helped me. 'Fear is the real enemy.'... It brought me back, too, from a real scary place."

The boy moves very close to the old man's side. "But ... why were you injured, Gramps? It doesn't make sense. How are there so many protective forces around us, even now, but you were still attacked, hurt? Why *you?*"

He clasps his hands together, with his gripped fingers interlaced, as if he can squeeze some truth from them. Gramps' face remains impassive. "I think ... don't know why, but I sort of think your injuries and our fears have something to do with one another. Is that right? Did our fears ... sort of ... attack you? Or maybe you battled against them *for* us?"

Inanna startles upon hearing these words. She starts to tremble. The girl knows that medicine men are often injured — sometimes badly — in ceremonies and healings. Fear, lack of integrity, people using the ceremony for selfish purposes or showing lack of respect … these things can be very dangerous. The medicine man can be punished by energies that demand to be honored; they can bear the physical brunt of any spirit's anger. And thereby a door can be opened to allow the Darkness in.

Inanna's been afraid all morning to ask herself the questions that Conan is now raising. To imagine that her fear could cause her beloved grandfather to suffer is more than she can bear.

She takes the cup from Gramps' good hand, then presses his palm to her wet cheek. Blame, shame and guilt are messengers of fear that walk among us, she knows. And yet…

Gramps adjusts himself in small inches of shrugs on the pillow. He tries not to grimace, tries not to worry the kids. He hisses, "No worries, no worries." What he does not tell The Three is that, yes, their fears had catalyzed the Darkness. Fear had drawn the destruction in. Gramps had allowed their projected fear into his own body, to protect them from as much of the fury as possible. Until his body had broken, ravaged by the malevolence. This is the fate of medicine people everywhere.

"Fear is cast out into wide circle," he acknowledges aloud, "… or it's thrown into atmosphere, like shards of invisible glass … like weapons worse than any devised by man." He cocks his head slightly, squeezing his eyes into a crinkled smile. "Inanna, tell these boys my Native name."

His granddaughter beams. "White Whirlwind. Gramps' medicine name is White Whirlwind, *Wamniomni Ska*." Conan and Leo look at each other, then at Gramps, bemused. "The elders gave it to him," Inanna goes on to explain. "They said when Gramps called spirits into ceremonies and lodges, a small but really powerful tornado, a white spirit-whirlwind, swirled around him every time he sang or drummed or started a healing."

She's startled to see that her words have a profound effect on Conan. The boy's expression goes from confusion to dawning awareness.

"*You* were the tornado! Gramps, that was *you* in my dream, wasn't it?!"

The old medicine man does not respond or alter his expression; he merely cocks his head to the other side as he meets Conan's eye.

Incredulous, yet totally empowered by the revelation, Conan tells Inanna and Leo about his dream before waking this morning. He describes the blue light exploding across the black-hilled horizon in myriad directions like shattered, sparkling glass. And then the small but devastating tornado that drove relentlessly toward the center of the Sun Dance circle, and the lone medicine man who gave up his earthly form to merge with the wind.

Gramps is nodding now.

"Why should you be surprised that humans could take elemental form, in same way they can shapeshift, if that is their calling?" he asks quietly. "You saw Meera battle the Hungry Ghosts, turning herself into tornado, am I right? Conan. That medicine man in your dream, maybe he prayed to go home to spirit world. Maybe he was hoping to help his people, and spirit world responded."

Conan folds himself into a cross-legged position on the floor next to Gramps' bed. He tries to calm the trembling in his hands.

Meera had told him he *already knows everything needed to know*. Now he understands what she had meant.

I was the boy at the edge of the ceremony, the medicine man's apprentice.

Inanna sits on the side of the bed next to Gramps, still holding onto his hand. The old warrior gives her a weak squeeze. "My children. The only one true enemy is the enemy within. Stay strong within, and no enemy can defeat you."

Leo has been looking out the window. He walks back to the bed.

"Until last night I didn't know that fear of betrayal was a string that tied all fear together for me, Gramps. I never saw it. It must be so ancient a fear, carried through lifetime after lifetime." He crosses his arms, shifts his stance.

"But the weird thing is that fear of betrayal shaped me, helped me become who I am in strange ways. I never recognized it, so I called it other things … good things, like, ya' know, 'duty' or 'co-operation.' But now I see that sometimes I did the 'right thing' because unconsciously it might protect me from betrayal … like, who's going to betray the guy who's always *there* for you?!" He mocks himself. "How often was I driven by *that* fear? And then last night," he shudders, "there it was … in a form I couldn't deny."

For Conan to hear his brother's fears, spoken out loud, is inspiring. And he realizes that his own fear of abandonment doesn't hold water when weighed against his brother's love for him, and their connection. *Leo and I will never, never abandon each other. Not even in death. That's what these past lives tell us. We find ways across space and time to be together.*

Aloud, Conan says, only partly in fun, "You know I'm always there for you, Bro!" The brothers laugh.

"Got your back, too, Bro!" Leo cheers.

Inanna feels a pang of longing, seeing the closeness the brothers share. It's underscored by her stomach-twisting anxiety about losing Gramps. She will not let his hand go, though she can tell her grandfather will need to rest again in a few minutes.

Leo sees the girl's concern for Gramps, and he agrees it's time to wrap up the talk. "All I want to say is, I guess … Gramps, I think I saw my True Self, last night. Or I mean, not really *saw* it, but got to feel and experience that moment when fear didn't control me, even unconsciously.

It was … like the infinity symbol. Fearlessness and choice became that energy continuum, somehow." He puts his hands in his pockets, shrugs self-deprecatingly.

"Yeah" his brother adds. "Fear is like that big hairy monster in the closet. When you're a kid, you never actually look in the closet, you're so sure that scary thing lives there. And then one day you grow up, or you get up the nerve and open the door, and you understand that you made it up in your own head."

Leo smiles and moves closer to the foot of the bed. "I'm only just, well, afraid that last night we projected out our greatest fears, and that resulted in injuries …" he places a hand on Gramps' blanket. "Not just in some energetic way we couldn't see. Last night, it *physically* hurt someone we love."

The old man shakes his head. "That is just your fear getting the better of you." He grins. His voice is crackled and weary, but he is resolute.

"You are past, present and future, you Three. You see, three dimensions live simultaneously in you. You will be tested … but as long as you stay together, the path is now laid before you. My three brave friends, my grandsons and granddaughter … You did not just learn any of this … truly you are *Remembering*."

Gramps coughs and grimaces, closing his eyes. Again, he waves off concern. "No time," he murmurs, frustrated with his own vulnerability. *No time to be weak.* Privately he curses dark spirits for the unexpected events of the past day and night.

"Inanna." The girl moves her head closer to his, and her grandfather opens his eyes to focus on her. "Inanna, today was to be spent … teaching … survival skills. Preparing journey. But … must rest. You know where supplies are. Get everything out. Sharpen knives. Get bows and arrows … clean the rifles … I'll sleep, then we continue … remember, *no fear!*"

The Three sit and watch Gramps rest for long minutes. Until Conan's stomach growls, and they quietly crack up. Inanna bends down, kisses her grandfather's cheek and gazes at him a few more moments.

At length, she gets up. "Okay, Conan, let's find some food for you. Guess those *three* helpings of oatmeal weren't enough." Her heart is heavy, but she maintains a light voice.

"Hey, it was hours ago," Conan defends himself as they move into the other room. "I'm starving! But I'm also dying to see the supplies Gramps has." He opens some cupboards, looking for crackers or jerky or nuts, or anything to snack on.

Gramps, dozing, hears some of their words from the next room. His heart is gladdened to hear them laugh. *So young … and so old, too. And for me …*

He whispers to himself a Lakota warrior pledge.
It's a good day to die.

Chapter 64
Weapons

When Gramps is fully asleep — and the three kids have snacked on peanut butter and crackers and some canned peaches they found in the cupboard — Inanna quietly leads the brothers back into the bedroom. She moves to a corner where a large army chest stands. It has occupied that position for as long as she can remember. Inanna unlatches it now, careful not to disturb the rusty hinges.

The boys stuff the last of the crackers in their mouths, wipe their hands on their jeans, and move to help Inanna with the trunk's lid. It's heavy. They realize they'd better move the chest into the other room so as not to awaken Gramps.

Considering the hefty weight of the trunk, Leo and Conan each take a handle and Inanna guides the side while they navigate the bedroom door, trying to be as quiet as possible.

When they've set it down near the dining table, Conan whistles. "*Wow!* That's a load! It's pretty antique, too, army green and all. I woulda' liked having that to store my art supplies and stuff!"

Leo rolls his eyes to Inanna. "His *junk*. He means to store his junk."

Conan hoots and reminds his brother of the many inventions he used to make from scraps. Before they can get into it, Inanna hushes the boys, a finger pressed to her rigid lips. She motions for them to help her lift the unlatched lid of the trunk. It takes the three of them to swing the top open on its rusty hinges, carefully, without it hitting the floor.

Looking into the cache, the kids find a multitude of supplies neatly packed and organized into compartments. Compasses, zip lighters and canteens are squeezed into every small space. There are three lightweight camouflage backpacks and solar-powered flashlights, and even a tightly-packed tent. Leo reaches in to test the batteries on one of the flashlights; to his surprise, it works. And there's a GPS device packed in its original box, unwrapped. Conan concedes, "Probably useless, old technology. And anyway, these only work if there's cell service." But he adds it to his pile.

It's clear that whoever packed the chest knew what he or she was doing. Every item might not be the latest style or brand, but everything essential is there. And most of what's there is new enough to still have sales tags dangling from leather sleeves or shiny zippers.

Inanna carefully lifts out a small tissue-wrapped bundle containing three hand-crocheted beanies. She holds them to her chest a moment. "Nonny made these, I'm sure of it." She disciplines herself to avoid sentiment, and proceeds to hand Conan a grey beanie, a navy one to Leo. The older boy takes off his red cap and stuffs it into his pocket, pulling on the navy beanie at the same time as Conan dons his. Inanna keeps the black one for herself. They smirk over the way Conan's curls stick out from under his cap in every direction.

Inanna reaches back into the trunk and tosses two sweatshirts to the boys, telling them to check for sizes. But when she sees what lies under the shirts, she lets out a yelp.

"*WTF!*"

The boys peer over her shoulder and spy the hunting knives.

"These aren't meant for spreading butter!" Conan is impressed.

Several hunting knives are packed tightly together. One has a ten-inch serrated blade, shined to perfection with a hilt of rich ebony wood. Another is smaller but with a delicately curved blade.

Conan pulls out a Bowie knife. He grabs it for himself before anyone protests. "This is a *beauty!*"

"It can't be the only one…" Inanna gingerly lifts the stash out of the trunk, and sure enough, they find two more Bowies. Each is inside a leather sheath with a band and a buckle for attachment to a limb or ankle.

Conan holds his carefully. "And what do we *do* with these?"

Inanna moans her disdain. She half turns, and in one swift twist of her arm, she flings her knife toward the closet door. She nails the center of the Eye of Providence poster pinned to the wood.

Leo lets out a yelp. "*Dang* girl, you are *always* a surprise!"

"Uh, Okay. Got it." Conan isn't as effusive — but there's no challenge in his voice, either.

There are three bows bent in perfect arcs and three rawhide quivers sewn with leather thongs and wrapped in deerskin so soft Leo feels it will melt in his hands. A dozen arrows, handmade in the traditional way from ash trees, are fastened with razor-sharp modern arrowheads. The boys don't know the process or history of such things as well as Inanna does. But they're bowled over by the obvious craftsmanship.

Conan says, "Well now, what the hell are we gonna do with these? I think I failed bow-and-arrow at summer camp." He holds his bow out in front of him awkwardly, stiff-armed.

Disgusted, Inanna shakes her head, turns the bow right-side up and places Conan's fingers on the string correctly. "You'd *better* be a medicine man," Inanna hisses under her breath. "Because you sure as hell aren't a warrior." Conan takes the taunt without complaint.

They start to line up their wares on the kitchen table, creating piles, assessing what's there and what may be missing that would be essential. Under the bows and arrows are Swiss Army knives and another Leatherman tool kit like the one Conan carries. There are army-issued cutlery sets that include tin plates, forks and cups and an entire layer of high-quality tarps, tents and sleeping bags.

And underneath it all, they find the guns. Three of everything, a cache of firepower that astounds the kids. First, they bring out the hunting rifles. Inanna says the Remington 7600 is Gramps' favorite deer rifle, but she's never seen a brand new one. The second one is a Ruger American, which she tells the boys is nick-named the "Predator." There are two other models the girl is not familiar with, but she points out the high-tech scopes and silencers. Three heavy bandoliers and a significant trove of bullets accompany each rifle.

Leo softly whistles. "These are some ... um, *killer* weapons." Conan and Inanna nod silently, taking in the gleam and power of the armory.

Conan turns back to the trunk and lifts another layer of guns. He barks, "*Whoa!* Are these what I think they are? *Glocks? Damn!*"

Heavy with their own metal weight and the extra heft of the kids' instinctive discomfort with such a weapon, the surprise in finding the Glocks gives them a tingly, mineral taste of fear in their mouths. The boys glance at Inanna questioningly. She shrugs. "No idea who would have wanted us to have these. But I can tell you there's nothing here Gramps wouldn't know about."

Inanna reflects on the power of all the weapons, and about their intended use. She shakes her head. "There's more firepower in this cache than I've ever seen. I know these hunting rifles, used 'em plenty of times, but I never shot a Glock. And don't plan to. You guys can keep 'em."

Inanna returns to the chest and unloads smaller, lighter pistols, impressed that all are in perfect condition. Only one is brand new; the others are well-oiled, cared-for older pistols. Inanna tosses one then another from palm to palm. She tightens and loosens her fingers and feels for balance and weight. She's clearly used to handling a pistol. She purrs, "Now ... these I like."

Conan squints at her. Then turns to Leo and twists his mouth and thumb in the girl's direction. "Remind me not to piss her off when she's got one of those in hand."

Inanna pretends not to hear him.

They stand back from the rifles and guns now displayed on the floor. They don't know whether to laugh, weep — or leave the weapons in the supply box.

"Well. This journey is suddenly looking to be an expedition into heavily-armed enemy territory." Leo points out the obvious. No one laughs.

Breaking the heavy mood, Inanna moves back to the trunk to see if there is anything left. She sees only three Army-issued blankets, which she pulls out and adds to their individual piles. Returning to the chest, she realizes there is yet one more layer that the blankets had covered.

"What the...? What is *that?*"

Inanna carefully lifts out a shoebox-sized, chamois-fur envelope, carefully tied with a leather strap. Intuitively she knows it's something very special. She tenderly holds it out at arm's length towards the boys, unsure if they should even open it.

"I think … that's *white buffalo* hide," Leo murmurs. He clears a space on the table for Inanna to set the bundle down.

She takes a long minute with the double-knotted strap encircling the package. When she has untied it, she still hesitates to fold open the hide. She brushes her fingers across the fur. She knows that the sacred white buffalo changes color four times, turning from white to tan, then to a burnished red before turning black.

Conan breaks the silence. "I agree it must be white buffalo skin. You can tell there," he reaches over to gently lift one corner of the hide, "it's leather on one side and fur on the other." He tells her that after the white buffalo sisters came to live with them at their ranch in California, he and Leo would gather the fur that fell when the sacred sisters shed in the spring. "Feels like home," says Conan quietly, giving it a caress. He is standing quite close to Inanna, who still has her hands on the bundle. He looks at her inquiringly. "So, what's inside? Can I unwrap it?"

Inanna takes a deep breath and lets her hands fall. "Okay. But unwrap it *super* slowly. Just in case …" She doesn't finish her sentence.

Leo moves in to join them in a close circle over the package.

Conan doesn't stand on ceremony. He quickly folds open the leather.

Inside the fur, The Three now see another layer of wrapping, this one a vintage calico fabric. And once that is unwrapped, a beautifully crafted, dark maple wood box, polished with age and care, is revealed.

Inanna holds up a hand, indicating for Conan to leave the box on the table. She stands back, her arms at her sides. "I … remember something that my grandparents told me about a wooden box. It was supposedly crafted to hold … a secret."

She tells the boys that, according to legend, the box was wrapped in a white buffalo skin. That it had been re-wrapped many times over centuries every time a White passed and the people who had the box could secure the animal skin. Only the eldest medicine men, like Gramps and his teachers, knew anything about it.

"They said the … treasure … was so old, it was beyond imagination. It seemed impossible that it could be true, actually. It was super secretive, like one of those stories that people never told all the way out. It was hinted at in Sweat Lodges in 'Lakota code,' which means somebody whispers a phrase, like, '*ahhh*, that box,' or a hint, 'from the Star Nation.' But no one ever claimed they'd seen it."

As the girl talks, the boys gaze back and forth between the gleaming wood of the box and Inanna herself, whose eyes never leave the treasure.

"When the U.S government forced our people onto reservations, most of the sacred objects were taken from what once were the five hundred nations of Native tribes. Lots of what was stolen was taken to D.C. and put in some vaults. Most has never been taken out except when super wired-in scholars, mostly white ones, want to study them. So — any unconfiscated objects our people managed to keep needed to be hidden." She finishes quietly by telling the boys that just a few years ago, her grandparents had told her about this mysterious box. "In case, they said, it ever came into their possession … 'cause if that happened, it would eventually come to me."

After a long moment, Leo puts his hands in his pockets. "If there's a Native sacred object in that box, it should be you, Inanna, who opens it."

Conan shrugs an agreement. "Yeah, sure." But clearly, he's disappointed. He stares hard at the box, then back to the girl, impatient to see what's inside.

"Back off," she says. She moves a couple of inches towards the table where the box lies unwrapped. "Not sure I should be doing this until Gramps is awake …" She hesitates again.

"Okay," Leo agrees. "I get that."

But Inanna's fingers get as itchy as Conan's. She says a quick prayer and opens the box.

A perfectly constructed, foot-long, curved blade without a hilt, like a gleaming slice of moon, sits on a cushion of fabric inside the box. *Awe and wonder.* Inanna can't make her voice work aloud. She lifts the box for the boys to see up close — but doesn't dare to touch it directly.

"What the *hell* is that?" asks Conan. "Is it a dagger? Or a sort of mini scythe? It looks so thin, and sleek … and made of … what?"

He asks if he can touch it.

Inanna responds in one breath, "Maybe — but I'm not sure." She adds that she doesn't know what the risk may be.

Conan either doesn't hear her concern or doesn't care. He runs an index finger gingerly down the length of the mysterious instrument, avoiding the sharp edge of the curve. "It feels like glass ... but there's something about it that reminds me of hyper-polished steel. Maybe it's a new alloy, or a kind of titanium or something. Like … whatever astronaut capsules are made of?" The dagger demands respect in a coolly seductive way. The silvery-blue blade is carved from one piece, clearly, whatever material that may be. "It's too beautiful to be a weapon," Conan whispers, as if something so special, so rare, must be respected with near silence.

As The Three huddle together and ponder the mystery of it, a shimmery wave vibrates along the length of the blade, humming on an esoteric frequency. It's as if being free of its protective layer brings it to life.

The kids shoot wary looks at each other. Inanna places the box back onto the table, and the boys move to surround it on either side of her, listening to the ebbing vibration.

Softly, still with reverence, Inanna observes, "*Some* of my people tell an origin story. They say our very first ancestors came to Earth millions of years ago from the Kuiper Belt region of the Milky Way. In the oldest stories, mostly forgotten now, the First People descended from a space between the stars. First Warriors brought the guardian spirits and the elements, four hundred and three sprits, I think, to guard the elements. And ... they forged the first knives."

She pauses. The boys look at her expectantly, but Inanna's eyes do not leave the blade. "The knives, it's said, were shaped like arcs. Later, they compared the shape to boomerangs of the Australian Aborigines, or old curved daggers of the Middle East." The intensity of her stare suggests she's searching the knife for a confirmation of its story. "The story is, that the warriors, being that they came from the stars, were ... kinda' like, you know, super-heroes. Highly skilled, super-agile. And they wielded their knives like extensions of their arms and hands. The weapons didn't need a hilt or handle."

Her heartbeat speeds up. She tells the boys it was said that the warriors forged their knives alone in long, personal meditations with the elements they brought from the stars — and the spirits of the elements — as their partners in the craft. The warrior, knife and elements became one frequency of creation. Together they wove a personal song, awakening the star power that forged the blade.

"But my people said that the last star knives, if they ever existed, were lost or destroyed." Inanna tilts her head. She wants to shrug and make light of such an unbelievable assumption as she is about to suggest — but she can't take her eyes from the scythe. "I ... *guess* one could have been hidden to keep them out of the hands of enemies."

The boys understand that they don't have the lineage or authority to comment on such a powerful possibility. They remain silent and respectful as Inanna speaks.

"But, anyway, no one would be able to wield the star knives except their original owners. Only they knew the vibration. And since those people lived thousands of years ago, it's really doubtful this can be used ... *if* it's a star blade." She reaches out to touch the lid of the box. "I mean, no one ever claimed that they saw one ... But if anyone would know about 'em, that would be Gramps." She carefully closes the box. "We'll ask him when he wakes up."

Inanna slides the box into the calico, then wraps the fur back around it, but leaves the leather strings untied until she can talk to her grandfather. She puts the bundle up on the mantle for the time being.

Conan is disappointed they can't hold the blade, and he's impatient to know more about why it was in the trunk. But he jokes that they'll just have to rely on the technology he knows about. He picks up the tools, easily figuring out how the collapsible shovel works. He worries about the solar energy needed to run the water purifier, and questions himself aloud on how to test it since there hasn't been much sun. He checks the Swiss Army knives and reports they're easy to open.

"He's a gadget guy," Leo smiles. "He loves to figure out how stuff works. He'll fuss with pieces of things that are basically useless. And, of course," he winks to Inanna, "Conan's answer to all broken things is — duct tape! I swear he used to have enough duct tape to hold up a house!"

"*Duct tape!*" Conan laughs. "Hell, what's an adventure without it?"

The three kids share a much-needed laugh. It feels good to let go of their tension and just enjoy being young — if not exactly carefree.

Chapter 65
Cobalt Light Promises

"Duct tape. There should be some in root cellar."

Gramps leans against the doorframe of the bedroom. He holds his injured shoulder tightly to his right side with his left hand. Braids askew, hair wisps loosened, face strained, his leathery veins are raised in channels coursing his cheeks and neck. Every day of his one-hundred-plus years, the rivers of his blood and fluids have run through his body's patterns, and today they do so still, if more slowly. His strength is low, but he flashes his broadest grin regardless.

The kids jump to his side. Leo brings a chair.

"No, I have to stand," Gramps waves the boy off. "Need to walk a little, get these old bones moving." He indicates a loose bandage. "Leo, bandage slipped when I got up. Need you to secure sling. Can you do that with me standing?"

Leo nods and finds loose gaps, gently reties them, all the while studying Gramps' face for any recognition of pain.

"Good." Gramps, in an easy manner, surprises the boy by gently kissing his forehead. Leo blushes and smiles. He accepts the kiss as intended, a blessing of one generation to the next.

As Leo helps Gramps forward, Conan moves behind them — and emits a small gasp.

"*Whoa!*"

A faint trail of cobalt blue light cascades behind Gramps, swirling itself into a circle to include all three of them in the doorway.

Conan whispers, "The light … it's as if it's *conscious*."

Inanna feels the light, its uniquely cool warmth and odd denseness, before she sees it. She's entranced, but not surprised. It hovers, forming circles of spinning sapphire blue that shimmer around all of them.

With Inanna and Conan now tucked in close, Gramps bestows kisses to each of their foreheads, too. None wants to leave the embrace of the moment.

The medicine man breaks the spell and asks Leo to help him get to the bathroom. "Gallons of tea you made me drink." He closes the washroom door behind him.

The cobalt light hovers in the room.

Conan paces. When Gramps emerges, he rushes to lend an elbow while jabbering a stream of consciousness. "Exactly what *is* that cobalt light, Gramps? Does it follow you?" The blue circle pulses and breathes around them. "Or does it exist within us? Okay, that sounds arrogant. But maybe … Or does it come just to us? Well, that sounds arrogant too." He guides the old man to a chair he places in front of the hearth. "But Gramps

… you had the blue powder in your possession for a long time before you gave it to me. Is it a tool of the healer's world …?"

The medicine man looks at The Three with an expression that is almost impassive but colored with approval.

"I think," Leo considers, "maybe, *long* ago, I knew how all the blue we've seen is connected. And why it's important. But," he shakes his head, "it's locked in the past."

Inanna suddenly feels jumpy with all this talk. She's starting to feel trapped by expectations. Whomever these boys are to her, whatever they may be tied to in her past, the undefined journey means she will leave her grandfather's house and live again among strangers.

But, she thinks, *I do want to be a part of whatever being The Three really means. I want adventure and I want to unravel mysteries. And yeah, just figure out shit.*

She doesn't allow herself to concede how much she wants to be accepted by the brothers. She hates the way her stomach tightens into a fist when she sways back and forth through options. Distrust, her companion for a long time, squirms through her even now, when a different future, one that speaks of trust and faith, calls her. Inanna had no emotional bridge in the hostile worlds that seduced her mother. Without Gramps and Nonny, she had lived inside herself. Only Bird-Girl had whispered to her, bringing dreams of guidance, love, and support.

I can't allow any slip into self-delusion or neediness, she warns herself.

Still, she can admit that she wouldn't have found the courage to face down her demons without the boys last night. And she can't deny the magical, mystical gift of their connection.

Inanna notices Leo watching her, casually but with intent, as if he's observing a not-quite-tame animal. She likes that. Believes it's a strength of hers, that others are wary of her. Yet, she craves this new feeling of familiarity and friendship — and in the next moment she judges those same cravings as weakness.

As the boys talk with Gramps, Inanna keeps herself busy with food prep. She fidgets and walks back to the supply table to distract herself from worrying. *I really don't want to give a shit if they include me!*

Gramps' evasive answers to the boys' questions tell her he wants Conan to remember and find his own truth. Her grandfather wants the boys to look within at their own karmic legacy. *This is Gramps' way*, Inanna knows. *He likes to keep questions coming and give you non-answers until you figure it out yourself.*

She pretends the weapons are suddenly and totally captivating, so she can stay close to the conversations. *This is how my crazy life has mostly been. Me hanging out on the edges of things.*

And then a flash of silver sparkles in front of her mind's eye. A filmy image of Nonny appears, just as Inanna remembers her, warm and encompassing … and teaching, always teaching. Inanna stops her nervy hyperactivity. And listens.

Trust comes to those who trust. Love, the essential element of trust, creates the sacred circle. To be loved, Inanna, love; to be trusted, trust and be trustworthy. To enjoy generosity, give until your heart bends. Deepen love and your heart will ache, but it will not break.

And then the image is gone.

Chapter 66
The Three

Inanna stands motionless over the table filled with supplies, her gaze fixed in the air. Gramps shuffles in his silent moccasins to her side.

She had long ago given up trying to figure out how her grandfather always seems to sense her inner thoughts. She shakes her head ruefully and looks at her feet.

Grandfather and granddaughter both know she has prepared and practiced for whatever is ahead. She descends from generations of what Nonny called, "the whole crazy quilt of healing and tradition." She's ready.

Yet Inanna had never heard about the *journey* when she was younger. Or if she did, she never accepted its meaning.

She's suddenly overwhelmed by a need to fight back against the inevitable. "Why wasn't I meant to *belong*, Gramps?" She whispers, unsure she wants the boys to hear. "I was always being prepared to *leave* when I wanted more than anything just to stay and serve with you and Nonny. Was everything you both taught me always just meant to prepare me to leave again?"

Brave, she hears in her head. She closes her eyes and commands herself to remember how she and the boys conquered their fears last night. She exhales and denies the choke in her voice. She commits to saying what is true for her. And loudly enough for the boys to hear.

"Was this the real point of all those years of training? To prepare me to leave for this 'journey?'" She blinks back tears. "...*our* journey. And whatever's ahead for the *three* of us."

The boys stop sorting their gear to listen.

Gramps knows that for Inanna to include herself with Conan and Leo, to say, "our" and acknowledge "The Three" of them is a terrible emotional risk for her. He decides, *Now is the time for what must be said, before it's too late.*

"Inanna," Gramps starts and shifts his eyes to include the boys, "there were many prophecies, as I said, and in many languages. But certain knowings were same; cataclysmic changes to Earth and its people could no longer be avoided. But importantly, rebirth is now possible." He sits at the table piled with supplies.

"Weeks before you were born, Nonny had a dream of a celestial being she called a 'sacred eminence.' A spirit form, born out of the highest and best intention of Universe. The dream told her the eminence had chosen *you* to carry right-intention and right-action forward. The eminence would be your personal guide and would appear to you as a Halfling — part human girl ... and part bird."

Inanna gulps a sharp, hard breath that sticks in her voice box.

Gramps insists, with the directness of his stare, that his granddaughter look at him with her full attention. She blushes and her eyes burn, but she holds Gramps' stare.

He tells her that Nonny knew that Halfling would claim their granddaughter for a mission to rebalance the Earth and its peoples. And, yes, this terrible, wonderful challenge would start with a journey.

"It was our task to prepare you to live on in a world that your Nonny and Gramps would not join. You are right, granddaughter, it was always your task to learn and leave."

He waits for Inanna to grasp that he has known of her secret guide, muse, and protector since before she was born. And for her to realize that Halfling is more than a childish dream-friend.

She asks in a whisper so low that Gramps has to lift his head to hear, "Are you *sure*, Gramps? Really sure?"

Her grandfather reaches out to squeeze her arm.

"Once Nonny had that dream, she never doubted herself or message. And then Meera came to confirm it. Yes, the day before you were born, she came to us, fully embodied." He chuckles. "Just when we think we understand ways of mystical happenings and how messengers of Great Spirit come to our assistance, along comes Meera, ancient and yet so young. And she hasn't aged from time Nonny first met with her. Can I explain that?" He laughs again. "*No!*"

Instead of feeling special or empowered in this moment, Gramps' revelation leaves Inanna feeling a loss of innocence.

"Granddaughter. Meera told Nonny that the Sacred One, Halfling, originally comes *only* to you. Later she will reveal herself to these brothers. And later still to others who will join you, especially and definitely The Fourth of prophecies. Yet her most vital connection, Inanna, is to you. I don't know why you, daughter. But Halfling will only reincarnate in relationship to *you*."

The brothers are listening without wanting to intrude, busying themselves with sorting their gear and stoking the fire. Inanna drops into a lotus position on the floor next to her grandfather.

"Inanna, you are serving by going forward. 'Come, stay, leave, go; what *I* want, *we* want,' are nonsense words. You already know this."

Leo brings Gramps his unfinished cup of tea from the bedroom, now cold, but still soothing.

"My task, as I've told you," the old man says between sips, "is to help you remember specific past lives and lessons. To help you understand what of past to take forward, so that you can move beyond fear."

The old medicine man apologizes to the three of them that he is so old at such a young time. At the birth of change and hopefully transformation of life on the planet. He says he has so little time to teach the lessons that require deep understanding. "But, Meera will be back. She and other teachers will come forward and inform you of secrets I cannot."

Conan sits on the floor next to Inanna, and Leo pulls up a chair next to Gramps.

"Greater movements are at play in the Universe than just wishes of one old medicine man. You saw this last night. There are powerful, conflicting forces fighting for dominance to control and direct future. But they are not here in any comic book way. There won't be movie-scene final battle of good versus evil."

A terrible cough rattles Gramps. His bones quake but he waves away their concern. Inanna gets up to add a dollop of honey to his cold tea, making him drink before he continues.

"This will be the greatest battle ever fought. It begins *inside* every being, each person. You experienced that challenge last night."

Gramps worries his words leave gaps. That there's too much unintended babble-mystery. He sits back and feels his long years in the weariness of his body. He silently damns old age and injury and yet dismisses his frailties too. *No victim. No defeat.*

"If we … start a new world …" Conan pursues an aching thought, "that means the world we know, or knew, isn't … well, *there.* Right?"

Inanna stands, stretching out a cramp in her leg. She walks around the room, looking at the semi-organized supplies: bedrolls, blankets, utensils, tools and tents on the floor and table. She waits, tensed. None of The Three had allowed specific thoughts on what's left of the outside world to settle into their minds until this moment.

Gramps' bones creak. He feels utterly weak and tired. He doesn't trust his voice to stay strong much longer. But his eyes are alert, and he misses nothing. He wants to inspire them but without any false hope. He prays aloud in muted Lakota that his guides will assist him.

"Conan," he says, after several minutes. "I can't tell you the answer. I don't know how much of the world has changed. Meera will know."

In the next moment, the old man's gaze shifts into an outward-looking but inward-seeing focus. His voice is pitched to a trance tone, as if he translates words of an unseen messenger.

"*Much is lost.* Entire continents have shifted … most boundaries are gone. Oceans have expanded, coastlines have crumbled under new seas. Many island systems are no longer visible. Others have risen from sleep after thousands of years underwater, wet with ripe vegetation on new ranges of mountains."

Gramps' tired ligaments scrape against cracked ribs and restrict his lungs, but his otherworldly voice seems not to be concerned with his body's shallow breathing.

"Volcanoes erupted in recent years that hadn't roared for eons. Tectonic plates shifted in ways that were unthinkable. Epic winds grew to colossal tornadoes that tore through deserts and plains. Monsoons couldn't stop the burning of dense jungles from endless droughts. The

Three Days of Darkness came when Earth tilted on its axis. Earth lost its bearings with Sun and Moon. Our own mountain that loved and protected us has spoken through its quaking that the shift is not yet complete. Convulsions of earth will continue to transform the planet. Death and re-creation are not over."

The old medicine man opens his eyes and returns his focus to the three young ones surrounding him. He sees the boys' youthful stubble on unshaven chins. He looks at his granddaughter's face, with its beautiful mixed-race influences.

"My children, I don't know what all this means for your journey. Until Meera is back, I can only give you outlines. But I do know there are others like you, young old souls, who were saved. These will be known to you. They are, like you, *the chosen who chose.* Like you, they carry their karmic pasts forward. But only you Three and one more, The Fourth, are responsible for the complete mission. The linking of your minds, and your history with the Sacred Bird-Girl, at least for now, are manifested only through The Three that become The Four."

To the boys, Gramps' words are mysterious, but they ring with hints of things that were shared in their family's community of wisdom seekers. The concepts of mythical creatures, spirit guides, angels and divine intervention are known to them. But the mystical depth of a Halfling, a sacred Bird-Girl is intriguing. Another mystery.

Inanna sits next to Gramps again and reaches to hold his hand, hiding a pang of shock at how slight it's become in the last twenty-four hours, how bony and cold.

In the next moment, the serenity of the room is shattered by the first ground-quake of the morning. The cabin shifts on its unwelcoming ground. Dust flies and the few dishes not secured in cupboards fall crashing to the floor. Leo's chair skids sideways, but he springs into quick action and grabs Gramps to help stabilize him.

Within less than a minute, the house groans and squeaks into a new position. The earth seems to re-settle itself. All four of the cabin's inhabitants remain still, waiting to see if this new tremor presages more violent rolls, or whether it is yet another in a series of inevitable aftershocks.

The old medicine man closes his eyes. *Spirits, you promised your help. Help us now. Give us protection for The Three.*

Gramps is so still, Leo reaches over to check his pulse. *It's shallow and weak,* the boy thinks to himself. He drops his head, listens to Gramps' chest. The truth of the old man's fragility is not a reality he wants to face in this moment. After another listen to the low thump and swish of the teacher's heart, Leo tilts his head to the other two. *Okay, just okay,* he indicates, giving them no false hope.

He props up Gramps' back and unfolds his chest from its slump, to free the lungs. Gramps pats Leo's hand and allows Inanna to give him another sip of the cold sweet tea.

With no new tremors shaking the ground under them, the kids wait to see if the medicine man wants to continue the lesson or whether they should get him back into bed to rest.

"Must ... give you messages of ... medicine bags." The old man lifts his head and sits up straighter in his chair. "Must be understood by you ... for Remembering to be realized."

"All right," responds Leo, "but for now, please just *rest*. We'll be okay, Gramps."

He's taken by surprise when the old man grabs his wrist in insistence.

"Each medicine bag tells a personal ... *and* linked story." The old warrior is suddenly stern. "My children ... you must stay *together*. You are each part of whole story and yet part of a larger ... necessity."

Leo concedes. He sits again in the chair next to Gramps.

"Leo. Fear of betrayal is your teacher... bring your *wisdom* to fear. Unmask it, and betrayal can be a friend ... *yes?* You learned this last night. All fears contain gifts."

Leo is nodding.

"My boy. A very important person is coming into your life. She will be a partner for you."

The three kids look at each other, wide-eyed. Leo blushes and almost laughs — but Gramps is perfectly serious.

"A woman with skills, karma and promise equal to yours. She is Fourth of prophecy." Gramps winces as a stab of pain makes a deeper breath impossible. Yet he will not allow himself to weaken. "... It will be test for you to accept someone as strong and capable as she. Those who fear betrayal, unconsciously look for betrayers. In your past lives, women betrayed you. She will not. But ... she is not ... *usual* woman you attract. Betrayal-fear brings ... tendency to love victims. Broken, needy women. As leader, this will not do. You need an equal. I tell this now, Leo, because the future needs you both to recognize the other."

Leo balances between expectation and surprise. The future world that may await him now has an added element of mystery.

Conan can't restrain himself from interrupting. "Leo attracts girls who are beautiful and smart, but dependent — and more than a little crazy, too! It really bugs me! To call 'em women with 'issues' would be an understatement!"

The younger brother laughs. Inanna looks uncomfortable.

"Hey!" Conan protests, with his classic cat-smile. "Why not admit it? They were all beautiful psychos!" Leo gives his shoulder a shove.

Conan presses his medicine bag to his heart as they all share the momentary levity. He thinks about what might be ahead for himself. He's nowhere near ready to chase after any girl. He is wholly focused on growing into his promised shamanic power. *It's a freakin' thrill!*

Gramps seems to read his mind. "Do not allow one minute of pride, Conan. Hold the energy of your medicine bag as it should be held … with full commitment of sacrifice and humility of medicine man."

The boy chokes and clears his throat.

The old man knows the temptations of those who carry within them the energy of the great mystics and medicine people. Conan, Gramps sees, is in the first flush of self-realization. In other circumstances, with more time, he would teach the boy healing techniques and spirit world calling. He'd instruct him in insight, protection and miracles, and the boy would naturally build responsibility.

Gramps closes his eyes, then suddenly opens them again. His obsidian orbs bore into Conan. "In the lessons of fear, you Three are alike. But for a medicine man, there is this difference … The power of medicine can turn against you, destroy you — and others — if fear and ego are not controlled. Hear my voice clearly, Conan."

The words of warning thunder through the boy. He feels his neck flush, his hands tremble.

The old medicine man's formidable psychic energy pierces the apprentice's defensiveness. "Medicine and mysticism misused or abused turns into deadly force. *Most* dangerous to medicine man himself."

Inanna drops her head, gulps down a frightening memory of Gramps' suffering at the hands of those whose disrespect had poisoned sacred energy.

The White Whirlwind will not back down. "Our medicine legacy, heritage and gifts are equal, yours and mine." Conan's look of amazed excitement at these words causes Gramps to drill his message all the harder. "I know the excitement and seduction the gift of this power can tempt. It is both blessing and curse, because medicine energy can turn into arrogance … and arrogance draws the Darkness." Gramps reaches out to put his good hand on Conan's head. "*Humility* must come first. Conan, you must understand *right now* what you learned over lifetimes … medicine comes to you, as it did to Merlin, as it did Horn Chips … to be of *service*."

He looks at each of them in turn. "Unless all Three of you are up for challenge of leadership, humility, responsibility, and unity … there is no future possible."

A silence descends upon the room again. Even the shifts of the dirt outside, or a random tree limb falling in response to the aftershock, can't disturb the right-intention of this gathering, and the full acknowledgement of the duty of The Three.

Leo shifts the mood with a deep breath. "Suit up, show up and hope there's a God to do the rest!" he laughs.

He gets up. "It's a lot to take in, Gramps; can't lie to you! It's been a lot, everything that's happened these past couple of days." He searches for words. "I'm sure we're here for a purpose. I have to believe

that." He shakes his head in wonder. "No lesson has been lost on me ..."
He looks from Conan to Inanna. "Not lost on any of us."

The day is fast darkening. The weak dusk light is slipping away
and a faint glimmer of what may be the moon peeks through the slate-grey
sky they can see through the window.

"Gramps, it's getting late," Leo says. "You're exhausted and in
pain. Let's break and get some food. We have tonight, all day tomorrow
... Yeah. So, let's get you comfortable and rested, and we'll work more
tonight."

But before getting up, Gramps tells them he needs to see if
they've sorted their supplies for the journey. He instructs them to divide
the gear into three piles, joking about how glad they must be he'd gotten
three new backpacks from the Army Navy store before the global changes
came.

"Gone now," he sighs, "all gone ... nice young couple ran Army
Navy store, Rapid City ... both served in Middle East ... chose each item
with me ..." He stops. There's no time for sentimental rambling. *Old man
chatter.*

Conan is already surveying the weapons cache. He admires a
Korean War machete, beautifully cared for and finely sharpened. Inanna is
reminded of the arc blade on the mantle. She moves to ensure it's still
covered and safe, making a mental note to talk to Gramps about it when
he's rested.

The three kids wonder about food for the journey; can they bear
freeze-dried army rations? "*Yuck!* For how long?"

Gramps notes hoarsely, "There's extra elk jerky stored in root
cellar. Grab flashlight. Stairs down are dark."

Inanna and Conan tease each other with favorite food fantasies.

"I'm sure there's chocolate cake mix down there, too, right?"

"Cake? Hell, I'm a sugar-holic, but right now all I want is a
steak, big and juicy..."

"Don't forget to get the duct tape!" Leo grins. The older boy
remains with Gramps, poised to help the old man back to bed while the
other two move to the cellar door.

When they try to open the door, however, they find it's stuck.
The earthquakes must have jammed the hinges. Conan finds a crowbar in
Gramps' toolbox under the sink and gets to work on the jamb. Inanna and
Conan push and pull at the door until they creak it open an inch at the top.

"It's totally stuck at the bottom," Conan grunts.

"Let me do it, I'm stronger than you!" Inanna puts her back into
it. "You *need* a steak, dude!"

"Okay, *geez!* On my count, lean your shoulder into the door, and
I'll pull..."

Leo holds Gramps' elbow and helps him out of the chair. As
they move slowly towards the bedroom, the old man murmurs, "So little
time left." He shakes his head as he shuffles softly, Leo at his side. "So

much has happened that we did not expect, my boy. Well ... Nonny's samurai father used to say, *Prepare for everything; expect nothing.*"

Behind them, the cellar door slams open with a roaring suck of yawning air.

Chapter 67
The Abyss

Inanna is swept off her feet, sucked into the deafening wail of the hollow abyss that was once the root cellar.

The blaring wind inhales her in the blink of an eye. As her feet leave the floor and the force of the void pulls her downward, Conan instinctively grabs for the arm nearest to him, her right arm — but all he can grasp is her shirtsleeve before she is suctioned into the breach. Her only tenuous hold is Conan's clenched fist on her cuff.

The boy lunges forward and grasps Inanna's wrist under the cuff. His hand is shaking. The girl's fingers wrap around his forearm as the full weight of her body hangs over the hungry hollow. Her feet feel like they are being pulled heavily downward toward the blind bottom of the void.

She screams. Her howl into the wind has an eerie echo. She hears the fear in it, and wills her throat shut. Inanna dares to shift her wide eyes down only once. She can't see the chasm's ground or sides — there are no rock holds or footing, no safe ledge. The bottom, if there is one, is miles away.

"Inanna! Try not to move! Just freeze and HOLD ON!!" Conan's voice falls in echoing, fragmented syllables plummeting down and around the black hole. She stares up at the face behind the arm, her lifeline. He seems a million miles away.

Leo is behind Conan in the short second it takes him to cross the room. He takes in the unfathomable reality of the crisis as the deafening wind pummels him. The air begs to suck the boys through the cellar door into the abyss along with Inanna.

The younger brother, holding the girl's wrist in a grip so tight he feels his fingers start to lose blood, wedges his heels against the two sides of the rotted doorjamb for leverage. He presses his shoulder against the flimsy wood frame to bolster his gripping arm. He denies the urge to panic, even as his mind demands to know, *How? How? How?*

"Hold on … *hold ON!!* …" Conan urges, willing both of them to stay strong and steady, praying his handclasp won't slip.

The older brother's rescue instinct propels him across the kitchen space to grab a rope from the supply table. Grasping the entire reality of the life-or-death circumstance, Leo has bare seconds to act. He trusts that Gramps, weak as he is, will have followed him and taken in the crisis.

Leo ties the rope around his middle, securing it with a swift sailor's knot and leaving a long loose end to make a lasso. He sees that Gramps is already behind Conan; he rapidly gestures for the old man to tie the other end of the rope around Conan's waist and then to the copper leg of the kitchen sink, stabilizing them both. Leo doesn't question how Gramps will do this, with his right arm barely useable, and he doesn't pause to verify that he's been understood. All he knows is that if he hesitates, he'll lose both Inanna and Conan.

The older brother moves to Conan's left side in front of the open, breathing door. The rope has been secured to Conan, and Leo tugs it taut as Gramps ties the end to the sink.

"Okay!" he yells over his shoulder, confident in the old medicine man. Leo inches closer to his brother's side and commands him, "Keep your eyes only on *Inanna*. Stay *strong!*"

The boy doesn't answer or nod or even twitch. Inanna's athleticism and Conan's lean strength are all that save her from sure death as she hangs, buffeted by the siphoning wind.

Leo balances his wide stance, pulls on the rope end around his waist and makes a wide loop with the loose end. He eyeballs his goal, widening the lasso. He tries out a swing.

The rope falls impotent into a blast of wind.

Won't work! His clear-thinking mind demands new action. *Need ... real roping lariat!*

Gramps is ahead of Leo. Supplies are cast to the floor as he shuffles through backpacks to find a well-handled cowboy lariat. He holds it up to Leo and the boy grabs it, relief already flooding him. He feels its appropriate stiffness, the heft of this cowboy's tool of the trade.

Leo positions himself next to Conan again. He extends the precise loop, guessing the distance and Inanna's body width, fighting the vacuum pull of the abyss while he prepares the lasso. He palms the rope to get a feel for casting a clean throw. He gauges the distance he'll have to clear. *Speed. Precision.* He narrows his eyes on the target, takes a short breath, and yells down to Inanna he's about to throw a lasso around her shoulders.

He realizes with a stomach-dropping shift that he will have to ask her to let *go* of Conan's hand at the *exact same* moment the rope descends, or the lasso will have no hold other than the girl's neck.

"Don't be scared. Keep your eyes on Conan," he tells her.

Inanna stares straight up, unblinking. Leo barely makes out the whites of her eyes. She's a rag doll blown by winds. And Conan can't hold on much longer, Leo knows. The doorjamb begins to splinter under Conan's heels. His brother's knuckles are white on the doorframe. He has no other protection than this flimsy wood — and the rope — to keep him from falling headlong into the canyon himself.

"Inanna." Leo drops his voice, keeping it calm and deep to soothe the girl dangling above the unfathomable depths of the earth's floor. "I'm going to throw the lariat down around your shoulders. When I do, and *exactly timed*, you have to let go."

Inanna hangs in circling view. Conan's eyes tear from the effort of holding her. His fingers cramp, his quadriceps burn, his calves tremble. The rope tightens around his waist. He counts his breaths and heartbeats to stay calm. No part of him can abdicate to fear or stress.

Leo straightens his spine, inches sideways and back. The rope tightens around his waist, forcing an outbreath. He wraps the lariat shoulder-to-arm. As he prepares to throw, he pitches his voice the way cowboys do when facing bad odds — slowly, laconically, matching the casually distracting talk with the determination to stay calm and diffuse tension.

"First time Dad let me catch a calf, I was what? Twelve?" He talks above the wind's howl, measuring the distance to Inanna without drawing attention. "Yup, twelve — about two years too young. 'Course that never bothered Dad. Damned steer pulled me half-off the horse. I woulda' flown into the fire pit if it wasn't for Smokes. *Hell* of a roping horse."

It has always suited Leo to speak this way, staying measured and calm in a crisis.

He inhales, exhales. With quick decisiveness, he throws.

Leo's lariat curls through the air and whips by Conan's head on its descent. But before he can call the signal for the two to let go of each other's hands, the rope catches a loose end of his brother's thick hair — and the lasso loses its trajectory and falls limply into the dark.

Inanna and Conan stare through the void at each other.

Leo doesn't allow himself to show alarm or disappointment or fear. "You and those damned curls," he says to his brother. He disciplines his voice into a rhythm again. "Been causing me trouble from day you were born."

Leo pulls in the lariat. He adjusts the length, squints at the size of the loop, and moves four inches to his left. *Can't risk another error.*

"Old family story." The older brother rambles about a time they were little when he'd cut his baby brother's then-golden curls because Conan got way too much attention for his great hair. All the while he is narrowing his mind on the rope-loop, grateful that Inanna and Conan hadn't let go before he gave a signal.

Now Leo re-instructs them on the precise timing. "Not one second before or after I tell you."

The abyss yawns below Inanna. Sweat pours down Conan's face and blurs his eyes.

From behind them, Gramps' gravelly Lakota pierces the air. He is humming, chanting. Inanna hears the words as if her grandfather had thrust a deluge of targeted prayer above the boys' heads and into the wind around her, like spears of invocation. She closes her eyes and follows the vibrations of Native words. Hearing the ancient knowledge fills her body with eagle energy and bird elements. She pictures smooth muscles perfectly attached to fine bones of tail and feathered wings. She wills herself to have the power of a raptor in flight.

Leo feels the communication, grandfather to granddaughter, White Whirlwind to Eagle Dancer, as he lifts the rope to prepare his throw. *Trust.*

He whips the lasso over his head.

"*Wait!*"

Leo sucks in his breath at Gramps' command, and lets the rope circle another circuit before Gramps yells, "*Now!*"

Inanna rises like a phoenix out of the black abyss, hovering in the air in front of Conan, just high enough for them to release their grip in perfect timing with Leo's directed loop.

It circles her chest, and Leo tightens the lasso. Fear waves through the girl as the rope pulls taut two inches down her shoulders. She's lost any ability to move her arms or hands. Her mind freezes against panic. Her body goes limp. Conan teeters on the edge of the void, his legs trembling, both arms now holding the rickety door jamb.

Leo pulls the rope backwards but doesn't yank. The rope is not far enough down her arms to assure he can pull her up without it slipping.

He has a quarter second to decide. "Inanna, *one more time!* Like an *eagle!*"

She registers the command, even as her body loses its resistance. Gramps chants louder. Eagle energy soars from her belly straight up her spinal column to the crown of her head in one red-hot flush. Raptor fire-power rushes through her human wings, tucked tight.

Halfling's prism eyes appear inches in front of Inanna. But the voice she hears in her mind is Meera's. *Those unafraid of entering the abyss are given wings to soar above it.*

For a fleeting instant, Inanna can see Halfling's iridescent wings flutter above the infinite chasm. And Inanna wills her body to lift, just high enough for Leo to slip the rope four inches lower, tight and safe.

From behind him, Leo feels Gramps tighten and tug the rope to help the pull. Slowly, with the most careful steps his large feet can take, he inches backward. He damns the slippery sweat pouring down his arms, hands to fingers. He grips the lariat with all his strength, pulling Inanna above the lip of the doorway jamb. He realizes the sucking wind could slam her into the frame, possibly crushing her. *Leverage! Need leverage!* Behind him, he hears Gramps' chant grow louder, each note as wide and deep as the abyss below them.

Cobalt light flies from the rafters and through the windows. It swirls into its now-familiar twisting circles, creating infinity loops and tornado patterns, energizing the air with its current. And through the charged atmosphere, Leo hears a familiar voice.

"*Dally-up! Damnit, dally-up!*" his father's voice hollers in his ear, just as if the big man was standing inches from his son.

The words bring instantaneous memory of his steer-roping past, of winding his cowboy rope around the horn of his saddle to create a determinative force against the angry animal fighting every effort to control him. In this moment, with Inanna's life literally hanging in the balance, he is without horse or saddle; and so, with zero time to think, he wraps the rope around his forearm and pulls hard for a tight line. His wrist bends to the point of snapping bone. Blood pounds in his ears and temples, hot sweat careens down his forehead and stings his eyes. But Leo follows his father's command. He tightens the lariat loop and with two quick steps backwards he uses all his strength to pull Inanna up and out of the hole.

Conan grabs the girl by the shoulders and holds her, leaning back until her legs and feet crest the doorjamb. Leo grips tightly against the drag on his wrist and moves all the way backwards until both Conan and Inanna are free of the doorway.

He'll swear the rest of his life that his Dad joined Gramps behind him to pull with them, barking orders at every step.

Leo yells, "*Step back from the door!*"

He's afraid that the suctioning air or another aftershock could still cause any one of them to lose balance and fall into the abyss before they can get the door shut. Leo stumbles back before righting himself, hitting the sink behind him and hearing a crash and thud of falling materials. But his focus is on the door. Before even loosening the rope around his body and wrist, he dashes forward and, with Conan's help, shoves the door closed. The shrill wind whips their tense faces as they push, as if jealous of their safety.

Once the door is tightly shut, Conan and Inanna fall to the floor right where they are, their terror and exhaustion completely overtaking any other possible response. Leo sinks to his knees and folds forward, breathing heavily, his head cradled in his arms.

Long minutes go by, no one speaking, their senses simply focused on slowing the spinning of their heads and the pounding of their hearts.

Leo gradually reaches down to untie his rope and set himself free. He drops the lariat, rubbing his swollen wrist. It balloons with bruising. The skin is torn, abraded and spotted with blood. His father's yelled commands are still fresh in his ear. He won't allow himself to ask from where the voice came. He closes his tear-filled eyes and says silently, *Thanks, Dad. Thanks.*

Conan lies flat out for two minutes, then coughs and rolls from his back to all fours. He breathes steadily again, but each breath feels like it weighs a hundred pounds. His head flops down, his arms shake. His stomach roils and he wants to vomit from relief. He tries to lift his head and stand but can't. His limbs won't respond to his brain's commands. He gives up and sits bent forward, head between knees, on the spot where he fell.

Inanna's ribcage shakes in upheavals that cramp and burn her lungs. Her adrenalin recalibrates, cooling and then warming, then chilling her again. Mind blank, she lies across the floor, face down. Her arm feels as if it has been pulled from its socket. Her legs tingle. The slackened rope rests on her shoulders.

After another minute of stunned silence, Conan unfolds painstakingly from his bent position. He flattens his back against the floor, arms spread out, sore legs splayed.

And he starts to laugh. Big, crazy, out-of-control belly laughs. The fear has drained from him, and relief and gratitude leave him so full, his emotions need to erupt. He laughs until he cries, and still laughs through his tears at the miracle of it all.

His brother looks up, momentarily shocked, but then he understands the release. Captured by the sheer freedom of it, he lets go, too — and Inanna picks up their euphoria and rolls onto her back in convulsions of gladness.

Unrestricted and carefree joy fills the room. The Three laugh the way kids do when no worries drive them, when youth and time and dreams are on their side.

They laugh like they did before the world fell apart.

Chapter 68
Consequences

Her body still vibrating with relief and release, Inanna rolls over and folds into a fetal position. She stays curled until her natural twitchiness insists on motion. She flexes her feet, then her ankles and calves, unwinding inch by inch.

She tries to sit up, feels her brain spin and drops back down.

Leo lifts his head from a final belly laugh, noticing Inanna's struggle. He leans over and gently supports her shoulders to elevate her. The spinning is less intense, yet the girl keeps her eyes closed as she tries to reduce her vertigo. Leo gently lifts the lasso off of her shoulders.

The Three sit in a tight circle and wait for their breathing to return to normal.

"Nothing like almost dying to appreciate life!" the older boy murmurs, wiping the tears of hysterics from his eyes.

"You should've *seen* yourself!" Conan erupts in another loud gasp of laughter. "Eyes bulging outta your head …" He gawps to imitate a popped eyeball. "But for real. *Damn*, girl! How did you hang *on?* Couldn't believe your grip. It's a damn *vise!* You are one strong string bean."

"*Me?* Hell, if my eyes were popping, it was because I was lookin' up at *you*, wondering how your scrawny bod was going to hang onto me!"

Leo fist-bumps Inanna, shaking his head.

Overcome with a full-body shudder, the girl tries to clear her throat. "Um … Conan," she begins. "I, uh … I owe you, dude." She gives him a side-eye and tries to sound casual.

"Sure thing," Conan is suddenly as uncomfortable as she is. He turns his head to his brother. "Leo, *whoa* … how did you think of *roping* her? I mean, you were never exactly king of the rodeo, ya' know! But what you did … *damn!*"

They are still reeling from vertigo. The rare kind that swirls in dizzying repeats, inside and out.

"For a second, I felt I was being dragged in myself." Leo's voice is not proud. "Guess I just visualized what Dad made us practice … It happened so fast. Couldn't stop and worry whether it was the best choice. And …" he pauses, head down. "Bro … I heard …" Leo lifts his head to look into his brother's eyes. "I heard Dad's voice, right in my ear. I heard him yell, you know, like he always did, 'Dally up!' I'd swear he was right there with me."

Leo's voice catches at the feel of his father's closeness and the timber of his familiar shout.

"Insane, but I *felt* Dad. It was like he reached out and pulled the rope in with me. And then Gramps pulled, too, at exactly the right time …"

Inanna shrieks beside him. "*Gramps!*"

Ignoring their sore and shaking limbs, the three kids jump up like one six-armed, six-legged organism. They turn behind them to the kitchen area — and see a jumbled pile of furniture, supplies and dishes, with a human form crumpled in the midst. The old man's back is pinned against the wall next to the stand-up sink. A chair lies broken under him, and one of Gramps' legs appears to be caught in its rungs in a twisted position. His already-injured arm has fallen from its sling, and the other one is folded in an unnatural position behind his back.

Blood seeps from his head.

Inanna, Conan and Leo shove aside the clutter surrounding Gramps and kneel next to him. Inanna begins to coo, gently caressing his bloodied face, praying she is not too late. She reviles herself for taking these long moments to recover from the abyss, instead of rushing first to check on her grandfather's safety. Both boys, too, are horrified they did not previously notice what had happened to the medicine man. Their delirium had confused and distracted them from duty.

"*Please* Gramps, talk to me. *Please*," Inanna whispers. She feels for a wrist-pulse while Leo searches for one on his carotid artery.

The old man is still alive. His heartbeat is very weak, but it's there.

Leo quickly takes charge. He checks Gramps' head, finding that the blood is seeping from a bad cut. He sends Inanna to get a clean cloth. He directs Conan to help retie the sling and they lift the medicine man's limp arm into its support with absolute care. Already, though, Leo can see it's a hopeless task. Gramps' brittle bones are broken in more places, now, than his frail body can heal. His left arm and leg appear to be shattered.

Gramps flutters his eyelids open a fraction. The usual glittering twinkle has gone grey, shot through with orange capillaries.

Sinking to her knees again by his side, Inanna presses a towel to her grandfather's head, caressing his face with her other hand. Gramps registers her presence with a grunt of gratitude.

Leo stays steady, but his self-reproach is obvious. He whispers to the others, "I yelled at him to tie that damn rope. I didn't even think about how he'd have to use his arm to do it. He must have sat in the chair with the rope wrapped so he could support us both, me n' Conan … that's how we both got tugged so tight."

He speaks softly to the medicine man. "I am so sorry, Gramps, I …" Leo's heart sinks, imagining how the old warrior must have fallen backward in his chair when they pulled Inanna up and the rope slackened. Leo himself had lost his balance at that moment. And in the fall, Gramps must have hit his head badly — and torn tendons from bones.

Gramps lifts two bent fingers of his right hand. Leo reaches out to grasp them and receives a faint squeeze in response. The boy bends down so that his ear is close enough to Gramps' mouth to hear the words he is trying to utter.

"Choice-less. Only … thing …to be done … is often best, son." He tilts his eyes up to Leo. "Was … good … work."

Leo is battling to stay stoic.

Inanna gets up to give Gramps water. Her own dry throat is tightly constricted. Her head is spinning again, and she finds it hard to maintain balance. Her feet slip when she turns around. She grabs for the sink to steady herself and notices a puddle of spilled water on the floor. She traces it to a large, overturned jug that must have fallen when Gramps toppled.

Resisting alarm at their low residual stash of fresh water, she hides her fear and grief behind a practiced, tight-lipped cloak.

She brings her grandfather a cup of water, though she doesn't try to make him drink until they can find a way to move him upright. The boys make room for her, standing back and mentally assessing what next to do to make the old man comfortable.

All of them are silently lifting up prayers for a saving answer.

The winds start again outside, whining past the flimsy shuttered windows. Loose rocks and tree limbs strike the cabin in the surge, and they hear a shattering of glass from the sole, un-shuttered keyhole window above the sink near where Gramps has fallen. Shards fly into the room.

Leo and Inanna both move quickly to protect the medicine man's head with their hands. A piece of glass cuts Leo's palm; he winces but doesn't complain as he picks it out. He looks up to examine the window — and sees that the blue light he'd noticed earlier is still hovering near the ceiling.

Gramps remains completely still. "Too still," Leo whispers, wondering how they are going to move him without inflicting excruciating pain.

"Cobalt light." Conan points to the ceiling, seeing the same glow his brother had just perceived. Inanna looks up and regards the blue glimmer for long seconds. Its presence gives them a strange peace even in the midst of their sense of foreboding.

"Protection," Leo breathes in a low voice.

"Do you think the spirits who were here last night are here again?" Conan asks.

Inanna nods a *Yes*, with more hope than certainty.

The boys gently push a folded blanket behind Gramps' shoulders. The medicine man barely registers their ministrations; his awareness seems to be out of body. Inanna offers him some water from a cup, holding it up to his lips, while Leo wraps his own hands around hers to steady the girl's shaking.

Gramps licks at the water. He can't swallow without choking and stops to catch breath.

Leo knows there is little hope to save the medicine man, who, for the boys, was first a stranger but has become a mentor, teacher, friend, and grandparent in just these few short days.

The granddaughter watches her beloved grandfather with devoted patience. Kneeling in front of him, she wipes away dribbles of water from his chin with the faded and stained kitchen towel. She brushes wisps of hair that fall from his braids and holds his face in the palm of her hand, speaking to him in Lakota all the while, its lyrical tonality flowing from her in a circular frequency.

Experienced as they are with rescue and emergency response, the boys recognize that Gramps must be moved to a more upright position, or he will be unable to breathe and take in water. They exchange a look. The older brother gives Conan a silent nod, and they move to either side of the fragile, broken old man.

Gramps closes his eyes, listening to Inanna's words and seeming to know he must brace himself for what's ahead.

Leo doesn't hesitate further. He signals to his brother, who deftly untangles the chair from Gramps' twisted leg at the exact moment the older boy scoops the old man up in his arms. Gramps' body is shockingly light. Inanna and Conan step back to clear Leo's path. The boy's wrist is throbbing, his hand is bleeding, but it's nothing compared to what the medicine man endures as he carries him to rest.

Chapter 69
Blessings of Trust and Distrust

Inanna and Conan rush ahead to straighten the bed with its woven Pendleton blankets, gifts, Inanna knows, from grateful families for her grandparents' endless service to tribe.

The old man is aware, but already preparing for his last hours. He doesn't heed his pain and suffering. The time for enduring it will be short.

His eyes are closing as Leo lays him down with care on the bed and the other two cocoon him in the blankets. Inanna carefully places Gramps' ceremonial flute next to his bandaged arm, tucking it in close to his hand; it will bring comfort to have his trusted instrument at his side even if he no longer has the ability to use it. Leo takes another look at the cut to Gramps' head, assessing that it has stopped bleeding externally – though the inner blood swelling to the injury site is of more concern.

Quietly moving back into the little main room, The Three take a moment to stretch their bruised and sore limbs. In the fast-darkening cabin, it's hard to get a good look at each other's wounds, but they set themselves to the task. Inanna thinks Leo's wrist is probably sprained, and she curses that they don't have ice to reduce the swelling. In turn, Leo checks the girl's arm and shoulder, considering it a miracle she hadn't popped a socket. Conan's leg muscles are intensely sore from balancing on the precipice. His shoulder feels acutely strained. And he discovers a raw bruise where Gramps had tugged the rope around his waist.

Inanna retrieves disinfectant from the supply pile for their skin abrasions. Conan clenches his teeth and swears at no one in particular as Inanna douses his forearm with the tincture. Leo puts a water-soaked cloth in a bucket outside the cabin door, telling the others, "Might get cold enough to ice the soreness."

No one wants to talk about Gramps. They silently agree not to worry aloud, or deny, or be delusional — but they can't bring themselves to state the obvious, either.

"Let him sleep," Inanna whispers, when Conan moves to the bedroom door and pokes his head in to check on the old man. "We should go and organize our packs." She hovers behind the boy, then moves to put her own head in the door. After taking a moment to assure herself that her grandfather is resting relatively peacefully, she sighs, blows a kiss in his direction, and closes the door behind her.

Seeing Leo wince as he lifts his backpack with his bruised hand, Inanna suggests a poultice similar to the one she made for Gramps. Both boys wrinkle their noses and grimace, remembering the smell; but Leo concedes he'd better give it a try. "Come to think of it, we'd better bring some of those herbs in our packs, Inanna. They may be smelly, but they help with wounds."

The girl shuffles through Nonny's herb and poultice cabinet, confidently opening mason jars and sniffing a variety of aromatics to mix into potions. She fills a small cook pot with a careful measure of water from the waning supply and watches the mixture simmer for long minutes, thinking all the while about the risk of going in search of fresh water, considering the dangerously shifted terrain. She decides to talk to the boys about that question after they've eaten. There would be time enough tomorrow to search for a stream from which to fill their canteens.

The pungent, sour odor of the herbal medicine fills the room. Inanna drains the water and prepares a couple of poultices. Carrying the first soaked wrap over to the boys, she instructs Conan to remove his shirt. He does so, a bit reluctantly. She then applies the hot compress to the shoulder and arm that had saved her life. The boy recoils for a moment at the surprising heat, but he soon becomes a dutiful patient when the medicinal poultice works its magic and he feels an immediate and blessed relief from his aches. Though he can't help blushing when Inanna massages his naked shoulder with a strong hand.

"How're your leg muscles?" she asks him. "If you've pulled something, that could be tricky for hiking. Could cramp up on you at the wrong time."

Is she suggesting he drop his jeans so she can rub his thighs? His embarrassment at the thought makes his voice crack when he replies, "Nah, I'm fine."

Inanna glances up and her face reddens when she recognizes his discomfort. "Yeah, okay. I'm sure you'll be okay," she says hastily. "But, um, try to stretch out those legs, yoga-style, spine against the wall." When Conan emits a short whine, she teases, "Don't be a freakin' baby." She rattles the direction with efficient authority over her shoulder as she turns back for the second poultice, making no eye contact — and he's glad of it.

Inanna moves to Leo. She wraps his purple wrist with the poultice. The older brother's age allows a certain emotional distance and comfort; he's eager for Inanna's help.

She chatters as she tends to him. "Unfortunately, the best way to heal a sprain is to rub it hard and apply ice *and* poultice. Unless I had acupuncture needles." She sees Leo's eyebrows shoot up. "Hey, no lie, I know how to use 'em."

He laughs as he peels off his shirt so she can check for any other bruises or strains. He is alarmed at his own thin-ness, seeing his bony ribs. But he's glad that his brand doesn't burn.

Distracting himself from the smarting of her aggressive massage, he grits his teeth and asks about their food supply. "Now we've lost the root cellar, what have we got left for provisions?"

At the mention of the lost cellar, the picture of the yawning abyss floods back for Inanna. She slows, then stops her work and walks to the sink. Leaning on her elbows, she drops her head. The reality of the last hour's events overtakes her. She fights her body's shaking.

The boys exchange a look of understanding. Conan removes his now-cold poultice, picking up bits of herbs from the floor and cursing aloud at his still-stiff legs. He pulls his two shirts back on as if they are one, then finds his jacket.

"*Wow!* That actually worked!" He twists his upper body at his waist, then gingerly reaches above his head and tests the shoulder. "Good job, Inanna. Thanks!" He sees the fire is cold. Throws on a stick or two. "Bro. Are you done lollygagging? We need to get more wood from outside before we can't see anything out there."

Before Leo moves to put his own shirt back on, Inanna turns from the sink and takes a deep breath. "Conan. I, ah … well. Like I said, you saved my life," she begins, looking at her hands. "I want to say … it's not easy for me to express. But it was both of you who saved me. I keep seeing that black endless hole. I'd be … dead, without you guys." She swallows, looks up, forces herself to meet their eyes, each of them. "I'm … not good at needing help. Trust is hard for me. But I just want to say, *thanks*."

Recognizing the emotional risk the girl is taking, Leo considers his words carefully. He puts on his shirt and says slowly, "We saved each other, Inanna. Told you this before — I wouldn't have found Conan without you. As big a pain as he is, I wouldn't want to lose him." Leo winks. "And then Gramps … and the medicine bags …" His entire being is infused with the sincerity of his words. He doesn't have to say much more. "So overall, I'd call it even."

From the corner of her eye, Inanna catches Conan's gaze as he crouches in front of the cold fire. He's obviously uncomfortable with this whole line of talk.

"Look, Inanna," the younger boy ventures, "I … I guess I don't like to trust, either. But right now, after these days with you and Gramps, I'm beginning to feel … like I *know* myself for the first time. Like, I'm, I dunno … comfortable in my own skin." He looks to his brother for help. Leo gives him an encouraging nod. "We're on shaky ground." Conan gulps a laugh. "Yeah, *literally*, I guess! What the hell, we don't actually know what's ahead or expected of us. I just know we're going to have to pull together. Hell, it takes a lot of trust to even walk out that door. So … you're welcome, Inanna. And Leo's right — thanks back to you, too."

The words come out right, but his brain loops on the words *trust, distrust*. It's a refrain he's heard all his life.

Leo gives his brother a high-five on his way to the door. He checks on the towel he put outside. "Wow. Almost icy! Perfect." He gathers a few of the logs that he and Conan had cleared from in front of the door earlier, carrying them into the house under one arm with the cold towel draped across his swollen wrist.

As Leo starts a new fire in the hearth, Conan and Inanna continue sorting their gear. It's clear their conversation has opened a rare door for Inanna.

"I had to relearn trust," she blurts out. "At least that's what the school psychologist said." They all share a brief laugh at that confession. The boys go on with their chores as Inanna rambles out her story. "Mom took me back and forth from my real home for years. Which was here with Gramps and Nonny. But when I turned ten, she had a major fight with Gramps and, well, she stole me. That's how I felt about it, anyway. For a whole year." She won't look up from her packing and organizing. The words tumble out of her. "I … stopped trusting everyone. Even Gramps and Nonny. I couldn't understand why they didn't just come for me, steal me back."

Her heart pounds. She's never been so emotionally vulnerable.

"… Not proud! I hung onto victim shit, and I would've stayed that way. But mom got pissed at life, some other dude dumped her, she made it about me and sent me back during the summer." Inanna tries to remove the tag from her backpack with her teeth, but she'll need to get a knife. "I was a bitchy wreck, all blameful … couldn't even be happy I'd escaped."

The fire has started to warm the room. Leo pulls up a chair as she talks. He wraps the cold pack fully around his wrist. Conan sits on the floor and stretches his aching quadriceps while he listens, giving up on the sorting of supplies for the time being. They are both attentive to Inanna's story. Their patient presence is both reassuring and confusing for the girl. She's not sure what the attention of these two young men means to her. Never in her experience has anyone simply been there for her, except for her grandparents.

Is this what friendship means? she asks herself. *How would I know?* Is her head's answer. *Will it last? When we're off the mountain, will Conan and Leo leave me, too?* She bites her bottom lip, feels the sting of tears. She tries to meet both boys' even, unthreatening gaze.

Suddenly edgy, Inanna gives up her packing task and moves to the kitchen area. She opens an herb jar, complains the lid is loose, tightens it with a huff. She takes down cups, puts the kettle on the fire with a bang and scrounges for tea. Muttering and fussing, she turns the honey jar over to extract a last dribble and curses the empty cracker tin. "What the hell will we eat?!" she asks no one and everyone.

She's hating herself for having blurted out her vulnerability and uncertainty, her issues with trust and distrust. The boys are probably silently judging her, she thinks. Or they'll laugh at her behind her back.

But instead, Leo says gently, warmly, "Each of us holds our stories differently — but Conan n' me, we've had people leave us, too, Inanna. We can relate to loss and grief."

The girl won't turn from the fire to face him, but the posture of her back tells him she hears his words.

"You know us so well by now, better than people we've known all our lives. Hell, you were there, in our minds, linked through those stories. We even shared each other's emotions. Anything you've seen or heard lead you to believe we'd abandon you?"

Leo considers how young Inanna really is. He's grown used to thinking of her as a peer, with all they've endured, but she is very young in years. Thinking about girls he'd known growing up in California, he tries to remember what they were like at fourteen. Faces float around him, their laughter and gossip, how they'd shifted from shy to bold, from self-assured to needy — almost universally tougher and wiser than any boy at that age. *Gone too fast. Where are they now?*

He's suddenly tired and dizzy.

"We're not going to abandon you, Inanna. We're in this together." Leo ties the cooled rag around his wrist more tightly to bind it. Then he gets up and moves to the hearth to retrieve the boiling kettle and make the tea. He finds three bowls, pours in some oatmeal, and tops each with some of the boiling water.

Conan stands to help Leo carry the bowls to the table, but his legs cramp when he rises. He yelps. Leo barks, "Sit and stretch out those thighs like Inanna told you!" Conan shakes his head, but does as ordered, eating his oatmeal with his back to the wall.

Inanna silently clears a space to eat at the table laden with supplies. Leo offers both of them sugar from a jar he discovers in the cupboard.

"Eat," Leo's voice is kind. "We'll be on the road soon enough. Better fuel up now." He watches closely until she turns her eye on the cooling cereal and reluctantly scrapes the rim of the bowl with her spoon.

The winds outside are starting up again. The early dark has driven out the last of the dim daylight. Leo gets out candles. He moves to the door to secure it against the wind — but remembers first to go out for a last load of sticks to keep the fire going.

With Leo outside, Conan looks at Inanna and notes, "Not going to be easy to sleep out there in that cold." She doesn't answer, looking down at her bowl with deliberation. Leo re-enters with a load of wood under his good arm, and kicks the door shut. After dropping the pile near the hearth, he pauses to lift the lid of the water kettle. He's sees it's nearly empty and moves to refill it from the water urn.

"We're almost *out!*" Inanna shouts. Her pent-up emotion finds an outlet. The issue of water holds the entirety of what she can't bring herself to say. She wants to respond to Leo in kind words, to *be* kind. She's heard everything he said, and also every compassionate intention that was unsaid, but she has no idea how to communicate thoughts and feelings too big to understand.

From his position on the floor, Conan is closest to the water jug. He peeks in, taking Inanna's outburst in stride. "Yeah. But there's enough for now, for tea or whatever. We'll have to worry about tomorrow when it comes."

He gets up carefully, stretches himself, and refills the kettle. Over his shoulder, he says casually, "It's the *three* of us, Inanna. Just like Leo says. Whatever's ahead for you and me and Leo, it's *The Three* of us in it together." He turns to look at her, and she meets his eye. "We're all in," he nods.

From the next room, the kids hear a bang. The wind is whipping the cabin again, and with the bedroom window only loosely boarded since they'd used it to crawl out this morning, they all three race to ensure that Gramps is safe and warm.

"Gramps," Inanna murmurs, at his bedside before the boys. She is already caressing his brow and tucking in his blankets. Leo brings a candle to see what caused the bang — and finds a fallen shutter. The boys move to cover the window again as best they can.

The old man is awake, and seemingly alert. His mouth opens to speak, but his throat is so dry he can't form words. Inanna leaps to give him her cup of tea, placing small spoonsful to his lips until he nods weakly and indicates *enough.*

"Three of you," Gramps coughs, his words scratchy and thin. "Here ... sit ... yes, close." He swallows with difficulty. *Don't know if eyes or voice will fail me first,* the old man thinks. He knows his hour is near. *We Elders wanted The Three better prepared, but there is too little time. This mountain which has served faithfully for a million years, she is after all so fragile.*

Aloud, the medicine man strains to tell them, "Had ... sleep-vision of tomorrow's dawn. You three ... still here ... otherwise, would've told you to leave ... hours ago."

In his mind, he continues his thoughts. *Should have known. No plan could be assured in these times. Three days to prepare The Three were never going to be enough.*

He coughs again. The pain of it causes him to try to hold it back, and he loses breath. *The Darkness will try, has already tried, to end their journey now, before it begins. Darkness will try to snuff out Meera, break her connection to them. Darkness will try to end the possible.*

"Extreme dangers ... require *martial* preparation," he says, closing his eyes to push the words past his pain. "Tomorrow ... was meant to ... prepare you." *To practice safety and weapons training for emergencies.*

Inanna props the pillows behind him, and Conan adds another blanket for his warmth. "But ... few hours ... left to us." *There are dangers they must know.* He tries to clear his throat. "Tomorrow ..." *Tomorrow was a treasured promise that is now lost.* He tries again. "Tomorrow ... meant to practice skills learned ... in past and in this life."

The man knows as White Whirlwind fights for the air to speak, but he's interrupted by half-swallowed, bloody phlegm that causes him to convulse in spasmodic coughing. The three kids try to comfort him, not meeting one another's eyes. There is little they can do for the dying warrior.

After a few minutes of silence, he manages to whisper out the words he wishes he could shout. "Now we know … mountain won't hold. You must *leave*." Gramps' eyelids collapse like heavy curtains. *To be fearless, one isn't served by half-truths.*

The Three are brave, but they are not foolish. Leo and Conan had learned early and young that the best way to maintain courage is to accept and confront the entire reality.

Inanna whispers Nonny's directive like a mantra, willing herself to hear the lesson in the treasured words. *Be grateful for the entirety. There are blessings in all things.*

Halfling floats in Inanna's inner vision, her prism eyes piercing right to the heart of the girl's fear and sadness. *Courage. Trust.* She closes her own eyes, breathing in the Bird-Girl's words.

"Teach me," she exhales in a whisper, her tears falling freely, "to see the blessings."

Faith, the Halfling whispers back.

Chapter 70
Way of the Warrior

The bedroom is dark except for the one candle. The boys leave Inanna with Gramps for a moment, each collecting a couple more candles that they light and bring to the bedroom. Gramps has opened his eyes again by the time they return, his weakened gaze falling steadily on his granddaughter.

"Bring … samurai sword," the warrior whispers.

The boys have no idea what he means, at first. Inanna knows. She straightens her back sharply, raises her head. But stands immobile until the old man repeats his request.

Nodding just once, Inanna beckons the boys with raised eyebrows and moves to the fireplace. The beautiful Japanese sword hanging from its red and gold silk cording rests in pride of place, only slightly askew from the cabin's displacement over the past day. Inanna indicates silently for Leo to please take it down. He does so with great care, noticing its pristine condition. The Three walk back to Gramps' bedside with Leo carrying the weapon. He's surprised at how heavy it is.

"Lay … at foot of bed. Good."

In the ensuing silence, the grandfather appears to speak to his granddaughter with more than mere words. His presence is somehow as commanding as ever, weak as his body and voice have become. And the girl understands his compelling gaze and realizes immediately what Gramps asks of her. She doesn't want to obey, dreads what is to come, but she knows protest is useless. And at the same time, Inanna feels the honor and fulfillment in this moment.

She and Gramps share the same silent thought. *It is as predicted.*

"Move … furniture. Make … clear," the old man hoarsely directs.

Following Inanna's lead, Conan and Leo move the bedroom furniture against the walls, stacking some pieces so they clear a 6-foot space at the bedside. The boys then stand near the window as Inanna moves into the open space near Gramps.

She picks up the sword and removes it from its enameled wooden sheath. It's razor sharp.

Less than two years ago, the girl thinks to herself, *Nonny told me that the sword would be mine one day. She'd said, The samurai tradition lives on through you.*

She takes a step back from the bedside, holding the weapon out in front of her in both palms, blade side presented. Inanna waits for her core of confidence, one heartbeat and two, then a third so forceful she feels the pounding must be visible. She feels Gramps' faith flow to her. She hears Nonny's voice. *Be flexible as you are strong, powerful as you are agile, quick as you are calculating. Reside in your breath and your deep center will hold. Courage. Trust.*

Inanna breathes a prayer of gratitude to Gramps, her sensei, Nonny and her samurai ancestors, male and female. And to the natural elements of the sword itself. The sword's power and history grounds and strengthens her, as it always has. She draws three slow, measured inhales, and bows low.

Then she steps like a fawn on light feet, and with one rapid delicate gesture she is poised. Shoulders squared, perfectly balanced, neck erect, she fully embodies the graceful warrior.

Inanna bends from her waist to Gramps, holding the weapon as if the sword has no weight whatsoever. She strides backward four paces, settling her energy into her lithe body, and glides into the slow initial series of practiced martial choreography. She sweeps the sword in front of her and stirs the stale air into life, then raises the sword above her head in wide arcs, each swifter than the one before. The girl's body flows like gossamer drapery in soft, rhythmic winds. Her every action is smooth, collected, almost balletic — and deadly.

Inanna picks up speed and spins into warrior poses, knees and elbows in precise geometry. Her arms are held away from her body by carved, lean muscles that ripple under the fabric of her threadbare shirt. She slays an invisible enemy as he falls to the ground, then in syncopated rhythm thrusts the sword over her head, legs bent wide in a dance of flowing triangles. Her black eyes gleam steadily all the while.

She parries the sword with ease, her long, tapered fingers wielding the weapon as if it's made of *papier maché* instead of tempered steel. She spins and jumps right-left with lethal precision driven by her low-growl outbreath.

Leo and Conan's mouths are agape. *Awe and wonder.*

On the third round, Inanna moves so quickly, her feet blur. The sword rises and falls just inches from her face which reflects a fierce concentration without a hint of tension. Her jumps are aerial exhibits. She leaps low to one knee, jumps up, dashes into a *fouetté* spin. Without hesitation, two feet above the floorboards, knees bent to her chest, she dives and slashes the sword, left-right in exact trajectories. Her agility and speed are breathtaking. The sword sings with her rapid-fire moves.

From a sheer standing position, she bounds a last time into the air. She twirls the sword hand over hand above her head and strikes an airborne pose, left leg bent and the other extended fully, executing a Siberian half split. She lands without a shiver of adjustment and holds the pose, sword arced over her head in her right hand as it rings in the steel-shimmered air.

Years later Inanna would fully understand the gift of that performance for Gramps. The hours he had devoted to her lessons and practice; the days and nights of the too-short visits when she had disciplined herself, wanting to please him; her tears over the demands made on her; all these challenges combined with the earth-changing temperatures and the plagues of mosquitoes that grew in size and ferocity in adaptation, had made her cry out to quit. Gramps had ignored her pleas.

Inanna had learned to love and hate the sight of the sword.

Tonight, the patience of her grandfather's teaching is rewarded, his faith in her vindicated. His own training in Japan and Korea, starting from his soldiering years when he had been a battle-weary foreigner walking into a city dojo straight out of the jungle war, comes to its fullest realization and achievement in this moment.

Inanna holds her final pose for a long thirty seconds, her sword arm held high without a tremble. Her piercing, golden-flecked black eyes flare with energy. Her essence is completely that of an imperturbable warrior.

Leo and Conan are stunned into a long, silent pause. Until they burst into applause.

The older boy is beaming, babbling *"Whoa! Amazing,* girl!! I'm just blown away! I think Conan must see why I was so *agog* when I saw you leap across the river!"

The younger brother's mouth is still open. He nods slowly, keeping his eyes riveted on Inanna. "Dude, I don't even know what 'agog' means, and I know it's the right word."

Leo turns to the old warrior and master lying in the bed, whose pride in the girl is evident in his teary eyes. "You've got all *kinds* of magic up your sleeve, Gramps!"

The boy recognizes this love, grandparent to grandchild. He's captured and moved by all that transpires between the old man and this unusual girl he has raised, trained and blessed.

Inanna drops her head, purposefully slowing her breath. Then she stands erect, soldier-straight, and presents the sword in both hands as if it's an offering to the gods of the samurai. She bows again.

She sheathes the sword, then turns with precision to replace it over the hearth – but Gramps' hoarse voice stops her.

"Inanna. Sword …. Goes … *with* you."

The words stop her, mid-stride. Weapon still held formally, the granddaughter turns back to face her mentor. Her legs quiver undetectably as she recognizes that she has now become responsible for the continuation of a tradition as powerful and profound as being chosen Pipe Carrier and Eagle Dancer.

Gramps understands every charged nucleus of her thoughts. At fourteen, to be given the unexpected responsibility to carry forth these traditions with their vast and intricate teachings, songs and music alongside the myriad, textured spirit layers stretching back to the mystical awakening of her people in the wind caves of the Black Hills … these charges are more than mere auspicious honor.

Her grandmother's predictions echo in her ears. *In times ahead, those gifted by the traditions will help shift the future into right-intention, right-action, and rightful position. Today's lessons are tomorrow's foundation. Responsibility for the life of the tribe falls to you.* The full meaning of that teaching was never clear until this exact moment.

She turns to face her grandfather. She bows low to the master, her teacher, and presents the sword before her. Then Inanna turns and bows to each of the boys in the same manner. They bow back awkwardly, neither sure of the tradition, but sincerely respectful.

Remember it all. Remember everything.

She wills herself to fix this hour in her heart.

Chapter 71
Never Doubt Me

Inanna walks to the table in the little main room and clears a
space for the sword. She stays there long moments, her head bowed over
the samurai blade, while the boys tiptoe out of the bedroom, leaving the
old warrior to rest.

The girl looks up decisively. She moves to a drawer at the end of
the kitchen area, rooting through her Nonny's fabrics and notions until she
finds what she was looking for: a thick piece of red velvet trimmed in
gold thread, shiny from ages of use. She wraps the sword in the fabric in
careful folds, then places it on the table again, unsure of how to pack or
carry the heavy weapon off the mountain.

The boys watch her in silence — until they are no longer able to
contain their questions.

"Do you know any other martial arts?"

"How long did it take you to learn that?"

"Did Gramps teach you?"

"What other weapons can you use?"

And the last the question is from Leo. "Can *we* learn?" He can't
yet fully process what he's witnessed, yet it resonates within him. *There's
a lot of art and beauty in how she executes this stuff*, he thinks to himself.
But is it a practical skill?

As if reading his thoughts, Conan blurts out direct questions.

"So, can you actually *fight*? I mean, don't get me wrong, that
was…" He searches for the right wording, so as not to piss the girl off.
"Great! It was a *great* performance, and with a sword that heavy, I mean,
it was really *amazing!* It's just that we did some martial arts, too, Leo n'
me, when we were little — me especially — Kung Fu, Karate … lots of
forms. No sword, I admit, but we still got to be pretty good. But then Dad
put us on Judo mats and into boxing matches and full-on contact football,
you know, with real opponents. It was little kid hand-to-hand battle!" He
laughs modestly, taking a seat at the table. "A totally different thing than
hitting a bag or doing a form, is all I mean."

His voice rises as he begins to worry he's said too much, but he
can't slow his words down. "You know, it's just that, *damn*, Gramps
warned us that the Darkness keeps watch. We're gonna face real danger,
and maybe soon. So, can you actually protect yourself?"

The girl stands with her back partially turned away from Conan
and Leo, all at once statue-still. She narrows her eyes as if to shutter her
inner thoughts.

In the next instant, she spins, leaps and dives to the floor with a
swiftness so shocking that the boys don't have time to see what she
targeted. She rises with one of the Bowie knives in her hand, and then,

like a young lioness on a kill, she springs up onto the table above Conan. Before he can blink, she twists the collar of the boy's shirt until his head is forced back and his throat is exposed to the knife tip now at his jugular.

Leo jumps to stop her. But seeing the tiny curl of Inanna's lip as the knife threatens to draw blood, he hesitates.

As quickly as she was on Conan, she's off, springing from the table in a balanced gymnast's landing. She whoops a great blast of irreverent crowing.

"Can I really *use* a weapon?" she snorts.

She tosses the knife casually back onto the packing pile. "Yeah. And I'm trained to use other weapons, basically everything in that giant footlocker. But I take your point, the only fighting I've done is with dummies and targets … until now." She grins.

Conan's face is red. He has to admit to himself that he'd asked for it. Literally.

Her training, Inanna tells them, was damned hard. It had started with silent meditation and disciplined inner work. And when she was three years old, too young to even sit still, Nonny and Gramps had taught her the Way of the Warrior, the techniques of the true samurai, and the skills of the Lakota braves.

"*Steady your heart-mind-spirit, because the only enemy is within.*" She repeats for them Nonny's continual lesson. The training from her grandparents had been ceaseless.

She pauses. "I guess … today is the day I begin to learn *without* Gramps by my side."

Embarrassed as he is, Conan still relates to her sense of loss. He rubs his throat tenderly. And Leo sees the entirety of Inanna's mindful legacy.

She reaches out a friendly hand to Conan, gently punching his upper arm. "Hey man. Sorry. Kind of." She smiles sheepishly. "Didn't mean to scare you. Just wanted to … reassure you that I'm not a wimp. Or whatever."

Leo laughs abruptly. "So …" he asks, "You're designated Sword Bearer? Just like you're also Pipe Carrier and Eagle Dancer? And … all of this has more significance than what we could really understand, right?" His question is sincere.

Inanna moves to stand in front of the broken kitchen window, staring up through the shattered glass into the lightless sky. She tries to fathom how to think of herself, to explain her role within her family's long ancestry. She debates whether further explanations of her life and her feelings would sound like bragging or complaining.

"Look, you know what I know." She turns back to them. "The three of us were 'accounted for' in the prophecies, like Gramps says. But *this* part, being Pipe Carrier, Sword Bearer, yeah, it has to do with, like, ya' know, the history of bloodlines, the legacies of all my people coming together. I just … never expected the prophecies were saying it was *me!*"

She tells the boys that Nonny's father and grandfather had been direct blood descendants of venerable samurai warriors. And her great-great-grandfather had actually fought for the emperor of Japan. The stories she had loved best had been about the few women samurai in Nonny's family.

"Gramps, when he was stationed in Southeast Asia, became, like, completely obsessed with Japanese warrior culture. You can ask him. I guess he was trying to understand battle, and all the questions and bullshit about war. He was stoked to go to Korea, but the war ripped apart his fantasies of heroism." Inanna tosses her curls out of her face. "He met Nonny's father at the R&R hospital, and after the war followed him to Tokyo to study. It's how they met, my grandparents I mean." She sighs, suddenly very tired. "Anyway, *stories, stories.* But yeah, whoever carries this sword, made by an original hero ancestor, carries the tradition of the samurai." Now it's her turn to blush. "And, shit. Don't laugh, but it's never been a girl!" She hoots. "Let alone a mixed-race Indian, biracial African-American with Japanese bloodlines and whatever else is thrown in! My great-grandfathers are turning in their graves!"

The boys nod silently, but their lack of words begins to unnerve Inanna. She shuffles around in the supplies to give herself something to do and to avoid their gazes. "We'd better eat and finish doing the packs."

She curses herself for the stupid move with the Bowie knife and returns to the broken window. She looks in the direction of her birth and reminds herself that she was born under the powers and protection of the Western Gate of the Native tribes, where the Thunder Beings reside. Her father's people, she was told, had come to this continent as captured slaves from Africa. But they had survived and endured and had learned to live as compassionate guardians of the true Christ consciousness. Her grandmother, meanwhile, had preserved the best teachings and traditions of the Daoists, the Shinto, and the Buddhists. Nonny had lived as a woman warrior in the samurai discipline, with fearless focus and compassionate dedication to all sentient beings and the full complement of the natural world.

I am all of this! Inanna reassures herself. She fills her lungs and finds courage. *I owe Nonny this, and Gramps: to be a true heir.* She sighs in spite of her resolve. *Buck the fuck up, girl!*

She puts her back to the window and straightens to full height. She tilts her head up and returns Leo's engaged and warm smile. She includes Conan, whose eyes are slightly hooded but wholly awake.

Pitching her voice in the B-flat of drums and ceremony songs, she tells them slowly, confidently and unequivocally, "Experience or no experience ... healer or warrior ... weapons or no weapon ..." She pauses to make sure she has their fullest attention.

"Never, *ever,* doubt me."

Chapter 72
Infinity

Leo and Conan do not respond in words. The looks they exchange reflect their certainty that the girl is assuredly not to be doubted. Inanna's astute listening, the rare kind that catches a mouse scampering in tall grass or a dipped owl wing on a still night, breathes in their responses, to be gnawed on later, when it suits her.

She turns to the task of packing food supplies. The brothers join her. They pull together dehydrated soup, stale crackers, and a little jar of peanut butter. They snack on some of the jerky while they pack; it tastes wild, delicious, and nourishing. Conan murmurs, "I can feel my blood turning red again."

"It's elk meat culled from herds that used to roam pastures on the far side of the river," Inanna tells them. "Every fall, the bulls would bellow for their right to hump the best females." She gives Conan a side-eye. "Uh, you know what that means, right?"

Both boys laugh. Leo reminds her they'd helped breed studs to mares along the hilltops of the Pacific Central Coast, and they'd run bulls to meet cows in the valley below during breeding season. They had learned to birth foals and calves, sheep, goats and pigs.

"Yeah I think we got the whole 'circle of life' thing down." Conan isn't embarrassed — but neither does he want to explore the conversation too far.

She returns his smirk with a lifted eyebrow. "Gramps bow-hunted only one elk per year. He and Nonny taught me to skin, gut and debone the elk into steaks, sausage, and stew meat. And whatever they killed, they shared with anyone who needed it."

Leo's thoughts circle back to her directive, *never doubt me.* He swallows his piece of jerky. "I can't remember knowing any girl like you before. You're ..." He searches for words that carry truth, but without false flattery. "You're, like ... a surprise in every way. I mean, you're still a kid — we are, too! — but you're your own person. I think you've got what our Aunt Sophia called 'pure grace.'"

The girl is momentarily at a loss for any rejoinder. Only her grandparents had ever spoken to her in such a way, in words that say: *I see you.*

Her response is interrupted by a startling sound emanating from the next room.

It can't be, they all think.

From the bedroom, a sound of ... *music* is floating on the air.

They look at one another, confused, before setting down their packing and swiftly moving to the bedroom door. Inanna is the first to enter. The boys are two steps behind her, but she abruptly throws a hand up to halt them, without turning to explain.

She's seen Gramps do too many astounding things over her lifetime to think, *not possible* — as the boys do now.

Conan whispers, "It just … can't be."

His voice raspy with sudden emotion, Leo says, "But it *is*."

Gramps is lying as they had left him, pillows supporting his head, one arm bandaged and the other inert under the blankets. But the weak hand of the arm in its sling is holding the sacred flute to his lips. His mouth is pursed above the musical instrument, yet not closely enough to encompass the entirety of the music pouring forth. The flute has resonance, as if a celestial orchestra is joining the one piece. The very air of the room takes on the vibration of his intention.

The flute in the old man's hand seems to be playing itself, accompanied by a river of unseen harmony, an ocean of natural sound.

Inanna lowers her hand and allows the boys to follow her in. As the kids move quickly to the side of the bed, the music increases in volume and accompaniment. The old medicine man doesn't move except for the trembling hand holding the flute and the quivering mouth willing itself to draw notes from the embouchure of the one-handed instrument.

Gramps' surprises and gifts seem to them never-ending.

His eyes meet Inanna's. Slowly, he holds out the flute to his granddaughter.

With eyes wide and a slow shake of her head, she comprehends his desire. She settles on the bed beside her grandfather. Inanna brings the small, cherished woodwind to her own lips, joining the celestial orchestra. The rough-hewn instrument that Gramps so treasures is gracing them all through her playing, now.

Conan gazes around the room, then back to Inanna. "Where's the back-up band?" he whispers. "I'm serious, music is *everywhere!*"

Inanna smiles as she plays. The girl's five senses calm into one stream of musical consciousness. She knows what she has always known. The music is hers, and not hers. It plays on with or without her. The old man's face isn't the deathly grey mask it was an hour ago. His cheeks are tinged pink, his black eyes have some of their former sparkle.

As she plays, she reaches over with her other hand to open the drawer of a boxwood bedside table. There she finds, as she knew she would, another, smaller silver flute. It's the instrument Nonny had played. She places this piece in her grandfather's still-trembling fingers, cupping his palm tenderly.

"Only Inanna, after today … will be able … to ask the flute spirits for protection … and guidance." Gramps sounds out the words slowly, hoarsely, but with utter calmness and direction. And then he brings the silver instrument up closer to his mouth. Its music joins the spirit orchestra and harmonizes with the melody his granddaughter plays.

The brothers, standing on either side of the bed, begin to feel the aches and stiffnesses that had plagued them since their experience at the door of the abyss begin to ease. It's as if the music is healing the very cells of their bodies. They stretch their shoulders, clench and release their fists to be sure they are not imagining what is happening.

Am I making this up? Conan wonders. *Maybe anything is possible in a world turned upside down.*

Winds whip outside the cabin, pounding some nearby boulders loose. A tumble can be heard behind the music, a rumble and slide somewhere on the far side of the little home. Tonight, the kids don't sustain the fear they had last night. The music offers them blessing, care and protection; they feel it in their bodies and souls.

Conan closes his eyes, thinking again of last night's cobalt smoke spirals. Images of circles and infinity symbols rise in his inner vision. Minutes pass before he feels Leo elbow him.

"*Look!*" Leo exclaims.

The blue smoke is not only in his mind — it spirals around the room and out the bedroom door, filling the cabin. There had been no powder to create the smoke. This time, Inanna's flute is singing the cobalt and silver and blue-purple spectrum of colors into being. Swirling in waves that merge to form a single mobius, the symbol dances apart again only to furl into a horizontal infinity figure. The loops of iridescent blue continuously ribbon and spool, alive and aware, moving to the rhythm of the music.

Leo and Conan watch in awe as the calling of the spirits unfolds. Inanna sways as she plays, with Gramps joining the symphony. Leo is flooded with a rush of déjà vu. *Seen this before. When?*

The girl is one with the music. Its color, legacy and promise will always sustain her, even in times of chaos, she feels assured amidst this mystical unfolding. Though Gramps can barely hold his silver flute, it joins Inanna's playing, and together they channel the celestial energy that is never-ending.

Leo is electrified and soothed, all at the same time. He can see her clear inner peace. Words come into his head, from where, though, he can't place. *When inside is out and outside is in … beginnings and endings become One.*

No discernable light illuminates the angry atmosphere outside the house. Darkness presses against the broken windows. Furious wind whips down the chimney to snuff out the dying fire in the hearth. The battered cabin groans.

But Gramps and Inanna play on, undisturbed and unconcerned. Smoky cobalt spools widen until they fill the room. Every inch of the craggy space dazzles in deep blue. The three students and their teacher absorb and reflect the dancing iridescent vapor.

Chapter 73
Ancestors

The music sings itself into a Native symphony, a forest of woodwind instruments. Not even Inanna, granddaughter to mystics and Native saints, has heard this orchestra. And yet, here it is, pouring out from the flute she holds in her hand. To the boys it sounds like a symphonic sigh through the pines of Colorado, a zephyr rustling the aspens in September. To every listener, the music has its own unique breath of sound and succor.

When it reaches a height and breadth that engulfs the whine of the outside wind, the four of them begin to hear a march of distant drums grounding the orchestra. The first beats resonate with the singular sound of kettledrums in the Sun Dance ceremony, until the thrum grows to an entire percussion ensemble.

Conan spins around. "Where the hell is that *coming* from?"

As he turns back, the wall behind Gramps' bed begins trembling. But only the one wall, not the entire cabin. The boys reflexively grab the bed to protect Gramps, though grandfather and granddaughter both continue to play their flutes as if nothing at all disturbs them. The girl, sitting close to the old medicine man on the bed, keeps rhythm with her free hand, tapping along on one bent knee with the drumbeat.

And all at once, the wall heaves an enormous respiration — and expands inward, blowing itself into a translucent blue bubble that bursts forth with a host of spirits in animated parade. Elders in full Native regalia with feathered warbonnets and decorated buckskin robes are mounted on regal-looking horses. They are followed by young braves who stride in or come trotting up on war ponies painted with symbols. Some of war and some of peace. All the men are strong-limbed and fiercely determined. Every one of the spirit figures stares straight ahead and past the humans, moving in pace to the flute and the drumbeat. Shades of blue encompass the procession, and all seem to be singing to the music of the two flutes and the orchestra that accompanies them. The Spirit Nation strides towards them from beyond the shadows of the mountain and the thickness of the night, behind Gramps and Inanna, and through them.

Animals appear in the parade; eagles and hawks soar over it. A family of bear ambles by, three coyotes dart ahead of a fox and a puma that saunters next to two raccoons and a mama skunk with her babies. And last come the buffalo — a cantering herd of them: calves racing to catch parents, bulls snorting to gallop ahead.

The brothers reach out to touch the buffalo spirits as the figures glide past, watching their own hands slip through the animals and the ghostly clouds of cobalt dust they leave behind.

Through the wisps of blue, a lone female buffalo appears at the crest of the otherworldly horizon. Small at first, she grows as the ground beneath her shortens. She is pure white, dazzling and lustrous, and majestically strong. By the time she reaches the room, her size is so vast it takes up the entire span of their vision. She alone of all the spirit beings pauses her stride. She lifts her noble shaggy head, and gazes upon each of The Three in turn with her wide-set golden eyes. And nods deeply. Then charges past them into the distance beyond.

All through the parade, Gramps and Inanna have continued their flute music. But as the White Buffalo moves past them, Inanna moves her mouth above her flute to sing in accompaniment to her own playing. She sings a song of gratitude to the Buffalo Nation in the beautiful vibrato that the brothers first heard on the porch, the morning of the heaven-sent ray of Light.

The boys see her face in silhouette, her high forehead covered in tumbling curls. She is openly weeping. As her flute flutters in a series of ending notes that her singing rejoins, the infinity loop of blue smoke draws itself together and spirals back into the body of the instrument.

Gramps lets his hand fall with the flute dropping gently onto the blankets. With the cessation of the music, his weakness returns and his face folds into the time-worn patterns of creases and lines that contain his pain. He is drained to the marrow of his bones. He feels his once-strong body, the agile limbs that had carried the world — from his dying comrades in battle, to his new bride across this very threshold, to the baby girl now sitting on his old bed — needing rest. The kind of rest that only eternity can provide.

The granddaughter rises and kisses her grandfather's forehead. The boys on either side of the bed stretch themselves, marveling again at the miracle of their healed soreness. Leo bends and straightens his wrist, shaking his head in wonder.

Gramps sees their amazement. He smiles with a crinkle of his eyes. "Trust … the vibrations … of healing. And of … of Inanna's … ability to bring this … forward."

The old medicine man's eyes close for a moment — but not his mind. A long pause follows, and the children draw nearer to the side of the bed

"Conan, Leo … your job is … suit up … and show up." His mouth twitches in a momentary grin. "Let God … Great Spirit … do the rest."

Leo knows that Gramps sees them better than anyone ever has before this moment. He is not sure it's the right time to raise the concern he's carried since the ant battle last night, but he also knows there might not ever be another opportunity.

"Gramps," he says quietly. The others look at him curiously, sensing there is something unexpected on his mind. "After the ant fight, I went outside to get some more wood … and I thought I saw the same …

black ooze that killed the elk. I'm not sure, it happened so fast. It went into the crack in the ground where we threw kerosene in. I ... don't know if it was real, or some fear-imagined shadow ... But I'm thinking now that the force in that abyss where Inanna almost fell today ... was pulling at us. I mean, it pulled at Inanna," he finishes. "It wanted a victim."

A silence falls. Gramps closes his eyes again briefly.

"Darkness ... doesn't sleep. Each time ... the Darkness rises ... it will come in different guises."

The peace of the music and the parade of infinite spiritual support give way for the time being to the chill of the room and the howling of the wind outside. The Three all at once feel a fatigue that mirrors the old man's.

Inanna leans in to give her grandfather one more kiss — and to tuck the flute she had played — his flute — into her grandfather's hand.

She closes his fingers around it and whispers, "*Infinity.*"

Chapter 74
Being Light

The three kids tiptoe out of the bedroom. They are so tired they almost drop where they stand. Everything the day had brought – from the joy of Inanna's rescue to the heartache of Gramps' condition and then the supernatural beauty of the music and its blue-circled miracles, finally catches up with them.

The boys pull out their sleeping bags while Inanna gathers bedding to make a comfortable spot on the floor next to Gramps. The hearth is cold, so all of them grab an extra blanket.

When they're settling and almost asleep, Conan leans up on one elbow. "Bro. How the *hell* are we gonna walk all the way home? Thousands of miles?"

Leo, looking up at the dark wooden ceiling, shakes his head. "Now would be a great time for a private plane."

"A helicopter! Yeah! This is the moment in the movie when the *Mission Impossible* helicopter flies over the mountain with a Secret Service detail and the Navy Seals jump out to save our asses!"

"Hell, I'd take a jet pack at this point. — Do those actually exist anymore?"

The boys quietly joke some more.

Silence falls.

Until again Conan startles Leo from his near sleep. "Remember that song I always liked?"

He croons softly,

Time will continue without you ...
So in the end;
It's not about you,
But,
What did you do?
Who do you love besides you;
beside you.
Many die in the name of vanity.
Many die, in their mind's eye, for justice
We die for you
And still do
So I say to you
This is nothing new
I will be light,
I will be light,
I will be light,
I will be light.

In the quiet following the last refrain, Leo murmurs, "Yeah. It fits what Gramps said. And with what we saw in the cobalt … and with that laser of Light yesterday morning. And the Light Beings."

He tries to make sense of what they experienced in feeling the Light by measures of science, assumptions of proof. He settles peacefully into acceptance of the beautiful mystery.

Conan hums the tune of his song again, trying a few more bars of lyrics.

His brother turns away on his side and folds an arm under his ear. "One thing I'm grateful for, Bro, is that you didn't plan to be a rock star. *Damn*, your voice is bad!"

The boys snort in the darkness.

After another long pause, the younger brother says with a familiar tone of wistfulness, "God, I miss it all."

Leo understands the entirety of what his brother is saying in those few words. He shares Conan's emotions, and knows that he has intuited them his entire life. He's always pushed the younger boy to be positive, to look past temporary feelings of sadness, to look forward to the future with excitement.

But tonight, Leo sighs, "*Home.*" He can't keep the longing out of his own voice.

"Yeah," Conan answers. "But not just our house. I miss my phone and laptop, I miss video games, music videos with beautiful girls! *Hell*, Leo, I just miss being a kid. Even with my crappy singing voice."

Smiling in the dark, Leo responds, "Well, me too. Miss it all." He flips to face Conan and reaches out an arm to his shoulder. "But if we think of what's lost for too long, fear and grief will take over faster than even the Light can appear. We can't fix the past. What we have is now. And the promise, scary as it is, of tomorrow."

He realizes by his brother's breathing that Conan is already asleep.

In the next room, Inanna too is fast asleep, curled up on the floor next to her grandfather.

Gramps' hand still clutches the flute. Wisps of blue smoke emanate ever so faintly from the mouthpiece. In his head and heart, the old spiritual warrior hears the music playing on. It's the music of his people, joined by that of Nonny's people. It resonates with Sun Dance songs and gratitude prayers and the sounds of chords first learned in the adobe homes of the Zuni and Hopi and on the deserts of the Apache and Navajo, joining the ocean music of the Tacoma and Chumash and the river songs of the Iroquois — and circling back again to Zen flute melodies that echo through the White Hills of Japan on a cold winter night.

Gramps prays to the Universe his gratitude.

PART V

Chapter 75
Where Will You Stand?

Before another leaden dawn wakes them, Leo, restless in his sleep, struggles to bring a dreamscape into focus. He's not the active, lucid dreamer his brother has become in recent years. But he knows to surrender to the flow between half-wakefulness and the unfolding story. He knows not to resist the truth of things, especially when it is confrontational, demanding attention.

*

Sophia!
Leo's heart jumps. But he remains still, to be able to see and understand.

His aunt, in profile, stands tall and straight, shoulders wide. Her abundant black curls with their few first strands of white are pulled into a loose ponytail that exposes her regal neck.

As a baby he had loved to wrap his chubby fingers in the tendrils of her hair and lose sight of his own flesh in her curls. He'd wind and unwind her hair continuously while she whispered in the ear he pressed to her lips and chin. His fingers flicker, feeling the comfort he did then whenever he was close to her. He yearns for one curl of her hair to touch now.

In his half sleep, hot tears push against his eyelids and demand attention. He tucks his longing away, so he's not distracted. *Is this a dream?* he whispers to his restless mind. *Or do I actually see her as she is now?*

Sophia stands at the edge of a large Spanish hacienda-style patio. She stands as he remembers her so often in recent years, poised, at ease, never rigid, always graceful. Yet focused and determined. As the lens of his dreamer's vision expands, he sees mountains rise behind the large house cantilevered over rolling, soft hills. His internal, dreamer's vision follows the cascade of hills down toward an enclosed horseshoe of water that seems to Leo like a small inland sea.

Is this the Pacific? Is it near home?
His vision moves back to his aunt. It's as if he stands next to her, and together they watch the morning fog lift off the small, solemn waves of the sea far below them.

Where is this? Leo asks himself. The rolling landscape is covered in familiar sagebrush and mesquite and dotted with sandy-colored boulders. He tells himself it looks like California, the central coast of his home. But no such natural inlet sea exists near home. He's puzzled and tries to deepen and sharpen his view.

As he does, Sophia turns and looks directly at him. He sees the crinkles of sadness around her eyes. *Mourning? Grief?* he asks himself. He concentrates, and understands she's concerned, and with more than a hint of worry. But she isn't anxious. And he sees no loss of faith. No anger. No fear.

Every fiber of his being wants to reach out and touch her. He whispers inside his dreamer's mind, *We're okay, Sophia. We're far away now, but we'll be back.*

He imagines that the loss of his Dad, her brother — and he and Conan, too, seemingly gone without a trace — would be the source of her sadness.

He wonders why he doesn't recognize this house and the secure-looking hills that support it. And he wonders how the house survived the Three Days of Darkness. But the questions are fleeting.

A colorful flash of motion interrupts his aunt's meditative focus. He sees her break into an enormous and almost jubilant smile as she bends down to welcome a small child.

Meera!

There she is, in a sari of gold and pink. A light melody of tinkling bells reverberates from her small frame, spreading into rings of music that match her laughter.

A heartbeat behind her come the boys, his cousins. They crowd the little girl and their mother; bumping and pushing, they tease and run, laugh and insist.

Alive! His exclamation echoes in his ears. The boys, older and bigger than he remembers them, are still easily recognizable. With the blanket covering his face, lying there on the floor of Gramps' cabin, Leo doesn't fight the tears that run down his cheeks.

Alive! Thank God, alive.

Yet something's not right. Sophia, though she is joyfully laughing with Meera and the boys, can't hide her deeper emotions from the dreamer. There's an unmistakable shadowing under his aunt's almond eyes, which are so like Conan's. And the corners of her beautiful full lips that are so like his own are turned down.

He counts the boys. The two older ones, the two younger ones are there. But where is the middle boy? And where is his uncle? He assures his dreamer's mind that of course they could be close by, just out of his line of sight. But he feels an absence detached from any story or explanation. And, in spite of his cousins' raucous play and the laughter he sees on their faces, he feels his aunt's aching heart.

Sophia would say when he was growing up, *You and I, our hearts have a very similar feeling sense. You have a tenderness for the world and its people, Leo.* He remembers that as if she speaks to him now, heart to heart. He breathes that truth in.

He feels again into the scene. And on the energetic wavelengths of family vibrations across space and time, he sends out love. Support. On the ethers of their shared sensitivity, he searches for meaning. What he's certain of is that something's missing.

Yes, more than just us and dad, someone, others, are missing. He and Conan, but who else? How much, how many, are gone? Who will not return?

He calls to her again in his sleep. *We're okay, Sophia, we're heading back. We'll be together, soon. Soon.*

*

Before first light, Conan wakes. Though groggy, he is urged to something like alertness by the sound of a flute. He closes his eyes and wishes the music would flow into his blood and brain, body and spirit ... and stay inside him forever.

"Being Light," he whispers aloud. The events of the night before fill him with faith and amazement. *I want the blue infinity to flow into my body, into every atom and cell.*

Conan sighs, exhales and rolls over. But he can't go back to sleep.

Leo, awakening next to his brother, thinks, *I wish I could connect with Sophia and the cobalt.* He desperately tries to hold his aunt in that heart-mind space, but his head nags him awake with awareness of today's duty.

He nudges his brother.

Conan resists Leo's prod and rolls away, wrapping himself more deeply in the sleeping bag. "Shhh ...*Listen.* Flute. Gramps," he whispers.

Leo understands what Conan doesn't. The ambient flute they hear is playing itself inside their bodies... and in gentle, sweeping circles around them. Leo sits up just enough to peer through the open bedroom door, confirming his intuition. Both Gramps and Inanna are dozing, though the old man's hand still clasps his flute.

He whispers to Conan's back, "Gramps is asleep. Lightly, maybe, but he's not really awake. Seems to be breathing into the flute ... and it's, well, playing *itself.*"

He lies back and thinks about his dream, of the inlet sea and the faces he loves and the promise of fragmentary return to the life they once had all together ...

And Meera!

But he can't bring the images back. He sighs and decides he'll wait to tell his brother the dream. *Maybe it's selfish to keep it to myself.* But Sophia had taught them, "Always honor the dream. It came to you for a reason. Don't give it away until you are sure why it calls you."

He nods to the memory of her voice in his head. *Yes,* he answers. But there's no response back from the dream.

Instead, his brother's voice muses, "Whatever happens Leo, to us, to Gramps ... we can't let his music die."

Leo is not sure either of them fully understand what Conan means, but believes his brother is right. He whispers back, "Yeah. Granny said that gain and loss always traveled together. But what we gained here, because of Gramps, we can't ever lose. Nothing gained is ever really lost, as long as someone remembers, right?"

Conan murmurs, "Yeah, and makes a story of it."

They lie like that for minutes more, their bodies begging for rest and motion in equal amounts of insistence.

At length, the younger brother rolls onto his back and puts his hands under his head, looking up at the ceiling. "I really miss the storytelling. Like, I miss the lyrics of music, the rap and hip hop. Bro — remember those 'Get Lit' poetry slams at the high school? And that amazing one, the last one I guess, when we went down to L.A with Mom? *Damn!* I loved it. I remember I came home and stayed up half the night trying to write a slam poem about riding the range and horses. *That* woulda' been a whole other kinda rap poem! ... I loved those stories. That was before all hell broke loose and we couldn't get down there again."

Another pause follows before Conan adds, "Where are all those kids? The ones in L.A., and the ones who came up from San Diego and down from San Francisco for the finals of the slam? What do you think happened to all of them?"

The unanswerable questions hang in the air between the brothers. And now they are restless and start to move into the day that calls to them ... but it's a day they also don't want to face. Neither boy wants to leave Gramps. Yet both want to find their way home.

The brothers say the words over one another's thoughts. Leo admits, "I need to see what's happened at home, in the world." At the same time, Conan sighs, "It's time to get home."

In their shared memories they smell the ocean, and the sweet dry sage bursting its fragrant seeds in the heat of the summer. They remember so easily the fog that creeps up from the valley floor and dampens old oaks hung with moss and mistletoe. They lie there and whisper in word-skipping short sentences and broken syllables, like they did as little boys from their bunk beds. Both brothers are wise enough not to question too deeply what is left and what will always remain as only memory.

In their connected hearts, they come to the same conclusion, spoken aloud, "We *must* go." The future is a mystery, but whatever is ahead, heading home has to be the goal.

"Gramps' mountain's not stable," Conan acknowledges, "and could get worse. But — on the other hand, maybe not. It's a huge old mountain. Come on Leo, we're from earthquake country. Yeah, it's pretty much been hell the last few days here but, ya' know, eventually it stops ... I think."

He doesn't say, *how can we leave Gramps?* He knows Leo is asking himself that question, too.

Conan's stomach growls loudly enough for both boys to hear. They know they have to get up. But the younger boy has to tamp down his worry first. "I just feel, like ... jagged with my thoughts going back and forth between gain and loss. Home sounds good, *so* good!" Conan heaves a sigh. "But the teachings are here, Leo! And, well, how will I learn anything else? I don't want to make this about me, but I need Gramps — and he's here. And I know his strength's gone and the mountain won't hold, but ..."

He sits straight up in his sleeping bag. A full minute goes by in silence while the boy tries to reason with his own crackling temper. Finally, he says between clenched teeth, "I'm pissed Leo. About ... all of it!"

Leo sits up, too, wrapping his arms around his knees. When Conan doesn't say more, Leo gently touches the younger boy's shoulder and says, "The fire's not giving off any heat. Let's grab some wood outside." He's thinking that the fresh air and a simple task will settle them.

The boys pull on their Levi's, crusty with weeks of dirt, and wriggle into their worn cowboy boots. As they tiptoe to the door, Inanna looks up from the floor of the bedroom and sees them going. She starts to sit up, but Leo waves her back to rest. "No worries, stay put," he whispers.

The brothers lean their weight against the door in order to push away the fallen timber and rocks again after last night's shifts. When they step out onto the remnants of the porch, they feel just how flimsy the cabin's position is. With their feet over the doorframe, the cabin shifts subtly. They can't help wondering if it's barely balancing over the chasm they know to be beneath them.

The boys survey the new damage to the terrain outside.

Leo mutters, "Bad as the quakes have been, I don't think I knew the cabin and the mountain were *this* precarious."

Conan's eyes flash his alarm. He has to breathe deeply so as not to freak out.

Carefully, gingerly, measuring each scrupulous step so as not to disturb the unsettled ground, they search for anything within near reach that will serve as firewood. They are suddenly hyper-aware that any forceful movement could cause the ground to stir. Inanna's face appears at the bedroom window for a moment, checking on their progress.

"Leo," Conan whispers, looking behind him to make sure he has enough distance from the half-closed cabin door to ensure they can't be heard. "I know what you're going to say, okay? But I want to hear you say it." He crouches nearer to his brother. "Leo ... you're sure about Inanna, right? I mean it's been only the two of us, until just the past few days. And I know she's, well, really good at stuff. And I know what she's done for us and what she's capable of. It's a lot! But still, there's a hell of a trip ahead. Do we need someone to be responsible for? I mean ..."

Leo drills a rare, hard-eyed stare at his brother. "What the *fuck* is up with you, Conan?" He's tired, frustrated and agitated. "This is at least the second time you've whined about her." He's got a headache and his dry throat irritates him. The Sophia dream continues to preoccupy his mind and sensitivities, alongside his worry about the mountain's stability. *And now this crap?* "What the hell should we *do?* Leave her here to die with Gramps?"

Conan's eyes fly open. He gapes at his brother. They haven't spoken of the real and unreal choices and the inevitability of Gramps' future until now.

Leo bites and spurts his words through clamped teeth. "Or *what,* Conan? Let her go off on a journey alone? Send her in a different direction? Are you kidding? Really? I mean, *really?* We're on a friggin' mountain ready to collapse from under us! We need *more* Inannas! We need, like, an *army* of 'em!" He pulls back on the throttle of his anger but can't reverse direction. "And how about what Gramps said about The Three, and how we need to stay together? I mean, I thought you wanted to be a medicine man, like he is? But what, suddenly you don't believe the things he says? Far as we know, we're among the few humans left in a disappearing world. And you want, what? Assurances!? ..."

He exhales, pauses and drains anger from his voice. "*There is no certainty!* We knew that before we even got here! And *now* ...?"

As if on cue, the mountain belches rocks and dirt that rain down on the flimsy, battered porch roof. The boys crouch and stare up at the dropping shingles, wondering if the rest of what's left will fall on them.

Conan widens his eyes at Leo. The older brother, out of nervous habit, cracks his knuckles and shakes his head as if to say, *need more proof?*

When the tumbling dirt and debris still themselves, the brothers stand. As calmly as possible, they check out the damage they can't repair.

Despite the scare, the conversation needs to be finished. Leo pitches his voice to be steady and calm. "Ya' know what Granny used to say? *Where will you make a stand when the ground is liquid?*" He puts a hand on his younger brother's arm. "Well, I choose to stand with you." He squeezes the arm. "*And* with Inanna. Linking our minds, choosing the pouches, seeing our connected past lives ... I mean, we share prophecies we've heard since we were kids! ... She saved our lives, Conan, and we saved hers. What *more* do you need?"

The older boy doesn't trust himself to say more. He turns to pick his way carefully across the broken porch pieces in search of more wood scraps.

Conan squints at him, taking his brother in. He sees Leo's clear-eyed commitment, but also his unusual impatience. He knows the rarity of it. And wonders whether Leo is as anxious as he and Inanna about the journey ahead.

Under his breath, on as light a step as he can take, Conan gets close to Leo and says, "Okay, *hey*, I get it. It's just that …" He sighs. "It's hard for me to trust someone else, Leo. With you, I know what to expect, I know you've got my back. I agree, she's, well, amazing. But she's also weird and temperamental." He's trying to convince himself, but now he can't grasp why he felt he needed to in the first place. His frayed nerves are so often bugging him, he doesn't notice — until Leo argues back — that he's anxious and tense and out-of-his-skin.

"Leo, I … I just hope she doesn't get all, ya' know, like I said, *unpredictable* … after we have to say goodbye to Gramps."

Leo wonders about the choice of those words. And whether Conan sees how much alike he and Inanna are.

Conan shifts from one foot to the other. He bends down to pick up a piece of split wood. Without looking up, he says, "She wouldn't be with us unless we're all supposed to be together. Okay! Got it. But you n' me, Leo, we've been in this together from the start, right?"

One frustrated heartbeat — and then Leo realizes, *Damn! Of course. Conan needs to be reassured that no one takes his place with me.*

The older brother reaches out and puts both hands firmly on Conan's shoulders. He notices how bony his brother has gotten. There's been too little food, for too long. "Bro. There's not much we can be sure of. But no matter what, the two of us are together." He wants to sound light and not worried for whatever's ahead. "You're the Merlin, right? You think I don't want that magic with me?"

"That's right," Conan smiles reluctantly. "You know I'm going to know some shit … eventually. And … you're right about Inanna. Even though she may *knife* me at some point." He rubs his throat with a smile. "Better get the wood inside before she comes looking for us."

Gazing on his brother, Leo remembers that the boy is only fifteen years old. *Just two years ago, when I was fifteen, what the hell did I have to worry about?* he asks himself. He'd have been stressing about losing a football game, or maybe breaking up with his first girlfriend and worrying what their friends would think. Or he'd have been sleepless over an A.P. Physics test. *My biggest fear was how a B grade would affect my GPA.*

They'd already been on the front lines of fires and rescues, two years ago. School had become episodic because of whatever was the latest pandemic, or tech breakdowns that led to rolling outages. Power shutdowns later became the "new normal," along with too many environmental disasters to count.

But they hadn't thought of those things as existential threats. Total disaster wasn't obvious to him. And, if they weren't obvious to him, as he prepared to be a first responder on the front lines, he thinks, *they sure as hell weren't to thousands of other kids trusting in a reliable future.*

But in the following twelve months, any hope of that future would be gone.

Conan's only fifteen. He didn't even have two high school years to be a teenager.

The brothers gather up the wood pieces they've collected. They are only half a dozen yards from the remnants of the busted-up door, but they take careful half steps to reach it.

The starless, moonless night still hangs on the edges of the thin, grey morning light. Leo shutters a sigh for the losses left behind and for the mysteries that lie ahead.

He watches Conan push the door open while balancing his lopsided armful of logs. Leo thinks of him as the little brother, needing protection. Yet the Merlin role is one of wisdom and equality. They need each other in ways understood and not yet known, too.

The younger boy pauses just before they enter to whisper, "Nothing breaks our tie, Bro."

In the cabin, Inanna has laid out a breakfast. She's arranged cereal bars crumbled into bowls, with powdered milk on the side and a handful of trail mix for each. She wears a sly, secretive grin.

Conan blurts, "Hey! What are you hiding?"

"What? *Me?*" she responds coyly, then brings out from behind her back a small honey jar. "Look what I found!" Conan drops the wood he's carrying and reaches for the jar, but Inanna whisks it away from his grasp.

"*So sorry!*" There's no apology in her tone. "Can't have any now. It's for later, when we need a shot of energy."

"Hey, I *always* need a shot of energy… how about a sugar fix for the road?"

She ignores him and secrets it into a hiding place in her backpack.

Conan turns to Leo and moans, "She's got all these damn titles, and now she's the *Sugar Carrier,* too?! — Wait. Is that a thing?"

Chapter 76
Never Stop the Music

Leo fist-bumps his brother.

"Inanna knows if you're in charge of honey, there won't *be* any. And I kinda think she earned her titles. You'll have to find one of your own before you're in charge of anything as precious as sugar."

"*Exactly!*" Inanna crows. Then pivots with efficiency and goes back to her cooking.

The older boy notices that there is an obvious shift in the girl. It's not anchored in her yet, he thinks, and not so strong as it will become when she's a fully developed woman. But her growing confidence makes her gifts more profound, her energy less edgy.

He whispers to Conan with an unselfconscious smile, "*The force is strong in her.*"

Conan knows his brother is in sales mode. He pounds his own chest in solidarity.

Leo erupts in laughter. "Yeah, let's make *Sugar Carrier* a thing," he declares loudly. "Only us around — we can make any damn thing we want into a thing!"

Conan whoops, "*Hell*, yes! Who's going to argue with us?"

Inanna gives them a thumbs up. "And," she says pointedly, "It's time you two made packing up a *thing.* And right now."

The boys jump in almost enthusiastically, still joking and fist bumping back and forth. Leo is glad the tension between them all is broken for now. But he knows they each carry a deep disquietude about Gramps' broken body, much as they keep their thoughts hidden while stuffing last provisions in their backpacks.

As The Three enter Gramps' bedroom, they see the medicine man's halo of golden Light expand and warm the small space. Even Inanna, a child of phenomena and mystical ceremonies, isn't accustomed to the strength this miraculous illumination seems to give her grandfather in spite of his failing body.

The kids move into the glow.

Gramps smiles. His hand grasps the flute that Inanna had played last night, the instrument he himself had played for most of his life. He beckons them closer to his bedside with a nod, then focuses his gaze on his granddaughter.

"Always ... keep music playing," he tells her hoarsely. And presses the flute into her palm. "Vibrations ... must forever ... be freed."

Inanna understands. She searches within herself for equilibrium, needing to hide her longing and sadness. The medicine of the flute is a powerful conduction of vibrations that only those who are truly humble and willing to serve can channel. Gramps is passing it on to her.

"The power ... exists within instrument itself. And ... within you," he tells her.

Inanna had learned to play under Nonny and Gramps' tutelage. The flute, she knows, sings in order to draw the spirit world to the earth. It's a healing tool, and a tradition to which one is born. She had been taught that a day would come — a day she had thought would be far distant — when she would take these traditions into the future, to preserve them and teach "those who choose the One-ness."

"Never ... stop ... the music," Gramps whispers.

The relationship of the vibrational medicine to Inanna, this child of many breeds, carries profound responsibility — a responsibility few have been known to bridge from to life to life. Unleashed, the right music can heal a broken mind. In a marriage ceremony, two separate souls become one when the music unites them. And it can call their newborn into the world. Yet, in the wrong hands, the power of such music can bring death and devastation. It can spin cyclones, and it can usher in war.

Part of her screams, *I'm a kid. I'm not ready! It's too much responsibility.* But she refuses to give that voice breath.

She bows her head in respect, keeping her eyes tilted up to her grandfather, and accepts the sacred flute, acknowledging the blessing and the command given from heir to heir in a long, sacred line.

"Inanna," her grandfather directs in his halting, ragged voice, "it is *you* ... who must teach Conan ... to play medicine music ... also. He will find ... cobalt notes ... within him." The old medicine man turns his eyes to the younger brother. "Son ... the flute, like Sacred Pipe ... heals ... protects ... guides. As medicine man ... you need that ... power. Live up to ... trust ... I have placed ... in you."

Conan feels a red-faced flush of concern that Gramps knows about the worries he harbors over taking Inanna with them. He feels a burning shame ... and then lets go of his doubt. The faith Gramps puts in him renews his faith in himself and in their journey.

"Gramps ..." Conan ventures after a long silence. "Now we're starting on this journey you've been talking about. So, today, it all begins. It's time. Is that right?"

The medicine man's laugh startles them. It is almost his deep, familiar belly-laugh. "Oh, Conan ... my new, young ... and *so* old ... apprentice." He gestures for the boy to lean forward so he can bless him. His shaky hand pats Conan's cheek, then moves to his forehead. Eyes closed, Gramps whispers, "Which journey?"

He lets his hand fall, opening his eyes and squeezing them in a smile. His black irises meet Conan's crystal-clear gaze.

"Conan ... there's no ... real ... start. Ever." It's clear that speaking is painful for Gramps, but he is determined to override his body's weakness in order to deliver his final lessons this morning. "There is no ... real ending. Today ... you leave ... for *this* life's journey ...

towards the home you know … in this life. But … today's journey is a continuation. Also, another chapter … of your very long story."

The old man coughs for long seconds. With the hand of his bandaged arm, he motions off their concern, even as he gasps for a clear breath he no longer possesses. But his presence of mind is keen and focused.

"This journey … is *part* but not all … of why you took … this incarnation … at this time. Choice … or choice-less … there are no mistakes … in Universe."

In the warmth of the room emanating from Gramps' aura of golden Light, The Three reflect on all of their teachings, today and throughout their lives, converging on this moment, this recognition that their individual stories are woven into the tapestry of the Continuum.

At length, Leo whispers, "I've been thinking about Aunt Sophia. She used to talk about how there are no beginnings and no endings, too." He glances at his brother, sitting on the edge of Gramps' bed. "Remember how she had that black and white mobius strip?"

Conan nods.

The older boy recalls how fascinated they were by the visual infinity of the strip, how the black became white and the white black, without end. Sophia had taught them how important it was to remember that silos, boxes, boundaries and delineations in life are not God-made, but man-made. She had said to them, "*Wolf-brothers, my nephews, children of my heart... in the vast plan of the Universe, there are no beginnings, no endings. There's only the next journey, and a new mission.*"

Sophia taught that the entire purpose of a person's life may be to connect greater truths, one to another. Christ lived thirty-three years, yet Christ-consciousness and the messages of love linked together essential truths that have lasted thousands of years.

Gramps smiles and rests his eyes.

"Yes. In one sense, my children … you have much to learn. In another … nothing to learn. That is the lesson of the Continuum."

Chapter 77
The Brand

The flute, now resting in Inanna's hand, still plays its mystic melody into the air around them. The four gathered together let the music fill their souls in preparation for all that the day must bring.

The old warrior opens his eyes after a long pause.

"Leo. It's time." The boy tilts his head in question. "Time now… to take off your shirt … show us gift … and burden … of your karma."

It's Leo's turn to feel his face flush. He can't pinpoint why he feels so confused and embarrassed about the mysterious images seared on his chest. *Trust. Faith.* He speaks words of courage to his heart-mind as he reluctantly wriggles out of his long-sleeved flannel, keeping his eyes on Gramps alone as he does so.

Both of the other children are unprepared for Gramps' command — but at the same time, their curiosity about Leo's tattoo has been an unspoken source of keen interest for them since it was accidently revealed. Their stolen glances at his marking, that first morning they had woken in the cabin, had raised countless questions they had not yet dared to ask.

Inanna and Conan turn their eyes now to Leo's bare chest.

"What the *heck*," Conan low-whistles.

"Who *did* this to you?"

"When did it happen? How?"

Words of shock and amazement tumble from them. Yet Leo begins to realize that what he sees as a disfiguring embarrassment appears to the others as a work of other-worldly beauty.

Conan whispers his admiration. "No *way*. Air-pawing dragons… and what are these?" he asks, pointing to a border of cross and sun shapes radiating with sharp spikes of yellow, "… Celtic symbols?"

Inanna stands back to take in all of the design. "*Wow!* Red flying horses … breathing flames! Same as you saw the night of the Rishi vision!"

On that last California dawn, Leo had had one short glance of the markings in a broken mirror. He admits to himself he'd been scared. He hadn't wanted to inspect the brand further, and then … events had prevented him from taking the time to do so. He realizes now how little of it he has actually seen.

But the primary question remains: *Who could have done this to him?*

His brother continues to murmur his appreciation for the detailed artwork. "*Exquisite.* This is like something you'd see in old European churches." Then he snorts. "Speaking as an experienced couch-potato historian."

He adds that the tattoo looks more sculpted than inked, as if the sculptor used Leo's skin to carve a bas relief. Each individual symbol crosses and ties to another. Inanna and Conan both marvel at how the separate scenes and symbols seemingly unite to tell one connected story.

Leo glances awkwardly down at his chest, then up to meet their inquiring eyes. Inanna and Conan talk over each other in a slam-barrage of questions, opinions, and observations.

"They're symbols of … What? Nobility, right Gramps?"

"Warrior kings?"

"Whoa, the closer I look, the more the symbols seem to rise up right at me."

Inanna studiously hovers over each image. "That's the … yeah! The Third Eye of the Rishi teachings! *Damn!*"

Conan nudges her, "And see that? It's the Pendragon, from the lineage of King Arthur! We've read books about him since we were in preschool, all that stuff about the Round Table and *Might Does Not Make Right.*" Conan stares again at his brother's flustered face. "Thought I knew you, dude, but …"

Inanna shakes her head, "That's why Meera held her hand on your heart, isn't it?"

"Bro! Musta' burned like *hell* when you got it! … Why the hell didn't you tell me?! Does it hurt right now?"

Conan traces the overlapping images with his artist's fingers, apparently not overly concerned with the answer to his own question. Inanna, too, itches to touch the brand. But when she gazes up at Leo under her curtain-thick lashes, she senses his embarrassment. And feels her own, suddenly. She leans back and presses her hand to her heart, instead.

Now that this moment of discovery has arrived, Leo wants to know from Gramps everything he can learn about the mystery of his marked flesh. After all, Meera had known about it, and so seemingly had Gramps. He locks eyes with the old medicine man, wanting to reassure himself that whatever force created it, the sign is not an omen of doom.

The old warrior's gaze is suddenly as piercing as ever. "I know… how it happened. Leo … awakened on the day … when *winds swept light from earth* … as predicted. The morning … Three Days of Darkness … descended." He closes his eyes again, as if seeing that morning on his own inner screen. "The burn … spread across Leo's heart … and chest … like it was afire. Yet … the boy did not cry out. He knew he had to get on with … rescues … he had to protect … others."

Pausing to gather strength from the flute music, Gramps swallows. "The brand, Leo … tells karmic story of your lives … *all* the lives you … have lived. That brand … was earned. No one else burned the brand … It grew … above your heart … from within you."

Gramps, Conan and Inanna watch the heavy lifting of Leo's chest and his long, slow exhalation of breath.

"*No ... mistakes ... in the Universe,*" the old man finishes. The effort of speaking causes him to cough in a long rattling sputter. Inanna wipes his mouth with a hand trembling from emotion. She reaches for her grandfather's palm and holds it to her cheek. He curls a small smile up to his granddaughter, whispering to her in Lakota.

Inanna interprets his words for the boys. "Gramps says, *we chose and were chosen.* The Darkness only succeeds ... when we fail to use our abilities for the greater good."

The old man's eyes wander above their heads as he whispers in his native tongue, his granddaughter translating. Inanna knows what the boys don't, yet: that when the flute gives up its secrets, when it chooses to tell a story or unravel mysteries, the human needs of the medicine man are of no importance or consequence. Her grandfather is able to give these last lessons because the music of the spirits is imbuing him with more hours of life than he would otherwise have left.

"He says," she goes on to translate his words, "The message from the flute last night was that the force field, the wall of energy, did — as we thought — protect you from the Darkness that killed the elk."

The old man seems to ask something, then, that the girl does not translate. Instead, she takes the small silver flute, the one that had been Nonny's, from the bedside table — and holds it up to her grandfather's mouth. He forms his lips into a small sigh, and all at once the flute begins to play a new story-song. A fresh, floating vibration lifts from the instrument as if carried on angel wings.

The medicine man bends his head in reverence and whispers, "*Aho.*"

The Three, poised for the next miracle, are captivated by the melody. It seems to Conan that the music contains a cat's low-pitched purr and also something like a whir of raptor wings. The flute's song without lyrics lifts them, expands their hearts and calms their minds. What they hear is the resonance of the single syllable of creation, *Om*: the vibration of forever, of ancient beginnings, and the ending of the Universe that will never come.

Chapter 78
Mystery of the Labyrinth

Gramps begins to shift into a trance state. His eyes flutter between closed and open; when open, they are wide and far-seeing, as if he sends this message back to the earth plane from the other side.

"Inanna ... you must Remember ... your Bird-Girl ... your Divine Protector ... she knows all the secrets of the Universe." Inanna leans over her grandfather, caressing his brow. "But, for reasons not revealed to me, she needs *your* human energy. Nothing is hidden from Her. She will ... guide you."

Again, the medicine man is silent so long that Leo takes his wrist in hand to feel his pulse. "The beat is there, but it's thready," he tells the other two in a whisper. The once-steady pulse of Gramps' blood flow is weakening into a shallow stream, as if moving away to a distant shore the boy can't reach.

The next instant, the four of them are rocked by a sudden jolt. The cabin seems to jump. The sound and movement are sharp and intense, as if the ground beneath the mountain had launched a single giant projectile.

Gramps slumps over at his waist. Inanna moves to shield him from any fallout from the lurch, ensuring the silver flute is near Gramps even as she rocks on her feet. The tone and tempo of the little instrument drops octaves lower into a barely audible hum. Her own flute, the one she had been gifted by her grandfather, still issues faint strains as she grips it tightly in her palm.

The Three balance themselves again, poised to act if the mountain shakes further, but for the time being it seems steady. They all lend a hand attending to Gramps, easing him back onto the pillows, trying to settle him in as comfortable a position as his broken body can allow.

A million questions dot and dart through their minds, meanwhile. Until Conan whispers to the others, "What about the labyrinth we saw? Should we ask Gramps again? He just confirmed the force field protected us from that black ooze. I mean ... do you think we should know more about that weird *heat* that came from it, and stuff ...?"

The old medicine man opens his eyes.

"*Chunkshi* ... your flute. You ... must find vibration to answer these questions."

The girl is momentarily taken aback.

Then, she lifts the silver flute from which the faint mystical music still emanates, at the same time pushing the other instrument nearer Gramps' weak hand lying on the blanket.

Praying within herself for wisdom and strength in the old ways of her people, she brings her flute to her lips. Her grandfather nods a blessing that assures her she is ready for this moment.

A complex and beautiful melody begins to emerge from her playing, a composition of such profound intricacy and serenity that the girl knows she could never have created the notes before now. The sound calls in other wind instruments, creating an elaborate orchestration of harmony. The player and listeners are certain the sound filling the cabin has so much depth that it must emanate from the very bottom of the earth under their feet. As if to underscore that particular imagery, a slow beat of drums grounds the heavenly wind instruments.

The music calls forth color and images before their eyes. Pictures flash and form in the room, floating in independent shapes all around them. Blue cobalt becomes the dominant color of the shapes, and then the blue frames configure themselves into columns that whip with increasing speed into horizontal and vertical planks.

Multiplying in number as quickly as they appear, the quadrangles begin to attach to one another like shimmery scaffolding, building themselves into a multi-beamed tower. The structure connects itself with such eye-blinking rapidity that before those witnessing the miracle are even aware of what's happening, it rises through the roof of the cabin in an infinite spire of cobalt construction. The iridescent superstructure contains a vast interconnecting complexity of bridges and tunnels and recesses. The entire glimmering battlement appears strong enough to hold up the sky.

The music plays while the four observers gaze speechlessly at the miracle. Inanna merely holds her flute in her hands; no longer does she need to physically play it. The other-worldly orchestra continues all around them as the framing builds itself upwards.

At the peak of its perfect, intricate construction, the tower quivers. In the next instant, as suddenly as it grew, the entire framing inverts itself — and with driving speed, it folds with a *whoooosh* through the floor of the cabin, reconstructing its cobalt quadrangles into the blackest depths below.

"*Labyrinth!*" All three kids exhale the same word, as one. They are hypnotized by the eerie formation as it lays down plank after plank.

The expanding symmetry under their feet forms an enormous assemblage of mazes. The four observers are looking down into a fathomless translucent framework, a beautiful and mesmerizing reflection of light and geometric fractals. Flares of heat and mists of steam fan up and out from the Labyrinth. The Three find that they are sweating, and the hair on their head is damp with the hot vapor that rises like a blue haze on a foreign planet.

Gong!

A single drum-strike rings from the depths below the Labyrinth, sending reverberations up their spines.

And through the steam, two young women arise from the depthless formation. They are running, growing larger as they come closer; they appear to be challenging each other across the dangerous gauntlet of connector planks. One girl, light of coloring and with fair hair, is dressed in a shimmering silver gown. The other, a dark-skinned girl with jet-black hair, wears a velvety magenta dress, the only note of contrast against the blue and silver shades of the bridges they cross.

The girls run together. It becomes apparent, their faces strained, spying anxiously over their shoulders, that they are running from a danger below them, behind them. The three observers feel a visceral ache to help, to reach out to them, to shout support.

Nothing is certain. The words ring in Leo's mind. He falls to his knees as an urgent need to reach into the Labyrinth and save these girls grips his limbs, lungs, and heart. With an altered-state sense of familiarity that is completely at odds with what he sees below him, Leo leans towards the scene.

His heart is thumping in his chest, his throat constricts with the rising steam. Cold and hot shivers of fear and courage drive confused shots of energy through him. The boy half-stands and pivots, looking desperately around him for a clue, a hint of some meaning or plan.

The Labyrinth's bridges create and connect themselves just a step ahead of the girls' fleet feet. It appears to Leo that with every stride, the runners risk a free-fall before making the next dangerous leap — yet they never slow their fast pace.

He rises, leaning towards the girls … and almost howls with the frustration that he seems to be outside of any range of possibility that he could help them. He has entirely forgotten that the flute's vibrations created the labyrinth and the girls. He feels sure he could run next to them, with them. If only he might drop into the Labyrinth, he could reach them.

An earsplitting roar explodes around the cabin and heaves it in the most violent shake. Gramps' Montana mountain is crying for attention, unable to defend itself against the earth's upheaval.

The vast and complex Labyrinth, along with its mysterious runners, folds instantaneously over and into itself, its cobalt columns and glimmering planks disappearing in clouds of steamy fog. The Three manage to lean forward, even as the ground is shaking, to try and touch the last sight of the elusive, beautiful girls.

Chapter 79
Into the Dawn

The Three are knocked out of their yearning focus on the Labyrinth and its runners by another sharp quake. The bed rocks in place, shivering and sliding into a right slant. Leo is off balance when the new jolt hits. He's tossed against the wall. Inanna's chest slams on the wood frame of the bed with enough force that she is propelled backwards into Conan. He grabs her arm in one hand and a corner of the mattress with the other, restabilizing them both.

The old medicine man appears to be unmoved by the roaring rebellion of the mountain and the tremulousness of the cabin. It's as if, for him, this is all part of his goodbye. His golden halo of Light reappears and warms the room.

Inanna steps closer to her grandfather's side again, caressing his forehead while she replaces her flute into the sheath that she vows will never leave her side for the duration of whatever this journey will bring.

Gramps raises the hand of his bandaged arm to grasp Inanna's. He gives it a squeeze, then points to the corner hutch.

"Granddaughter ... bring me ... what is left ... in the drawer ... there." The golden Light gives Gramps a much-needed infusion of stamina, replacing the music and imbuing him with the last strength needed for this hour of consequence.

She nods, steps to the hutch, opens the rickety drawer, and removes two small leather pouches a quarter of the size of the medicine pouches they already wear around their necks. The last item in the drawer is another flute, a small and roughly hewn wooden one.

She brings these three items back to Gramps' bedside, carefully laying them on the blanket next to his good hand. The boys gasp when they see the little pouches. They look at each other, astonished.

"Recognize them?" the old man murmurs with a crinkle of his eyes. The bags are a soft, cordovan leather with long, thin leather cords woven into their closures. The brothers hesitate only a moment, looking to Gramps for his okay before Conan reaches for the one he knows to be his own, his childhood totem pouch. He smells it, remembering the summer he'd thought it lost. Leo takes his, too, and holds it high, Gramps' golden Light infusing it with a new warmth.

"Your Granny ... made sure ... the bags would be here for you," Gramps whispers affectionately. "Don't open them now ... wait until you are down mountain ... and safe ... and can look at each treasure ... with new eyes."

Next, the old man gestures to Nonny's silver flute, the one he'd been playing this morning, and instructs Inanna, "Teach Conan with this flute ... the one you learned on when you were little. When he ... earns it

… trade it for the one I gave you. Each… carries a certain power… Only give him yours … when he's proven himself worthy of it." Conan stiffens and reddens under Gramps' stare when the old man adds, "Too much medicine … in that flute … will overpower you … until you're ready."

Feeling on the blanket for the small wooden instrument Inanna had just placed there, Gramps finds it and tremblingly holds it up.

"Inanna … you carved this flute … when you were seven years old." The rough wood of the instrument is whittled with baby birds and crooked, notched initials. "Leave this smallest one … with me, daughter … I will sing you Three … down the mountain."

The Three have known this moment would come. They had known when they woke this morning that the day would be about getting started on their journey — and leaving Gramps behind. And yet, all three of the kids sense they'd been somehow yearning for a magical transportation or intervention, so as not to say goodbye to the old warrior. Now, as Gramps prepares to play the music that will accompany their farewell, The Three find themselves almost unable to move.

They wait. They wait to see if there might be something that will change. Into the ensuing silence, Gramps breathes one deep inhale and rattling, bumpy exhale. The Light around him responds in synchronized circles of gold that continue to grow until the entire cabin and their own bodies, hearts and minds are filled with the glow of it.

"Inanna," he finally says with deliberate effort, "Take them up… across river at source … It has … changed … don't be fooled … follow your instincts and listen for flute. Vibration … will find vibration." He beams a broad smile, though every bone and muscle of his being is clearly spent. "There is … purpose … in everything, daughter." His eyes move to take in The Three. "*Do not stop for anything.* Understand?"

The old warrior's sudden insistence shakes them from sentiment.

"Yes, understood," Leo answers for them all.

The golden Light pulses around Gramps' head as he studies their faces. "Speak only when necessary … in lowest voices. When you cross a second stream … you will be off … this mountain …" His throat catches. "*Off* … but … not safe … don't stop … until day is lighter … noon … you'll be in valley … there will be trees … there you will rest … but not long! Don't … make camp … until night. Star Portal will guide … follow energy wave."

Leo and Conan shoot looks at each other. *Star portal?* Conan is tempted to ask, *Really?* But thinks better of it. Gramps catches his eye and smiles. "Enter … The Remembering … and you answer your own questions."

The wooden flute in the medicine man's hand begins to flow with low, single-note vibrations of music supporting the golden Light that surrounds Leo, Conan, and Inanna, illuminating every corner, from the dust-covered rafters to the tattered windowpanes and creaking floorboards. The medicine man closes his eyes and curls his hand to bring the mouthpiece closer to his lips. The single-note ambient music begins to increase in volume, and The Three know this is the time. The goodbye they had all been fearful of — Inanna most of all — has come. The Light and the celestial music give them the strength they need, to trust and move forward.

Inanna bends to kiss her grandfather, and the old man's eyes flutter open. Before praying a Lakota blessing, the girl reaches into her pocket and removes Nonny's necklace from its velvet pouch. She secures the necklace's clasp around her neck. A prism of color sparks off the crystals and semi-precious stones spacing the necklace's talismans.

The warrior's eyes smile when he sees his wife's favorite jewels on their beloved granddaughter. "Good ..." he murmurs. "You wear ... your Nonny's protection." He seeks her eyes. "And ... you found ... the knife of the Spirit elements, my daughter ...?"

The girl straightens, holding her hand to her mouth. "OH, my gosh! I almost forgot! I was afraid to pack it, it's still on the mantle! I wanted to ask you about it, but ... everything has been happening so fast!"

The boys are as curious as Inanna about the arc knife. They lean into Gramps as he tells them, "It ... was from ... First Warriors."

The Three want to ask, *how did you get it? How did it come here?* But time is too short for such questions now.

"It was ... given to you ... for safe-keeping, Inanna. The person ... who brought it to me ... traveled far ... to make sure it would be with ... our people ... and with you, my daughter."

"But — I have NO idea how to use it. What am I supposed to do with it?!" The girl is suddenly agitated.

"The person... who brought it to me ... I pray he will find you ... eventually. He will be able to tell you ... more."

"But how will I know that person?!" she exclaims.

After a long pause during which the old man's gaze does not waver from his granddaughter, he whispers, "He is ... your father, Inanna."

Find your center, she commands herself within. The questions screaming in her head make her dizzy. She sits on the bed and puts a hand to her chest to still her heartbeat.

The brothers circle closer, the low music surrounding them creating a rhythmic pulse in the Light. But before Inanna can give voice to her thoughts, Gramps raises the hand holding the notched flute. "Enough. You must ... have trust. Judgements ... will hurt you more ... than the person you are judging, my *Chunkshi*."

He closes his eyes once again.

The boys move now to bless Gramps. Leo leans in to place a kiss on the old man's forehead, quietly thanking him as he does so for all the knowledge that has been bestowed by the teacher on his students. Next, Conan leans in to kiss the hand holding the wooden flute. And finally, Inanna rises.

There is no more to be said. She knows her grandfather will countenance no argument, no hesitation, no doubt, and no concern for the weary and broken body that begs to be released from its earthly form. Inanna disciplines her tears to wait.

She gives her grandfather a blessing that contains the same words of prayer he had used to tuck her into bed when she was a child.

"*Wakan Tanka.*"

With a final kiss to his familiar, wizened, noble cheek, she moves to the bedroom threshold. When she turns back to look at Gramps one last time, the old warrior has already closed his eyes.

She straightens her shoulders and goes through the door to join the brothers.

Chapter 80
The Mountain

In the next room, Leo and Conan are zipping their backpacks. There's so much to be said, but no way to express the weight of it.

They let the flute music accompany their thoughts.

Leo stares at his red hat for a moment. He almost removes his beanie in favor of the familiar cap but decides no one is looking for his rescue signal now, and maybe it draws too much attention anyway. He folds the red cap into a side pocket of his bag.

He turns to Inanna with a gentle look as she comes into the room, meeting her eyes for a brief moment of mutual courage and strength before shouldering his pack.

Conan is tying his trusty drover's coat to the straps of his backpack. Leo notices its bulk and raises an eyebrow, telling him, "I'm leaving my ratty old jacket, bruh. Wearing this nice down one from the trunk, instead."

His younger brother retorts, "Really, with the tags still on, and all?"

Leo smiles to himself, deciding Conan will be happy to have both coats when the nights get even colder. Besides, he realizes, the drover's coat, its flair and uniqueness, is suited to Conan as no ordinary down jacket, after all, could be.

Inanna moves to the hearth and takes down the box holding the arc knife. She pushes it deeply into her own pack, next to her skater shoes. Then she squeezes the velvet-wrapped samurai sword into the other side. Like Leo, she puts on the down jacket — but she decides to wear it covering her black cape. She lifts out the hood and adjusts it so it covers her beanie.

Leo glances at the girl to gauge her emotional strength before moving to the door with his equipment.

Conan takes a last long look around the room. He adjusts his pack, securing a rifle tip. "Wonder if the 'Remembering' comes with weapons training?" he murmurs with a hard swallow. "Because we don't have magic wands or flying brooms or light sabers or invisibility cloaks. Not even a damn rocket pack."

"Yup." His brother nods. "No cell service or devices ... Just a couple of compasses and a whole lot of weaponry. But ... we're together. And we're as prepared as we'll ever be."

He meets his brother's eye and they both look to Inanna. The girl has heaved her heavy backpack up onto her shoulders. Under any other circumstances, the boys would laugh at her ensemble: moccasins, witchy cape under puffy down coat, glittering gemstone necklace, and a load of accessorizing weaponry. Now is not the time for that perspective, however.

From the bedroom, the music shifts in pitch and tempo.

"Courage," Leo whispers to Inanna from the open cabin door.

She closes her eyes and lets the flute melody fill the space of all that's been said. "Yes, courage."

Inanna purposefully places one foot in front of the other until she reaches the door. And crosses the threshold of the cabin.

The Three feel that Gramps' presence is no longer merely in his body, but with them, through the flute music and the Light pouring out the windows and open door of the old home, accompanying their steps.

They move as one until they come to the crest of the cabin's hillock. There, they pause to survey the desolate terrain. No living green seems to remain. The tumbled ground is a mass of rocky, unrecognizable brown. Trees are ripped from their roots, dead warriors of a once-noble, high mountain retreat. The enormous boulders that had safeguarded the cabin are buried under the avalanche of debris, barely jutting out of their former homes in the soil or rocked askew in wrong directions and odd angles. The landscape is lifeless.

All the years of her family's care and blessing were not sufficient to protect the mountain from the planetary rebellion, Inanna sees. The guardian spirits were not able to shield it from this kind of assault. Her grandparents' beloved retreat has been pulverized. She's shocked but not surprised; the protections were put in place to guard against invaders, not the destruction of the very foundations of the Earth.

Torn in every direction, Leo observes in silence. North to south, east to west. He'd seen it when he and Conan were gathering wood, but now that their journey is starting the scope of devastation hits him harder. Up and down the hillsides as far they can see, leafless trees are split from their trunks, branches bent and peeled of their leaves.

"Damn," Conan whispers. "Gramps was right. This mountain is shredded."

Inanna glares at him to stay silent. Leo waves a hand indicating for them to continue forward. There's no choice but to get down the mountain. The directive they were charged with from Gramps was to *keep moving*.

Shorn gravel and loose stones slide and roll under their every step. The Three have to measure each foothold, balancing and rebalancing their loaded backpacks as they negotiate the treacherous slope. *Should've practiced carrying this equipment*, Leo notes, and marks it down as another lesson in survival leadership he has to master.

In the silence of their slog down the slippery, muddy mountainside, all three kids' thoughts are on Gramps, on the old medicine man's acceptance of his earthly journey's end — and on the precious days they'd had with him. What they'd learned from Gramps since arriving on this mountain just three nights previously had been more than a lifetime of experience could measure, under normal circumstances; but nothing had been normal for these Three, for too long.

The inconstant ground requires their complete and careful attention. Gramps had told them to stop for nothing, to observe silence, and to be off the mountain by noon.

Conan's inner dialogue circles as he gulps strangled sorrow and clambers over the next boulder. *I hope I can be what Gramps expects of me, I hope I can 'live for the people'... and be a White Whirlwind. Someday, Gramps, I will be like you. I will. I promise.*

He rebalances his load and stops for breath. As he does, the boy tilts his head to catch the flute music still reaching their ears over the sounds of the wind and water. Leo and Inanna pause, too. All three nod silently to each other, encouraged by the transcendent notes that accompany them even as far from the cabin as they now are. All three kids, feeling the depth of Gramps' unceasing gifts, are filled with *awe and wonder*. It's not our imagination, Leo thinks. *The old medicine man is conducting us over the mountain with his flute, just as he promised.*

The music seems to drive renewed power and balance into their limbs. Conan asks himself again, as he pushes forward, whether the frequencies of the instrument had manifested the parade of ancestors last night. And whether the vibrations of Gramps' drum had lifted the cabin, the night before. Had saved them. He wonders, too, what it will take for him to learn the flute, to play the way that Inanna and Gramps do. The old medicine man believes in him, he assures himself. He must hold onto Gramps' confidence until he finds his own. When the White Whirlwind sings a ceremony, he rocks the house and all the spirits want to visit him. *Will I be able to do that, too? Will the spirits find me?*

Conan has to stop his brain from teasing his imagination in order to concentrate on the pace Inanna sets. He reminds himself of Gramps' warnings. To be injured out here at the beginning of his journey would be unthinkable. He pays closer attention to the extreme tilt of the steep grade. Until, after another half hour or so of footslog, his brain floats up another question.

Am I worthy to be weaver of mystery? Like Gramps? Am I worthy to be Merlin? Or medicine man? Gramps said so, but ... He suddenly feels too small for that promise. And in the next moment, he hears a whispered word, a single charge in his ear. *Remember.* Conan whirls around. Inanna and Leo are several feet ahead of him; the word could not have been their utterance.

The music directs him to press ahead.

Okay. Maybe I'm worthy enough for now, he grins to himself.

His brother looks back to check on Conan. But Leo is wrestling with his own private thoughts. He's feeling as much of a direct calling, a command to lead, as he's ever known in this life — even while Gramps' last instructions point to the paradoxes that he worries are still nagging him. Their enlightenment from Gramps' teaching is not a light bestowal.

Yet both Gramps and Dad had said, "Suit up and show up," in their different ways. That makes sense, Leo thinks. Dad had pushed his boys to their best efforts every day. "Don't say you've come to play unless you come with your A Game, every damn time! No excuses," he'd drawl.

Leo shakes his head to focus on the immediate. He's less than a yard behind Inanna, but it's as if she skips across the broken earth unaware of the barriers and dangers. She seems unstoppable. The boy laughs at his own relative clumsiness, and that perspective breaks up his heavy thoughts on the responsibilities of leadership for a span of minutes … until the theme repeats itself in his head as if placed there by an outside source. It brings to mind his Uncle Richard, who had started life on the concrete of inner cities and had brought that asphalt anger to an early career as a head-busting boxer. Overcoming substance abuse, his uncle had directed his energy into helping others, and in time Richard became what his grandmother had called "The Bodhisattva of Gold's Gym." A true spiritual warrior who led troops of young addicts to redemption and a sense of purpose, Richard had preached, "To be your greatness, understand your darkness; they ride the cyclones of transformation together."

Fears of betrayal draw those who want to betray you, Leo reminds himself. *That's what we saw the night we battled our fears. The best leaders aren't confused by their own fears, and they aren't surprised by the people who don't stand with them.*

Only he can't yet fully reconcile himself to the darkness and bloodshed he'd seen in his past lives. He knows that a leader has to be prepared for battle — and sometimes for fights in which others would be injured or die. Even a righteous war kills people, and often the victims are the innocent. *War is a failure of moral imagination. Aunt Sophia taught that. I just can't make sense of why I am called to this role.*

An unexpected barrage of images suddenly flashes into Leo's consciousness. Flames, speeding horses, screaming refugees cross his inner screen, just as he had seen them on the night he and Conan were blown away to Montana. Then scenes of fire ants, Native warriors, and the pounding circle of the Last Encampment circle in his mind. He has to stop for a breath to clear his head before taking the next step down the steep hill.

You Three are chosen, he can hear Gramps say. *Not because you were born in the right "tribe" or because this life is a magic fairy tale. You were chosen because, lifetime after lifetime, you chose The Good Red Road. You chose paths of righteousness, courage, integrity, right-intention, and right-action.*

Though they don't know it, Gramps' lessons are echoing concurrently in the minds of The Three. Inanna's heart is heavy with grief, yet her grandfather's words give her purpose. *Choice and chosen.* She keeps her head high, guided by the music of the pipe. She never slows her pace. She narrows the lens of her vision so her focus will be stronger. She knows she can't risk a look back.

As they finally approach the river to cross at its source, Inanna sees that it has changed, just as Gramps had warned her. Where before there were rocks to jump across, now there is only a narrow collection of broken branches lying across the higher water. The branches might serve as a wobbly bridge, she decides. She puts her pack down at the shore, testing the wood for a foothold, and finds that the sticks are tangled thickly enough to hold her weight. She nods to the boys, shoulders her pack again, and starts across the sodden but safe viaduct. The boys follow, one at a time, Leo taking up the rear.

The music of the flute can still be heard when they pause on the far bank, as if it's guiding and protecting their way, flowing towards them on its own watercourse of smooth, sustaining sound. The Three look at each other in smiling wonder.

At what feels like noon, difficult to assess according to the full haze of the sky, they cross the second stream. Leo high-fives the other two kids. *Right on time*, he notes. This second small bridge is formed of slippery, moss-covered rocks. Inanna goes first again, familiar with the rock leaps and comfortable in her moccasins. She springs easily from rock to slippery rock. The boys' cowboy boots are a liability; it takes them twice as long to cross. Conan almost falls into the water at one point, without any traction — but he catches himself and rebalances before he takes a tumble, equipment and all.

At this point, the kids realize they are off Gramps' mountain. They don't recognize the terrain. The place where the river had forked on their ascent, just days ago, is no longer discernible. But they can gauge the general area of where Gramps' mountain begins, and they pause for a moment to silently reflect on all they had faced and survived since climbing to find the old medicine man.

Leo is prodded by Gramps' warning: *stop for nothing*. He nudges the others from their reflections, and they move on. The tempo of the flute music slows, and the level of the melody grows softer as they progress across acres of accordion-folded land squeezed by the movement of the Earth's tectonic plates. They watch for Gramps' promise of a "valley with trees" where they could safely rest for a brief time, but there is still no living greenery in sight.

Chapter 81
The Valley of Safe Keeping

The hazy noon light stretches across the horizon as they come to a conical hill. It's clear they are now going in a different direction from where they had started when waking up after the Three Days of Darkness.

Inanna climbs ahead of the boys, and at the peak of the hill, she turns to Leo and Conan. With her finger on her lips, wary of drawing the attention of any energy or being that might be lurking in the shadows, she points down into the valley on the other side of the hill.

Reaching her side, the brothers gaze at a vista of three hills, two of them covered in sharp and irregular agate, one a sheer vertical rock face. Together the hills guard the valley below, a refuge of green in the otherwise desolate landscape. A small forest of trees stands in the valley, seemingly the last sentinels of living verdure. Willows and silver-leaved cedars line a narrow stream running through the miraculously undisturbed grove, and a small copse of fir trees lines one end of the valley.

The Three descend into the lush little haven, reaching the fir thicket where cones have dropped in a thick scattering over the ground. The wondrous signs of natural life in the little forest bring them such unexpected joy and respite, it's a brief balm to their sadness and fatigue. They lift off their packs and stretch.

"As long as we are careful to whisper ... we can speak a little, now," Inanna says in a low voice.

"Keeping our eyes open for danger," Leo adds.

Conan's elation in the presence of actual plant life is contagious. "Awesome!" he whispers with a wide-armed gesture of euphoria.

They get out their canteens and some dried fruit and jerky from their packs, and sit gratefully on the soft, cool ground.

"I don't remember ever being here before," Inanna admits. "I don't think I was ever on this exact route before today. This is ... a miracle. Gramps ... knew it would be here for us, a place to rest." She looks up at the sky.

They are all asking themselves unanswerable questions. Did Gramps know this valley from his travels? Was it part of the flute's story, drawing them here, even if he never actually came here himself? But they'd learned from Gramps that they shouldn't get stuck on looking for answers at every turn in the road. They'd learned that sometimes you just have to stay in the flow.

"It's like what happens when we remember our stories, even the ones hundreds of years old — or thousands of years old, like the Rishi ones," Leo reflects. "Sometimes we just have to accept that there are ... miracles and mysteries."

Inanna crushes a handful of pine needles and smells the lush, woody aroma.

"Damn," Conan sighs. "We sure need any miracles we can get!"

The three kids laugh wistfully. Their giggles threaten to become too loud. Leo puts both his palms over his mouth to indicate they should lower their volume. The other two immediately mimic him, clapping their own hands over their mouths, fighting back their hilarity until they're almost sure they have their emotions under control.

But Inanna can't resist a jibe out of the side of her hand. "Great job keeping up with me on the way here, *not!*" The boys guffaw, covering their faces with their arms to keep quiet.

"Are you kidding me?" Leo hisses. "I'd be flat on my scrawny ass if I tried to keep up with your ninja leaps."

"Hey, Leo's got some moves," Conan teases in a hushed voice. "Don't laugh, Inanna! I just don't know where they're hiding!"

Inanna high-fives him, then flops to her side, one arm under head. "Hey. Uh, look Conan." She hesitates, looking down at a pinecone she toys with in her free hand. "Ahhh … sorry I … uh, pointed that knife at your throat. No, really! I … pulled that stunt in middle school, once. My third school in a semester, actually. *Anyway*, what happened was, I made my first real friend. A smart, super-kind girl — but she got bullied a lot for her weight. Like, bad. Probably because the rest of the girls were effing idiots, nasty chicks who basically dominated that shitty excuse for a school." She spits the last words out. "They brutalized her every day for sport. So, one day in the cafeteria some bimbo, ya' know, probably the kind of chick you guys like, all fake and platinum perfect, but *anyway*, she was queen of the lunch benches, and she starts in, making fun of the 'new Goth girl,' meaning me. I wouldn't give a damn, but then the bitch calls out my friend, like, *Hey, Blimp, hey Fatty!*"

Inanna shakes her head at the stupidity of life in middle school.

"… And I had to do it!" She spits out a pit from a dried peach and growls, "I went for her throat with a plastic cafeteria knife."

Both boys' fight to control a howl of laughter at the mental picture of Inanna jumping from table to table, leaping and diving with the plastic weapon in her hand.

"I mean, come *on*! A plastic knife? Like it could do any damage, couldn't even smear the greasy make-up off her face, woulda needed a freakin' cement trowel for *that* job! *Anyway*, I got suspended. That's when I started hanging with the skaters. They didn't care who I was or how weird, or whether I was the only girl. Anyone was in, as long as you could skate." She has averted her eyes, but now Inanna gathers her courage and looks squarely at Conan. "I … shouldn't have done that to you, Conan. I was proving something, I guess. Damn if I remember what. I'm sorry."

Conan rubs his larynx and busts out in a rolling belly laugh, so rare for him. "Shit! No defense I tried on a bully was ever as *genius* as a plastic knife attack!"

Inanna stands and dips an exaggerated bow.

No stranger to peer cruelty, Conan reflects that bullies aren't separated by gender. Most of the time, his brother had been there to defend him or tell him to step away. But other times, he hadn't been so fortunate. He'd have been glad, he says now, for Inanna's fierce friendship.

Leo smiles, watching the two of them. He knows that much of Inanna's past is amazing; her education in healing methods, herbology and the natural environment; her flute playing, her weapons training, her familiarity with ceremony and symbols — as well as her gift of Sight — are all astounding. But he also knows she's had a crazy-painful childhood, and revealing her vulnerabilities does not come easily to her. Sharing this story with them now, with an apology, is a very good sign of her growing trust, faith and courage.

They are silent for contemplative minutes.

Until their attention is arrested by a shift in the air. The flute music which had accompanied The Three all the way down the mountain and even, faintly, into this small verdant space of valley, abruptly stops. They shift their eyes to one another, alarmed. Unconsciously they had felt it lift their spirits and guide their steps. The sudden cessation of the gentle, supportive hum creates a void in the atmosphere, as if the sound had been swallowed whole.

The kids jump up as one. "*Gramps!*"

Leo, Conan and Inanna scramble to ascend the hill they had just come down, frantic to understand why the music had stopped. They slip and slide on the gravel-strewn slope, struggling for toeholds, often climbing on all fours until they crest the summit of the conical hill again.

Just as they reach the top and look towards the elevation from which they'd descended that morning, an earth-shattering blast, a boom as deep as if they'd broken through a planetary sound barrier, erupts around them.

From Gramps' mountain, in the distance, boulders fly in every direction like rockets competing for air space. The kids can no longer see where they'd crossed the two rivers. The slopes are indecipherable under the deluge of high-flying dust, stones and scree. They gasp, then cover their mouths, trying not to inhale flying debris. The blast had knocked them to their knees, but they scramble to their feet and stand shoulder to shoulder, trying to understand what they're seeing.

A second rumble and boom rattles the ground again. A reverberating thunderclap echoes throughout the terrain in deep rolls.

In the next moment, as Leo, Conan and Inanna stand witness atop the conical hill, Gramps' entire mountain collapses into itself. It *drops*, falling into a canyon the size of an ocean. The once-majestic mountain drowns in its own rubble. What was once a Rocky Mountain majesty, thick with snow in winter, sprayed with wildflowers in summer, orange and yellow-leafed in Autumn, supporting so much and so many for a millennium — is *gone* within a span of seconds.

Holding onto each other for safety and salvation, the kids watch the final sigh as the abyss sucks the remaining dry air, dirt and rock, with every boulder and watercourse and mineral that had constituted the eminent mountain, into the vastness of its void.

Where the ten-thousand-foot peak had stood there is now only an expanding cloud of mile-thick dust.

Coughing, spitting, wheezing, the kids clutch one another and fight to stay upright.

Leo is the first to look up and see the golden Light that begins to rise. He squeezes the shoulders of his companions and points to the sky above the dust. They all see it now: a halo is ascending from where rivers once ran, from where birds flew over the canyons and peaks of Gramps' cabin refuge. The Light circles itself, building like a dawn of glorious sun, growing into a helix that spans the entire expanse of the sky above them. It pulses like a breathing entity of conscious radiance. The halo's center is poised above and exactly where the small cabin on the old mother mountain once stood.

For an unforgettable moment, they see a familiar smiling face in the heart of the golden glow, a beaming, transcendent vision of their teacher, with his high, wide forehead, chiseled cheekbones and eternally wise obsidian eyes.

"*Gramps!*" Conan and Leo and Inanna, voices choked with awe, with joy, with the enormity of the illumined brilliance, exclaim as one.

And then the golden Light descends in a showering of brilliant particles. The kids turn their foreheads towards the sky and hold their palms out to welcome the rain of shimmering, glittery teardrops of love and legacy, as the last vision of the old man known as White Whirlwind scatters over The Three in a blessing of golden stardust.

Chapter 82
Star Portal

Standing together on the crest of the hill, The Three feel their entire beings trembling with the magnitude of what they've witnessed. The weight of truth hits them forcefully: the loss, grief, and shock of the mountain's destruction, set against the miracle of Gramps' spirit rising and showering them with Light, leave them unable to form clear thoughts for long minutes.

There's so much that needs to be said, Leo understands. *But ... not now.* Although his head pounds with the ebb and flow of emotion, he hears Gramps' warning that they need to move on. They cannot linger here.

He won't deny his tears. But the boy commands his body to act. Turning from his companions to look down into the green valley where they had rested, he finds that his legs are so wobbly he doesn't trust them to hold him upright for the downhill trek. He opts to slide down the slope on his butt. It's not a comfortable descent, but he gets to the bottom and starts picking up their food and canteens and packs. He calls up to his brother to lend a hand — but gives Inanna her space alone at the summit of the hill.

When he and Conan have silently packed up and reorganized their backpacks, Leo feels his legs starting to regain strength. He makes the climb back up the hill, where he finds Inanna in the same place where she's stood since the mountain was swallowed. He steps to her side and takes her hand without speaking and waits with her in the sustaining silence.

In time, Leo bends his head to engage Inanna's dark eyes, so like her grandfather's. He nods gently to let her know he's going to guide her down. Leo has seen this before, how grief can cause a body to freeze.

Conan is waiting for them on the cool, piney valley floor. He has sliced up small bites of jerky for Inanna, giving himself a task he hopes will bring the girl some nourishing comfort. He hands a few pieces to Leo, who offers one to Inanna, cooing that she needs to eat something. She shakes her head once, but he slips a bite into her mouth, like he would feed a baby bird fallen from a nest. Then the older boy lifts a cup of water to her lips, while Conan adds raisins and nuts to his brother's palm. Inanna accepts a few from his outstretched hand but doesn't eat.

Leo judges more than half an hour has passed in the valley. They have to get going. He quietly directs his brother to fill all their canteens at the stream.

"It's getting colder, Inanna. Zip up that down jacket, all the way to the neck." She obeys without engaging his eyes and without comment, not seeming to care that her cape bunches under the down jacket. *She's on autopilot*, he observes. He lifts her backpack onto her shoulders and adjusts the straps. He wants badly to hug her, to wipe her tears, but he knows she'll reject any effort at comfort. He wants to respect her need to grieve the way she must.

When Conan returns from the stream, he hangs Inanna's thermos on her waist. Leo helps his brother heave his backpack on and mutters, "Damn! That's a heavier pack then you've ever volunteered to carry. You must've muscled up since becoming a medicine man."

Conan retorts, "Ha! You need help with yours, Captain America?"

The older boy just shakes his head with a rueful smile. In truth, he aches to stay among the living trees and the clean water. But he's vigilantly aware that night will fall too early, so he leads them forward.

As they cross the valley floor, Leo and Conan collect some pinecones and dry tree branches for tonight's campfire, tying and tucking them into their pockets and packs.

"Won't bring much warmth," Conan whispers.

"We'll need it, all the same. And carrying more would be dangerous," Leo responds quietly.

Inanna stares ahead of her, silently, never breaking pace.

The brothers find themselves listening for flute music as they hike, forgetting for a moment the impossibility of it. Inanna's head is down while she walks, her focus completely inward.

The brand above Leo's heart suddenly and unexpectedly burns. He registers its power but chooses to believe it's a reminder of the mountain and the man and the promises of his own future that Gramps had shared with him. He blinks his eyes closed quickly and glimpses a vision of the small, lean old warrior. Gramps was a man fully contained, complete, within and without, like Crazy Horse, like Horn Chips and Sitting Bull, and like his Marine Corps brothers who'd given their lives for their country.

The boy tucks his medicine pouch inside his shirt and gathers strength from the memory and the image of his teacher, whispering a prayer of gratitude and farewell.

Then Leo turns his attention to best route out of the valley. Three steep hills guard the vale on the opposite side from where they had entered. Each option looks pretty treacherous from where they are now. Hoping to find an old deer trail once they're closer, he guides his companions toward the right-hand hill.

The other two follow him without comment for less than fifteen minutes before Inanna slips silently to the lead. Leo holds up a hand to Conan, motioning for him to let the girl alone. She doesn't turn and look at them, only charges ahead at a determined pace. The boys trot to keep up. After five minutes or so of traveling in the direction Leo had set, Inanna makes a sharp turn to her left and heads toward the hill of sheer, steep rock that looks to be the most dangerous of the three slopes.

The boys exchange a quick look. They have to trust that Inanna's grief isn't clouding her instincts or skills. The rocks that form the vertical wall feel to them like a veneer of slick granite. The stones chip and crumble under their boots; the boys progress very slowly, hardly gaining any territory with so much slip-back.

"Intense!" Conan huffs aloud. He's getting pretty frustrated, especially because Inanna hadn't asked their opinion before choosing this hill to climb.

A jutting ledge appears a few yards ahead. The girl bolts forward, scaling the slippery divots as easily as if it's a rubberized rock-gym wall. She waits there for the boys to catch up; they are climbing one slow foot at a time, slipping backwards nearly as often as they catch a toehold.

Inanna shakes her head impatiently and points to their feet. "Boots!"

She had known at the beginning of the day that until they saw their limitations for themselves, she wouldn't be able to talk the boys out of wearing their familiar cowboy boots. "Damn *boots*," she grunts.

Conan is sweating by the time they reach her. "Yeah, sure. But... anyway, whatever. We're here. And it's all we've got."

The girl crouches and opens her pack. She digs her hand into a deep inner pocket — and takes out two pairs of plain, beautifully-stitched moccasins. They are exactly like the pair she wears herself, only larger.

The boys gape. "No way!" Leo grins.

"You ... brought *moccasins?*" Conan blinks.

She doesn't have to convince them to make the change. Their sore feet are crying for help, loudly. The brothers perch on the ledge and pull on their moccasins, surprised at how thin and flimsy the soft second-skins feel. They tie their boots to the outside of their packs and resume the ascent behind Inanna.

It's not quite as impossible, now. The boys feel their arches stretch and relax, and they're able to navigate the narrow outcrops more securely. But one way or another, it's still a nasty challenge. Their packs are overstuffed and there's no easy pathway over the sheer wall.

In short order they need another break to sip water and readjust their packs. Conan can't help himself from scanning the other two hills that guard the valley they'd just left.

"Inanna. What's up with those two slopes over there? I mean, this one here is about the hardest hike I've ever taken! Could we get where we're heading by going over one of those hills, instead ...?"

Leo interrupts him, seeing the glare that forms on the girl's face. Before the two of them get into it, he says quickly in a reasonable tone, "Gramps wouldn't send us in this direction if it wasn't right. So, what are we not understanding about this route you chose, Inanna?"

With her voice tight and her lips in a straight line, the girl faces them. "Figure it out. This one takes us where we actually want to go.

That's why I chose it." She seems numb, not caring whether her words sound harsh.

Conan suddenly gets it. If Gramps had wanted them to go this way, there *must* be a reason. He remembers his words of direction, and the term he'd used.

"Star Portal!" he blurts.

Inanna nods.

She turns back to the granite wall and points in several directions. "Look for oddities," she instructs. "Look for what's hidden in plain sight."

She tells Leo to go wide to his left and scan that area, while Conan should look center. She goes to the right. They climb simultaneously, each searching his or her field of vision as they slowly ascend. Being careful not to yell and create an echo in the canyon, they have to communicate in strained whispers.

"Portals can be real tricky to find," Inanna guides. "Look for something that's just a little bit … off. A ledge that's weirdly crooked, or an odd angle of rock that looks a little different than the rest. They can be in places that look extra dangerous, too, like there's been a rockslide, or something was busted up in the granite-face. They always look to me like they almost fit, but not quite."

Their eyes burn from their minute scanning of every detail in the rock face.

"Keep your eyes soft and wide, see what can't be seen," Inanna tells them. She's sure that if one does exist here, it will be in a place most people couldn't easily reach.

After another ten minutes of concentrated, exhausting effort, Conan suddenly points to a lopsided crack in a cleft of the canyon wall about twenty feet ahead and to the left. It's barely an indentation, but with perspective, it resembles a small door knocked off one upper hinge; it casts a slim, crooked shadow diagonally across the rock face.

Inanna half-smiles, impressed with Conan's careful observation. "Maybe."

All three kids start moving toward the shadow. Inanna goes slowly at first, knowing the boys will take longer to reach the goal with their slip-backs on the granite and shale. She easily climbs past them after a few yards and then redirects them to stay behind her so they can see where she grabs the divots. She moves like a mountain goat across the rock, from narrow ledge to narrow ledge. The boys notice she doesn't take one false step.

Inanna closes in on the wrinkle in the sheer face of the hill, and at that point, about a dozen yards below the marking, she waits for the boys to move in and perch at each side of her.

"Star Portal?" Conan scrutinizes the crack in the rock wall.

Inanna's mood has shifted. She is pensive, but less withdrawn. "I traveled the Star Path with Nonny and Gramps just a few years ago. They taught me that Portals are always in impossible places like this," she reflects in a soft voice. She gives the area another close scan. "Yup. I think that's it."

Together they climb up until they are all three facing a tall, oblong sheet of notched stone that has an aspect of being slightly ajar.

"Escape," Leo breathes.

"Pray first," Inanna whispers, again reminding herself — and the brothers — to stay aware of what's not seen. Squatting on the ledge, she removes a pinch of tobacco from her leather waist pack, holds it in the air and turns to the four directions, supplicating the spirits in Lakota all the while. The boys listen with reverence. Conan touches his medicine pouch.

When the prayers are over, Inanna gives the boys firm instructions.

"*Inhale* right before you enter. Hold that breath in your lungs, and when you pass into the frequency, you will feel the air change around you. Then you exhale, and the same frequency will carry you the rest of the way through."

She tells them they'll feel a "whoosh" of quiet but forceful energy.

"Whatever you do, don't wobble! Don't fight the current, or back away or get scared. You do, and it's a freefall of fifty yards, straight down and we won't be able to save you."

The boys redden. But Leo nods solemnly, and Conan says, "Okay, got it," in a voice that betrays only a small tremble.

She nods back to them. "Remember: *Faith. Trust. Courage.*"

Inanna scans both their faces to determine their resolve before giving them a thumbs up.

"I'll go through last, just in case one of you needs me to help you start through."

They agree that Leo should go first. He swings his backpack to the front, so it won't bump behind him.

"Face the wall now, right there where you see the crack," Inanna directs. "Wait for my signal. And then once you start, don't turn back. Got it?"

The boy inclines his head once, willing his heartbeat to stay steady.

From behind him, Inanna concentrates on the spot she believes hides the Portal. When she is sure the moment is right, she gives him the go-ahead. "*Now.*"

Leo inhales deeply, holds the breath — and steps forward. He doesn't look back.

And then he's gone.

Seeing his brother disappear into the rock, Conan has a moment of tremors.

"I can't see him! How do we know he's okay?!"

The boy is fearful that he's lost his brother. And yet, he knows that to resist or leap forward could be fatal. Either choice could send him in a direction that could determine his death. But to take this step of faith requires a massive amount of trust and courage.

There isn't much time, Inanna thinks, to explain or quiet Conan's nerves. If there is doubt on the part of anyone stepping into the Portal, its frequency won't respond. From behind the boy, she simply repeats, "*Trust. Faith. Courage.*" She prays that all Conan has been taught will be enough to give him the strength needed for this passage.

The boy slides his eyes back to her for confidence before turning once more to face the rock. Inanna sees the back of his head nod. Conan closes his eyes and silently asks Gramps for help. Like his brother, he takes an enormous inhale, then steps forward. And disappears into the Portal.

Inanna counts to ten to ensure she's given the boys time to clear the other side, while allowing herself to anticipate the thrilling rush of the ride. With her head held high, arms relaxed at her sides, she surrenders gladly to the current.

She feels the familiar sizzle-chill of the gentle electric waves. The current runs from her feet to the top of her head to the curlicues of hair standing straight out from her scalp. The energy floods her spinal column, surging across and down her limbs. A sphinx-like smile spreads across Inanna's dark, gold-flecked skin. She glides through the terrain in an eyeblink, meeting the boys across the distance where her toes gracefully step out on the outer rock ledge on the other side of the Portal.

Leo and Conan are waiting breathlessly for her to appear. Scrutinizing the crack in the mountain from which they have just emerged, they see her come through. They cannot hold back their flood of wonderment.

But Inanna immediately hushes their questions with a finger to her lips. *Later*, she mouths. She wants to hold onto every molecule of the Portal's energy. "You'll probably feel a buzz for a couple of hours," she whispers with her eyes closed.

When the whirring vibration inside her quiets to a hum, Inanna opens her eyes again to find the boys waiting, watching her with anxious expectation. For the first time since leaving the green valley, she laughs aloud.

"Oh wow, you two! You've got your panties in such a bunch you aren't enjoying the view."

The boys turn around and encounter a wide, coppery plateau. They must have come out of the Portal so far below where they entered it that none of the terrain now matches Montana's Rocky Mountains. The rock face behind them isn't the same granite. This mountain is colored in shades of ochre and sand. The land ahead of them is a rugged mesa banded by distant hills. The charged energy of the Portal had carried them through the enormously thick wall of the slope, over the high ground and across a rocky chasm.

"Hope you enjoyed the ride," Inanna smiles.

The boys feel themselves released from the fatigue of the day, and relieved of their heavy hearts. Their nerves are calmer than they've been for days. Their minds are fully awake and alert.

Incredulous, the brothers exchange words of astonishment.

"Bruh! That was *epic!*"

"Fan-fucking-*tastic!*"

Taking satisfaction in their enthusiasm and confoundment, Inanna turns toward the downward trek to the flat valley.

"Glad you liked it." She bows as deeply as possible without the backpack sliding forward and hitting her head. Leo laughs. Conan is enthralled.

"There are other Portals around, but all of 'em are rare and hard to find."

She starts forward.

"Now we'd better get going, or we'll miss the rest of our daylight while you two stand here *blah-blahing!*"

To herself, she whispers, *Thank you, Gramps and Nonny. I mean, what other little kid ever got to fulfill prophecy and travel by Portal?*

The boys can't see her wry smile.

Unencumbered by their previous fatigue, Conan and Leo follow Inanna down the slope to the plateau, held in the pure heart of awe and wonder.

Chapter 83
Awe and Wonder

The Three descend from the rock-strewn hill in an hour, faster than what should have been possible, and stop at the base to scan the long flat valley they'd seen from the hilltop. The canyon floor is scattered with water-starved fir trees. There are no pinecones to salvage from the dry branches of the undersized conifers. The kids are grateful now to have gathered the few they had for feeding campfires.

They are not dispirited as they take in the barrenness. The journey through the Portal has renewed their faith, refreshed their spirits and refocused their purpose. The impossible again seems possible.

They pause for brief minutes to chug canteen water, readjust packs, and check compasses before progressing across the wide valley plateau towards the mountains ahead of them.

At the base of the next elevation, Leo, Conan and Inanna stare up at the high, crescent-shaped peak. Abiding Gramps' warning, no one speaks. The nods they share between them acknowledge that the next challenge demands equal parts climbing skill and courage. Yet what should be a long, dangerous ascent goes without a stumble and with surprising speed.

"The portal power?" Conan asks Inanna, as he gives her a hand over the lip of the crescent. "It gave us extra energy, right?"

She returns his smile.

Leo has climbed a yard higher and ahead of them to the peak's summit. He upheaves his backpack and sighs satisfaction with their achievement.

"Let's stop, hydrate, grab a handful of trail mix. Doesn't feel like we even *need* a breather, right?" The others, distracted by canteens and shuffling through packs for food, agree with nods and thumbs up.

Until Conan turns to face the direction they are headed.

"Whoa!" He muffles his shock and points to the horizon.

Inanna and Leo turn to stare at the view, silent.

They stifle any thought of being overwhelmed, refuse any exhale that might give away a slip of belief in their shared abilities. But neither do they allow delusion.

As far as their eyes can see, countless miles of folded hills and shadowed mountain ranges stand in profile. Silhouetted against the silver-grey bare light of the sunless sky, the craggy heights and ponderous slopes fill and define the entire skyline. And the vistas they see ahead of them are also desolate. Dead and crumbled earth. Destroyed forests. Clogged rivers and lakes.

Before they can be discouraged or dispirited at the sight, Leo leads their thoughts.

"We've been through enough challenges to know *this* journey is just another one. Distances and destruction haven't stopped us yet. And won't now."

Inanna unlatches her waist pack and takes out a pair of small field binoculars. After a long look, she hands the binoculars to the boys.

"A lot is destroyed," she says. "But not all."

The brothers study the horizon, each in turn.

"Yeah," murmurs Leo. "Small signs of life in places."

"But, damn and holy shit!" Conan tilts up the lenses to examine the endless outline of mountains. "So many miles to cover." He hands the glasses back to Inanna. "And no sure path," he adds.

They fall silent again in the shadow of the looming ranges. It's as if the mountains had grown there to protect themselves and their elevated comrades against any plan to cross them. For the first time since dawn, the kids absorb the enormity of the challenges they face on their long journey home.

Leo squints into the coming night. "A worthy journey, Dad said, should be one that has a purpose. A mission." He deepens his voice to mimic his father's gruff cowboy talk. "And no mission is worth taking unless at the start it seems impossible."

Within each mind and heart, they vacillate between possible, impossible. They silently mull over mission. Promises made. And the vast landscapes that brought them to this moment in time.

Finally, Leo concedes to himself that the beautiful terror of the shaded row upon row of mountains staggers his imagination.

He turns to his companions, however, with fresh determination.

"It was only the three of us who fought the black ooze. Only us, fighting the fire ants and the winds and the quakes, and the abyss under the cabin. Only us fighting our own demons of fear, the night we faced them in the circle. And Gramps' teachings lie within us, forever. Like the spirits that lifted the cabin, he will be here when we need him." Leo places his palm over his heart.

"Yeah," Conan says softly. "I thought we didn't have a choice, those times, except to do what we had to do. But we did. We always do. Right?"

Leo gazes into the horizon and imagines the Channel Island vistas that dot the Pacific Coast, and how the fog hides them for days at a time until the sea winds lift the mist and it's as if the islands come to life.

"Courage," he says, "can be hidden. Under cover within us, until we need it."

He shivers. He glances over his shoulder and detects darkening swirls of clouds gathering in the distance behind them. The hazy grey formations remind him of Hungry Ghosts. Harbingers of the Darkness.

Inanna's curls blow softly in a light wind. Her acute instincts pick up the shift of energy. Conan, too, sniffs out the concern rising in the shared quiet. He turns in a slow circle and scans the nebulous sky from every angle.

"*Vigilance!*" Inanna's demand grabs their attention exactly as she wished it would. "Vigilance keeps animals alive in the wild. A constant state of vigilance." She meets Leo's eyes and holds them.

He nods. Silently, he rechecks each pack and rebalances them for the umpteenth time. He slides the velvet cover down on Inanna's sword. Then he secures the pistol holstered at his hip.

"Vigilance," he repeats. "Guns ready? Loaded? Safety on?"

"Yep. Easy to get to," Conan nods.

"Good. We're as ready as we can be."

"Cowboy up!" Conan declares. Then raises an eyebrow. "Can we say that, wearing Indian moccasins?"

All three kids bust a laugh of relief and pump chests, filling their lungs with new breath and resolve.

The Three, Gramps called them. Together they hold the prophecy, only barely understood, tucked up close to each of their hearts where memories hum.

For a future to be possible.

Inanna whispers, "Not more than an hour or two left in this day. Better set our compasses."

Conan wishes aloud again for a working GPS. "Or a superhero who can fly us over the mountains. Maybe Spiderman and his webs…"

The girl cuts him off. "Like you said, big boy, better *cowboy up!*"

Leo shakes his head with a grin. "Spiritual warriors? Or teen romantics?"

The others *ugh* and look away.

Still wearing a smile, Leo points a finger at the mountains ahead. The peaks of shadowed watchfulness and crowns of foreboding majesty are set against the day's last attempt at casting light without requisite sun. The effect is breathtaking.

Without any more assurance than their belief in one another and in new beginnings, they repeat, "Trust. Faith. Courage."

Then they face the mountain ranges and the future.

And together they enter the next valley.

Credits:

~**A Place in Space** collected essays, by Gary Snyder (2008)
~Poem **A Ritual to Read to Each Other** by William E. Stafford (1998)
~Song lyrics from **I Will Be Light** by Matisyahu (2008)

Made in the USA
Las Vegas, NV
11 January 2023

65365672R20243